Blood-Borne Series

~BOOK TWO~

A Blinding Winter

C.R. QUINN

Designed by C.R. Quinn
Cover created by C.R. Quinn and Tony Leone
Front cover photo by Zoe Rochelle
Back cover photo by Chris Jupin
Spine photo by Brendan Lally
www.flickr.com
www.creativecommons.org\licenses\by-nc\2.0\legalcode

Printed in the United States of America

Library of Congress
ISBN-10: 069238832X
ISBN-13: 978-0692388327

A Blinding Winter

For Mama, because together we beat the odds.

And no, you were not the inspiration for Shelby.

Chapter One

Cameron

The backseat of the SUV was cramped, especially with Alexander nearing seven feet tall sitting next to you. Of course he was all muscle, which was exactly the reason my Vampire father, Victor, had Turned him. He was exactly what the Warrior coven needed, intimidation. But as my fellow Warriors knew, he was one of the kindest men you would ever meet. Unless of course you threatened him, Kyla, or anyone else he cared about or was supposed to protect.

"So how's Brianna feeling? Kyla said she was still a little under the weather," he asked, trying to shift his body closer to the window to allow me more room.

"Is she still vomiting?" my older brother Devin asked from the front passenger seat, causing Connor, another Warrior, to look curiously into the rearview mirror while he drove.

"Yes," I replied with a sly smile, "every morning in fact."

Both Alexander and Devin turned to me, expectant smiles on their faces.

"So…" Alexander prodded, causing me to laugh lightly as I looked down at the floor.

"So…" I began slowly, drawing out their anticipation, "she promised me she would take a pregnancy test today."

I could not help but smile as the words crossed my lips. I was ecstatic. Brianna Morgan was having my baby. I was almost positive she was.

"I've been tellin' her for weeks she's preggers," my youngest brother Jared said from the comm's other end. "I told her there's no way a concussion would affect her this bad for over a month."

Devin gave an audible harrumph as he pressed into his comm unit, "Jared, what have I told you about eavesdropping on the comms *before* the mission."

"I believe we talked about me not listening in, but I don't think we actually agreed on it."

Everyone in the SUV tried unsuccessfully to stifle their laughter, except Devin who did not laugh at all. Even though Jared was being nosey, he was absolutely right. It had been nearly five weeks since Elaina and her coven attacked the Warrior manor where Brianna had sustained pretty severe injuries, including a bump on the back of the head. She had deemed her sickness a product of her head injury since it was too early for any kind of morning sickness. However, my theory as well as Kyla's was that my Bri was indeed with child. My child!

Over the last few weeks Brianna made many an explanation for her illness other than being pregnant and I knew exactly why. She was scared, and rightfully so. Her life before she met me was fraught with heartache and abuse at the hand of her now deceased husband. She had suffered many miscarriages over their fourteen year marriage, though I was not sure of the exact number. Losing one child was enough to bear, and I should know since I had lost my own son the night I was Turned. So Brianna was definitely scared of losing another baby, but I believed she was also scared at the prospect of having a hybrid Vampire child. Although she was a hybrid herself, it was probably not something she would necessarily wish on anyone in these troubled times. Hybrids were still being hunted by a Vampire named Elaina, and we hadn't been able to stop it.

Elaina was the very reason we were on a mission tonight. Her coven had expanded and branched into various territories - kidnapping, experimentation, and in many cases murder. When Elaina's coven had attacked the Warriors last month, we had captured several of her surviving hybrids and a few of her Vampires. To date, only two survived. The hybrids became erratic and ended up killing each other. Four of the Vampires chose to burn to ash from silver and sun rather than turn on their former master. But two remained, though barely after the tortures our Warrior prison master Julian had subjected them to. At first they divulged what we already knew – Elaina was experimenting on hybrids and using their blood to gain powers. Those hybrids that either did not possess significant powers or did not respond well to the experiments were used as blood bags and left for dead.

The only new information Julian was able to get out of them was the location of one of their laboratories near Salinas, which we were now only minutes from.

"Ersch…Devin One this is Eagle Stud, perimeter team has landed. Over," Jared said in a deep voice and successfully irritating Devin.

"Jared, if you cannot be professional…" Devin began loudly.

"Whoa, whoa, calm down, Dev, I'm just joshin' you. Perimeter team is on site. They're seeing movement inside, but they're waiting for you and the other team. I'm opening the comms now," Jared said lightly, but we all knew he was upset that Father had not allowed him to come on the mission with us. Instead he was forced to work tech support, which there was no one better. But being a former Army Ranger, Jared would rather be part of the action than supporting it miles away. Victor, however, was still reluctant to allow him on missions after the near fatal injuries he sustained during the manor attack. That was the unfortunate thing about being the baby of the family. When you got hurt, Father became overprotective.

"Rrrroger that, Eagle Stud. Red Leader is a go," Alexander answered teasingly.

"Are we finished?" Devin snapped.

"Rrroger that Devin, we're finished. Rrroger, over." Jared laughed, but then quickly switched to business. "Perimeter team just set up the satellite link, starting to download infrared now."

"Affirmative, Jared, I am seeing images now," I said looking down at my cell phone and seeing the cold forms of the perimeter team surrounding the large warehouse. "It appears there are ten subjects inside, temperature readings seem to indicate hybrids. I do not see any Vampires on site."

Damn.

"With only ten hybrids and no Vamps our numbers are more than sufficient," Devin added as we pulled up next to the perimeter team's convoy.

"See, Jared, you're not missing anything," Alexander said comfortingly into his comm.

Jared broke in already laughing, "Well, if those hybrids are anything like the others, you guys have your work cut out for ya. Bring me back somethin' nice. Hoo-rah, brothers."

"Hoo-rah!" Devin and Alexander shouted back.

"Ten-four. Over and out," I said kiddingly.

Alexander and Connor, laughed but Devin groaned as we all exited the vehicle while the secondary team pulled in behind us. Once everyone was gathered, Devin pulled rank.

"Everyone listen up, infrared is showing only ten hybrids in the building, no Vampires. The perimeter team will stay positioned outside the building and handle anyone who escapes from inside or tries to penetrate the line from out here. Jared is downloading the infrared images to your phones so use them wisely since we're going in there blind. And by all means, do not underestimate these hybrids. If they're anything like those we encountered last month, they are far from ordinary. Skylar, Vincent, and Uri, you take the northwest corner. Connor, Maxim, and Vanessa enter through the loading dock. Cameron, Alex, and I will come in through the front. Remember, we're considering this a rescue mission so hybrids are not to be killed."

From behind me I heard Skylar mutter, "Let's see if he takes his own advice."

"Just use your judgment," I interrupted. "We know some of Elaina's hybrids are dangerous to themselves and others. So Skylar, if you are unable to handle one of them on your own. I am sure Devin will be able to save your ass. Again."

A hint of a smile started at the corners of Devin's mouth as the other Warriors began to snicker behind me. No one disrespected my brother, especially not a cocky bastard like Skylar.

The group dispersed, passing the members of the perimeter team as we made our way to our designated entrances of the warehouse. The building was dilapidated, and even from outside you could smell the distinctive scent of decomposition. Once everyone was in place, Devin gave the signal and Warriors from various sides entered the building, but the warehouse was eerily quiet. I looked down at my phone and gestured to the next room where it appeared two hybrids were sitting almost motionless. Devin and I moved forward, while Alexander covered our backs.

Once we rounded the corner, the stench of urine and feces slapped us in the face. There was no longer a door to the room where the hybrids were located; at some point it had been ripped from its hinges. Devin stood shoulder to shoulder with me as we entered the room and found the two extremely emaciated hybrids sitting silently on the floor covered in their own filth. I knelt down in front of one of the young male hybrids, touching his shoulder gently. Slowly his eyes rose to meet mine and I could see the electrical burns on his face and neck along with track marks stretching up both his arms. Carefully I offered him my hand, but in the blink of an eye he leapt from his position and knocked me to the floor. I was completely taken off guard by his strength and was thankful when Alexander pulled him off of me. I glanced over to see Devin struggling with the other male hybrid, but only a few seconds later the young man went limp in Devin's arms.

"Devin!"

"I didn't kill him! I was just restraining him when he…dammit!"

Devin's frustration was muffled by the echoes of other Warriors seemingly having the same difficulties with the hybrids that we were.

"Son of a bitch," Alexander yelled in his deep voice from behind us as he thrust the hybrid firmly against the wall. "The little shit bit me. Cam, come take a look at this. He broke the skin." I stepped over to Alexander's side, seeing a trickle of blood that had escaped from his now healed bite wound. "How can a hybrid break though Vampire skin?"

"I do…not…know," I said as I cautiously brought my fingers closer to the hybrid's mouth to examine him. Just as my index finger lifted the hybrid's upper lip, he gnashed his teeth and hit Alexander hard in the neck. Alexander dropped him to the floor where he scurried into the hallway like an animal.

"Devin with me," I shouted over my shoulder as I hurried into the hallway. Devin was at my side a second later, but there was no sign of the hybrid. Perpendicular from where we stood, Vanessa began screaming as another hybrid clawed and tore at her hair and back. Devin bolted over to help her just as my missing hybrid jumped down from the ceiling onto my back, wrapping his legs and arms around my neck and waist. His teeth easily sank into the skin of my neck, prompting me to turn my back and crush him up against the wall. The hybrid's legs and arms immediately went slack. I stepped away from him as he slid down the wall and I could hear the sound of his heart beating irregularly, and then stop altogether.

Alexander stepped out into the hallway just in time to see me press my fingers against the hybrid's neck verifying that he was dead.

"Heart attack?"

"Possibly. Why would you think that?"

"Devin was right. He didn't kill the one in there, his neck isn't broken. So I assumed heart attack. They look like they haven't eaten in months. The number of electrical burns they have could have stressed the heart and combine that with overexertion could explain a heart attack."

As the sounds of the Warriors' struggles began to die down, Devin stepped into sight. "Cameron, Alex, you need to come with me."

We followed Devin down the corridor which opened up into the main storage room of the warehouse. The massive room was like a scene from an old science fiction horror movie. There were rows and rows of medical tables with various plastic bags and tubing hanging down in front of them. Only a handful of the tables were occupied. The smell of decomposition was overwhelming, even Connor and Maxim had to cover their mouths and noses while they searched each table for survivors.

"Connor, start sending images of everything to Jared," Devin began. "Jared, do you copy? Other coven leaders need to see this. This really kicks everything into high gear."

Jared acknowledged over the comm as I walked to where two large sliding glass doors led to a darkened room. The smell of decomposition was sucked into the dark room as I pushed opened the doors causing the rancid smell to combine with the stinging smell of rubbing alcohol and industrial disinfectant. The walls were lined with tables of cruel looking medical instruments, tubing, and electrical equipment with exposed wires. Whereas the previous room was more of a holding area, this room was where the actual experiments and procedures took place. There were only three metal tables in this room, and only one of which was occupied. I quickly stepped over to the far end of the room to find a young woman no more than twenty strapped to a table with only tattered cloths covering her private regions. As I stepped closer I could hear the faint sound of her pulse. Not wanting to startle her, I came around the table and gently placed my hand on her shoulder. "Miss? Miss, can you hear me?"

With great effort the young woman opened her eyes slightly. Her lips were severely cracked from dehydration but she was able to whisper, "Hhhelp...me."

"We have a live one here," I shouted to my brothers who were still in the holding area. While I ripped the hybrid's wrist and ankle restraints, Alexander and Devin came running into the room with Maxim and Uri close behind. Carefully I lifted the young woman into my arms and could feel her trembling against my chest.

Devin extended his arms as I came closer. "I'll take her, Brother. I've got the medical kit in the truck."

As I tried shifting the young woman into Devin's arms she screamed suddenly and kicked herself out of Devin's hold. When she tried to run, Maxim grabbed her violently around the waist, lifting her up off the ground while she continued to scream and flail about.

"No, Maxim, no! Let her go," I shouted at him, afraid she too could have a weak heart. He released her at my urging causing her to fall to the floor and scurry to the far corner of the room. "Surround her. We will contain her until she calms down," I ordered. The five of us in the room formed a line in front of her while she cowered and shivered in the corner like a trapped animal.

"She doesn't look like the others," Devin whispered next to me.

"Well, if we do not scare her to death, maybe we can actually save this one," I said firmly. "Miss," I began softly as she peered at me from underneath her arm. "What is your name?"

She lifted her head slightly, her eyes still looking frantically between the Warriors who surrounded her. Her cracked bottom lip trembled as she said, "Nnnn...Nikki."

"Nikki, no one will hurt you. My name is Cameron, and this is Devin. He is going to take you outside so he can treat you," I said in the calmest tone I could manage.

Unfortunately when Devin took a step toward her, Nikki grabbed one of the larger bone saws from the table next to her and began swiping it in front of her as she screamed. Devin took another step in her direction causing her to sidestep around him and run into me, wrapping her arms tightly around my waist. Bending down, I gathered Nikki back into my arms, turning so that Devin could remove the scalpel from her hand. Her breathing began to slow and as I lifted her head it appeared she had passed out.

Everyone in the room parted ways to allow me to exit with the only surviving hybrid of the evening. All other hybrids had either died from overexertion or were killed in self-defense, making the mission a failure in my eyes. Everyone else would stay behind to continue to gather evidence and clues regarding where Elaina's coven may have run off to while Devin, Alexander and myself drove Nikki to the Facility for treatment and further observations.

As we drove away from the warehouse she did not regain consciousness, however, I was unable to remove her grip from my combat gear without risking breaking her fingers. Alexander looked back at me at the scene of Nikki curled into my chest while she lay across my lap.

"You better hope she wakes up when we get to the Facility, otherwise Brianna's getting a surprise for her birthday."

Shaking my head I responded in an annoyed tone, "I am sure Nikki will come to her senses once we get to the Facility. She was terrified in there and I was the first face she saw. That is normal. Right?"

Alexander snickered. "Cam, just from her reaction in there, don't be surprised if she has trouble letting you go." It was hard not to sigh at the prospect. "Jared, this is Alex do you copy?"

"Rrrroger that, Eagle Stud is here, over."

"You asked us to bring you something nice, well Cam has a nice gift-wrapped crazy hybrid girl just for you."

"No thanks. I've had my fair share of crazy hybrids. She's all yours, bro. If we're done, I'm gettin' ready for the party. Guess you guys are gonna be late?"

"Only by about a half hour," I replied, hoping it was the truth.

"That is if Cameron can peel his new hybrid off of him," Alexander chided.

About to challenge him, I stopped when Nikki stirred and wrapped her arms around my neck and nuzzled her face deeper into my chest. When I tried removing her arms she simply put them back. To the snickers from the front seat, I simply responded, "Ah, hell."

Chapter Two

Brianna

Basically, my life sucked. Well, no, that wasn't exactly true. I had escaped from my abusive husband, met the love of my life, connected with my birth father and stepmother, had been welcomed by the Warrior Vampire coven, and had even gained a few close friends that had become more like family. One of which was pacing outside my bathroom door while I peed on a pregnancy test. The test and a few other things were making me think my life sucked, and now that I thought about it I felt like I was just being overdramatic. Really I was taking all my fear and frustration out on this pitiful piece of plastic that would tell me what I already knew - I was pregnant. I didn't want to admit it because of the complications it brought to my already complicated life.

For instance, how could I raise a child when I wasn't even allowed to leave the manor? How would I go to the doctor, have the baby even. Kyla had to purchase the at-home pregnancy test for me, which really just irked me. I knew it was dangerous for me to be out in public because Elaina was still out there somewhere looking for her next opportunity to take me. And if I was pregnant, it meant that some of my scarier dreams would be coming true sooner rather than later. Oh that's right, I should add that to my life sucks list – my dreams, more like nightmares, come true. They were only about me, and sometimes the details were fuzzy, but overall they always came true. Cam and I had tried to find ways to prepare for the events I dreamt of, but how did you prepare for being kidnapped by a crazy Vampire and have her hold you down while she did a crude C-section.

"Come on let me in, you have to be done by now," Kyla called from the other side of the door.

"Yes, I'm done," I announced as I placed the test stick on the counter and vigorously washed my hands, watching through the mirror as Kyla bolted into the bathroom. "It's not an instant test, Ky. We have to wait about five minutes."

"No fair, I want to know now."

"I'm sorry, my friend. But hey, at least you'll know what the result is a few seconds before I will," I said encouragingly, referring to her power of seeing into her future by several seconds. Taking the hand towel from its rack I dried my hands and sank to the floor, feeling the butterflies in my stomach fight with the nagging nausea I could not get over today.

Kyla sat down next to me, placing her cool hand on my cheek in order to help keep my sickness away. "Everyone is so excited about coming to your party tonight."

"Ky, why do you insist on calling it my party?"

"Because it's your birthday, silly."

"Yes that's true, but everyone is coming to celebrate *your* birthday, not mine. So it's really your party that just happens to be on my birthday."

"What can I say? No one wants to have a birthday party on a Tuesday. Parties are meant to be on Fridays and Saturdays, *your* birthday happened to be on a Friday this year. The timing is perfect."

"Who all is coming?" I asked as I brought the back of her hand to my other cheek.

"Just a few people from my old coven, a few people from here, and then of course the boys once they get back from Salinas. BTW did Cameron give you your present yet?"

"BTW?"

"Hel-lo, it means by-the-way."

"Then why didn't you just say that?"

"OMG it's how humans are speaking now, Bri. You need to get with the times."

"You've been spending way too much time with Jared. And no, Cameron has not given me my present yet. He said I had to wait until tonight. God only knows what that means. And don't even pretend you don't know what he got me because the two of you are as thick as thieves when it comes to shopping for me." Kyla gently took her hand from my face and crossed her arms in front of her chest. "So these people from your old coven, they're like your family?"

Kyla paused for a moment, twisting her lips back and forth. "IDK…"

"I.D…what?"

"*I don't know*," she replied annoyed. "It's kind of hard to explain. Really they're not. They were all Turned by Vivienne, she's the coven leader. But I was actually a solitary that they took in. Of course I got close to some of them. I mean really, who doesn't like me, but I never felt like I belonged there. So when I met Alex it was easy to leave. Well, at least at first. Then I realized there were no real girls in the manor so I had to make do with Cameron."

"Why didn't you feel like you belonged?"

"Vivienne's coven is made up of all these artsy people. They're all really talented in dance, music, theatre, and well…art. So, really I just marveled at their talent, and always wished I had some of my own."

"Now Ky, that's complete nonsense. You're very talented."

"Really, how?"

I paused for a moment, having to think of a real answer. "Well, you can spend money faster than anyone I've ever seen."

"Now I take offense to…" she began but suddenly stopped, gasped, and then bounced up and down from her position on the floor. "Check it! Check it," she shouted.

"Why bother? I think I know the result," I replied, hearing my cell phone ring from the counter above my head.

Kyla handed me the phone as I pushed myself up from the floor. "It's Sera. Do you think she knew?"

"I try not to be surprised by either of you anymore. Hey, Sera," I said quickly, changing my tone to one appropriate for my stepmother.

"Bonjour, ma petite chute, I have bin waiting all day to congratulate you," Sera said cheerily, calling me her little cabbage as she always did in her thick French accent. "I am so happy for you!"

"So I guess that means it's positive?"

Seraphina gasped and became very quiet, making me feel a little guilty. She was the true prophetess of the family. I could only imagine the control it took on her part *not* to tell you every aspect of your future. "Zut alors! You have not taken zhe test?"

"Yes I have 'taken zhe test', just didn't look at the results yet. I don't really have to now, do I?"

"Oh, petite chute, I am so sorry. I have ruined everyzhing."

"Ser…uh, Mom, you didn't ruin anything. Actually Kyla did."

"Hey!" Kyla shouted defensively from my closet (which worried me).

"I will say nozing more zhen. Your fazer wants to speak with you. Je t'aime!"

I could hear the phone being passed clumsily from Sera's hand to my father's and I could honestly say I was a little nervous to speak with him. He had been less than thrilled with Victor regarding the attack on the manor and every time I had spoken with him since then he pressed me to move in with him and Sera where I would be safer. Obviously I refused, but not without a tremendous amount of arguing. As his voice crackled through the phone I made my way into the bedroom hoping for some support from Kyla if the argument got ugly again.

"Bella sera, mia figlia," Eris said happily into the phone in *his* thick Italian accent.

"Dad, we had a deal. You promised no fake accent if I beat you in a challenge. And I won, remember? Or should I give you the play by play."

"Daughter," Eris replied in his real voice, "I told you it would be difficult for me since my accent has been a part of me for so long."

"*Fake* accent," I reminded him

"Happy birthday, my Brianna Marilena, and what a wonderful birthday gift it is to find out you are with child. I am so…" he began, but his speech faltered from emotion as he cleared his throat. "I am so happy to be a grandfather."

"Don't get too excited. I don't have a particularly good record in this department. I've never made it past the first trimester."

"This time it is different," he said firmly. "It is to be. I have told you this, your stepmother has seen it. Did you get my gift?"

I turned to the wall near the bedroom door where my father's gift stood. A female's suit of armor, actually, fully equipped with a breast plate meant to hold actual breasts. Along with the armor came a plethora of daggers. To an outsider it would appear that my father had stolen a museum's historic weapons cache, but in all honesty they were all from his personal collection. The gift not only sent a message to me that my father had no idea how to shop for his only daughter, but it also sent a message to Cameron and Victor, effectively pissing both of them off. Which was probably Eris's agenda in the first place.

"Yup, got the gift, Dad. Thank you."

"I think you should consider wearing the armor, Daughter."

"Funny, Dad."

"It was not a joke."

"It was to me."

"*Brianna...*" he snapped.

"*Eris...*"

"I do not wish to ruin this joyous day. I love you, daughter."

"Love you too, Dad. Or should I say, Grandpa."

Eris's laughter was light, but happy all the same. When he hung up I could feel Kyla's hand on my shoulder. She had actually been in the room when I ended up a sobbing mess after speaking with my father the last few weeks. Eris meant well, but his old violent ways were hard for him to completely get rid of.

"So are you going to call Oliver to tell him the news?" Kyla asked.

"No, I'll call him tomorrow. Daddy O's probably asleep by now."

"So I guess that means you're going to call Renee?" she asked, walking back toward the closet.

"Yes, Kyla," I answered, rolling my eyes at her jealousy of my only other friend. "Why wouldn't I call her? She's my best friend."

"One of!" Kyla shouted as her long orange hair swirled around her when she turned back to face me.

"Yes, one of! Don't know what I was thinking," I replied defensively.

Kyla nodded affirmatively and walked into my closet again, making me really worried at what she was doing in there. But I didn't have the time to think about it since I wanted to talk to Renee before she too went to sleep. The east coast/west coast time difference made it difficult for me to keep in contact with her and Daddy O. If I had only been allowed to get the pregnancy test myself earlier in the day, rather than have to wait for Kyla to do it, I could have had all my calls over and done with hours ago.

Not only had a lot changed for me since I met Cameron, oddly enough things had drastically changed for Renee at the same time. She had always been a serial dater, and had no interested in being tied down to anyone. That was, however, until she met Dr. John Ryan. Needless to say, he was perfect for her. He was established, smart, employed, dealt with all her quirks, and didn't stand for her bullshit when she spewed it. I would honestly call him a saint. Handling Renee wasn't always the easiest job, but he seemed to be doing it well. Not only did he convince her to move in with him a few months back, he recently convinced her to move to Boston where he had been offered a position in the ER of one of the city's largest hospitals with only two weeks' notice. More surprising, she went. Today was their move-in date and I had no idea which Renee I would find on the other line – the sweet I-miss-you-so-much-Renee, or the how-could-you-have-abandoned-me Renee.

It only took half a ring before she picked up the phone. "Well if it isn't my best friend whose face I can't remember."

Ah, how-could-you-have-abandoned-me Renee it was.

"Hey, snotty pants. You've been in Boston for what, fourteen hours and you're already a bitch?" I said jabbing her attitude back at her. Today I was in no mood.

"Honey, it took less than two minutes for it to settle in. Happy birthday, by the way. Couldn't getcha anything since I have no idea where you live. But hey, I don't even know where I live. So there you have it, I already hate it here," she said miserably to which I heard Dr. John yell at her that she was lying. "I do too hate it," she yelled back at him, forgetting to take the phone away from her ear.

"And thank you for making me deaf."

"Sorry. Hey, aren't I supposed to call you on your birthday?"

"Well, my friend, I think you totally failed on that one."

"Crap, Bri, I'm sorry. This move just killed me. Mom hasn't stopped crying, I don't have a job, I don't even know where to find a grocery store, there's not a single parking space in the entire city, and John starts work tomorrow. The only thing that has worked out was this apartment, and that was a miracle from God. Although I'm not sure where John's sleeping since my shoes fill our entire bedroom." From somewhere in the apartment Dr. John shouted at her again that her shoes would find themselves on the street before he slept anywhere else besides their bed.

"So where in Boston is the apartment?" I asked, trying to move the conversation along before Renee began yelling through the phone again.

"It's in the South End."

"Ohmygod, Renee, isn't that a bad part of town? That's like where Marky Mark's from?"

"You are such an idiot sometimes," Renee replied flatly. "That's Southy, not the South End. So no, I do not live with Marky Mark or the Funky Bunch. The South End's historical or some shit like that. All I know is that I've never climbed so many freakin' stairs in my life. There's a flight of stairs to the door, and then two sets in the apartment alone. Hey at least I'll have a nice ass." And yet again Dr. John provided commentary that she already had a nice ass. "Bri, I'm sorry, I have to call you back."

"Oh, ok," I said, completely disappointed and crushed that I hadn't gotten a word in since I called her. Within seconds of hanging up the phone, my cell phone rang in my hand displaying that the incoming call was from Renee. "Er...hi?"

"Happy Birthday, Bri! Girl, you have no idea how much I miss you!"

"You need medication, Re."

"Don't think John hasn't offered to write the script. Look, I needed to start from scratch. I'm sorry I was a total downer earlier. Totally wrong of me, and don't worry, John had your back. He was giving me the stink eye the whole time. So seriously, why did you call me?"

"Oh ya know, just wanted to call you and tell you I was preggers. Same old stuff."

Renee was quiet for a moment before she asked, "It's Cameron's, right?"

"Actually I'm not sure. Since I've moved into the manor I've become a total Vampire slut. I'll probably have to go on a talk show and find out who my baby daddy is." I took a moment to let my sarcasm sink in. "Of course it's Cameron's. Now who's the idiot?"

There was another pause before Renee began screaming and cheering in the phone. I could hear Dr. John telling her to be quiet, but she didn't really seem to care. "Bri, this is so great. I'm so happy for you." And then her voice changed as she started to cry. "I wish I was there with you."

"I..." sniffle "know, Re. I miss you too." Now we were both crying and sniffling through the phone. "I'll come see you soon. I promise."

"Don't make promises you can't keep, Bri."

"I'll make it happen, Re."

"'Kay. I'll ah...call me like every day. I have no life anymore."

"Well neither do I, so it's a date. Every day. Love ya, sweetie."

"Bye, my friend."

I wiped my eyes as I took the phone away from my ear, my heart feeling suddenly heavy. When I turned around, Kyla was sitting on the couch in front of the fireplace, wiping away watery red tears from her eyes with a tissue. "Kyla, why are you crying?"

"Because you are."

"Kyla, I cry all the time. You know this."

"It's just that you miss her so much and I feel bad that you can't see her."

"Well then it's a good thing I have you. Don't we have a party to get ready for?" I asked, not wanting to think about how there was no way I'd convince Cameron or anyone else in this house to let me out of it while Elaina roamed free. Meaning I had just lied to my dearest friend. Again.

"I picked an outfit out for you," Kyla said with a forged smile.

"Of course you did. You know, I was completely unaware that I was unable to dress myself before I moved in here. Really, it's amazing I got through life without you or Cam to pick out my clothes."

Kyla raised an un-amused eyebrow at me. "Is this how you're going to be through your entire pregnancy? Or are you saving it all for me?"

"You wanted to be one of my best friends. That's what you get."

"Well you better be in a better mood tonight when you meet my friends. A few of them are kind of famous."

"Like, how famous?"

"Like you're totally going to shit your pants famous."

Chapter Three

Brianna

So Kyla was right, I almost shit my pants. Seriously, how would you feel if all of a sudden you were shaking hands with three major film stars, one of which was supposed to have died fifty years ago, and the other two just released one of the biggest box office smashes playing very convincing Vampires. Go figure. There were also a couple of musicians, one which was also supposed to be dead and spent his time making money hand over fist impersonating himself. I'll admit I felt a little out of place amongst the talented people in the room, and I could now see why Kyla felt inadequate living with these people on a full-time basis. However, you would never have known that she ever felt inferior to them while she basically held court amongst the members of her old coven.

Thankfully since the party started a couple of hours ago Jared was at my side. The other few hybrids and Vamps that I knew from the manor wished me happy birthday, but I knew they were really there to see the celebrities, and that was ok. Well, it had to be. The boys hadn't returned yet, and I was getting worried even though Jared assured me that everything had gone well.

"Beebs, cut it out," Jared said annoyed and snapped his fingers in front of my face. I blinked hard, startled to attention and looking at him quizzically. "I told you everything's fine. Now stop worrying."

"Who said I was worrying?"

"I know I haven't known you that long, but I've come to recognize that when you get all catatonic and start to stare into space, you're worrying. Can I get you somethin' while I'm up?" he asked as he rose from the couch with his empty glass that still had a red film from the blood that had previously been in it.

Just as I shook my head no, the door to the sitting room opened, its doorframe filled with Alex's large silhouette. Kyla squealed with excitement as I jumped off the couch only to be disappointed by the sight Alex and Devin *without* Cameron.

As my face fell, Devin interceded since Alex couldn't break away from Kyla's welcome home kisses. "Brianna, have no worry. Cameron will be delayed only a short while."

I nodded my head, but bit my lip almost to the point of drawing blood. Everyone in the family could tell me Cam was fine, but until my arms were around him *I* wouldn't be fine. Ever since Elaina had attacked the manor there had been five missions that took him away from me. And every time he left I felt my heart being tugged out of my chest. Today, however, it wasn't only the fact that Cameron may be taken away from me, but now from our unborn child, or possibly children if my stepmother's visions were correct.

After another few minutes of Jared trying to get me to eat a piece of birthday cake, I saw that Alex had finally been freed from Kyla's loving arms. While he poured a glass of warm blood for himself, I tapped him lightly on the shoulder and tilted my head toward the door. Taking his glass with him he followed me into the hallway and quietly shut the door behind him.

"Ok Alex, go ahead and tell me the truth. How bad is he really? Where did you take him to heal? Does he need blood?"

The gentle giant furrowed his brow as he answered in his deep voice, "Bri, Cam's fine, really. We're not lying to you."

"Then where is he?!"

Alex took in a slow breath allowing my overwhelming emotions to die down. "He's at the Facility with the hybrid we rescued tonight."

"Why did he have to stay and not you?"

"The hybrid is having a little trouble adjusting and trusting anyone but Cameron."

"Well the fact that he survived at all is a blessing. How messed up is he?"

"*She* is quite messed up, although we don't know what all has been done to her. She won't let anyone examine her and she'll only talk to Cam. She went into hysterics when we started to leave and began throwing things at the medical staff, so Cam decided to stay until they could sedate her."

Feeling the nausea begin to rise within me, I pressed myself up against the wall and bent my head down in order to get the blood flowing into my head again. Alex gently put his hand on my shoulder.

"I'm fine," I said, waving him away, but then decided to put his cool hand on my cheek without giving him any kind of explanation or choice. "So the warehouse was bad, huh?"

"It was the worst we've seen. Nikki was the only survivor, and we're not even sure how she was able to manage that. The equipment we found…"

"That's good, Alex, I don't need to hear anymore," I interrupted, pushing myself off the wall and seeing a mischievous smile on his face. "What?"

"Nothing," he replied, shaking his head and opening the door to the party.

Once inside, I plopped myself back down on the couch in front of the fireplace. Jared quickly sat next to me with one eyebrow raised. "So did Alex tell you anything that I didn't?"

"Well you didn't tell me Cameron was at the Facility with some girl."

"Cuz I'm not a moron. I heard she was a little crazy."

"Ah, just your type," I responded kiddingly, but then regretted it. I knew that Jared was still not quite over the fact that the last woman he had feelings for aided one of Elaina's Vamps in trying to kill him. "Wanna play cards?"

"'Bout time you let me win my money back."

"Ha! As if you could ever win against me."

As always, playing cards helped take my mind off of the nagging worries that kept echoing in my head. Of course it didn't hurt that I was also winning gobs of money, though Jared didn't know I wouldn't accept a dime from him. It wasn't until another hour had past when Kyla handed me my third piece of cake and my need to play cards vanished. Cam was home.

"It's about time," Kyla shouted at him when he came through the door.

"My sincerest apologies, Kyla," he said giving her a quick kiss on the check before I flew from the couch and into his outstretched arms.

My body was suddenly showered in goose bumps as his cool lips gave me soft quick kisses on my neck before he whispered, "Forgive me, love."

"You're back safe, so there's nothing that needs forgiving."

"I am late to celebrate your birthday. There is a lot I need forgiving for," he said stealing a kiss from my lips and then lingering for a moment. "So, anything you would like to tell me?"

I ran my fingers through his hair, twirling one of his dark curls while I took in his hopeful smile. Just as I was about to answer, Kyla's cheerful voice broke through our little romantic moment as she brought the party to order.

"Ok, now that *everyone* has finally joined us," Kyla began, giving Cameron a quick wink, "I'd like to thank you all for coming tonight. It always excites me when both my covens can come together. I have such great people in my life, and I would like to propose a toast to the newest member of our family, my very best friend, Brianna Morgan. Even though it is her birthday today, she has given me the best birthday present ever."

Cameron draped his arms in front of my chest as he stood behind me and whispered, "I thought you were waiting until Tuesday to give her your present."

"I am," I whispered back and then realized in horror what Kyla was about to do.

"I know she's going to be angry with me but..." Kyla began.

"Kyla don't," I said over her, stepping out of Cameron's arms but it was too late.

"She's making me an auntie!" she squealed as she jumped up and down clapping her hands.

Cameron wasted no time and lifted me up from the ground as he twirled me around while members of our family cheered loudly. Once he put me back down on the ground he looked over my shoulder and said, "Kyla if I was not so unbelievably happy right now, I would be angry at you for not letting Brianna tell me herself."

"Well I knew you'd be happy, so I took a chance," she replied slyly, slinking into the safety of Alex's arms. "Now go celebrate the happy news."

"Yeah, bro, it's not like you can get Beebs any more knocked up than she already is," Jared laughed.

In a quick second I took a deep breath, lowered my guard, and allowed myself to see the essences of the Vampires in the room. When I looked in Jared's direction, I concentrated on the bright halo around his head and Pushed him to the floor. My family laughed, Jared yelped in pain, and Kyla's friends stared in shock.

"Beebs, I was just joking," Jared whined as he brushed himself off.

"That's what you get for being a jackass, Jerry," I said snidely.

"Well I believe that is our cue to leave," Cameron said lightly as he tucked me into his chest and drew me toward the door.

But before we could leave, Kyla pulled me from Cameron's arms and into hers, looking for forgiveness. "Bri, don't be mad. I just couldn't help myself I'm so excited."

Spitting out the many strands of her bright orange hair that had been thrust into my mouth by her intense embrace I replied, "I know, Ky. I'm sure we'll figure out a way for you to make it up to me."

"I feel a major shopping binge coming on."

"Well if you can convince Cameron to let me out of this house then we'll be even."

Kyla pulled away, twisting her lips back and forth across her mouth. "That's going to be a hard one."

"Kyla, the father of my child found out I was pregnant the same time everyone else did because of you."

Kyla paused and then sighed in resignation. "Fine, I'll work on him."

After a quick kiss on the cheek, Kyla released me back into Cameron's arms and we bid our goodbyes. Our walk down the corridor was quiet until we reached the wretched staircase. But before I could even groan, Cameron scooped me up and began carrying me up the stairs.

"You totally spoil me."

"It is my job, my love. And in my opinion I do not spoil you enough," he said, kissing me gently as he raced up the stairs causing the scene around us to blur and take focus on the inside of our bedroom a few seconds later.

Since I wasn't allowed to leave the manor for the time being, the majority of my time was spilt between the training room downstairs and our bedroom. If I had to describe Cameron's room when I first moved into the manor with one word, it would be cold. Not literally since it had been summer, but there were no pictures, no history, nothing that would tell you who Cameron Burke was unless you went into the massive closet and saw almost every stitch of clothing he had owned in his entire three hundred years of life. So I took matters into my own hands and added a few blankets, a rug, and the three pictures I had managed to obtain so far. One, my favorite of course, was of me and Cameron dancing together at my Claiming ceremony. The second, a selfie of Kyla and I being our silly selves, and the last taken only last week while the boys played their traditional poker game before a mission, of which I had not been allowed to play. All three pictures were framed and set on the mantle of the fireplace that stood in front of the couch and chaise where Cameron and I would lay and read and snuggle those rare times when we actually got to spend a whole evening together. Tonight, however, I didn't feel like reading.

"Why do you smell like honeysuckle?" I asked as I nuzzled my face into his neck.

"Because that is all we have in our shower and I desperately needed to wash the smell of the warehouse off of me."

"Alex told me it was bad."

Cameron nodded. "I cannot even begin to describe what it was like. It only makes my worry for you grow when I think about you leaving the manor."

"I'm not sure the honeysuckle smell is you," I said, wanting to change the subject from a topic we often argued about.

"I agree, but I was desperate to smell nice for you on your birthday."

"And I appreciate that since we have a lot to celebrate. I'm sorry that Kyla just blurted it out like that. That's not how I wanted…"

"Then let us pretend that this evening never happened, and I have just returned home and fled into your arms."

"Well, I thought that maybe I would start by…"

I pulled his face down to mine and kissed him gently on the lips. He eagerly responded by opening his mouth and teasing mine open with his cool tongue. I ran my fingers through his thick black hair, pulling at the curls in the back and loving his pleasured breath waft gently against my face. Without a second's delay, I pulled his shirt from within his pants and shrugged it up and over his head, enjoying the view of my lover's masculine chest in front of me.

Cameron smiled lovingly at me as the back of his fingers traced the side of my face down my neck and to the front of my chest where he slowly untied the thin ribbon of my scooped-necked blouse. He bent his head, gently caressing my neck while his fingers pulled my blouse down from my shoulders exposing my bare breasts to him. He moaned at the sight of them and pulled my legs around him, crushing my chest against his and with it causing me to gasp in pain.

"Are you all right, love?"

"Sorry, just be careful with the girls. They're a little sore," I responded, taking the pressure off my breasts.

"I will do everything not to ruin this spectacular way of telling me that you…"

"Not yet! You don't know yet, remember?"

"Oh yes, terribly sorry. What am I to do now, my love?"

I squeezed my legs tighter around his waist, placing my arms around his neck. "You are unable to control your lust for me any longer, and you must take me to our bed."

"That should not be difficult for me to portray," he said smiling crookedly at me. As he carried me to the bed he pulled away the thick comforter before lowering me down on the soft mattress. Cameron brought the blankets over him as he slipped underneath them, placing the weight of his pelvis on mine. I could feel his growing desire as I fiddled clumsily with the button of his pants, but then I felt something that seemed out of place.

"Cameron, you're vibrating," I said, feeling the jarring vibration on the inside of my thigh.

Cameron lifted himself up on one elbow and pulled his cell phone out of his pants pocket, took a quick look, and then placed it on the nightstand. By the time the cell phone finally stopped vibrating against the table's surface, both of us had shed what little clothes remained and were entangled so tightly it was hard to know where one of us began and the other ended. Though Cameron was always a few degrees cooler, whenever our bodies met there was electricity generated between us. The radiating heat made Cam feel human and quashed any reluctance I might have had about making love to a Vampire. For in this moment I didn't care what he was. I loved him, and we had created a miracle.

When it seemed obvious that both of us were ready to be taken by the other, I pulled away in order to look deeply into Cameron's eyes.

"Do you remember…" I began as the cell phone on the nightstand began vibrating again. I could see Cameron trying to ignore it, but it was annoying me. "Maybe you should get it."

He reached over me, took another glance at the cell phone, and sent the call to voicemail. Then in a move that surprised me, he reached back and took the house phone off the hook.

"Cam, it could be important."

"Nothing is more important to me than you," he said firmly, taking my hand in his and kissing the backs of my fingers in a loving gesture he had performed so many times since we met. "You were asking me if I remembered something."

I sighed but then continued, "Do you remember the first time you made love to me and you told me that you would never hurt me?" He nodded as I took his hand and pressed it against my stomach. "And do you remember you also asked me if I believed that one day, right under your hand, I would carry your children?"

"Yes, my angel, conceived in all the love I have you for," he said softly as he kissed me, not daring to close his eyes for a second.

"I believe, Cam, I believe it all. You have never hurt me, ever. Nor do I think you ever will. And I believe it because right here, right underneath your hand I am carrying your child. Just like you said I would. And even though I'm a little scared, I can't tell you how happy I am that we're having a baby. A little baby Burke."

Cameron slid himself down and placed his lips where his hand had just been resting on my stomach. As he kissed my skin where his unborn child rested in its early stages, I could feel a little burning from within as if my child was somehow acknowledging its father. Cameron looked up from his position, his eyes smoldering with love and desire as he moved his way back up to be hovering just above me.

"Brianna Marilena Morgan, you made me the happiest man alive the day you told me you loved me. I did not think it possible until this moment to be happier than that day, but I...I am overcome with joy that I will be a father again." Cameron's head dipped as he cleared his throat of the emotions dredged up from his past. I couldn't stop the tear that escaped my eye since I was wiping away the reddish one from his face. "I love you, Brianna. And I love that you are carrying my *babies,*" he said with a devilish smile.

A worried laugh came out of my mouth as I looked skeptically at him. "Let's not push it. I'm scared enough as it is."

Cameron furrowed his brow as he shook his head. "Do not be scared, my love. I will be with you every step of the way. Whatever is thrown at us, we will handle together like we always do. Always."

I looked into his eyes seeing just how adamant he was and my fear left me. He kissed me hard on the lips while his hand traveled up my abdomen and massaged my breast.

"Ooh! Not the boobs, babe," I gasped.

"Sorry, sorry, angel. Just habit."

"There are plenty of other parts you can explore," I said seductively as I pulled all of his weight directly on top of me and I fully opened my legs to him.

Cameron smiled and moaned into my mouth as he pulled himself up on his forearms and entered me, but only a second later he froze. Before I could ask him what was wrong, the door to our bedroom flew open.

"Brother," Devin shouted as he bolted into our room, "why aren't you answering your phone."

"This is not happening," I groaned with Cameron still poised above me, anger all over his face as he pulled himself out of me.

"Dammit, Devin, what have I said about knocking," Cameron shouted as he sat on the edge of the bed, pulling the sheet around his waist and allowing me to hide behind him.

"You're not answering your cell or the house phone."

"There was a reason for that," Cameron snapped.

"Lanashell is calling from the Facility. She needs you back there immediately. That hybrid is going crazy again."

"Lanashell has a capable staff. The hybrid is her responsibility now, not mine."

"Nikki has already attacked several of the staff, and Lanashell is making her our responsibility since we brought her there."

"Then have someone else go. I do not work for Lanashell and I am not at her beck and call when things go awry with a hybrid."

"You may not work for Lana but since Nikki seems to only listen to you, Father wants you at the Facility in twenty minutes. You can take your objections up with him. I am only the messenger." Devin took two steps toward the door before turning back around as he said, "Oh, and congratulations on the baby."

"Get out, Devin," Cameron said flatly. Once Devin closed the door behind him, Cameron's head fell into his hands. "I am so sorry, love."

"It's times like these I wish we had a place of our own."

Cameron lifted his head from his hands and turned to face me. "And I would gladly give it to you, angel. I cannot believe I have to leave you right now. I hope you realize I do not have a choice."

"I know," I replied as my chest began to constrict. "How long will it take you to get to the Facility?"

"Ten minutes if I drive inhuman speeds, as you say."

"Then drive inhuman speeds," I said, pulling him back down next to me.

As he stretched his long body down the length of mine, he pulled at my leg that was draped across his torso, sliding me on top of him. "Nineteen and a half if I Project."

I bent my head down to kiss him as he gripped my hips firmly. "Then you better hang on," I said playfully, "it's gonna be a fun and fast ride."

Chapter Four

Cameron

I stared heartbreakingly at my love wave her fingers goodbye to me as the black mist of my Projection began taking me away from her and to the Facility. Seventeen minutes and thirty-eight seconds was not near the amount of time I wanted to make love to Brianna. It might have been ample time for a mortal man, but I am no mortal. I was more than capable of going for hours on end, and I desperately wanted to take Bri until she begged me to stop out of sheer exhaustion and pleasure. Unfortunately seventeen minutes and thirty-eight seconds was all I could afford in order to have time to hold her, kiss her, dress, and Project without a second to spare.

Speaking of my Projection, I was not yet at the Facility because my concentration was definitely elsewhere. Concentrate Cameron! Or you will never get yourself back together. Picturing the tall glass doors and rich mahogany furniture, the black mist began to thin and reveal the lobby of the Facility with the addition of an irritated Madelyn Forebush in her night robe and slippers. Madelyn had the title of a receptionist, but for all intents and purposes she really did keep the Facility running along with Lanashell. It took several seconds for the scene around me to focus completely, which was unusual but explainable by fatigue and lack of blood. In other words, it had been a long day.

As the last wisps of black smoke faded around me I walked toward Madelyn who was eyeing her watch. "Twenty minutes to the second, Mr. Burke. You couldn't come any earlier? You have no idea what we've been going through since you left."

Not stopping to respond, I passed by her and into the open atrium which was relatively vacant at this hour. "Maddy, I am sorry for your troubles but I wanted to spend as much time with Brianna as possible before leaving her a second time on her birthday. I am sure you can understand."

Madelyn pursed her lips as she struggled to keep up with my pace. I could have slowed down, and normally I would have but my angry energy was propelling me.

"Well happy birthday to Miss Brianna, but this is a crisis, Mr. Burke."

"Maddy," I said angrily and then hated myself for it. I stopped abruptly to take a calming breath. "Madelyn, forgive my tone. I just do not understand why I am here. Lanashell has a very capable staff. I do not understand how they cannot handle one disturbed hybrid."

"Mr. Burke, if there was anything else we could think of doing besides calling you we would have. The fact that I'm standing here in my night clothes in the middle of the building tells you something. This girl is a hellion. Once the sedation wore off she bit one of the doctors, threw a chair at a nurse, and began breaking the equipment. Once she calmed down, two of Lana's guards escorted her to her room where she attacked her roommate, began throwing furniture across the room, and then started cutting herself when she realized that would keep the guards back. Now she's cornered herself in her room and anytime anyone comes to talk to her she either throws something or cuts herself again."

"What makes you think I will do any better?"

"Because she's been screaming for you ever since you left. So yes, Mr. Burke, I think you'll do better."

I raked my fingers through my hair and exhaled deeply in frustration. This was not what I wanted or needed, life was complicated enough. But unable to turn my back on a young woman who was obviously in great pain, I acquiesced and gestured for Madelyn to show me to Nikki's room.

Even before the elevator doors opened on the fourth floor I could hear the commotion coming from the other end of the hallway. When I rounded the corner with Madelyn I was shocked at the scene of broken furniture scattered amongst other debris in front of an open door where several guards and Lanashell stood trying to negotiate with the screaming woman inside. Lanashell glanced in my direction and immediately came to my side.

"Cameron, thank you for coming. I know this must have been an inconvenience, but as you can see we have been unable to control your hybrid."

"She is not *my* hybrid, Lanashell," I corrected.

"Cameron," Lanashell began in a guarded tone, "you may not be her Gatherer but you brought her here. She has alienated and attacked my staff and several of the other hybrids in the short time she has been here and I will not stand for it. With the current state of things I cannot throw her in the street, but if she does not begin to behave herself and follow our rules, I will force Victor to take her. The Warriors brought Nikki here so they will have to be responsible for her if she continues to behave this way."

"Lanashell, I will speak with her and try to calm her down, but be ready for a fight if you try to force Victor to take her in."

"Trust me, Cameron, I am more than prepared to fight the mighty Victor when it comes to protecting my other hybrids."

I shook my head as I walked into Nikki's room and was startled when a small table crashed into my chest.

"Enough!" I shouted at Nikki once the dust began to settle around me.

Nikki lay crouched on the floor between the two beds in the room. Peeking out from underneath her elbow she quickly rose and threw her arms around me, squeezing my waist so tight it was almost uncomfortable. The fact that she was inflicting even the slightest amount of pain and had just thrown a wooden nightstand made me believe that some of Elaina's experiments had increased her strength.

I looked behind me to see Lanashell and Madelyn standing in the doorway, waiting for some kind of confirmation of my next actions. Truly not wanting to get any more involved with Nikki, but conflicted by her obvious suffering, I reluctantly said, "I will take care of her."

Lanashell nodded curtly before she left the doorway with the guards following behind her. Madelyn stayed for a second longer only to give me a cautious look. "Be sure to tell Miss Brianna happy birthday. I'm sure she's missing you."

I nodded and understood her inferred warning. Nikki was attached to me, literally, and that certainly was not good for me at this moment. Reaching behind me, I pried Nikki's hands from around my waist, pulling her away so that I could talk to her. Her eyes were bloodshot and sullen with dark purple circles underneath. She looked so frail underneath the clothes she had been given that were too big for her. If I had not just witnessed her strength, I would not have thought it possible at the sight of her.

"Nikki, why did you do all of this?" I asked and lowered her to a seated position on the bed behind her that she had stripped of all pillows and linens.

Her eyes were lost in thought as she surveyed the destroyed room around her. When she finally looked back up at me, she shook her head fearfully causing two tears to streak down the length of her cheeks. I nodded as I sighed and turned toward the door.

"Don't leave me!" she screamed as she bolted from the bed and began pulling on my arm in a panic.

"Nikki, ssh," I said in a soothing voice, "I am not going anywhere. I am simply going to clean up the items in the hallway so I can close the door. Ok?"

She nodded slowly as her hold on my arm loosened enough to where I could remove her hand without breaking it. I lowered her back down onto the bed before swiftly bringing the broken furniture, linens, and other debris in from the hallway. I had a feeling Madelyn would be grumbling if she were to find the mess still there in the morning. As I closed the room door behind me I noticed that Nikki had not moved from her position on the bed and looked as though she was in shock with her hands still shaking in her lap. I lifted the comforter from the floor and wrapped it around her.

"Why did you leave me? I woke up and you weren't there."

Knowing I needed to be calm with Nikki in her current state, I took a deep breath and began stretching the linens across the bare mattress while I responded, "Nikki, I have a home and family of my own. I left you in the capable hands of the Facility. As I explained to you earlier, they are here to help you. No one will harm you here."

"That's what they told me, too," Nikki replied as a chill went through her body.

"They?" I asked as I picked up several of the pillows from the floor and tossed them toward the headboard.

"The Vampires at the warehouse."

"Did you go with them voluntarily?"

She nodded as she climbed up to the head of the bed and curled up on the pillows with the comforter secured tightly around her. "The blonde woman told me she'd help me, make me even stronger. B-but...but they didn't help me. It was all a lie. If she was lying about helping me, why should I trust the people here?"

"Why do you trust me?" I asked as I sat on the bed opposite her.

"Because you took me away from there," she said letting her tears soak into the pillow. "When they told me you left, I just got so scared. It felt like I was back at that horrible place. Those people downstairs wanted to take my blood and run tests, then they were holding me down and I started freaking out and everyone was yelling at me and I was just trying to get away…and then…and then I just couldn't think straight. I just did whatever I could to keep them away."

Nikki sat up quickly as she began to cough through her dry throat. I stepped into the bathroom and a second later returned with a glass of water which she accepted gratefully. "I didn't mean to destroy the place. I know cutting myself was really stupid, but they backed off once I did it so I just kept on doing it."

I took the empty glass from her and placed it on the surviving nightstand next to her. "Nikki, we should go to the medical wing and have them examine the cuts you made."

"No need to. See," Nikki replied as she rubbed her forearm under the lamp revealing only thin pale scars.

"These are from this evening?"

"That's why that blonde woman said she wanted me. She called me a Healer. Watch."

In a sudden movement Nikki took a shard of glass from the floor and quickly cut down the length of her forearm. Bright red blood rose out of the large gash causing my throat to burn. I locked down my jaw and turned away looking for anything that I could use to stop the bleeding.

What was she doing? She would bleed out with an injury like this. Ripping the pillow case off of a pillow on the bed behind me, I returned to Nikki's side as she giggled softly under her breath. I reached for her arm where her wound was stitching itself together right before my eyes. Within seconds the thick wound was only a pink scar leaving a thin trail of blood on her arm.

The sight and smell of the fresh warm blood made my throat burn fiercely. My fangs were piercing the inside of my bottom lip as I clamped my mouth tightly and handed her the pillowcase in my hand with which to wipe her blood away.

She took the pillowcase from my hand, but lifted her bloody arm to me. "You can take it…I can tell you want it."

My eyes widened as she placed her arm up to my mouth and suddenly my tongue was halfway up her arm before I realized what I was doing. I thrust her arm away from me and turned my back to her, clamping my hand down tightly around my mouth and nose. Through my fingers I struggled to say, "Forgive me. Please wipe away the rest."

What had I done? This was not me. I did not lose control like this. To take the blood from a vulnerable hybrid was disgraceful and in a small way a betrayal to Brianna.

"Sorry, Cam. It's gone now," Nikki said softly behind me.

"Nikki, my name is Cameron, not Cam, and you must never cut yourself like that again. Understood?" I said as I turned back around. She nodded tentatively and I looked down at the pillowcase still wadded in her hand but saw no blood soaked into its threads. "Nikki, where's the rest of the blood?"

"I drank it," she said softly, suddenly seeming ashamed. "Is that wrong?"

"No. I...I guess not. What I did was wrong. I should not have taken your blood."

"But I gave it to you."

"Which you should not have done. I...I must leave, Nikki. I have to get back to my..."

"Please, Cameron," she yelled as she crawled down to the edge of the bed and took hold of my arm. "I'll never be able to sleep without you here. Please stay, please help me, they'll come for me, I know it."

I could smell the fear radiating from her body as she hugged my arm tightly to her chest and soaked my sleeve with her tears.

"They will not find you here."

"The nightmares are just as bad," she cried. "You don't know what they did to me, you have absolutely NO idea. Every time I close my eyes I see them torturing me, please don't leave me alone, please, please, Cameron. I'm begging you to stay, just until I'm really asleep, please!"

I looked into her eyes and saw the absolute fear behind them. I had seen that level of fear in the eyes of my beloved the night her ex-husband brutally attacked her and I did nothing. Nothing to help her, soothe her, or take away any of her pain. How could I let myself do it again and still consider myself to be a decent man? But then again, how would I explain my absence to Bri? How could I look at myself in the mirror tomorrow morning knowing I could have helped another vulnerable and abused woman?

"Just until you are asleep, but then I must go," I replied reluctantly.

"Thank you, Cam," she said softly as she crawled back toward the head of the bed.

"My name is Cameron," I corrected again.

While Nikki tucked herself into her blankets I turned all the lights off in the room and slumped to the floor with my back up against the opposite bed. This was a bad idea. I knew it was. I could feel it nagging and gnawing at the back of my mind. But after a few minutes of sitting in the quiet darkness I heard Nikki's breath begin to find a slow and constant rhythm meaning sleep was near. My head fell backwards onto the edge of the mattress while I concentrated on the sound of Nikki's breathing. I closed my eyes and still felt a hint of burning in my throat. I was exhausted and needed to feed, which was out of the question at this moment. But while I waited for Nikki to succumb to her own exhaustion I could rest myself. I only needed ten or fifteen minutes and then hopefully Nikki would be asleep and I would be on my way to wrapping myself around my Bri. The plan was simple and easy, and a first for today.

Chapter Five

Cameron

"Hmmm?" I mumbled as my left buttock began to vibrate and the muffled sound of an Irish jig made my eyes flutter open. In front of me Nikki lay curled up as I left her, but something was different. The light in the room was different. Looking past Nikki I noticed a stream of light hitting the cream colored walls. With sudden realization I jumped from the floor and turned to the window to see the morning's sun peeking through the drapes.

How could this have happened? I shut my eyes for ten minutes and slept all night? Shit. Deep shit. Not wanting to waste any more time, I took one last glance at Nikki who did not stir and quickly shut her room door behind me as I stepped into the hallway. Using the strength I had gained from recharging myself, I sped down the hallway and took the stairs to the main level of the building. Even with the amount I had slept, with the level of burning in my throat it was more than evident I would not be able to Project to the manor. I would definitely have to drive, and since I did not come in a car I would most likely have to steal one from the parking lot outside. This morning was already a moral nightmare.

The atrium with its glass ceiling was extremely bright, making me wish I had my sunglasses. My lack of blood was affecting me greatly and I had no one but myself to blame. This was part of my punishment – a morning walk of shame. Thank goodness the lobby doors were only a few feet away.

"Good morning, Mr. Burke," Madelyn said from her receptionist's desk as I passed. I did not stop, but when I peered over my shoulder I could she was giving me a disapproving look over the top of her reading glasses. I did not need her to add to my already overwhelming guilt.

The tall glass doors swished opened as I approached, revealing a cool September morning. The air felt nice and refreshing against my face as I traveled across the large parking lot in search of a vehicle. Actually there was one in particular I was hoping would still be here before I broke into someone else's. Only a few months ago I had brought Brianna to the Facility and had been forced to leave with Devin. I had not even been allowed to gather my things, and had not bothered to do so since then.

I breathed a great sigh of relief when I looked three rows ahead and saw the black sports car parked in the exact spot I had left it. Although it was dirty and covered with pollen it was a sight for sore eyes. As I approached the car I could see my former traveling bag in the backseat along with my leather jacket, which I knew held my old pair of sunglasses. Thank goodness. Maybe today would get better after all. The car door was unlocked and the keys still hung in the ignition. I guess I was a little preoccupied the night I brought Brianna here, but my previous mistake was today's godsend. I reached into the backseat and slid my thin leather jacket on. Not that I needed it, I just liked wearing it and had missed it from my wardrobe. I could hear Brianna laughing at me now.

I pulled the silver aviators from the inside jacket pocket then roared the car to life, letting the engine warm up before pushing it to its limit racing home. Both Facility security gates barely had time to open wide enough to let me pass I was driving so fast. Thankfully my vision was not affected like the rest of my body was by the lack of blood. Just as I turned onto the main road and really tested the engine's abilities, my phone rang.

"Alex?"

"Cam, where are you?" Alexander said in a hushed tone.

"Long story. On my way home now."

"On your way home? From where? Wait, hold on…Kyla, just a minute," Alexander said, pulling the phone away from his ear. The muffled sounds on the other end made me think he had put his hand over the speaker as well while he talked to his wife. Then the line began to thump and shuffle as though there was a struggle for the phone. And I was correct on that point when Kyla's voice came through.

"So you answer the phone when it's him and not me?"

"Is Brianna awake yet?"

"How should I know? I haven't been to your room all night because I wanted to give you two some privacy and then we just saw Devin who said you left last night to go to the Facility to see that crazy pants Nikki girl. Are you telling me you're just leaving from there now?"

"Kyla, it is a long story."

"Well you better hope Bri's not up yet. WTF, Cameron?"

I took a breath before speaking, hearing the leather steering wheel groan slightly at the tightness of my grip. "Kyla, I do not even have the energy to figure out what WTF means. I will be home in seven minutes. Do *not* say anything to Bri if she wakes and starts looking for me. I want to explain everything to her myself. Goodbye, Kyla."

"But wait Ca..."

But I did not wait. I hung up on her. Another un-gentlemanly thing I had done in the last ten hours. But I could not dwell on it, there were other pressing matters. Such as explaining my whereabouts to Brianna, begging for forgiveness, and somehow make up for my unacceptable behavior.

The trees around me eventually gave way to homes and buildings as I sped toward the shore and up another set of winding roads that led me directly to the manor. The front gate stood tall and grand with the Warrior's circular golden coat of arms displayed at the top. The guards at the gate waved me through and I pulled the car into the first available spot in the large gravel driveway located in front of the house. I wasted no time getting inside and did not even stop to remove my jacket and sunglasses as I made my way to the kitchen. Though I desperately wanted to run to Brianna's side, I would be dangerous to her in my current condition. Blood needed to come first.

I stepped around the corner and found Christine, the head of our kitchen staff, placing large platters of fresh eggs and bacon on the main island for other members of her staff to bring out to those humans who were already awake. Not wanting to get in her way, I stepped over to the industrial refrigerator marked "For Vampires Only" and pulled out one of the many bottles of blood located on its shelves.

"Christine," I asked tentatively, "where may I heat this up so that I am not in your way? It is a bit of an emergency."

Christine looked in my direction but did not stop her cooking. "Well the blood warmer is full unless you want to use the microwave. But I know how you all hate the taste after it's been nuked. Actually, Devin's bottle is ready to come out. If you think he wouldn't mind you taking his, I'll put in a new one for him."

Without saying another word I stepped over to the blood warmer, removed Devin's bottle, and replaced it with mine. It only took me three and a half seconds to drink a little more than half the bottle. I could feel the burning in my throat begin to subside as the warm blood flowed down and into my stomach, taking away much of the edginess I felt.

"Thank you, Christine."

"No thanks needed, Cameron. I should really keep an emergency stash heated and ready to go. You all are keeping me on my toes these days," she said as she placed the last of the hour's hot breakfast items on the island.

As I placed the bottle to my lips once again, I could see Devin walking toward me through the darkness of my aviators and the green glass of the bottle.

"That better not have been mine," Devin growled.

"Here, Brother," I said as I pushed myself off the counter and handed him the half-empty bottle. "Do not blame Christine. I took it without permission."

Christine gave me a sly wink as I brushed past Devin and headed out of the kitchen.

"Brother, wait," Devin called after me just as I entered the back stairwell to the living quarters. When I did not stop, he pulled at my elbow to turn me around. "Why are you just returning now?"

I signed as I reluctantly stopped my assent up the stairs and faced him. "Because it has been days since I fed, and between the mission and the Projections I ended up falling asleep and losing track of time."

"You're being careless, Brother. We cannot afford…"

"Yes, Brother, I take full responsibly for neglecting myself. I had planned on feeding once Brianna went to sleep but someone came barging into my room in the middle of night. Oh wait, that was you."

"Lana insisted it was an emergency and Father pushed me to find you. My hands were tied. If the hybrid would have let anyone else help her…"

"I know, Brother," I said putting a frustrated hand through my hair. "Lanashell stated to me last night that if Nikki continues to have these outbursts, she will force Father to take her."

Devin looked stunned. "I'd like to see her try and force Father to do anything. I wouldn't worry, Brother, every hybrid comes around eventually."

"Therein lies the problem, Brother. Nikki trusts no one. She would not even let the medical staff examine her."

"She trusts you."

"And that is problematic for me."

"Perhaps not," he said tapping his index finger on his lip. "Nikki is the only semi-coherent hybrid we have ever come across. She could be the key to helping us find out what Elaina is doing, where she is, and who is working for her. If she already trusts you then let's use that. We could certainly use the help."

"Help with what?" Kyla said from two landings up.

I looked back at Devin, grabbed the bottle of remaining blood, and finished it in three gulps before I said, "No. I will not use Nikki."

The truth was I did not want Nikki becoming even more acquainted with me, she was already too attached. I handed Devin his empty bottle of blood and began my assent to Kyla.

"Brother, we are not finished," Devin said behind me as he followed me up the stairs.

"Yes, Brother, we certainly are," I replied as I reached the landing where Kyla stood with her arms crossed and foot tapping lightly on the stone floor.

"Please tell me you didn't do anything with…" Kyla paused as her eyes unfocused for a spilt second. "Ok, I believe you."

"Do you need me for this conversation, or may I go now?"

"Hey now, Brianna has a hormonal excuse for her rude sarcasm. You do not. I only wanted to know if you'd done something stupid, and then I saw that you answered you didn't. Ok, stupid boy?"

I raised my eyebrows to her and shook my head as I replied, "It does scare me when you start talking like Brianna."

"Well you deserve it. Now go, I don't want you blaming any of your neglect on me."

"Brother wait, we need to discuss what to do with this hybrid," Devin interrupted before I could turn away.

"No. I am not going to discuss Nikki anymore today if I can help it. I am going to my room and hope that Brianna is still sleeping." I turned my back leaving Kyla and Devin standing on the landing, but then quickly turned back. "And Brother, one last thing. You know how much respect I have for you. But if you ever barge into my room without knocking and interrupt me and Brianna like that again I will rip your head off. Show me the same courtesy I would show you if you were with someone."

Devin's eyes dropped to the floor and nodded at my request. As I turned to walk down the hallway I could hear Kyla scolding Devin as they walked down the stairwell and it certainly brought a smile to my face. When I got to my room, I lifted the handle and slowly pushed the door open hoping to find Bri curled up in our bed, but as I poked my head into the room she was nowhere to be seen. The comforter and sheet looked as though she had thrown them off of her making me look towards the bathroom. The door was closed and I could hear her fumbling around inside.

"Cam? Is that you?" she asked over the sound of running water.

"Yes, love. Do you need me?" I answered as I stepped in front of the bathroom door.

"No. Just brushing my teeth. I'll be right out."

With a sigh I walked over my nightstand and opened its drawer. From within it I removed a ring box I had been hiding from Brianna and placed it inside the pocket of my jacket. Next I grabbed the stack of crackers that had somehow made it to my side of the bed, walked back over to the other side, and waited. Painfully waited. Dreadfully waited. The water went on, the water went off. The water went on again, it went off again. How many times was she going to brush her teeth?

Finally the bathroom door creaked open and my pale angel padded back into the room wearing her favorite jersey knit pajamas and thick woolen socks. Her dark hair was matted on one side while the other lay limp and clinging to her neck. She was still the most beautiful thing I had ever seen. When she stepped through the archway she stopped and caught her breath, causing me to immediately step over to her. "Bri, what is it?"

Brianna just stood and stared up at me while I searched her face. Her eyes were slightly glassy with tears as she touched my cheek with her warm fingers.

"I just haven't seen this Cameron in a while. You look like you did the day we met."

"And I still take your breath away?"

"Dressed like that you do. Of course, as usual I look like crap."

"I beg to differ," I replied reassuringly and removed my sunglasses in order to kiss her.

"Not yet," she said, putting her hand up against my mouth. "I think I still have puke breath."

"Nothing kills the mood like the word puke."

"Well, Mr. Smarty Pants, all I have to say is that you did this to me. So it's your own damn fault." Though her tone was serious, she gave me a loving smile.

"Let's get you back to bed," I said, pulling her to the bed and wrapping the blankets tightly around her. "Cracker?"

Brianna smiled sleepily as she carefully took a cracker from the stack and held it to her lips. "Angel."

"Certainly not today," I replied, placing the stack of crackers on the nightstand and then sitting on the edge of the bed. "An angel would have remembered to give the love of his life her birthday present."

Brianna took a bite of her cracker as her eyes widened with excitement. "Do I get my present now?"

"Yes, love," I said, laughing lightly at how adorable she was. I reached into my jacket pocket, pulled out the small ring box, and held it out to her. Her breath caught in her throat at the sight of the box and her excitement quickly changed to dread. Suddenly remembering what an unsympathetic idiot I was, I quickly opened the box. "No need to panic. It is not that kind of ring." Brianna relaxed once she laid eyes on the circular sapphire and diamond ring. "I was not sure what to get you, and I remembered how much you liked the onyx ring and how upset you were when we had to destroy it. And then I remembered you liked the sapphire earrings Father gave you and well here you go." I paused and took a breath, confused by my sudden anxiety. "Can you tell I have not given a gift to a woman I love in a long time?"

"Cam, it's beautiful. It's…it's perfect," she said and held out her left hand.

"Oh no, right hand, my love. You told me very specifically I could not buy you a replacement ring for your left hand," I said teasingly and placed the ring on her right ring finger.

"Well, just not yet," she smiled and held her right hand up to her face, admiring her gift. I felt nothing but relief. Brianna placed both hands on my cheeks and brought me down to her lips. They tasted of crackers and toothpaste, but I certainly did not care. I was simply enjoying the feeling of her warm lips pressing against mine. Unfortunately I was enjoying it too much and my fangs extended quickly. Abruptly I pulled away so that they would not nick Brianna's lips.

"When did you last feed?" she asked with worried eyes as she traced her thumbs lightly underneath my eyes.

"Just a few minutes ago."

"It wasn't enough. How long has it really been? I know you haven't…um…taken it from me in a while."

"Only because I knew you were with child. Even though you would not admit it, I knew. With your…delicate history…I did not want to jeopardize the pregnancy in any way."

"And I understand that, but that doesn't mean you shouldn't take care of yourself. So I ask, for the third time mind you, how long has it been since you really fed?"

I looked down at Brianna's hands. "About two weeks."

"Two weeks! Cameron Jackson, what were you thinking?"

"I was not thinking. Things have been so chaotic and I kept getting pulled away in so many directions that there was not time. I would drink a little here and there, but I never seemed to find the time for what I truly needed."

"Here then," Brianna said as she placed her wrist up to my mouth.

"No, you need your strength."

"So do you," she pressed. "You look exhausted. You have circles under your eyes and your fangs came out right away. All signs that you need to rest and have my blood." I shook my head and lowered her wrist from my mouth but she continued with, "Let's be honest. We both know I have *great* blood, and you're always stronger when you drink from me. So here's what we'll do, I was supposed to train with Devin today and I can tell you that's not happening because I feel like crap. You're weak and need rest, so you're going to drink from me and then we're going to play hooky."

I knitted my brows together. "What is hooky?"

Brianna laughed at my ignorance. "Hooky is where we skip what we're supposed to do and do absolutely nothing else."

"I doubt Father will approve of that."

"Well what good are you to him like this?"

She did have a point. I was basically useless in my current condition and the blood I had just ingested seemed to have little effect. Seeing in my eyes that I was considering her offer, Brianna raised her wrist to my mouth again. Her eyes were pleading me to feed from her and the thought of having her blood made my fangs extend once more.

"Just take it," she said sweetly, "I know you want it."

Just as I was about to pierce Brianna's skin her words rang sourly in my head. Her words were so close to what Nikki had said to me that my entire body was shaken with guilt. Angrily I rose from the bed, ripped my leather jacket off, and threw it on the floor.

"W-what did I do?" Brianna asked painfully.

"Love, you have done nothing. Absolutely nothing. I..." I lowered my head and turned to her. "I need to tell you about something that happened last night."

Brianna's face lost what little color it had. "Ok."

"I know you are aware that we rescued a hybrid from one of Elaina's warehouses last night." Brianna nodded, but looked away from me. "This hybrid we rescued, Nikki, she is very troubled which stands to reason since Elaina tortured her. And though she has not gone into details about what was done to her, the abuse is evident. And...well..." I stuttered, unable to speak at the sight of Brianna breaking down in front of me. "She cut herself in front of me."

"Cut herself?"

"She took a piece of glass and cut down the length of her forearm. There was a good amount of blood and she put her arm right up to my face...and...and I lost control because I had gone so long without a proper feeding and I drank a little of her blood."

Brianna was frozen, simply staring at me and blinking her eyes. Finally she raised her brows and said, "Is that all?"

"Well...no...afterwards I...she asked that I stay until she fell asleep. I was only planning on staying fifteen minutes and then the next thing I know the sun is up."

Brianna was silent for another moment before raising her brows again. "And?"

"And? And then I came straight home to you."

"So you didn't sleep with her?"

"Of course not!" I replied and stepped quickly to the bed, taking her face in my hands. "I would never betray you that way. Is that what you thought I was going to say?"

"What else would I think, Cam? You scared the crap out of me. You took a little blood, big deal. You're a Vampire, it's what you do. Yes, I'd prefer if you didn't drink directly from others, but that's unrealistic sometimes. Do I like the fact that this girl put her arm right to your face? No. Do I blame you? Not really. You lost a little control because you were weak and I think that Nikki is a little bit crazy. Let's just not make it a habit, ok?"

I nodded and kissed her softly, loving every ounce of her caring and forgiving heart. When my lips released hers, my fangs extended once again as she lifted her wrist to my mouth.

"Now open up, big boy."

I smiled slyly and pulled her over to me, letting her straddle my side and nuzzle her head into my neck. Brianna flinched when my fangs pierced the skin of her wrist but then melted back into me as the relaxation of my bite took control of her. The blood filled my mouth and left a warm trail behind as it flowed down my throat and into my stomach. From there I could feel the power in her blood radiate and pulse through my body to the same rhythm of her heart that was beating strongly against my arm.

"Better?" Brianna asked sleepily as she twirled my hair between her fingers.

Even with the small amount of her blood I had ingested my body felt one hundred percent better. Not wanting to take even the slightest amount more than I needed, I retracted my fangs from her wrist and licked the puncture wounds closed.

"Much better," I sighed and kissed the top of her head. "A little different, actually."

"Bad different?"

"Heavens no," I responded, brushing her forehead with my fingers and tucking her bangs behind her ear. "I think it must be the hormones. Your blood is much more potent today. My body feels…I can only describe it as…warm? Like a radiating heat."

"Just another freaky thing to add to the Brianna Morgan list."

"I love every freaky thing there is about Brianna Morgan."

She laughed lightly in my ear as I wrapped my arms around her and closed my eyes while her blood continued to flow and pulse with heat. We sat together for several minutes just enjoying the feeling of one another, not saying a word, more so just being Brianna and Cameron. These moments were rare these days, and I could not take them for granted.

Just then someone rapped lightly on the bedroom door.

"I am knocking, Brother," Devin said from the other side.

"I'm making you tell him I'm not training today," Brianna said as she pushed herself up from her nuzzled position.

"If I must," I sighed dramatically as I opened my eyes to see Brianna stretch her arms above her head. "Oh my god!" I shouted as I stood quickly from the bed.

"What is it!" Brianna shouted at the same time Devin burst through the door ready to strike.

"Brother, what happened?"

I whipped my head between Brianna and Devin, mesmerized by the halos of light surrounding their heads. Devin's was a bright, pure, white light while Brianna's light was crimson red.

"Is…is this what you see, Brianna? The lights?" I stuttered as my hand made a circular gesture around the top of my head.

Brianna's eyes were wide and still frightened by my outburst. "You mean you can see Devin's light? A white halo?"

"Yes, exactly. I…I can see it, and yours, too."

"What do you mean, mine too?"

"Yes, Brother, what do you see," Devin interrupted. "And how are you seeing it?"

"I just had some of her blood. This has never happened before. Devin, your light is bright white, but Bri…yours is red…this is what you see when you need to Push someone." Brianna nodded. "Tell me how."

"You want to use Devin as a guinea pig?"

"Absolutely," I replied, smiling widely.

"Now wait a minute, I did not…" Devin began.

"You let me try this on you and I will forget what happened last night."

"Maybe you will," Brianna grumbled.

Devin stood with his hands on his hips, debating whether the prize was worth the pain if it worked. "I have your word we won't speak of it again? I can't take another round with Kyla."

"I give you my word, Brother. Now Bri, what do I do?"

"Ok, well what I usually do is try to think of my mind actually pushing his light away. Lana always explained it as a tentacle reaching out from you to him. And then sometimes I'll actually thrust my arms out too, it seems to help make the Push bigger. So first step, concentrate on his light. Then just think about reaching out to him, and touch him."

Devin stood a few feet away from me, his body braced for whatever would come. I looked intently at the bright white light surrounding his head and then just as Brianna had instructed, imagined a tentacle extending from within me and pushing Devin away.

Apparently a Vampire with this power needed to use a more gentle touch. In my head I imagined only tapping him, but unfortunately Devin flew back the entire width of our bedroom, hitting the stone wall behind him. When he fell to the floor I felt so bad that I thrust my arms out in apology, but it caused him to fly into the wall again and create a Devin-shaped divot. The Warrior Assassin was none too pleased and quickly began to charge. Afraid of what else I might do, I lowered my arms and prepared for the impact.

"Devin no!" Brianna shouted as she stepped in front of him, thrusting her right arm out and holding it there. Devin's body froze in mid-air, his face contorting in pain while Brianna held him in place. Again I was amazed at what I saw. From the red light that surrounded Brianna's head there was a thin red string of light stretching out and touching Devin's white halo.

"Amazing," I whispered under my breath.

Brianna released Devin from her hold and effectively dissolved the connection between them.

"Amazing what?" Brianna said with worry.

"I could actually see your power leaving you and touching Devin."

"But how? I have never seen lights around hybrids. How are you able to see it when I can't?"

"Maybe it is my enhanced sight capabilities."

"But why now?" Devin asked, still trying to shake the pain and bits of stone from his head. "You've had her blood before. Why would this power suddenly appear? What's changed?"

Brianna's hand floated gently to her stomach. "The baby?"

Devin's eyes grew wide as he stepped to stand between the two of us. "Perhaps the child's powers are already showing themselves. That would be...remarkable. Think of how strong the child will be when he is fully developed."

Brianna's face creased with worry at Devin's statement. I offered her my hand, but she pushed it away and sat at the foot of the bed.

"Thank you, Brother, I think you should be going."

"But we should try and test all that you can do with this new blood. This is something we've never seen before. It could give us an idea of the powers of the child."

"No, no, no!" Brianna shouted from her seated position on the bed, her head resting on her knees. "No tests. No experiments. Just leave it alone, Dev."

"But Brianna…"

"Brother, no more. Brianna and I are going to hooky today."

"Play hooky, babe. We're going to *play* hooky," Brianna said from her lap.

"Oh, well Brianna is ill and must rest, and as you pointed out to me earlier I have been neglecting myself. So today, neither Brianna nor I are to be disturbed. It is for the health of us both. Well, the three of us," I corrected as I knelt down beside Brianna and slid my hand onto her stomach.

Devin sighed and stepped around me to head out of the room. "I will make sure no one bothers either of you today. Including me."

Once Devin secured the door I placed my hands on Brianna's knees trying to get her to look at me.

"Angel, are you all right?"

Brianna lifted her head, tears streaming down her face. "Devin's right. If this is what's happening now, what will happen in eight months? If Elaina finds out…we'll never be safe, Cam."

Brianna's emotions took the better of her as she rested her head on my hands and cried deeply into them. But only a minute later she suddenly looked up, her skin pale and slightly green. I knew that look. In an instant I lifted her from the bed and carried her quickly into the bathroom where she shooed me away before the sickness came out of her. Wanting to give her the privacy she desired, I closed the door and slumped to the floor, feeling useless. As the sounds of Brianna's sickness subsided and then began again I could not get her previous words out of my head. *If Elaina finds out we'll never be safe.*

Elaina. All this time I thought Elaina wanted Brianna for her blood and powers. On the battlefield Elaina even said she wanted what was inside of Brianna. What if Elaina had meant the baby? But how would she have even known? Brianna's dream might be more on target than we thought. If Elaina found out that Brianna was with child, she would be in even more danger. More to the point, if Elaina found out that the child was already showing signs of abilities, there would be no stopping her. I had to protect my love and my child from an enemy I knew nothing about, but one person had survived after being captured and tortured by Elaina. Thankfully, I knew exactly where to find her.

Chapter Six

Brianna

The night was cool and clear with stars shining above me like diamond. Cameron's fingers were gliding gently up and down the back of my arm while he held me against him swaying slightly, almost dancing. The back of my head rested on his shoulder allowing me to look at the city skyline that shimmered in front of us. The scene was beautiful as the lights flickered against the floating autumn leaves carried by a gentle fall breeze that smelled fresh and rustic, similar to the Vampire whose arms were wrapped around me. I didn't recognize the city expanding in front of me, but the scenery wasn't nearly as romantic as when Cameron twirled me around revealing a small beautiful candlelit table for two.

Cameron took my hand and the kisses he gave me on each finger caused goose bumps to rise all over my body. He looked up from my hand, giving me his crooked smile, as always enjoying when he was able to produce this reaction. He rose and turned to lead me to the table, but after two steps I tugged gently at his hand.

Honestly I could have just stood there and stared at how wonderfully masculine he was. His tailored black suit and opened white dress shirt only enhanced his tall, slim, but muscular physique. Cameron's smiling eyes were as dark as his suit and grew curious while I continued to stare at him.

"You humble me when you look at me like that, my love."

"I...I need to ask you something," I stuttered, squeezing his hand in mine.

"Anything, angel," he replied, taking a step back to me and placing his

hand on my round baby belly.

"Will...well someday, n-not today but someday down the road...will you...marry me? Someday?"

Cameron's mouth dropped while his eyebrows rose in shock. "Of course I will marry you, Brianna. I...I would have certainly asked you if I thought for a moment you would have said yes," he said as he swept me off my feet and spun me around our little private tent. His excitement was still obvious after he carefully lowered me to the floor and began shaking his head.

"Cam, what's the matter?"

"This does not feel right without a ring. I wonder if I have anything that will..." he said as he began patting down his pockets.

"But I have a ring," I said and pulled my sapphire ring from my right hand and offered it to him.

He took the ring and gently raised my left hand to his chest and slid the ring onto my finger. He looked at me longingly, holding my left hand flat against his heart and pressing his lips against mine. But after only a moment his lips went still. I pulled away from him and found two cold black eyes staring back at me. His body was rigid and all the love he previously showed in his face had melted away.

"Cam?"

"I must leave," he said unemotionally as he took a step back.

"What do you mean you have to leave? Wait, I'll come with you," I said, reaching out to him as he continued to step back.

"No, Brianna."

"No? What do you mean no?"

From behind him the rooftop door opened and a slim, black-clad figure slinked out from the opening, her long silky black hair billowing all around her. Jazlyn.

"Cameron, what's going on? W-why's she here?"

I was terrified at the sight of Jazlyn striding toward us and eventually taking position next to Cameron.

"I am not who you think I am," Cameron said flatly.

"Wait, what?" I said and placed my hand protectively on my stomach.

"You are not the only hybrid in my life, Brianna."

"What the hell are you talking about? Stop this, Cameron. Stop this right now!"

"Come, Cameron," Jazlyn said, pulling on his elbow, "we must go."

"Get away from him," I shouted at her while trying to remove her hand *from Cameron's arm.*

Jazlyn grabbed my left hand firmly, crushing it to the point of breaking. "Brianna, not all is what it seems."

I clasped my bruised hand to my chest after Jazlyn released it. With another tug on his arm, she led Cameron to the rooftop door.

"Cameron, no! No!" I screamed at him, but he continued to walk away from me.

Just before he disappeared behind the door he turned back to face me, his face still absent of all emotion as he said, "Remember, love, I am not who you think I am."

"NO!" I screamed at the top of my lungs and ran to the door, pulling on the handle but unable to open it. I kicked the door and began banging on it while I screamed, "No, Cameron, no! Come back, no, no, no!"

"Brianna!" someone shouted as firm hands grasped both of my wrists.

I continued to struggle as I opened my eyes to see Victor standing in front of me trying to restrain my hands.

"S-s-sorry, ohmygod, I'm sorry!"

Victor nodded once he felt my muscles relax and gently released my wrists. "Bad dream?"

"You could say that."

"Would you care to discuss it?"

His tone was sympathetic and slightly curious, but in no way did I want to discuss what I had just seen. When I didn't answer, Victor ushered me toward the couch and turned on the gas fireplace that stood in front of it. It was a tender gesture that I certainly didn't expect from the leader of the Warrior coven, but then again I hadn't had that many encounters with him. However, this was certainly the first in my pajamas. The realization made me a little self-conscious. Just as I fidgeted in my seat on the couch, trying to cover what my little white cami exposed, Victor draped the blanket from the adjacent high-back chair over my shoulders. When he stepped around the arm of the couch he glanced down at my left hand. This of course made me look down as well.

"Oh dear, Brianna, I have injured you," he said apologetically and a little fearful. My left hand was slightly swollen and a dark bruise was quickly forming on the back of it. A brown and purplish outline was forming in the shape of thin fingers wrapping themselves around my hand. Then my eyes focused on my sapphire ring that was staring back at me from my left ring finger. That's when I realized my dreams were becoming way too real. Cameron had placed the ring on my left hand, and Jazlyn had almost broken it. And now here I was sitting on the couch with a bruised hand, my ring on the wrong finger, and Victor looking at me like I was crazy.

"This wasn't your fault," I said softly, holding my hand to my chest now that it was starting to throb.

"Has my *child* injured you?"

"Who? Cameron?" I could see little sparks of fury flicker behind his eyes. "No, no, of course not. How would that even be possible, I've barely seen him in the last three weeks." Victor nodded though I could see he was a little uncomfortable with my admission. Well it was the truth. I'd barely seen Cameron since the morning after my birthday, and frankly it was Victor's fault. "No, this is from my dream, a new occupational hazard it seems."

"I heard you screaming for him, Brianna."

"I'd rather not talk about it."

"If it involves Cameron I'd rather we did."

"Like you said, it was just a bad dream that…unfortunately involved a great deal of sleepwalking since I made it all the way over to the door. Trust me, if the dream had any really important stuff in it, I'd tell you."

"Considering your reaction I would say the dream had…"

"Not gonna happen, Victor."

"Brianna this is not…"

"No."

"Are you just as impertinent with Cameron and your own father?"

"Worse," I laughed, causing his firm scowl to stretch into a smile. "Actually there is one dream I wouldn't mind having your input on."

Victor sat in the high-back chair and crossed his legs while bringing his cheek to rest on his hand that was propped up on the armrest. This must be his *ok, I'm listening* pose. "As I said to you once before, I will always be here to listen to whatever you'd like to share with me."

Shifting again on the couch, I pulled the blanket tighter around me since this topic made me feel uneasy. "There is a dream that I keep having, and usually when I have the recurring dreams, those are the ones that come true." Victor nodded, but didn't interrupt at my revelation so I continued. "So remember the day before the manor was attacked and I accidently projected my dream to the entire manor? Well I know everyone only saw a piece of it, and I've actually never told anyone the whole thing before. Er...well Cam knows I guess. Anyway, the fact is Elaina kidnaps me." Victor's fingers fell from his face as he sat up to interrupt but I continued, "I don't know when, and I don't know how. Um...ok, I guess I kinda know when since in the dream I look a million months pregnant, but I don't have an exact date or time if that's what you were about to ask." Victor sighed and sat back in his chair, propping his head back onto his hand. "The reason it worries me even more now is obviously because I'm pregnant."

"Do you recognize any of your surroundings in this dream?"

"No, just that it's an older structure, kind of like the manor."

"And what about people? Do you recognize anyone else besides Elaina?"

"Just...just Jazlyn," I said timidly.

Victor's lips tensed and became thin while he sighed through his nose. But finally he said, "No others?"

"There are, but I'm actually in labor at the time and can't seem to concentrate on anyone else."

"So if this is to happen, we are to assume it is at the end of your pregnancy? That at least gives us something to go on I suppose."

"Here's the thing," I started, but paused as my hormones kicked in and I became quite emotional. "I don't mean to cry in front of you but I'm scared, Victor. I-I don't want to finally carry a child to term only to..."

Unlike Jared who ran from a crying woman, Victor rose from his chair and sat next to me, carefully placing his arm around me and allowing me to use his shoulder to cry on.

"Brianna, I have always hated using the despicable modern slang, but I will tell you that I will not allow...that *bitch*...to touch my grandchild. Are you aware this will be my first?"

"N-no," I sniffled.

"The thought of being a grandfather never interested me, honestly, but now that the opportunity presents itself, I am remarkably overjoyed. Of course if any sire of mine were to have children it would be Cameron. Come to think of it, he is the only one of my children who was ever a father in his mortal life."

If Victor had seen my earlier dream, he might have reconsidered his statement. But quickly I pushed the thoughts out as I tried to focus on one emotional breakdown at a time. I pushed myself off of Victor's shoulder and wiped my eyes and cheeks as I said, "But my question is, why does she want them? Why does Elaina want to take my babies away from me?"

"*Babies?*" Victor said raising both his brows at me.

Crap.

"Rumor has it, well, more like Sera's futuristic visions say I might be having twins."

Victor's face hardened as he rose from the couch. "Brianna, I cannot answer why Elaina wants your children so badly. Unfortunately, I feel that only time will develop that answer. However, if you are having these dreams, I should speak with Alex regarding your security for the outing. Today is a big day."

"Yes, first doctor's appointment *and* first day out of the manor in how many months?"

"You are Rapunzel trapped in a tower until the evil Victor lets you out, is that it?"

"Let's just hope Cameron isn't late breaking me out," I responded, giving Victor a sly wink.

"I cannot see anything pulling him away from you today, not even me."

"Since you've been ordering him to the Facility day and night for the last three weeks there's a good chance that…"

"The Facility?" Victor interrupted, looking extremely puzzled. "Why would I order Cameron to the Facility?"

Victor's statement slapped me across the face. Thankfully I was sitting down. "Because of that hybrid, Nikki. He's been at the Facility with her, I assumed that you…" I said but couldn't finish. I merely pointed in Victor's direction.

Victor licked his lips and held his hands tightly behind him. "I am sure that Cameron's reasons for being there are honorable. I have heard she is having difficulties adjusting, perhaps…"

"Yes, perhaps," I said, cutting him off. I didn't want to hear another word.

Just then a knock came at the door at the same time it opened and Devin peered inside. "Brianna? I am knocking first, like you asked."

"You're getting better, Dev. Next time wait until I say it's ok to come in."

He sighed heavily as he stepped inside the room and then stiffened when he saw Victor sitting next to me. "Father, is everything ok?"

"Yes, child, I was just leaving. I assume you are training Brianna today?"

"Yes, Father," Devin answered stiffly.

"Well then, Brianna, I will bid you good morning. I must consult with Alex on enhancing your security today."

Victor began crossing the room to the door when I said, "Wait! Why were you here? Before, when you found me?"

Victor smiled sheepishly. "I always seem to be at the right place at the right time I suppose. It has always been my gift, among other things of course. I guess fate decided this was an important moment for us."

In a flash Victor left the room closing the door behind him before I could ask anything else.

"Is that true? Or do I have to worry about him being a stalker?"

Devin's previously puffed out chest lowered as he laughed. "He is right. He does seem to have a gift for being at the right place at the right time. Doesn't seem quite fair."

"How's that?" I asked, throwing the blanket off of me.

"Every Vampire has a quirk, their own special gift in addition to what their maker gives them. Father's is that he is always somewhere at the most opportune moment. I, however, am stuck with the sixth sense of feeling when someone's about to die or already dead."

"Well, you are the Warrior Assassin, Dev. I guess it kind of goes hand in hand."

"I'd rather be an opportunist."

"And I'd rather be a figure skater. I don't think either is ever going to happen."

Devin stared me down, trying really hard not laugh. "Get changed, we're training today. No excuses."

"Throwing up everything including my toenails is not an excuse?"

"I'll get you a bucket. Now change."

If I hadn't wanted to hit something so unbelievably hard I would have made a big stink about skipping my training today. Thing was, if anyone could handle my aggression today it was Devin. Not wanting him to think that I was going to train just because he said so, I stamped my foot and dramatically stalked off into the closet. Unfortunately my dramatic exit was cut short when I had to quickly veer into the bathroom for my usual spell of morning sickness. Devin would certainly need more than a bucket. An industrial sized hamper seemed more appropriate.

"Brianna! What is that god forsaken song you're singing in my head!" Devin shouted as he whipped his daggers around, hitting mine and causing them to fall on the mat.

"Sorry, I heard it on a commercial and now I can't get it out of my head," I said wearily as I picked my daggers up.

My grand idea of being able to pummel Devin in order to get out some much needed frustration completely backfired. It had been several weeks since I'd trained, and it certainly showed. Devin was more than willing to tell me over and over again how much I'd forgotten. Funny enough he did keep his promise, at the edge of the mat was a bucket which he mandated I use since he wouldn't allow me to stop training. I loved Devin, but I don't think he took into consideration that the others training around us wouldn't appreciate me puking while they worked.

I looked up to see Devin shaking his head at me. "Brianna, stop thinking of silly songs and concentrate. You keep turning your wrists down, you are better than this. Now pick up your feet, your footwork is a mess. Let's do it again, and concentrate."

The others in the room glanced at us while Devin yelled at me. I just wasn't in the mood. All my anger from before had turned into a mushy hormonal breakdown. His shoulders fell when he saw the tears escape down my face.

"Please stop crying," he whispered guiltily.

"Then stop yelling at me."

"I wasn...never mind. Let's just try it one more time. We only have a few minutes before Cameron comes to get you."

The thought of Cameron coming for me brought on another wave of something I couldn't describe, but it came with a boost of energy so I used it. I thrust both my daggers at Devin who quickly hit them away but lost his balance slightly when I began thrusting questions in his head.

Did you know that Cameron's been spending all his time at the Facility?

Devin didn't respond and instead swung his daggers around. With three powerful bursts I Pushed him across the mat and hit back with my silver daggers. I gripped the rounded handles tighter in my hands, feeling the swirls of pearl and silver melt into my palm.

Did you know he's spending his time with that hybrid?

"Her name is Nikki."

"I don't give a shit," I shouted out loud and continued my assault on Devin. *Did you know that he's there on his own? Victor didn't order him there?* I screamed in his head causing his eyes to squint in pain as he deflected my dagger away from his shoulder.

"Brianna, concentrate," he growled as we spun around with our daggers entwined. He was avoiding my question. It made me so angry that I Pushed harder against his essence to thrust him away and untangle my daggers from his. Devin came back at me with full force without a second's hesitation. As he raised his daggers to hit me from above, I hit his thrust away and lunged forward as I shouted in his head, *Is Cameron having an affair?*

Devin was taken completely off guard and his block was completely useless which allowed my dagger to sink into his abdomen up to the hilt. In a panic I released my grip on the dagger, forgetting to take it out, and dropped my other to the floor as my hands flew to my mouth in horror.

"Dev, I'm sorry. So sorry."

Devin was silent as his chest rose and fell while his nostrils flared. "Just take it out," he growled.

With a shaking hand I grasped the silver handle and slowly pulled it out of his stomach. His face grimaced and snarled until the tip of the dagger was finally out. I kept telling him to put on some kind of armor or chainmail. But no! The mighty Warrior Assassin liked to practice without it. So it's his own damn fault. He turned away from me and walked to the edge of the mat and continued to pant in anger while the wound closed. Everyone's eyes were on Devin and they were all asking the same question: What would he do now?

Finally Devin's breathing began to slow and he suddenly realized that everyone was looking at him. In a deep authoritative voice he said, "Unless you all want to challenge me right here and now I suggest you get back to work."

Everyone in the room scrambled back to training. No one wanted to challenge Devin, including me. When he turned around, the anger was still evident on his face but melted away by the time he stood in front of me.

"Brianna, I know my brother, and he would *never* do such a thing to you."

"I haven't seen him in two days, Dev. Literally two days, me-him-no-see. Why would he…I never thought he…then Victor said…ugh I can't even think straight."

Devin placed a comforting hand on my shoulder and squeezed it gently.

"Cameron is working hard like all of us to find Elaina. He and I believe that Nikki could be the key, but she will only talk with him. I know it has been difficult for you, and trust me it has been for him as well. But I see Nikki coming around soon and life will get back to normal." I actually snorted at his comment which also made him smile a little. "As normal as our lives can be. Our time is up anyway. Any second now Cameron will be coming through that doorway and all of this will seem silly to you. I guarantee it."

Devin absolutely believed what he was telling me, and in a way I believed him. My loneliness and hormones were becoming a dangerous combination. Releasing a deep sigh I wiped down my daggers before Devin escorted me toward the door. As we approached, Kyla stepped into the training room with a tense look on her face.

"We have to get going, you only have ten minutes to get ready. Victor changed a few things and we need to leave a little earlier than planned."

"Where's Cameron?"

Kyla looked over my shoulder at Devin before saying, "He called a few minutes ago. He…said…he'd meet us at the doctor's office."

I whipped my head around to face Devin, looking to see if he still believed what he had told me earlier, but he gave me nothing. I pushed past Kyla who tried to look encouragingly at me. When we reached my room I jetted for the closet, pulled out a pair of jeans and a sweater and headed into the shower. Once the shower door closed I heard the bathroom door creak open and Kyla's orange hair peek through the opening.

"Ky, I want to know everything he said. I mean everything."

Kyla stepped fully into the bathroom, choosing to sit up on top of the sink's counter while I threw bottles of shower gel around trying to find one that had even a remote amount left to use. I wasn't mad at the soap or Kyla or Devin. I was mad at Cameron. It didn't happen very often, but right now I was furious at him. All I really wanted to know was why Miss Tricky Nikki was so much more important to him than me. I doubted that Kyla had the answer hidden in the few words she shared with him when he called. I also wasn't sure I would be able to stand listening to any explanation he may have. I just didn't have the patience today.

To me it was simple. He should be here with me right now and he wasn't. Nothing really happened at the first doctor's appointment, but that wasn't the point. Cameron promised me he'd be with me every step of the way. So far, my footprints were well ahead. Alone.

Chapter Seven

Brianna

When the time comes for most women to choose an obstetrician they consider things such as the doctor's credentials, number of births, acceptance of unique birth plans, and in some cases the size of their hands. I seriously doubt that few chose their doctor based on the number of entrances and exits within their building, clear evacuation paths, and not being a member of the Vampire network. Who knows, maybe they do. Dr. Peter Saunders's practice was small but catered to the elite and those who needed to be discreet. I'm sure some people even used aliases, as I did, leaving no trail whatsoever. All things I never really thought about when it came to having a baby. But life was different now.

Kyla and Alex sat on either side of me in the chic waiting room. Alex of course was getting the usual stares from the others in the room while he read a parenting magazine, and Kyla couldn't stop telling me that Cameron would be walking through the door any minute. I looked pathetic turning my head every time the door opened and revealed someone other than Cam.

I was mad and getting madder at every passing second. When we left the manor and played our shell game with multiple SUVs, I kept telling myself that Cam would make it. He wouldn't break my heart like this. He loved me. He was my Cam. However, when the black sports car he'd been driving for the last few weeks sped past us going in the direction of the manor my doubt took over. I had seen the quick glance Kyla and Alex gave each other when the car passed, but neither looked back at me. I knew they were hoping I hadn't seen it, so they chose not to acknowledge it. Very Southern of them

I'd say. If you don't acknowledge it, it doesn't exist.

"Joanne Jones?" a nurse said as she stepped through the doorway that led to the examinations rooms.

I was so lost in thought that Kyla elbowed me when I didn't answer. "Come on, *Joanne,*" she said, bugging her eyes at me.

I rose from my seat with Kyla right behind and followed the nurse down the hallway. Joanne Jones was my grandmother, otherwise known as Mama Jo, before she married Daddy O. I figured someone would have to go digging to pull up that information. Jared had told me to pick something random, but I couldn't see myself answering to something I didn't recognize. Now I realized I didn't answer to something that was familiar either. I was a moron.

The original plan was Cameron would be with me in the room, Alex and Kyla in the waiting room, the other three Warriors at strategic spots within the building. When my name was called and Cameron was still not there, I guess Kyla had decided she would be in the room with me. She was my friend, don't get me wrong, but I almost wanted to be alone rather than have a replacement for Cam.

Within minutes my blood pressure, heart rate, and temperature had been taken. All normal, but on the low end. Duh, half-Vampire. A few minutes later Dr. Saunders introduced himself and mistook Kyla for my lesbian lover.

"Um no, this is my...my sister, Kyla."

"Oh yes, I can see the resemblance. It's the eyes more than anything," Dr. Saunders said before flipping through my chart. "So Ms. Jones, you're here because you think you're pregnant. Is that correct?"

"Yes!" Kyla squealed from her chair next to the examination table.

"And your sister seems very happy about that," he laughed lightly.

"You have no idea," I replied and rolled my eyes.

"Since we don't have your full medical file I must ask, is this your first pregnancy?"

I swallowed hard knowing the question would come up at one point. "No."

"How many children?"

"None," I replied, suddenly having to clear my throat. "I tend to miscarry within the first trimester."

"How many miscarriages have you had?" Dr. Saunders asked while he took copious notes.

Kyla snuck her hand over mine as I tried keeping in the emotions that were starting to flood over me. "Twelve."

Dr. Saunders quickly looked up from his notes. "Twelve in what kind of time period?"

"Over fourteen years, but five in the last two. The last one was five months ago."

Kyla's hand squeezed mine even tighter, digging my sapphire ring into my finger. It was painful, but it was the only thing that kept my tears from coming.

Dr. Saunders continued, "All the same father?"

"Those? Yes. This one, new guy." Who wasn't here.

"Well first thing's first we should make sure you're pregnant which we'll do with a simple blood test and we'll do a full work up. Now will the father be involved?"

That was certainly a loaded question. I was about to open my mouth when Kyla interrupted instead, "Yes he will be. He was unexpectedly detained today."

Unexpectedly detained? Unexpectedly detained! I felt like my head was going to explode. Or maybe it was just my hand since Kyla was squeezing the crap out of it causing me to finally pry it out of her grip.

"Well, Ms. Jones, with your history you'll need as much support as possible. Also, with the number of miscarriages I am obviously concerned with getting you to full term. Therefore diet, exercise, and more specifically a reduced amount of stress are vital." Well that was easier said than done. Kyla even let out a nervous laugh. Either Dr. Saunders didn't hear her or ignored it as he continued, "I will send the nurse in to draw your blood and she'll give you some vitamins and some material regarding diet. We'll get the test results by tomorrow and if it's positive we'll schedule a future appointment for an ultrasound. Sound good?"

"Yes, thank you, doctor," Kyla said standing and shaking his hand. I could only look at her in awe. I wondered if she would just have the baby for me as well.

"Good day, ladies. Ms. Jones, I'm sure we'll see you in a few weeks."

As soon as Dr. Saunders closed the door behind him Kyla was squeezing me tightly around the neck. "I'm sorry, Bri."

I patted her arm lightly. "You're choking me, Ky."

Kyla released me and I could see a tiny red tear bubbling up in her eye. "I didn't know that you'd had…"

"Don't want to talk about it," I said, cutting her off and wiping my sweaty palms on my pants.

"Are you ok then?"

"No, I'm not. He missed it, Ky. He couldn't pull himself away from Nikki for an hour?"

"I'm sure he has a good reason for not being here."

"It won't be good enough."

Kyla put her hand on my shoulder to calm me and opened her mouth to speak, but just then the door opened. Both of us looked expectantly at the doorway but were completely dejected when the nurse entered the room.

I didn't say a word while the nurse took my blood and then sent me on my way with pamphlets and prenatal vitamins in hand. Kyla held me firmly around my waist as we exited the waiting room. Alex stood protectively in front while the other Warriors filed in around me as we squeezed into the elevator. If I didn't love Alex the way I did, I would have forced him to take the stairs. Elevators were not made to fit a man of his size and have other people be able to fit as well.

The elevator's display began ticking down when Alex turned his head and said, "Bri, why don't you do a scan before the doors open."

I nodded, closed my eyes, and with a deep breath I stretched my mind out as far as it would go, looking for any other Vampires other than those who were cramped around me. Just before we reached the first floor my eyes flew open and I gasped.

"Vamp! Vamp in front of the door."

I could see a Vampire's essence waiting and coming in line with us as the elevator sank to the first floor. Everyone in the elevator tensed and Alex's muscles bulged under his shirt as he braced himself for whatever awaited. I was completely hidden behind him, and Kyla's grip was firm around me until right before the doors opened.

"Everyone can relax," she said just as doors opened and revealed a relieved Cameron. Kyla and Alex turned to me with encouraging grins on their faces, but I wasn't having it.

Cameron's hopeful smile faded when I didn't run to his arms. He was even more surprised when I stepped out of the elevator and walked right past him toward the doors. My entourage was a little confused as well and didn't know whether or not to follow after me or stay with Cameron. No one expected me to walk away from him, especially Cameron.

When I actually stepped outside and started walking down the stairs toward the parking lot everyone came running. The next thing I knew I was surrounded by Warriors with Cameron standing in front of me and Kyla barking orders to everyone else.

"Right, so Brianna you'll go with Cameron, and the rest of us will follow you in the SUV."

"No, Kyla, I'll be going with you. Alex, can you pull the truck around?"

Alex glanced at Cameron whose face was scrunched with confusion.

"Now, Bri," Kyla chimed in sweetly, "don't you want to…" she began but I turned on her and gave her a murderous look. "Ok we'll go get the truck."

As soon as Alex and the entourage had stepped off the sidewalk Cameron immediately started in with the apologies. "Bri, angel, I'm sorry. It has been a difficult day and a few things landed in my lap."

"Was it Nikki? Did *Nikki* fall into your lap?"

Cameron was shocked at my accusatory tone. "Love, I sincerely apologize for being late. Maybe the doctor can talk to us both now that I'm here."

"There's nothing more to talk about. I have everything I need to know," I said, waving my pamphlets in the air. "But maybe you could speak with Dr. Saunders and he could tell you about how much support I need because of my history, and then maybe you could explain to him how you'll never be able to give that to me because you're a big stupid jerk."

"Excuse me?" Cameron said angrily just as Alex's SUV pulled up next to us. "Brianna, you have no idea what happened today."

"Then why don't you tell me. Why don't you tell me what was so much more important, Mr. Burke," I said, opening the passenger door to the SUV not caring that our fight was now public. Cameron glanced at the passengers in the truck and became suddenly quiet. "Nothing? I get no explanation?"

"Bri, I do not want to do this here. We can talk while I drive you home."

"What is it you're going to tell me that you don't want them to know, Cam? Does it have anything to do with you speeding back toward the manor? I saw someone else in the car, Cameron, I'm not blind." I turned into the truck and found Alex and Kyla gapping at me. "And don't think I didn't see you guys notice him too."

Cameron's lips tightened as his chest began heaving slightly. Finally he gave up his fight and said, "I had to bring Nikki to the manor." The passengers in the SUV shifted uncomfortably in their seats while I stared dumbfounded at Cameron standing before me defeated with his hands resting on his hips. "That is why I was late. Nikki has been getting out of control again and Lanashell demanded that I take her to the manor. After fighting with both Lanashell and Father, I got Nikki settled and I rushed here hoping I would make it. I truly am sorry, Bri. I did everything I could to get here. Honestly I did."

"So you're telling me that the girl you've been spending all this time with, time away from me, is now living in our home?"

"I had no choice," Cameron answered and took a step toward me, but I put my hands up in front of me.

"You're such a liar."

"Brianna, no, that is…"

"Anyone else could have done it, Cam. How many other Warriors are there in the manor? How many people work at the Facility? All you had to do was ask someone else to do this. That's all it would have taken. But no, once again little Miss-I'm-Needy takes you away from me and you can't help but be at her side. Who cares that you missed the appointment, right? No big deal, right? It was a big deal for me, Cam. Every step of the way, huh? Well you must have meant being there for someone else because it certainly wasn't me. I can't believe my friggin' dream was right."

"Now wait a minute," Cameron shouted, grabbing me around my elbow as I turned to step up into the SUV. "Everything I am doing right now is for you and the safety of our child. Do not even begin to assume that I do not think of you every second that we are apart. All of this is for you, Brianna. I missed the first appointment, forgive me, there are larger things at stake here. And truly, what all did I miss?"

Stupid, stupid boy! I was so angry at him that I could feel the blood rushing to my cheeks.

"Even Sam made the first appointments, Cameron."

Fury burned behind Cameron's eyes. I had hit a nerve and I wasn't sorry for it. I turned and stepped up into the passenger seat but when I went to pull the door shut, Cameron's hand grabbed the door and held it open.

"How dare you compare me to him! That is NOT fair," he shouted.

"The truth isn't always fair," I snapped. Cameron stood with the door open and continued to fume but no more words came from his mouth. "Can we go now, please?" Alex turned his head and glanced at Cameron seeking approval. "Don't look to him for permission. I'm asking you to take me home. Please, Alex."

Alex turned back to the steering wheel and put the SUV in gear. Without saying another word Cameron slammed the door and watched us pull away.

"I didn't mean to yell, Alex."

"It's fine, Bri," he replied, reaching back with his arm and patting me gently on the knee.

The rest of the ride was silent which initially was fine but then it became uncomfortable. My life was crumbling around me and I had no idea how to stop it. As the manor drew closer all I could think of was that somewhere inside was Miss Tricky Nikki, laughing and licking her chops. I didn't want to go home. A panic started burning inside me; I didn't want to go home with her there. But just as Victor had said earlier, I was Rapunzel and I was being driven back to my tower.

"Are you going to answer that, sweetie?" Kyla asked softly from the front seat.

My cell phone was ringing from within my purse and again I was so deep in thought I wasn't hearing anything around me. I ruffled through my purse trying to find the phone, although I assumed it was Cameron, but I was actually surprised when I saw the number.

"Dad?"

"Bonjourno, mia figlia," Eris said cheerfully. His cheerfulness was a little harsh against what I was feeling at the moment.

"Not a good time to talk. I…ah…"

"Yes, daughter, I know," Eris said in a softer tone doing away with his thick Italian accent. "I wanted you to know that the jet will land at a private airfield in San Francisco in about twenty minutes but you can leave whenever you like. I'm sending you the information now. The flight is only an hour and ten minutes. Sera has even prepared a room for you. We cannot wait to see you."

"W-what?"

"You are coming to see us, daughter. Sera had the vision this morning. It is what you need, Brianna - some time away to relax and gather your thoughts."

I sat dumbfounded in the seat. Kyla turned in her chair staring intently at me. I did hate that I could never have a private phone conversation with Vampires around. My father was right though, it was exactly what I needed. Time away. Time for Cameron to get his shit together and not take advantage of the fact that I was always there laying in waiting. I'd become complacent again and that was unacceptable.

"I'll see you in a couple of hours then, Dad."

I could hear his excitement as he hung up the phone. Kyla on the other hand was quite the opposite. "What do you think you're doing? You can't leave the manor! You can't...you can't leave..."

"Cameron? And actually I can him, but that's not what I'm doing. I just need to get away from everything right now. And yes, maybe this'll teach Cameron a lesson. I refuse to always be second fiddle, especially now. Besides, I should be allowed to go see my father when I choose to."

"You will have to get Father's permission," Alex said from the driver's seat.

"Then I will get permission. And if Victor says no, then he'll have to deal with Eris."

That certainly shut everyone up and I meant every word I said. At times like these I was grateful for having a feared Vampire for a father. In a few short hours I would be sitting on my father's balcony overlooking the ocean and...and...and what? Crying that Cameron was slipping away from me? That I might be pregnant and alone? Yup that sounded about right. At least the view would be nice.

Chapter Eight

Cameron

When Brianna drove away I was furious. Furious at her for comparing me to Sam, furious at Alexander for driving away, and furious at myself for everything I had done to cause Brianna such pain. As usual she called me out on my faults and I had more than taken advantage of the trust she had for me. I was too arrogant to believe that our love would ever crack or be tested as it had been these last few weeks. In no way was I prepared for it to shatter as it did in front of members of my family. Brianna's wrath would be nothing compared to what awaited me from Kyla. She may have known me longer, but Brianna was her dear friend and only real female companion at the manor. Hurting Brianna meant hurting Kyla, which was bad news for me.

After Glamouring Dr. Peter Saunders into telling me the same information he had given Brianna, I pushed the sports car's engine to its limit for the third time within the last couple of hours. The smell of citrus still filled the cabin and wafted from my clothes. It had been difficult to pry Nikki off of me when I left her at the manor, and the sting of her lingering lemony fragrance burned my nose, making me resent her even more. Brianna had been right, I could have forced Nikki to go with someone else, but I found it difficult to be cruel to her after all she had been through. As the manor drew closer I could feel that difficulty lessening.

After I had passed through the manor's tall black gate, I was puzzled at the sight of Alexander's SUV parked in front of the main entrance along with several other manned vehicles preparing to leave. What had happened?

How had a mission been commissioned within the last hour? I sped up to the front of the driveway and then spun the backend of the car out causing an immediate stop and a spray of gravel and dust to float in the air.

I leapt from the car and came to Alexander's side just as he stepped down onto the driveway. "What has happened? Did Elaina surface?"

Alexander's face was shadowed by the sun that his body eclipsed as he stood in front of me, but through it I could still see the sadness in his eyes. "No, nothing to do with Elaina."

"Then why the escort?"

"Cam," he sighed, his face contorting in conflict, "you need to talk to Brianna. Right now."

His firm tone caused my stomach to drop and a sudden panic to erupt within me. As I fled up the first two steps toward the main entrance to the manor I closed my eyes and Projected myself into my bedroom. Brianna saw me immediately as she stepped out of the bathroom and handed a bag to Kyla.

"Ky, can you take this downstairs?" Brianna said. "I'll meet you at the car."

"Brianna, what are you doing?" I asked, taking a step closer to the bed where my large red suitcase lay open.

"She's being ridiculous is what she's doing," Kyla shouted as she took the bag from Brianna's hands and turned to leave the room, her face streaked with watery red tears.

After Kyla slammed the bedroom door behind her, I stepped alongside the bed and took Brianna's hands in mine, stopping her progression of filling the suitcase with clothes that were scattered around it.

"Brianna stop, what are you doing?"

"What does it look like I'm doing, Cam? I'm leaving," she replied flatly, ripping her hands out of my grip.

"Leav...leaving? Where are you going to go?"

"I'm going to see Eris and Sera."

"For how long?"

"For as long as I need to be away from here."

Brianna stuffed the remaining items into the suitcase but became flustered when the zipper would not close. I tried closing my hand around hers to get her to stop her assault on the suitcase, but she slapped my hand away and then cursed herself from the pain it caused. I took her by the shoulders, turning her body to face me and in her eyes I could see the anger that stirred behind them.

"Brianna, I know you are angry with me, but I cannot let you leave. It is too dangerous out there for you and…and I will not let you go until we talk about this like adults."

Brianna's face softened slightly and she took both of my hands in hers. The fire inside of me began to fade and I actually exhaled with relief.

"Cameron," she began in a calm voice, "this is happening. I'm going to see my father and you can't do anything to stop me."

Brianna threw my hands away from her as I stood shocked at the words that came across her lips. She took the suitcase from the bed, not caring that the zipper was open at the top.

"Angel, stay," I begged as she brushed past. "Do not separate us like this. Think of the baby."

Brianna whipped back around, the anger once again burning behind her eyes. "I *am* thinking of the baby." Tears began to trickle down her face. I took a step closer only to have her take a step back. "I can't stay in this house and be constantly reminded that so many other things are more important to you than me."

"There is nothing more important to me…

"Then where have you been the last three weeks, Cam? Certainly not with me."

I sighed as I put a frustrated hand through my hair and tugged at the ends of it. "I have been working with Nikki in order…"

"I don't even want to hear her name, and I refuse to stay here with her under the same roof. God only knows what will happen now when all you have to do is walk down the hall to see her."

"Brianna, are you excusing me of something?" I asked through tight lips.

"All I know is that she was twenty minutes away and you were with her day and night. What will it be like when there are only a couple of floors separating the two of you?"

Though I did not need the air, my breath began to quicken with her accusation. "I swear on my late wife and child that I would *never* betray you like that. Besides, in no way do I even find her remotely attractive."

Brianna bit her lower lip and closed her eyes tightly. Another tear trickled down her face and her voice waivered as she said, "Maybe you don't, but you kowtow to her every need. I'm…I'm just too tired to compete with her."

"There is nothing to compete for, Bri. I am yours and no one else's.

Please do not push me away like this."

Brianna's tears suddenly stopped. "Me? I'm pushing you away? You've abandoned me for weeks, Cameron! I can't keep doing this. Sam neglected and hurt me for fourteen years. I'm not letting it happen to me again."

Brianna turned away from me, suitcase in hand, and began walking to the door. Only letting her get three steps away I grabbed her elbow and turned her back around. Warm tears streamed down her cheeks and over my hands as I placed them firmly on either side of her face. "I. Am. Not. Him."

Her bottom lip trembled as she opened her mouth to speak through her sobs. "B-but you're…b-breaking my heart and…I'm just as alone."

Her sorrow overwhelmed me. I loved her with every ounce of my being and yet she did not believe it. Without thinking I crushed my lips onto hers, I did not know what else to do. Brianna kissed me with great passion, only removing her lips to take gulps of needed air. I could feel her sadness and longing in every movement of her lips and tongue. Her tears continued to flow and began to drip onto my face. When at last I thought I had won her back, she Pushed me with her mind projection, but only enough to make me step away from her.

"I can't do this," she whimpered as she turned away from me again and opened the door.

"Brianna, no," I shouted at her as she stepped into the hallway. Just as I crossed the threshold I was thrust backwards into the bedroom, my head pounding with the feeling of Brianna's mind projection rattling inside. Shaking the pain out of my head, I got up and ran into the corridor to find that Brianna had already made it halfway down the stairs. She looked up to see me following after her and within seconds I was flying backward again. Her second Push was more intense and painful than her first. She did not want me to follow her, but I would not stop fighting for her. Though my head was weak with pain, I closed my eyes and Projected myself into the foyer of the manor just as Brianna stepped out the main entrance.

"Brianna, I am begging you to stay," I growled as I wrapped my fingers around her arm. "Think of all we have been through together, please just give me one more chance. I cannot bear to be without you or our child. Our baby, love, please stay with me for our baby's sake."

Devin stood just inside the doorway, his arms outstretched defensively toward me, ready to pounce if Brianna gave him the word. Brianna turned her head slowly and met my eyes. I could tell she was conflicted. Her body was pulling away from me, but in her eyes I could see she was on the cusp of staying. I just needed to keep eye contact with her for a few moments longer and I knew her body would respond.

"Cam, what's going on?" I heard Nikki say behind me. The fragile connection I had with Brianna was lost at the sound of another woman calling me Cam.

"Let me go, Cameron," she said angrily. She tried pulling her arm away and I squeezed it harder, regretting the pressure with which I was holding her, but still unable to let her go. "Devin, make him let me go."

There were no more tears flowing out of Brianna's eyes, only anger and betrayal. She had all the proof she needed. Devin stepped between us and wrapped his hand around my wrist while placing his other on my shoulder.

"Brother, let her go."

"N-no."

"Do not make me hurt you in front of her. Let her go," he said in a gentle tone.

"I cannot," I whispered unable to move my fingers from around Brianna's arm.

Devin's grip around my wrist tightened though his tone was still even and soft. "I am here for you, Brother. I will help you, but you must let go of her. It is what she wants."

I looked into Brianna's eyes one more time and whispered that I loved her. A single tear slowly traveled down her cheek before she slipped her arm out of my grip. She turned and walked out the door of the manor and into the arms of Kyla. Devin held me by both shoulders while I struggled against him, trying to run to her. The last glance I had of my angel was of her sobbing in the SUV's backseat before Alexander sped away.

I screamed in agony when they disappeared out of the gate. Devin's hold on me tightened as I slumped over, placing my hands on my knees. The room was spinning similar to the way my life was spinning out of control. A million emotions came flooding into my head and I slowly rolled up to be eye level with Devin. My chest began to rise and fall in deep heaving breaths. I could feel the anger rising inside of me and Devin could see it, mainly because I was acting just as he often did when his anger consumed him.

"Steady, Brother," Devin warned.

I turned my head to see Nikki standing apart from the other humans that were escorting her. They pulled at her arms unsuccessfully as I stepped slowly toward her. I could feel Devin hovering at my heels, afraid of what was going through my head. I was only inches away from Nikki, and I towered over her.

"You have stripped me of everything I love and hold dear. There are only two people in my life I allow to call me anything but my true name, and you are not one of them. Because of you, the mother of my child believes that I have been unfaithful. If you ever utter that name, or come near me again, so help me I will hurt you and accept Victor's wrath proudly."

Nikki shook fearfully in front of me when finally one of the humans took her by the arm and led her away. Now it was only Devin and I standing in the entranceway which only caused the anger and loneliness to flood over me. My chest began to heave again and I felt as though I was going to explode.

"How could you, Brother," I shouted at him as I grabbed his shirt collar and thrust him up against the tapestried wall. "How could you let her go? You know the dangers that are out there for her. Father will be furious to know you just let her walk out of here."

"Brianna received Father's permission to go," he replied in an oddly sympathetic tone and did not fight against my grip on him. "Since she was going directly to Eris's, Father felt the dangers were minimal. He demanded that we comply with her request, so my hands were tied. And frankly, Brother, she's not happy and had every right to go."

I stepped away from him and felt the room closing in on me. The long entryway table hit the back of my legs and in a flash I swept the entire table clean of vases and other decorative trinkets causing them to crash loudly onto the stone floor.

"Feel better?"

"Not in the slightest," I replied, looking down at the shattered glass and ceramics on the floor and seeing the similarities of how I felt inside.

"Let's hope that wasn't one of Father's favorite Ming vases."

"Thankfully for your sake it wasn't," Victor said tersely from a few feet down the hall. "Both of you, with me."

Devin gave me an apologetic look, but I knew whatever scolding Victor needed to give me I most likely deserved. Now that oxygen was finally reaching my brain I could see that my behavior had been less than admirable, and nothing in the way a Warrior of Victor's coven should act. We followed my father down the main corridor toward his private study which was just off the large ballroom. Just passing the ballroom reminded me of holding Brianna in her beautiful white dress while I danced with her the night of her Claiming. With the memory came another piercing pang of grief in my stomach as the fear of never holding her in my arms again took hold.

Devin saw that I was more than preoccupied and steered me into Father's study. Victor sat behind the desk in his specially made chair that elevated him to a height that would make anyone forget his small stature. Devin stood strong behind me, showing me his support, but I knew he was really behind me in case I got out of control again.

"Today has not been a good day," Victor began matter-of-factly, his voice rough with age and authority. "There are many things I do not appreciate, and one of them is having to defend myself against Brianna this morning while she screamed the words 'No, Cameron, no. Come back, no, no.' She was having the most terrifying dream which she refused to share the details with me. Regardless, it obviously had something to do with you, child, and I am wondering if you have any insight."

"No, Father," I responded, although I did recall Brianna shouting something at me while we fought in the doctor's office parking lot about her dream being right.

But I was unable to ponder the thought further when Devin said, "Father, if I may interject, during my training session with Brianna this morning she stated she had fears that Cameron was having an affair."

Victor's eyebrows rose. "Are you, child?"

"No!"

"And I told her as such, Brother, but she believes you are having an affair with Nikki."

"That hybrid you brought to the manor today?" Victor asked and I nodded. "Ah, I see. Well that certainly does lead me to my next point. I take responsibility when someone is angered by my actions. Therefore, I do not appreciate being disliked when I have not earned it. Needless to say I was quite confused when I learned that Brianna was under the impression that I had actually given you an order to stay at the Facility, hence blaming me for your neglect of her."

My head fell into my hands as puzzling parts from earlier in the day began piecing themselves together. "I assume you told Brianna that I was there on my own, so when I missed her appointment because I was bringing Nikki to the manor that basically solidified her suspicions."

I felt Devin's hand squeeze my shoulder while I massaged my temples.

"Let us move to the next item I did not appreciate today," Victor said as he stepped down from his chair and slowly walked around to the front of the desk. "I *truly* do not appreciate being told what to do, especially from one such as Lanashell. Needless to say I am furious at being forced to take a hybrid into my home - especially one who seems so troubled and disrespectful. Obviously the girl, N-Nikki, is it?" Victor snarled slightly when he said her name.

"Yes, Father," Devin answered. "Nikki Williams is the name she gave the Facility."

"Well, in exchange for taking this hybrid I have demanded Lanashell's resignation."

"What?" Devin and I shouted at the same time.

Victor was surprised by our shock. "What would you have me do? Lanashell is unable to handle a troubled hybrid, a group of rogue Vampires blew up and broke into the Facility which has endangered our hybrids even more. It was really only a matter of time until the heads of the other covens demanded her release."

"Who will take over?" I asked.

"Nothing for you to worry about, child. Now let's discuss the last element of this horrid day. I really didn't appreciate being thrust in the middle of the relationship between two of my Warriors."

"Father, I am sorry. I never meant…"

"I certainly hope you didn't mean for any of this happen, but it has. Brianna is in a delicate state right now. The last thing she needs is the stress of infidelity. I had no choice but to grant her emotional request to leave the manor. Besides I would rather not have to deal with Eris if I denied it. I can only imagine how much he is gloating at this moment. Now what I want to know is why, child? After all you have sacrificed to be with Brianna, why are you suddenly walking away to be with this Nikki girl?"

"That is not what I am doing," I shouted as I stood up and then felt Devin's hand squeezing my shoulder uncomfortably. "I love Brianna, Father. I love her more than anyone in the world."

"Then why, child? Tell me why."

"Because…I…I…"

"Say it, child, say it!"

"I was scared!" I roared, causing Devin push me back down into my chair.

Victor paused, allowing time for the tension in the room to diffuse. "My Warriors are scared of nothing."

"Your Warriors are not having a child."

Devin released my shoulder as he said, "But you have been a father before."

"I was a human father to a human child. Not the father of…" I stopped to allow my head to fall into my hands again. "Eris calls me practically every day to remind me that Brianna and her children are somehow the key to our future, not that any of us really know how. I look at Brianna and I am instantly consumed by fear of not protecting her from Elaina. That is why I have been spending so much time with Nikki. I was desperate to find out anything I could that would help us shut this down. To make this whole ordeal even worse, Nikki has given me nothing. And if I was not already terrified enough, Brianna has had a recurring dream where she is taken by Elaina and I am nowhere in sight. Her dreams are already predicting that I fail her and if that happens, our race will be in jeopardy according to Eris. This is all I have been thinking about since Brianna became pregnant.

"There is so much expected of the babies and they are not even born yet. How am I qualified to be their father? The only Warrior without a true specialty. The only Warrior who was not a fighter or a soldier in his human life. I…I am just Cameron Burke, the son of a farmer. I am not some…I am not anyone."

My admissions hung in the air and I felt the weight being released from my chest. At first I was afraid of Father's reaction, afraid that he would consider me weak. But when I felt his hand on my shoulder, I looked up into his eyes and saw a caring and concerned father.

"Cameron, I have lived a long enough life to realize that there are things at work that none of us can see. I have always believed that invisible forces play a more active role in our lives than any of us ever wish to believe. For instance, similar to you, I came upon Devin quite by accident. Instantly I had a feeling about him and when I saw his skill I knew that he was to be in my coven. And look at him now, a fierce and unchallenged Warrior.

"Then take you. I had that same feeling one night nearly three hundred years ago on the streets of Boston. I had actually been there scouting a soldier who just ended up being a violent drunk, but my gut told me to walk down this random street that night. If I had chosen to ignore that feeling I would have never come across you. I would never have been moved by the grief and love you felt for your family and my instincts would never have urged me to Turn you. If I had never Turned you, you would never have been a Gatherer and in turn never met Brianna. Think of your life before you met her. It is difficult for me to admit, but I know you were not content, always looking for the next thing with which to distract you from your sadness. But look at you now, I have never seen so much life within you.

"Now as you told me once, Seraphina has had visions of Brianna's destiny since the day Brianna was born. So for thirty-two years it has been seen that Brianna and perhaps her children will change our future as a race. Of all the Gatherers and other Vampires that could have crossed her path, it was you, Cameron Burke, son of a farmer, who has now fathered her children. If fate isn't at work here then I don't know what is."

Victor's eyes were fierce as they bore themselves into mine. "Child, I never want you to forget your human father, but what you must remember is that you are also the son of a Warrior. My blood also flows through your veins and with it strength and determination. The one thing it does not have is the ability to truly love someone within the depths of your soul. You, however, have that power. No, there is a reason why you are here in this coven of mine, and that is because it is your destiny to lead and protect and to be a father to my grandchildren.

"That said," Victor continued, changing his tone abruptly and walking back around to sit behind his desk, "you must get Brianna back and I do not care how. Do as the mortals do, send flowers and letters, I've never fully understood chocolates but use them if you have to. You get her back here and I mean pronto.

"Now for this troublesome hybrid. Devin, assign someone to oversee her, but make sure whoever it is understands that Nikki is to be kept away from Cameron. I do not want any repeats of today. Also I want her drilled harder. She *must* know something about Elaina's intentions. Pull Julian in if you have to. I will be having a conversation with her as well. In no way will I tolerate the behavior she displayed at the Facility. I will sooner throw her out on the street than have her behave that way here. We all know what we need to do?" Devin and I nodded. "Good. Be vigilant, my sons."

Victor was out the door before I could even acknowledge him. As I watched him blur around the corner I realized it was the first time that he had called any of us anything other than "child". His term had always been a way to show us that he was in control and we were merely his children, Turned to do his bidding. But he had called us his sons. A term I had never heard him use. Perhaps the thought of being a grandfather had changed him, softened him maybe.

As I thought about Victor being a grandfather the rush of reality came back over my body. Brianna was gone. She was gone because I had been afraid of losing her to Elaina. Now I had lost her to Eris instead.

Devin patted me roughly on the shoulder. "What can I do for you, Brother?"

"Nothing. You cannot imagine how I feel right now."

I stood from the chair and walked swiftly toward the door, but was met with Devin pushing against my chest.

"But I can, Brother. The person you love is still alive, mine is not. You actually have the opportunity to beg for her forgiveness and hold her once again. I will never have that with Tao. My loss is forever, and yours is only a blink of an eye. Do not wallow in sadness, fight for her. Your battle is not lost. I know she loves you. She will come back if you fight for her hard enough and are honest. What you said to Father is exactly what you need to say to her. Brianna deserves to know why you did what you did and that in no way was it to hurt her."

"That seems easier said than done."

"I never said it would be easy. Brianna is the most stubborn person I have ever met. You definitely have your work cut out for you." I could not help but laugh at my eldest brother and the feeling lightened my chest slightly. "Perhaps it would make you feel better if you hit something, hit me even. I'll let you get in a few good shots, just something to release the tension."

"You are on."

Chapter Nine

Brianna

It was another beautiful day - the sky was blue, not Carolina blue like at Daddy O's, but still stunning. I always found the view at its peak around this time in the afternoon. The sun skipped over the peaking waves and it was a few hours before the noise of the tide became overwhelming as it crashed on the craggy rocks below. My father's balcony and panoramic ocean view was just as it had been in my dreams, only now I had seen the view in person for almost three weeks now. Well I guess the first two days didn't count since I spent most of my time lying in bed crying like a broken-hearted teenager.

My first night without Cameron brought on spells of uncontrollable sobbing, catatonia and a late night snack of homemade onion rings from Seraphina. Who knew long, thin, fried onions could heal the heart. Well, honestly they couldn't, but fried food, Sera's soothing touch, and Eris's ability to put me to sleep helped me get through the night. After that, Eris only let me sulk for one more day. To him my behavior did not embody a true daughter of Eris.

Since then I had read five books, taught Eris how to play poker, and learned to knit, though very badly. The activities and the view were certainly helping me sort through all the crap that was floating around in my head. Though I think sitting outside and listening to the sounds of the ocean relaxed me more than anything. My life had been such a nightmare the last few months and being here on my father's private island certainly gave me hope that life really could be this beautiful.

So today was like so many others – sitting in a cover up and big floppy hat with a cool glass of ginger ale. My nausea had thankfully been limited to the mornings or when I woke from a nap. I was already showing, which was unusual for me this early, but was probably natural if you were having twins (if, if I was having twins). At least the pregnancy was confirmed by Dr. Saunders, although I had no idea when I'd be going back for my follow-up appointments. I couldn't think that far in the future. At least not yet. I felt like an addict, I was just taking it one day at a time. However, sometimes that was hard when each day I received an email from Cameron, but only after he had left me a voicemail. I hadn't listened to one message or read one email. I wanted to, but I knew that just hearing his voice or seeing his words would make me crumble. Today, however, I felt like maybe the strength was within me when the subject of his email today was "I was scared". Short, simple, honest.

Just as I was about to open the email I heard a gentle coo coming from the kitchen located through the open balcony doors behind me. Sera was making her way outside, a tray and napkins in hand, which meant it was 2:30. Snack time. Just like in school, except I never had a chef like Sera. Today's afternoon snack was homemade guacamole and toasted pita chips. I had developed a craving for avocadoes, and Sera made the best guacamole I had ever had.

"Here we are, ma petite chute," Sera announced as she placed the tray on the table in between our two patio chaises.

"Sera, you are going to make me the fattest pregnant lady ever," I said as I brought a pita chip sagging with guacamole up to my mouth. She liked being motherly and being able to take care of someone other than my father. "Can I ask you something?"

Sera nodded as she wiped the corner of her mouth with a napkin. "Oui, I do believe you should return home to Cameron."

Well she was direct if she was anything.

"Um, well not quite what I was going to ask, but I guess I know where you stand."

"I only mean zhat I believe you are ready, and zhat he is as well. Have you not read your message today?"

"Not yet. I haven't read any of them, actually."

"I zhink you should. Not zhat I won't miss you, but you know how important it is for children to have both of zheir parents."

Touché, Sera.

"Actually," I began, but had to pause so I could stuff the chip in my mouth and swallow, "what I wanted to ask you is really personal, and if you don't want to answer you certainly don't have to."

"Absolument, ask me anyzhing."

"Have you always been ok with...I mean is there a reason you never...sorry, I can't even think of a way to ask it."

Sera sat on the edge of her chaise and patted my hand gently. "You want to know why your fazer has never Turned me?"

"Uh, yeah," I said relieved. "Does it bother you that you age and he doesn't? I mean in a few more years he'll look like..."

"My son? And zhen my grandson?" I looked down at the ground, embarrassed by how forward my question was. "It is alright, Brianna, do not be ashamed to ask me. It is a valid question. Your fazer has wanted to Turn me many times and only so zhat we would be togezer forever. But if he Turned me, what would happen to my visions? What if zhey disappeared? Zhough I have worried many times that your fazer would not want me once I reached a certain age."

"I don't ever see that happening," I said, stuffing another full pita chip into my mouth. "Eris loves you so much. I'm not sure how he'd survive without you."

Sera patted my hand again, but looked away toward the ocean. "He would survive as he has for zhousand of years."

"But he would be miserable."

"As would Cameron if he were to lose you."

"Cameron's resourceful. I'm sure he'd find someone else."

"And you believe zhis because he has had so many ozer true loves?"

"Touché again."

"Zhere was a first?" Sera said winking at me. "Read your messages from him. Men, especially our Vampire men, have difficulties admitting when zhey are scared and cannot control what happens to zhose around zhem. Your fazer has great difficulty with zhis."

"Eris afraid of something? Please," I scoffed as I scraped the last of the guacamole from the bowl with my finger. There weren't any chips left, what was I supposed to do?

"Brianna, your fazer is only afraid losing moi, toi, and les petits-enfants."

"Say again?"

She smiled. "Losing me, you, and zhe grandchildren.

"But he will lose us all someday."

"Hopefully to old age," Sera said, taking the bowl away from me so that I couldn't lick it clean.

"That's my problem, Sera. Cameron's already lost a wife and child. I don't see how he could cope if it happened again and I don't want to be a Vampire."

"And what's wrong with being a Vampire?" Eris asked as he stepped out onto the balcony. He was dressed in his usual linen vacation attire, his shoulder length dark wavy hair pulled back in a tight ponytail. His voice was absent of his thick Italian accent, since I demanded he be his true self in my presence and not the character he played in front of everyone else.

"Nothing," I said, adjusting uncomfortably in my chaise. "I just want to be a real mother to my child."

"*Children,*" Eris stressed as he pointed to my popping belly.

"It hasn't been confirmed yet, Dad."

"I do not need a doctor to tell me that you are carrying the little boy and girl from Sera's visions."

"Either way," I replied, slightly annoyed, "I want to be a real mom. A real mom with soft warm skin and breast milk and regular teeth and not one that has to worry about bloodlust or aversion to the sun or even being afraid I'll crush them when I try to hold them."

Eris sat down next to Sera and both of them had looks of concern on their faces.

"Petite, have you spoken with your mozer?"

"Uh, no. I think that ship sailed a while ago, Sera. Shelby doesn't ever call me. Daddy O said he told her I was pregnant, but he didn't tell me what her actual response was. That usually means she said something that he didn't want to repeat."

Eris's nostrils flared and I could see Sera squeeze his hand. "Daughter, you are nothing like your mother."

"Do you know something I don't?"

"I am only saying that being a good mother has nothing to do with being human. I don't want you to associate becoming a Vampire with being similar to Shelby."

"I don't associate it that way," I lied. "I'm just saying that right now I want to live and die the same species I was born."

The lines around Eris's eyes squinted and flinched before he was able respond with, "So even if becoming a Vampire meant saving your life you would still refuse?"

"Yes. That's why I was asking how you dealt with the age thing. By the way, this was a conversation between me and Sera and now that you've butted your nose into it, I'm going to my room."

"Daughter, wait. I did not mean to..."

"Too late, Dad, you've ruined the mother daughter moment." Sera eyes fluttered at my statement and suddenly filled with tears. "Don't be so surprised, Sera. You know you've been a mother to me, especially since I've been here. The hugs, the tissues, the onion rings, all things Shelby would never have given me."

Sera stood and hugged me tightly only for a second before she turned and left to go back inside the house, wiping her eyes with her back turned so that neither Eris nor I could see.

"I didn't mean to upset her," I said softly as I grabbed my laptop and stood from the chaise.

"Quite the contrary. You are the nearest thing she has to a child, a sacrifice she made when she became my wife. And now you have said that you think of her as a mother, something that she has only dreamed about for the last thirty years."

"Why did Sera have to sacrifice having children? It's not like you can't make more."

Eris sighed deeply as he stood up against the wide balcony railing, staring out at the ocean. "After everything I went through with your mother, I found it difficult to even think about doing it again. Although I would have loved to have a child with Sera, I was afraid that other Vampires would hunt our child down as well. Would you wish your fate on a sibling?"

"Absolutely not."

"Precisely. With our current situation being what it is, we obviously made the right decision. Although I believe your love for her makes it easier for Sera to handle that decision. So have you started thinking of names for the children?" Eris asked, obviously wanting to change the subject.

"Too early, I think. I want to get further along before I start any of that. I haven't gotten past my longest duration yet."

"You will not lose these babies, my dear."

"Thanks for being positive, Dad. But we'll have to see." Our conversation paused, both of us deciding that the ocean was definitely more pleasant. Finally I said, "Speaking of names, where did my name come from?"

"I believe it came from your great-grandmother," Eris said, stepping over to the wide balcony railing and propping himself up on his elbows.

"Yes, Grandmamma Lizzy was Brianna Elizabeth. But what about Marie? Or I guess I should say Marilena."

Eris's smile faded slightly as his gaze returned to the ocean breaking loudly below us. "I know I have told you about the woman I was secretly betrothed to before I was Turned." I nodded. "Your mother's likeness made it hard not to be reminded of my past. Shelby wanted your middle name to be Marie, which was just common, in my opinion. My former lover's name was Orlena, and I often called her Lena. So basically I pieced them together to make Marilena, something that would be unique and honor her. I guess your mother had other ideas when she filled out the birth certificate."

"Well, Dad, if I'm ever able to get to a Social Security office, I'll have it officially changed. Ok?"

Eris knitted his brows together. "Why must you go to an office? Marilena is your name. I do not need a piece of paper to tell me that."

And that was the end of this discussion apparently.

"Ok, then. Well I'm going to read an email and take a nap. Wake me for dinner?"

Eris nodded and I gave him a quick kiss on the cheek as I passed him with my laptop in hand. Everyone around me was acting like an adult, it was finally time for me to as well. Seraphina was right, I of all people knew how important it was for a child to have both parents in their life. Cameron was obviously trying, so maybe I should give him a chance. Besides I still loved him, there was no question on that.

Just as I stepped through the balcony doors that led to my bedroom I heard Eris call to me. "Mia figlia, one question before you go?"

"Sure, Dad. What's up?"

"Who is Aidan?"

"Don't call me Shelby, Bri Bri, I am your mother," Shelby shouted at me as we stood in the center of Daddy O's foyer.

"Could have fooled me," I snapped back and turned to walk into the

living room of my grandfather's home. Shelby's hand gripped the back of my arm and spun me around to face her.

"Bri Bri, you listen to me. That man is a Vampire. And one thing I know about Vampires is that they don't love anyone but themselves."

"Cameron does love me."

"He loves this," she said, picking up my arm and slapping the veins on my wrist. "They only care about where their blood is coming from. That's all you are to him, Bri Bri, a blood bag."

"No, it's not true. He loves me, and nothing you say will make me think otherwise. I'm having his children."

"It doesn't mean anything, don't you understand that? He's taken what he wanted. Now he's going to leave you just like your father did."

I shook my head vigorously from side to side as I bit my lip. "Eris loved you and all you could think about was becoming a Vampire. I am nothing like you. I have a man that loves me."

"Then where is he? Where is your precious Cameron?" Shelby smiled when I didn't answer, her voice victorious when she said, "You don't know, do you? Trust me, Bri Bri, you're going to end up just like me - alone with a baby you don't want."

"That's enough," a man shouted from behind me, and from past experience I had expected Eris, since this was where he had stopped my dream before. But when I turned around I saw a tall, broad-shouldered, sandy-blonde haired Vampire standing in the doorway. "Now I told you that I'd let you come here as long as you didn't upset Brianna. Now you've just gone too far. You have exactly three seconds to get your boney ass out of here before I..." But then everyone froze as if someone pressed the pause button. Well everyone but me and the beardless Jesus-looking guy stepping out of the kitchen.

"This man, mia figlia," Eris said as he stepped next to me and gazed upon Aidan standing in the doorway. "Who is this man here?"

"That's Aidan,"

"I thought you said you didn't know an Aidan."

"Well now that he's standing in front of me I know him. He's one of Cameron's old Gatherer friends or something like that."

"Why is this man in your dreams, daughter?"

That was certainly a question I wouldn't mind having answered. And why is he handsomer than I remember.

"Brianna, you know I can hear your thoughts when you are sleeping."

"Ok, dream's over. Get out of my head, Dad."
"But we need to discuss why…"

I opened my eyes, refusing to discuss why Aidan was in my dream. It made me confused and conflicted and desperately wishing I had woken up with Cameron lying beside me. I hadn't had the Shelby dream in a while, or at least that I could remember. But when I did, Cameron always seemed to know and would hold me and rub my back until I got back to sleep. Tonight I was on my own, and I hated it.

I had read his latest email this afternoon and it prompted me to delete all the others. It wasn't that I was mad, I just didn't need anything else to convince me. His words were honest and to the point and I could tell that he had had difficulty writing them. The note was filled with heart and truth and absent of flowery subject skirting language. I had meant to call him after dinner, but apparently I fell asleep without knowing it since it was now almost midnight.

The moon was full and lit up my room in a pale silvery light that allowed me to find my cell phone without having to turn on a light. The phone barely rung once before Cameron answered.

"Hello? Bri," he said quickly, but then there was a loud bang and shuffling sounds while Cameron shouted for me to stay on the phone. Finally a few seconds later he came back on the line, "Sorry, sorry, I dropped the phone and then Jared had to kick it under the table because he is an ass." I heard Jared shout that he didn't do it on purpose, but we all knew he did. "Bri, hold on for one more moment, I am going to leave the room." Through the phone I could hear the wind whipping past so I assumed Cameron ran full speed to go wherever it was so that he could talk to me in private. "Love, are you there?"

"Yeah, Cam, I'm here." There was silence on the other line, so quiet in fact that I thought I'd lost the call. I took the phone away from my ear and saw that the call log was still ticking away. "Cameron? Are you there?"

"Yes. Sorry, love," he said, sounding like he was sniffling. "It is wonderful to hear your voice."

"I m-miss you," I cried, unable to keep my emotions hidden any longer.

"Brianna, you have no idea how much I have missed you. I think Alexander has hired Devin to take me out. Jared keeps calling me a whiney…well I will keep that to myself. How are you feeling?"

I took several gulps of air, unable to control my breathing as my emotions were getting the best of me. "F-fine. I ate guac-guacamole," I sobbed.

"Angel, you are tearing my heart out, why are you crying?"

"B-because I w-want to come h-home."

"And I want you to come home. Come home to me, angel. Please, just tell me when and I will come get you."

"Would it be ok if I came home tomorrow?"

When he came back on the line I could hear that his voice was a little shaky, showing similar signs of emotion, though obviously not as dramatic as mine. "Tomorrow is perfect. Unless you can get on a plane right now."

"That would involve sneaking out of here and I'm not sure how well that would work with a psychic in the other room."

Cameron laughed lightly which made me smile. "So honestly, how angry are Eris and Seraphina at me?"

"Surprisingly not as angry as I wanted them to be," I replied jokingly but causing an awkward silence between us.

"Brianna, I meant every word I said in my note today," Cameron began but I cut him off in my true Southern way.

"Cam, it's late and I really want to talk about everything in person. Can you promise me we'll have some private time together tomorrow?"

"Yes. Wait. Dammit! We have a mission scheduled for tomorrow night. I was in a planning session when you called. We are not scheduled to leave until 9:00pm so that Jared can go with us. But that means we will have all afternoon and most of the evening. No never mind, I will find someone who can take my place. I have plenty of time to get someone else up to speed."

Cameron's tone was quickening and I could hear the frustration in his voice. He was already being pulled in two directions and we'd only been on the phone for three minutes.

"Cam, did Victor ask you to lead this?"

"Yes," he answered tentatively.

"Then you need to go."

"No, I will find someone else. I am not going to ruin your homecoming."

"Babe, calm down," I said firmly. "The flight is short, I'll be sure to come home by one. Hopefully we won't need eight hours to talk."

"But Bri…"

"Cam, I can't be mad because Victor didn't foresee that I would finally come back tomorrow after three weeks."

"But I need to hold you in my arms, love."

"Eight hours isn't enough?"

"Definitely not," he laughed. "Home by one, then?"

"Yes, unless Eris freaks out and says he won't let me use the jet."

"I will swim there myself if I have to."

"I'll meet you halfway then. Or more like waiting for you on the shore, I'm a horrible swimmer plus I've put on a few pounds."

"Must be that guacamole."

"You have no idea. Tell Christine to stock up on avocadoes."

There was a brief silence before Cameron spoke again, his tone changing to one of longing and loneliness. "Brianna, I am miserable without you. I cannot seem to find my way when you are not with me."

"The way I left…was…was awful, I know. I shouldn't have left like that."

"No, love, you did what you needed to do to protect yourself. There is much we need to discuss, but like you said we should talk in person. It is late my angel, you need your rest, and Devin is about to rip this phone from my ear."

I heard Cameron place his hand over the microphone of the cell phone while he and Devin grumbled something back and forth. "Love, I apologize, but I must go. I will see you tomorrow."

"Yes, tomorrow. I'll let you know exactly when I leave. If I can get home sooner I will."

"I will be waiting, angel." Cameron paused again and then said, "Do you still love me?"

"Always, Cam," I responded immediately, and only because it was true.

"Goodnight, my love."

"Goodnight."

Reluctantly I hung up the phone, but knew that it was necessary. Cameron didn't need to be pulled at any more than he already was. As soon as the phone left my hand my eyelids closed. They were heavy, but my chest was light, feeling as though I hadn't breathed in three weeks. Cameron was the air that my lungs needed, and now that I had spoken to him they were filled.

I didn't want to think about the uncomfortable discussion that Cameron and I would have tomorrow. All I wanted to think about now was his voice in my head whispering goodnight to me. As the dark around me began to deepen and swirl, I concentrated on what I wanted to dream about, and that was my man in black, my love, my Cam. I only hoped that he wouldn't suddenly appear sandy-blonde.

Chapter Ten

Cameron

"I'm totally stoked to kick some Vampire ass tonight," Jared announced as he undocked his laptop from his "command center" as he liked to call it. Jared had been cooped up inside and prevented from going on any missions since the manor attack. He was more than chomping at the bit for some action tonight.

"Jared, do you have the photographs?" I asked, urging him back to the topic at hand.

"Printed them in a glossy finish, bro, gives them a little something extra, dontcha think?" he said with a wide smile as he placed four 8x10 photographs on the small round table we were sitting around. His excitement was contagious, but I was bursting at the seams not because of the mission but because any minute now my Bri would be walking through the door of the manor. While Devin took everyone through their duties for this evening, I was still debating on exactly what to say to Brianna and how to say it.

"Cameron, do you agree?" Devin asked as he kicked me under the table. I had not heard him and he knew it. He was slightly sympathetic with my current plight, but had no patience for my lack of concentration.

"Ye-Yes," I began as Alexander caught my eye, pointing to the photos and then to his cell phone. "I do think we should send these photos to everyone's phone so that we can all study them before we get to the site."

Devin squinted skeptically at me and then turned his head faster than Alexander could put his phone down. Everyone around the table snickered, unable to stop themselves from enjoying the moment at Devin's expense. He, however, was less appreciative.

"Brother," he said annoyed, "I need to feel assured that I have your full concentration on this mission. I can't have you distracted."

"You have nothing to worry about, Brother. This mission has my full attention."

"I doubt that," he replied smugly as he pointed to my knee that was unknowingly bouncing up and down a million beats per second.

"Dev, Cameron's got this. We've all got this. It's not like we haven't gone over this a b-gillion times," Jared chimed in to my defense.

"We are presenting our plans to Father within the hour and I want to make sure we have covered every avenue. He is none too pleased with the fact that for the last few weeks our missions have produced nothing but empty warehouses and residences. He is sick of us coming back empty handed, and frankly so am I. What I don't understand, Brother, is how you of all people don't seem concerned."

I took a breath before I spoke, trying to remember Father's plea to me about working more harmoniously with Devin. However, at times like these I found it difficult when my brother's tongue was sharp and provoking.

"Brother, I assure you we are all more than frustrated with the results of our missions of late. If it would make you feel better about this evening, let us go through the plan one more time. Alex, how about you take us through it again."

Alexander nodded and began going through our plans one step at a time. There were only six of us going since we were only raiding a home we suspected housed four of Elaina's followers. Jared, Connor, and Maxim would be our perimeter tripod outside the home while Alexander, Devin, and I converged inside. The plan was relatively simple. Get in, get out, and get home hopefully with four Vampires of the enemy clan in the backseat.

Once Alexander finished the "b-gillionth" debrief, he held up the photos we had attained from cameras in the area – four men, late twenties/early thirties, one blonde while the others were dark headed. "These are the four subjects in question. Jared was able to dig up some info on this guy," Alexander said, pointing to the blonde-haired man. "We believe his name is Rowley. We're pretty sure we caught him in the footage from the manor attack, and as Connor pointed out yesterday he believes this is the same Vamp who bit his ear."

"I don't *believe*, Alex, I know. There was a lot going on that day, but that dickhead bit my ear. You don't forget something like that," Connor grumbled as he crossed his arms in front of his chest. "We'll just see how he likes it when I rip his right off."

"I will give you fifty bucks if you come back with his ear, man," Jared said as he fist bumped Connor. Slowly but surely Connor was becoming a more trusted member of our little family. I wondered, however, if Maxim was feeling a little left out. Of course one would never know it. Maxim barely said three words a week.

Devin cleared his throat causing Jared and Connor to snap back to attention and Alexander to continue with, "We're pretty sure we've got the right guy and our surveillance shows him with these three gentlemen, of whom we have nothing on. That said we are going in slightly blind since we don't want to spook them and give them time to get out before we've made it over to Modesto. We have a basic floor plan of the house, but we don't know what weapons or powers these four possess. Like Devin said, we'll be sending these photos to your phones, so burn their faces into your brains in case we have to take them down outside the home. Got it?"

"This is going to be awww-some," Jared squealed just as the door to his room opened. I could not imagine trying to fit anyone else in his tiny room. It was difficult enough sitting around the table in his limited space, but because of the daylight hour it was the only room where he could really be comfortable. I caught Jared's worried expression as he stared at who was coming through the door, but I did not need to turn around to know who it was when the stinging citrus smell wafted around me and made my jaw clinch.

"Skylar, dude, we're in a meeting," Jared said while rising from his chair.

"You told me that Nikki could come by and get one of the refurbished cell phones."

"I didn't mean now, man, you know we're busy doing totally awesome superhero work here and you just couldn't stop from coming by because you're jealous that you weren't invited."

It was hard to keep a straight face since Jared's statement was absolutely the truth. Though it was not gentlemanly for Jared to rub it in Skylar's face that he had replaced him, but it was satisfying all the same.

While Jared fished out a cell phone from the large stores that he had, I felt a hand squeeze my shoulder.

"Hi, Cameron," Nikki said in a tentative voice.

Only my brothers knew that Victor had ordered that Nikki be kept away from me, and until this moment it had not been a problem. Both Devin and Alexander were looking at me intently, their eyes widening as they wondered what my next actions would be. I turned toward Nikki in an effort to get her hand off my shoulder, but unfortunately it only made her squeeze it harder.

"Good afternoon, Nikki."

Nikki smiled a little too enthusiastically and my stomach sank. "I can't believe I haven't seen you since that first day. I mean, I'm totally different here, keeping my cool and everything. Right, Skylar?"

Skylar gave an exhausted smile as he nodded his head.

"I am glad to hear you are adjusting," I said, finally removing her hand from my shoulder and turning back around in my seat.

Before I knew it, Nikki's arms were around my neck, her chest pressed awkwardly against the side of my face as she said, "I knew you couldn't stay mad at me."

Quickly I removed Nikki's arms from around my neck when Devin rose from his seat. I knew Nikki was trying to be nice, but Devin would not see it as such. The last thing we needed was to have a scene in front of everyone in the room. As I gently pushed Nikki away, I gestured for Skylar to come and take her away.

"Skylar, we must really get back to work. I am sure you and Nikki have some work of your own…"

"I know those guys," Nikki interrupted as she shook her arm out of Skylar's hand and stepped closer to the table. She leaned over the photos that were splayed and gently rubbed her fingers across faces of the men staring back at her.

"*How* do you know them," Devin replied as he pushed me aside.

Nikki stared at the pictures on the table, almost in a trance. Finally she picked up the photo of the blonde male. "This is Raleigh or Rowley, something like that, right?" she asked as she looked up at Devin for confirmation. When Devin nodded she swallowed hard and slowly placed the picture back down on the table. "He's uh…he was always with Elaina when she would visit the lab where you guys found me." Her hand shook as she picked up the picture of one of the dark haired men. "His name was uh…Carl…no, Cart…Carter, I don't remember the others. Any time they showed up, the doctors – well I guess they really weren't doctors, but they would always show these guys the latest…things…they were doing to us."

"You're sure?" Devin pressed.

Nikki tightened her lips together trying to keep her composure. "Yup. I remember they wanted to…see me heal. More like they wanted to see what I couldn't heal from. Are you…are you going to get these guys?"

"I expect my Warriors to bring me their heads on a platter," Victor said from the doorway of Jared's room. My father's light expression changed once he saw that Nikki was standing only a foot away from me and because of it he gave me a questionable eye.

"Nikki has just identified another one of our suspects, Father," Devin interceded. "This more than proves that we are on the right track. This could be the very break we've been looking for."

Victor stepped inside, causing everyone to adjust in order to make room at the table.

"How long since they have been seen on surveillance?"

"This morning, Father," Devin confirmed.

"So if this is our big break, I do not wish to delay the mission until this evening. We could lose the only chance we have of taking these four men and interrogating them. That said, I want you to proceed with the mission in the next hour."

"The next hour!" both Jared and I said at the same time from opposite sides of the room, and for two very different reasons. Victor did not flinch at our objections, he merely stood composed as he fanned through the pictures that lay on the table.

"Dad, if you move up the time then I can't go. That's…you…can't. You just can't," Jared shouted as he stepped over to Victor.

"And why can't I?"

Victor's challenging expression made Jared's nostrils flare and his jaw tighten. He tried keeping Father's gaze, but eventually he backed down and his eyes found the floor.

"You gotta let me go, Dad," Jared whispered sadly.

"There will be other missions, child," Victor said flatly.

"Father, please," I said, leaning over the table, "Jared is fully prepared for this mission, we cannot lose him."

"Then have Connor take his place," Victor said pointing at Connor who suddenly looked confused across the table.

"Uh, sir, I'm already going," Connor replied awkwardly.

"Ah, then you will take Skylar. He's already here, and has been on past missions. No hybrid duty for you tonight, child," Victor said to Skylar's relief.

Jared sat defeated in his chair at the table as he stared venomously at the laptop's screen. The light-hearted feeling that previously filled the room was gone. No one knew what to say. We were all disappointed at the change of plans, but there was nothing you could say or do to change Victor's mind.

"Cameron, any further objections you'd like to present?" Victor asked, daring me to complain.

"No, Father. If this is the change you wish to make…"

"Yes it is. There really shouldn't be any changes in the plans, just the time."

"And the people," Jared grumbled, though Victor ignored him. "Bibi's convoy just pulled in, bro."

I glanced over at Victor who surprisingly met my eyes. "I'm sure your brothers can bring me up to speed."

I smiled widely, unable to help myself as I pushed Devin and Nikki aside and ran into the hallway. The tapestries and paintings blurred around me as I made my way down the back hallway. When I was only around the corner from the foyer I stopped in front of a large mirror to adjust my shirt and hair, ensuring I looked presentable. But even though my sweater lay flat and clean against my chest, I could not help but fidget with the collar of the shirt underneath. I was unbelievably nervous about how Brianna would greet me. Would she be cold, or longing and loving like she was last night?

"How was your trip, angel?" I whispered into the mirror but hated the sound of it. "Bri, my love, how I have missed you." And how unbelievably pathetic I sounded.

The front doors opened around the corner and I had officially run out of time. This was Brianna, my angel with whom I was never at a loss for words. When I saw her they would just come to me as they always did. Besides, knowing Brianna she would be able to tell that I had practiced. I would just say the first thing that came to mind when I saw her beautiful face.

As I took one last breath in, her sweet honeysuckle scent filled my chest, reminding me of how much I missed her. I rounded the corner to see Kyla shutting the front doors. When she noticed my worried expression at not seeing Brianna next to her she pointed down the main corridor at Brianna walking quickly toward the main stairwell.

"Bri?" I said shakily, afraid in some way that she was trying to run from me. Startled by the sound of her name, she turned her head quickly around causing her long bangs to fall into her eyes as they so often did. She slowly turned the rest of her body towards me as I stepped closer to her and said the first thing that came to me.

"You are showing."

Brianna smiled brightly and laughed as she placed a gentle hand on her stomach. She was glowing and more beautiful than I had ever seen her.

"I know. Usually I have a little more time before I have to break out the fat girl pants. Of course I don't have any, and actually had to borrow this shirt from Sera so that it would hide the fact that I couldn't button my jeans," she said lifting her hip-length blouse.

At the sight of her skin I closed the distance between us and could not help but place my hand on her abdomen. My life had returned, and somehow the warming sensation that was suddenly radiating throughout my entire body was originating from my hand that was resting upon my children. As Brianna's eyes met mine, she knitted her brows together and removed my hand.

"I don't even want to know why that just happened," she said as she curled her fingers around mine.

Unable to help myself, I pulled her into my chest, holding our entwined hands between our hearts while I kissed the top of her dark brown hair. She tilted her face up to mine and I grazed my lips over hers ever so slightly, silently asking her permission to kiss her. Her heart began to beat faster against the back of my hand and I took that as permission granted. With my other hand I cupped her face and neck as I kissed her with weeks of passionate longing. Neither of us cared that we were standing in the middle of the main corridor, kissing one another in a way that was reserved for when we were alone in bed. When Brianna's breath seemed desperate, my lips finally released her and I squeezed her tightly into my chest. Her stomach pressed against me, and the feeling was wonderful.

"Well if she wasn't pregnant already, she would be now after that," Kyla said kiddingly behind me. She tapped me on the shoulder and held out her hand which held several tissues. I smiled at her, because as always Kyla knew what someone else needed and at this moment it was Brianna successfully soaking through both my shirts with tears. I took the tissues from Kyla's hand and began dabbing Brianna's eyes as she looked up at me.

"Sorry, I'm a bag of hormones."

"But you are the most beautiful bag of hormones."

Brianna gave me a skeptical eye at my comment, but it was the truth.

"So," she sighed as she took a step away from me, "can I grab something to eat before we start having the most uncomfortable conversation in our entire relationship?" A tight laugh escaped from my mouth as I put a hand through my hair and diverted my gaze to the floor. "Well is that a no to me getting food, or us talking?"

"Love, this is utterly beyond my control..."

"What happened now?" she sighed.

"Father literally told us minutes ago that he wants us to leave within the hour instead of this evening."

"I thought the point of leaving later tonight was so that Jared could go?"

"Yes, well apparently Father is still reluctant to let him fight. But this means I will be home earlier, and we will have a whole night together. I will not have to leave your side once I step through those doors, I promise you this." Brianna began biting her bottom lip, and worried me further when she looked over my shoulder at Kyla. "Please, love, tell me you understand. Otherwise we will have to have the most uncomfortable conversation of our relationship in the truck on the way to Modesto in front of Devin and Alexander."

"No, no, it's fine. Kyla wanted to take me shopping anyway."

"No malls, I promise," Kyla said quickly. "She'll never leave my side, and I'll take some security with me. You have to let me take her, Cameron. I can't let her stand here with her pants undone, and I know your skin is crawling over it."

Kyla was correct, though I had initially been overtaken by the sight of Brianna's baby bump, the fact that the mother of my children was standing in front of me with her pants partially open did make my skin crawl.

"Angel, please spend every dollar I have. I never want you to be in public ever again with your pants open. Can you promise me that?" Brianna smiled as she kissed me softly on the lips and wrapped her arms around my neck. I nuzzled my face into her hair, once again inhaling all that was her. "I am yours tonight, my angel. We will talk."

She lifted her head and pressed her warm lips against mine once more. "And maybe we can do a little more than just talk."

I was startled at the feeling of my buttocks being pinched as Brianna stepped away. Brianna had never been so forward with me, especially in the presence of others. I caught her eye as she looked back from Kyla's guiding arm. Her smile and tiny wink were enough to make me want to carry her to the nearest room I could find to lay down on top of her. But keeping my control intact, I clamped down on my desires and simply placed my fist over my heart and lowered my head. It had always been a Warrior's sign of respect, but it had become a symbol of my undying love for her.

Within seconds Kyla had shuffled Brianna out the door and the only evidence remaining that my love had actually come home was the sight of her luggage (actually my luggage) sitting by the front door. Grabbing the suitcase and matching overnight bag, I walked up to our bedroom where I could drop off the bags and change into my battle gear. At first, the trip upstairs was as lonely as it had been the last three weeks, but then I was flooded with the feeling of anticipation for tonight. I no longer had doubts that she would be coming home. She *was* home, and now merely going shopping with my sister-in-law. It seemed so normal after such a horrific time.

When I stepped through the door of our bedroom I thought to myself that life could only get better after today. But for some reason, whatever god existed and looked down upon us decided to rein havoc on me. As soon as Brianna's luggage hit the floor next to the door, my nose detected the scent of citrus. My eyes rose slowly to see Nikki sitting up from my bed holding the comforter around her chest revealing only the straps of her bra.

"Nikki, get the hell out of my bed." As soon as the words came across my lips, anger filled me. She was lying in the bed that I shared with Brianna, actually lying in my lover's place. The sight of it disgusted me and when she remained in place I screamed at her again. "Either remove yourself from that bed, or I will pull you out myself."

Nikki paused before seductively removing the comforter from her chest and rising from the bed wearing a white cotton bra and panties.

"Although I do like the idea of you coming in after me, we can certainly do this standing up. With Brianna back and all we really don't have that much time to take our relationship to the next level."

"Nikki, we have no relationship," I said as I backed away from her approach. "You need to put your clothes on and get out of here. Now."

"Oh Cam, putting clothes on would defeat the whole purpose of me being here," she said as slipped her bra straps off her shoulders. "Why are you being so resistant?"

My heels hit the back of the bedroom door. I felt like a trapped animal. If I left, there was no guarantee she would leave as well, but staying was also not the best option.

"I do not wish to hurt you."

"I'll heal," she replied and launched herself at me, trying to hold my face in place with her hands while she kissed me. Quickly I took her arms from around my neck and threw her down on the ground. The action itself made my stomach turn.

"Get. Out. Now," I growled at her as I picked up her clothing from the floor.

"You know, Cam, the problem with being a healer is that you never show scars. You never show cuts or even bruises. So even without evidence people have to believe you when you tell them a story about being attacked by a certain male Vampire."

"What are you implying?"

"All I'm saying is that if Victor suddenly found me crying on his doorstep claiming that his precious Warrior named Cameron has sexually assaulted me, what do you think he'd say?"

"He would not believe you. He trusts me certainly more than he will ever trust you."

"And that's exactly what I'll tell him you said while I sob at his feet. Oh, and what will Brianna say when she finds out?"

"What do you want from me?" I asked, keeping my hands wrapped in her clothes versus around her throat.

"I want you," she replied as her hands pulled at my shirt trying to un-tuck it from my pants.

I threw her clothes down and grabbed her wrists. "That will never happen."

"A kiss then. Just one toe curling kiss and if you don't totally want to bend me over this couch then I'll leave."

"And if I refuse?"

"Well, it could be me at Victor's door, or naked pictures of me hidden in Brianna's closet, my lipstick and perfume on your shirts. Oh it could be so many things, Cam, you'll be constantly looking over your shoulder wondering what I'll do."

"Stay away from Brianna," I said angrily. "One kiss, that is all."

My chest began to rise and fall with anger, my hands flexing with frustration over being blackmailed. Ten minutes ago I was holding Bri in my arms welcoming her home, and now I was struggling with whether or not I could kiss another woman in order to protect her from further pain.

"If that's what you still want after you kiss me."

"I will never want any part of you."

Nikki snaked her arms around my neck again being sure to press her breasts firmly against my chest. I sighed and concentrated on not breathing in any amount of her perfume mixed with the pheromones she was emitting. Taking her shoulders firmly in my hands I closed my eyes tightly and kissed her. Nikki's tongue flicked inside my mouth, making me squeeze her shoulders harder in order to keep myself from biting down on it and ripping it out of her mouth. The pain I was causing her seemed to make her more aroused since her hands began scratching and pulling at my hair and neck. Unlike her I felt completely disgusted; my fangs did not even extend. Only a second longer and this would be over.

"Listen, bro, you gotta talk to..." Jared began before the black mist of his Projection had dissipated around him. Immediately when I heard his voice I pushed Nikki away from me, but the damage had been done. "What the fuck is going on?"

Jared stood looking between me and Nikki, complete shock on his face. With a shake of her head, Nikki's demeanor and posture changed dramatically. She suddenly became self-aware of her actions and lack of clothing. With tears that came out of nowhere, Nikki picked up her clothes from where I dropped them and ran out of the room muttering choked apologies.

"It is not what it looks like, Jared," I said softly as he stood and glared at me.

"So you weren't just standing there kissing that girl."

"No. I mean, yes I was but..."

"The same girl Bri thought you were having an affair with. So what, you've been lying this whole time? You've really been screwing around on my sister?"

"Jared, I did not have sex with that girl. I...I had to kiss her..." But I was unable to finish my sentence before Jared's fist broke my jaw and I hit the floor.

"I'm not an idiot, Cameron. No one is forced to kiss someone like that. I looked up to you, you son of a bitch. The minute I saw you and Brianna together I was jealous of what you guys had. Now you're just a cheatin' bastard. You don't deserve Bri and she doesn't deserve being lied to."

Jared turned on his heels and headed towards the door. My jaw was still knitting itself together when I leapt from the ground and pulled at Jared's arm to stop him from going out the door. "Whe ou oin?" I said painfully while my jaw continued to reconnect.

Jared's eyes were murderous as he ripped his arm from my grip. "I'm going to find Bri and tell her what a lying, fucking douchebag you are."

When he turned to leave again I stepped in front of him, pushing him back slightly with my hand against his chest. "J-jared," I said stretching out my mouth and jaw, "you are too angry right now to even listen or understand what really went on here, and I know it looks terrible but I promise you I am not being unfaithful. You have my word that I will tell Brianna what happened, but I want to be the one to tell her."

"I will not lie for you," he replied as he shoved my hand from his chest.

"I am not asking you to. I only ask that you let her hear about this from me."

Jared paused, his nostrils still flared with anger as he looked everywhere else but at me. "Fine. But if she asks, I have no control of what'll come out of my mouth." I nodded as I took in the waves of hatred Jared was sending in my direction. Finally he took one last look at me and said, "Don't ever fucking talk to me again."

Jared stepped around me, and this time I let him go. When I heard the door close behind me it sounded like the walls were falling in around me. What the hell had just happened? I looked around the room and noticed the bed was still rumpled where Nikki had been. Quickly I made the bed and pulled off the pillowcase that smelled like her perfume. Within seconds the gas fireplace was on and the pillowcase was burning. I looked down at myself and noticed the edges of my shirt hanging down from underneath my sweater where Nikki had un-tucked it. Her body had touched my sweater, it smelled like her and made me rip both shirts from my body and throw them into the fire along with the pillowcase.

I stood shirtless in front of the fire for several minutes, watching the items burn until they were ash. Watching the flames lick up the sides of the fake logs I wished that somehow I could get the fire to burn away the horrid taste of Nikki still in my mouth.

"I am so screwed," I whispered.

"How can that be? You're the only one in the room."

I turned to see Devin standing just inside the door dressed in full Warrior battle gear, an awkward smile on his face that fell when I did not reciprocate.

"Sorry, Brother, I was just trying to make a joke. I didn't knock because I knew Brianna had left with Kyla. Are you okay?"

"Yes," I replied as I cleared my throat trying to shake away the demons from the last few horrifying minutes and get my head into battle mode.

"Everything's fine. Bri went shopping with Kyla, just a little worried about her being in public."

I could not be sure if Devin believed me or not, but he simply carried on as if the awkward tension was not surrounding us. "Very well then, get dressed. We need to start loading up."

Without saying a word I walked into my changing area and quickly began pulling on my gear. Just as I zipped up the new protective vests we had purchased after being ripped to shreds by Elaina's last hybrids, I heard Devin call from inside the bedroom, "Brother, why does it smell like lemons in here?"

Chapter Eleven

Cameron

"Perimeter team, confirm position?" I whispered into my comm with no response. "Perimeter team, this is Cameron, do you copy?"

When no one responded I began backing away from my position, but suddenly froze when the brush began to rustle behind me. Either the perimeter team had been taken out and the killer was now approaching me, or the comms were down. I sincerely prayed for the latter of course and my fears were quenched as soon as Devin burst through the bushes in front of me.

"I copy you, Brother, but only because I was right behind you. I think Uri turned the comms off. What possessed Jared to assign Uri of all people to run tech?"

I shrugged, though I had a feeling it was to punish me somehow. "Text Uri, we need to...oow god damn it." Devin and I ripped out our earpieces as the high pitched feedback rung in our heads. Even with the earpiece hanging down you could hear the muffled bickering of the other members of the team. "I guess Uri turned the comms on."

Devin was not amused. "I'm going to throw Jared in the sun for this."

"Brother, be gentle with Jared. You know how upset he is."

"Be gentle my ass. Um, no, pretend I didn't just say that. Everyone confirm positions," Devin said, clearing his throat and avoiding all eye contact with me as he backed away to get into position.

"See you inside, Brother."

Devin pumped his chest before disappearing into the brush. If our enemy did not know about our presence before, they may certainly know now. That was always a major issue with raiding a Vampire hideout – it was hard being quiet enough to where a Vampire would not hear you.

The hideout in question was a small ranch-style home located on the outskirts of Modesto hidden among the trees of an area park. In some respects hidden in plain sight, but far enough away from snooping neighbors. Thankfully the woods provided us some cover, but there was most likely some kind of surveillance and we had little time to search for it.

After placing the earpiece of my comm back in my ear I checked my watch. Two minutes left until Devin would give the signal to Project to our positions on the sides of the house. Two minutes for me to continue to see flashes of Nikki standing half-naked in my bedroom and Jared screaming in disappointment. Now a minute and a half left to imagine the hurt and sadness in Brianna's eyes when she finds out what I have done. The hope I had felt earlier this afternoon when she came home to me had dissipated and the worry of her leaving me again was settling in. One minute left to think about what I was going to do once I got back to the manor. Who all would I tell, how would I mend things with Jared, how would I keep Brianna from leaving again. Less than one minute left to…

Tap.

I looked at my watch again. According to it I still had thirty-two seconds left to wallow in self-misery. But I heard Devin tap the mic of his comm. Two more taps and it was time to Project.

Tap.

Tap.

Devin's watch must be fast. Taking a deep cleansing breath, I shot away all my nagging thoughts and doubt, and Projected to the backdoor of the little house. From the look of the windows it appeared my entrance led into the kitchen. Devin was taking the front, and Alexander was going to make a door of his own through the side of the house.

The mist around me faded as I crouched into position up against a set of concrete stairs. Now all I had to do was wait for three more taps in my ear. Like I said before, it was hard to sneak up on a Vampire. You could not give out an order verbally and not have a Vampire hear it when you were this close to them. So we had become accustomed to tapping the mic on the comm since it was silent to anyone who did not have an earpiece jammed in their ear.

In the seconds that passed waiting for Devin's signal to storm into the house, a sickly sweet fragrance began wafting around me. The smell was distinctive and undeniable - Vampire blood. In fact more like dead Vampire blood. When the first tap came through my earpiece I braced myself for whatever was located on the other side of the door.

Tap.

Tap.

In one quick movement I leapt from my crouched position and burst through the backdoor causing shards of glass and wood to fly around me. Even before the debris hit the ground the smell of a dead Vampire was overwhelming and the source was lying right at my feet. As I knelt down beside the beheaded Vampire I heard the sounds of my brothers searching the house, or tearing down walls in Alexander's case.

"I have Rowley," I announced as I lifted his head by his blonde blood-crusted hair.

"I have two dead in the living room," Devin responded.

That was three. I stood and walked out of the small kitchen and turned into the hallway. "And here is the fourth," I said, looking down at another decapitated Vampire lying on the floor in the direction of the kitchen, seemingly trying to escape along with Rowley.

Alexander came from within one of the bedrooms and said, "The rest of the house is clear, Cam. I'll have the perimeter team look for any trails and evidence leading away from the house." He turned and left through the large hole in the back wall that he had created. I looked up to see Devin shaking his head, his eyes conveying the frustration and anger of being beaten again.

"How did Elaina know we were coming?" Devin shouted and then punched a hole in the wall in front of him. "The blood is relatively fresh so they were killed maybe an hour or so ago. An hour! For weeks we have been just a half step behind and I am tired of it. If we have another traitor among us I will rip his head off, sew it back on just so that I can rip it off again!"

"I see Devin is handling this well," Alexander said as he came up behind me while Devin continued his ranting and destruction of the area around him.

"Walk the scene with me?" I asked in order to let Devin cool off.

Alexander nodded and we began recreating the havoc that happened prior to our arrival. Based on the side by side position of the bodies in the living room, it seemed as though they were killed at the same time. We knew the body in the kitchen was of Rowley, and we soon identified the Vampire in the hallway as Carter. The difference between the dead Vampires in the living room and Elaina's cohorts was that the latter two appeared to have been trying to escape, but from whom was the real question. Someone had gotten away alive.

"Perhaps this fifth Vampire had been tipped off that they had been found out," I speculated to Alexander and Devin who had finally calmed down enough to join us. "There would not have been enough time for one Vampire to kill all four at once. So perhaps Carter or Rowley killed the first two..."

"And the fifth Vamp killed the two of them?" Alexander asked as he walked the path from the hallway through to the kitchen.

"Think about it, Carter and Rowley think they are two of Elaina's most trusted allies. So they killed the peons in the living room, but it was only when they realized that they too were on the kill list did they run."

Devin nodded in agreement and headed into one of the bedrooms. "So what we really need to do is find this fifth Vampire. He has to be pretty highly ranked in Elaina's coven to do this and be trusted with everything he took out of here."

The house had been trashed even before Alexander and Devin destroyed the walls and a few pieces of furniture. Power cords and other wires dangled from outlets and monitors within the bedrooms. It was apparent that several computers had been taken along with items from a small overturned filing cabinet. A shredding machine's trash bag was overflowing with thin slivers of paper and photos that had been shoved into it before the culprit finally left. The perimeter team had unfortunately only found a small trail of blood leading from the house to the driveway where the Vampire most likely drove away with the evidence of what this specialty team of Elaina's was doing. Victor would be furious.

Because the location of the home was near a residential area I needed to call in a clean-up crew. Within an hour they would have all evidence of death and destruction gone, along with placing Glamours on any neighbors in the surrounding areas if appropriate. There was a coven specializing in practically everything. The Cleaners, as they were commonly called, were the only Vampires summoned more often for help than the Warriors. Anyone associated with their coven specialized in Glamours and human manipulation, and of course cleaning up the messes we Vampires so often created. They were essential in keeping our race hidden, though in modern times it had become increasingly difficult. Just as the crew's white van pulled into the driveway, Alexander called me into one of the bedrooms.

"Take a look at this," he said as he handed me a ripped corner of a photograph. "It got jammed in the shredder. Look familiar?"

I squinted at the small black and white picture in front of me and saw only a pair of legs from the knees down of a slim male in front of a vehicle.

"What am I missing, Alex?"

"Cam, look at the shoes, look at the pants."

I narrowed my eyes again, concentrating on the figure in the picture. "Is that me?"

"I think so," Alexander replied as he pulled several thin shreds from the underside of the shredder. "And if we put it together with a few of these…" he said as he placed the pieces together to form a larger piece of the photograph.

"This was when Brianna and I were fighting in the parking lot at the doctor's office. How did you recognize that?"

"The rims of my truck, and well, Cam not many people wear black skinny jeans like you do."

I tried to laugh at his jab, but I was more frightened at the fact that these men who were so close to Elaina had been so close to Brianna. "After all the evasions and protective measures we took, she still found us. We might as well hand her over to Elaina with all the good we are doing."

"I'm going to take that as the anger talking. Don't give up, Cam. You didn't let me, and I'm not letting you. Even though this tells us they were there, Brianna is still with us. She's still safe."

My eyes widened at the realization that Brianna was out in public and exposed to a threat that was closer than any of us had known.

"Call Kyla," Alexander said quickly as the realization hit him as well.

I pulled my cell phone from one of the cargo pockets of my pants and quickly dialed Kyla.

"This is girl time, no time for boys right now. Call back later please," Kyla answered cheerily on the other end of the line.

"Where are you," I said gruffly.

"Around the corner from the manor, what's up your butt?"

"Brianna is all right?"

"Of course she is. She's sleeping right next to me. I completely wore her out."

"Make sure you are not being followed and get her in the house right away. Elaina's been a little closer than we thought."

"Got it. We're pulling up to the gate now, so no worries here. We kept a look out and Brianna kept scanning her little head out which is probably why she's so tired. We didn't see anyone and Brianna didn't feel any other Vampires but us, so I think we're safe."

"That is certainly a relief," I sighed in the phone.

"Now tell Alex I'll be waiting for him and that I have a scantily-clad surprise he's going to love."

"I will not."

"I would tell Bri something like that if you wanted me to."

"I would not want you to. Oh for heaven's sake." I took the phone away from my ear and handed it Alexander. "Talk to your wife."

While Alexander and Kyla conversed about their evening's sexual escapades I walked out of the house while the cleaning crew began disposing of the bodies. Once outside I could hear Devin screaming into his cell phone. Just as I came alongside him he hung up the phone and threw it into a bush.

"Useless, absolutely useless!" he shouted at the bush.

"And what has the bush done to you, Brother?"

Devin turned to face me, utter disgust plastered all over his face. "I called Uri to pull up any satellite or surveillance footage we could find from the last few hours. What does he say to me? Guess. No, you'll never guess because it's so ridiculously asinine. He says to me, 'I don't know how to do that, Devin.' Can you believe that? Jared puts someone on this team who can't remember to turn the comms back on, can't upload the photos I sent him of the scene to our servers, and now tells me he has no idea how to get into the satellites. Like I said, useless."

"Not everyone is Jared, Brother," I said patting him on the shoulder.

"Then Jer had no business leaving the team. This is inexcusable," Devin shouted and stepped away from me in search of his cell phone.

"Brother, he is mad and upset about not being able to come with us. Try and talk to him when we get back and tell him that you will speak with Father."

"Why would I speak with Father?"

Sometimes talking to Devin was like talking to a selfish child.

"You need to speak with Father about not being so protective of Jared."

"You think Father is being protective?"

It took all my strength not to shake him. "Yes, Brother. Have you not noticed that Father is continually making excuses and changing our plans so that Jared is unable to come with us on missions?"

"I usually don't question Father's reasoning. That's your job apparently," he chided as he plucked out a leafy twig that was wedged in his phone. "Why would Father purposely prevent Jared from going on missions?"

"I think Father got scared after Jared was burned so badly during the manor attack."

Devin shook his head. "Father doesn't get scared. He's lost soldiers and Warriors all his life. Why would Jared getting hurt affect him?"

"Why did he spare my life after I disobeyed him? Why does he only argue with you in private? Why are some Warriors allowed to live outside the manor's walls and others are not? It is because we are all different to him. Every one of us has a unique relationship with him. I think he is protective of Jared because he is the newest and youngest of all of us. Father needs to let Jared be a Warrior again, not keep him locked in the manor."

"I can see your point, but why do *I* need to speak with Father about this."

I paused for only a second and I could tell that my delay in answering caused him to have silent questions of his own. "I believe Jared would appreciate it more if it came from you. And Father might listen to you because he knows that you are usually not emotionally tied to these sorts of things."

"I'm not emotionally tied to this," he said flatly.

"Devin, this is Jared, our little brother. You are tied to him as much as I am and we both know it. Think about it this way, if you do not speak with Father, Jared may never help us again. What happened today with Uri could be a regular occurrence."

That got him. He nodded vehemently at the realization of not having Jared on our side any longer, and the conversation left me exhausted. Not only did I have to try and pull at Devin's non-existent heartstrings, I had to convince him to do this good deed for our brother since Jared would not take kindly to me speaking to Father on his behalf. If I did, it might look as though I was trying to buy his silence, which I was not. I was helping him through Devin because I loved my youngest brother and I would do anything for him even though now he thought the worst of me. However, within the next couple of hours he would not be the only one. Soon enough I would be telling Brianna that I had kissed another woman. To hell in a hand basket, that was where my life was going today. I only hoped I was a good enough swimmer to save it.

Chapter Twelve

Brianna

"Wake up, sleepy head," I heard Kyla cooing softly in my ear as a cool breeze hit my face.

Had I fallen asleep?

Slowly I stretched my eyes open finding that I was in the last position I remembered being in before I apparently passed out. The baby was zapping all my energy, and though it was annoying I would sleep every hour of the day if I had to. Kyla offered me her hand and helped me down from the tall SUV, her arms full of our treasures from a very successful shopping trip. Since the last two times I went shopping ended with me running for my life, Kyla and I had decided to make this one count. I had enough clothes to last me several pregnancies. No matter how big I got, I had a shirt that would cover me, and pants that would stretch far enough that I would never need to walk around with them unbuttoned. Cam would be thrilled.

With bags in tow, Kyla wrapped her arm around me and pulled me up the stairs that led into the manor. Home. Well, kind of. It was the closest thing I had to a home, and though I was happy with Eris and Sera, I felt like a guest. This was where my heart wanted to be – surrounded by stone and thick carpets and large hanging tapestries. I was surrounded by history and strength and most importantly, family.

"Why are you looking at me like that?" Kyla asked as we stepped into the foyer.

"Sorry, just thinking about how much I missed this place."

"*And?!*"

"And you too, of course. Especially you. I cried myself to sleep every night because we were apart."

"LOL you did not," she said, placing her hands on her hips and causing the shopping bags to fall and hit her legs.

"Ky, I know I'm not all up to date on today's lingo, but I don't think you're supposed to actually say that you're laughing out loud, you could probably just laugh out loud."

With an exasperated sigh she turned away and began walking down the main corridor. "Do you need to eat?"

"Were you not there when I ate my weight in French fries?" I asked as I tried to catch up with her.

"Yes and you also threw up most of them up. So food, yes or no?"

"No, I'm going to go see Jared and give him the shirt we bought. Ya know, just try and pick his spirits up."

While we were shopping the two Warriors who had escorted us began talking about how they had heard through the Warrior gossip grapevine that Jared had ended up refusing to do the mission altogether. My baby brother was upset, and I was hoping that a vintage concert t-shirt would help.

"No fun," Kyla pouted. "I thought we could unpack all your new stuff and play dress up."

I pouted and replied, "Kyla, I'm exhausted. I'm just going to see Jared and then probably pass out again. I'm not even sure I'll be able to stay awake until Cam gets home. Besides, don't you need to grease yourself into that dominatrix outfit you bought for your wild naughty night with Alex?"

"Ok, fine," she sighed and then hugged me tightly. Just before I released her she whispered in my ear, "Please don't leave like that again, ok?"

I pulled out of her embrace, taking the bag that contained Jared's shirt from around her wrist. "I didn't want to leave, Ky, you know that. But I think Cam got his shit together while I was gone. At least I hope he did."

"He did!" she shouted quickly. "He was miserable without you, trust me we all wanted to slap him a couple of times." I laughed softly which made Kyla smile. "I'll take the bags to your room, go see Jared and then into that comfy bed of yours where you'll cuddle with Cameron all night and make up and make more babies."

"And where would I put them?" I laughed as I rubbed my hands over my bulging belly.

After another tight hug Kyla turned and quickly disappeared up the stairs while I headed downstairs where my favorite strawberry-blonde Vampire was most likely pouting and feeling sorry for himself.

When I was only a few feet from his door I said, "I don't see a sock on the door, so I'm assuming you're alone. Either way, I'm coming in."

Just as I approached his door, Jared stepped out from his room, his shoulders slightly slouched but there was still a smile on his face. "Good grief, Bri, you're huge."

"I am not!" I said as I squeezed my arms around his neck. "I've been gone for three weeks and I get Bri? No Bibi, no Beebs? Who are you and what have you done with Jerry Smith?"

Jared glared at me over using his real name. "I finally call you something you'd rather be called and you rank on me for it? Hormonal much?"

"Oh you don't even know the half of it."

"Well...ah...you...er...it was good to see you. You'd...ah...better get some rest or something," he said and turned to go back into his room.

"Hey, I can't come in? Are you mad at me or something? I know I didn't say goodbye to you when I left, but I...."

"No, no, it's not that," he replied quickly, but his tone was still sad. "Um, my room is a mess."

I stood in front of him sunken in my hip with my arms crossed in front of me. "Jer, your room is always a mess. You gotta girl in there or something?"

"No..."

"Well, I need to sit down," I said, pushing my way through the door uninvited, but then stopped suddenly. Now I had been in Jared's room many times and I was used to seeing dirty clothes and electronics strewn all over, but this was frightening. "Jer, what happened in here?"

"It's been a really shitty day. That used to be a table," he replied, pointing to a pile of splintered wood in the middle of the floor.

I stepped further into the room, being careful not to trip over the carnage of wood and plastic electrical pieces. "Had a little tantrum, did we?"

Jared only half laughed as he made a clean patch on his bed for me to sit.

"I say spring cleaning. We don't have a single extra cell phone or computer now."

"Well if you say so. Here, I bought you something," I said handing him the small plastic bag.

Jared lifted the vintage black shirt and without caring that I was sitting in front of him he removed his shirt and pulled the new one over his head and smoothed it down his chest.

"I have no idea who this band is, but the shirt is great. Thanks, sis."

He bent down and hugged me tighter than I would have expected for a new shirt. There was almost a sense of urgency that I rarely felt from him and I thought it could only be about one thing.

"Have you tried talking to Victor?"

"Talk to Dad about what?" he responded and walked around his equipment-filled desk to sit behind one of his many monitors.

"I know you're upset that you couldn't go on the mission tonight, *hence* the state of your room right now."

"Talking to Dad doesn't really work."

"What if you asked Cam to talk to him? Maybe he could convince…"

"No."

Jared didn't yell, he growled. Having experienced the brunt of Jared's anger before, I decided not to push the topic of why Jared was obviously angry with Cameron.

I rose from the bed and kicked away what looked like half of a table leg out of my way as I leaned over Jared's monitor. "So what's the story with Nikki? Is she still here?"

Jared kept his eyes on the monitor and began typing on the keyboard. "Yeah, I've seen her around."

When a silence extended between us I pressed. "Seen her around whom?"

"Just around. She came in for a cell phone today with Skylar."

"So Skylar's her latest victim?"

"Hardly," he muttered, keeping his attention intently on the screen in front of him.

"You?"

"No!"

"Cam?"

Jared's eyes shot up at me, and my stomach starting to sink. His worried stare made me afraid that whatever fries I hadn't thrown up were unfortunately going to shoot out into Jared's face.

"I really don't want to go there, Bri."

"Jer, please, you're making me think the worst."

"What would be the worst?"

"That something happened between Cameron and Nikki while I was gone." Jared didn't respond and a lump formed in my throat. "D-did something happen between Cam and Nikki?"

Jared sighed as he looked at the floor. "I saw them kissing."

The blood ran from my face. Jared shot up from his chair and helped me over to the bed where he lowered me down slowly. A second later he disappeared into his small bathroom and returned with several tissues.

"Look, I'm learning. Tissues instead of alcohol."

"When did you see them?"

"This afternoon."

The tears stopped. "*When* this afternoon?" He didn't answer. "Jer, please tell me the truth, when did you see them?"

"A little while after you got back. I went to talk to him about Dad and that's when I saw them."

I was at a loss for words. Cameron, my Cam, the supposed love of my life, father of my child dared to put his lips on another woman. Not just any other woman, Nikki. Miss Trick Nikki was once again messing with my life. But was I overreacting? Cameron had been so happy to see me when I returned home today. Why would he turn around minutes later and throw everything away?

"Was she throwing herself at him, or was he really kissing her?" Throwing herself, throwing herself, please say she was throwing herself at him.

"She was in her underwear and had her arms around him. He certainly wasn't pushing her away."

"Well he's had that problem before," I said, remembering when Melanie kissed him my first night at the Facility. Was this my life? Would my future with Cameron be filled with women kissing him at will? I don't know any woman who could compete with that. I *wouldn't* compete with that. My tears were replaced with anger and yet again, betrayal. If Cameron thought he could just do whatever he wanted when I was away then he had another thing coming. Did he think he could keep doing this to me? Was it because I lived in *his* home, and used *his* money.

"I'm not a gold digger."

Jared scrunched his face together. "Never said you were."

"Sorry, I meant to yell at Cameron in my head. Can you do me a big favor?"

"Totally, since I feel like a complete asshole right now."

"Kyla said she would drop off the stuff I bought in my room, can you grab those bags and bring them in here? And if you happen to see a suitcase and an overnight bag can you grab those too?"

"Ah, sure," he replied questioningly, but didn't push. Once he stepped out into the hallway I grabbed my purse and started digging for my cell phone.

"Bonjourno, mia figlia," Eris's cheerful voice came over the line. "Miss me already?"

"Dad," I whimpered, and then had to cover my mouth to hide my emotions. Even though I hated to admit it, I had become a daddy's girl with my actual father.

"What has happened," he demanded, his cheery voice changing dramatically at the sound of his daughter breaking down.

I took in one big sniffle before I answered, "I really don't want to talk about it, and I know it's a lot to ask but I was wondering if you could send the jet back to San Francisco?"

"Of course. Come back home."

"Dad, I don't know where I'm going yet. I just can't be here."

"Whoa, where the hell are you going?" Jared shouted as he struggled to get through the door with all the bags and suitcases.

"Daughter, I do not think it wise for you to go anywhere where we cannot watch over you."

"Dad, please just trust me when I say I need to do this. I need to get out of here and be by myself. Please, Dad."

I heard the phone shuffle around but Eris's voice returned shortly after. "Sera says to send the jet, but I still say it's dangerous."

"Sera will know if I'm going to get into trouble. I know it's a lot to ask, but I hope you'll understand."

I could hear the reluctance to give me his assurance, but finally he said, "I trust you, daughter, but also understand my concern. The jet will be there in an hour, but Vlad will need to know where to take you."

"Th-thanks, Dad," I said, struggling to swallow the lump in my throat.

"Be careful, daughter, and you let me know if I need to straighten anyone out. One Warrior, the whole coven, I will take them all if I have to."

When I hung up the phone I was startled by the sound of Jared dropping all the shopping bags and suitcases on the ground.

"First of all, you have way too much shit. Second, WTF?"

"Ok," I said as I stood and put my hand up in front of me, "I hate when Kyla does that so I really hate when you do it. Use your words."

"Fine, Miss English Major, what the fuck are you thinking? You can't *go* anywhere? Are the hormones making you crazy or something?"

"Cool it with the hormone talk, ok? You just told me that..." but I couldn't even say it and the tears started to come again.

"Oh come on, you know I hate it when you cry." Jared stepped through the scattered bags and patted my back as he allowed me to rest my face on his chest. "Although I hate it more when you ruin my new shirt."

This time I laughed into his chest, though it was half a laugh and half a cry. I raised my head and could tell that even though he wanted to help me, he was worried about what I was choosing to do. "I need to sneak out of here and I can't do it on my own, but I hate to ask you because I know you'll get in trouble with Victor, and Cameron will be furious with you."

Jared shook his head. "Screw 'em, especially Cameron."

I wiped my eyes with the remaining tissue in my hand and began sifting through the bags to find something I could change into since I was still in my unbuttoned pants.

"I'm going to change and then I have to unpack and then repack, but it should only take about fifteen minutes."

"I'll get a car and pull it around to the side entrance." Jared turned to leave but then stopped. "You know I hate this right? I hate that you're leaving, I hate why you're leaving, and I especially hate that you'll be out there all alone. What if Elaina finds you? I'll never forgive myself."

Taking a step over to him I threw my arms around his neck and hugged him tightly. "I'll be careful. And if something should happen, all of this was my decision. I made you do this, you had no choice."

Jared pulled my arms down from around his neck and shook his head again. "It just scares me that I may never see you again. I…I love ya, sis."

"Don't do that or I'll start crying again." He laughed lightly but looked up at the ceiling instead of keeping eye contact with me (or trying not to cry, although he would never admit it). "Make sure you avoid Kyla, she'll know something is going on."

"You do realize she's going to go ape shit when she finds out, right?"

"Yep." Especially since only minutes ago I promised her I would never leave again.

"Ok, fifteen minutes and I'll be back. Be ready to go, no primping or anything."

"Wait," I said, turning back to him before he closed the door. "I'll need one more thing."

"What could you possibly be missing?"

"I need my daggers."

Chapter Thirteen

Cameron

"So you actually ripped Rowley's ear off?" Alexander asked, looking over at Connor in the driver's seat.

"Yeah, got it right here," Connor smiled and pulled out the bloody remnant of the dead Vampire's ear. When he glanced in the rearview mirror and saw that both Devin and I had disgusted faces, his proud expression faded. "What? He didn't need it anymore and the Cleaners were going to burn it anyway."

"Even I don't keep trophies, Connor," Devin said smugly.

"That's because there's never enough left when you're done with them," Connor fired back. Even Devin joined in laughing at Connor's accurate depiction of the Warrior Assassin.

The drive home from Modesto had been relatively quiet, mostly on my part. The others dabbled in polite conversation, none of us truly happy with the results of our mission. It would be another failure in Father's eyes and no one wanted to present that information to him. Unfortunately what we did find only made my anxiety over Brianna's safety grow, although it was not limited to the surveillance photo we found. As the manor drew closer the deepening pit in my stomach was becoming almost unbearable.

"Brother?" Devin asked, tapping me lightly on the shoulder.

I snapped my head in his direction, coming back from wherever my mind had wondered. "Sorry, what?"

"I was saying to Alex that I think we should present our findings to Father as soon as we get in. Do you agree?"

"Brother, although most times I would agree with you, since we do not have the best of news to present to him I think we could wait until early morning." Devin opened his mouth to protest but I continued, "I have to spend some time with Brianna and speak with her about...things and it simply cannot wait. She will not miss me in the early morning hours and hopefully Alex will no longer be...er...otherwise engaged."

Alexander turned around in his seat quickly. "She told you something, didn't she?"

"She started to, but I refused to listen which was why I gave you the phone."

"Oh that woman!"

If Alexander could have blushed he would have. Kyla was unfortunately very open about their sexual activities, to all our dismay.

"Brother, perhaps this will give you an opportunity to speak with Jared," I suggested.

"I still don't understand why I have to do this. This is more your territory than it is mine."

"Consider this a learning exercise. I am helping you grow your leadership skills."

Both Alexander and Connor laughed at my statement and Devin's eyes narrowed at me. He could tell there was a reason I was asking him to do this for me, but he was choosing not to ask and I was thankful since I was not up for telling.

The remainder of the ride home was relatively quiet and when the four of us entered the manor we all parted in different directions – Connor to preserve his trophy, Alexander into the arms of Kyla, Devin to see Jared, and me to speak with my angel. As I approached our bedroom door a sense of dread and foreboding flooded over me. Brianna would be hurt tonight, this I knew and it killed me. I only hoped that she would listen and not immediately dismiss me as Jared did. One could hope, but when raging female hormones were involved nothing was guaranteed.

Taking one last deep breath, I turned the door handle and quietly opened the door in case she had fallen asleep. The bedroom was silent and still, and even through the darkness I could see that Brianna was not in our bed.

"Brianna?" I called, stepping further into our room and looking over at the sitting area near the fireplace. Nothing. "Bri?" I called with more urgency as I walked into the changing area and peeked into the dark bathroom. Nothing. I stepped back into the bedroom and my panic exploded when I saw the absence of Brianna's luggage on the floor where I had left it. The room did not even have a hint of her smell.

Not wanting to jump to any horrifying conclusions I began searching the manor and the grounds for her. Again, she was nowhere to be found. After twenty minutes I finally gave in and knocked on a door I had been trying to avoid.

"Busy," Kyla said annoyed from inside.

"Do you know where Brianna is?"

"She's not in here. Try your bedroom."

"I did. She is not there or the training room, the kitchen, the library, the garden, the courtyard…"

"I don't need a play by play," Kyla said as the door flew open. She was tightening the robe around her and giving me a murderous glare.

"Kyla, I apologize, you know I would never dream of interrupting you but I cannot find Brianna and I am worried."

"More like freaking out. She said she was going to see Jared, she's probably still down there. You know how those two are. Why are you looking at me like that?"

Because my worst nightmare might have just come true. Without waiting another second I used every bit of energy I had to propel me down the hall and stairs toward Jared's room ignoring Kyla's shouts behind me. In the few seconds it took me to get to Jared's room, I said a hundred silent prayers that Brianna was not with him. The combination of her going to Jared's room and her luggage missing sent panic pulsing through every nerve in my body.

Without knocking I burst into Jared's room to find him standing with a garbage bag and speaking with Devin who turned as I came into the room. Jared's expression instantly changed and he was furious. "Get out, asshole. I so don't want to talk to you right now."

"Where is she?" I asked impatiently as I looked around the room and then saw a pile of her clothes on his bed and the sight of a broken table and electronics strewn all over the room. "If you have hurt her…"

"If I?" he shouted, throwing his garbage bag down on the floor and pushing against Devin. "I'm not the one who cheated on her."

"Where is she!?"

"She's gone, dude," he replied with a sly smile.

"What do you mean, she's gone?"

"Did I stutter? She's not here, douchebag, she left."

"Who left?" Kyla asked as she came through the door with Alexander.

Jared answered before I could. "Brianna's gone. I took her to the airport an hour ago."

"You did what?" I growled as I stepped toward him, only to have Alexander step in my way.

"I told you I wouldn't lie for you," Jared replied, trying to remove Devin's arm from in front of him.

"And why would Cameron need you to lie for him?"

The room went silent and all eyes turned to see Victor standing in the doorway, his raspy voice cutting through the chaos in the room.

When no one answered, Victor stepped further into the room. "I will not beg to be told why two of my children are fighting. One of you better start explaining what is going on here."

Once again Jared beat me to the punch. "Brianna's left again."

Father raised his eyebrows and looked in my direction. "Has she decided to go back to her father's?"

"No. Brianna told him she wasn't going back but she didn't tell either of us where she was going. Probably so that we couldn't be compelled to tell."

"You stupid prat," I shouted as Alexander slowly backed me to the other side of the room. "You have just fed her to the wolves."

I could see Jared's cocky attitude fade slightly as he shifted uncomfortably from side to side when Victor stepped in front of him. "Child, what have you done? What would possess you to take Brianna from the safety of our home?"

Jared looked over Victor's shoulder and glared in my direction as he said, "Why don't you tell 'em, Cameron? Why would Brianna want to leave the manor so badly that she would beg me to sneak her out so that she could fly away somewhere where you'll never find her?"

All eyes turned on me, but I could not say it, not with everyone in the room.

"Child, we are waiting," Victor said, moving Alexander to the side so that he could speak to me directly.

"Father, it is a misunderstanding," I began but was interrupted by Jared.

"Oh yeah, screwing around with Nikki was all a misunderstanding."

"I DID NOT SLEEP WITH HER," I shouted, letting my temper get the best of me. "After Brianna left with Kyla today I came to my room and found Nikki in my bed. She kissed me and I threw her down on the floor." I put my hand up to stop Jared from cutting in. "She threatened that she would tell Father that I had assaulted her sexually unless I kissed her, and if I refused she would find a way to drive Brianna sick with worry that we were having an affair. I felt like I was backed into a corner, therefore, I kissed her so she would leave us alone. That was when Jared Projected into my room and he neither felt the obligation nor the courtesy to listen to any kind of explanation, so all I asked was that he not tell Brianna what he saw since he would tell her what happened out of context and I wanted to tell her the truth."

"Bullshit," Jared said under his breath.

"No, Jared, what is bullshit is the fact that you believed I would blatantly cheat on Brianna the day she returned from a three week absence. Not only do you have her thinking I have been unfaithful, you have exposed her to our enemy that we discovered only tonight has been following her more closely than we thought. For all we know they have followed her to wherever she has gone and her dream of being kidnapped by Elaina will now come true. For all we know the Vampire who killed four of Elaina's cronies is now after Brianna, and good news for them, she no longer has an entourage of Warriors around her. Smart move, Jared, you have just sent your sister to her death."

The room was silent for a moment before Victor turned away from me and said to Devin, "I take it there is information from the mission you need to share with me?" Devin nodded. "Jared, since you lost Brianna I suggest you find her and bring her back here."

Jared's chin stiffened as he looked Victor dead in the eye and said, "No."

All noise and movement ceased. Surprisingly, Father's tone was even as he spoke. "You are trying my patience, child. Now I will say it again, find where Brianna has gone off to and bring her back."

"No," he replied. "I will not help *him* drag Bri back here."

"And why not?" Victor demanded.

"Because she is not a prisoner like I am."

Victor's face and tone softened as he said, "No one is a prisoner here, but it is a matter of safety when it comes to Brianna. I am surprised that Eris even agreed to this."

"Sera has her back," Jared mumbled.

"Seraphina cannot help Brianna if she is thousands of miles away. Right now I am asking you to find out where Brianna has gone, but in three seconds I am going to be ordering you and I will not show restraint."

Jared's lips tightened and nostrils began to flare, ready to fight, but for the first time that evening I was able to speak before Jared could. "Father, do not force him. I will find Brianna, she is after all more my responsibility than his."

"Very well," Victor said in a huff. "I want to be debriefed on tonight's activities in fifteen minutes and every member of the team better be present. I want answers for yet another failed mission and no one is above reproach tonight." He turned in a sweeping motion and disappeared into the hallway.

The air felt stagnant as my family and I looked around the room at each other wondering who would break the awkward silence. Not able to look at any of them a second longer I turned on my heels and moved toward the door. Suddenly Kyla was standing in front of me, her arms crossed in front of her chest, hurt and disappointment etched into her smooth skin. Before I could open my mouth to give her words of apology, she slapped me hard across the cheek. So hard in fact that I lost my balance and reached for the wall.

"Kyla!" Alexander shouted from behind me and then pulled Kyla away from the door by her wrist. "Cam, I'm sorry."

"Don't apologize for me, Alex Hunter!" Kyla shouted as she pulled her wrist from her husband's grip. "He deserved it, and don't even try and tell me that one of you believe he didn't. Jared stuck up for Brianna and so am I. If she were here she would have done the same thing or used her mind trick to knock him down. Cameron, you know I love you, but how stupid can you be? There were ten different things you could have done other than kiss that skanky girl."

"Then you should have been there to tell me what they were," I snapped. "Now if you will excuse me, I need to call in a favor."

This certainly had to be one of the worst days of my long life. After being physically slapped in the face by Kyla, my team and I were verbally slapped by Victor for over an hour. He was furious that his coven may have another traitor within its midst. To Victor, not only did this person threaten the security of the Warriors, they were threatening the safety of his grandchildren. *My* children. The thought kept circling in my head as I sat on the floor with my back pressed up against my bedroom door with a bottle of cold blood in my hand. If I were human it would have been a bottle of bourbon or scotch, and just as I was doing now I would not be bothering with a glass. I was drunk with over indulgence, my stomach bloated and uncomfortable as I continued to forcibly drink the rancid red fluid.

My bedroom never seemed so stark and cold. I chose to sit in the dark since the lights displayed my harsh reality - I was alone. Brianna's absence was even more devastating now than it had been in the weeks prior. At least when she was with Eris I knew she was safe. Now, I knew nothing. Elaina could have taken her already and I was none the wiser. I hated myself for what I had done. Kyla had been right, there were probably other options than the one I chose but it was too late now. This was the consequence of my actions and it was painful.

For hours I sat up against the door, picturing in my mind the sight of my angel lying in our bed and being fascinated at how the moonlight would glow against her skin, somehow making her even more beautiful than she already was. My fingers ached to run through her dark hair as I would often do while she slept. It was awful to think that I might never see Brianna again.

Just when I thought my hopelessness would consume me, I felt my phone vibrate from my back pants pocket. Thankfully I was the only one in the room, as I must have looked ridiculous kicking my legs out and rolling over to get to my phone only to have it slip through my fingers like a bar of soap. I felt utterly human. Looking at my phone my stomach fell when the call was not coming from Brianna.

"Good morning, Oliver."

"Son, what in tar nation is goin' on over there?"

"Have you spoken with Brianna?" I asked, eagerly hoping Brianna was with him.

"She called me last night after midnight and she knows better. When you get a phone call after nine o'clock, somebody's dead. 'Bout nearly had a heart attack when I heard her voice. A course I could barely understand what she was sayin' with all the cryin' she was doin'."

"So she is not with you?"

"No, son."

"Have you spoken to her since?"

"Naw, and she said she wouldn't be able ta call for a while."

"What did she tell you?"

"Like I said, I couldn't really understand her she was cryin' so much, but she said sumpin' about you carryin' on with another girl and that she was leavin' San Francisco for a little while. Now, I think a ya like a son, Cameron, but if yous a foolin' around on my girl…"

"Oliver, I assure you I am not."

"Then what's goin' on with ya? Now 'Lil Bri don't tell me specifics, but I know you ain't been around and that just don't make sense to me. What's goin' on in that head a yours? It's like someone's controllin' yur mind. Pregnant women can be downright crazy and you can't…"

"Wait, Oliver, what did you say?"

"About pregnant women bein' crazy?"

"No, before that."

"That you're acting like someone's controllin' yur mind?"

"Oliver, I apologize I need to go."

"Oh, alright then. Well, just one more thing and I'll letcha go," he began, although I was itching to hang up. "She's hurtin', son, and I stayed quiet way too many years when she was with Sam and I ain't gonna do that again. So I'm tellin' ya now, you better make this right and straighten up or I'll be at yur door with somethin' silver that's got yur name on it. Ya hear me?"

"Yes, sir. Quite well."

Even though he was most likely serious, I could not help but smile a little. We said our goodbyes and I raced out into the hallway and headed down the stairs to the lowest level of the living quarters. When I opened the door to Jared's room I found that it had been cleaned of all debris, and Jared sitting behind one of his computers with a quizzical look in my direction.

"I need your help."

"Dude, I appreciate you sticking up for me in front of Dad, but I'm still not going to help you find her."

"No, no, not with that. I already have someone working on it," I responded and made my way around the desk and pulled a chair up next to him. "I want to run something by you, and if it sounds…wait are you trying to hack into the CIA?" I asked pointing to the monitor in front of him.

Jared smiled sheepishly as he replied, "It's the only government network I haven't been able to crack. Whenever I'm upset or mad I just hack away. So what do you want?"

"I know this will sound as though I am making excuses, but I think I am being set up."

"Come on, man, you don't actually expect me to believe that."

"Just hear me out and if it sounds ridiculous then you can kick me out." Jared turned off the monitor and turned his chair to face me with his arms crossed in front of his chest, daring me to continue. "So think back to when we raided that warehouse. They obviously knew we were coming and the only hybrids we found alive were unbelievably damaged and emaciated, and then there was Nikki. The damaged hybrids were practically on death's door, but Nikki was not injured or suffering from starvation like the others."

"Yeah, but she's a Healer," Jared interrupted.

"True, but what if she was a plant?"

Jared leaned back in his chair. "Ok, but why?"

"To infiltrate our coven and eventually get to Brianna, or even perhaps get Brianna *away* from us." Jared's eyes flashed at the possibility. "Elaina convinces Nikki to stay at the warehouse and tells her to get into our coven to break the bond between Brianna and I, which would be the only way that Brianna would distance herself from the Warriors. When I found Nikki myself, I walked right into her trap. When she found out who I was she latched onto me and would not let anyone else help her, even when we got to the Facility."

"It seems a little farfetched, bro."

"Ok then, the night of Brianna's birthday I had to go back to the Facility because Nikki was being violent with the staff. Nikki was just inside her room when Lanashell said that if she did not control herself I would be forced to bring her to the manor. So for the next few weeks she continued to act out."

"Yeah, but you kept going to the Facility on your own. No one made you go," he said, pushing his seat away and stepping into the middle of the room.

"I know," I admitted with regret, "but it was only because she was our only connection to Elaina. With Brianna being pregnant I became obsessed with trying to find out anything I could that would lead us to Elaina so that we could put a stop to this madness. But even with all the time I spent with Nikki, she really just kept luring me in with a little hint of information here and there to keep me interested, but nothing of real importance.

"The day I brought Nikki here was the same day I had told her that I would no longer be coming to see her. I knew I had been neglecting Brianna, and Nikki was not giving me anything. So I told her that she would need to learn how to adjust in the Facility without me. Nikki flipped out and became so violent that Lanashell forced me to take her, which I think is exactly what Nikki wanted to happen. After the whole fiasco at the doctor's office, Brianna was half out the door, but I had her, I could see it in her eyes that she was going to stay, that was until Nikki interrupted us. It was on purpose, Jared, I truly believe that.

"Since then I have not seen Nikki until this morning when she came into our meeting. She saw our plans for the attack, even saw who we were attacking. What if she was able to warn Elaina that we were coming? Even missions before today have failed, she could have found out about those too, maybe even from Skylar who cannot help but brag about himself and the missions he is going on. She could have asked him some simple questions that would look like she was just curious but really she was gathering information so that she could warn Elaina."

Jared was now pacing the floor in front of me debating whether or not my theory had merit. "But what about today? You were standing there kissing her in her underwear, bro."

"This is something that has been nagging at me all day. Brianna had been gone for weeks, and not once did Nikki come to my room like that. Nikki was there when you said that Brianna was pulling up. I left right away and I am guessing she left soon after. She most likely went right up to my room and waited. It was the most opportune moment to do the most damage, and obviously it worked since you are furious with me, Kyla slapped me across the face, Father thinks the worst of me, Oliver is threatening to stab me with silver, and Brianna has left me and is out there somewhere with absolutely no protection providing the perfect opportunity for Elaina to take her without having to worry about battling us."

Jared stood in the middle of the room, rubbing the back of his neck with his hand. "So if you're right I just served Brianna on a silver tray."

I paused, making eye contact with him in silent affirmation, but unable to take his guilt. "Aidan will find her and though I would never tell him to his face, he really is one of the best Trackers I know."

"So what do you need my help with?" Jared said as he came back around to his seat in front of his computer.

"Find out everything we can on Nikki. Monitor her phone calls and watch her while she is here without tipping her off that we suspect her. She told me that Elaina took her in herself, so see if we can find out more about her family, who her parents are, what her life was like before, during, and after she was taken."

"Phone calls and research on her family I can do, but I can't find out about her life from a computer."

"I know it is a lot to ask," I said, urging him to make the conclusion on his own.

"What, you want me to pretend to be her friend?"

"Or perhaps make her think you are interested in her."

"So you really do think I'm a man whore, don't you?" If he did not have a smile on his face I would have thought I had offended him. "I'll do what I can, no promises though."

"I appreciate whatever it is you can do."

I stood and extended my hand to him and he shook it, though only half-heartedly. It was difficult not to ignore the awkward tension that still hung between us.

I turned and headed to the door when Jared said, "I know it was your idea to have Devin talk to Dad for me."

"Why would you think that?"

"Because Devin said, and I quote, 'Cameron thinks I should talk to Father on your behalf.'"

"He is not the best at being discrete, is he? I did not think you would appreciate it if I spoke with Father. I was afraid you would think that I was…"

"Trying to buy me off?"

"Something like that," I responded, giving him half a smile and uncomfortably rubbing my chin with my index finger. "Jared, what I did…what you saw…"

"Listen, bro, I really don't want to talk about it again. You screwed up big time and although we're having this little bonding moment, what you did was shitty even if she threatened you. Bri made me promise not to look for her and I hope you can understand why I won't help you. You need to work to make this up to her."

I nodded. "I know. And I hope you understand that if something happens to her because you took her out of here that I may never be able to forgive you."

Jared licked his lips and I could see that he was conflicted on keeping his promise. "It was her decision to leave, she knew the risks."

"Believe me, if something happens I will not be able to forgive her either."

Chapter Fourteen

Brianna

"I am not who you think I am," Cameron said with an expression as flat as his voice.

"How can you do this to me? To all of us," I shouted as I placed a hand on my swollen stomach, silently begging the babies to stop kicking.

"You are not the only hybrid in my life, Brianna. There is another who is in greater need than you."

"What the hell are you talking about? Stop this, Cameron. Stop this right now."

"Come brother we must go," Jazlyn said as she curled her arm around Cameron's elbow and pulled him toward the door.

"Get away from him," I screamed as I reached to rip her hand from his arm but she crushed my left hand and shoved me away. "Brianna, not all is what it seems."

I clasped my hand into my chest and Jazlyn led Cameron to the rooftop door.

"Cameron, no! No!"

I woke with a start, almost falling into the floor of the jet and yelping in pain as I caught myself with my swollen left hand, effectively pissing me off more than I already was. Out of the eight hours we had been in the air, I slept only a total of two and a half and every minute was filled with that dream cycling over and over again. The other waking hours were filled with tears and doing anything to keep myself awake so that I wouldn't have to hear Cameron's words or watch him walk away from me."

"Please fasten your seatbelts as we prepare for our descent," Vlad announced over the speakers.

I wiped a tear from my face. "You know, Vlad, you could just as easily turn around and tell me to put my seatbelt on."

Vlad kept his back to me as he replied, "But then I wouldn't get to use my trusty microphone. It is part of the fun of being a pilot."

Vlad, short for Vladimir, was my father's personal transportation specialist as he liked to call himself. After we had first met I couldn't help but think that with a name like Vladimir it seemed like it was his destiny to be a Vampire. He was tall and muscular like Devin, but sweet like Alex and funny like Jared. Vlad had known my father during his self-proclaimed indulgent years and was extremely fond of the way Sera had calmed his ways. Vlad's words, not mine.

My ears popped as the plane began its descent into Connecticut making my heart jump into my throat. Of all the places I could have chosen, Connecticut came out of my mouth. Not Jamaica, Barbados, or North Carolina even. No, Connecticut. Gray, rainy, cold, home of bad memories, Connecticut. I wanted a fresh start and I couldn't do that without shedding my former life as Mrs. Brianna Lewis. In the eyes of the law I was still married to Sam. I had had over eight hours to think about what I would do, and now that I was out of time I had absolutely no plan. I didn't even know how I was going to get out of the airport. The private airfield was in Middle-Of-Nowhere and I had to get to Upper-Butt-Crack. Sweat began to bead on my forehead and my stomach began to flutter. It could be the babies kicking, or it could have been nerves or maybe even gas.

I wiped away the sweat with the cuff of my sleeve and patted the slim rectangular leather pouch sitting next to me. Vlad had given it to me the moment I boarded the plane, telling me it was a little "cushion" from my father. Cushion? It still made me laugh. A cushion would have been a hundred dollars, not a hundred one-hundred dollar bills. My fingers shook as they rubbed against the crisp bills inside the pouch. Instead of being worried about carrying around that much cash I kept wondering how many people would hate me when they had to try and break one of them.

The plane began winding its way through the airfield trying to find, I don't know, a parking place? The sun was peeking over the horizon and I was reminded that I had lost four hours flying to the East Coast. I needed a bed and a shower and I had no idea how I would even find my way to a hotel. Once the plane had finally stopped, Vlad came through the cabin laughing as I tried taking my suitcase out of the overhead compartment.

"Are you sure I cannot escort you on your travels?" he asked as he pushed me lightly to the side and handed me the smaller overnight bag.

"I'll be fine as soon as I can figure out how to get a rental car."

"Maybe I'll stay with you until you find one?"

"Deal," I replied gratefully as I followed him through the cabin and toward the door. Just as Vlad lowered the small set of stairs to the ground a large black town car pulled alongside the plane causing us both to tense and freeze.

"Stay here," Vlad said firmly.

He certainly didn't need to tell me twice, and I ducked to the side of the door but continued to peek around enough to see Vlad approaching the car. From my position I could see the driver roll down the window, but I could hear Vlad shouting at him to get out of the car. The young man couldn't have been more than twenty, and looked as though he might actually shit his pants when Vlad pulled him from his seat. While holding the young man up against the car with one hand, Vlad quickly dialed his cell phone. After only a few minutes he released the driver and turned toward the plane gesturing for me to come out. He offered me his hand as I stepped slowly down the stairs and onto the tarmac.

"A gift from Seraphina," Vlad said with a smile. "He's paid up for three days and is ready to take you wherever you need to go." Vlad's smile grew as my eyes glazed with tears and I found it hard to swallow the big lump in my throat. "She really is a remarkable woman, isn't she?"

I nodded. "She's a really great mom," I replied weakly, trying to fight back the tears.

Vlad smiled as he stepped past to grab my luggage. When he made his way back to the town car the young driver stepped away giving Vlad a wide berth. Poor kid.

I, however, stood frozen in place. This was it. The choice and its consequences lay ahead of me in the form of a black town car. I didn't want to go home, I couldn't, but I was having difficulty finding the courage to take the step forward toward the car. By this point both the young driver and Vlad were looking at me questioningly. I'm sure I looked like a crazy person just standing there frozen in front of the plane.

Ok now listen up you big fat booger baby, get yourself together, my inside voice began. You chose to do this, so get on with it. You are a Warrior for cryin' out loud and you're wearing the pin to prove it. What would Victor say if he saw you like this? He would say you were weak. You can't be weak, you are a daughter of Eris. You have you're big girl panties on, now start walking in them.

I took a deep breath and slowly took my first step toward the car. After that first step, the second, third and fourth were much easier. I was finally on my own, taking steps toward the unknown, on my own.

Vlad opened the car door as I approached and touched my elbow. "You're positive about this?"

I nodded and smiled. "I am sure, and you can tell my father that you begged and begged, and yet I still got into the car."

Vlad smiled back after having been caught. "If you ever need a ride home just tell Eris and I'll be wherever you are. For your father's sake, do be careful. I don't know how he'd react if he lost you only having just found you."

Smiling with tears in my eyes (again), I kissed Vlad gently on the cheek and then nodded as I ducked into the car. I watched him walk away, unable to help but think of him as Uncle Vlad. It had a weird ring to it, but he seemed as close to Eris than anyone besides Sera. But before I could even start thinking of Sera and her gift, the young driver cleared his throat from the front seat.

"Good morning, Ms. Dubois, where can I take you today?"

"I'm sorry, who?"

The young driver turned quickly around in his seat, his eyes wide and worried. "Oh my god, please don't tell me I picked up the wrong person. It's only my second day, please tell me you're Ms. Dubois, Sera Dubois?"

"Ah," I said as a light bulb went off in my head. "Sera Dubois is my mother. She was just using her name to try and protect me."

"Was that guy trying to protect you too?"

"Um, yeah, sorry about that. He can be a little over zealous."

"Overzealous? The guy's a steamroller. I haven't even been employed long enough to pay for that dent. Oh crap, I'm sorry. I shouldn't be saying any of that in front of you, ma'am. I'm really sorry...it's just my second day," he blurted out as he turned back around in his seat.

"First of all, don't call me ma'am, that's just...well...weird. Second, you're absolutely right, Vlad is a steamroller and I will certainly pay for the damage to your car, it's only right. And you are doing a great job for it only being your second day. Now, you can call me Brianna, what can I call you?"

"Jonah."

"Ok, Jonah, I'm going to tell you right now, today is going to be a very boring day for you. I need some sleep, but will need a ride around town this afternoon. I hope you don't mind waiting around a lot today."

"Not at all, I am at your service," he smiled widely in the rearview mirror. "Where to?"

"Upper-Butt-Crack, Connecticut, on the double."

Chapter Fifteen

Brianna

The Honey Maple Inn, or known by locals as Ms. Mable's, was the only bed and breakfast in town. Being the tail end of leaf-peeping season I was lucky to get a room, especially since I needed it immediately and with an open-ended stay. Of course that could have been because I had gone to church with Ms. Mable for years and the fact that she was the only other Southern woman I knew in this area. Like me, she was a transplant, though I didn't know the circumstances of why she came up north. Over the years we had shared our troubles over living with Yankees with their harsh demeanors and their "soulless cooking" as she often said and didn't care who heard her. If you weren't staying at Ms. Mable's you were certainly eating there in the evenings or coming in from the cold for afternoon tea or apple cider and her famous cookies and cakes. The smell of which was wafting through the little bed and breakfast as the afternoon strolled in.

I had slept a few hours and took my time soaking in the large claw foot tub before my stomach began cramping and grumbling at how empty it was. My children were starving. I was already a horrible mother and they hadn't even been born yet. I loved hormones; they made you feel so warm and good about yourself. Giving my hair a final brush, I dabbed on a little lip gloss and headed down the stairs to the large sitting room only to find young Jonah sitting on the Victorian-styled couch in his black chauffeur's suit reading a textbook of English literature.

During the hour and a half drive from the private airport I had learned that Jonah was finishing his degree in English online after having to come home to help support his mother and younger sister when his father passed away last spring. He was a good boy, a good boy who had to become the man of the house and find the extra money to finish school. His mom had found her husband's death difficult to get over and was often too depressed to handle a full nursing schedule at the hospital. It was a difficult situation for anyone, let alone a twenty-year-old boy. But looking at him you would never know the trials he faced at home because he didn't wear it on his sleeve. He didn't want anyone's pity, it was his life and he accepted it. I needed to take a lesson.

Jonah looked up from his book and came quickly to my side, offering me his hand as I stepped down to the floor. His cheeks were rosy against his fair skin and his hands were warm from sitting in front of the fire for so long. I did feel guilty for having him wait around, but sleep was absolutely needed. Jonah had insisted that he was required to wait in the car per company policy. However, Ms. Mable had different ideas. After bringing him a cup of hot apple cider she all but dragged him into the house. A true Southern woman.

"Did you sleep well?" Jonah asked as he followed me into the sitting room.

"Yes, actually I did. Did you finish your homework?"

"Almost. I keep getting distracted."

"And why's that?"

"I hate short stories, don't ask me why, and this one is really boring. Plus it doesn't help that Mable keeps bringing me cookies and these, I don't know what you call them, but these little squares that taste like syrup. She must lace them with crack or something because I've eaten like twenty of them."

"Oh that would be her famous maple cake." Just the thought of it made my stomach growl loudly and I even had to wipe a little drool from my mouth. "That cake brings in top dollar every year at the church auction, and yes, it is laced with crack."

Jonah laughed behind me as we made our way through the dining room where a few other lodgers were enjoying some of Mable's treats. I swiped a large chunk of the maple cake from the buffet table and had finished it by the time we reached the kitchen where Mable and the other cook were busy fluttering around in preparation for the official teatime and dinner crowds that would be filtering in only a few hours from now.

Because all lodgers were asked to park in the back, they were also asked to come in and out of the house through the back door which was located in the kitchen. It was a bad design in my opinion with everyone going through your kitchen during all hours of the day, but Ms. Mable always thought of her bed and breakfast as a home versus a business. She wanted you to feel like you were staying with your favorite Aunt Mable, and family didn't come through the front door. Plus if "family" parked in front they would take up the spaces she had for the dinner crowd. She might be your favorite Aunt Mable, but she still had to be a business woman.

As Jonah and I stepped toward the back door Mable spun around in her flour covered apron while she stirred what looked like another batch of maple cake in a large bowl tucked under her arm. Mable was in her late fifties, her face wrinkled with every year of her age. She wasn't unattractive by any means, but she had earned every gray hair on her head as a B&B owner and a single mother of two college-aged boys.

"Mrs. Lewis, you certainly look refreshed. I hope everything was to your liking?" she asked. Although she and I had been in Connecticut about the same amount of time, she had retained her Southern accent, unlike mine which only came out when I was mad or talking to Daddy O.

"Yes, everything was perfect," I replied, although the sound of being called Mrs. Lewis sent shivers down my spine. "I'd forgotten how much I loved your maple cake. I think you've made a believer out of Jonah."

"Well, Mr. Jonah, there's plenty more out there if you want it."

Jonah shook his head slightly. "No thank you, ma'am. You've been generous enough."

Mable shrugged as she turned back to the kitchen counter, setting down her bowl and wiping her hands. "Well, get some now or forever hold your peace because there won't be any left once the teatime crowd gets here."

Jonah's face crinkled with conflict and I couldn't help but smile as he struggled with what to do.

"Jonah," I whispered, "a Southern woman won't bother tellin' you twice." Without another word he stepped back into the dining room and began loading a napkin with treats. "That boy may eat you out of house and home."

"Naw, he couldn't do more damage than my sons when they come home on the holidays. 'Sides, I love to see a boy with a good appetite, especially for my cookin'. So, Mrs. Lewis, what are your plans while yur in town?"

I took a breath before I answered, "Well, I plan on not being Mrs. Lewis anymore for one thing."

Mable turned her head slowly while she nervously wiped her hands on her apron. "That will certainly get the town gossip goin'."

"Yes I suppose so," I responded, fiddling with the purse strap on my shoulder. "I'm sure you'll be getting calls from the gossip brigade."

"Already have," Mable answered slyly. "That Gayle Davis knew the minute you crossed into town. No tellin' what she'll say when they see you walkin' around with that belly of yours."

My hand instinctively went to my stomach, rubbing it protectively. "Frankly it's none of their business."

"You got that right," she replied, but then cleared her throat. "And it certainly isn't any a my business either, but since Mr. Lewis has been missing for so long, I assume he isn't the father of that precious one?" I shook my head and felt twinges behind my eyes as they prepared for another downpour of tears. "Thank goodness for that. It's none of my never mind, but Sam Lewis is an ass, always was, always will be, so be thankful you found yourself someone else."

I concentrated on biting the inside of my cheek trying to prevent myself from breaking down in her kitchen. Now that the dust had settled and I had slept, my reality was even more terrifying. Just then Jonah returned to the kitchen, his previous napkin replaced with a small paper plate in order to hold the weight of the food he had piled on.

"Ma'am, I hope your offer didn't exclude these crunchy doily things," he said as he took a large bite of one releasing the licorice smell into the kitchen and causing a little nausea to rise within me.

"Now don't go eatin' all my anise cookies!" Mable cried as she eyed the pile on the plate.

"But don't spit it out," I shouted as I saw the thought cross his mind and his jaw open.

"Warry, warry," Jonah apologized with a full mouth.

"Now will you be joining Mrs. Le…um Ms. Brianna for dinner? You gotta tell me now because I'm certain I won't have enough food if you're gonna be eatin' with us tonight, Mr. Jonah."

Jonah turned to me. "I've been booked to drive you around all day and night, so whatever it is you…"

"Oh no, Jonah, I won't need you tonight. You have to get back to your family, I won't have you carting me around all night."

"But…"

"But nothin'," I said firmly. "Besides you have homework and I will not have you being delinquent on my account. Now let's get going before Mable throws us outta her kitchen."

"Nonsense," Mable laughed. "Now, Mr. Jonah, the next time yur up here, you bring your family in for a bite?"

Jonah's face fell slightly as he shook his head. "Thank you ma'am, but nowadays we don't really have the money for things like that. I'm really trying to save whatever I can so I can give my mom and sister a decent Christmas. But thank you for the offer."

I could see Mable had a lump in her throat about the same size as mine.

"Now listen, child, I wouldn't be tellin' ya to bring your family here and make you pay, what kind of Southern woman would I be? Now the next time you wanna take your family for a nice home cooked meal you come see me, my treat." Jonah nodded his head but couldn't find the strength to thank her out loud. "Now go on and get Ms. Brianna into that car before she plops that baby down on my nice clean floor."

"Yes ma'am," he responded quickly, opening the door with his free hand and walking down the short set of stairs to the back parking area.

As I started after him, I felt Mable tug on my arm. "Ms. Brianna, I don't want to be forward or anything."

"What should stop you now?" I replied with a smile.

She laughed lightly but then her face grew serious. "Like I said before, it isn't any a my business, but there's always sumthin' up when a mama-to-be is traveling around by herself, especially without a ring on her finger. Not that there's anything wrong with that, but there are a lot of people who'll just say mean and horrible things about you. So don't you listen. You don't need a man in order to be a good mama. Yes it's certainly easier and I'll testify to that, but not all of us get the happy ending, which is why I think God made us women so strong. Sometimes we just have to do things on our own, and it ain't a party, but you get through it and raise two boys and turn your Victorian dream home into a business in order to pay the bills after your no good husband leaves ya stranded in Connecticut of all places."

I laughed, causing a tear to escape down my cheek. As I brushed it away, Mable gave me a gentle hug and patted me on the back before sending me on my way. Was my situation and grief plastered on my face? I thought I was doing a great acting job. I needed to up my game if I was going to get through what I expected was going to be a very long day. When I stepped outside, Jonah was already alongside the car holding the back passenger door open.

"I can't sit up front with you?" I asked, but he didn't answer and just stood stoic holding my door open. We stood staring at each other for almost ten seconds before I finally stuck my tongue out at him and stomped into the backseat. With a cute and victorious smile he walked around to the driver's side and loosened his tie before closing his door.

"Where to?" Jonah asked into the rearview mirror.

"Hang a left, that'll take us to Main Street. I need food and then I have to stop in and see a friend. That means you'll have more time to finish your retched short story."

"Oh thanks," he replied sarcastically as he turned out of Mable's driveway. "So can I ask you something?"

"Of course."

"I was just wondering if you thought Mable was really serious about me bringing my mom and sister up for dinner one night."

"Absolutely. Already making plans, huh?"

"Yeah…uh…it's just that my father's birthday is Thursday and I'd really like to do something nice for my mom. She'd like Mable's, don't you think?" Jonah looked in the rearview mirror for an answer and said, "I'm sorry, was it something I said?"

"No, I cry at everything," I replied, wiping away more tears. "Don't take it personally, I cried at a coffee commercial while I was getting ready. But yes, to answer your question, I think she'd love it. It's very sweet that you think of doing that for your mom."

"Wouldn't you?"

"My stepmother, yes. My mother, not so much."

"Wow, it's usually the opposite, isn't it?"

"Well, I'm really not a traditional kind of girl."

I had ordered the Main Street Café's roasted turkey club sandwich since it opened ten years ago and today was no different. Unfortunately what was different about today's turkey club was that as soon as I bit into it I had to spit it out. The turkey actually tasted so rancid I took it back up to the counter and asked for another one, only to spit that one out too. When this happened, the owner came from around the counter, I'm sure afraid of having a lawsuit on his hand but I set him at ease when I assured him it was most likely because I was pregnant rather than his café having expired meat. So I ended up having just a toasted tomato and mayonnaise sandwich and it was unbelievably delicious. So much so that I had them make me another one for the road, or really just the sidewalk since I was only going to walk down to Roger's bookshop a few doors down.

I had left Jonah in the car, unable to convince him to come inside while I ate and I didn't push. But when I left the café eating my second sandwich, he quickly exited the car and came to walk alongside me.

"Jonah, you don't have to escort me all over town. I am perfectly capable of walking on my own."

"Yeah, but I've been thinking about what you said earlier."

"And what was that?"

"Well you said that your stepmother and that guy were trying to protect you, so then I thought if they were trying to do that then it probably isn't safe for you to walk around alone."

"I'm sorry to say that you can't help me against what I need protection from."

"We'll just have to see about that," he said with a cocky smile but I grabbed his arm tightly and turned him to face me.

"Jonah, I'm not joking. There are people after me and they will not care that you have a mother and sister that need you. So if I tell you to run, you need to run no questions asked, ok?" Jonah stood frozen on the sidewalk, I was scaring him. "There are just people who would really like to get their hands on me." And my babies I said in my head and rubbed my stomach again.

Jonah was still frozen in place so I took advantage of the silence and continued down the sidewalk stuffing the final pieces of my sandwich into my mouth. Jonah caught up to me just as I stepped in front of the large picture window of Books 'n' Such and Roger the owner came bursting out the door.

"Well slap me with a wad of cash and call me greedy, Brianna Lewis is back in town! And we've been naughty," he said touching my bulging belly and then looked next to me at Jonah. "And robbing the cradle."

Jonah's eyes widened and I released a laugh that was both humored and panicked. "No, no, Roger, this is my driver, Jonah. Jonah this is my friend Roger whose imagination tends to run rampant and directly into the dirty section."

"I do not," Roger replied, trying to sound offended. "Now come in, come in, we have so much to catch up on."

Roger opened the door to the shop and I followed but turned to see Jonah backing down the sidewalk.

"I'll wait for you in the car," he said.

"Not surfing on the web or downloading music, finish your homework. I shouldn't be long."

"Like hell you won't," Roger said, this time sounding offended. Jonah turned and began walking back to the car as I ducked under Roger's arm into the bookshop. The smell of the new books was so inviting and comforting, another thing I had forgotten how much I loved. Roger led me to the sofa that was located perpendicular to the counter and had a perfect view of the street outside littered with yellow, red, and bright orange leaves.

As I sat down on the couch it was hard not to think about the last time I was in here – the first time I had spoken to Cameron, the first time I had smelled his rustic autumn scent, the first time he had touched me.

"Do you need some water? You look green all of a sudden."

"Sorry, just some morning sickness," I said as I sat down.

"It's two in the afternoon."

"Don't judge me, book boy."

"Ooh, I missed you," Roger said as he stepped over to the door and flipped the sign to closed.

"Speaking of being two in the afternoon, aren't you a few hours early for closing up shop?"

"Oh please. At this time of day people in this town are either getting their Botox injections or making their daily gossip calls, which I'm sure you're the main topic of today."

"And why would that be?" I asked coyly while rubbing my belly.

Roger walked around to the counter laughing and came back with bottled waters and yes, a box of chocolates.

"I've saved these for just this type of occasion, or a slow Tuesday. So really I have only one question – what the hell happened? Here one day, gone the next. Your husband disappears and then you suddenly reappear, and in the family way of all things."

"I thought you only had one question," I said and then scoured the chocolates for the perfect one.

"There was only one question in there. The others were factual statements that if you wanted to expand on I would certainly lend an ear."

I narrowed my eyes at him as I bit into my chosen chocolate. Cherry, ugh. I still swallowed half the chocolate down and wrapped the other half in its small brown wrapper.

"There's not much to tell. Sam had hit me for the last time and I found someone to get me out of there. Now don't give me that surprised look, you must have known Sam was abusive."

Roger looked out the large window while he chewed several chocolates at once. "Renee told me once when I noticed a bruise through the pound of cover-up you had on your neck one day. But it was your secret to tell, so I didn't pry. You'd tell me if you wanted me to know, although every time I saw Sam Lewis I'd give him a dirty look in your honor. So tell me who this mystery knight in shining armor is who carried you safely away."

"Knight in a black leather jacket and silver aviators is more like it. You might remember him, he came into your shop the day I left."

I could see Roger search his memory and then his eyes widened at the recollection. "You mean Mr. Tall-dark-and-let-me-have-your-baby? Oh my god, you are having his baby, aren't you!" I nodded with effort. "Oh, and he's not here with you because…"

"Because apparently he wanted something else, or really *someone* else."

Roger's eyes were sympathetic and patted my hand gently as he said, "Usually this is where I tell you that he's an idiot and he's not worth it and other junk like that. And he may be an idiot, but I'm sorry, he's totally worth getting back up on that horse, and I mean that literally."

He was trying to make me laugh, but the smile didn't even reach my eyes. "It never quite works out that way now does it?"

"Oh sure it does. He lays down and then you climb…"

"Bababa, enough," I interrupted, leaning over and placing a hand over his mouth and this time I was able to laugh.

Roger took my hand from his mouth and kissed the back of it. "I just wanted to make you laugh. So what brings you here? Planning on moving back and raising your child in beautiful and historic Podunk, Connecticut?"

"Actually I'm going to try and figure out how to divorce Sam."

"My sister is a lawyer. I'll send her your way, so check that off. Next?"

"Um, er…" I hadn't really thought about anything past that. "Do you happen to know what happened to the house?"

"I heard through the grapevine that a week or so after Sam went missing the bank took control. But it's not on the market, the security lights are on at night, so I have no idea what they're doing with it. Best bet is to call Jim Davis."

Jim Davis, Sam's best friend and drinking buddy, was also Sam's boss at the bank. Roger was right, if anyone knew anything it would have been Jim. Unfortunately he was the last person I wanted to call, especially since his wife, Gayle, was the head gossip honcho in town.

"Can I use your phone?"

"Of course, but it'll cost you."

"Oh yeah? How much?"

"Dinner tonight. Somewhere where everyone will see us and start rumors all over town that I'm your baby daddy. It'll be a night to remember."

"Deal. But no climbing onto the horse analogies," I laughed.

"Oh honey, I have the Kama Sutra memorized. There are definitely other analogies I can use. What if Jim isn't in the office today?"

"I have a feeling he'll be expecting my call."

"And why's that?"

"Because Gayle is staring at me through your window with a cell phone glued to her ear."

Roger turned to see exactly what I was referring to. Gayle's eyes were wide while she frantically spoke into her cell phone. I stood and waved, turning profile so that she could see my baby bump in its full light. Roger stood as well and kissed me on the forehead while rubbing my belly. We were having way too much fun, but it quickly ended when Gayle gave us a nasty look and walked away. After one last laugh I sighed and walked to the counter to use Roger's phone.

"Jim Davis, please," I said once the bank's receptionist came onto the line.

"May I please ask who is calling?"

"Brianna Mor...um Brianna Lewis."

"Ah yes, he's been expecting your call."

"I'm sure he has."

Chapter Sixteen

Brianna

"I really think I should go with you," Jonah said, looking at me through the side of his eye while I leaned over the front seat.

"No, I'll be fine," I replied, trying to convince myself.

"But the police are here."

"It's just one cop. If I was in real trouble the entire police force would be here. And by police force I mean the other two cops in town."

I grabbed my purse from the seat next to me and secured it on my shoulder before taking a big breath. My palms were sweaty and the butterflies were jumping on a trampoline in my stomach. Not only because I was in front of the hell house I had finally escaped from, but yes I was nervous that there was a cop towering over Jim Davis in the driveway. I truly felt that I hadn't done anything wrong, but my luck being what it was they'd probably put me in handcuffs if my hair blew in the wrong direction.

"I could just go back down the driveway," Jonah said breaking the silent tension in the car while I tried to find the courage to move.

You can do this, you can do this, it's why you're here. Sam won't be beating you down anymore. Now pull up your pants and, "get out of the car."

"Oo-k," Jonah said startled as he unbuckled his seatbelt.

"Oh, no. I meant me. No, you stay in the car, I'm going. Here, take my phone. If the cop pulls out handcuffs then call my dad, his number is under Dad."

"Wow, I don't think I could have figured that out."

"Quiet, smartass. Don't turn the phone on unless I'm in trouble."

"Last chance to go back to Mable's," he said, turning around and taking my cell phone from my hand.

The thought of sitting in front of the fire in my cozy bedroom at Mable's was so enticing, but I felt a tiny flutter in my stomach urging me to get out of the car. "No, I'm ready. Besides I know the only reason you want to go back is to get more food."

Jonah smirked. I'd caught him and he knew it. I took one last breath before Jonah opened my car door and offered me his hand. I'd only known the kid for a few hours, yet there was such an odd bond between us. He was the best driver ever. Oh for goodness sake, Bri, don't start tearing up now.

Finally, after what seemed like an eternity, I took my first steps up the driveway toward Jim and the police officer.

"For a moment I didn't think you were going to get out of the car," Jim said as he closed the distance between us and then noticed my baby belly. "You...ah...look well."

"Oh don't look too shocked, Jim. I'm sure Gayle already called to tell you about my condition."

"Frankly, I don't listen to half of what she says, but when she said that Brianna Lewis was back in town I finally paid attention. Listen," he began as he tentatively placed an arm around my shoulder and escorted me further up the driveway toward the policeman, "since you called me I'm guessing you know that Sam has gone missing." I nodded. "Because his case is still open I had to call the officer in charge. They've been looking for you and wanted to ask you a few questions. I hope you don't mind."

"I don't really have a choice, now do I?"

"Not really, no," Jim replied then stepped away from my side and gestured toward the officer. "Officer Reynolds this is Brianna Lewis, Sam's wife."

The officer extended his hand and I shook it firmly. "Nice to meet you, Mrs. Lewis."

"Please just call me Brianna."

The officer gave Jim a curious look but then turned and gestured toward the house. "Why don't we go into the house so we can discuss your husband's disappearance and subsequently your whereabouts the last few months?"

"Officer Reynolds, I don't mean to be rude but I'm pregnant and my hormones have been making me cranky lately. Let me save you some time because there's really nothing to discuss. Back in April I left Sam Lewis because I was tired of him beating and violating me."

Jim stepped in front of me, "Now wait a minute, Sam had his faults but I can't believe he would…"

"Did you ever report this abuse?" Officer Reynolds chimed in, placing a hand on Jim's shoulder.

"No I didn't because Sam controlled every aspect of my life including never letting me go to the hospital let alone be unsupervised long enough to go to the police. And if you don't believe me you can go into the house and see that there are cameras all over where he would monitor my every move. Most people in this town thought I was some crazy recluse, but the truth was that Sam rarely let me out of the house and many times it was because he was too stupid not to hit me in places that were visible. There was always a bruise or a swollen eye or even finger marks on my throat where he would choke me when he…w-when he would rape me. As a matter of fact, *Jim*, the last time he did that to me was because your nosey gossip-starting wife called you and told you that I had the audacity to say hello to another man."

A flash of recollection crossed Jim's face and he suddenly looked down at the ground.

"I couldn't leave the house for two weeks after that, and finally when I did I connected with a women's shelter that could help me escape from here." I had remembered that Renee told the police something similar, so this would support her statement. At the notice of Officer Reynolds' nodding his head, I had a feeling my lie was successful. "Unfortunately the night I tried to leave, Sam got here before I could get away and he actually t-boned my SUV, pulled me out and dragged me up the driveway right where you two are standing. He dragged me into the house and tried to kill me and the only reason I'm standing here today is because the contact I was supposed to meet got worried when I didn't show up so he came to the house and saw the accident in the driveway. He broke into the house, punched Sam a couple of times in the face and then got me out. I haven't seen or spoken to Sam since, and frankly I hope I never do. The only reason I came back was to find a way to get a divorce from him and maybe grab a couple of things I had to leave behind."

Both Jim and the officer were quiet while I wiped away a tear that had fallen down my cheek. If my performance was fake I would have won an Oscar, but unfortunately it wasn't since I couldn't help but remember the night that Cameron broke through the door and changed my life forever. My

Cam. Another tear crested over my lower lid and I wiped it quickly away as the wind began to whip by, giving me a chill. I crossed my arms in front of my chest, pulling my thin cardigan closed.

"And when you left, where did you go?" Officer Reynolds asked as he wrote something down in his little policeman pad.

"I've been in San Francisco ever since."

"And you never heard from or saw your husband again?" he asked, looking intently into my eyes, trying to see if I would waiver in the slightest.

There was a little voice screaming in my head, *he's dead, he's dead, I don't know where he is, but he's dead and I know who killed him.* Through very controlled lips I responded, "Nope."

Officer Reynolds once again stared me down for several seconds before finally giving up and saying, "Just one last thing, and then I'll leave you with Mr. Davis. The last call your husband made was to an Oliver Morgan, do you know him?"

"He's my grandfather, but I'm sure you knew that."

At least he smiled a little on that one. "Yes, well the call was only a few seconds long and hit towers near where your grandfather lives. Were you aware that your grandfather had received this call?"

"No, he didn't tell me anything about that." And that was the truth. "I'd ask him about it."

"We did, actually."

"So, what does that mean?"

He sighed and tucked his little notebook back into his pocket. "It means we have nothing and your husband is still missing. Because of the placement of the call we believe your husband traveled down to North Carolina thinking you might have fled to your grandfather's house. The authorities down there have done a cursory search and found nothing."

"Where does that leave the investigation?" Jim interrupted.

"The investigation will remain open for now, but unless we get a break or find a body it'll eventually go into the cold case files unless there are other family members that push to keep the investigation going?"

I shook my head. "Sam's mother died a few years ago, and he never knew his father. Sam can rot for all I care, but Jim if you…"

"No, I guess not. We'll just let this run its course."

My entire body sighed with relief.

Officer Reynolds extended his hand and I cringed a little, preparing for him to slap on the cuffs as he took my hand. "Thank you for your time,

Brianna, and even though it is my job to find Mr. Lewis, it should have been my job to protect you against him. I am sorry we were unable to do that for you, but it looks like you're one of the lucky ones and have been able to move on," he said gesturing to my stomach.

Officer Reynolds bid goodbye and Jonah adjusted his car to allow the police cruiser down the driveway. Jim turned to me and fought with himself on what to say. I could tell his statement was right on the tip of his tongue, but I interrupted before he could speak.

"Look Jim, I don't want to take up anymore of your time, I really just want to take a look around the house and maybe take a few things."

"Actually, Brianna, let's go inside, we do need to talk about what to do with the estate."

The estate? It sounded so formal, like my house had magically become the Kennedy compound. Yes, on the outside its cream-colored stone looked almost majestic, but within them there had been so much evil and hatred and suffering. I didn't want to have to talk about anything regarding this house, I just wanted to wave goodbye and never have to see it again. Unfortunately Jim didn't give me much of a choice as he herded me toward the front walkway.

"I have a key to the front door, unless you know the code to the garage?"

"We can try it, but Sam may have changed it since I left."

I ducked out of Jim's hold and walked over to the garage door and pressed in the code on the slim black number pad. 1-2-3. That was the code. 1-2-3. It was true that Sam was an idiotic jackass, and the fact that the security code to our house was 1-2-3 proved as much.

Once I finished pushing in the ultra-secret passcode, the garage door opened loudly in front of us. The butterflies in my stomach started making me feel nauseous and the feeling was definitely not the babies. My garage bay was of course empty, but the one thing that was still there was the sign hanging in front of me – *Reserved for Brianna M. Lewis*. Blood rushed to my cheeks as my butterflies melted away and anger took over. The sign was my resolve and in some ways my strength. It signified everything I hated and everything I would never let happen to me again.

"I always thought that was so funny," Jim said next to me as he pointed up to the sign. However, his smile quickly faded when I gave him the stink eye.

"I'm glad you thought so," I said nastily as I looked past him at the other three garage bays that all held similar signs that said *Reserved for Samuel A.*

Lewis. Only the last two were occupied with a motorcycle he never rode and his baby, the fully restored silver 1969 Chevy Camaro with black racing stripes down the front. I had only been allowed to ride in it three times even though he'd been restoring the car for the last ten years. The bratty kid inside of me wanted desperately to go over to it and leave fingerprints all over its shiny paint.

It took me a few seconds before I realized that I was standing alone staring at the car and Jim was standing in the doorway that led into the house. Ok, let's get this over with. Putting one foot in front of the other I walked up the three wooden steps and followed Jim inside. The house smelled stale and my shoes echoed loudly in the eerily quiet hallway. I couldn't help but pause at the door of my study, even brushing my hand along the handle. Later. There would be time. I'd make the time.

As I walked into the large open foyer I noticed that Sam had repaired all signs of Cameron's attack. There wasn't a mark or a scratch anywhere. Even the large Sam-shaped dent in the wall next to the staircase had been repaired. Jim was standing in front of the kitchen island pulling a folder from within his briefcase unaware of the chaos that had occurred only inches from where he stood. No one would ever have known what really happened here if they walked in, except me of course. I could feel the various scars on my body start to burn and ache, and not just the ones I had on the outside.

"Jim, do you mind if we sit?" I asked, gesturing to the living room as a mixture of nausea and light-headedness came over me.

"Oh, of course. Do you need some water? I've made sure to keep up on the utilities."

"A glass of water would be great. There are glasses in the...well the cabinet you already have your hand in. I forget you've been here before."

I plopped down on the large couch that sat in front of the wall of windows that revealed the sprawling side lawn which melted into the surrounding woods. Most of the leaves had turned, many of them scattered on the ground creating a multi-colored carpet. While I gazed out the window, my eyes narrowed on three thin brownish smears on the glass. I had seen them before. I was actually surprised Sam hadn't seen them and wiped them away. It was blood, my blood actually, and the sight was what had propelled me off this very couch to leave this god awful place. The sight didn't affect me as it once had, but I still didn't want to look at it. Whereas before I had only seen my blood, now I saw Cameron's eyes staring back at me through the window. Wanting to wipe both away, I pressed my fingernail up against the window and scraped the smears away.

"Everything ok?" Jim asked, bringing my attention away from the window as he handed me my glass of water.

"Yeah, just a little something on the glass. Thank you for the water." It was cool and refreshing and my dry mouth thanked me by drinking almost half the glass in one sip. Thank goodness the utilities were still on, I would definitely need a bathroom soon enough. "So what did we need to talk about?"

Jim came around to the other side of me, placing the folder he had in his hand on the large ottoman and pulling it over in front of us. "First I think we should discuss…" Jim began, but then paused as he rubbed his face roughly and sighed. "Bri, I've known Sam for over ten years, and when he disappeared your little red-headed friend was very vocal about…she was accusing him of horrible, horrible things. I'd seen his temper, but never thought he could do…*those*…kind of things to you."

"Jim…"

"Please let me say this. Sam was my best friend, and I thought I knew everything about him. No secrets, we used to say to each other. Well, after he went missing I searched his office and found the video monitor that was showing the different rooms of your house. When you mentioned earlier about the cameras and him watching your every move I'm thinking that maybe I didn't know him as well as I thought. And then when you're friend…um…Renee?" I nodded. "When she started claiming you were abused, I told Officer Reynolds that it was all lies, but then after a while I began to recollect comments Sam would make about keeping you in line, teaching you a lesson, and honestly I thought he was just kidding around like every other miserable middle-aged married man. But…I guess…I guess not. Bri, I'm sorry."

"Jim, Sam did those things to me, not you."

"Well I certainly didn't help."

"That I will agree with."

Jim licked his lips and sighed loudly before he said, "I've been telling my wife for years that the nonsense she spreads is going to get someone hurt one day, and well it has. I promise you she'll never do it again, to you or to anyone, even if I have to permanently put a gag in her mouth. I might actually have some peace and quiet for a change."

I smiled, and couldn't help but laugh a little. "Jim, you have no idea what kind of relief that will give this entire town."

This time Jim joined me in laughing before he opened the folder in front of him and began organizing the papers from within. "Shall we get down to business?"

I nodded reluctantly, afraid of what he would bombard me with.

"When Sam went missing and we discovered you had disappeared, I took over what I could to keep things up to date. Thankfully there isn't a mortgage, I'm sure you're aware?" I nodded. It was one of the few things I knew. "But of course there are the usual monthly expenses – utilities, taxes, insurance, stuff like that. So we've been funneling money from the Trust in order to cover those."

"The what?"

Jim blinked and looked at me curiously. "The Trust. Sam's trust fund."

I shook my head. "I have no idea what you're talking about."

"Huh. I can't believe he didn't tell you. Right before his mother died she told him that his father had left him a trust fund. He was furious of course since he had basically lived in squalor with her. So after she died he took control of it and made me power of attorney."

All this time I had thought Sam was ashamed of his mother and demoed her trailer so that people would never find out about his upbringing. Really, he was just angry at her for making him have to live in that situation and giving him the excuse that she didn't know who his father was. Finally a family more screwed up than mine.

"But now that you're back you'll need to decide what you want to do with the estate."

"Jim, you've said that a couple of times, but I'm not sure why it's my decision. You have power of attorney, isn't everything up to you?"

Jim looked at me curiously again and cleared his throat before speaking. "Brianna, everything is in your name."

His words slapped me in the face. My cheeks were stinging and flush. My name? What the hell did he mean my name? "That's not possible, Jim. Sam made it very clear I lived in *his* house and that I had nothing he didn't provide for me."

Jim paused, again uncomfortable with learning who Sam really was. "I'm not sure what to say, Bri, but it's yours. The house, the extra lot, the vehicles, everything. The only thing that's not in your name is a new SUV he purchased shortly before he disappeared. Sam never had you sign anything? Paperwork? Loan agreements? Nothing?"

"He would put papers in front of me to sign, but I never knew what they…wait, what extra lot?"

"Years ago Sam started buying the surrounding land, several acres a year."

"Total?"

"You have fifteen acres around the house, and then another four acres across the street," he said as he shuffled a few of the papers in front of him and handed them to me.

"Can I sell everything?"

"Of course. There are probably some developers who would love to come into this area, you could do very well. I'm sure the Camaro will go pretty fast since it's in mint condition."

"You want it?"

Jim laughed which seemed to lighten the mood a touch. "I'd love it, but I'd never hear the end of it from Gayle, and I try to make it a point not to have to hear her." Jim stood from the couch and gathered his papers together placing them neatly in the folder and handing it to me. "These are yours now. Well I guess they were always yours, but now at least you know about them. Let me know if there's anything else I can do, and I mean anything. I feel like I have a lot to make up for."

"I'll try and set things in motion over the next few days, but if you could keep handling that Trust thing?"

"Well, I have to, actually. It's the only thing you don't have access to." He was trying to make a joke, but he was never really good at it.

"I wouldn't want it anyway."

He cleared his throat again and patted down his jacket before saying, "I'll head out then. Again, call if you need me to handle anything. Not sure how long you're in town so I can pop over every now and then until the place is sold, make sure everything is still working and whatnot."

"Thanks Jim, I appreciate that. Give my best to Gayle."

He smirked knowing I was being sarcastic and then left, leaving me alone in the house. It was too quiet and cold, and there was absolutely no spark of life. The house was as stark and gray as it was outside and you could feel that a storm was about to break, and not just out there. I came for a few things I'd left behind and came out with an estate. I finally had something in my name and now I couldn't wait to get out from under it.

I pushed myself up from the couch, my stomach already growling again. There wasn't much else I wanted to do today besides go back to Mable's, have a little dinner with Roger, and call it a night. Everything had changed in a matter of minutes and I was exhausted. My body was tired and a headache was starting to pulse at my temples.

Ready to finally call it a day, I walked over to the coat closet and found exactly what I was hoping for - my white winter coat. It was a pain to keep clean, but I never cared, it was my favorite coat and lucky for me it buttoned high in the chest and flared slightly below. It was now a perfect pregnancy coat, at least for another couple of months.

After buttoning the coat I was resolved to the fact that I wasn't saying goodbye to the house, more like see you tomorrow. Boy that sucked. I walked down the hallway toward the door that led into the garage and once again passed my study's door. Without realizing it my hand was already on the door handle. My heart was beating a little faster as I pressed down and opened to reveal chaos. Sam had been able to conceal his anger in every room in the house but this one. To him, he was destroying what he knew I loved most, but now it was just a room with books and pillows and blankets ripped up and strewn all over the floor.

Stumbling slowly inside, I kicked books and papers out of my way as I crossed the room and came upon a duffle bag with clothes hanging out of the opening. I knelt down beside the bag and knew it was the one I had packed the night I left. Removing a cotton shirt that was wrinkled and wrapped around a pair of pants, I found the toiletry bag I had packed that night and tucked it underneath my arm. With all the scurrying to get out of the manor I was stuck with the remaining items I'd had while staying at Eris's, which wasn't much. I searched the rest of the bag, thinking back on the night that I had packed it and what all was going through my head. Not a whole lot of sense apparently since I'd packed a million pairs of socks and only three pairs of underwear. With my tote of toiletries underneath my arm, I steadied myself and pushed up from the floor. The bag toppled onto my foot revealing the end of a wide red ribbon. I kicked away the bag and saw that it had been resting on top of a few books that had fallen out of the red ribbon's tie.

Tears flooded my eyes as Cam's first gift to me was splayed out in front of me. The bag and the books had been in my truck right before Sam crashed into me and I had left them behind. Sam must have taken them out of the SUV before disposing of it. I wondered what he must have thought when he took everything out of the car, or why he even did. But today was proving that Sam had more surprises and secrets that I didn't care to know.

But so did Cameron. Secrets and lies were bombarding me from all angles and it was all way too much to handle.

Unable to stop myself I bent down and took the books in my arms, wrapping the loose bright ribbon around them as I walked out the door. I wanted to throw them in the garbage, but I knew I wouldn't. I couldn't. Even after everything that had happened, even after his lips touched another woman's, I still loved him. My heart was aching at how much I missed him and it had been less than one day. I was a loser, a hopeless loser.

Tears were still coming down my face while I waited for the garage door to open. Through the opening I could see Jonah's legs walking toward the garage and when his face came into full view concern was written all over it. What must I look like right now? Dark circles under my eyes from lack of sleep and crying, cheeks flush with upset, and sniffling loudly.

"Holy shit, what happened in there?" Jonah shouted as he walked quickly to stand in front of me.

"N-nothing you need to worry about. You don't h-happen to have any tissues?"

He patted his pockets and shook his head. "Wait, I think there's some in the car." Before I could say anything he ran to the car and began rifling through the front seat until he pulled out a small box of tissues and returned to me. "I think the last guy to have the car left them in there, but I'm sure they're clean."

"Your confidence is overwhelming," I said as I wiped my eyes and blew my nose.

"Better?"

"Hardly. Sorry you have to see this."

"I'm used to seeing women cry, I live with two of them, remember?"

"That'll certainly help when you're older. Do you mind taking me back to Mable's?"

"I'll take you to Maine if you want me to. I told you I've been paid to drive wherever no matter the time or the distance."

"I told you I won't need you in the evenings."

"But you have me if you do."

Gosh he was stubborn, but he was an amateur compared to me. "Call your boss and see if I can extend your contract until Saturday, oh unless you have days off or something. I'm not really sure how this works."

"Don't worry about me. I'd rather have the extra money. Do you need to do anything else here before we go?"

I smiled as I looked behind me.

"Can you take down that sign?" I asked, pointing above my head to the Brianna Lewis parking sign above my head.

"Er…yeah, I think so," he replied. Thankfully Jonah was really tall and could easily lift the sign enough to where the hooks came free from the eye loops. "Is this you? Brianna M. Lewis?"

"I used to be her."

"Did you often need help to find where you were supposed to park?"

I couldn't help but laugh. "No, my ex wanted to make sure I always knew my place."

"Oh, he sounds like a winner. What do you want to do with the sign?"

Well that was a really open ended question.

Chapter Seventeen

Brianna

To say it plainly, Roger was a miracle worker. Not only did he have a sister who was a lawyer, but he had a cousin who was a real estate agent. It was all a little too easy and I was certainly waiting for the other Brianna-Morgan-Bad-Luck shoe to drop. Within two days my house was on the market, and I had officially filed for divorce. Unfortunately I had a feeling that both actions would cause flags to rise as to my whereabouts. I knew I couldn't stay in town very much longer. I was pretty sure I could handle Cameron, but Elaina or a member of her coven could be a different story. I hadn't trained in almost a month and my stomach was a disadvantage that made me weak and slow.

I'd taken to doing mind scans every half an hour no matter where I was, looking for even a sliver of a Vampire's essence. The scans were exhausting me, but it didn't matter, they were absolutely necessary. I'd also sewn in a thin long pouch on the inside the liner of my large purse that would hold one of my daggers. It was a good thing I loved big bags. I couldn't just walk around town with my dagger harness strapped to my back. It might draw some unwanted attention.

"You wanna soda?" Jonah asked as he came back through the front door with sweat circling the collar of his green t-shirt. For the last two days he picked me up in his black suit and changed the minute we walked into the house, and then changed back before he dropped me off. The car company required a suit, so they saw a suit when he came to pick up the car and drop it off.

Jonah was another life saver. He probably lost ten pounds helping me box up everything and then lug it out of the house for two days. Today Jonah had boxed up all the salvageable books for Roger, though he had put aside a small pile for his sister, Katie, as he did for most things. Everything was either something for his mother or his sister. I had never met a young man his age who was so selfless, but in ways it worried me. He needed to be reminded that he was important too, he deserved presents too. Jonah was working so hard to support his girls that he was forgetting about himself.

"Do you want a soda or are you just going to sit there staring at me?"

"Sorry, no I'm fine. You'd better take it all with you today since I'm leaving in the morning."

"Yeah, I still don't get that. Why did you pay for the rest of the week if you were just going to turn around and leave three days later," he asked as he walked into the kitchen and pulled a can of soda from the fridge then quickly began rifling through today's picnic basket from Mable.

"Jonah I told you…"

"I know, I know. I just can't believe you have people after you. You're like the nicest lady ever. Wanna piece of cake?"

He held up a plastic container packed to the brim with sweet maple cake.

"I wouldn't dream of taking any of it away from you."

He smirked and stuffed almost an entire piece of cake into his mouth. "Wheywefins wout, wow wha?"

"Yeah, no idea," I said as I pushed up from the couch and made my way into the kitchen.

He swallowed hard, having to take a swig of his soda in order to push the cake down his throat. "I said, everything's out, now what?"

"Cross your fingers that the house will sell."

"I can't believe you'd want to sell this place."

"Did you ask your friend about the Camaro?" I said, changing the subject like the pro that I was.

Jonah nodded as he wiped his hands on his jeans causing the mother within me to cringe. "I did, but he said he didn't have the money for it right now. But you could totally put up online, I'm sure a collector would want it, it's totally in prime condition. Why not just keep it?"

"I need to get rid of everything that reminds me of Sam." Jonah nodded again, not wanting to push for more answers. He'd actually been pretty good about that. Just then, a fabulous and clever idea hit me. "Hey, do you have a dollar?"

Jonah pulled out his wallet and handed me a crisp one dollar bill. "May I ask why you want a dollar? It's not like there's a vending machine around here."

I took the bill from his hand and gave him a devilish smile. "You just bought yourself a car."

"W-wwhat?" he said loudly while his eyes bugged out of his head. "NO! No, give me my dollar back."

"Sorry, it's my dollar now and your car."

"But...you can't just...Jesus! Please give me my dollar back."

"Why? You said you liked the car, so it's yours."

"No, it's too much," he said annoyed and walked out of the kitchen to stand in the open living room. "Why would you do that? That just makes me feel shitty."

"Why!? Roger took the motorcycle off my hands, which by the way is really a scary thought. Now all I need to do is get rid of the car before I leave. I'm allowed to sell you the car for as low as a dollar and so I did. What's the big deal?"

Jonah turned back to me, his hands resting frustratingly on his hips. "I-I don't want a hand out, Brianna, or a pity party."

I waited a second, letting the statement hang in the air and the tension die down a little. "One, I'm not giving you a handout, you paid for the car. Two, I'm not throwing you any kind of party, let alone a pity party. If you hate the car so much, turn around and sell it. I just want it off my hands and you're the only one here. If I had another driver named Stanley I'd be asking him for a dollar too. Don't read too much into this and take the damn car before my hormones make me say something snotty."

"Like you haven't already?"

"Jerk."

"Preggers." Jonah's hands fell from hips as we both laughed and I could I'd won. "I guess I could turn around and sell it. Then I could totally get Katie a car."

"Or you could keep it and give Katie yours."

Jonah shook his head. "My car is a piece of crap, not nearly safe enough for my sister to drive. Besides I could get her something small and maybe even have some money for Christmas."

"Is it always about everyone else?"

He sighed. "My dad always used to say 'Joey, a real man does whatever he can to take care of the women in his life and make sure they feel safe and loved.' Safe and loved. That's just what I'm trying to do. He's not here anymore and I…I just want to make him proud."

"There's no way he wouldn't be," I said and wiped my eyes before he could see. "How are you doing with tomorrow?"

He shrugged. Tomorrow was his dad's birthday, the first without him. "Trying not to think about it. The manual labor has been helping," he said with a smile.

"Want to talk about it?"

"Not really."

"Want to take your new car for a drive?"

"Now you're talkin'."

I opened the empty drawer in front of me, picked up the small ring with the two thin metal keys and threw them at him. He caught them right out of the air and a childlike smile spread widely across his face as he threw his suit on the kitchen island. Within five minutes we were sitting in the muscle car while Jonah savored the moment of roaring the engine to life.

"Ooooh, baaaby," he cooed as he gingerly stroked the steering wheel. Jonah sat lost somewhere in his mind staring at the dash in front of him. From my seat next to him, I could see his eyes glazing with tears. I placed my hand on his upper arm and squeezed it tenderly. Jonah cleared his throat and pressed his thumb and index finger into the inner corners of his eyes. "Sorry."

"Don't be. How many times have you seen me practically hysterical?"

He smiled. "But you're a girl."

"I'm glad you noticed. You ok?"

"I was just thinking about how my dad would have loved this car."

I rubbed his shoulder gently. "Well, I'm sure he's with you right now enjoying the heck out of it."

Jonah smiled again, but only one corner of his mouth lifted. I bit my lip and looked away, unable to stop seeing Cameron's crooked smile from flashing in my head.

"I can't wait to take my girls out in this tomorrow night."

"Girls? Katie's coming too?"

"Yeah, she asked this morning. I told her no on the boyfriend which I thought would be the kicker, but she said she still really wanted to come. It'll be nice just to have the three of us together." Jonah put the car in gear and slowly began backing out of the garage. "Boy I love this car already."

"Second thoughts?"

"Nah. Katie really needs a car. It's been hard to get her around everywhere since I can't always count on Mom with her schedule. Plus if Katie has her own car I won't have to constantly hear about the boyfriend."

"It's a shame you're going to sell it. This car is totally a chick magnet," I said coyly as he backed onto the street.

"What makes you think I'm not a chick magnet?"

"Are you?"

"No. I never have time to actually see a chick, much less magnetize her. But speaking of, you seem to play the field."

"What is that supposed to mean?"

"Well, I've been keeping my nose out of it, but since you're leaving tomorrow and you know so much about me and my family, I think it's only fair that you spill your dirty little secrets. I mean, you were obviously married to this guy Sam, but I have a hunch he's not the only guy in your life."

I pulled the flaps of my coat over my slightly exposed belly. I was much happier learning about Jonah than having to tell him anything about me. "Sorry to disappoint you, but there are no dirty little secrets to spill."

He laughed. "You're so full of crap. Who's Cameron?"

My head whipped in his direction. "W-who?"

"Oh I think you know who he is. You say his name whenever you're taking a nap. So who is he?" I couldn't answer but my hand rested on top of my belly. "Oh, is he the father?"

I nodded and turned my head toward the window so he wouldn't see the tears beginning to crest over my lids. "I've only been with two men in my life. I don't consider that playing the field."

"Just two people? You're whole life?"

"Why are you making it sound so bad?"

"I don't know," he shrugged as he turned onto the main road leading us into town. "I just can't imagine only having sex with two people."

"Then you haven't had great sex."

"And you have?" he asked with a questionable look.

"Only with Cameron, and yes it was phenomenal."

My last words were a little shaky as flashes of every kiss, every caress, every push, and every feeling of pleasure flooded over me.

"So where is he?"

"It's a long story."

"Well there is almost a full tank of gas, and I have no plans of turning this baby back around until it's almost empty. We have time for a long story."

A little laugh escaped my lips as I finally turned away from the passenger side window. "With the V-8 that's in this car we may not have as much time as you think." Jonah looked a little shocked as his head turned slowly toward me, his eyebrows raised. "Oh don't give me that look. Just because I'm a girl doesn't mean I don't know that this car has a V-8 engine. I'm not completely helpless."

"I could have told you that," he said, giving me a little wink. "I knew that within five minutes of meeting you. So seriously, where's this Cameron guy? Why'd you leave him?"

"What makes you think I left him?"

"Because there's no way anyone would leave *you*. Well, unless they were a complete loser."

I took a tissue from my pocket and dabbed my eyes. "He's not a loser. It's just really complicated."

"That's what the back roads are for."

Jonah sped up, letting the engine stretch its legs. As we bounced around on the scenic back roads of my quaint New England town I told him almost everything. I obviously left out the blood-letting and sharp fangs. Don't ask me why I opened up, but once I started I just couldn't stop. My lips kept moving and words spilled out of my mouth until I could barely breathe from all the congestion trapped in my nose.

Jonah was quiet the entire time, just letting me vent until I was completely empty. When I had finally finished, his only word was, "Asshole."

We were both right. Cameron wasn't a loser, he was an asshole. And yet I loved him.

Chapter Eighteen

Brianna

Today began like almost every other this week. I woke rested, ate breakfast with Jonah in Mable's dining room, and then sat comfortably in the backseat while Jonah drove me around. However, today instead of driving to the hell house, I was going to the train station. My bags were packed and it was bittersweet. I had truly enjoyed my time at Mable's and being able to catch up with Roger, but it was time to go and I needed to keep moving. I didn't have a plan and my brain seemed so foggy lately that even when I tried to sit down and think of what to do, I'd get sidetracked, a headache, or just fall asleep.

Jonah had been pretty quiet today so far, and I assumed it was because it was his father's birthday. I was also very quiet today, but it was because I was scared shitless of being so exposed.

"Do you want me to go in with you and wait?" Jonah asked, looking at me through the rearview mirror.

"No, just drop me off."

"But you could be waiting for hours."

"Or I could be waiting fifteen minutes. I'll know when I get in there."

"I feel like I'm abandoning you," he replied as he pulled into the parking lot of the train station.

"Jonah, you're not abandoning me. You're dropping your client off at the train station just like every other driver would do." I'd probably insulted him a little with that since he didn't respond or look back at me in the mirror. "I didn't mean that to sound so cold."

"It's alright. You are my client and I am your driver and if you want to sit in a train station all day that's your business. Just know that I might be waiting in the bushes until you leave to make sure you get off."

"No!" I shouted a little too loud which caused him to slam on the breaks and the seatbelt to lock into place across my chest and stomach. "Ow."

"You scared the shit out of me, what's wrong with you?"

"Jonah, please listen to me. You need to leave as soon as I get out of this car. I don't want you to know where I'm going so that if anyone tries to compel you to answer you really won't be able to."

"Compel me to…Brianna, you're being ridiculous."

"No I'm not. You have no idea the kind of people that are looking for me."

"Then let me help you."

"No, Jonah, you can't. And even if you could I wouldn't want you to. I don't mean to hurt your feelings…" But I already had and he was out of the car. I grabbed my purse from the seat beside me and put it over my shoulder while Jonah held the door open and looked past me. It pissed me off. It didn't take much these days. I stepped out of the car and allowed Jonah to close the door behind me before I laid into him.

"Now you listen to me, Mr. Poopy-pants," I began, pointing my index finger up in his face. "I know you want to help me, and I really appreciate it, I really do. But I don't want you to get involved in my crazy messed up life. You have a mother and a sister who need you, and I would never forgive myself if anything were to happen to you because of me. I have people that can help me and won't get hurt doing it and I know that doesn't make any sense to you but it does me and I'm not even calling them right now because I'm trying to do this on my own just to see if I *can* do this on my own. And then in some freakish kismet kind of thing I meet you and we became friends within five minutes of meeting each other, which rarely ever happens, and now I have to leave and we'll probably never see each other again and I'd rather not have a big childish fight before I go. So can you just put away your man card for two minutes, pretend that you're my friend, tell me that you'll miss me, and then tell me goodbye before I break down and sob like a little girl."

I was a little out of breath. I hadn't had diarrhea of the mouth in a while.

"Sorry, I tend to do that when I'm upset."

"It's cool. I've just never heard anyone talk so fast and have so many thoughts come out at once. But you're right, we do have this freakish bond, and I am your friend and I will miss you which is really weird. Just please don't cry, I've really seen enough of that this week."

We both laughed and I still had to wipe my eye.

"Oh, I almost forgot," I said as I dug into my purse, trying to hide the dagger's handle that was slightly sticking out and handed Jonah an envelope. "This is for you. Now don't open it until I'm gone, but I am telling you now this is for you. Not your mother or your sister, you. I know you want to take care of everyone, and you are doing a wonderful job. But you won't be useful to them if you don't start taking care of yourself too."

"Brianna, I can't..."

"You don't even know what it is, so don't start saying you can't take it." I shoved the envelope in his hand and he sighed deeply as he put it in his pocket. "Now give me a hug so I can go, this'll be the part that sucks."

Jonah laughed as I wrapped my arms around him, silently saying prayers for his safety and happiness. He was such a sweet boy and deserved so much.

As I released him he put his hand in his coat jacket and pulled out a small piece of paper and handed it to me. "This is just my email address and cell. If you're ever back in town and need a ride, just call me. Or you can email me or something and say hi. Or not, just thought I'd give it to you anyway."

I took the small piece of paper and placed it inside my purse. "I may not be able to email for a while, but I definitely will when I can. Thank you for...well just keeping me company the last few days."

I hugged him one more time and then took a couple of steps away.

"Wait, Bri, just one more thing," he began, stepping in front of me but looking down at the ground instead of directly at me. "I really have no business saying this to you, and you can totally smack me for saying it, but last night after I dropped you off I started thinking about everything you said about Cameron and what happened. I'm not in any way saying what he did was ok, but maybe...well..." He paused and scratched the back of his neck roughly and then looked me in the eye and said, "I miss my dad every day. Every freakin' day. And even though he absolutely had his faults, I would give anything to have another minute with him."

"Jonah, what are you trying to say?"

He sighed. "What I'm really doing a bad job of saying is that I think you should talk to Cameron. Every kid deserves to know his father, even if he made a really stupid choice. Who knows, sometimes things aren't always what they seem." My eyes flashed with surprised at his statement and my jaw went slightly slack. "I'm out of line, aren't I?"

"Uh, no. I've just…er…heard that before."

"So you'll talk to Cameron?"

It was my turn to sigh. "I'll think about it, Jonah. I promise I'll think about it."

With one last hug we finally separated and I headed across the wide brick walkway toward the train station. I couldn't help but laugh to myself when I heard Jonah shout, "Holy shit!" behind me. He must have opened the envelope I'd given him with an extraordinary tip. Afraid to look back, I quickened my pace a little, pulling my large suitcase behind me. I'd been spoiled up until now, never having to carry my own luggage, and I was definitely paying the price since it was so damn heavy.

Today was the start of something new, and it was a little scary. What I had said to Jonah was true - I needed to see if I could do this on my own. Today there was no Jonah to drive me around, or Vlad to fly me wherever I wanted to go, or Warriors surrounding me for my protection. I had to be my own protection today, my own problem solver. And the first thing I needed to solve was how to buy a train ticket. Now I know that sounds just plain dumb, but when you rarely traveled to begin with and then were swept away and hauled up in a mansion for six months you forget how to do certain things.

When the wide doors to the train station parted a gush of warm air hit my face while a flurry of people scurried in front of me to their trains. My right arm was already groaning at the weight of my suitcase while I stood dumbfounded just inside the door, so I pushed through the crowd and made my way to where people were congregating near little machines. I almost hit myself upside the head when I finally asked a gentleman where I could buy tickets and he looked at me like I was the village idiot and pointed to the big signs that read "Buy tickets here" with a big red arrow pointing down to the actual machine. So far my little excursion in self-discovery had only proved that I was blind.

While I stood in line waiting for my turn to make a fool of myself in front of the ticket machine, I kept scanning the building for any Vampires. I ended up scaring the crap out of the guy in front of me when I sucked in a gallon of air at the sight of a white light shining in the distance. I tried to remain calm when the light began moving closer, but I didn't want to move an inch in case it brought attention. So I white knuckled the handle of my suitcase and kept my head down while I waited nervously in line.

When it was finally my turn I stepped forward dragging my heavy suitcase behind me and kept my "eye" on the Vamp. He was closer, at least I thought it was a he, but in my heart I knew it wasn't Cam. I couldn't tell you how I knew, I just did. That was good and bad, but I didn't have the time to analyze it further since the woman behind me was clearing her throat loudly, obviously annoyed by my delay in getting my tickets. Ok, Bri, you can do this, although I'm sure a five-year-old could do it faster.

Question one – Where do you want to go? Answer – Boston.

Question two – What time do you want to leave? Answer – uh, now? The times displayed on the screen and by some wondrous stroke of good luck there was a train leaving in seven minutes. Print, print, print, where was the damn print button? Oh, I should probably pay for the ticket first. I could hear the groans behind me when I struggled with trying to hold my suitcase upright with one leg while rummaging through my purse for my wallet, trying not to expose my weapon. There was a Homeland Security agent just a few feet away with a semi-automatic. If my dagger was seen, or heaven forbid was to fall out, I'd be labeled a terrorist and locked up for sure, never to be seen again and probably sent to Gitmo. Ok Bri, a little dramatic and off track, focus you silly girl.

By the time I slid my bills into the machine my suitcase was sliding down my leg threatening to fall completely over and I had lost track of the Vampire. While I waited for the machine to process my payment and print my ticket, I closed my eyes and gasped loudly. Not only because my suitcase fell over onto my foot, but also because the Vampire was only a few feet behind me.

"Print you stupid thing," I whispered harshly to the machine while I bent down to grab the handle of my suitcase, my belly getting slightly crushed and causing the babies to flutter. Just as I stood up, a long piece of thin card stock flew out of the shoot and I grabbed it and walked quickly toward the terminals.

Unfortunately as was always the case, my attempt at trying to blend in completely failed when I tripped over what must have been a speck of dust, since there was absolutely nothing there, causing me to fall on my knees and my gargantuan suitcase to tumble on top of me. A gentleman behind me who almost toppled over me caught himself against the wall and then offered me his hand to help me up. Mama Jo would have bonked me on the head with a hymnal if she saw that I barely thanked the man before grabbing my suitcase and taking off down the long corridor. But my fall had

168 ~ C.R. Quinn

definitely caught the Vampire's attention since I could now see his light coming through the crowd in my direction.

Running down the chrome tunnel that led to the tracks I was suddenly struck dumb. What timing! I needed track nine. Nine! Where the heck did that fall in the number scheme? Did it come before or after thirteen? There was track fifteen, thirteen, twelve, wait what happened to fourteen? For goodness sakes, Brianna Marilena, who gives a crap about track fourteen you need track nine you stupid girl. I kept running and looking behind me to see that the Vampire was gaining on me.

Finally I rounded the corner and saw signs for tracks ten, eight, and five. Who the hell designed this freaking place?! I walked past the entrance to track eight and was grateful to see a sign for track nine directing me around the corner. My elation, however, was only short lived when I came face to face with a tall flight of stairs.

"You have to be kidding me," I said rather loudly to myself, causing a few stares. Grabbing the handle of my suitcase I began pulling it up the stairs, slowing my progress down significantly as it banged loudly up every step. I could feel the Vampire's presence getting closer and now that I was only half way up the stairs I knew that any minute he would be coming around the corner and I would be a sitting duck. I didn't stop moving up the stairs as I closed my eyes, feeling his light only a foot or so away from the staircase and said into his head, *Sorry, I hope you're not on vacation.*

With a deep breath, I Pushed the Vampire away just as his light came around the corner. I was absolutely out of practice since instead of trying to hold him back until I could get up to the top of the stairs, I tossed him through a family of four and into the opposite wall. Oops. Well I didn't have time to worry about it since he got up just as I was able to close the heavy glass door behind me.

"Last call for Boston!" a conductor yelled as he hung from the small set of stairs between two train cars.

"Me! Me! I'm coming!" I yelled like a complete moron as I tried running toward the train while my suitcase hit everyone in sight. The Vampire was already sprinting up the stairs when I Pushed him again and even with my human hearing I could hear the chaos of a body falling down a flight of stairs and bringing others down with him. I felt guilty, I didn't want anyone else to get hurt, but I couldn't stop running toward the train.

Thankfully the conductor was waving me toward him and grabbed my suitcase from me so that I could get up the stairs and into the car. Once safely on the train I grabbed my suitcase from him and began wheeling it down the aisle. Through the windows I could see a man scurrying out from the stairwell's doorway and onto the platform. At the end of the aisle I could see a sign for a bathroom and I ducked into it, barely able to latch it behind me with the size of my suitcase in such a tight enclosure.

I pressed myself up against the wall, trying hard not to imagine all the germs that were probably growing on it, and stretched my mind out to feel the Vampire outside. Just as I found his essence, the train lurched forward causing me to lose my balance and fall to my knees, catching myself with my hands. Gross.

Not having any time to worry about the diseases that were now on my hands, I closed my eyes again and quickly saw that the Vampire was just outside the moving train and keeping pace with it before he finally stopped and the distance between us began to grow. I pushed myself back up to my knees, placing a hand on my stomach.

"Are you ok?" I asked my babies frantically, hoping I hadn't done anything to harm them. But how would they answer? Some magic telepathy? Just about the time a panic attack was coming on I felt my stomach flutter. "Oh thank god!"

Not even having a second to wipe the tears from my cheeks a sudden wave of nausea came over me and I barely made it to the toilet in front of me. As I wretched uncontrollably, a trainman began knocking on the door looking for tickets.

"Morning sickness!" I shouted between wretches. My declaration didn't stop his banging. I was so pissed off that I rose from the toilet without even wiping my face, grabbed my ticket from where it had fallen on the floor and opened the door dramatically to see the trainman scowling at me.

"Here," I snapped and handed him my ticket, making sure the putrid vomit smell from my breath wafted in his face. "May I please continue with my puking?"

The trainman placed his hand over his mouth, ripped my ticket, and walked away. That's right Mr. Trainman, you walk away. I am woman, hear me roar! I just out chased a Vampire, you run you mere human! Brianna Morgan, Vampire out-runner-girl. Nothing can stop me now.

"Oh crap," I said as I latched the door and flew to the toilet to empty my stomach. Perhaps there was one thing that could stop me.

"Brianna, wait!" Aidan shouted at me as I pushed past him and ran out of Daddy O's kitchen and into the foyer.

"Where's Cameron?"

Aidan wrapped his hand around my arm, pulling me to a stop and turning me around to look at him. "After everything he's done, why do you care?"

"Where did he go?"

He sighed and pointed toward the front door. "He left, Bri. Just let him go."

"I...I can't," I stuttered as I ran out the front door and just in time to see Cameron opening the door to a large SUV. "Cam, wait!" I shouted as I waddled down the stairs.

Cameron paused, but stayed behind the truck's door. "Brianna, I really must go. I think we've said everything that needs to be said."

"No, Cam, this isn't how this ends."

"Why not? It's ok for you to leave me but not the other way around? That's not exactly fair, now is it?"

Stepping around the car door I placed my hands on either side of his face. "Cameron, please don't make me beg. I love you and I know that you love me and that you're scared. But stay, please, for all of us," I pleaded as I removed my hands from his face and placed his hand on my stomach hoping that the babies would kick and pull at his heartstrings, remind him of the miracles we had made together.

"It's not what I want. You're not the only hybrid in my life anymore and she needs me. You'll be safe here and I'll make sure you'll want for nothing."

"I don't want your money!"

"That is all that I can give you now. If you don't want it, you'll be left with nothing."

"Brianna, don't take it," Aidan said from behind me. "Stay with me. I'll take care of you, better than he ever could."

"Aidan's right. He can give you what I can't."

"Or won't," I cried.

"Brianna, step away," Cameron said coldly.

Aidan pulled me away from the door, holding my arms down at my side. "Brianna, stay with me," he whispered into my ear.

"Cam, I know you love me."

Cameron slammed the door shut and a second later Aidan stood in front of me, crushing me to his chest in order to protect me from the gravel flying from Cameron's spinning tires as he sped out of the driveway.

"Let me go," I sobbed, "Please, Aidan, let me go."

Aidan moved his hands from around my back and placed them firmly on either side of my face. "Allow me to love you, Bri. I promise I will never hurt you."

Aidan lowered his face and rested his lips lightly on top of mine. A moment later he lifted his face and looked deeply into my eyes before he crushed his lips against mine again, forcing his tongue inside my mouth.

I woke with a gasp, sitting up so quickly in my seat it caused a head rush and little stars to sparkle around me. Everyone within the vicinity turned in their seats staring at me with mixtures of annoyance and curiosity.

"Sorry," I whispered apologetically while picking my coat up from the floor where it had fallen.

"I always found that was the worst," said a woman sitting across the aisle from me.

"Oh? You mean humiliating yourself in tight public places," I replied, placing my cool hands on my hot cheeks.

The woman laughed. "No, the dreams. I always had the craziest dreams when I was pregnant. Sometimes they were so embarrassing I couldn't even tell my husband."

I smiled, laughing to myself at the fact that I didn't need to be pregnant in order to have crazy dreams. And if the woman was having the kind of dream I had just had, then I hope she didn't tell her husband. "It's good to know I'm not alone."

"Boston! Boston next," the conductor said over the intercom. I couldn't believe I was here already. The trip was only two hours with a handful of stops, but it seemed like my dream went on forever. Though in all actuality it most likely only took five or six minutes for me to kiss a man I barely knew.

Another twenty minutes passed before I was finally able to walk out of the train station, and once again I had to ask myself, now what? I looked out at my surroundings, individuals being mobbed by loved ones, business men and women fighting over cabs to get to their corporate offices, and then there were the tourists like me who had no idea what they were doing or where they were going or how in the world they were going to get there. So instead of trying to figure out how to get a cab I started walking. It was a good thought at first, I liked the freedom of walking down a sidewalk by myself in a new city.

My walk didn't last long, however. The problem with Boston's sidewalks was what also gave the city its charm. They were made of brick and stone and were narrow and uneven. It was incredibly difficult walking down them dragging a two ton suitcase behind you.

"Fine, I'll get a cab," I grumbled to myself and like I had seen on TV, I stood at the curb and held my hand up. And well…nothing. There had to be more this. I tried waving my hand, standing further in the street, even rubbing my belly for sympathy. Just about the time I was going to give up hope, a cab slowed in front of me and popped the trunk. I truly thought I was going to get a hernia trying to lift the suitcase into the trunk (thank you jerky cabby) but once secured I was in the warmth of the cab holding my hand over my mouth from its musty sweaty smell. The last thing I wanted to happen was to puke in this man's cab. I would be traumatized for life.

"South end, Dwight Street please," I said confidently and proudly.

The only reason I remembered that Renee and John lived on Dwight Street was because it reminded me of one of Daddy O's favorite embarrassing stories about me when I was a child. When I was three years old Mama Jo felt it was time for me to share in her annual Christmas tradition of watching *White Christmas* in front of the fire on Christmas Eve. After watching intently for almost an hour snuggled in Mama Jo's and Daddy O's arms I finally asked, "Mama, where's Dwight? You said this was Dwight's Christmas, where is he?"

It was a story that had been repeated many, many times during my life. After a while both Daddy O and Mama Jo referred to the movie as Dwight's Christmas instead of its true title. So because of this one random story I was able to remember where Renee lived.

Boston was beautiful. Of course I hadn't been to many other places in my life, but even through the cab's window I could feel the city's rich history surrounding me. It was hard not to imagine horses pulling carts in the street while women in long thick skirts and gentleman in waistcoats and tights lined the sidewalks. At one point I even imagined seeing a tall well-dressed man with black curly hair holding little Christian Burke's hand as they shuffled around the hustle and bustle of the busy city. I had really chosen Boston to see Renee, although now I had a feeling Cameron would eventually find me here. If I wasn't at Daddy O's, Renee's was the next logical place. It wasn't smart of me, but if Renee ever found out I was only two hours away from her and didn't come to see her I would never hear the end of it. But I wasn't just here out of guilt, I missed her terribly and I needed my friend.

After another ten minutes the cab turned onto Dwight Street. It was at this moment another worry began to come over me – what if Renee wasn't home? It wasn't like I could call or anything. I really hadn't thought all of this through, but it was too late now since the cab stopped.

"There's a car behind us, so you'll need to get your suitcase yourself," the cab driver said annoyed.

"Uh, not if you want a tip," I replied flatly.

The driver groaned as he exited the cab and walked around to the trunk of the car and all but threw my suitcase on the ground. I pulled my other two bags over my shoulder, threw the driver some money, and then wheeled my suitcase over to the sidewalk trying not to hit the cars that lined the street.

I rolled my suitcase a short distance down the uneven brick sidewalk, using most of my strength to keep the suitcase upright. When I finally came to stand in front of Renee's brownstone I about had a heart attack. A set of stairs rose in front of me that were so steep and tall I thought there was no way I would be able to climb them without toppling down head over feet, especially with having to carry this big-ass suitcase.

Taking one step at a time, I dragged the suitcase up, not caring that it made a horrible thump when it hit each step. If the suitcase didn't trip me, the two bags I had over my shoulder kept sliding down every other second. I was an accident waiting to happen. When I finally reached the top I had a feeling of accomplishment, almost as if I had just crested the summit of a very tall mountain and I was just as out of breath.

Looking at the metal box next to the door I had to rack my brain to remember which apartment number she and Dr. John lived in. Hey, I remembered the street and the house number, was I expected to remember everything? Apartment number two was the only one that didn't have a name penciled in next to it so I took a chance and pressed the call button and waited. When she didn't answer, I pressed it once more before her distinctive voice came over the intercom.

"Yeah, I heard you. I only know two people in this town and the milk man doesn't come until tomorrow and the other person just left. So whatever you're selling you can just turn right back around because I'm not buying anything and if you're a religious sect you might as well leave because trust me when I say in no way do you want me to be a part of your cult."

She obviously hadn't changed a bit. I pressed the intercom button, "First of all, it scares me that you have a milk man. Now get your sarcastic redheaded butt down here and let your pregnant best friend in."

There was no sound coming from the other side of the intercom, but through the thick brick walls I could hear Renee scream loudly from her apartment and then the sound of thick platform shoes clomping loudly against wooden steps. Within seconds, Renee's crimson red hair was billowing behind her as she ran to the front door, flung it open, and threw her arms around me causing me to let go of everything in my arms in order to hug her back. Renee's tears were running through my hair and down my neck, and they were matching my own. The only thing that made us stop crying was the sound of my suitcase toppling down the stairs.

"Ok, I lugged that thing up here once already, it's your turn."

"So because you're pregnant you think you can push me around?"

"Yeah, that's pretty much what I thought." We laughed as we hugged again. It didn't seem real to actually be standing in front of her. We had spoken many times since I left, but it absolutely wasn't the same. I finally felt complete being with my partner in crime.

"Crap," Renee gasped as she looked at the front door. "I left the key upstairs. I'll get the suitcase if you can buzz apartment number one. Mrs. Mitchell will let us in."

"Are you sure she won't mind?"

"She's used to it by now. She has to let me in at least three times a week." Renee lifted the suitcase from the ground and almost toppled over as she tried getting it up the first step in her massive heels. "These are certainly the wrong shoes to do this in."

"Do you ever really wear the right kind of shoes? For goodness sakes it's only Thursday afternoon and you're almost wearing stripper heals. Who were you dressing up for since you obviously didn't know I was coming?" I said as I pressed the button for poor Mrs. Mitchell.

"Just because I..." slam "moved into snotty..." slam "old Boston doesn't mean," slam "I've lost all my," slam "fashion sense. Good grief what do you have in here?" Renee huffed as she slowly brought the suitcase back up the stairs.

"About two months' worth of pregnancy clothes."

"And a full set of dumbbells?"

"Oh, there is a stick of deodorant."

"That must be it," she smirked and then looked at Mrs. Mitchell as she came to the front door. "Sorry, Mrs. Mitchell, forgot my key again. This is my very best friend B...."

"Joanne," I interrupted as I extended my hand to the scrawniest most miserable looking woman I'd ever seen. She didn't shake my hand, just turned and walked away causing me to leap forward in order to catch the door before it latched closed again.

"Isn't she a peach?" Renee asked, dripping with sarcasm as she finally made it to the top of the stairs. "I missed you."

"Can't miss me anymore, I'm standing right in front of you. Can we go inside? I think my shoulder is going to fall off from these bags."

"Yes mother, but you're going to have to help me get this semi-trailer you call a suitcase up the next flight of stairs."

"I forgot you said you had so many stairs. Your ass does look great."

She turned her backside to me and posed. "Thanks for noticing, but you do know I don't swing that way."

"Well if you did, you'd be alone in this relationship."

We laughed and made our way up to her apartment's door to tackle yet another unbelievably steep set of stairs. It took us almost ten minutes to get up them with the suitcase, even with each of us taking a side. Renee lost her balance once and almost took us both down. We would have been able to see the gravity of our situation if we weren't laughing hard enough to make ourselves pee.

Once we reached the first landing there was a living room that immediately opened up to my right, and another set of stairs that curved up and disappeared to another floor.

"Please tell me I can stay down here," I whined.

"Yes," Renee panted as she rolled the suitcase into the living room. "There's actually a guest room right off the kitchen. It's full of crap, but dropper-inners can't be picky. I think that's how it goes."

"Sorry, sweetie, it's not even close, but you never were good at analogies."

"Well you can't be good at everything, and there are so many other things I am good at," she said and disappeared into a doorway off of the kitchen.

"Sweetie, you know I love you, but there is something else you're not good at."

"And what's that?" she shouted from inside the bedroom followed by the sound of a loud crash.

"From the sound of that I'm guessing you hadn't unpacked in there either."

There were boxes everywhere. Some were opened with items hanging out while others weren't touched because there were other boxes on top of them. Renee about fell out of the guest room, items from whatever had fallen down following her out into the kitchen.

"Don't judge me, Brianna Marie. It takes time to unpack a home."

"You've been here three months, Renee Alexandra, and you don't have a job."

"Unpacking takes time away from job hunting."

"And reality TV watching."

"That too," she laughed. "I'll take your coat, you want something to drink?"

"Water would be great," I said as I handed her my coat and then melted into the couch.

Renee's eyes bugged out of her head. "To quote Daddy O, good gosh a-mighty, you're huge. Did you eat a toddler or something?"

"It is a miracle my self-confidence is as strong as it is with a friend like you. I'm not that big."

"Then you need glasses, Bri. Are you further along than you thought?" she said as she handed me my glass and sat down beside me.

"There's a lot I need to tell you, Re."

"Do I need to get chips and French onion dip, or chocolate crème cookies?" My stomach growled louder than a full symphony orchestra. "Ok I'll get both. You're a hungry baby aren't you?" Renee laughed as she tickled my stomach, causing the babies to flutter inside. I guessed they loved their Auntie Renee already. "I'll get the food, you start talking. John's not home until tomorrow morning, so we have a whole day to ourselves," she said as she rose from the couch and headed back into the kitchen.

"Great, we'll eat for a few minutes and talk, and then we'll tackle the boxes."

"Bri, no."

"Re, yes. My body is literally cringing at the sight of them."

"Then I suggest you don't go into the bathroom," she said snidely as she pointed to a doorway in front of me.

Immediately I pushed myself off the couch and ran into the bathroom. "Are you freakin' kidding me?" I shouted at her and then walked back out into the living room to see her laughing hysterically with chips, dip and cookies in her arms. "Renee, your shower is full of boxes?! That's the first thing we're working on today, I mean it," I said firmly as I sat back down on the couch.

"Yes mother, now sit, eat and spill. Oh, wait, let me get the phone."

"Why?" I asked, grabbing her arm before she could leave the couch.

"Don't worry, I won't call Cameron."

I let go of her arm and tried to act nonchalant. "Why would you think I wouldn't want you to call Cameron?" I wasn't really successful.

Renee raised one eyebrow at me. "Because I'm not an idiot, Bri. When your best friend's baby daddy calls you every day for almost a week it makes even the most uneducated think something's up. I was actually getting the phone in case John called on his break. So are we going to tackle what the hell happened between you and Mr. Wonderful first?"

Not wasting any time I opened the bag of potato chips and began digging into the dip.

"How about we start with something simpler. Like, Marilena."

"Mary what?"

"I changed my middle name. Actually, I guess I've changed it back to what it was supposed to be."

"Why the hell would you do that?"

"I did it for my dad."

"The guy with the weird name, right?"

"It's not that weird."

Renee shook her head. "I don't like his name and I don't like your new middle name, Mar…whatever it is. Change it back."

"Good to know you're still able to compromise."

"I told you I was good at everything."

Chapter Nineteen

Cameron

"Boston! Father she is in Boston," I shouted as I burst through the doors of Victor's private study and then instantly regretted my intrusion. "Oh, forgive me. I was not aware you had a guest. Good afternoon, Maddy, I apologize for the interruption."

Madelyn Forebush turned in her chair and gave me a warm smile. "No interruption at all, Mr. Burke, it is always a pleasure seeing you."

"And you as well," I said, bowing deeply in front of her.

"Hey," Jared said from a chair in the far corner hidden from the sun, "don't be hitting on my girl."

Madelyn giggle from her chair, but Victor rolled his eyes.

"Jared, I would not dream of encroaching on your territory. Father, I apologize again, I will return later."

"No need, Mr. Burke," Madelyn said as she rose from her seat. "I think we're done here, don't you agree, Victor?"

Victor's expression was anything but amused. "Yes, I believe we are. Cameron, Madelyn was just explaining to me how the Facility can longer run without Lanashell and that I must get her back immediately."

Madelyn nodded. "Harrison means well, but he is useless. The staff is fed up with him, hybrids are being boarded three and four to a room because he can't get everything together to open up the new wing, and he completely dropped the ball with the Cushlin girl. We're lucky she doesn't have parents, otherwise we'd be sued up to our necks. She'll be in the hospital wing for weeks with her injuries. I don't want to force the issue, but none of this would have happened if Lana were here. If you don't get her back, you will have my resignation. I'm almost seventy years old, I can't do everything over there."

"Amen, sista," Jared said from the corner, receiving a deadly glare from Victor.

"Madelyn," Victor said as he lowered himself from his elevated chair behind his desk, "I hear your message loud and clear, and I assure you we will come up with a solution to the leadership issue at the Facility."

"As long as the solution is Lanashell. Have a nice day," she replied and began walking in my direction with her arms outstretched. "Always good to see you, Mr. Burke. Oh, and Jared asked me to drop this off for you."

Madelyn handed me a thin manila folder with the name *Williams, Nikki* handwritten on the top tab. It was Nikki's file from the Facility – intake forms, medical exams, personal history.

"Thank you, Maddy. I will be sure to get this back to you as soon as possible."

"Keep it. I'd rather not have anything associated with that girl in my files. Jared, will you escort me out?"

Jared leapt from his chair, careful to stay in the shadowed path on the outskirts of the room. "A gentleman always walks his girl to her car," he said formally and winked in my direction. "Of course I'll have to jump around a bit, there's still a lot of daylight around."

"Oh you sweet boy, I always forget. No need to skip around for an old lady like me."

"Old? You're perfectly aged," Jared replied as he offered Madelyn his elbow and opened the door for her to exit. "Hey bro, if you pull the shades I'll come to your meeting room and we can go through that file."

I nodded at my brother and with one last wave Madelyn left Victor's study on Jared's arm.

"That woman is exhausting. How can an elderly human woman have such power?" Victor asked in his low raspy voice.

"She is quite a woman. At least the solution to the problem is simple enough. Lanashell will have the Facility up and running within hours of returning."

Father twisted his lips as he sat back in his chair and folded his hands in his lap. "It would be simple if we knew where Lanashell was."

"She has gone missing? I was not aware."

"Only a few know of this. The problems at the Facility started the day after she left. When it became obvious Harrison was unable to manage, I unnaturally tucked my tail between my legs to contact Lanashell, only she's practically disappeared. No one has seen or spoken with her since she left."

"Do you think she's simply gone to a private island, or do you suspect some kind of foul play?"

"I hope for the first, but feel it is the latter," he responded, rubbing his chin with his forefinger. "I am going to ask Alex and Connor to do some searching. The Facility certainly can't last much longer in the incapable hands of Harrison, and even more so it can't survive without Madelyn."

"Unfortunately that is an absolute fact."

Victor came around to the front of his desk and looked down his nose at me. "May I ask what the file is?"

"It is Nikki's Facility file."

"How is all of that going?"

I shook my head in frustration. "Slow. It is as though she did not exist until a few months ago. Jared thought the file might give us something, but I hold little hope."

"Child, sometimes hope is all we have. Speaking of, you have news of Brianna?"

I could not help but smile with relief. "Yes. Aidan just contacted me. Apparently he initially found her in Connecticut just as she was getting on a train. She took out a dozen people throwing him around the station. Apparently he did not have the opportunity to identify himself before she started using her mind projection on him."

"At least we know her pregnancy has not affected her ability to defend herself."

"Thank the heavens," I sighed.

"I assume you are planning a trip then?"

I nodded. "Yes sir. I hope to leave this evening after I wrap up a few things. I can only hope she will not greet me the same way she did Aidan."

"I may not be the expert on love affairs, but I know my Warriors and I know for sure that Brianna loves you very much. She has every right to be angry with you, but deep down I have a feeling she cannot be without you. Much in the same way you have become almost useless without her." He laughed lightly, although it was the truth. "Everything is falling perfectly into place. Since you are going to Boston you can take care of some business that has just landed on our plate."

"Of course, Father," I replied proudly, feeling relieved that after all the upheaval I had caused in his home he still considered me a trusted asset.

"It is readily known that the Facility is overcrowded. What is not known is that all the coven leaders have just agreed to build a second hybrid facility, however, this time on the East Coast and also not solely funded by me."

"I am sure that took a bit of convincing."

"I am sure the others would call it more like threatening. But the Warriors shouldn't be responsible for funding everything, the others need to be more involved. I have also petitioned them for more volunteers for Gatherers. The group has become extremely short-handed and with everything going on with Elaina I cannot afford to spare any more of my children. With a new Facility on the East Coast it will basically cut the country in half and create less travel time for everyone."

"It is definitely a long time coming, Father. What is it you need me to do?"

Victor took a black leather portfolio from his desk and handed it to me. "Here are all the financials, what we've agreed on for total spending, amount of square footage, amenities needed, etc. The city of Boston has been the most endorsed because it is populous, easy to get to, and Dante's coven is based there. He has offered to oversee the operations of the new Facility East and I will monitor Facility West. What I need you to do is find potential sites and present them to the coven leaders. Dante has offered to provide you with resources to help you through the process."

"Although I know Dante's coven specializes in negotiations, I am confident I can handle a real estate agent, Father."

Victor smiled slyly. "I have no doubt. You will, however, need help with the coven leaders. If I didn't know they were Vampires I would think they were children. Every time we conference I want to gouge my eyes out."

"Duly noted, Father. Anything else?"

"Bring back my newest Warrior."

"I will try my best, Father."

Victor's voice became low and very serious. "Do not try, child, just do."

That was easier said than done. The first hurdle was to get Brianna to even speak to me, the second to bring her home to the manor. Unbeknownst to my father I was willing to sacrifice the second. "I will update you on my progress, Father."

I stood from my chair, leather portfolio in hand, and headed toward the door.

"Cameron," Victor began just before I was out the door, "how are you with going back to Boston?"

"Fine," I lied. "I have visited several times over the years."

"I know you have, but only for short periods of time. I want to make sure your past will not cloud your judgment." Though his words were all business, his tone was caring. He knew that I was always somewhat affected whenever I went back to the city where my family had died several centuries ago. My will would definitely be tested.

"I will not fail you, Father," I nodded and closed the door behind me.

Putting the portfolio and Nikki's file under my arm, I raced to my meeting room and flipped the switch to lower the shades for Jared and then turned on the gas fireplace. In no way did we need the light or the heat from the flames, but it was more of a habit. Just as the shades clicked securely in place there was a knock at the door.

"Since when do you knock, little brother?"

"Since I am not your little brother," a voice said as the door opened slowly.

"Good afternoon, Nikki," I said as politely as I could, though she did not deserve it. "I am expecting someone momentarily. I must ask that you leave."

Nikki sighed deeply and shifted her gaze to the floor as she stepped further into the doorway. "Cameron, I know I am the last person you want to see."

"You are correct."

Her eyes shot up to meet mine for only a moment before they found the floor once more. "I just wanted to apologize for that day…for what I did."

Before I could answer, a cloud of black mist thickened in front of her and took the shape of my youngest brother. Once he was fully formed he noticed the tense expression on my face and quickly looked behind him to see Nikki standing in the door.

"Aww-kward. I can come back later."

"No," Nikki said before I could speak, "I'm leaving. I was just apologizing for, well you know."

"Oh good," Jared smiled uncomfortably. "My timing is awesome."

"Jared, we need to get started," I said firmly, wanting nothing more but for Nikki to be out of my sight.

"Yeah, I'm going. I really am sorry, Cameron." Nikki took a step into the room and placed her hand on Jared's arm and whispered, "See you tonight?"

Jared nodded, and gave her a quick kiss on the cheek. "I'll find you."

A moment later Nikki closed the door behind her and Jared turned to face me looking sheepish.

"Have I missed something?" I asked slowly. "Are you…dating her?"

"Don't look at me like that, it's your fault."

"And how is that?"

"You told me to get close to her. And underneath the lying and blackmailing and overall craziness she's actually a pretty cool chick."

"I told you to get close to her to get information so we could find out if she's working for Elaina, not so that you could fall in love with her."

"Whoa, whoa, no one's talking about love here, and you didn't put down any restrictions."

"You gave me so much grief about her, and now you are dating her. I cannot believe this! You know that when Brianna finds out she will be furious with you. Do Alexander and Devin know?"

Jared burst out laughing as he walked toward the table. "Hell no. Can we get this over with, I need a nap. The sun hits this place the worst around this time. Hey, I said stop looking at me like that."

"Sorry, I am just in shock." Trying to shake away the reality of Jared and Nikki together I opened Nikki's folder. "Nikki Williams, born July 8, 1989."

"False. I've search under Nikki, Nicole, Nicolette, the letter N, no one by that name was born in the United States on that date. I also looked in the Social Security database. There are Nikki Williams' of course, but they're just born, old, dead, or in one case previously a man. Oh you should have seen him, bro, in no way should he have ever decided to become a woman. His nose for one thing…"

"Jared!"

"Oh, yeah. Sorry. Nikki Williams is a false name, that much I know."

I read down the rest of the form, most of it was blank except for her parentage. "Father, unknown. Mother, Marla Williams."

"Nope. That's a false name too. What's that scribble?"

The words Charles Cushlin and a question mark were scratched into the margins. "Lanashell must have added that. Look here under siblings, it says none, but Lanashell put the name Natasha Cushlin." Again with a question mark. "I met a Charles Cushlin once, and I thought I heard that he had two girls. I wonder if this Natasha Cushlin put down that her parents were Marla and Charles Cushlin and Lanashell got suspicious and somehow put this together. Perhaps the two girls have similar powers."

Jared took the folder from my hands and flipped through a few more of the pages. "Well Lana is a sneaky bitch. I wonder if she saw an image in both of their heads."

"Good thinking, little brother."

"It's bound to happen sometime," he laughed. "I'll do a search on Nikki Cushlin and see what comes up."

Just then another thought struck me. "When Madelyn was complaining to Victor she mentioned something that had happened to a Cushlin girl. She must have meant this Natasha. Do you know anything about her?"

Jared shook his head. "Not much. All I heard was that there was a hybrid that could actually create fire, like seriously, fire coming from his fingertips like a superhero."

"They are called Firestarters, little brother. They are very rare."

"Whatever, that's an awesome power. Shooting fire, now that would be something..."

"Jared!"

"Sorry dude, having an ADD moment. Anyway, fire boy got it on with this Cushlin chick I guess, and apparently he like spontaneously combusted while they were having sex. Talk about a climax."

"Jared, it is not funny. Is she ok?"

"Maddy said she got burned pretty badly, but if she's related to Nikki I'd think she'd be a mega healer."

"Maybe there is only so much one can heal from. Pull whatever you can about Natasha and when you are with Nikki tonight mention the fire incident, see if she reacts in any way."

"You got it. Are you going to leave tonight?"

"There is usually an evening flight, I am going to try and get on it. I will charter a private plane if I have to."

"Give her a hug from me, will ya? Can't wait for her to come home, I miss her something fierce, well...uh...nothing like you I'm sure."

"I will agree with you on that. Actually, there is something else I need to talk to you about."

Suddenly the door to my meeting room burst open, only a blur of orange hair was visible as Kyla ran inside. "You found her? You really found her!" Kyla threw her arms around me, almost making me topple over the back of the chair behind me. "When are you leaving? Can I go with you?"

"Good grief, Ky," Alexander's deep voice sounded behind us. I pulled Kyla's arms from around me, pulling a large chunk of her hair out of my mouth and then seeing Alexander and Devin coming through the door.

"Aidan found her in Boston. She is staying with Renee." Kyla's face fell and her previous smile was replaced with a pout. "I am actually glad that you are all here, I need to tell you something that might come as a surprise." I shifted uncomfortably where I was standing, choosing to use the table for stability while my siblings looked on with curiosity. "You all know that I completely messed up things with Brianna, but I am willing to do anything it takes to get her back. Unfortunately if that means…"

Kyla gasped, and the look that crossed her face would have killed even the strongest of Vampires. "I can't believe this!" she screamed as she fled the room through the door that led into my bedroom.

Jared turned to Alexander as he said, "Dude, I know she's a Vamp and all, but somehow she's able to have some wicked PMS."

Alexander raised an eyebrow at him. "Jer, I've been married to the woman for seventy-five years, you think I don't know that?" From the rumblings coming from my bedroom I knew she was rummaging around in there and it made me quite nervous as to what she was doing. "So Cam, what are you planning on telling us that's causing my wife to go into hysterics?"

Both Alexander and Devin stepped further into room, Devin shutting the door behind him before joining Alexander next to Jared. All three of my brothers were standing before me and every moment we had together flashed before my eyes. It was hard not to choke up at the prospect of not making new memories with them.

"Like I said, I am willing to do whatever I need to do in order to get Brianna back. That may mean staying in Boston, or somewhere other than here." The room became deadly silent as all three of them displayed utter disbelief on their faces. Devin's chest began to rise and fall quickly; it was only a matter of seconds before he would explode. "Brother, I need your support on this."

"Absolutely not!" he yelled. "You're leaving? You're leaving the manor, us, your brothers, our father! Have you told him of your plans?"

"No not yet. Brianna may very well want to come home. I am only preparing those closest to us if she does not."

"Don't you know what this means," Devin yelled even louder, taking a step forward into my face. Alexander placed a gentle hand on Devin's chest, but I shook my head at him. I knew Devin would take it the hardest.

"Tell me, Brother, I want to know."

Devin's eyes were flaring with anger while his chest continued to rise and fall at an intense pace. "It means that…if you're not…Father will not let me lead without you."

Of all the things I thought would come out of his mouth, that was not it.

"Brother, you are the most capable of all of us to lead our coven, Father cannot deny that. He would never…"

"He has told me this himself, Brother. He tells me all the time. The future of our coven is in the hands of both of us, not just one."

We balanced each other. Father had even said that to me once. Devin and I balanced emotions and violence, caring and duty, love and war. He obviously did not want one without the other.

"I won't let you do this," he shouted grabbing my arm and squeezing it to the point that the bone began to crack under the pressure.

"Brother," I said through clenched teeth and placing my hand over his, "my decision is not meant to hurt you. I have to make Brianna and our children my first priority. Trust me when I say I am not making this decision lightly, this is one of the hardest things I have ever had to do."

"You have been at my side for three hundred years, Brother. How…who…"

"Brother…"

"Fuck you," Devin growled and walked toward the door. Just before he left the room he said without turning around, "Tell Bri we love her."

Alexander bit his lip, but Jared could barely keep his laughter inside. "Our future leader needs some therapy," Jared joked. Before I could chastise him he turned and held Nikki's folder in the air. "I've got some research to do."

I smiled. "Yes, please let me know what you find out about your new girlfriend, Nikki." Jared froze for only a second when he heard Alexander shout in surprise, but then quickly ran out the door. I looked at Alexander and shook my head. "That was pretty much my reaction as well."

"Hopefully she'll fade away just like all the others. Listen, Cam, I apologize for Kyla and even Devin. I don't want you to leave, but if it were Kyla instead of Bri I would be doing the same thing. They'll come around, you'll see. Father may not," he smiled as he extended his hand. I took it gladly, and we patted each other on the back, though my arm barely reached around him. "Do you want me to take Kyla out of your room?"

"No, I will try and talk her down."

"Good luck with that," he laughed and left the room.

When I stepped through the door to my bedroom I was definitely confused. Sitting on top of my bed were multiple open suitcases with various levels of fullness while Kyla flew in and out of the wardrobe room.

"May I ask…"

"No you may not," she snipped as she threw several of my black sweaters into the largest of the suitcases.

"Kyla, I know you are upset…"

Kyla stopped in her tracks, wisps of her brightly colored hair hanging wild across her face. "Upset? Why would I be upset? This is the best news I've heard in weeks. I'm just helping you pack up your things so that Alex and I can move in. I'm just happy I get a bigger closet."

"Kyla…"

"You'll definitely need to put some things in storage, unless you just want to transfer some of your stuff into our old room. Do you want me to pack the sheets and comforter? It's not really my style."

Not allowing her to object, I hugged her tightly to my chest. Her body tensed at first as she hit me lightly on the back to let her go, but after a few seconds she relaxed and I could feel her tears soaking into my shirt. Good thing I generally always wore black.

"It may not come to this. Brianna may very well want to come home."

"Yeah right," she responded and pushed herself out of my chest, wiping her eyes with the cuff of her ruffled turquoise cardigan. "She's not going to want to raise the babies here. Stone floors, stone walls. Think of all the weapons around here, the blood, the fangs! What if they took a cup of blood thinking it was juice? Having them here could be a disaster. You're never coming back, I just know it."

"There is no way I can stay away from here permanently, you know that. You all are my family, this is not goodbye in any way."

More watery red tears trickled down Kyla's face, and I found it hard not to get choked up in front of her.

"It's not fair."

"I know. I do not think any of us thought things would turn out like this."

"Oh not that," she snapped, rolling her eyes at me. "It's not fair that Brianna goes running to Renee. How come Renee gets to be with her and I don't even get one phone call or email, nothing! I'm her friend too! I would have flown out with her and kept her company on this ridiculous trip of hers. But no, she has to run to Renee, apparently her number one BFF. I mean WTF."

I stood frozen while she threw her little tantrum and spoke in letters instead of actual words as was her annoying new trend. I had yet to understand the jealous feelings Renee and Kyla felt for each other even though they had never met.

"Kyla, my dearest sister, you must remember that Brianna has not seen Renee since she left Connecticut, and you have. You have been able to share so many things with Brianna that Renee has been left out on. It is only fair for Renee to have some time with her friend, too."

"But it's been days. She hasn't even called me!"

"Jared told her if she called anyone they could track her. That is why she has not called you. I think, however, you have forgotten that she did not leave *you*, she left me. I should be the one upset here."

"But you deserved it, I didn't," she replied, standing with her arms crossed tightly in front of her. I would never win this argument, there was never a chance in hell that I would.

"May I finish packing then?"

"I've practically done it for you, but we need to talk about the black V-neck sweaters. You really need to move on. I believe you are stuck in a fashion rut."

"But they are already in the suitcase," I responded and gestured to the pile.

"One more smartass remark and you'll be lucky if I don't fill your suitcases with clown clothes when your back is turned."

"I will make sure that Brianna calls you right away."

"It's not Bri talking to me that you need to worry about. The hard part will be getting her to talk to you."

Unfortunately I knew this all too well. Thankfully I had a long flight to think of how I would approach her. This would be our second uncomfortable reunion in a week, and I knew for a fact that this one would not go smoothly.

I felt Kyla's hand on my arm. "Have you eaten?" I shook my head. "You finish packing and I will bring you up a bottle. Just please don't get any on the bedspread, I'd hate you to ruin it before I get any use out of it."

She turned and began walking toward the door.

"I thought you said it was not your style?"

"Unlike you, my style changes."

"Within seconds?"

"Clown clothes, Cameron, clown clothes."

Chapter Twenty

Brianna

"Seven!" I shouted at Renee who was fumbling around in the kitchen while I unpacked box number 4,375, although that could be an exaggeration. "I knew you were lying to me. I can't believe you have seven miniature tea sets. Are you expecting to entertain a circus of gnomes? Fairies maybe?"

Renee stuck her tongue out at me, and then flipped me off the same time a pan crashed into the sink. "I told you my mom used to buy those for me when I was little."

"Yes, sweetie, but that doesn't mean you keep them when you're thirty."

"Well maybe I'm keeping them for when 'your' kids come to 'Auntie Re's' house to play," she said with fingers flying. I forgot how much I missed her air quoting in person. It just didn't have the same effect over the phone.

"I'm having two kids, not an army."

Another pan clanged against the stove and the smell of burning food began to waft into the living room.

"Oh yes, I forgot, you're like a Vampire physic now."

"I swear you never really listen to me. You hear the word Vampire and then you don't hear anything else."

"Well, it's kind of hard to concentrate on anything else after you hear that, honey," she said while struggling to scrape off whatever she had burned onto the pan.

"Are you sure you don't want me to cook?" Oh please for the love of god let me cook. I don't think I could stand another whatever-I-have-in-the-pantry casserole. Thankfully right now she wasn't cooking for me, she was making, or more so trying to make breakfast for Dr. John when he came home any minute now. I worried for the man's health if he were to eat whatever it was she was making for him.

"I told you no the first time you asked. So, I'm listening, you're not a Vampire, I know that."

"Yes, and I'm not a physic."

"Then how do you know you're having twins? Oh that's right, Daddy Dearest told you so in some dream, right? See I listen. I don't believe half of it and it confuses the hell out of me, but I listen."

The floor shook slightly as the exterior door to the brownstone closed down below.

"You haven't told John anything, have you?" I asked quickly when I heard his key go into the lock of the apartment's front door.

"I told him you were here."

"No," I replied frustrated, "about...you know."

Renee rolled her eyes at me. "Of course not. He'd check me into a mental institution. Now just stay clear of the path to the bathroom, he'll be charging through here in three, two, one."

And right on cue Dr. John Ryan came barreling up the stairs and through the living room without a word to either of us as he made his way into the bathroom. I laughed as Renee did her best of impression of him lumbering through. A second later Dr. John flew out of the bathroom, his eyes wide with fear while he held up his loosened scrubs in his hands.

"Oh my god, Re, we've been robbed. Why didn't you call me! Call the police, are you ok?"

Renee stepped out of the kitchen, her hands raised in front of her as she tried to calm Dr. John down. I just sat on the floor and watched the show.

"What are you talking about? We haven't been robbed. Bri and I have been here the whole time, I think we would have noticed."

"But...the..." he said flustered gesturing toward the bathroom, "the...shower. It's....it's empty."

Renee rolled her eyes as she turned back toward the kitchen. "You're such an ass. Thank Bri, it was all her. Look around, honey, you know full well I didn't do all of this."

Dr. John's eyes widened even further while he looked around the apartment, as if seeing it for the first time. He held up his index finger and scuttled back into the bathroom. Several minutes later he came back out and knelt beside me, hugging me fiercely against his chest.

"Thank you, thank you, thank you," he whispered as he squeezed me tighter with each expression. "I think she's a hoarder."

I held my hand against my mouth, trying unsuccessfully to hold my laughter in. He joined me as he pulled away and I was met with his unbelievable bright blue eyes. I was struck by the realization that although he and Renee had been dating for so many months this was only the second time I had seen him. This time, thankfully, he wasn't picking gravel out of my bleeding back.

Renee cleared her throat. "John, could you meet me in the kitchen if the two of you are done laughing at me."

John smiled as he squeezed my arm one more time and looked seriously into my eyes. "Has she been cooking?"

"All morning, but I think you're safe. Most of what she tried to make went in the garbage."

"One can only hope," he sighed and then stepped toward the kitchen. "Welcome, by the way. Oh, and congratulations," he said pointing to my stomach.

When John reached the kitchen Renee quickly pulled him to the area that was hidden from the living room. I didn't need to see what was happening to feel incredibly lonely. But it was my choice to be alone, so I couldn't complain since I only had myself to thank. Unfortunately neither my hormones nor my dreams were helping.

Rolling over onto my knees I used the edge of the couch to help me up the rest of the way. I was barely pregnant and already having trouble getting up and having to stretch my aching back.

"Bri?" Dr. John asked as he squinted his eyes at me. "How far along are you?"

I turned profile, showing him the full view. "Thirteen weeks, why?"

"Really? That's all?"

"Are you saying I'm fat?"

"Uh...no...I..." he stuttered and stepped back into the living room, his face full of guilt.

Renee laughed as she placed a gentle hand on his shoulder. "Honey, she's kidding. Bri 'thinks' she's having 'twins.'"

"You *think* you're having twins? What did the ultrasound show?"

"Actually, with all the traveling I've been doing I haven't been to the doctor. It's on my list of things to do, I promise."

"Brianna, if you think you're having twins you should definitely get an exam. Twins come with their own set of complications and I know that…um…you have had…problems in the past."

A lump was forming in my throat from the reality I didn't want to deal with. "John, I will. I've just been so busy."

Dr. John looked at me skeptically. "Still won't let me be your doctor, will you?"

"Why start now?" I replied jokingly, but he was not impressed.

"Ok look, I won't force you, but I really think it's best. I'll make it really easy for you, I have to go back to the hospital tomorrow and the OB/GYN on call is a friend. I'll call in a favor and you'll be in and out in no time, and you'll certainly get me off your back."

Renee looked over his shoulder and said in a kind voice, "Cathy really is nice, Bri. She's one of the few doctors I've met, you'll like her."

"Fine," I groaned as I flopped down on the couch. "Now can I call you Dr. John?"

He smiled and laughed lightly as he gave Renee a kiss on the cheek and then turned to the stairs that led up to the top floor of their apartment. "If you must. So how's Cameron? Ow!" he shouted as Renee punched him in the shoulder.

"Do you ever listen to me?" she shouted at him.

"Sorry I forgot, Brianna I didn't mean…"

I put my hands up to stop him. "It's fine, really."

"Well this doctor is going to bed before I get into any more trouble," he said as he rubbed his shoulder.

"We'll make sure to stay quiet, honey," Renee said.

"I seriously doubt that. 'Night ladies."

After I heard the bedroom door shut upstairs I said, "It has to be weird sleeping during the day."

"Says the girl who lives in a house of Vampires."

"Shh! He'll hear you."

Renee scoffed. "Please, he probably didn't even make it to the bed."

"But still, it has to be weird for you, too."

Renee rolled her eyes, more so in frustration (and this knowledge only comes from years of knowing her and her many shades of eye rolls). "His schedule is so crazy, and he's so tired all the time. He says once he straightens out the department it'll be better, but now he's just trying to pick up the slack."

"You two are really cute together."

"I know," she responded proudly as she slumped down beside me on the couch and then placed her hands on my stomach. "Do the babies like Uncle John, too? You do, don't you. He's your favorite Uncle John, isn't he? Are they kicking?"

I released a deep sigh while my stomach fluttered. "Yes, of course they're kicking. Just like every other time you've talked to them. They won't do it for their own mother who is their personal incubator, but they'll do it on command for Auntie Renee."

Renee smiled from ear to ear. "Isn't that great! I'm already the favorite Aunt."

I knew she was referring to Kyla, but in no way was I going to get into that ridiculous argument. So instead I went back to work since there were still tons of boxes to unpack. Renee grumbled for the first few minutes, but after a while the living room became quiet except for the TV. That was the great thing about a really good friend. You didn't always need to fill every waking moment together with endless conversation. You could sit next to each other and not say a word for hours, and it wouldn't feel awkward. The more time I spent with Renee, the more I realized how much she knew me better than anyone.

This was very evident when an hour or so later she blurted out, "Thinking of Cameron?"

I tried giving her a look of confusion and surprise, but with a raise of her eyebrow I caved. "How did you know?"

She shrugged. "You started biting your lip so you wouldn't cry. So spill."

"I was thinking that if I go tomorrow, it will be the second doctor's appointment I'll go to without him. I'll see our children for the first time and he won't be there."

My nose began to tingle with emotion and I knew the tears weren't far behind. Renee handed me a pillow and I hugged it to my chest.

"Now Bri, you know I love you and in no way do I think what Cameron did was cool. But don't you think at this point you should call him? Even if it's to tell him off?"

"No!" I shouted and then cursed myself, remembering that Dr. John was trying to sleep. "No," I repeated in a hushed but tense voice as I awkwardly stood from the couch, throwing my pillow behind me. "I don't think I should call him. He...he...I can't believe I'm hearing this from you. He cheated on me, Re."

"He kissed another girl, that's all you know, and you didn't even bother to give him a chance to make up some lame ass story. You ran because you didn't want to deal with it."

"I did not run away."

"Bullshit, you did too. When you find out your boyfriend is cheating on you, you burn his clothes in the front yard, put a baseball bat through his windshield, or put hemorrhoid cream in his toothpaste."

"Personal experience?"

Renee ignored me and continued, "You don't run to your dad's tropical island for three weeks without talking to him. You don't run away for another week to Connecticut and not talk to him. This isn't you, Bri. You're the one always telling *me* not to run away from things, or in most cases men."

"And the one time you finally took my advice you ended up with a great guy."

"Then take your own advice you stupid girl. You gave Sam a million and one chances, which was completely asinine, and yet you don't give Cameron even the slightest chance to explain himself. Sometimes things just aren't what they seem."

"Why do people keep saying that to me?"

I was unable to keep my volume at a whisper. I was livid and my cheeks were on fire as I pulled out a chair from the small dining table that sat at the far end of the living room. I sat with my elbows resting on the table while my hands supported my aching head. Tears began streaming down my face when I felt Renee's hand touch my arm.

"This is Cameron we're talking about, Bri. The guy who broke down your door and saved you from Sam like a damn superhero. Cameron who alienated his whole family in order to be with you and got really messed up, right?" I nodded. "Cameron who called me in the middle of the night looking for John to see if there was anything he could do for you that night you miscarried. Did he tell you that?" I nodded again, this time my head falling onto her shoulder. She rested her head on mine as she rubbed my back while I sobbed. "That first night he brought you to my condo I knew he loved you, whether he knew it or not. And yeah, he's been a total ass lately, but he wouldn't call me every friggin' day looking for you if he didn't love you, sweetie. It just doesn't work that way."

I raised my head from her shoulder, wiping away the tears from my cheeks with my hands until Renee offered me a tissue from the end table behind her. I tried pulling myself together, but it was difficult doing so. I had told Jonah everything that Cam had done, and I wasn't near as emotional. Renee was challenging me and I hated it. This wasn't the Southern girl way. Ignoring everything was just easier, you certainly didn't cry as much. You also didn't heal. The wounds just stayed on the surface until someone nicked them, and then it all came pouring out a hundred times worse. Like right now. The Southern girl way definitely had its faults.

"Why does this hurt more? Sam hit me all the time, and yes there were times I thought I was never going to heal. But this," I sobbed and buried my face into my hands, "sometimes I feel like I can't breathe. This hurts more than anything Sam ever did to me."

Renee knelt in front of me, once again pulling my hands away from my face and squeezing them as she said, "It hurts more because you love Cameron. It's always worse when someone you love hurts you. Take me and John, we'll have an argument and I'm actually affected by it. I even listen when he tells me something I did hurt his feelings. And I care!" A snotty laugh came out of me, which made Renee laugh too. "I mean before, if I had a fight with my boyfriend I would say, 'ok, we're done, now get out of my apartment', or 'hey, stop crying it makes me hate you more', but now if John says or does something shitty it actually upsets me because he's the only guy I've ever really cared about. You still love Cameron, and trust me, honey, he loves you, he really does. You just need to talk to him."

Renee handed me another couple of tissues and I wiped my face once again, feeling that my eyes and nose were already raw. "But what if it's true? I keep having this dream he leaves me, Re. What if..."

"It's just a dream, Bri."

"But mine come true! I left Cameron so that he couldn't leave me. And now I was miserable."

Renee rubbed my arm again, letting my emotions die down a little before she said, "Didn't that Freud guy say something like sometimes a dream is just a dream?"

"I think it's a cigar."

"What do cigars have to do with dreams?"

I shrugged knowing trying to explain it to her would be a lost cause. "Nothing, I guess."

"So, are you going to call Cameron?"

I shook my head. "Not yet." Renee sighed and rolled her eyes. "Look, I will. I just don't want to call him and be this blubbering mess. I'll call him tomorrow, maybe after the doctor's appointment, ok?"

Renee shrugged and I knew it wasn't the answer she wanted. She wanted me to make up with him and everything to be happy and merry, as did I. But if I were to call him right at this moment I would give in to him, and that was something I couldn't do. When we talked I needed to stand my ground, show him that he couldn't do this to me.

"Are there any cookies left?" I said after blowing my nose.

"It's barely ten o'clock, and you want cookies?"

I circled my face with my index finger. "Look at my face, I believe it says it all."

Chapter Twenty-One

Brianna

Let's talk about leggings. Leggings to a developing pregnant woman were wonderful. They were forgiving, expandable, and thanks to some fashion guru of late, in style. Combine them with a tunic and warm fury boots and my comfortable ensemble was complete.

"It's going to be a good day, Morgan," I said to myself in the mirror.

"Bri, are you talking to yourself?" Renee said from the kitchen on the other side of my door.

I had lost my mind so many times in the last year, the fact that I was talking to myself seemed the least worrisome. I grabbed my coat from the bed and made my way into the kitchen to see my best friend giving me a wide-eyed look.

"Don't look at me like that, Re. I know for a fact that you talk to the people on Judge Judy like they're your friends."

"Damn that Dr. John, isn't anything sacred anymore?"

"Not when you're holding a bag of potato chips in front of a man who hasn't eaten in more than fifteen hours."

"You are a worthy opponent my round brunette nemesis."

"Why are we talking like we're in a comic book?"

"Don't look at me. You're the one talking to yourself."

"Ready?" I laughed as I put my arms through my coat and buttoned up the front.

Renee chugged down the rest of her coffee and made a satisfied sound before she said, "Yep. Cab should be here any second. Let's go."

She stepped out of the kitchen first and I took a step with her, but then stopped as I suddenly became filled with anxiety about leaving the apartment. Renee stopped herself when she got to the landing of the stairs and noticed that I wasn't behind her.

"Sweetie, I know you hate doctors, but I promise Cathy really is cool and she'll keep everything confidential."

I shook my head. "It's not that," I sighed as I stepped in front of her and grabbed her hand. "Look, I know you block out half the things I say when it comes to all this Vampire crap, but I need you to understand that there really are people after me."

"Bri, come on…"

"Re, I know you don't want to have to process any of this, and honestly I don't blame you. All I'm asking is that if I tell you to run, I really mean run. Don't argue, don't try and help, just run."

Renee jerked her hand out of mine and placed her hands on her hips as she glared murderously at me. "Brianna Marrr…lawdy-lah Morgan if you are in 'trouble' I will fight to the death to help you."

"Renee this isn't some movie where the Vampire feels sorry for you and takes you sightseeing through the trees of Oregon on his back. This is real life. These Vamps will kill you and not give a shit a second later. Please just promise me that if I tell you to do something you will."

Renee's stink eye was one of legends, and I was certainly getting a good view. "You do know that whenever someone tells me to do something I make it a point not to do it, right?"

Boy did I. Renee thought I was either joking or exaggerating and there was no way I could convince her otherwise. The harder I pushed, the further she resisted, that's just how it was.

As we traveled down the two flights of treacherous stairs to our awaiting cab my mind was fully open and scanning every inch around us. I tried not to panic when I saw a Vampire's essence in the vicinity, though when I looked around there was no one on the street. When the cab pulled away I concentrated on this particular Vampire, and though he or she did not follow, I had a sinking feeling that my proclamation of a good day might have been a little premature.

Dr. Cathy Taylor was just as Renee had described her, cool. She wasn't uppity or brash and certainly didn't have a god complex. I knew I liked her when she patted her mechanical examination table and said, "Hop on, we're going for a ride."

Of course I had actually gone on the ride already since Renee made me get on the table before Dr. Taylor came in so that she could play with the buttons. Renee stayed with me during the ultrasound since she had bet me that I was wrong about having twins and that I was just fat.

Before I knew it there was slimy gel on my stomach and Dr. Taylor was moving the ultrasound wand across my belly while black and white images smeared on the screen.

"Well here you go, there's your baby," she said as she turned the screen toward me. It was peanut, a little mutant peanut and I was totally in love. Renee squeezed my hand as I wiped a tear away from my eyes. "Would you like to know the sex?"

"Yes!" Renee answered before I could. Dr. Taylor smiled but looked to me for approval. I nodded, although I was already pretty sure what I was having.

Dr. Taylor moved the wand at different angles, trying to get the best view when she finally said, "It's a boy, see here," she pointed to what she could somehow tell was genitalia, though to me it looked like every other blob on the screen.

A boy. I was having a boy. One down, one to go.

"Do you see anything else?"

"Oh yes, the twin theory. Let's look around." Dr. Taylor continued to move the wand, going back and forth and honestly she seemed a little frustrated. "Well this little guy does not want to give up the limelight. You may not have twins after all."

Renee had a smug smile on her face, she thought she'd won. Maybe she had. Not having twins would surely be easier at this point. It would mean that all that crap I had dreamt about wouldn't come true. But it didn't feel right. I knew there were two in there somewhere. I just couldn't be this fat.

"Hey Re, talk to the baby," I said and got an eye roll in response. "Oh please, you talked to my stomach the whole cab ride over. Just do it."

She did as I asked, asking the "fake baby" to stay where it was so that Auntie Renee could win the bet. The fluttering started immediately and you could even see my baby boy move on the monitor and just as I was about to give up hope, Dr. Taylor announced success. "There we are. Big brother was hiding this one. Would you like to know the sex?"

"It's a girl," I answered softly as I stared at her on the monitor now nestled beside her brother.

Dr. Taylor blinked slowly as she stuttered, "Er…yeah, it's a girl."

"Crap!" Renee shouted, but it didn't faze me. I was staring at my twins, my little ones – a boy and a girl who would grow to become the charming curly-headed children of my dreams. The thought immediately brought tears to my eyes. Joy and sorrow wrapped into one, squeezing my heart as hard as Renee was squeezing my hand.

Pictures began to print while Dr. Taylor wiped the gel from my stomach and handed me a tissue. "So just a few things before we wrap up. I want to urge you to stop traveling so much if possible and get on a regular schedule with a doctor. Everything looks fine and healthy, but with a past like yours we consider you a high risk pregnancy." Dr. Taylor rose from her stool and stepped away to stand in front of her computer. "Based on what you told me, it looks like the due date is around April 20th, however, twins tend to come a little early. With high risk pregnancies that can be pushed even sooner, and that means the babies will need neo-natal care. So again…"

I put my hands up in concession, "I know. Reduce travel, see a doctor."

"Stay away from stress and over exertion," Dr. Taylor chided.

It was always so easy for a doctor to say those things. Just stay away from stress. That's like saying just stay away from chocolate. Both seemed to magically fall in your mouth. Wait, maybe not the best analogy, especially since now I really wanted to chocolate. And a bag of corn chips. And guacamole. Oh I missed Sera. Good lord, my mind was like a five-year-old child's.

"Thank you, Dr. Taylor. Maybe if Renee doesn't kick me out too soon I'll come and see you again."

Dr. Taylor smiled as she walked toward the door. "I look forward to it then. Renee, sorry about the bet."

Renee waved goodbye in defeat, though she immediately grabbed the pictures and began looking at my twins. My precious little mutant peanuts. Baby 1 – boy. Baby 2 – girl. Instantly names began to run through my head, though it didn't seem right. It seemed wrong to think of names without Cameron. My stomach sank as nausea and hunger came over me at the same time, it was a weird combination.

"Earth to Bri," Renee said annoyed and waving her hand in front of my face.

My eyes fluttered as I returned to the present. "Sorry, just spaced out. Hungry?"

Renee nodded as someone knocked on the door. In an instant I scanned the other side, but thankfully saw nothing.

"Knock, knock," a familiar voice said from the other side.

"It's ok, Dr. John, we're descent," I said as I awkwardly hopped down from the table.

"What's the fun if everyone's descent?" A green scrub-clad Dr. John came through the door with his stethoscope hanging around his neck. He looked so...doctorish? Important? Impressive? Looking at his outfit for some reason I couldn't get the thought of fresh guacamole out of my head.

Renee walked over to him, giving him a quick kiss before she said, "You're pretty sick, you know that right?" Dr. John nodded happily. "By the way, I lost the bet. Bri really is having twins."

"Really!" Dr. John cheered as he hugged me to his chest. "Identical?"

I shook my head. "No, fraternal. Boy and a girl."

"That's perfect. One of each and only one set of stretch marks," he joked.

"And that's our cue," Renee said rolling her eyes. "We're going to lunch and then I'm spending your money on baby clothes for my niece and nephew."

Dr. John smiled as he petted Renee's dark red hair and kissed her gently on the lips. "I was pretty sure I was in trouble when I noticed my credit card missing this morning." Renee batted her eyes, looking coy. "Have fun you two. I should actually get off at a descent hour tonight, so maybe we can all grab some dinner?"

Renee and I nodded and then Dr. John bid farewell. Renee took one last look at the ultrasound pictures before handing them to me and putting on her coat. "So is it real to you now?"

Thumbing the picture that captured both my babies I nodded. "I'll call Cam tonight."

Renee wrapped her arm around me and led me through the maze of hospital hallways.

"Now remember, if he's still a big fat jerk we'll call in the big guns."

"And what guns are those?" I inquired as we stepped into an elevator.

"I hate to admit it, but if Cameron still acts like a dick, then you'll need to call in Kyla. She has access to his clothes and I'm sure she can scrounge up a match or two. If she's really your friend she'll burn his clothes on the front lawn in the formation of the word 'dick' in a blazing inferno."

"You know she might," I laughed.

When the elevator doors opened and we made our way to the main exit Renee looked over to me. "Feel like Mexican?"

I smiled from ear to ear. "And that is why you're more like a sister to me than just a friend."

Renee crooked her arm through mine and practically skipped through the main doors. "Ya know, Bri, we're kind of like our own set of twins. Except, of course, I'm the younger more voluptuous one."

"Hey now, I'm not too far behind. Look at these things," I said sticking my own chest out and looking down proudly at the pair I'd started to grow. "I mean they actually bounce a little when I walk. I've never had that, it's so cool!"

"Bri," Renee whispered, "stop staring at your chest. People are looking at you."

"I can't help it, they're mesmerizing." When Renee hit me in the arm I finally stopped looking at my bouncing breasts and closed my coat to prevent temptation. "By the way, you may be the more voluptuous twin, but you're only two months younger."

"Two months is two months," Renee said proudly as she stepped in the street to hail a cab. "You do remember my birthday is this Saturday, right?"

"Yes of course I do." Holy crap it seemed everyone had a birthday lately. "And no, I haven't gotten your present yet."

"Why not!"

"Because we've been together since I got here."

"Well then you should have gotten it beforehand."

"Renee…"

"Some twin you are."

"Renee!"

"What?!"

"Cab's here."

Renee huffed as she ducked inside and I followed, closing the door after I settled in. Renee rattled off an address and the cab sped away.

"So how long did you wait to get Kyla's birthday present?"

"I think I got it two days before, and I had to get overnight shipping. Happy?"

Renee crossed her arms in satisfaction. "Yes, very. And now that we're twins I'm even happier."

Even the cab driver looked in the rearview at that comment.

"You know what, *twin,* when you and Kyla finally meet I am going to rub it in your faces when the two of you realize how much you have in common and how quickly you become friends."

"Won't happen."

"Will happen."

Renee stuck her tongue out at me. "But I'm your twin and she's not, so I win."

As we bounced along the narrow city streets the ultrasound pictures crinkled in my coat pocket making me take them out so I could place them in my purse. When I had looked at them earlier I realized that in some ways I too was acting childish. Renee was right, I had been running. I would call Cam tonight in my most comfortable PJ's and curled up in the tightest ball possible with the biggest box of tissues I could find. Honestly it would take that long for me to rustle up the courage.

With my large gray purse on my lap, I opened it up to place the pictures carefully inside, forgetting that my long silver dagger was nestled inside. I tried closing it quickly, but Renee had already seen it and her eyes were bugging out of her head.

"Please don't ask," I begged as I placed the purse in the floor.

"Oh yeah, I'm totally going to ask about that shit."

Chapter Twenty-Two

Brianna

"I still can't believe you ate that entire bowl of guacamole," Renee said snidely as we stepped out of the restaurant.

"It's my only craving so far, and besides I'm eating for three," I replied. "What's your excuse? That burger was as big as your head and you ate the whole thing."

"I didn't want you to feel self-conscious," she laughed and took my elbow to turn me in the right direction.

Since we were going to do a little shopping we had decided to forgo the cab and tour Boston on foot, and honestly I didn't mind. It was a beautiful autumn day to see a new city show off its bright red and orange leaves while gabbing with my friend. We ducked into a shoe store where I fell in love with a pair of black platform heels that no pregnant woman should wear, but yet I still bought them with Renee's urging. Unfortunately the elation I felt over new shoes was quickly vanquished when I scanned the area around us and saw a Vampire's light in the distance. I didn't want to startle Renee so I kept it to myself. In a city this big there were bound to be dozens of Vamps walking around.

It wasn't until we stopped in to a second store did I get nervous. When we stepped inside, he waited a few feet away. When we left, he continued to follow behind us. I wanted to nip this in the bud if someone was really following me, and I wanted to do it before we reached Renee's. Thankfully she was blabbering next to me, unaware that I wasn't listening to her and actually concentrating on the Vampire. If I turned around now it would be obvious that I was watching him. So I let Renee continue on her rampage which had something to do with swimming pools and mayonnaise, though I may have that wrong. What can I say? It was hard to pay attention to her and the Vampire that was taking two steps for every one of ours.

It wasn't until Renee turned us down a side street through a neighborhood which looked much like her own that I became really worried for our safety. As Renee walked casually along the sidewalk lined with brownstone after brownstone still conversing about mayonnaise (I swear), the Vampire was narrowing the gap with every step. Casually I interrupted Renee, asking her to take my shopping bags while I searched for something in my purse. I rummaged around inside, pulled out a tube of lip balm and then placed my purse on my left shoulder so that I could retrieve my dagger with my right hand at the precise moment. In no way did I want to tip off the Vamp, I needed the element of surprise on my side.

Just as we approached a narrow alley between buildings, the Vampire was only inches away. Shoving Renee slightly forward I screamed for her to run as I latched onto the Vampire's light and threw him up against the alley's wall. Just as bits of brick and dust flew around him I whipped my dagger from inside my purse, slicing the strap and causing it to thump on the ground beside me. Still holding his essence firmly against the wall I quickly pressed the dagger to the Vamp's throat, hearing his skin sizzle as the silver burned into it. His gray baseball cap had fallen in front of his eyes, but I didn't need to see them to know what he was.

"Brianna, what are you doing!" Renee screamed as she threw the bags in her arms down on the ground and stood beside me.

"Renee, I told you to run, you have to run!"

The Vamp started to open his mouth and I slammed his head back into the brick wall causing his hat to fall down onto the bridge of his nose.

"Bri, I can't just….holy shit he's got fangs," she screamed and then picked up a rock and held it up in front of her.

"And what do you think that's going to do?"

"I don't know! It's not like I have a big ass knife in my bag like you do."

"T-thank god f-f-for that," the Vamp hissed while my knife sunk deeper into his throat.

"Shut up," I shouted as I squeezed the inside of his head causing him to grunt in pain. "Who are you? Tell me what you want or so help me god I will cut off your freaking head."

"Fuck me, when did you grow a set of balls!"

"Shut up, Renee," I shouted as I felt my hold on the Vamp feign slightly when my babies started doing backflips inside me. "Last chance, asshole."

"C-Cam," he coughed, "Cam s-sent me."

Renee gasped as I pulled my dagger from his throat. Instantly he bent over at the waist and coughed a few more times, placing his hand against his throat. His baseball hat fell to the ground revealing a head of sandy blonde hair. When he finally stood upright he wiped the remaining blood away with the cuff of his jacket revealing only a thin red line across his throat.

"Damn it, woman, that fucking hurts."

"Aidan," I said breathlessly. The babies instantly stopped kicking as my dagger clanged loudly on the ground.

Renee still held her rock in attack as she said, "You know this guy?"

"It was you at the train station, wasn't it?"

He bowed his head slightly and placed his baseball cap back on. "Oh yes. The Anderson family thanks you for throwing me into them like a bowling ball."

"You deserve it, you jerk."

"How am I a jerk? You're the one who keeps throwing me into things. Do you know how painful that thing you do is? Holy shit, I've never felt anything like it."

Ignoring his complaining I sheathed my dagger back into my purse and tucked it underneath my arm since I had sliced the strap cleanly in two.

"Aidan, why are you following me?"

"And Cameron told me you were smart." With a blink of my eye I Pushed Aidan's light back into the brick wall. "Damn it again, woman."

"Stop calling me woman," I growled.

"Yeah, stop calling her that or she'll do that physic thing again."

"Re, you're not helping. And seriously, put the rock down."

"Look," Aidan interrupted, "Cameron called me when you flew the coop. Stupid move if you ask me."

"No one's asking you," Renee and I said at exactly the same time giving him the same one-eyed glare.

Aidan pointed to both of us. "And that is why I'm single."

"That's not the only reason," Renee said triumphantly.

"Ok, red, why don't you scurry along with your rock while I take care of business."

I put my arm in front of Renee in order to stop her from pouncing on Aidan. "And what business is that?"

Aidan's face softened slightly as he tucked his hands into the front pocket of his jeans. "Hey, I'm not one to get mixed up with all the emotional drama shit, but Cameron sent me to find you, and I did. He thought it might be easier for me to confront you first versus giving you the chance to run the minute you saw him."

"Cameron's here? In Boston?"

"Er…well you're in Boston, where did you expect him to be?"

I swallowed hard as my heart began to race, feeling as though it would punch through my ribs. "Well you found me, now what?"

"You have a choice – one, tell Cameron to shove it. Two, let me take you to his hotel. He's my friend and all, but I've already been paid so really I could care less which one you choose. I just need to know what to tell him."

"I…I don't know."

"What!" Renee yelled. "Stupid girl, go see Cameron. You were going to call him tonight anyway."

"Yeah, but that was tonight," I said weakly as I turned away from Aidan.

"Don't run," she whispered to me. "I know you're scared, but this is your chance, it's fallen in your lap, now take it. She's going," she announced over my shoulder to Aidan.

"No…wait, I don't have any of my things."

"You go with blondie and I'll pack your stuff. Just have Cameron come by our place and pick it up."

Aidan shrugged and gestured to me. It was my choice and I was nervous as hell, but my big girl panties were fitting snuggly today.

"Fine. I'll go with blondie."

"I'm not sure I like being called blondie," Aidan scoffed.

"I don't think anyone gives a shit what you want, blondie," Renee replied and then threw her arms around me, crushing my shoulders against her chest. "Now remember, if he's still a jerk we go to plan B. 'Kay?"

"I'll call you if I need you."

Renee hugged me again. "Call me even if you don't. I wanna know how you are. Love you."

"Love you too, twin."

Renee gave me a wink, sneered at Aidan, and strutted off down the sidewalk only wobbling once when her heel got caught in between two uneven bricks. Both Aidan and I laughed as she swore and quickly rounded the corner.

"So shall we get this over with?" I asked, gathering the shopping bags from the ground and handing them to him.

"Am I your mule now?"

"Do you want to go up against the wall again?"

Aidan narrowed his eyes but smiled slyly as he took the shopping bags from my hands. "I should get hazard pay for tracking you."

"Don't mess with a pregnant lady."

"Pregnant? Really? I just thought you were getting fat."

Not thinking, I hit him in the arm and then clasped my hand to my chest in pain. Aidan couldn't help but laugh.

"For laughing at me, you're calling a cab."

Aidan shrugged unfazed as he directed me toward a busier street where he could hail a cab. "So, may I ask what plan B is?"

I laughed. "It entails matches, Cameron's clothes, and the correct spelling of the word dick."

Elaina held my arm tightly and forced me to the ground, although it didn't take much. The Vampires surrounding me cheered as I fell, thinking it was caused by Elaina's grip, however, the truth was the momentum to the floor was my own as another contraction came over me. Elaina brushed away the hair stuck to my forehead from the sweat that had formed on my brow and gave me a wicked fanged smile.

"It is time to bring these babies into the world," she shouted triumphantly. She snapped her fingers and as she had every other time, Jazlyn stepped through the crowd and handed Elaina a long knife. Jazlyn came around me, taking me by the shoulders and lowering me down to the floor while Elaina lifted the white gossamer gown over my swollen belly. I flinched and kicked while trying to pull the gown back down, though I knew I was only wasting energy.

"Hold her down," Elaina commanded and Jazlyn obeyed by holding my wrists above my head. I could feel Elaina teasing my skin with the cold blade of the knife while she cooed, "This will hurt, my little hybrid."

I began to scream and writhe, not caring that I was exposing more of myself in front of Elaina's coven.

"Let's get this over with," Jazlyn shouted as she leaned over me, covering me with her thick black hair.

I could hear the bones in my wrist creaking under her pressure, but the noise was soon drowned out by my own screaming when I felt someone's hands on my ankles, holding them down firmly on the floor. Tears streamed down my face as I stared into Jazlyn's black Vampire eyes.

"You're just like her," I whimpered helplessly.

Jazlyn's eyes narrowed slightly before she nuzzled into my ear and whispered, "Not everything is as it seems."

Jazlyn's grip softened as she lifted her veil of hair from around my face, just in time for me to see Elaina raise the knife above her head. A second later Jazlyn pushed off my wrists like a tigress and leapt over my head, tackling Elaina into the wall across the room. The knife clanged loudly on the stone floor the same time my ankles were released by my other captor. I looked up to see a blur of brown and black flying toward me, bringing with it the searing pain of the knife slicing my stomach open.

I sat upright in the bed, taking a moment to realize that it was me screaming in the room. When I opened my eyes it took yet another moment to recognize Cameron's hotel room, which he was now standing just inside the doorway, my suitcase toppled over behind him. The room was dark and though the hallway lights illuminated Cameron from behind, I would know him anywhere. Clumsily I turned on the lamp next to me and saw Cameron in all his masculine glory standing ready to fight with Aidan standing just behind him.

I waved my hands in front of me, still unable to speak, but wanting to give them a sign that I was ok. Cameron nodded silently and turned to Aidan, assuring him that everything was fine. While they shook hands and spoke in tones too soft for me to hear, I quickly removed the sheets that were twisted around me and lifted my tunic to reveal a thin red line up the middle of my lower abdomen. I traced the wound with my index finger, sucking in a small amount of air at the twinge of pain. Previously the scar had been in the shape of an upside down T because Elaina had been able to fully cut me open, whereas now it was only the stem. Things were changing.

"I take it this was not the Shelby dream?" Cameron asked from above me. I hadn't noticed he was standing in front of me. I hadn't even heard the door shut I was so entranced by my injury. My cheeks were flush and my heart quickened just from a whiff of his smell. My eyes traveled up to see that his familiar black sweater was replaced by a tailored light blue patterned button up shirt and dark denim jeans.

"This is new," I said gesturing to his outfit. My babies stirred slightly which gave me some relief after such a horrible dream, but I knew they were stirring because their father was here. I was feeling the same way as my eyes finally found his and he gave me the one thing that could melt me instantly – his crooked smile.

"This is Kyla's doing," he replied softly and I could feel that he felt just as awkward as I did. Tentatively he reached out with his fingers, brushing away a strand of hair that was stuck to my forehead, much in the same way Elaina had in my dream which caused me to flinch. Cameron took it as a sign that I didn't want him to touch me and sadly lowered his hand. "Let me get you some water," he said turning toward the minibar against the wall behind him. "I put some crackers in the nightstand drawer if you need them."

My heart sank at his gesture, and it sank even further when I opened the drawer and noticed they were my favorite kind. Some people may think that crackers were crackers, but I actually went through four different kinds before I found the one that calmed my nausea. And here they were, staring and laughing wickedly at me – *He cares, he really cares, and you acted like a big fat whiney bitch, ha ha ha ha ha.* I felt light headed.

"Love?"

I was startled to see Cameron standing in front of me again, holding a bottle of water out to me. Taking the water, I tried to keep my hand steady to show that I wasn't affected by him, but I was. Every nerve ending felt like it was on fire, every muscle pulsing and thrumming to throw myself into him. This was exactly what I didn't want to happen. If we had spoken on the phone my hormones wouldn't be affecting me as badly as they were now. His lips, his eyes, the smooth, cool, pale skin of his exposed forearms that made way to his well-defined biceps that were hiding underneath his shirt. Every inch of his body was calling to me. Immediately I removed the cap from the bottled water and drank until my body cooled itself off.

Stupid hormonal girl, stand your ground. Remember what he did to you.

Cameron's eyes were piercing through me, waiting for me to say something, anything. And in true Brianna Morgan fashion I said, "I ate guacamole."

Cameron smiled, letting out a sigh of relief and relaxing his shoulders slightly. "I am beginning to think you eat nothing else."

I laughed lightly, but then my chest fell as I realized I had said the same exact thing the last time I had come home to him, right before he kissed Miss Tricky Nikki. My body finally remembered what he had done to me, every emotion, and every tear. My lungs filled with air and I held it for a spilt second, closing my eyes and opening my mind to my gift. When I opened my eyes, Cameron's light was glowing brightly like a halo around his head. With the release of my breath, I Pushed his light to the floor, imagining that I had slapped him across the face.

Cameron fell as though his legs were kicked out from under him. Slowly he rolled to his knees, pressing himself up onto his hands while shaking his head. "I deserved that. Will you please let me explain?"

I stood from the bed and pushed my feet forward so that I wouldn't drape myself around him. "I'm taking a bath."

The Southerner in me was taking over, and right now I needed to diffuse the situation. It was a coping mechanism when you were completely falling apart on the inside. I was tired of holding myself together. Cameron had torn me to pieces and now he would either help me put myself back together, or blow away what was left.

Chapter Twenty-Three

Cameron

When Brianna slammed the bathroom door I could feel the floor shake slightly beneath my hands. She had Pushed me harder than she ever had before. Of course she had every right to be angry with me, but I hated when she shut me out. Unfortunately it was her way of coping and regaining control. I was certainly on shaky ground at this moment, but I could only tread water for so long before I lost my temper out of frustration.

I rose to my feet when I heard the bath water running and went to my own suitcase where I had packed a small bag of Brianna's common toiletry items including her favorite honeysuckle body wash. She had been away for over a month, I assumed she would have run out by now, but it was also a little selfish on my part. I loved the way she smelled when she used it, and honestly it reminded me of easier times with her. At this moment this bottle of yellow soap was probably my only way into that bathroom.

Standing in front of the door I took a deep breath before turning the handle and stepping inside. I looked to my left and saw that Brianna was already in the bath, bubbles climbing up her stomach not quite reaching her chest.

"Cameron!" she shouted in an irritated tone as she covered her breasts with bubbles. "When the door's closed it usually means to stay out."

"I thought you might want this," I said placing the body wash on the edge of the bathtub and trying to sound unfazed by her tone. "But I see you found something else to use."

Brianna bit her bottom lip and scrunched her face before she muttered,

"This stuff doesn't smell as good though."

"I have to agree." She held my gaze only for a second before she sunk down further into the tub and rested her head and neck on its ledge. "Bri, I want to talk about what happened with…"

"Nope, not ready."

"Love, please…"

"Don't call me that," she said flustered as she leaned forward to shut the water off. "It's not fair, Cam. I'm sitting here naked, the most vulnerable I can be, unable to go anywhere. If we're going to talk I want it on equal ground."

"Fine then," I replied and began unbuttoning my shirt.

Brianna's eyes grew large, her lips parting in surprise. "Wh-what are you doing?"

She swallowed hard as I removed my shirt and dropped it to the floor.

"You wanted equal ground, so I am giving you equal ground."

I removed my shoes and socks and then my jeans, catching Brianna struggling to look away. It was not until I finally removed my boxer briefs and stepped toward the large oval tub did she turn her head to face the wall, placing her hand securely over her mouth. I could hear her heartbeat quicken as she tucked her legs up toward her chest when I stepped into the extremely hot water. Her free hand was resting on the edge of the bath and I touched her fingertips lightly as I said, "I am now just as vulnerable as you are."

Brianna moved her hand away from mine. "I haven't even shaved, Cam."

"I have seen your unshaven legs before."

"Not this bad you haven't," she replied and smiled slightly and I returned it, but then something passed across her face and the smile faded, allowing the tension to return between us.

When I could not take the silence any longer I finally asked, "Why Connecticut?"

Her heartbeat quickened once again and for the first time I worried about her answer. Had she done something in retaliation? She had left thinking I had been unfaithful, would she have been unfaithful in response? Could she? This was something I had not even considered until now and the length of time she was taking to answer was making me even more fearful.

Brianna pushed herself into an upright position. "I filed for divorce from Sam. I wanted a fresh start and that meant making things official."

"That is wonderful, angel."

She ignored my compliment and continued over me, "Come to find out that everything is in my name, so…"

"Wait, what do you mean?"

She sighed. "Everything I thought was his was really in my name. Don't ask me why he did it, but he did. So I sold the vehicles, put the house on the market, and donated everything inside."

"I am sorry you had to handle all of that alone."

"Oh I wasn't alone," she answered snidely with a daring brow raised.

"O-oh, I see."

"Yes, I met a charming young man named Jonah. I couldn't have done it without him. He rarely left my side all week."

She was punishing me. The tiny smirk on her face was more than enough evidence. Reflexively my hand went through my hair and I knew she could see my worry.

"Do you have," I paused with fear, "feelings for him?"

She waited before answering, drawing my fear out as long as possible. "No. It would be like trying to have feelings for Jared. But it would serve you right if I did."

I could not hide my relief as a smile stretched across my face, but it faded a moment later when I looked Brianna in the eye and saw the pain that lingered in them.

"Please, love, let me explain…"

"Nope, not ready," she snapped, letting her head fall back onto the edge of the bath.

My frustration was not hidden from her as I exhaled loudly, but I knew pushing her further at this very moment would not help. So I took another approach. She was so close and trying desperately to keep her legs from sliding down and touching me. When her foot slipped again I took it in my hands and began massaging it before she could wretch it away. She lifted her head to protest but as I pressed my thumbs deeper into the arch of her foot her face relaxed, her eyes closing slightly in pleasure.

"You're playing dirty, Mr. Burke," she snickered as she rested her head back down, but thankfully kept eye contact with me.

"I will use any and all advantages I have," I replied. Brianna was silent for another moment, playing with the bubbles in between her fingers as she let her body relax at my touch. "Kyla sends her love."

"I'm sure that's not all she's sending. I'll be surprised if she ever talks to me again."

"I think it will be very difficult for her *not* to speak with you. She misses you terribly."

A flash of guilt came over Brianna's face and I could see her eyes becoming glassy with tears. "How's everyone else?"

"Fine," I lied, not wanting to burden her with all the trials and tribulations of late. "Even Devin sends his regards."

Brianna's eyebrows raised in surprise. "He's getting soft these days."

"Only for you, and only in front of us," I winked.

"Is Victor furious with me?"

I laughed softly. "Not in the slightest. His anger is completely directed at me." Brianna smirked. "And I deserve how happy that makes you. Thankfully I am still in his good graces as he has asked me to take control of finding the location for a new Facility on the East Coast."

"New Facility?" Brianna asked as she lifted her left foot out of my hands and replaced it with her right, which of course I took gladly and began massaging. "Are they closing the old one?"

I shook my head. "No, just expanding. Facility West will remain, and then there will be the addition of Facility East."

"Facility East. It sounds like a health club. So who's buying Facility East? That's got to cost a pretty penny." Brianna's eyes fluttered slightly as she asked, "Are you? Do you have to run the new Facility?"

"No, no, love. The coven leaders will put up the money. I am just the third party bringing the proposal to the table. Dante will oversee Facility East as a whole, similar to how Father does, and then the leaders will elect someone to run the day to day activities."

"Like Lana," she replied with a hint of disdain.

"Yes, like Lanashell." Who was still nowhere to be found and causing Victor great turmoil, I thought to myself.

"Who's Dante?"

"Dante is the leader of a major coven in Boston. They specialize in mediation and negotiation for both human and Vampire affairs."

"Let me guess, they're called the Mediators."

"Close," I laughed, "they're called the Negotiators."

"Vamps aren't very creative, are they? The Warrior-ers, The Negotiate-ers, The Clean-ers. What do they call Kyla's old coven, The Entertainers? Or The Artist-ers?"

"I have never thought of it that way. We are rather unoriginal."

Brianna lifted her foot from my hands and rested both of her feet on my chest. Gently I caressed the tops of them with my fingertips, reveling in the joy of having her near me once again and feeling her skin against mine. As my fingers traveled down to her ankles and then to her calves where the bubbles were disappearing and dripping back into the bath water I saw the reasoning behind her earlier embarrassment. "You are right, my angel, you have not shaved in quite some time."

Brianna laughed loudly, and the sound of her laughter filled my heart. I had not heard her laugh like that in so long, not just in the month she had been away but also in the months prior. But even as her laughter still hung in the air her smiled faded once again.

"You know what, no. No!" she shouted as she removed her feet from my chest and plunged them back into the bath and then stood up in front of me. "You do not get to do this. You don't get to be all charming and funny and make me forget what you've done. I'm mad at you, Cameron Jackson. I look at you and all I can think of is…is you…"

Brianna stood stuttering and pointing down at me while the bubbles slowly dripped down her body revealing her enlarged breasts and bulging stomach. Even with her eyes squinting in anger she had never looked so beautiful. It was difficult to form thoughts with her standing naked and wet in front of me.

A frustrated yell came through her clinched teeth as she stepped out of the bath and I offered her my hand for balance. It was reflex, and she took it as she placed her second foot on the bathroom floor but then shoved my hand away. "I can do it on my own, Cam. I've been doing everything on my own for the last month. With-out-you. You tore us apart!"

Her words were biting, as they were meant to be. She grabbed a towel from the shelf next to the sink and began wrapping it around her.

"Brianna, please," I began as I rose slightly from the bath and then quickly sank back down realizing that the brief moment Brianna had stood in front of me had aroused me. In a word I was mortified, no better than a teenage boy. She was absolutely furious with me and if I were to stand up in my current state there was no telling what she would do to me. I called to her once again before she hurried into the bedroom and slammed the bathroom door behind her. I, on the other hand had to close my eyes and think of things that would reduce the erection that was painfully reminding me how long it had been since Brianna and I had been with each other.

I pictured such scenes as Connor removing a dead Vampire's ear from his pocket, the sight and smell of Elaina's abandoned warehouse, the feeling of thick silver chains being ripped out of my body, splattering the walls with blood and tissue. I turned on the bath's cold faucet and splashed my face for good measure before exiting the tub and wrapping a towel around my waist.

When I exited the bathroom I found Brianna standing in front of the bed in a pair of pink jersey pajama bottoms, her back turned to me as she pulled a thin white tank top over her head. In some ways I was grateful that she was dressed, I was unsure of my control.

"I'm still not ready to talk about it, Cameron," she said angrily as she threw her towel onto the floor.

I came to stand behind her, holding tightly onto my towel as I said, "Brianna, I know you are angry with me, but we need to talk about this."

"No, we'll talk about it when I'm ready."

"Well I am ready, Brianna."

"Who says this gets to be on your terms," she shouted with her back still to me.

"Because I do not wish you to think I am guilty of things I am not," I snapped.

Brianna whipped around to face me, the wet edges of her hair sticking to her neck and chest that still glistened from her bath. She crossed her arms in front of her chest and I could tell that her wrath would be forthcoming. Her eyes were blazing with anger as she said, "Ok, Cam, let's talk. Did you or did you not start neglecting me and spend most of your time with Nikki?"

I blinked slowly. "Yes, but…"

"Time and time again, didn't you choose her over me?"

"It was not that simple…"

"And after begging me to come back, did you or did you not kiss her?"

My next word felt like burning silver as it came out of my mouth. "Yes."

Brianna's bottom lip began to tremble, her face flinching while trying to stop the tears. "So what am I supposed to think, Cameron? Put two and two together and you and Nikki are living happily ever after and laughing at my expense."

"No," I answered firmly. "That is not what happened. Let me…"

"Jared told me!"

"He told you what he saw, not what he knew," I said raising my voice again. "He did not know the circumstances…"

"The circumstances were that you got caught."

My grip on the edge of my towel tightened as I turned away from Brianna and hit the wall with the palm of my hand. Brianna could push me like no other woman had in my long lifetime. I took a cleansing breath in order to regain control. My fingers began rubbing at my lower lip and chin as I slowly turned back around to face the woman I loved. A fearful expression was etched into her face, her hand resting on her exposed stomach. Knowing that my child was within her while we yelled at one another stripped away all remaining anger and frustration.

Taking another deep breath, I spoke to her in a low soft tone, "What you have not asked, my angel, is did I or did I not agonize over your safety once you found out that you were pregnant. The answer is yes. Did I become obsessed with trying to find Elaina? Yes. Did I panic when you continued to have the dream about being tortured by Elaina, yes I did, and I still am since from your earlier screaming I believe you are still having it.

"Unable to get those images of you being held down while Elaina cuts open your stomach, did I stupidly run to the only person that could give us some information on Elaina? Yes I did and I am sorry for it. I was scared and wrongly let my fear consume me and I hurt you, the one thing I promised I would never do. I am sorry, love, I am truly and utterly sorry for not being there for you like I should have been. I was going to tell you all of this the day you returned from your Father's, but I did not get the opportunity because I...because I am an ass. But an ass who loves you more than you can ever imagine."

Brianna stood motionless. Tentatively I took a step toward her and she did not object so I took another, and then another until I was able to take her hand gently in mine and stare into her eyes as they filled again with tears. An hour before I might have thought her mind Push was my punishment, but now I realized that seeing her like this was the actual torture. I had broken her fragile and vulnerable heart, and I deserved to watch every tear fall down her face because of it.

I lifted my hand to wipe away the tears from her cheeks, but she took a step away and slowly sat down on the bed, choosing to wipe her tears away herself.

"Why did you have to kiss her?"

I knelt down in front of her, catching her head on my shoulder while she cried, feeling her tears drip down my chest. "Brianna, when you left with Kyla that day I returned to our room and Nikki was already there waiting for me." Brianna slowly raised her head from my shoulder and looked into my eyes with a trembling bottom lip. "Nikki threatened that if I did not kiss her she would go to Father and tell him that I had..." I stopped, finding the words difficult to say. "She said she would tell Father that I had forced myself on her."

Brianna's tears stopped as her brows furrowed together. "She…she was going to say…"

"That I raped her, Bri. That I raped her and beat her, and that Victor could not refute it because she is a Healer and there would be no evidence." Brianna wrapped one arm around her stomach and pressed her other hand to her lips as though she was going to be ill. "When I still refused she said that if I did not give her what she wanted she would make you insane with suspicion that she and I were having an affair. I felt I could defend myself against her when it came to Father, but I did not want her anywhere near you. So I gave in, thinking that if I did what she wanted she would just walk away and leave us alone. That was when Jared Projected into our room and saw me kissing her. He was so angry that he did not let me explain and I prayed that I would have the opportunity to speak with you before he did, but obviously that was not the case."

Brianna sat silently in front of me, blinking slowly as she processed everything that I had told her. She seemed almost in shock.

"Angel?" I prodded gently as I folded her hands in between mine. "Brianna, please say something."

She sniffled and cleared her throat before she said, "Your towel fell off."

I looked down to see that yes indeed my towel had fallen completely free from my body and was lying in a circle around me on the floor. Who was the vulnerable one now? As I grabbed the towel from the floor and stood to tie it around me, Brianna stood from the bed and walked toward the couch that sat just beyond the foot of the bed.

"Why are boys so stupid?" she muttered. "Girls lie, Cam, especially crazy ones like Nikki. Whether you kissed her or not, she wasn't going to stop harassing you or me, that's how they work and guys always fall for it. She found a way to get what she wanted and you walked right into it."

"Bri, I know," I answered, walking to stand in front of her. "I know that now, but it took all that chaos in order for me to see the truth."

"Which is?"

"She is a plant."

"Is that some kind of new hybrid power?" she asked flatly and I pressed my lips together trying unsuccessfully to keep my laughter inside. "Why are you laughing at me?"

"I apologize, love, what I meant to say is that we suspect she is working for Elaina."

"Can you prove it?"

"Not yet, but we have a close eye on her." Brianna nodded slowly, though I could see thoughts still churning inside her head. "Please do not give Nikki another thought. I need to know if you forgive me." I knelt down in front of her again, coming eye level with her pregnant stomach, unable to stop myself from placing my hand upon it. Within seconds I could feel the heat building from underneath my palm. "Brianna, you and our child are the most important things in my life right now and I could not bear it if you were to leave me again. I need you, angel. I need you at my side and our child in my arms. Please do not make me live without that."

Brianna's face softened slightly, although she took my hand away from her stomach.

"Glad to see that the freaky heat thing still happens when you touch my stomach. I so missed that," she said sarcastically as she stepped away and walked around the couch to her purse with a strap that was oddly tied together. She unzipped an inside pocket and removed several pieces of paper. I stood as she walked back around the couch to stand in front of me. "Cam, what you did was really stupid and has damaged my trust in you." I lowered my eyes to floor, afraid of where this was going. "While we were apart there were times I kept screaming that I never wanted to see you again. But even on my darkest day I still loved you. I do love you, even after everything that has happened, I still love you. You need to win my trust back, but I will be there at your side while you hold our son in your arms."

My eyes flew up to Brianna's and then to the small black and white photo with the words "Baby Boy Burke" written in her handwriting in the border. I knew ultrasounds existed, but I was amazed at seeing my child, my son, from inside the womb. It was hard to tear my eyes away from the ultrasound photo, but Brianna cleared her throat and looked at me expectantly.

"However, you will need to make room in those arms for your daughter," she said happily as she held up another ultrasound photo with the words "Baby Girl Burke" written in the border.

My eyes rose back to hers, happy tears beginning to crest over her lids.

"Twins?"

She nodded as I took the photos from her hands, rubbing my thumb over the sight of both my children. A second later I pulled Brianna into me; crushing her against my chest and feeling her hot tears trickle down my skin. "This is really happening then."

Brianna did not answer, but merely sniffled loudly against my chest. Our future and our children's future had never been so real than in this moment. The ultrasound photos had clinched any doubts either of us may have had about what would happen next. As she shook in my arms I knew she was just as terrified as I was. Brushing her hair over her shoulder I began rubbing her back and swaying ever so slightly in order to calm her, and in affect me as well.

"We will get to Elaina first," I whispered, though I could hear my own skepticism.

Brianna raised her head, messily wiping her tears away with her fingers. Her eyes burned into mine. Then the anguish I saw in them was transferred into a kiss as she feverishly pressed her lips against mine. She was giving me everything; her fear, longing, anger, sorrow, desire, and I took all of it. I was greedy and drunk with lust for her as her tongue flicked inside my mouth and her lips kneaded against mine. It was not long before I felt the prick of my fangs extending and then a sudden breeze against my backside.

"Um, Cam, I think this towel has a mind of its own."

Honestly I did not care that I was standing completely naked in the middle of my hotel room. I was finally holding my love in my arms and I could feel the heat building again in between us as her stomach pressed against mine. It was something neither of us could explain, but we knew it had something to do with our children's connection to me. It did not occur with anyone else, and the fact that it still happened even after being apart from one another for so long comforted me.

Brianna pulled out of our embrace first, and I caught her taking a peek at me before finally turning away. "Put some clothes on, would you? That was what got me in this condition in the first place."

"And I do not regret it, my love," I said and turned to the armoire for a pair of silk pajama bottoms. Brianna had often teased me about them, but I was choosing comfort as she had after such a trying day, or months actually.

"So what happens now?"

"Whatever you would like to happen, love," I replied as I tied my pants securely and closed the armoire.

"Well first I need a new purse since I destroyed mine today attacking Aidan."

"Again?"

She shrugged sheepishly and sat down on the couch. "Nowadays I feel a Vamp, I Push first and ask questions later."

"I whole heartedly agree with that approach. What is second on the list?"

Brianna rested her chin on the back edge of the couch. "I can't say that I haven't been thinking of going home and sleeping in our bed, especially now that Nikki's gone. I mean now I can finally relax without having to worry she'll come walking around the corner."

I froze next to the bed, my back turned away from her but knowing with absolute certainty that she could see everything I was trying to hide.

"Cameron? She's not still in the manor, is she?"

I turned around, hands up in front of me, begging her to let me explain but my hope was lost.

"Cameron Jackson Burke, what the freaking freak! How…wh…why?"

"Brianna, it is not the best of situations, but by keeping her in the manor we can keep an eye on her and monitor everything she does. Eventually she will lead us to Elaina and the more she thinks we trust her, the sloppier she will be."

Brianna stood from the couch, shaking her head violently from side to side. "I can't, Cam. I refuse to stay under the same roof as that tramp. I won't, Cam, I won't go back if she's there."

I stepped in front of her, combing my fingers through her dark hair to calm her. "Bri, I understand. We will not go back until you are ready."

"But what about the other Warriors? What about Kyla? Nikki could get everyone killed."

"Love, we are handling it. Trust me when I say Jared is keeping a really close eye on her."

As if she could read my thoughts she narrowed her eyes at me and extended her hand. "Phone please."

"You know it is only one o'clock in San Francisco."

Brianna quirked an eyebrow and I quickly retrieved my cell phone for her. From where I stood I could hear the phone ringing and my youngest brother answer groggily. "Jesus, bro, it's the middle of the afternoon."

"If I could reach through this phone I would throw you outside," Brianna shouted into the phone.

"Beebs! Holy…"

"Don't Beebs me, you horny little shit. I cannot believe…"

Knowing there was nothing I could do to save him, I stretched out on the bed while Brianna laid into Jared for almost thirty minutes. Though he was my brother and I loved him as such, I was happy that someone else was getting Brianna's wrath. I never said I was not selfish from time to time.

Chapter Twenty-Four

Brianna

Life was better in the four days after I reunited with Cam. Some of the anger I felt towards him had been transferred onto Jared now that he was sleeping with Nikki. Good grief that girl got around, and it infuriated me that she was with Jared. He was so in the doghouse right now, even if he was just using her for information. But I tried not to dwell on things that were out of my control. I had enough trouble as it was, and like I said things were certainly getting better. It wasn't perfect of course, but there were fewer tears, although my hormones weren't helping. Cam had taken to changing the TV channel when a coffee commercial came on, however, we had to add phone commercials and movie previews to a growing list.

I missed Cameron. I couldn't deny I felt more complete when in his arms. Smiles were sometimes followed by tears when I thought of him with Nikki, and he could instantly tell when the thoughts crossed my mind. He was patient with me, knowing that trust was not just a word for me but linked to how comfortable I could be with him physically. Kisses were one thing, but I hadn't found the strength to make love to him. When he kissed me, my body would scream for me to give in to him whereas my mind definitely had other ideas.

Now that I was back in the presence of a Vampire my dreams were running rampant. Some I confided in him about and others I didn't. But there was one theme that was constant throughout all my dreams – not everything is what it seems.

There were so many possibilities of what that meant that it made my head pound while I stood in the kitchen of a three-story brownstone in an affluent part of Boston. My feet were killing me from scouting buildings for the third day in a row searching for the new Facility East. We had looked at abandoned schools, factories, and corporation buildings alike, however, the brownstone confused me. But I certainly didn't want to ask questions, I was only along for the ride. I just wished the ride had a chair.

I propped the back of my elbows on the large center island of the kitchen that had a small eating and sitting area opening to its right and a formal dining room to its left. A moment later Cameron came strolling down the hallway that dissected the kitchen from the dining room with the realtor who quickly excused herself and walked down the stairs to the first floor.

"So? What do you think?" Cam asked with a questioning smile on his face. As usual he was immaculately dressed, but today he was wearing a black tailored suit with a crisp white shirt, no tie, and the top buttons were undone. Be still my heart.

"I've already told you a million times today, I think you should wear a suit every day. You told me once how much you missed it."

He smiled as he wrapped his arms around to my back, kissing me gently on the forehead. "I have to admit I do not mind having to dress up. Today is an important day. I must look as professional as possible."

"Yes, yes I know, you're meeting with Dante today."

Cameron pulled his arms away from me, adjusting the collar of his shirt and then pulling at his jacket. "It is a rare occasion that I am nervous for anyone other than you, my love."

"I gathered that this morning when you said, 'Love, would you mind wearing something other than leggings today?'" He laughed at my impression of him while I adjusted his shirt collar back to where it needed to be. "Babe, you'll be fine. Dante can't be nearly as scary or intimidating as Victor."

"You are certainly correct there, *babe*." Cameron still didn't fully approve of my nickname for him, but too bad, nothing else had fit so he was stuck with it. "I want to ensure that I represent our coven in the best way, and in turn keep Father's confidence in me."

I rose to my toes and gave him a soft kiss on his cool lips. "Like I said, you'll do fine, Cam-er-on."

My sass earned me a crooked smile and it melted my heart as it always did.

"Now, Brianna, may I ask again, what do you think of the home?"

I stepped away from the island and circled around to the large stove. "Well my first question is why would anyone put the kitchen on the second floor?"

It was true. Living room and master bedroom on the first floor, with the kitchen, dining area, and three bedrooms on the second, and a forth bedroom on the third floor. Cameron merely shrugged and opened the French doors at the far side of the kitchen which opened up to a small balcony that overlooked the street below. As I stepped onto the balcony, the setting somehow made me think of Paris, not that I'd been there, but I could imagine sitting out on this narrow balcony at a small round table enjoying a croissant in the fresh morning air.

"The place is beautiful, Cam, but it's a little small, don't you think? Unless they're planning on buying the whole block."

Cameron was quiet for a second, taking my hand and rubbing it gently with his thumb as a gentle breeze rustled the yellow and orange leaves that still hung from their branches in front of us.

"You are correct, love, this is definitely way too small for the Facility. I was actually thinking that perhaps..." he cleared his throat, "that perhaps it was the perfect size for us." My eyes bulged out of their sockets. Cameron placed both our hands on my stomach. "And our children."

I must have swallowed for two minutes straight while a million thoughts ran through my head. Instead of speaking, my brain moved my feet to bring me back inside. I heard Cameron close the doors behind him and I didn't have to turn around to know he was waiting for me to answer. His hands began to rub my arms gently and I let my weight fall back into him.

"We will handle each question one by one. I am here, love, let it all out."

He knew me too well.

"You want to stay in Boston? What about the manor? It's our home."

Cameron sighed. "Yes, it is our home, but Nikki is there and you said yourself you would not return until she left. Since we have no idea how long that could be we might as well put some roots down. I figured you would want to stay in Boston because Renee is here."

I stepped away from him, turning back to look into his eyes. "But what about Victor? He'll be furious with you. I couldn't take it if..."

Cameron placed his hands on either side of my face as my voice rose and quickened with fear. "Brianna, let me worry about my father. Yes, I am positive he will be upset at first, but he will come around."

"You're too optimistic."

He laughed. "No, not optimistic. I have seen my Father's face when he speaks of his grandchildren. I will simply tell him the truth. The manor is no place to raise two young children. Having one Vampire in the house is dangerous enough, let alone thirty at varying levels of bloodlust. This is not just about Nikki being in the manor, I am thinking of the safety of our children."

"But what about your brothers? And Kyla? Good grief she's going to flip out about this."

Cameron brushed the hair out of my eyes, his fingertips skimming my forehead ever so slightly. "Do not worry. I prepared them for this before I left San Francisco."

"You've been planning this?"

He shrugged. "I know you."

I took Cameron's hands from where they rested on my shoulders, squeezing them slightly as I whispered, "But it's Boston. Where...you know...stuff happened."

"Boston is a city like any other," he replied stiffly while his jaw tightened and flexed. "Come," he said pulling me gently back down the hallway. "Three bedrooms up here, one for each baby and a guest room. Or the twins can share a room for now, and the other two can be used as guest rooms for Oliver, or Devin."

"Or my Dad and Sera?"

"Unless of course your father would feel more comfortable in a hotel," he said, quirking his brow at me. I knew he was somewhat kidding, but only somewhat.

"Kyla and Alex?"

He pointed up to the third floor. "Keep them away from the rest of the house."

"Jared?"

"There is a coat closet downstairs," he laughed. "Only kidding. There is a full basement downstairs, no windows. But it will be difficult for him to travel across the country, so his visits may be rare until his sun sensitivity lessens. Living here does not prevent us from flying to San Francisco from time to time. But I can see that is not the biggest worry you have."

"How can you tell?"

"I told you, I know you. What is it, love? We can handle whatever it is."

I fidgeted with my long black sweater that fell to the hem of my dark purple printed dress he had made me wear. "Can we afford this?"

Cameron seemed relieved as he hugged me tightly to his chest and kissed the top of my head. "Yes, angel, we can certainly afford it."

I pushed myself away from him slightly. "And by we, you mean you."

Cameron scrunched his brows together. "It is our money now. You have just as much access to it as I do, you know that."

"But it's still yours, Cam. You put it in that account, I certainly didn't. The house may be ours, but you'll still be paying for it."

"What would make you feel more comfortable?"

"I want to be equals in this. When it comes to our house I want us to be partners, straight down the middle."

Cameron adjusted his stance, crossing his arms in front of his chest and rubbing his chin with his index finger while his feet were planted firmly to the floor. He was ready to negotiate. "Agreed. However, first things first, do you like this place?"

"Oh crap, did I forget to say that? Ohmygod, I love this place. It's beautiful and perfect and I can see our babies taking their first steps." Cameron reached into the inside pocket of his jacket and handed me a handkerchief. He should buy a value pack of these things. "So yes, I want this place. How much is it?"

"It was just recently reduced to two-point-five."

"Million!" I shouted and then put my hand over my.

"Yes, love, but I can probably get them down from that." I tried to hide my fear and surprise, but Cameron wasn't fooled. "Bri, you are my partner in this whether you put a dime in this house or not. I can write a check today and both of us will be on the deed, I promise you. This is awkward I know. We have never spoken about finances like this because the situation has never presented itself. I know you do not possess this kind of money, and I do not expect you to. I swear to you I will never flaunt what I have, and if I do you can knock me to the floor again."

I laughed through the tears that were collecting in the corners of my eyes and dabbed them with the handkerchief. Just then an idea hit me like a ton of bricks.

"Ohmygod!" I shouted, startling Cameron and causing him to place a protective hand on my stomach. "No, no, I'm fine, sorry. I've got it. You buy my place in Connecticut." Cameron cocked his head to the side in confusion. "Sorry, not you personally, but the coven leaders could buy my place and use it for Facility East."

"The house is a decent size, but still…"

"No, tear the house down for all I care. I own all the land around it and some across the street. You could build a brand new building right on site and have plenty of room around for training and things. Plus, it's tucked away from everything unlike the places here in the city."

I could see the wheels churning in his head as he thought about my offer. "It has merit. I certainly would love to level that house. What is it listed as?"

"Debbie listed the house and all the land at just under two million. I'd sell it for half that if it meant getting it off my hands. I can't believe that a big house on nineteen acres sells for less than this apartment."

Cameron smirked. "Welcome to living in a big city."

I nuzzled myself underneath his chin, pressing my belly against his in turn using all tools at my disposal. "If they buy my house I'll have the money to put into this one. I mean I can't give you the money today obviously, but…"

He placed his finger underneath my chin, tilting my head up to look at him. "I will present the offer to Dante when we see him today, but I do not want this place to slip through our fingers. How about I put in an offer now and if it is accepted we will buy it outright. Whenever the house in Connecticut sells you can use that money to furnish and renovate our new home."

"Boy you're good," I swooned. I didn't even mind the heat rising from my stomach when he placed his hands on it. The babies were kicking and I completely agreed with them. This was a happy moment for all of us, a budding little family buying their first home together. We were unconventional to say the least, and I'm not even talking about the fact that Cameron was a Vampire. "Fine," I said, "go put in an offer."

In a graceful move he lifted me from the floor, my feet dangling at his shins while he kissed me five times in quick succession before placing me back down. He was beaming, his smile stretching from ear to ear. This meant more to him than he ever let on, trying hard not to sway my decision in any way.

"I love you, Cameron."

"Always, angel."

He took my hand, kissing it one last time before turning away to find the realtor to put in our offer. Looking around it was hard not to get attached. I turned around to face the first bedroom and knew instantly it would be the nursery. We could paint the walls light yellow or green to accommodate a boy and a girl and it was certainly big enough to hold two cribs.

"Is this your bedroom, my little ones," I cooed to my belly. It felt like bubbles were popping inside as my babies kicked for me. "I like it too."

As I stepped over to the window to see the view, my sweater's pocket began to vibrate. I reached in and pulled out my cell phone, surprised to see Aidan's name come across the screen. "Hh-ello?" I answered tentatively.

"Yeah, I may have put my cell number into your phone," he said smugly.

"When the heck did you do that?"

"While you were in the bathroom in the hotel room. I told you to call me if you needed anything, remember? How did you think that was going to happen?"

"I don't know," I shrugged to myself. "I'd just call 1-800-Find-Me-An-Arrogant-Vamp."

"Is that an international number?" he laughed.

"So what do I owe this honor?" I asked as I exited the proposed nursery and took a closer look at the other bedrooms.

"Just checking in. The last time I saw you, you were screaming like a banshee."

My head fell in my hand. "Yeah, sorry about that. It's the price I have to pay sometimes for sleeping."

"Usually I hear women screaming for other reasons."

"Ah yes, inappropriate as ever," I replied, feeling my cheeks blush with embarrassment.

"So whatcha up to?"

"Why so interested in me all of a sudden?"

"Just being a friend, Morgan, just being a friend."

"I didn't know guys like you had friends."

"Well, there's a lot you don't know about me. I'm full of surprises. Are you taking care of yourself?"

"Yes, I have to nowadays."

"You certainly do. You're carrying precious cargo."

"Awe, you do have a heart," I joked.

"Hey now, careful who you say that around. I have a reputation to uphold."

"Of what, an asshole?"

"There is a long line of women who would agree with you there."

"I have no doubt. So are you still in Boston?"

"Yeah, not for much longer. Everything's good with you and Cameron?"

I smiled. "Things are great, really great."

"No matches or gasoline?"

"Not so far," I laughed.

"Brianna?" Cameron asked as he stepped into the room.

I waved at him happily as he came closer to me, concern on his face. "Hey, I've got to go," I said quickly into the phone.

"Yeah, yeah. Say hi to Cameron. Take care of yourself, and if you do need a match just call me."

"Who was that?" Cameron asked as I hung up the phone and placed it back into the pocket of my sweater.

"It was Aidan."

"And why would you need him for matches?"

I laughed awkwardly and replied, "Inside joke. He was calling to make sure I was ok. Kind of weird, but it was nice of him."

"He can be a good man when he wants to be."

"Unfortunately that's not very often." Cameron laughed as he extended his hand to me. I wrapped my hand around his and followed him out of the bedroom. "Offer in?"

He nodded. "The offer is in. Now we wait."

"Ugh, that's the worst part."

"You will have plenty of time to be distracted at Dante's."

"Still nervous?" I asked, tugging on his arm as we slowly made our way down the stairs to the first floor foyer.

"I can tell you are enjoying this," he said, crooked smile in full affect.

"It's not often I see you like this, so yes. Yes I am."

When we opened the front door another cool breeze swept across causing the leaves to dance and twirl around on the street. Unfortunately the breeze did not have such a glamorous effect on my hair and caused a large section to fly into my mouth causing me to choke and have to spit it out in a very unladylike way.

Cameron chuckled to himself as he held me up on my feet, helping me remove the strands of hair from my face. "Have I told you how beautiful you look today?"

"Quiet, smartass."

"It is good to see the pregnancy has not affected your foul mouth."

"Keep this up and I'll change into a pair of overalls and talk like an ignorant hick in front of Dante. And don't put it past me to make up some story about how my family tree is more like a wreath and we're naming our children Vam and Pire."

"I do not think it possible to love you more," he said proudly, squeezing the side of my shoulder into his chest and guiding me down the sidewalk.

"So when do you think we'll hear something about the offer?"

"The realtor said the clients are eager to sell, so hopefully we will hear something relatively quickly." Cameron looked down at me as we rounded the corner of the street onto a busier intersection full of small shops and restaurants. "I have not seen you smile like this in a long time."

"I am just so excited. That could be our house, our street. Look there's even a park right over there where we can take the kids. It's all just coming together."

"Do you need another handkerchief?"

"Very funny," I replied and pretended to look up to enjoy our surroundings in order to keep the tears inside my eyes. Just as we began crossing the street I felt my cell phone vibrating in my pocket.

"Is Aidan stalking you now?" Cameron asked as I pulled the cell phone from my pocket.

"Ha, he's the least of my worries," I laughed as I looked down at the screen and answered the call. "Hey Kyla."

"So you *do* remember my name."

Cameron smirked as I rolled my eyes. "Of course I remember your name. I remembered it when I called you two days ago, and the day before that."

"Well you never know what can happen in two days, or even two minutes when it comes to you."

"Ky, I told you I was sorry fifteen times."

Cameron leaned into my ear, "Actually twenty-two and a half if you count the time she interrupted you."

"Cameron says hi."

"Oh I heard him," she replied annoyed.

"So I take it I am still being punished?"

"Yes you are. So what are you guys doing?"

"Um…" don't say looking at houses, don't say looking at houses.

Chapter Twenty-Five

Cameron

We were standing at the front door of the Negotiator's headquarters which honestly looked like any other Bostonian multi-storied home overlooking the bay. Brianna had teased me about my nervousness over meeting Dante, but the meeting was not the only thing that had me unable to stop fiddling with my shirt collar. I had told her that it was also because I wanted to represent our coven to the best of my ability, and that was certainly the truth. But deep in my soul I had a feeling that this was a test for the path my father hoped I would take. Cameron and Devin, the future leaders of the Warrior Coven, two parts of the whole, the heart and the weapon. If I wanted it, that is. Devin certainly did, and Victor would not let him obtain that goal without me - I was the lynchpin. Whether I accepted the challenge in the future, Victor would have to ensure that the other coven leaders were comfortable with the shift of power. Covens rose and fell at the change of a leader, and if the Warriors collapsed it could mean chaos within our race.

My shoulders suddenly felt extremely heavy. Brianna kept reminding me to be myself, and that was exactly what Victor wanted and why he did not send Devin. I loved my eldest brother, but he did not possess any kind of diplomacy. If Victor wanted to pass the coven on, he would need the support of someone who would be able to ease the other coven leaders into the idea. That person was Dante, a centuries old mediator who could size up a person within seconds of meeting them. Or so I heard.

"Cameron, honey, you have to stop fidgeting," Brianna said lovingly, though slightly annoyed as she pulled my hands away from my collar. "Goodness I feel like I'm in *Pretty Woman*."

"What is *Pretty Woman?*" I asked looking down at her and receiving a flabbergasted look.

"Only the best chick flick ever made. Prostitute meets filthy rich business man, he climbs the fire escape at the end and they live happily ever after."

"This is a movie?" When Brianna rolled her eyes at me I said, "Am I the prostitute or the business man?"

"Ohmygod, just leave it alone. You've ruined my whole point," she replied angrily. I gave it only another few seconds before she started crying. The hormones were tougher to manage than I had expected.

"I am sorry, love, I...."

"She fidgets ok? She fidgets all the time in the movie and he keeps asking her not to. Can we just drop it? Gosh!"

Yes, hormones were definitely a challenge for the mother of my children. Doing the only thing I hoped would not set her off, I placed my arm around her shoulders and gently kissed her temple. Thankfully the gesture did not seem to irritate her. Afraid to bring my hand anywhere near my collar I took her right hand in mine and kissed the back of it before glancing down at the large sapphire ring that I had given to her on her birthday. The stone was so beautiful against her pale skin, but I could not help but notice how incredibly dirty it was. As if she read my mind, she jerked her hand out of my grasp.

"Don't even look at it, it's so dirty, I know."

"I was merely admiring the ring on your finger, love."

"I never take it off, so it's just caked with crud," she replied as she dug her nail into the edge of the setting.

"So we need to buy gloves and ring cleaner?"

"Why gloves?"

"Because your hands are almost as cold as mine are."

She shrugged and stopped her attack on her ring. "Just put your hand on my stomach and give me a hot flash. That fixes everything," she said and rang the doorbell impatiently. "Where are these people?"

Carefully I pulled her hand away from the doorbell and thankfully a second later the door was opened. We were greeted by a short, slim Vampire with an irritated look on his face. "May I help you?"

"I am Cameron Burke. I have an appointment with Dante."

The man's expression lightened as he opened the door wider. "Oh yes.

Master has been expecting you. Please come in."

Brianna squeezed my hand tightly as we stepped through the doorway into the grand foyer. The Negotiator's headquarters was much smaller than the manor but it was certainly more extravagant with its grand white marble staircase expanding in front of us which matched the opulent columns and decorative gold leaf ceiling. Brianna's eyes were wide in awe as she took in her surroundings. Through my history I had been in many well-regarded homes, but I had to admit in some ways this one intimidated me almost as much as it did Brianna. Thank goodness I wore my best suit today.

While we waited in the center of the foyer, other coven members bustled around us speaking into phones while others flipped feverishly through large stacks of papers in their arms. Brianna began rubbing her lower back, her lips twisting slightly in pain. She had been on her feet for hours and I knew her body was punishing her for it. Gently I brushed her hand aside and began massaging my thumb and forefinger on either side of her lower spine, feeling the muscles heat and relax at my pressure.

"Has no one offered you a chair?" a voice spoke from the tall staircase. I looked up to see a thin young man, no taller than Victor, make his way down to meet us. "Some people just don't have manners," he said as he cupped Brianna's hand in his and placed it on his chest. "Please don't take this the wrong way, but I seriously hate the fact that your hair is naturally this straight. I got tired of using a straightener so I finally cut off all my hair. Hopefully the style lasts since, well, I'm stuck with it for goodness knows how many more centuries. But who knows, perhaps they'll develop extensions for buzz cuts someday, or maybe I could start wearing wigs.

"Oh I cannot tell you how nice it is to meet you, I have heard so much. Actually, rumors more than anything, but girl let me tell you that you are rockin' this whole bun-in-the-oven look. Celebs eat your heart out, here comes Brianna Morgan."

Nervously I looked around to see several Vampires stop what they were doing and look in Brianna's direction. Her cheeks were flush, most likely because a total stranger was doting on her, something I myself was not all that fond of either.

The young man shifted his eyes quickly between me and Brianna before finally saying, "I'm sorry, I didn't mean to say that out loud."

Brianna shook her head. "No, it's fine. I'm just not used to someone knowing who I am, especially when I have no idea who you are."

"Girl, I have simply lost my head. My name is Fabiani, but everyone calls me Fabi." Fabiani released Brianna's hand and then extended his hand to me. "That especially goes for you, Cameron Burke. I don't answer to anything but Fabi, so you should simply put that in your head." I raised my eyebrows at him. "Oh don't look surprised. People talk, and they say you actually fought a Vampire twice your size before agreeing to call him a name other than his given one. And the fact that they also said you were an incredible specimen of man, I'd say they were right on both accounts. If I were human I'd be having a hot flash right now you're so damn handsome, but of course you're straight," he said pointing to Brianna's stomach. "The good ones always are."

Fabiani rubbed his thumb against the back of my hand as he gave me a sly wink. I was completely taken aback and unprepared.

"You are homosexual."

"Cameron!" Brianna shouted, hitting me in the arm with her purse and then placing her hand over her eyes. "Fabi, I'm sorry. He doesn't have much experience with this sort of thing."

Thankfully Fabiani did not seem offended as he laughed and said, "No apology needed, Brianna. And yes, Cameron, I am gay, a total flame sometimes if the mood suits me and everyone knows it, so no harm done. However, I'd work on your delivery. Any other queen might have just smacked you across the face. But alas I cannot, it is too damn cute. Anyway, Master should be down any second now to greet you."

Brianna leaned into me as she whispered, "Does he mean Dante?"

"Yes," Fabiani answered. "I'm sorry, that's what we refer to him as. Do you Warriors call your maker something different?"

I nodded. "All of Victor's sires refer to him as Father."

"So very family oriented, those Warriors. Who would have thought? Well, only the Master lives upstairs in the residence. You are standing in the center of the most prestigious mediation company in the world, known only to those who can pay the high price for it. Though we do a significant amount of pro bono work to keep the government off our back, but they only do it in order to get a discount when they really need us."

"And I only give it to them when they grovel," someone else replied from above.

My gaze went to the top of the stairs where a Vampire I assumed was Dante stood very erect, his thick black hair coiffed high with sideburns growing down his jaw. The light from the large chandelier above us refracted off his shiny white suit as he glided down the marble stairs. I clamped my lips tightly together, afraid of what would accidently pass them.

Brianna, however, forgot. "Liberace?"

Of course Dante heard her and my stomach dropped. Somehow both of us had forgotten to install our social filters. This was not quite how I pictured today going. I could only imagine what Dante would report back to Victor.

Dante stepped down from the final step and walked gracefully to stand in front of us. "You know, Ms. Morgan, few people see the resemblance nowadays, but he truly took my style and embellished it to suit his needs. I do miss him so, he was truly a wonderfully talented man. But I digress, I am of course Dante and it is an honor to have a daughter of Eris in my home," Dante said as he bowed deeply in front of Brianna, then kissed the back of her hand as he rose. "And I see the rumors are true, you are glowing with child, my dear."

Brianna placed a protective hand on her stomach, though she smiled at Dante's compliment. "Glowing with twins, actually."

"Double congratulations then, my dear," Dante replied and then began shaking my hand excitedly. "Wonderfully done, my boy."

"Thank you, sir," I replied as I placed my hand into my inside jacket pocket and removed the two small ultrasound photos. Brianna rolled her eyes at me as I handed them to Dante. "Brianna feels I show too many people the photos of my children."

"Cameron, you showed the pictures to the cab driver this morning."

"I cannot help but be a proud father."

Dante handed me back the photos and patted me on the shoulder as he said, "As well you should be. So I see you have already met Fabi, shall we go inside for a conference? We have much to discuss."

With arms wide, Dante herded the three of us through a set of wide double doors and into what was originally built as a large living room with a fireplace tall enough to stand in. However, in order to support the business need, a wide oval conference table was placed in the middle of the room surrounded by corporate-looking chairs and the latest in video and audio conference equipment.

Immediately I pulled out the closest chair for Brianna and she graciously fell into the thick leather upholstery. I kissed the top of her head before pulling out one of the conference chairs next to her and placing my black leather portfolio on the table. The portfolio had all the details of the properties for the coven leaders to review, except for Brianna's. I would need to sell the fact the property just came on the market and that it in no way had a personal connection.

Dante remained standing near the head of the table while Fabiani lifted the lid of a laptop whose screen projected onto the large plasma TV above the fireplace.

"Now that you have met Fabi, I would like to explain his purpose during these proceedings," Dante began. "You see, because I am a coven leader myself, I must be part of the decision making process and appear impartial during what I can only say will be the most painful negotiation process you will ever be witness to." Brianna's breath caught in her mouth. "Oh, my dear, I did not mean to frighten you, it was more of a figure of speech. I would so like it if you began breathing again."

Brianna sighed in relief and I offered her my hand for support which she took gladly while the other rested comfortably on the crest of her stomach.

"As I was saying," Dante continued, "I must look impartial to my colleagues. Therefore, I have asked Fabi to support the negotiations and mediate the difficulties I know only too well will occur during the next few days. I do not wish to make you a sacrifice to the wolves, my dear boy, and Fabi is one of my best pupils. I do hope that this experience will give you both the exposure to our race's leaders you so deserve. Now then, I have said my peace, what is it they say? On with the show?"

Dante gestured dramatically to the screen before taking a seat only several down from my own. As I opened my portfolio to the first property, Fabi displayed the online listing on the screen. With a deep breath and a squeeze of encouragement from my Bri, I began walking Dante through each of the properties I had selected for the proposal. One by one Dante picked apart different aspects of each property in order to prepare me for what was to come from the other leaders. He was teaching me the ways of an excellent communicator. In a word he was, amazing. There was not enough space on the print outs for the amount of notes I was taking. My writing became so small even I had difficulty reading it.

Once our discussion of the final property had been completed, Fabiani lowered the lid to the laptop, however, Dante held out his arm and gestured for him to open the laptop once more.

"So, dear boy, do tell me about this last property and why it is the only one you have not sent beforehand?"

I was stunned. It was difficult to fathom how he knew what I was withholding from him. "Yes sir, there is actually one more I would like to show you," I said, rising from my chair and walking over to Fabiani's computer and typing in the web address that Brianna had given me only moments before walking through the door. I could see from across the table that Bri's lips were tight while she bit the inside of her cheek when the photo of her former home flashed on the screen.

Dante was quiet while I explained the details of the property, but mostly about the endless possibilities with the amount of land and the ability to customize Facility East to our needs versus retrofitting a current structure.

"And this property is in Connecticut? Not here in Boston where it would be easier for me to oversee the operations?" Dante asked rhetorically. It was the hurdle I was expecting.

"Yes sir, however, it is nestled in a small remote town where there would be less attention drawn to it unlike here in the city. This would mean less Glamours, fewer media and government entities asking questions. It is less than two hours from here by car and only a short run on foot. And although you would not be able to oversee day to day operations directly, hire the right person to run it and you will not need to. Victor has had little to do with Facility West over the years due to Lanashell's skills."

"But when a person such as Lanashell disappears it is imperative that a leader be close by."

My eyes would have naturally diverted to the floor at his point in defeat if they were not currently being bored into by Brianna's. By her shocked expression I realize now I forgot to mention the fact that Lanashell disappeared.

Dante turned in his chair, choosing to face Brianna instead as he asked, "May I ask, my darling girl, how this particular property is connected to you?"

Brianna's widened eyes and blank expression gave her away instantly. "I'm not sure what you're referring to. Um…sir."

Dante stood from his chair, taking position next to me and placing a hand on my shoulder while he spoke to her. "But, my darling girl, you absolutely know what I'm referring to. Your face says it all, just as it did when the picture came up on the screen. I have to say it is a beautiful home, but your earlier expression was one of disgust. Whatever your connection to this house is you wish to be as far away from it as possible."

"H-how did you know that?" Brianna asked astonished.

"I told you, my darling, your face. None of us can help making even the smallest expressions when it comes to our emotions. I am just gifted in seeing the signs that are written there, that's what makes me and my pupils so talented in the ways of mediation. We see what people won't or can't say."

Removing another handkerchief from within my pocket, I placed it gently into her hands as she said weakly, "I used to live there with my ex-husband."

"Ah yes, that's what I'm seeing. He was horrible to you, wasn't he?" Brianna lifted her head and nodded, tears gathering at the corners of her eyes. "And from the look the two of you shared, correct me if I'm wrong, this wonderful boy took you away from all of that and now the two of you have a new and loving life together with children on the way. Sometimes I do miss the fortune telling days. Can your story be any more romantic?" Dante said happily while handing a handkerchief of his own to Fabiani who caught several reddish tears from his eyes.

"Thank you, Master, it is quite romantic," Fabiani sniffled and locked eyes with Brianna as she too wiped a tear from her eye. "If the covens don't buy your house from you I'll take up a collection and buy it. I got your back, girl," he said still whimpering slightly.

Dante looked between the two whimpering individuals in the room, and then sighed as he looked at me. "We seem to be the only ones not weeping, my boy." Dante gave Fabiani another second before finally giving him an eye to stop. "Back to work, pupil. It appears we do have a slight conflict of interest here, not that the situation bothers me in any way, but other coven leaders may disagree. They could look at this as a financial advantage for a Warrior, or even a way for Victor to somehow have control because of his connection to you. I know this isn't the case, Cameron, but you must negate all feelings you have about this property, clamp them down, and make them non-existent."

Brianna squeezed my hand, bringing my attention down to her. "Yeah, babe, just act like Devin."

I raised a brow at her while Dante clapped his hands together triumphantly.

"Very well, my boy, I believe we are ready for tomorrow then. You seem well prepared and Fabi will aid you when the bickering begins. Let us hope we all survive unscathed." Dante stepped to stand directly in front of me, shaking my hand vigorously before turning his attention to Brianna and kissing her on both cheeks. "My darling Brianna, I cannot wait until I have the pleasure of your company again."

A second later Dante gracefully flitted out of the room, his white suit glittering behind him. It was amazing what the material of his suit could accomplish without sequins.

"So, Mr. Hottie, we have a big day tomorrow," Fabiani said from my side, although I was still watching Dante's suit as he traveled through the foyer. When I did not give Fabiani my full attention he rose to his toes and whispered in my ear, "He has thirty replicas of that suit in almost every color imaginable. It's almost hypnotic, isn't it?"

I blinked myself to attention and gazed down at Brianna. "With that said, I do not want to hear any other condescending remarks regarding *my* wardrobe."

"Obsession, Cam. You need to call it what it is. That's the first stage in dealing with an addiction."

I turned to Fabiani, who for some reason was sniffing my suit jacket. "You are right, Fabia...ah Fabi, tomorrow is a big day. Will you be able to restrain yourself from smelling me during the presentation?"

Brianna snorted behind me while Fabiani beamed, completely unfazed from being caught. "Don't worry. I'm getting it all out now. Tomorrow my lust for you will fade as it does for so many others. For your own sake don't fall in love with me, Cameron Burke, I couldn't bear it. Brianna, you'll have to work your womanly ways in order to get me out of his head, but I know you can. We both need to be at our best tomorrow. So long, my friends."

With a quick wave and a smile, Fabiani Projected to places unknown.

"I like him," Brianna announced. "What I really like is the fact that he can make even the most stoic of Vampires somehow blush."

"You are referring to me?" I said kiddingly and offering her my arm. As she began to rise, I wrapped my arm around her waist and pulled her to a standing position.

"You'll need to do that full time in a couple of months," she said with a smile.

"And I will love every second of it," I replied and guided us across the foyer and through the front door.

The afternoon had given way to cooler winds and warm yellow street lamps lining the walkways around us. The city lights hid the stars trying to shine through the darkening sky while the moon hung low and glowed in amber tones. The night was setting itself up for a beautiful showing, and my love snuggled underneath my arm trying to protect herself from the coolness of the winds that whipped around us.

"Shall we return to the hotel for some dinner, love?" I asked, squeezing her firmly into my body, though I knew I could produce no body heat for her which pained me.

"No, I've decided that you're taking me on a date."

"Am I now?"

"Yes, since we have never been on one since we met and I think I deserve it since you've knocked me up. Twice, actually. It's the least you could do."

"That goes without saying, angel. One problem, I have never taken anyone on a date. What exactly...do I do?" She looked at me quizzically as I steered her around the other pedestrians navigating the sidewalks. "Bri, you must remember that in my day a man courted a woman through letters and supervised visits for only a short time before marrying her. Our situation is altogether new for me."

Brianna pushed herself away from underneath my arm and entangled her fingers with mine. "Well, let's not go crazy here and just go out to dinner because I could eat a whole cow I'm so hungry."

"A romantic dinner I can do."

She shook her head. "It doesn't even have to be romantic. The place just has to serve an inordinate amount of food."

My laugh was interrupted when my jacket pocket began vibrating causing Brianna to release my hand so that I could retrieve my phone. As I stared at the screen I never thought I would be so happy to see two lines of text.

Offer accepted. When can u move in?

"Angel, how hungry are you?" I asked as I locked the phone and slid it back into my pocket.

"Was the cow reference not effective enough?"

"Could you wait another thirty minutes? We need to drop off a check."

Brianna looked confused for only a moment before she threw her arms around my neck, squealing loudly on the streets of Boston. Her excitement reflected my sentiments exactly. We officially had a home of our own. Now all it needed was a family and we were well on our way.

Chapter Twenty-Six

Brianna

It was like a scene from a movie – a quaint but high end Italian restaurant, beautiful view of the city, candles on the tables, couples whispering words of love to one another over bruschetta. Ooo, bruschetta! My mouth was watering over almost everything on the menu, which I had been scanning for almost ten minutes, unable to make up my mind. Cameron was humoring himself by trying to make small talk about what looked good. Now that we were sitting in a restaurant, reasons why we had never been out to dinner began to surface. Cam couldn't eat. Duh. He must have needed to fake it before, right? Of all the questions I had asked him over the last months, this was not one of them.

"Do we need more time?" the waiter asked next to me.

"No, no! Starving pregnant lady here," I replied quickly, though I still hadn't decided between two things. "I…will…have…" Eenie meanie miney moe. "Bruschetta chicken." Whew, that was actually quite difficult. Tomatoes, garlic, basil, yum, yum, yum.

The waiter jotted my order down and then looked to Cameron. "And for you, sir?"

"What would I like, love?" he asked and raised his brows slightly, urging me to order for him. Oh! That meant I could get the other item I wanted. Best of both worlds! I loved going out to dinner with Cameron. I would never have to make up my mind again.

I smiled broadly up at the waiter. "He'll have the fusilli and broccoli rabe."

The waiter turned to walk away but Cameron held up his fingers. "Would you be able to prepare that without the garlic?"

"Yes of course, sir," the waiter said politely while I pouted.

"But Cam…"

Cameron sighed and shook his head. "Apparently I like garlic more than I think I do," he said to the waiter who gave both of us a curious look before taking our menus and walking away. Cameron leaned over the table, pulling my hand in his. "Do you want me to sleep in the next room tonight?"

"I'm sorry, babe, I just have such a craving for garlic. Which is so weird considering what I have growing inside me," I said. "I'll take a shower and even scrub with mouthwash." Cameron gave me his crooked smile and when I tried to lean over to kiss him my stomach hit the table, not allowing me to get any closer. Seeing my pleading eyes, Cameron smiled and moved his chair to sit on the side of the table next to me rather than across. Once he sat back down, he leaned into me, brushing my hair from my face before kissing me lightly. Unable to stop myself, I placed my hands on either side of his face to keep his lips on mine.

Cameron cupped my hands, gently pulling them from his face and leaning away from me. "Angel, you tempt me more than you realize."

"Sorry," I replied embarrassed, "trying to get in as much as I can before dinner."

He laughed, pulling my hands down to the table where he began stroking them soothingly. With each stroke I felt all the tension leave my body. Even though we had spent almost a week together, between looking at properties and Cameron working well into the evenings finding new ones, we never had time to just be with each other. Finally there were no more demons standing between us. I felt completely safe with him, safe enough to get lost in his big black eyes.

"What are you thinking about, my angel?"

"Oh just hoping that the babies have your eyes."

"My eyes are almost the same as yours."

I shook my head. "Nope, yours are better, but I think we can compromise. My son can have yours while…"

"My daughter has her mother's eyes?"

There was wave of emotion that flashed across Cameron's face.

"How great did that just feel?"

Cameron placed one of his hands on my stomach and immediately there was a fire stirring underneath it. "Wonderful, but in some ways frightening."

"Frightening? You're not the one who has to push two babies out of a hole the size of a golf ball."

"Forgive me, love," he laughed lightly and removed his hand. "I am nervous about raising a daughter. They have so many…different…things." My eye squinted into my best stink eye. "Not that. I mean dolls, tea parties, boys. Good heavens, boys."

"She's not even born yet and you're already worrying about boys? And what about our son?"

"Boys are different."

"Says the man."

The waiter broke up our little debate when he placed a basket of bread and a dish of rosemary and olive oil down on the table. The poor boy barely got his hand away before I dug into the thick crusty bread.

"So what is it we do now on our date?"

"Wewelworwies," I said, spitting a piece of crust over his shoulder. Mama Jo would be mortified. "Sorry," I coughed as I forced the bread down my throat. "We tell stories. You know, funny things that happened in our lives, or secrets we've never told anyone. Stuff like that."

"All right, so tell me a secret no one knows."

"But you know all my secrets."

"Ok, your favorite childhood memory," he asked, taking a slice of bread and breaking off a small piece and rubbing it between his fingers until there was nothing but dust falling onto his bread plate.

"Snow days," I replied, taking another piece of bread.

"Snow days?"

"Mm-hmm. Snow days were great because Mama Jo and I would cook all day. Even though I was only seven she would prop me up on this chair and wrap an apron around me. No doubt we would always make big batches of Mama's famous cornbread. Her trick was to beat the batter with a slotted spoon for eight minutes. Not seven, not nine, eight minutes. I would whine after the first two and she would stand behind me and wrap her hand around mine and help me the rest of the time. Snow days were always just Mama Jo and 'Lil Bri time. It was one of the things I missed most when Shelby took me away. To her, snow days meant she had to take a day off to watch me, and that just pissed her off. What about you? What's your favorite childhood memory?"

"It was so long ago, it is difficult to remember," he said while he took a moment to flip through centuries of memories, and I seized the opportunity to soak my bread into the oil. "Perhaps it was bath day."

"Huh?" I groaned, leaving the piece of bread hanging half out of my mouth and then swallowing it hard. "Day? You only had one?"

"I did not judge your story, love," he scolded and lowered his voice. "Hygiene was very different back then. Some people would rarely bathe more than twice a month let alone every day. However, Ada...er, my father, insisted that we bathe weekly. Even though he was only a farmer he expected me and my sister to conduct ourselves as though we were from the richest of families. He was quite staunch with his rules actually, except on bath day. It was the one day that my sister and I could do almost anything we wanted and get completely filthy and muddy until all you could see were the whites of our eyes through the layers of dirt."

"What color eyes did you have?" I asked.

"Just brown. Not that much different than today."

"Your father's name was Thomas, right?" Cameron nodded, though he looked at the table. "And you called him..."

"Ada."

"Why Ada?"

He shrugged. "My mother said it was because when I was a baby my father would lift me up or pull me into his lap and always say 'A-da boy.' It just stuck I guess."

"I think it's sweet."

"Silly really."

"So you're telling me that if your son or daughter started calling you Ada you would think they were just being silly?"

"No. I see your point but..."

"But nothing, Cam. I'm thirty-two years old and still call Daddy O, Daddy O. Now how silly is that?"

"I am much older than you are."

My stink eye returned. "You weren't always this old, well then again maybe you were. Ok, moving on. Tell me your scariest moment since you were Turned."

"How do you come up with these, my love?"

"It's a gift," I winked.

Once again Cameron went deep into his memory choosing to disintegrate the remainder of his bread and then place the dust back into the basket.

"The scariest moment would have to be only a couple of years after Victor Turned me. We were living in Savannah and quickly found it was difficult to keep a low profile as we had up North."

Cameron lowered his voice once again, leaning in closer to me so that no one else could hear. "Unfortunately a Warrior was caught feeding on a girl in the woods of a neighboring plantation. Superstitions being what they were, a large angry mob came to our home with their crosses and blessed water and started to burn it down.

"Victor ordered everyone to run outside to basically prove we were not what they believed we were, which was fine for everyone but me. I was still sensitive to the sun, so everyone running out to the mob of people acted more like a diversion so that I could be hidden away until nightfall."

"Obviously the plan worked."

"Yes, and Jazlyn did not let me forget that she had to carry me over her shoulder for ten miles through the woods until we found a cave we could hide in."

My face fell, and he certainly noticed the change in my demeanor. "Jazlyn? As in crazy, selfish, Jazlyn?"

I could see the conflict in his eyes, and honestly it worried me a little. "She was not always the way she is now. Jazlyn stayed with me for three days. Running at night and watching over me during the day until we were able to meet up with Father again. I miss who she used to be."

His longing for Jazlyn made me extremely nervous. The flashes of my dream where he left with her arm in arm suddenly had a bit of possibility.

"Of course if I saw her now she would be dead within seconds," he said a moment later and I laughed to myself. Maybe my dream didn't have any merit after all.

Only a few minutes later and our waiter was placing our plates of wonderfully smelling food down in front of us. As the drool began to form at the corners of my mouth I knew there was a possibility that I could finish both plates. I began cutting through my chicken, making sure to have the right proportion of chicken to bruschetta in order to form the most perfect bite. And oh boy was it perfect. Although I was loved my food, I couldn't help but be entranced by Cameron using a fork. It seemed so odd to see him push the pasta around on his plate.

"You do know I have used utensils before."

"Sorry, was I staring?"

Cameron laughed as he loaded his fork and held it in front of my mouth. "Yes, but only for the last twenty-two seconds."

"Oh my god, I don't know which dish is better," I moaned.

"Good thing you do not have to choose since they are really both yours," he said happily as he loaded his fork once more and placed it in my mouth. "So, my love, when you are on a date is it customary that your dearest friend come along?"

"Huh?" I replied confused, but followed his finger as he pointed over my shoulder to Renee knocking on the window and waving wildly at the two of us while John tried to pull her away. "I think our dinner just turned into a double date. Do you mind? I don't have the heart to send her away."

Cameron didn't answer but smiled and waved at the two of them to come inside, and then waved the waiter over to our table. Thankfully it was large enough to fit two more chairs, but I could see a few of the people that were still waiting for a table give Renee and John dirty looks as they came in.

"Ohmygod!" Renee shouted as she entered the dining room and ran over to us almost knocking the waiter down as he placed two more chairs at our table. "See we really are twins! Even in this big ass city our psychic connection pulls us together. This is so weird. We've been trying to get in here for the last couple of weeks but the wait is always so long. How did you get in?"

I smirked. "Cameron tipped the hostess."

"See, John," Renee said as she smacked him in the shoulder, "bribery! That's what we're doing wrong. Oh Cameron, you remember John, right?"

"Yes of course," Cameron replied as he stood from his chair and shook John's hand. "Good to see you again, Dr. Ryan."

"No Dr. Ryan among friends, please just call me John. Wow, Cameron, you need to get the circulation going in these hands. Is our New England weather getting the best of you?" Renee's eyes bugged out of her head, but Cam just laughed as he rubbed his hands together pretending that it would do some good. "Look, I'm sorry we interrupted your dinner, we're not staying."

"Like hell we are," Renee corrected as she sat in the chair next to me.

Cameron gestured to the other empty seat. "John, by all means join us. Otherwise I will be sitting at this table alone since we both know these two will be preoccupied with one another."

"Not true," Renee and I said at the same time and then laughed since we knew it was the absolute truth.

"Cam, do you mind if we trade meals?" I pretended to beg.

"Ohmygod, Bri, I'll take it. That looks fabulous," Renee interrupted and I didn't flinch when she took the plate from my hand and I placed Cameron's in front of me.

"Re!" John said flabbergasted. "You can't just take their food."

Renee turned to John, not stopping her attack on the chicken. "Trust me, he's not going to eat it. Plus I'm starving because I waited to eat until you got home like a big idiot."

"Why are you an idiot?" I asked and smiled when Dr. John rolled his eyes.

"Apparently," Renee began in a huff, "my cooking is so bad that hospital food is better than mine. So Dr. Smartypants over there decides to eat at work before he leaves so that he won't have to eat my food and didn't think I would catch on. Which I did!"

"Oh boy did she," Dr. John moaned, looking to Cameron for support. "So, Cameron, what brings you to Boston?"

Renee dropped her fork loudly onto the plate. "Because he finally got his head out of his ass."

"Re!" Dr. John growled, giving her a stern look, but as always Cameron stayed cool and collected and patted John's shoulder.

"Renee is right, John. I did get my head out of my ass. And thank you both for taking care of Brianna in my absence."

"Of course, anytime. Well, hopefully not…uh you know what I mean. Oh, and congratulations by the way. Twins, wow, that has to be intimidating."

"Only when I think about it," Cameron laughed, and then reached into his inner jacket pocket. "Have you seen the pictures?"

While the two of them began diving into a conversation regarding the ultrasound pictures, Renee leaned into me and said, "Things seem to be going ok."

"Yeah, great actually."

"So you're free to roam the city by yourself now?"

"Ha! You're funny. If Aidan can find me, others can too. So Cameron's always with me, and then there's the addition of a bodyguard that Cam doesn't think I know about." I peered over at Cameron who glanced in my direction, a little surprise in his eyes. I winked at him and he smiled as he turned his gaze back to Dr. John.

"Bodyguard? Where is he? Is he cute?"

"He's outside, I think. And I'm not commenting on his looks."

"So he'll be following you guys around?"

"I guess so. Cameron has some business to take care of the next couple of days so I think this guy is going to babysit me. Oh wait, how about you come and hang out with me? Room service, movies, the works, all at Cam's expense."

Renee placed her hand on Dr. John's, politely interrupting the boy's conversation. "John, honey, you're working tomorrow, right?"

John nodded. "Yeah, tomorrow and Saturday."

"Great, I'm going to stay and babysit Bri while Cameron's working."

"Don't worry, John," I said leaning across the table. "I'll make sure to give her back for Saturday night. I don't want to mess up any birthday plans you have for her. And no, Re, I don't have your present yet. Don't yell at me."

"Yeah, uh that's sounds great," John replied, shifting uncomfortably in his seat. "Just as long as I have her back for Saturday night. Big birthday plans, you know."

"See Bri, at least *someone* plans ahead for my birthday," Renee chided. "So Cameron, what business do you have to take care of? Or am I not allowed to ask?"

Cameron smiled, never surprised by Renee's forwardness. "My family is looking to open up a training facility for our security firm. We have one on the West Coast, and are now looking to expand in the Northeast."

"Are you looking here in Boston?" John asked, unaware of the staring contest Renee was having with the side of my face.

"Yes, in fact we have several properties in mind."

"You know, Cameron, you should buy Bri's house. She's got all that land out there," Renee said, thankfully taking her eyes off of me. "And it would really be justice for Bri's new man to buy the house of her ex-husband."

"And that, my friends, is why Renee is my twin," I laughed. "Ohmygod!" I shouted causing Cameron's hands to fly to my stomach and John to jump out of his chair in full blown ER doctor mode. "What is the matter with you two?"

"Are you ok?" Cameron said in a panic with John just over his shoulder.

"I'm fine! I just remembered that we hadn't told them we're moving to Boston."

"Ohmygod!" Renee shouted, leaping from her chair and hugging me tightly around the shoulders.

"Brianna, never do that to me again," Cameron scolded as he straightened up in his chair.

"Sorry! I was just excited. John you can sit down, honestly I am fine."

Dr. John shook his head as he returned to his seat muttering something that only Cameron heard which made him smile slightly, but only slightly since he was still quite upset with me.

Renee, however, somewhat came to my defense. "You two are ridiculous. I knew nothing was wrong, you guys just haven't figured out the different levels of 'ohmygod.' That was the 'ohmygod I'm so excited about moving to Boston that I forgot to tell my twin about it the minute I saw her.' You boys can just sit your butts in your chairs and I'll tell you when she really needs you. 'Kay? So seriously, you're moving here?"

Cameron nodded. "We purchased a place this afternoon."

"You're shitting me!" Renee shouted causing the entire restaurant to look over and John's head to fall into hands.

"We're totally getting kicked outta here," he grumbled as he rubbed his eyes with his fingers.

"Ok, drama queen," Renee replied, rolling her eyes and digging into the last piece of bruschetta chicken. "So, when are you guys moving in?"

I looked at Cameron since I had no idea. "The house is ours, so we can move in as soon as we get it furnished and transfer a few things from the house in California. Maybe a couple of weeks?" he said as he looked at me hopefully.

"A couple of weeks? Really?" John chimed in. "That has to be the fastest closing on a mortgage ever."

"Actually, no mortgage. We paid for it out right," Cameron replied, and then was covered in bits of bruschetta chicken as it flew across the table from Renee's mouth. But Cameron took it in stride while he wiped his face and shirt clean, and waved for the waiter to give us our check. I think he was really letting the restaurant know that we were leaving since it was only a matter of minutes before they kicked us out. My first double date was a rousing success.

The restaurant was certainly happy to see us go, and Cameron made sure that the waiter was tipped well. Once we stepped outside we all said our goodbyes with hugs and promises of calls the next day. Renee snuggled under Dr. John's arm as they turned and began walking in the opposite direction. Cameron stepped into the street, his arm up ready to hail a cab when I tapped him on his shoulder.

"Can we walk instead?"

Cameron turned, unsure if I knew what I was really asking. "Are you sure? It is about ten blocks, you must be cold."

"Then give me your jacket."

In a flash his suit jacket was off and wrapped around my shoulders. I held the jacket closed with one hand and tucked myself under his arm while we walked down the sidewalk. Now I was warm, surrounded by his comforting scent, and taking an evening walk with the man I loved. It was the perfect end to our date. The only thing it needed was a kiss. I turned my face to him, nudging his side slightly and he immediately responded with a kiss. On my nose.

"Is my breath that bad?"

"Unfortunately the pungency is not just in your breath."

"I might have some gum," I said while fumbling around in my purse.

"Garlic and spearmint? Even better," he replied smugly. Knowing that hitting him in the ribs would do nothing, I simply breathed heavily in his face. His eyes fluttered from the stench, causing him to wave his hand in front of his face while he said, "So you know about Hugo."

"Who?"

"Your bodyguard. His name is Hugo," he replied nodding his head to the Vamp across the street. "So how did you know?"

I looked up him. "I saw you talking to him earlier and then I kept seeing him wherever we went. Is he part of Dante's coven?"

"No, he is a former Warrior trying to win back Father, you might say." Since the man was only a few feet away and could hear every word we were saying, I didn't want to push on getting the scoop on what he'd done to upset Victor. "So, angel, are you going to tell me the reason you wanted to walk?"

"Wanting to be held by you while we enjoy a beautiful night together isn't enough?"

He squeezed me tighter into his side, kissing the top of my head. "It certainly is for me, however, I know there is another reason."

"How do you know these things?" I replied flustered and then sighed in defeat. "Ok, I really want something sweet. Now don't judge me, I know I just ate a truckload of food, but seriously I need something sweet and something salty. These kids are already driving me crazy with cravings. And neither of them wants the same thing."

"I am sure that the hotel will have something that will suffice."

"Ugh, I've already eaten their food. I want something different."

"Of course you do."

"I said no judging."

"Yes, angel."

"Now that's more like it."

"I would not get used to it."

"Please! Who are you trying to kid? You are always a pushover when it comes to me."

Cameron continued to look straight ahead and tried not to smile. "You are my only weakness."

"For now. This little girl is going to have you wrapped around her little finger."

"Just like her mother," he replied lovingly and kissed me lightly on the temple.

"Oh look! There's a place," I said pointing down a small side street to a bakery.

We were definitely in one of the historic districts of the city since the sidewalks and the street were nothing but brick and cobblestone. As I began to cross the narrow street, Cameron pulled on my arm. "Bri, are you sure you would not rather go back to the hotel?"

I looked back at him confused. Didn't we just have this conversation?

"I'm sure, Cam. It'll just take a second and then we can catch a cab if you want."

Cameron sighed as he helped me cross the street but when I went to open the door to the bakery he suddenly looked uncomfortable.

"You go ahead, I need to speak to Hugo for a second," he said, taking his jacket from my shoulders. After he stepped away from me, walking towards Hugo who was now coming down the sidewalk, he quickly turned back to me still preoccupied with something. "Do you need money?"

"Uh, no. I have money. Cam, are you ok?"

"Fine," he replied and turned away again.

Yeah, well that was a big fat lie, but he walked away so fast that I couldn't call him out. The smell of chocolate was somehow seeping through the walls and pulled me through the door. The shop wasn't large by any means, but had a bakery case that spanned the length of the store and several small round tables piled high with displays of gift wrapped chocolates and other confections. Could they wrap up a whole table if I asked nicely?

"Is there anything I can help you with?" the young girl asked from behind the bakery case. She couldn't be more than eighteen, and didn't weigh more than a hundred pounds. I hated her. Not really, but in my current state I kind of did.

I stepped closer to the brightly lit bakery case and suddenly my brain began to panic over the number of choices that I had.

"There is no way I'll be able to make up my mind before you have to close. I need something sweet but want something salty."

The young girl smiled and waved me over to the far side of the case. "Maggie likes to call these the pregnant lady special."

She reached into the case with a thin sheet of paper and handed me a long chocolate covered pretzel stick. It was almost as though she was handing me the Holy Grail. As the pretzel crunched in my mouth, the salt mixed with the chocolate in perfect harmony.

"I'll take a dozen, please."

The young girl laughed as she grabbed a box from behind the counter and began filling it with the pregnant lady special. Once she finished, she waved me over to the register just as the little bell rang announcing another customer.

"These really are wonderful," I said. "You should have a gift box prepared for expectant fathers."

"That's what I told Maggie," she laughed as she rung up my order and I handed her my money. "Uh, sir? Can I help you?"

I looked to my left to see Cameron standing only a couple of feet away staring up at a narrow wooden staircase that led up to the second floor. The sight hit me in the face causing my cheeks to flush with realization. The wide wooden planked floor, the low exposed beams and antique windows that gave the shop its historic look also brought its troubling past to life.

"No, he's with me. He...uh...has a thing for stairs," I said, trying to joke with her since I could see she thought Cam was some weird creepy guy. She smiled half-heartedly and handed me my bakery box and change, still uncomfortable with Cameron's comatose state in front of the stairs. Carefully I wrapped my hand around his, pulling him gently toward the door. His body came with me, but his head was still staring up at the door at the top of the stairs.

Silently we left the bakery and began our walk down the sidewalk toward a busier street where Cameron immediately hailed a cab. Once inside I was grateful for the heat, but the silence from Cam was still giving me a chill. Not knowing what else to do I opened my bakery box and began devouring my second chocolate covered pretzel. My fingers were still entwined with Cameron's, but the butterflies flared in my stomach when his thumb began to gently caress the side of my hand. He was coming back to me, there were finally signs of life returning and I couldn't help but rest my head on his shoulder. There were so many emotions silently passing between us that it was almost unbearable.

"I love you, Cam," I whispered, squeezing my eyelids together to hold back the tears that were forming as he kissed my hair and rested his head on top of mine.

"And I am a better man for it, my love."

Cameron's body began to relax as the cab put more distance between us and the bakery. And though the lid of the box in my lap said Maggie's Bakery and Sweets in bright scrolling red letters, I knew without a doubt that it was also known as the former residence of Cameron and Chloe Burke.

Chapter Twenty-Seven

Cameron

My suit was perfectly pressed, charcoal striped shirt neat and crisp, shoes highly shined. However, nothing could raise my spirits today. It would be a long and trying day of negotiations, but an even more emotional morning that would affect me to my core. Today I would finally close the door to my past. If I were human I would be vomiting about now.

Brushing my hand through my hair one last time, I nervously pulled at my collar before turning away from the mirror within the armoire and closing the doors securely. Brianna muttered something unintelligible as she rolled over in the bed. I knelt down in front of her, placing my head where she had shrugged off the sheets, exposing her round belly bulging out from underneath her thin camisole.

"Be good to your mother today, my precious ones," I whispered and kissed Bri's stomach softly. She stirred slightly but did not wake as I rose and kissed her on her forehead. Dante was right, she was glowing. I had to kiss her once more, pressing my cheek against hers as I whispered, "I love you, my angel. Hugo is right outside."

"Mmm-hmm," she moaned sleepily. "Yugo is on the slide."

I smiled, realizing how Brianna could always pick my spirits up. When I let her, of course. I completely shut down last night and it was unforgivable, especially after everything I had put her through the last couple of months. Her amazing silent understanding solidified my decision to make a stop before heading to Dante's. It was time.

After one last kiss on her forehead, I tucked my leather portfolio under my arm and headed to the door. I was leaving Brianna in Hugo's care, and although I did not know him particularly well, he was once a Warrior. It also helped that Devin vouched for him. Hugo had fallen from Victor's favor over sixty years ago for becoming a hit man for the mob. He of course was quite successful at it, unfortunately causing it to come to Victor's attention. Victor always felt that his circle of Vampires had to kill for the protection of others, but were not in the business of killing. Hugo was one of only three Warriors that had not received a visit from Devin after they had upset Victor. But Hugo was an interesting case because he continued to try to be reinstated in our coven. Many had told him that Victor would never grant such a request, but Hugo was determined and he certainly had the time to wait Victor out.

"Coming out," I said softly before opening the door and finding Hugo in the same black suit and dark sunglasses I had left him in the night before. He was tall and fit like most Warriors, but he had extremely broad shoulders and thick muscular legs. Overall he was not as intimidating as Alexander, but most people would choose to turn around and walk the opposite direction rather than have to pass by him. Our hotel room was at the end of the corridor, strategically selected since few people would come this far down the hall and also because there was an emergency exit right across from the door.

"Good morning, Hugo," I said quietly as the hotel door clasped behind me.

"Good morning, Cameron. Brianna isn't going with you today?"

"No, not today. And although she hates it, she knows to stay inside. The only people that should be coming down this way are room service and possibly a friend of Bri's named Renee Snider. She is the red head who joined us for dinner last night."

"Very good then. Will you only be gone during the day?"

I sighed. "I am hoping to be back by this evening, but I will not guarantee it. Hugo, I know you are good at what you do, but my entire life is in that room."

Hugo removed his sunglasses and then extended his hand to me. "And I will protect her with mine. You can count on me, Cameron." I shook his hand and reluctantly pushed my feet forward. After taking only three steps Hugo asked, "Do you really think this will help me get back in?"

I turned my head slowly, shrugging slightly as I did not want to lie to him.

"Hugo, you know how Father is. But protecting his grandchildren has to account for something. I will be sure to put in a good word for you, on my honor I will."

Hugo nodded again, placing his sunglasses back on and then clasping his hands low in front of him as he settled into his bodyguard posture. My feet felt like lead as I made my way down the hall. Just as I approached the elevator I felt my pocket vibrating with an incoming call.

"Good morning, Jared," I answered.

"Not for me, bro, I'm getting ready to go to bed," he laughed.

"I am getting into an elevator, I may lose reception."

"Oh bullshit, that's such an..." the elevator door shut "...ol...Cam...there...C...ron...what...the...got...be...ki...ing...me..." Jared continued his rant as I traveled slowly down to the lobby of the hotel. When the doors finally opened I heard him say, "Seriously are you just messing with me?"

"Jared, I assure you I am not."

"Were you encased in lead or something? For fuck sake take the stairs next time, my time is precious and I charge by the hour."

"I thought it was by the minute, actually."

He laughed as I stepped out of the hotel and began walking with many of the other Bostonians making their way to work.

"Are you outside now? It's so loud all of a sudden. Doncha have that big meeting with the snooty coven people?"

"Yes that starts at nine, but I am going to the bakery first."

Jared paused before he spoke. "Like just an ordinary old bakery, or the bakery, *bakery*?"

My youngest brother always did have a way with words. "Yes, my former home that is now a bakery."

"Is Beebs with you?"

"No, I thought it best to do this myself."

"Bri would understand, bro, you know she would."

"She has enough to worry about right now. I do not wish to burden her."

"You all right?"

"Yes...no. No, I am not, but I will be."

"Well, you know that if you need to talk, you can always call Alex. He's there for ya, bro," he laughed.

"So, little brother, since your time is so precious, why have you called? Do you have information for me?"

"Dude, I am the keeper of some major intel. It's amazing the funds I lose helping my brothers out. I need to rethink the family discount." I cleared my throat trying to get him back on track. "Ok yeah, so after you left I went to Maddy and had her pull Natasha Cushlin's file to see what she had down for her family and contacts and stuff. Plain as day, mother and father listed as Marla and Charles Cushlin, and one sister – Nikki Cushlin."

"So Lanashell did put them together somehow," I said as I stepped off the curb and took a gamble at crossing street without getting hit by a speeding cab. Not that it would hurt me, but how would I explain the damage to the car?

"Yeah, Lana proved my girlfriend is a liar."

"I cannot believe you call her your girlfriend. She is not there with you now, is she?"

Jared laughed. "Please, bro, I can't have her spending the night in my crib all the time. That's just way too much commitment for me. Besides she kinda snores when she's sleeping, and then there's this thing she does with the covers…"

"Jared," I said firmly.

"Crap! Sorry."

"Nikki is a liar about her family, what else?"

"Yeah, so that night I started telling her that I'd heard the story about this girl Natasha who got really hurt down at the Facility, and you were right, dude. She totally got interested and almost started to cry when I told her what happened. So with that I started digging into DMV records and Social Security."

"And you found everything?"

"That's just it. I didn't find anything. If she is working for Elaina, they wanted to make sure no one knew she existed."

"Has she been making any phone calls?"

"Nope, I'm tracking it. I also slipped a tracker on her. Two, actually."

"Two, why two?"

"Totally pulled an Elaina and put a tracker in Nikki's ring like they did with Beebs. Figured that if she goes back to them they'll be looking for it and they'll probably find the one in the ring and be done with it. So I put a subcutaneous tracker in a place she'll never see, and she'll never let them look."

"Nice work, little brother."

"Doncha wanna know where it is? Come on, bro, ask me!"

"Really, Jared, I…"

"Under her butt cheek! Isn't that awesome?"

"Jared," I sighed, "how can you do these things to her and still call her your girlfriend?"

"Bro, I heard enough of that from Beebs the other day."

"I know you did, but has it not crossed your mind that she may be using you just as much as you are using her?"

"Of course it has."

"Then why let her get so close to you?"

"Because you told me to."

"I did not mean close to your heart."

"I'm waiting to be proven wrong, ok? She's not a complete sociopath."

I could not help but shake my head. Jared had fallen for her, and there was no use pushing him any further. He had made up his mind, and only physical proof of her betrayal against us would convince him she was doing so.

"For your sake, Jared, I hope we are proven wrong. I must go, I have arrived at the bakery."

"Ok, bro, uh listen if you do need to talk once you're done, you know you can call me. I was just kidding before."

"Thank you, Jared, I know."

"Shit, I almost forgot. I totally cracked the CIA, can't believe I didn't tell you."

"Be careful with that," I warned.

"Trust me, they keep me on my toes. Anyway, I got access to their facial recognition software."

"How does that help us?"

Jared sighed into the phone. "Do I have to explain everything?"

"Apparently."

"I took the images we have of Elaina and put a search out for her."

"Seriously? You…you can do that?"

"Well, it's more like by location. I don't want to set off too many bells. So I've put a search out in Boston since you guys are there. If she pops up on any cameras I'll get an alert on my computer. It's pretty fucking awesome if you ask me."

"Yes, little brother, that is awesome."

"Go on, say it like you mean it. I know you want to say it."

"Fine, it is *fucking* awesome. May I go now?"

"Yeah, good luck today...on...uh whatever it is you're doing."

"Thank you, Jared."

"Bye, bro."

After ending the call I placed the phone in my jacket pocket and took in a deep breath before opening the door to Maggie's Bakery and Sweets. The images were still fresh in my mind of Brianna standing only inches from where I laid unconscious before being dragged up to the second floor and killed. My past had finally caught up with me. It was time to put an end to it all, and the pain would be excruciating.

The door chimed as I entered, and I noticed that the same young woman from last night was behind the counter giving me the same scared look.

"Can I help you, sir?" she asked.

"Actually, I need to speak with Maggie."

The girl raised her eyebrows. "Is she expecting you?"

"Probably not, but it is quite important." She sighed and walked down the length of the bakery case and into the back room. Although she was whispering I could still hear her as she said, "Maggie, Maggie! Remember that creepy guy I was telling you about?"

"Yeah," Maggie's familiar voice replied.

"He's here and asking for you."

"Great, why are creepy guys always looking for me?" she replied. "Why can't some drop-dead gorgeous millionaire come through that door and marry me instead?"

A second later Maggie came bursting through the curtain that separated the back room from the rest of the store. "Maggie, all this time I thought you were already married."

"Mr. Burke!" she shouted as she began feverishly wiping her flour covered hands on her apron before shaking my hand. "Debbie, this is Mr. Burke, *my landlord*, Mr. Burke."

The young woman, now known as Debbie, stood just behind Maggie with her eyes wide while waving awkwardly at me.

"Mr. Burke, what do I owe the honor? You did get my check, didn't you?" she asked, suddenly worried.

"Yes of course, Maggie. In ten years you have never been late, but that is not why I am here. I am doing some business here in Boston and wanted to come in and make sure everything was still running well."

Maggie nodded her head. "Oh yes, everything is fine."

"That is good to hear," I responded uncomfortably and finding the floor.

"Would you mind if…I…went upstairs for a few minutes?"

"Yes of course. It's your place, you can do whatever you want. There are a bunch of boxes up there, feel free to move anything if you need to."

I thanked her as I placed my leather portfolio on the counter and then turned slowly to the stairs behind me. A shutter went through my body as memories of my shattered leg thudding up each step echoed in my ears. I had only come back here a handful of times, and each time I relived every second of my last moments as a human with absolute clarity. I could feel Maggie's and Debbie's eyes upon me as I entered my former living quarters and closed the door behind me.

"Seriously, Maggie, that doesn't creep you out? What the heck is he doing up there?" I heard Debbie ask through the thin floors.

"I choose not to judge. He's the best landlord a girl could have. Even though he lives out in California, if there's anything that needs to be fixed it is done immediately, and the rent is dirt cheap. So if all he asks is to go upstairs, I honestly don't care. He could tell me that he wanted to go up to the roof and slide down the drainpipe naked and I'd let him as long as he doesn't up my rent. Didn't you say his wife was with him last night?"

"Wife or baby mama, one of the two. What do you think went on up there?"

"Debbie, it's none of our business. Now get going, those muffins aren't going to put themselves in the case."

There were other mutterings but I tuned them out as my surroundings began to cave in on me. There were large cardboard boxes all around me, but I knew what lied beneath. I was numb and working on autopilot as I walked to the far end of what used to be my living area. There were boxes piled high in front of the fireplace and one by one I moved them to stand up against the wall. The floor was aged with centuries of dust and grime, but I could still see the dark discolorations within the grain where my family and I bled to death. Not caring about my suit I knelt to the ground. My hand shook as my fingers rubbed the wood, bringing up splinters of the blackened floor.

"Chloe," I whispered as I flattened my palm onto the floor where she had been tied to a chair and killed. "My shy Chloe. I am so…so sorry."

My voice waivered as years of grief filled me and watery red tears dripped to the floor. I reached into my inner jacket pocket and removed one of the many handkerchiefs I had for Brianna's hormonal moments. Just the thought of her solidified why I was here – to finally lay Chloe and Christian to rest.

Taking a deep breath I licked my lips and nervously ran my fingers through my hair. "Chloe, when I was with you I was the happiest man alive. Things were easy and quiet for us, and I did love you, so very much. I should have been here that night." I placed my palm back down on the floor as if I could transfer my feelings into the stain. "I should have died…with you, instead of you. I have never forgiven myself for not being with you, not protecting you…" I paused as another wave of emotion hit me, "a-and our son. I have tortured myself over what you must have gone through that night, and I have never given myself a reprieve. But now…I think Victor is right. There are greater things at work here.

"I…I have met someone. Her name is Brianna, and she…she has saved me, Clo. I have become a better man because of her. We are having twins, and for the first time I absolutely believe fate brought us together specifically for these children. They are destined for great things, and I feel it, Chloe, I really believe it now. But I cannot be a father and a husb…or whatever Bri will have me as, without…" Another tear began to streak down my face and I let it fall as I bent over and placed my head to the floor, allowing two centuries worth of pent up emotion flow out of my body and into the floorboard. "I-I have to let you…go, Chloe. You need peace, and I want…need to love Brianna with all that I have. She is my love in death as you were my love in life. I will never forget our life together, but I have to move on."

With my forehead still on the floor, I twisted it to my right as I stretched my right arm to another darkened area of the floor. "My son," I said breathlessly through the wet bloody tears leaking into my mouth. "You were my greatest achievement. You will always be my f-first born son. My brave boy. I was always so…so proud of you. I struggle with how scared you must have been that night, wondering where I was and why I was not there to…to…"

My emotions finally consumed me and I did not count the minutes that went by as I released the painful hold my love and guilt had on me. When the tears finally stopped, I wiped my face once more and sat back onto my knees.

"Goodbye, my loves," I sighed deeply, wiping my face with the handkerchief once again. "May your souls be at peace."

I brushed myself off as I stood from the floor, taking one last look at the discolored floor before putting the boxes back in their place. Next to the door hung an old cracked mirror which allowed me to make myself presentable before heading back downstairs. I looked around the room and now no longer saw the images of my tortured family. Instead I smiled as I envisioned little Christian running through the room, a bright smile on his face while Chloe cheerfully chased after him. When their ghostly images faded, I said goodbye for a final time and opened the door.

Walking down the stairs I could feel the weight being lifted from my chest. Everything that I had held onto out of grief and guilt had finally dissolved. There was only one last item to take care of in order to cut all ties to my past.

"Maggie?" I inquired as I stepped off the last step in time to see her walk through the back room's curtain.

"Everything ok, Mr. Burke?"

"Yes," I answered softly, but truthfully. "Yes, everything is fine. Do you have a few minutes to talk business?" Maggie swallowed hard and nodded. "Do not worry, I am not looking to raise your rent."

She laughed uncomfortably. "What makes you think I was worried?"

"The floors are thin," I replied as I pointed up to the ceiling and noticed her cheeks flush with embarrassment. Maggie opened her mouth to apologize, but I cut her off. "Maggie, I have decided to sell the building."

Maggie's face fell. "Sell? B-but why?"

"I need a change. This place has been in my family for generations." And generations, and generations. "I have been reluctant to let it go, but like I said, I need to makes some changes. Of course, I would like to offer it up to you before I place it on the market. Is that something you would be interested in?"

"Oh, Mr. Burke," Maggie sighed as she nervously wiped her hands on her apron. "If it were any other year I'd find a way."

"I will sell it to you for one dollar," I interrupted. "My…wife of sorts, did a similar thing a few weeks ago with some of her property." Maggie was speechless and frozen to the floor. I stepped over to the counter and opened my black leather portfolio, removing the latest copy of the deed. "Now your rent was mainly going towards maintenance, taxes, insurance and whatnot. Since you were able to keep up on your payments you should not have any trouble going forward. That is of course if you even want to stay here. If not I can…"

"No, no, Mr. Burke, of course I want to stay here."

"Good. Then sign here."

I offered her my pen and she took it with a shaking hand.

"Mr. Burke, I...I can't. This isn't fair to you."

"Maggie, you are giving me a gift by taking this building away from me."

The pen shook in her hand while she signed below my signature. A second later the pen fell to the floor as she threw her arms around me and began to cry in the crook of my neck.

"Th-thank you, thank you. I will never forget this," she cried as she lowered herself back down to the floor. "Anytime you're in town, everything is on the house, for the rest of your life. Oh, and your wife too!"

I laughed. "That is a tall order, Maggie. We are thinking of moving here and she is having twins. She may just put you out of business."

"She got the pregnant lady special, didn't she?" I laughed and nodded. "Debbie, wrap up another box of chocolate pretzels with the biggest bow you can tie. I hope red ribbon is ok, it's all we have."

"Maggie, you do not have to do this."

"Like hell I do. You just gave me a building, the least I can do is give you some pretzels for your pregnant wife."

I paused, reveling in the sound of Brianna being my wife. I glanced up at the upstairs door one more time and then said, "She loves red ribbons."

I had spent more time at Maggie's than I had expected to, so now I was hurrying to Dante's with my portfolio under my arm, a dollar in my pocket, and a white box of chocolate covered pretzels tied up beautifully with a bright red ribbon.

Just as I stepped onto the crosswalk, my jacket pocket began vibrating. Honestly I was not in the mood to speak to anyone, but when I noticed Victor's name come across the screen I knew I did not have a choice.

"Good morning, Father."

"Therein lies the problem," he grumbled. Even though he did not have an ounce of sun sensitivity, he still hated being awake during the day. "Why does it sound like you are outside?"

"Because I am outside, Father. I am walking to Dante's now."

"You're not there already?!"

"Father," I responded calmly, "I still have a few minutes before the meeting. Dante has prepared me well. I assure you everything will be fine."

"Ha," he scoffed, "just wait. You will have to restrain yourself from strangling the phone like I have to. Now why is it you are just going to Dante's now?"

"I stopped by the shop this morning."

"Why? Why on earth would you do that on a day like today? You know how important this is."

"I sold it, Father."

"Oh, I see. Very interesting," he said slowly in his low raspy voice. "So you have sold your past, and now Brianna is trying to do the same."

"I do not think I follow, Father," I lied.

"Do not be smart with me, child. Dante forwarded all the property materials a couple of hours ago. Don't think I didn't notice the property in Connecticut. I know its Brianna's."

"Father, you know I cannot divulge any specifics. You have to be impartial just like everyone else." Everyone else except me, Dante, and Fabiani.

"This is why I do everything myself. I hate being in the dark."

"Father, you are never in the dark and you know it. Everything will be fine, have a little faith in me today."

Victor sighed deeply into the phone. "Cameron, I have the utmost confidence in you. I always have."

"What about Devin?" I asked and shocked even myself.

"What about your brother?"

"Do you have as much confidence in him as you do in me?"

"Of…of course I do. Child, where is this coming from?"

"I think you need to tell him that, Father."

"Devin knows I trust him."

"He thinks you will only let him lead the family if I am by his side," I said, lowering my voice so that the people around me could not hear.

"That is my preference."

"But it is not mine, Father. I have a family now, or will in a few months' time. I cannot see myself dropping everything to lead the Warriors. Devin should not be made to feel that he is not good enough simply because I do not share his desire. You hurt him more than you know, Father. If you truly have the kind of faith in him as you do me, I am begging you to tell him."

"Are you finished?"

"Yes, Father," I replied just as the phone line died. That went well. I did not even want to think about what his response would be when I told him that I would not be coming home. But that would need to wait for another day.

As I turned down Dante's street, the cell phone began vibrating in my hand. Goodness I was popular today and truly did not want to be.

"This is Cameron."

"Cameron! Thank god I caught you, it's John Ryan. How are ya?"

"Good. Is everything all right?"

"No, actually. I am shit up a creek, man, and I'm hoping you can help me or else Renee is going to cut my balls off."

I laughed. "I will certainly do what I can. What is the issue?"

"Well," John laughed nervously, "I thought Renee's birthday was next Saturday, not tomorrow Saturday. I've been working so many hours lately I barely know what day it is and got my weeks mixed up. I made dinner reservations at this hoity-toity place that she's been bugging me about that takes weeks to get into and they can't change the date. I'm screwed, man, and I don't know what to do. I haven't been here long enough to call in any favors and I thought maybe you might have some kind of connections, anything that may be able to help me."

I felt for him. With someone as high-strung as Renee, there was no room for error.

"John, I will be in meetings all day today, but I will enlist the help of my sister-in-law, Kyla."

"You mean, *the* Kyla?"

"Yes, that one. She is the only person I know that could make something happen."

"We should probably not tell Renee that Kyla was involved."

"Have no fear, she and I will work together and in the strictest of confidence."

"Cameron, buddy, this has to be special, I mean really special."

"Of course, but may I ask what makes this birthday so unique?"

John adjusted the phone loudly, seemingly cupping his hand around the receiver as he whispered, "I'm going to ask her to marry me."

Chapter Twenty-Eight

Brianna

The crisp autumn night was beautiful from the rooftop, the city lights reflecting off the sheen of an earlier rain. Cameron's cool fingers were gliding gently up and down the back of my arm while he held me tightly against him swaying slightly, almost dancing. A small candlelit table for two was set behind us tucked inside a quaint three-walled tent that allowed for a stunning view of the city.

Cameron turned to lead me to the table, but after only two steps I tugged gently at his hand urging him to turn back to me.

"You humble me when you look at me like that, my love."

"I...I need to ask you something," I stuttered, squeezing his hand in mine.

"Anything, angel," he replied, taking a step back to me and placing his hand onto my round baby belly.

"Will...well someday, n-not today but someday down the road, will you...marry me? Someday?"

Cameron's mouth dropped as his eyebrows rose in shock. "Of course I will marry you, Brianna. I...I would have certainly asked you if I thought for a moment you would have said yes. Oh Bri, my Bri," he shouted as he swept me off my feet and spun me around. His excitement was still obvious as he carefully lowered me to the floor and began shaking his head.

"What's the matter, Cam?"

"This does not feel right without a ring. I wonder if I have anything that will..." he said as he began patting down his pockets.

"But I have a ring," I said as I looked down at my sapphire ring, noticing for the first time that my form fitting dress was the same color – Cam's favorite color. Easily I removed the ring from my right hand and offered it to him.

He took the ring and gently raised my left hand to his chest as he slid the ring onto my finger. I took both of his hands and placed them on my pregnant belly as he lowered his head and pressed his lips against mine. From underneath his hands I could feel my stomach stretch and expand to look like I was many months pregnant.

Cam's lips went still. I pulled away from him and found two cold black eyes staring back at me.

"Cam?"

He didn't even blink as he stared blankly into my eyes and abruptly removed his hands from my stomach.

"I must leave," he said and took a step backward.

"What do you mean you have to leave? Wait, Cameron, I'll come with you."

"No, Brianna."

"No? What do you mean no?"

From behind him the rooftop door opened and a slim figure slinked out from the opening, her long silky black hair billowing all around her. Jazlyn.

"Cameron, what's going on, w-why's she here?"

"Remember, love, I am not who you think I am," Cameron said flatly as Jazlyn came to stand next to him.

"Stop this, Cameron, stop this right now!"

"Come, brother, we must go," she said as she curled her arm around Cameron's elbow and pulled him toward the door.

"Get away from him," I screamed at her while trying to remove her hand from his arm.

Jazlyn grabbed my left hand firmly, crushing it to the point of breaking. "Brianna, not all is what it seems."

I woke with a start, tears streaming down my cheeks while my babies fluttered feverishly in my belly.

"I'm sorry, I'm sorry," I said in a panic as I rubbed my stomach trying to sooth them, my hand throbbing where Jazlyn had squeezed it. My heart was racing and I felt small beads of sweat drip down the back of my neck. The babies were in a panic because I was, and I felt unbelievably guilty.

My cell phone was beeping from the nightstand, yelling at me that it was low on battery. Grabbing it quickly I immediately called Cameron. It was day two of the negotiations from hell and I wouldn't dream about interrupting, but I needed him to talk me down.

Cameron answered before the first ring was even finished. "Bri! Are you all right?"

"The babies are fine, but I need to talk to you."

"Let me get into another room," he said with the sound of strong voices behind him. A second later the voices were gone, and I heard the clicking of a door shutting. "I am alone now, angel."

"Cam, I'm sorry you know I'd never…" I tried say, but couldn't finish as I became weepy with tears.

"Please, love, do not cry. Do you need me to come to the hotel?"

"No, no, I just had a really bad dream and needed to talk to you, but if you need to get back…"

"I will not go back until you tell me what is upsetting you."

Just hearing his voice was calming me down. I tugged on the blankets and pulled them securely around me as I asked, "Have you seen Jazlyn lately?"

"Of course not. Why would you think…was that part of your dream?"

"She made an appearance."

He sighed. "I am going to tell Dante I need to go to you."

"No, don't. I just needed to talk to you. I'm fine really."

Cameron sighed. "Is Renee still with you?"

"I kept falling asleep so I told her to go on home. She said she had to leave anyway. Apparently Dr. John has some big plans for them tonight. And thank goodness for that, I still haven't gotten her birthday present. I'm such a horrible friend."

"I told you last night I had Renee's gift taken care of, remember?"

I groaned. "No. These babies are sucking my brains out of me. I'm sorry, Cam. I really didn't want to bother you."

"Are you sure you do not want me to come to you?"

"I'm sure. I'm going to try and go back to sleep, these babies are kicking my butt today."

I could hear Cameron chuckling. "Sleep, my love. I am hoping to be done here within the hour. I will come bearing gifts, and lots of love for you. Please call if you need me, everyone will understand if I need to leave. Fabiani is the one really doing the work now."

"Wake me up when you get here, ok? I love you."

"Always, my angel."

Just as I hung up the phone a soft knock came from the door.

"I'm ok, Hugo."

"Very good, ma'am," he replied.

Ma'am? Yuck! I was going to be a mom, I guess I was officially a ma'am. My head was suddenly very heavy as it sank deeper into my ultra-soft pillow. Though I was afraid of what I might see I couldn't stop my eyelids from closing.

"Bri Bri, you listen to me," Shelby said firmly in the scolding voice. "That man is a Vampire. And one thing I know about Vampires is that they don't love anyone but themselves."

"Cameron does love me."

"He loves this," she said, slapping the veins on my wrist. "They only care about where their blood is coming from. That's all you are to him, a blood bag, Bri Bri."

"No, it's not true. He loves me, and nothing you say will make me think otherwise. I'm having his children."

"It doesn't mean anything, don't you understand that? He's taken what he wanted. Now he's going to leave you just like your father abandoned me."

"Eris loved you and all you could think about was yourself and becoming a Vampire. I am nothing like you. I have a man that loves me."

"Then where is he? Where is your precious Cameron?" Shelby smiled when I didn't answer. "You don't know, do you? Trust me, Bri Bri, you're going to end up just like me - alone with a baby you don't want."

Suddenly I felt the cold silver handle of my dagger in my hand. There was a burning in my stomach, but it wasn't the babies. It was thirty-two years of anger and hatred and resentment for the tiny blonde woman that stood in front of me.

"That's the difference between you and me, Shelby. I will love my children, whether Cameron comes back or not. I would give my life for them if I needed to and not just to blackmail someone into making me a Vampire, unlike you." The dagger in my hand began to shake as the thought of how Shelby had slashed her wrists and tried to stab herself in the abdomen so many years ago. "Let me help you finish what you started," I shouted as the anger consumed me and my dagger disappeared into her stomach.

Shelby's eyes flashed with shock and then slowly emptied with life as her blood drained onto my hand and arm.

"Dad! Dad, help me! Please, Eris," I screamed while my mother's blood continued to gush from her wound.

The scene around me finally dissolved in a spinning whirlpool of colors until I was sitting on a long deck chair surrounded by the sight and sound of the sea. My father's arms were wrapped securely around me as he held me close to his chest. When my breathing finally calmed, I lifted my head to see Eris's concerned eyes looking at me and his brown wavy hair hanging uncharacteristically loose around his shoulders.

"I killed her, I...I'm going to k-kill my m..."

My stuttering became unintelligible as I began sobbing again, my head falling back into my father's chest.

"You do not know that for sure," he said softly.

"Have I ever been wrong?"

"You have not always been right."

"Places are wrong sometimes, but the actions are always the same. I-I c-can't believe I...Has Sera seen anything?" I asked, lifting up to see him shaking his head. "Were you busy? I didn't mean to interrupt anything."

Eris put his fingers to my lips. "I will always come to my daughter if she needs me. That's what a father is for. It is odd that this has never been the ending to this dream, I wonder what has changed."

"Maybe the hormones are throwing my dreams off," I replied and wiped my eyes, allowing me to look out at the ocean. "I miss this view."

"And it misses you," he winked at me. "But not as much as me and Sera."

I rested my head on his shoulder. "I'm sorry I haven't called. It's been a little crazy lately, but things should be calming down now."

Eris gave me a skeptical look. "And why is that?"

"Cameron and I bought a house," I said proudly.

"Oh you and Cameron? I take it things have been resolved?"

I nodded my head and sighed. "I'm sorry, I told you things have been crazy, and I've been an awful daughter. Sera must be so mad at me. I'll call her tomorrow, or maybe tonight..."

Eris held up his hands. "Brianna, do not worry yourself. We are fine, missing you of course, but I'll admit I check in on you from time to time."

"Stalker," I said, nudging him in the shoulder.

"Stalker and father sometimes must be the same man. So you have bought a house with the Warrior. Where may I ask?"

"In...Boston," I answered tentatively.

Eris's face fell slightly, but he tried to hide his disappointment. "Show me."

"Huh?"

"Think about your new house, and show me around."

"Oh, duh," I replied and quickly thought about the kitchen of my new home. Boy that sounded good. A second later I was standing in front of the island in the open kitchen, the balcony doors open causing the sheer white curtains to billow inside.

"This is the kitchen, dining room through there," I said pointing to the adjacent room and then grabbing my father's arm and walking him down the hall to the bedrooms. "This will be the twin's room. Oh god, I didn't tell you I was having twins."

Eris looked confused. "Of course you are having twins. I have been showing them to you for months."

"Well, I mean it was confirmed by the doctor. A boy and a girl." Eris didn't look surprised. "Ok moving on then, this room will be a guest room, and so will the one next to it until the babies get a little older. So which one do you want?" My father scrunched his brows, not understanding. "I'm going to need you and Sera here when the babies come. They have to meet their grandparents, don't they?"

Eris was quiet for a second, a smile struggling to form across his lips. He wasn't angry or anything, more like emotional but trying not to show it.

"I believe Sera would like the view of the gardens."

"So you'll come?"

"The second you ask, daughter," Eris answered and hugged me tightly,

my bulging stomach pressing up against his. "Are you staying healthy?"

"Yes, but the dreams aren't helping."

"I can help with that."

"I know you can, but I don't...they're important. Otherwise I don't know what's coming."

I gasped as a heat started growing in my stomach.

Eris stood in a panic. "Is it the children?"

"Sorry, no, they're fine. Cameron's home," I answered and then noticed my father's confused look. "I'll explain later."

Eris kissed me gently on the cheek. "The house is lovely, my dear."

"Don't say anything to Victor about it. He doesn't know."

"Your secret is safe with me," he replied with a devious smile.

"Give Sera my love."

"I certainly will," he said as his figure began to dissolve.

"Mmmm," I moaned as I woke feeling Cameron's lips caressing the lobe of my ear while his arms held my back firmly against his chest with his hands petting my stomach gently. "How can I sleep if you're giving me hot flashes?"

He laughed softly as he whispered in a low voice, "Because when I miss you this much, I cannot help myself."

Cam's lips traveled down my neck, his tongue flicking teasingly against my skin until he reached the soft muscle. I released a sigh as he began lightly sucking my lower neck, feeling the little nip of his fangs. It sounds completely sadistic but I missed his fangs. I missed the feel of them as they grazed my skin before pricking it.

"Sorry," he whispered before licking the tiny nip closed.

"Do you need it?" I asked, reaching up behind me and running my fingers through his thick curls.

Cameron took my hand from his hair, kissing my fingers before wrapping his arm around me again. "I will feed tomorrow at Dante's. I left as soon as we were done and did not get a chance."

"You don't have to wait, Cam, just take it."

Cameron squeezed me tightly against him as he rested his cheek on top of mine. "No, you need to keep all your strength."

I turned my face slightly, seeing him looking down at me through the corner of his eye. "Please? I had the most horrible dreams today, and when you drink from me it takes all that stress away."

"Bri, if you were not pregnant…"

"But I am, thanks to you," I replied, pushing him back so that I could turn around and face him. Placing my hands on either side of his face, I pulled his lips down onto mine. His cool lips felt refreshing on my raging hot skin, but I could tell he was holding himself back. I crushed my lips against his, trying to pry his mouth open and weaken his resolve. When his hand traveled to my breast I knew I was wearing him down. His lips opened ever so slightly, enough for me to be able to slip my tongue into his mouth. Purposely I flicked my tongue against one of his fangs, causing it to get nicked and drip a little of my blood into his mouth.

He pulled away abruptly, a bit of anguish in his eyes. "Why do you do this to me?"

"I know when something feels wrong, and this doesn't. If it does, I'll stop you, but I really want this. Please," I begged and kissed him again, still feeling his reluctance. I pulled his hand back up to my breast, squeezing it as much as I could handle without it being uncomfortable. His breath filled my mouth as he moaned softly, tucking his index finger into my newly developed cleavage. Slowly he released my lips, tilting his head up slightly allowing his fangs to fully extend. I ran my fingers through his hair, grabbing and pulling a handful of his curls and taking in his look of pleasure before he lost control and buried his face into my neck.

The prick was quick, and the relaxation immediate as my blood flowed into Cameron's mouth. With each suck my stress and fear was drawn out of me allowing me to melt into his body. Unfortunately the feeling was over way too quickly as he retracted his fangs from my neck and licked the two wounds close. Still holding me he rolled onto his back, pulling me under his chin and lazily brushing his fingers through my hair.

"Better?" he said, though I could hear a little bit of annoyance.

"Mmm-hmmm," I cooed as I tilted my head up. "How about you, pinky?"

Cameron raised a brow at me. "I truly dislike when you call me that."

"Well if the cheeks are pink."

"I also do not like being pressured into doing something that could affect your health," he said sternly.

"Cam, I'm fine. The babies are fine. Wait a minute," I said propping myself up on my elbow and pointing to my forehead. "Do you see a red halo like the last time?" Cameron nodded slowly, tracing his fingers on my brow. I took his hand away as I removed the thick comforter from my body and placed his hand on my belly. "Can you see them?"

Cameron's eyes traveled slowly to my stomach, his hand almost shaking as he traced a path over my shirt. "They are so small."

"And yet I am so big."

"You are amazing," he said with his eyes still drawn to my belly. "I cannot believe I can see them floating around in there."

"They're kicking now, can you feel them?"

"A little, I think," he said mesmerized as he leaned over my stomach, still tracing his fingers where the babies were.

I love you, my precious ones, his voice echoed in my head as he kissed my stomach.

The babies started bouncing like they were on a trampoline. "And they love you, too."

"You heard that?"

I nodded. "So did they apparently, can you see them jumping around in there?" Cameron smiled and nodded. "See, they're happy and healthy, nothing to worry about."

"When will you see the doctor again?"

"Not for a few weeks."

Cameron's face became extremely serious. "I will not miss another appointment, I promise you."

"Damn right you won't."

Cameron stretched up the full length of my body, cupping my cheek with his hand and kissing me gently before saying, "I do not wish to rush this moment, but we need to get ready for our evening tonight."

I bit my lip, not knowing what he was talking about as he pointed across me. Following his arm I noticed he was pointing to the armoire against the wall which had several dark garment bags hanging from the door with a designer's name sketched across it.

"We're going out?"

"Yes, we are helping John celebrate Renee's birthday."

"Ohmygod, but we don't have a present!"

Cameron held his hands up. "Yes we do, but it is a surprise." I pouted, but he wasn't fazed. "I hope you like what I picked out for you to wear tonight."

Stepping out of the bed I padded over to the armoire and slowly unzipped the first garment bag.

"This is for me?" I asked looking back and enjoying the triumphant smile on Cam's face. "Babe, it's beautiful," I said turning back to the dark blue satin dress. I pulled back the rest of the garment bag so that I could see the dress in the full light, running my right hand down its smooth front. My heart jumped into my throat when I noticed my ring disappearing into the rich sapphire color of the dress. Without thinking I ripped the dress from its hanger, throwing it onto the floor and crying hysterically.

"I hope this is not just about a dress," Cameron said as his arms wrapped around me and held me to his chest.

The buttons of his dress shirt scratched my cheek as I shook my head.

"It's hap-happening…again," I choked out.

"What is happening again?"

"Dreams are coming true, Cam," I whimpered as I lifted my head. "We're having dinner on a rooftop tonight, aren't we?"

Cameron froze. "We will handle whatever it is, just tell me everything that happens in the dream."

I took in a staggered breath and said, "We're having this great romantic dinner on a rooftop, I'm wearing a beautiful blue dress which matches my ring which is why I freaked out. We're talking about…our…future and then you go all rigid like a robot and then you don't want to be with me anymore and then Jazlyn comes in, takes you by the arm and…you leave with her. You leave me for her. That's the dress, this is the ring, your face tells me I'm right about dinner, so now I'm just wondering when Jazlyn's coming." Cameron's face was stoic as he stared at me silently. "You're mad."

"Of course not," he replied, softly tracing his fingers down my cheek. "I am just wondering why you are continuing to have dreams where I am either leaving you or not in the picture at all. I had hoped we were past all of that."

Cameron's frustration took hold of him as he stepped over to the couch and sat down with his head in his hands.

"I'm sorry, Cam."

"Love, there is nothing for you to be sorry about. You are not the one who…" He stopped but I knew how the statement ended, and I could see all the thoughts crossing over his face as he lifted his head and began rubbing his chin and bottom lip roughly with his index finger. "The dream with Jazlyn is why you called me this afternoon?"

"Yeah," I replied and sat down next to him, curling myself into his side and pulling his arm around my shoulder.

"Bri, I assure you I have not seen or spoken to Jazlyn, and I would certainly *never* go anywhere with her. If I ever see her again I will punish her for the betrayal against our family and against you. But Jazlyn I can handle, the fact that you are having dreams of me leaving you...I...I have had to live weeks without you and there is no way I will ever leave your side unless it is to protect you. I could never willingly abandon you, or our children. Please tell me you believe that."

"I want to, Cam, and in my heart I do. But it's hard when I keep seeing the same things over and over again."

My voice started to break again, causing Cam to hug me tightly against his body. I could feel his love radiating through him and into my skin. How could my dreams be true when we had moments like this?

"I am going to tell John that we cannot join them tonight," Cam said gently.

"No," I replied, pushing myself up from his side. "It's Renee's birthday and she'll kill me if we don't go. But since I've had such a traumatic day of dreams, I think you should tell me what you got Renee for her birthday."

He sighed. "Since it looks like all my surprises are going up in flames, I got us all tickets for the ballet tonight."

"No seriously, what did you get?" Cameron raised both his eyebrows, showing me that he was serious. "Seriously? Seriously, you got ballet tickets for all of us to go. Tonight."

"Why is this so hard to believe?"

"How did you even know Renee liked the ballet?"

"You told me last night that Renee was complaining that with John's schedule they never get to go anywhere and she said, and I quote, 'I finally live in a city where's there's a fucking ballet company and I'll never get to fucking see it', end quote." I stared at him, blinking slowly in shock. "Why are you looking at me like that?"

"Well one, you actually used three contractions and swore in the same sentence."

"I was quoting you quoting Renee."

"Still, it's a shock. Also, I can't believe you actually remembered, more so even listened."

Cameron tilted his head seeming a little insulted. "I listen to everything you say to me."

"Ok, but most men wouldn't take that random statement and use it to buy their girlfriend's best friend's birthday present."

"I am not most men," he replied cockily. "Are you sure you feel up to going out? I am sure Renee would understand."

"I have been cooped up in here for two days. We're going out. I think you'll need to grease me up in order to get me into that dress."

He laughed. "The woman said the dress can stretch to fit a woman with six months of pregnancy."

"So I should just fit then, right?"

"I am not stupid enough to even think about answering that. It will fit and you will look stunning, though you really do not need to try. However, the car will be here in less than an hour, so you will need to hurry."

"Less than an hour!" I shouted, jumping up from the couch and running toward the bathroom, but whipped back around as soon as I hit the doorway. "Ohmygod Cam, I'm so sorry, how was your day? Negotiations go better than yesterday?"

"My day was fine. We will be wrapping everything up tomorrow, but I will not bore you with details. Now go on, angel, you know you will be in the shower for at least thirty minutes."

"I take offense to that."

"Do not challenge me to time you."

I stood straight in the doorway, shoulders back, challenging eye contact. "I will take your challenge and beat it by five minutes."

"Not if I come in with you," he said seductively.

"Ah hell, if that happens neither of us will get out of here. Now you just keep that cute butt of yours on that couch, no sabotaging me."

I only caught a glimpse of Cameron's crooked smile as I turned and shut the bathroom door behind me. While I stripped down and entered the hot shower I realized that I wanted him to come into the shower with me. I wanted to feel his cool body pressed against mine as we melted into one another. It was the first time since our reunion that I trusted him enough to give myself to him.

Even with all the dreams and their awful images and messages, I loved him. Despite what my dreams kept showing me, I was meant to be with the Vampire in the next room and have his children. Though things had been rocky between us the last couple of months, our love brought us back together, and would keep us together with whatever was thrown our way.

As I lathered the sweet smelling bath gel up my arms I noticed a distorted dark-clad figure through the steamy shower glass.

"Don't think I can't see you. Don't even think about coming in here, I'm winning this bet."

Before my eyes the figure disappeared as the door to the bathroom opened.

"Brianna?" Cameron said from inside the door. "Who are you talking to?"

My heart skipped a beat as I clamped my jaw down tight to keep myself from screaming. There had been someone there, I swear.

"Just seeing things I guess," I replied.

Chapter Twenty-Nine

Brianna

"She l-lied," I grunted as I sucked in my breath. "The bitch lied!"

Cameron chuckled behind me as he fought with the dress's zipper. "I might have underestimated the size of your breasts."

"Ya think?"

"You are not helping, my love. Are you able to adjust them higher, perhaps?"

Cool! I'd never had big enough boobs to do that. I LOVE being pregnant. Once I pulled my breasts up and in, Cameron was able to zip the dress the rest of the way up which thankfully squeezed and held everything in place. When I turned around to face him his wide-eyed expression said it all.

"I look good, don't I?"

Cameron licked his bottom lip before answering, "There are no words for how beautiful you look."

"Well I have to compete with you," I said teasingly as I fixed the collar of his white dress shirt.

"Brianna, there is never any competition when you enter a room."

"You say that now, but wait a couple of months when I'm so big I can't get *in* the room."

"Only more of you to love," he replied, kissing my temple and handing me the soft black shawl and matching clutch he'd purchased for me. "I know we spoke about it before, but I still think you should reconsider wearing those heels."

He was speaking of the beautiful black four inch heels that I'd bought with Renee on our day of shopping. "But they make my legs look great."

"Your legs do not need any help, but your feet will after wearing those tonight."

"That's what I have you for."

He smirked as he opened the door to our hotel room to find Hugo standing protectively with his back to us. On Cameron's arm and with Hugo in front of us, I felt like a movie star walking into the elevator. Well, maybe more like the movie star's pregnant girlfriend that no one could remember the name of.

Just as the elevator doors closed, Cameron leaned in my direction and whispered, "Are you wearing lipstick?"

"Oh crap, I forgot to put it on," I replied and opened my clutch. Before I knew it, Cameron pressed me up against the elevator wall, his lips kneading mine within an inch of their lives as I gasped for air. His fingers were tangling themselves in my hair while he pressed his body up against me. While my knees trembled I wondered if we really needed to go to the ballet after all. Renee would understand. Ok, well she wouldn't, so I'd have to fake like I was suddenly feeling ill. I wanted Cameron to rip this dress off of me and take me right here up against the wall. I didn't even care that Hugo would get a free show.

But just as quickly as it started, Cameron pulled away right before the doors to the elevator opened. I could see the longing in his eyes when he gestured for me to exit the elevator first. With a dramatic breath I patted down my hair and stepped past Hugo who was holding the elevator door open. I had trouble making eye contact with him.

"Sorry about that."

Hugo shrugged. "Happens more often than you think. Most likely because of the hormones you're giving off."

Now I wanted to bury my head in the sand.

Cameron smiled at my embarrassment as he took my hand and pulled me down towards the lobby of the hotel. "You do not smell, Brianna."

"What would make you think that I thought that?" He raised his eyebrow at me. "I don't smell, do I? I'm already fat and moody, I don't think I could be the stinky girl."

Cameron pulled me to stop, bringing my hand up to his lips before saying, "You are not fat and you smell wonderful, too wonderful in fact."

"You didn't say I wasn't moody."

"Because I would be lying. Do you mind? I need to warm my hand," he asked as he placed his hand on my stomach. From the hot flash that was coming on combined with the episode in the elevator, no way would my deodorant last through the evening.

"Why do you need to warm your hand?"

"Holy boobs, Batman!" Renee said loudly as she and Dr. John walked across the lobby toward us.

"Why don't you say it a little louder next time," I groaned as I hugged her and noticed Cameron shaking Dr. John's hand. That's why his hand needed to be warmer. "Happy birthday…again."

"Ohmygod Bri, this is the best birthday ever!"

"How is that? It hasn't even started yet."

Renee took a step back, holding her index finger up to me, her head cocked with attitude. "Tell me the last time a man bought me a dress like this, let alone on my birthday. And let's not forget the fact that it actually fits and I like it."

Renee's bright red cocktail dress was beautiful and hugged every one of her sensual curves and tiny waist. But never would I believe that Dr. John picked it out for her which made me take a side glance at Cameron who gave me a tiny wink as he patted Dr. John on the shoulder. Whatever was going on between the two of them, Cameron was being very attentive to an oddly nervous Dr. John.

"Cam, are you sure we'll all fit? Do we need to get two cars?"

Renee scrunched her face at me. "Seriously, Bri, what are you smoking? If the four of us can't fit into a limo then we all need to go on a diet."

"Well how was I supposed to know we had a limo?"

"You sent it, ya crazy," she replied with an eye roll.

"Re, honey," Dr. John interrupted, "could you please stop yelling at the pregnant lady? People are staring, and we are going to be late."

"To what, to what?!" she shouted, jumping up and down like a little girl.

Dr. John smiled adorningly at her as he tucked her under his arm. "I'll leave that up to Bri and Cam, it's their present."

"Um, is Hugo going with us?"

Renee pointed behind me to where Hugo was standing with his dark sunglasses. Cameron took my arm, urging Renee and Dr. John toward the sliding glass doors.

"Yes, he will have to join us."

Renee smiled and winked over my shoulder at Hugo. "That's ok, it makes us look even more important. Well let's get shakin' here. I don't need to get any older than I already am."

As Renee pulled Dr. John toward the doors, Cameron and I followed a few steps behind them with Hugo in tow.

"So Dr. John can call you Cam now, too?"

Cameron took in a deep breath. "I was wondering if you caught that. I just do not have the heart to correct him tonight of all nights."

My eyes flashed at him, knowing he was keeping something from me. "What's so special about tonight?"

"It is Renee's birthday," he replied teasingly. "I would think her twin would know these things."

"Ouch! Mr. Burke is hitting below the belt in order to cover his lies."

"Surprises, love. Surprises, not lies," he corrected as we stepped through the door to a cool night's breeze and a long stretched black limousine.

"I think you're right, twin, there's no way all of us are going to fit in this thing," Renee said smugly as she ducked into the car followed by Dr. John.

"You know, Cam, you could have told me you got a limo rather than making me look like a jackass."

Cameron shrugged apologetically. "Kyla just told me it was a car. I did not know until you did."

"Kyla?" I whispered.

Cameron nodded, putting his index finger up to his lips, gesturing for me to keep quiet and I knew exactly why. After a quick kiss Cameron ducked into the limo, offering me his hand once he was seated.

I lifted my leg to get into the car, but the short hem of my dress stopped me. I tried to sit down without exposing my fine china, but my big belly got in the way. Was this really happening? Unfortunately it was and Renee was laughing at me.

After several attempts at different angles and directions, Cameron finally said over my shoulder, "Hugo, grab her legs."

"What!" I barely got my protestation out before Hugo picked me up by the ankles while Cameron's hands cradled my back and pulled me into the limo. Both Renee and Dr. John were shocked into silence until Hugo shut the door, and then everyone (including me) burst into laughter.

Besides being in a limo with a bodyguard in the front seat, everything else about tonight felt right. Four friends going out to celebrate a birthday, it seemed so normal and that was something that hadn't happened in my life in a long while. I only hoped that my dream was wrong, we really didn't need a fifth wheel named Jazlyn.

Renee was beside herself when Cameron handed her tickets to tonight's ballet performance. She was rarely sentimental about anything, but when Renee was five years old her father had taken her to see a performance of the Nutcracker and she loved it. It became a father-daughter tradition only to be cut short by his death eight years later, but she never forgot the experience of watching graceful ballerinas gliding across the stage while being lifted in the air by muscular men in tights.

Unfortunately tonight's ballet performance was only fully enjoyed by Cameron and Renee. Dr. John fell asleep as soon as the lights went down because he had only had a couple hours of sleep. I at least made it through the first thirty minutes before my eyelids were too heavy to manage. Even a snack during intermission didn't help and the sleeping beauties were designated to sit on the outside while Cam and Renee sat together. I did feel bad that Cameron spent money on tickets when Dr. John and I would have been happy to sleep in the limo.

Speaking of which, getting back into the limo was easier the second time when I made Renee and Dr. John look away while I stepped into the car with my skirt hiked up. From the ballet we went to a late dinner and I was squeezing Cameron's hand so hard that if he hadn't been a Vampire it would have broken. But as was always the case, Cameron was calm, kissing my hair and whispering words of encouragement while I silently searched for any Vampires on the rainy streets of the famous North End of Boston. Surprisingly the only Vampire I found was the one sitting next to me since Hugo had been sent ahead to scope out the restaurant in case Jazlyn was indeed already there. Even with a text from Hugo claiming it was all clear, my heart was still beating out of my chest as we rode up the old rickety elevator to the rooftop of an area restaurant.

"Scan the area if you need to, angel, she is not here nor will she be."

Closing my eyes I took a deep breath and pushed my mind as far out as I felt it could go and returned nothing. Reluctantly I stepped from the tiny elevator and walked up the few stairs to the rooftop door. My breath caught in my throat when I saw an exact recreation of the dream scene in front of me – a small white three-walled tent and a gorgeous view of the city's brightly lit skyline. The only difference was instead of a table for two, it was a table for four and I took it as a sign. Maybe that one change made all the difference.

The night continued smoothly with good food and great conversation while both Renee and I stole glances and ate from Cameron's plate. But as the evening progressed Dr. John became seemingly more uncomfortable and continually had to wipe away sweat from his brow.

"Cam," I whispered, leaning over to him, "can you ask the waiter if they can turn the heaters down? I'm afraid John is going to have a heatstroke or something."

Cameron gave me a peculiar smile as his eyes bore into mine with untold secrets. A second later he waved over the waiter who had spent most of the night under the watchful eye of Hugo.

"Yes sir?" the eager young man asked.

"I think we are ready for the champagne," Cam announced to the glee of Renee and to my disappointment. "And a ginger ale for her," he said sympathetically as he rubbed a gentle hand on my stomach.

"Don't forget to ask him about the heaters," I whispered to Cam after the waiter left too quickly.

"I think John will be fine in a minute, love," he said secretively and then gave a quick nod to Dr. John who looked white as a sheet.

"For crying out loud, John, could you sweat anymore?" Renee said annoyed as she wiped his forehead with another clean napkin.

Dr. John gently took her hand away as he said, "Uh, Re…I, uh…"

"Uh, John…I, uh can't believe you graduated med school with that vocabulary," she said sarcastically.

Dr. John sighed deeply and took Renee's hand in his. "Renee, on our first date I thought you were the craziest, most spastic girl I'd ever met, and yet I couldn't stop thinking about you after that night. And since then you have made me laugh, cringe from your cooking, want to die from embarrassment at how forward you are…" Cameron cleared his throat bringing Dr. John back to attention to see Renee's murderous glare. "Er, what I mean to say is that we hadn't known each other very long before I got offered the job here in Boston. I know you left everything to come here to be with me, and honestly I'd be miserable here without you. I think of you every minute I am away from you and for the last few months I have tested every possible route in Boston to get home to you faster."

"I thought it was to get to the bathroom," she replied and I kicked her under the table. "Bitch," she whispered. "I'm sorry, John, you were rambling?"

Slowly John reached into his suit pocket and pulled out a black box and Renee's eyes grew to the size of saucers, as did mine. "Renee, I want you to know how much you mean to me and from the moment we met I knew I never wanted to be apart from you again." Renee's hands were clasped tightly around her mouth as Dr. John opened the small black box to reveal a sparkling oval solitaire diamond ring. "Marry me, Re. Give me years to find ways home to you."

Dr. John barely got the words out before Renee shouted a resounding yes, her hand shaking while he placed the ring on her finger. A spilt second later she flew out of her chair and wrapped her arms tightly around him before the two of them melted into a world of their own. Wanting to give them a moment of privacy I stood from my chair and walked to the edge of the rooftop, looking around at the stunning view.

The trees swayed slightly with the cool autumn breeze while the leaves whistled and twisted slowly to the ground. The rain had stopped earlier in the evening leaving behind glassy streets and sidewalks that reflected the city lights back up into the sky. When Cameron's fingers grazed the side of my arms I couldn't stop my body from stiffening. Immediately I turned to face him and instantly felt guilty at seeing the hurt in his eyes.

"I'm sorry, Cam, that…wasn't meant for you."

"Is this when Jazlyn joins us?"

"In a little bit," I replied, sneaking my arms inside his jacket and around his waist. Unfortunately my heels were so high I couldn't tuck myself under his chin so I had to settle for his shoulder. "You knew he was going to propose, didn't you?"

"I might have."

"And you did all of this for them?"

Cameron shrugged, causing me to lift my head. "He needed my help and she is your dearest friend. How could I refuse? Although I cannot take all the credit, Kyla took care of most of the details, but that of course is to be kept secret from Renee. Oh, angel, why the tears?"

I took the handkerchief he offered me and wiped my face. "I just love you so much and you're so good to my friends."

"I would hope they are our friends now."

"Of course they are," I laughed, causing a couple more tears to escape down my cheeks.

Cameron cupped my face between his hands, kissing the tears' tracks before whispering, "It always amazes me how the world's most dangerous creature can be rendered useless at the sight of his loved one's tears."

Cam's loving eyes pierced through me and in that moment I knew I wanted them to look at me like that forever.

"I have to ask you something, but I'm really scared to and Jazlyn's supposed to come through that door any minute."

"Forget about Jazlyn, and only concentrate on what it is you need to ask me."

My bottom lip wouldn't stop quivering and Cam's charming smile did not help. "What I wanted to know is if maybe…" but I stopped immediately at the sight of a woman's hand sneak into the crook of Cameron's arm.

"Ohmygod!" Renee shouted as she pulled Cameron away and ran into me so hard I thought we were both going to topple over the ledge of the rooftop. "I'm engaged! I'm engaged, can you fucking believe it?"

"If you hug me any harder I think you'll squeeze these babies out of me."

Renee jolted back, and bent down to my stomach. "You're happy for your Auntie Re, aren't you, you little rug rats?" As she tickled my belly the babies summersaulted inside me making me place a steadying hand on Cameron's chest.

"And you," Renee continued as she stood and turned sharply to point at Cam, "I can't believe you helped John do this. You are one sneaky bastard. Now come on we have some wedding stuff to talk about."

Renee wrapped her hand around Cameron's arm and pulled him toward the table. Just as his back turned to me I saw the rooftop's door slowly begin to open. It was coming true, right here and now. It wasn't Jazlyn who took Cameron away from me but Renee. That meant Jazlyn was the one coming through the door.

"Hugo the door!" I screamed, startling him to attention and causing Cameron to whip back around, grab my arm, and pull both Renee and I toward the edge of the tent. Dr. John sat frozen at the table, drink still in hand while he watched the confusing scene unfold.

A moment later Cameron pulled us to a stop the same time Hugo announced an all clear and stepped away to reveal the terrified waiter with a tray of champagne and a ginger ale.

"I am such an asshole," I said breathlessly as my heart continued to pound. Cameron didn't say a word as he quickly walked over to the waiter to diffuse the situation. I'm sure there was Glamour involved, but really I didn't want or care to know. I was too embarrassed. John still sat in his chair, however, now he was downing the remainder of his bourbon. And although Renee's eyes felt like lasers hitting my face she too didn't say a word as she brought me to the table.

As soon as I sat down I felt Cameron's cool fingers squeeze my shoulder before helping the dazed waiter place the bucket of ice and champagne in the center of the table.

"I'm so sorry," I said to Renee, almost on the verge of tears.

"Bri, it's fine. You're psychic voodoo magic can't work all the time."

Cameron snickered while Dr. John sat looking completely confused. "So," he muttered, "now that all the pressure's off and I have a few drinks in me, can I ask about the security guard and maybe about what just happened?"

Unfortunately I couldn't find a single word at the moment, and neither could Renee nor Cameron apparently since the three of us just looked at each other hoping the other would say something.

When Dr. John didn't get an answer he continued with, "Is this still about your ex-husband? I thought he went missing or something."

Cameron opened his mouth, but Renee interrupted, "John, for cryin' out loud, for someone as loaded as Cameron you have to go out with a bodyguard sometimes. And even though I love me some Hugo, I'd rather talk about the wedding."

"Renee, you've been engaged for less than ten minutes and we're already discussing the wedding?"

"Sorry, maid of honor, but this affects you."

"Maid of honor?"

"Considering you're the only real female friend I have, yeah, maid of honor," Renee said happily and then gave me a worried look. "So here's the thing, and don't hate me, but I want to get married right away. There's no point in waiting. So we're thinking, March, as in this coming March."

"As in a month before my due date, March? Are you freakin' kidding me?"

"Bri, listen…"

"No way am I going to walk down an aisle a million months pregnant."

"But Bri…"

"Why March? That's just ridiculous! Why so fast?"

"Because I can't let John realize he's marrying a crazy woman."

"Re, I know that already," Dr. John laughed but then cleared his throat and shifted uncomfortably in his chair when Renee slowly turned her head and glared at him. "Brianna, this is really my fault. You see, my parents are actually living abroad while my father is a guest lecturer in London. His only break right now is in March and they already have their tickets. We either get married now, or wait another year or so."

"And I don't want to wait," Renee said firmly. "Please, Bri, do this for me, please?"

I shook my head vehemently. "I love you, but let someone else do it."

"There is no one else, and you know it."

"I will be ginormous by then, if I even make it that long."

"And if you don't, then the babies come to the wedding."

I glared at Renee, furious that she thought it would be that simple, but then Cameron's fingers entangled themselves in mine. "Brianna, you will be beautiful no matter how pregnant you are."

"Ha! Wait until I waddle down the aisle looking like a sumo wrestler. Please don't make me do this."

Renee pouted, widening her already large green puppy dog eyes. "You have to be up there with me. You're my twin, remember? Please say yes, you have to say yes."

"This is so unfair," I whined and sipped my ginger ale hoping it would relieve the sudden onset of heartburn. With a reluctant sigh I said, "I will not wear pink, or ruffles, or gloves. And by then I'll probably have ankles the size of canned hams and I'll have to wear flip flops and you'll like it."

Renee squealed with delight and she hugged me tightly around the neck. Afterwards we toasted to Renee and Dr. John's upcoming nuptials, and although I was still unhappy about being in a bridesmaid's dress while being eight months pregnant with twins, I was ecstatic. My little Renee who was so stubborn and defiant on almost all aspects of life had found her true love. And thankfully tonight mine was not taken away as I had seen, but that in fact my dream was just a bunch of bullshit. It would be nice if that could be an ongoing trend.

Chapter Thirty

Brianna

Maybe if I switched my weight to my other foot...ow, ok maybe not. The balls of my feet were throbbing while my heels burned and strained under my weight. My grip on Cameron's arm tightened as we traveled up the elevator, unfortunately having to stop at several floors for other guests. Hugo had taken the stairs to do a search of the area and our room before we got there. He was so sweet, not Alex sweet, but sweet enough. Oh I missed Alex. And Jared, and Kyla, and Devin. Good grief I missed everyone so much and now I was moving here. My nose began to tingle and run at the thought of not seeing them. Cameron did not miss the familiar sound and handed me a handkerchief.

"Tears of joy or sadness?" he said softly as he gently petted my hair and squeezed me into his side.

"I miss our family," I replied weepily.

"I know you do. We will see them soon, I promise we will."

"Have you told Victor about the house?"

Cameron's delay in answering and screwing of his lips gave him away before he opened his mouth. "I am hoping to do it tomorrow. I was waiting until the negotiations were finished before laying it on him."

"You think they'll be done by tomorrow?"

"I certainly hope so. I cannot take listening to all of them screaming and debating with each other over the most minute and insignificant details."

"So...does it look like they'll be bidding on my property?"

"It looks good, yes," he replied without giving any firm promises. "We are starting very early tomorrow in order to accommodate Father's schedule."

"Victor has a schedule?"

"Not really," he laughed lightly. "He is just complaining about the daytime hours. Honestly it is just another way he tries to assert his authority around the other coven leaders."

"And that works?"

"Apparently. We are starting at 3:32am."

I looked up just in time to see him rolling his eyes at his own statement.

"Not 3:31?"

"Absolutely not," he responded, pretending to be serious. "Whereas Father is demanding an early morning hour, Vivienne is demanding the two minutes in order to irritate Father."

"Vivienne, that's Kyla's old coven leader, right?" He nodded. "She and Victor don't get along?"

"They thrive on aggravating one another, which they do quite successfully."

A moan escaped my lips when the elevator doors opened and the hallway leading to our hotel room seemed to stretch for miles.

"Cam?" I whined, shifting my weight again.

"Do your feet hurt?"

I hated to say it out loud, so I pouted and batted my eyes. Without hesitation Cameron scooped me up in his arms, relieving my feet of their torture.

"How long exactly have your feet been hurting?"

"Since the ballet."

"Brianna," he groaned and stepped out of the elevator, "you could have said something earlier."

"But that would have meant saying you were right, and I just couldn't do that so early in the evening."

Cameron shook his head, knowing there was no winning. Just as we approached our door, Hugo stepped out and smiled when he saw me in Cam's arms. "You're all clear, Cameron. It was certainly an eventful night, wasn't it, Ms. Morgan?"

"Hugo, I'm so sorry about that."

"Nothing to worry about, Ms. Morgan, it kept me on my toes. Have a good night, you two," he said and held the door open while Cameron carried me into the room.

"Shall I remove thy lady's torture devices?" he asked as he gingerly placed me on the foot of the bed.

"You are loving this, aren't you?"

"Of course I am. Do you need me to rub your feet?"

"Is that a rhetorical question?"

He laughed and carefully took my shoes off one at a time. My feet had a heartbeat of their own, but Cameron's cool fingers were fighting the swelling away as they dug into my arches and heels.

"Brianna, there is something I have been meaning to tell you."

"You've decided to quit the Warriors and become a masseuse. Sure, babe, I fully support your decision."

Cameron's hands stopped massaging my foot, causing me to open my eyes and see his eyebrow raised at me.

"Are you done?"

I nodded apologetically and he thankfully began massaging my foot again.

"Actually, I wanted to apologize for my behavior the other night." I scrunched my brows together. "The other night after dinner when you stopped at that bakery, I was short with you and I feel terribly guilty about it. I...I was unable to," he paused both with his voice and his massage, "...you were standing in..."

"In your home," I interrupted, trying to stop his obvious pain.

He blinked in surprise. "You knew?"

"Not at first," I answered and gently brushed his brow with my fingers. "It wasn't until I saw you looking up at the stairs that I realized why you were acting so weird. I didn't want to say anything because I didn't want to upset you. If you need time..."

"No, Bri, I do not need time, that is what I am trying to tell you. When I saw you standing in the shop I fully realized how much my past still had a hold on me."

"I promise I won't go in there anymore."

"Brianna, of course you can go there. I want you to go there, you loved those pretzels and Maggie said you can have a lifetime supply."

"Not that I want to squawk at the offer, obviously since I finished that last box you gave me in like an hour, but why would she do that? Do you...know her, or something?"

Cameron pursed his lips together and put his hand through his hair. "Love, up until yesterday I owned the building. After I was Turned I kept tabs on it. And a generation later I purchased it when it came up for sale. Whenever I would visit the area I would go there so I could hold on to the fading memories of my family. The other night my past and future collided and I did not know what to do with myself. So I followed your example and I sold the building to Maggie. I said goodbye, Bri. I finally let Chloe and Christian go."

"Oh Cam," I said breathlessly, "you didn't need to do that."

"Yes I did. I realized I could never devote myself to you and our children if I was still being held down by my sorrow. And I want to apologize for not doing it sooner. I let that part of my life define who I was and I think I was afraid of who I would be without it. I was ignorant not to see everything that I had in front of me. We have had so little time together lately that I want to make sure you know how committed I am to loving you and being the very best father I can be to our beautiful babies. And despite what your dreams show you, I will never leave your side unless it is…"

"To protect me, I know, you said that."

"And I will keep saying it if I have to." Cameron kissed the back of my hand before placing it over his heart, resting his hand on top of mine. Nothing was said between us for several moments and I found myself getting lost in his black eyes. "You humble me when you look at me like that, my love."

Oh crap here we go, I thought and my stomach sank. So much for my dreams being bullshit.

"I…I need to ask you something."

"Anything, angel," he replied, placing his hand on my round baby belly and resting his knees down on the floor.

The butterflies in my stomach started to rise and fall in waves. How did men do this? No wonder Dr. John was sweating so much tonight.

"Even though I kind of know how this whole conversation goes, I want to know if…well someday, n-not today but someday down the road, will…you…marry me? Someday?"

Cameron's mouth dropped, but the rest of him was so still he looked as though he had been carved from stone. For a moment I was afraid that my dreams were altogether wrong, but finally Cam said, "Of course I will marry you, Brianna. I…I would have certainly asked you if I thought for…"

"If you thought for a moment I would have said yes. Yeah, yeah, I know. Now kiss me," I said over him since I'd heard him say it so many times.

However, Cam didn't kiss me as I asked, but instead stood and began patting down his pockets. "This does not feel right without a…"

Before he could finish I took the sapphire ring from my right hand and held it up to him. "But I have a ring."

"You should have a real engagement ring."

"But I already have this one."

"You deserve diamonds."

"This ring has diamonds, and you bought it for me. So we're practically there. Now come on, I think I deserve an answer."

With his eyebrows raised he took the ring from my fingers and knelt down on one knee, taking my left hand and hovering the ring around my ring finger. "I, Cameron Jackson Burke, engage my heart…no, my soul to you. As long as I am with you, it will be my mission to make you as happy as you make me each day. I long for the day I can call you my wife, my Brianna Burke."

As he slid the ring down my finger I could almost hear it clicking into place. Both of our hearts were finally free of our pasts, and our future grew inside me. How long a future that would be depended on so many things, but tonight, in this moment I didn't care. I was engaged to a man I loved with every ounce of my soul, and I knew without a doubt he felt the same way. A tear trickled down my face at the sound of my name married with his.

"However," he began and my stomach dropped, "I reserve the right to buy you a traditional diamond engagement whenever I choose."

Cupping his cheek and loving the smirk on his face, I brought his lips to mine. His cool tongue flicked inside my mouth as he lifted me to a standing position, placing a firm hand on my back while his other stretched my newly ringed hand out slowly, dancing me around the room to music only the two of us could hear. Slowly I pulled my hand from his, nervously pulling his jacket away from his shoulders and letting it slide down his arms onto the floor.

This would be the first time we had made love since the night I told him I was pregnant, and it almost felt like it was our first time. My hands shook as I began undoing the buttons of his shirt and like his jacket, I pulled his shirt from his shoulders and let it fall to the floor. Cameron's hand traveled up to the nape of my neck where he began sensually kneading his fingers into the curves of my neck.

Wrapping my arms around him, I pressed my cheek into Cameron's sculpted chest, always struck by the silence of his heart. Even though it didn't beat, at least some of the blood flowing through him was mine. We were connected in more ways than one, keeping each other alive in non-traditional ways. But nothing about me and Cameron was traditional, it never had been nor would it be. I looked up to see Cam's dark eyes, and every nerve in my body fired at once. With a sudden fire I crushed my lips onto his and fumbled with the belt of his pants.

Cameron suddenly removed my hands and twisted his lips away from mine. "Angel, what are you doing?"

"I think it's pretty obvious."

Concern and confusion came across his face. "Brianna, I cannot make love to you."

My head flinched back. "W-why not?"

"Because you are with child," he replied in a shocked tone.

"What does that have to do with anything? Cam, just because I'm pregnant doesn't mean we can't have sex."

"Of course it does!"

I had to smile. He was from such a different time.

"It's safe, Cam, I promise it is."

Cameron shook his head, still not convinced. "What if...what if I poke one of them or something? One of our babies could be born with a misshapen head and it will be because of me."

I placed my finger over his lips so he couldn't continue, honestly because if he did I wouldn't be able to control my laughter.

"Cameron, I love you so much and you are a truly gifted lover. But you're not *that* well-endowed."

Cameron sighed, rolling his eyes in frustration as he put his hand through his hair, and then finally looked at me with uncertainty.

"Cam, I promise you this is safe, but I understand if I'm not turning you on looking like this."

In one sudden movement Cameron gripped the rounded neckline of my dress and ripped it completely in half, letting it fall to the floor among the other clothing victims. I stood in front of him shocked and slightly self-conscious in only a pair of underwear.

"Cam, my dress!"

"I will buy you another one," he responded and pulled my legs up around his hips.

The second my skin touched his smooth flat abdomen a fire ignited within me. My baby belly prevented me from getting as close to him as I wanted to, but my legs tightened around him as he walked us toward the bed, relentlessly attacking my lips. Each kiss was so intense I was taking in gulps of air while being mindful of the fangs that were now extending. The feeling of his tongue in my mouth, his arms wrapped tightly around me, and the growing desire beneath his pants caused my lady parts to pulse at the same speed as my racing heart. The feeling was so overwhelming I moaned loudly with pleasure.

Unfortunately the combination of relaxation and arousal caused me to let my guard down and accidently Push Cameron into the nightstand causing the lamp and phone to crash to the floor while the two of us burst into laughter.

"Everything is fine, Hugo," Cam said in the direction of the door.

"I'm so sorry, Cam," I laughed loudly while kissing his forehead.

"That has never happened before."

"I've never been *this* aroused before. Must be those hormones," I said teasingly.

"Absolutely," he replied and carried me to the bed, able to hold me with one hand while the other tore his pants from his body. Within another few seconds there wasn't a stitch of clothing between us as we fought each other over who would be taking whom.

I won.

Straddling him I could see his face conflicted with pleasure and concern as I grinded up against him, feeling all of him reaching up into the depths of my body. Cam moved his hands from squeezing my breasts to massaging my inner thighs to pulling my face down to his, unable to decide what he wanted more. The passion between us was so disorienting that I could barely breathe while I continued to bring myself down on top of him, feeling the muscles inside me begin to twitch and respond to the quickening rhythm we found together.

"Bite me," I moaned and brought his mouth to my neck.

Cameron shook his head, choosing to crush his lips against mine, forcing his tongue deep into my mouth. I pulled away and began kissing his neck until I reached the lobe of his ear and sucked it into my mouth. Cameron moaned and breathed heavily in my ear while gripping my hips with his hands and manipulating them in wavelike motions to draw him in deeper and faster. Oh. My. God.

My chest burned with quickening breath while my insides began to pulse and spasm, and yet I wanted more.

"Bite me," I said once again, even more breathless than before, and once again Cameron shook his head and leaned me back in order to take my breast into his mouth. Grabbing a handful of his thick black hair, I pulled his head back roughly as I shouted angrily, "I said bite me!"

Cameron's fangs hung prominently from his mouth as I pulled harder on the back of his head causing him to release a feral sounding growl from deep in his throat. Just as my entire body flashed with pleasure, Cameron's fangs pierced the skin of my breast causing my vision to blur and be flooded in red.

I love you, I Pushed softly into his mind as he continued to drink from me, not being as cautious as he had been earlier in the evening.

Always, Mrs. Burke, he replied.

Chapter Thirty-One

Cameron

My cheeks still felt warm from Brianna's blood. It tasted like no one else's - so sweet and warm, and flowing with such power. I took more than I should have, but it was extremely hard to stop. The latter half of the evening was completely unexpected to say the least. I was taken off guard when Brianna asked me to marry her. Though marrying her was something I desperately wanted, I honestly never thought it would happen after what Sam had put her through. But now I knew her trust in me was restored, and I could not be happier knowing she would share my name one day.

Our love making had exhausted her, and with good reason. The hormones had made her extremely aggressive causing a similar response in me that I worried if I left bruises. But even worse was when post-coital snuggling turned into round two. As I pulled down my black cashmere sweater I could still feel her back pressed into my chest, her hand reaching behind to grab the back of my hair while I pushed myself into her from behind. No wonder she lay limp in the bed.

Just at that moment Brianna turned over, causing the sheets to pull back and expose her round belly. I knelt down and gently placed my hands on her stomach and said, "Oh my precious ones, may you never know what I did to your mother last night, or have deformities from said activities."

I could have looked at Brianna sleeping all day, but unfortunately our extra-curricular activities had left little time before having to change and prepare to leave. The only good thing about leaving today was that it would be the last time I would have to. An agreement to buy Brianna's property in

Connecticut was almost settled, hopefully only an hour or so and I could slip back in bed before Brianna woke. Perhaps she would never know I had gone.

Before leaving, I nuzzled into Brianna's ear and whispered, "I will return soon. Please remember to charge your phone, love."

"Barge the dome, dove," she mumbled into her pillow.

Shaking my head, I sighed deeply knowing I needed to leave now, otherwise I would be late for this joyous day. With one last kiss I whispered to my fiancée that I loved her, tucked my portfolio under my arm, and walked to the door.

"Coming out," I whispered to Hugo just before opening the door to see his back moving away in order to let me pass.

"Good morning, Cameron. A vigorous night, eh?" he said with a smirk.

The advantage of Vampire hearing was also a curse if you ever wanted privacy.

"The hazards of a hormonal fiancée, I suppose."

"Yes, congratulations are in order. I am sure Father will be happy for you."

I could hear the longing in his voice to be recognized by Victor once again.

"Hugo, this could potentially be the last day I will need your services, but I want you to know that I will speak with Father. You obviously have an endorsement from me and Brianna."

Hugo smiled. "I will be grateful for any help you can give me. It has been an honor, Cameron," he said and placed his fist over his heart in the traditional Warrior salute.

I patted his arm and looked him straight in the eye. "Soon enough, brother. I will see to it."

Hugo gave a curt nod before I released his arm and continued my way down the hall to the elevator. It was now 3:15 and if I walked at human speeds I would be late and the distance would cause a draining Projection. Being it was so early in the morning I could potentially run down side streets undetected in order to get to Dante's on time. Besides, it would feel good to stretch my legs.

Running like the Vampire I was, it only took five minutes and forty-two seconds to finally come upon Dante's door. Surprisingly I was greeted by Fabiani rather than the regular doorman.

"Cameron, we must stop meeting like this," Fabiani teased as he gestured for me to enter. "I told you, we're through. You really have to stop embarrassing yourself like this. What will Brianna say?"

"I am sure my *fiancée* would not have many good things to say," I replied, quirking a smile.

"Get outta town! No wonder you look so happy. You must have gotten some major…"

"Yes, yes I am very happy," I interrupted. "I see you too have gone with more casual attire today."

"We rarely have clients on Sunday, but honestly I'm just coming in from Red. I am happy to see that you agree with a man wearing skinny jeans," he said posing in several positions that accentuated his dark jeans, gray vest and colorful wide scarf that he draped loosely around his neck.

"What is Red?" I asked curiously

"Wha…what is Red?! It's only the hottest Vampire club in town."

"Dante does not object to an open Vampire club?"

"Well, really it's a club for humans who pretend they are Vampires. We real Vamps are so popular and everyone wants to know where we got our fangs. Oh if they only knew! You should come down with us sometime. It's the easiest way to get fresh blood around here. I'm surprised you haven't been down there yet."

"I really do not think Victor would approve if I were to frequent such a place."

"Why? You don't have clubs like that in San Francisco?"

"Definitely not in Victor's territory. We are to stay the myth everyone assumes we are."

"Good thing Victor isn't my master. Before you go back I'm taking you to Red for our first date," he said waggling his eyebrows.

"I thought we had broken up. But perhaps my brother…" I caught myself, though from his expression he did not miss my slip. "Speaking of red, has Dante completely redecorated in the few hours we have been away?"

The previous white and gold foyer was now covered in bright red and yellow draperies that hung from the tall wide windows, gathering in large billows on the floor. The couches and chairs had been replaced by long Victorian lounging chaises and thick velvet upholstered chairs.

"Master often redecorates once everyone has left for the day. There have been times when I've turned around and left thinking I was in the wrong place. But let's go back to more important things, you have a brother?"

Devin would kill me.

"Cameron has many Warrior brothers," Dante said from the top of the stairs, his shiny white suit replaced with a pair of red satin pajamas with black Japanese-style embroidery.

"Yes I have many siblings, but I am only close to three of them."

"I can only imagine the carnage that must occur when all of Victor's children come together," Dante said as he glided down the large marble staircase.

"Which is probably why we are rarely together except in times of battle."

"Such a difference between the Warriors and my sires. My coven would try and debate each other until they were drained from exhaustion," he smiled and for the first time I noticed he was carrying a small gift bag. "No Brianna this morning?"

"It is a little too early for her."

"Oh yes of course," Dante said dismissively. "How I forget about a human's needs sometimes. I was hoping to give this to you both. It isn't much, just a little something from Uncle Dante."

With a wide smile Dante handed me the gift bag which had small ducklings printed in pale pastels. It was a baby gift.

"Dante, sir, this is very thoughtful, and actually our first baby gift."

"Cameron, it isn't anything much, just a little token for those two sweet babies. I do hope you'll visit whenever you're in town."

"You can count on it, sir. Shall we call into the conference? We are approaching 3:31, and I do not want to give anyone an opportunity to start today out on a sour note."

"By all means," Dante replied and directed us into the main conference room where a fire burned high in the large fireplace. And though I would certainly visit, I hoped this was the last time I would be in this room for a long while.

"So we are all in agreement that we will place an offer on the property in Connecticut for $1,282,000.03," Fabiani said with every ounce of control he had. Honestly I was ready to throw those three pennies through the phone. "Each of the coven leaders will deposit an equal share into a designated Grand Caymans account where a third-party financial manager will oversee the account during the building of Facility East."

Fabiani paused for just enough time where the other callers would think they were being prompted to voice any objections, but not enough time to make any. Just as I heard the beginnings of my father's voice, Fabiani continued, "Yes, Victor, your objection has been noted. We all acknowledge the fact that you and others within the vicinity have solely funded and maintained Facility West for the past four years, and object to being responsible for donating the same amount as the other coven leaders. And Vivienne your objection to Victor's objection has also been noted."

This time Fabiani paused long enough to roll his eyes. It was the first time in four days that Fabiani looked weathered, even with having fed only a few hours ago.

"If our offer of purchase is accepted," Fabiani began, giving me a leading glance as I nodded that Brianna would indeed accept our offer, "then the demolition of the current home, subsequent new construction, and all pertaining contracts will be mediated and managed by Dante or someone within his coven. Vivienne, your objection to the fact that we are purchasing a property that requires us to demolish and then rebuild has been noted. Victor, your objection to Vivienne's objection has also been noted.

"Facility East will be overseen by Dante as Facility West is overseen by Victor. The remaining coven heads will be consulted as needed, and plans for ongoing funding for both Facilities will begin next year. Construction of Facility East will begin once all contracts and permits are in place, and completion is set for three months after. Are there any other objections or concerns I have not addressed at this time?"

The phone was silent and Dante gave us both a thumbs up as he said, "Very well then, we have an agreement. Formal contracts will be created and emailed to you. I am expecting to have signatures received back within the hour. Thank you all for participating, and may I give kudos to both Cameron and Fabiani for spearheading this entire project, and frankly having to deal with all of us."

Thankfully there was laughter before the leaders began to drop from the call.

"Victor, may I trouble you to stay on the line?" I asked as I rose from my chair

"Of course, child," he replied and then continued with his goodbyes to his other colleagues.

Just as I placed the conference phone on mute, I felt Dante's hand on my shoulder. "Fabiani and I will give you some privacy, but I hope you will celebrate with us after."

"Actually, Dante, I was hoping you could stay. I am about to give Victor some news he will find quite distressing and I was hoping you could put your tremendous skills to use?"

I could see the surprise in Dante's face as he nodded. Fabiani's only comment was, "I certainly have to stay for this."

Dante gave his sire a stern look. "Forgive my unsympathetic pupil, we will certainly help you in any way we can."

I nodded and reluctantly took the phone off mute as Victor began calling to me. "Sorry, Father, we are here."

"We?"

"Dante and Fabi are with me as well."

"All right, child, what is it you have to discuss with me?"

Just as I was about to answer, my cell phone vibrated loudly against the table. Quickly I forwarded it to voicemail when I saw that is was Alexander. He would have to wait.

"First of all, Father, I wanted to inform you that I have sold the shop."

"The shop? Your former home?"

"Yes, sir."

Victor paused for a moment, purely from shock I am sure. "Good for you. This is a great step for you."

"I could not agree with you more," I replied and then cleared my throat. "I have also purchased a new property."

"It is always smart to have future investments, especially ones not as emotionally tied."

"Actually, Father," I began to the sound of my phone vibrating again.

"What is that infernal racket?" Victor shouted angrily.

"I apologize, Father, Alexander keeps calling me." What could he want? There was no way I could muster the courage to do this again. "As I was saying, this new property could potentially be just as emotionally connected. You see Brianna and I bought a home together. Here. In Boston. Massachusetts."

"I am aware of where Boston is, child," Victor replied in a strained voice.

Dante took the opportunity to speak up. "Cameron, I think it is wonderful that you and Brianna have decided to settle down, especially with two young ones on the way."

Father was quiet for another several seconds before saying, "Am I to understand you are choosing to stay in Boston?"

I took in a deep breath and counted to five before answering, "Yes, Father."

Dante and Fabiani stole a glance at each other, avoiding making even the slightest noise. They realized now why I had asked them to stay. The only sound in the room was my cell phone announcing that I had a text. Allowing Father to continue his silence, I looked down at a three word text from Alexander – WHERE ARE YOU?!

"So, child, after 268 years you are going to throw away your career as a Warrior and leave your family behind?"

"Father, I am not throwing away anything," I responded carefully while I texted Alexander that I was conferencing with Victor. "I am merely choosing to raise my children outside of the manor."

"Away from your family, your duty!"

"Away from a house full of Vampires."

"You are a Vampire, child, do not forget that."

"I am aware of what I am and it will be challenging enough. I do not need to worry about twenty other Vampires."

Father began breathing heavily into the phone as he became angrier, cuing Dante to intercede. "Victor, this is perfectly natural…"

"Dante, I urge you to refrain from speaking," Victor threatened. "Cameron, I cannot believe what I am hearing. This is why you have been counseling me on Devin. You have been planning this for some time, haven't you?"

"No, Father, it stemmed from Brianna not wanting to return while Nikki was in the manor."

"Then I'll dispose of her."

"Victor," Dante interrupted kindly, "disposing of someone is not the answer here. Cameron and Brianna have obviously planned out a future…"

"As have I!" Victor shouted.

"Those are your plans, Father, not mine. I have tried to be diplomatic, but you force my hand."

"Child, do not say something you might regret."

"I relinquish my seat on the Elite Council. If you wish me to leave the coven I will, but I ask you to think of your unborn grandchildren."

"How dare you threaten me, child." Victor was infuriated, but I did not expect anything less. Just then I heard other voices come into the room. "Alex, this is not the time."

Now I could hear Alexander's deep voice coming through the phone. "Father, are you still on with Cameron?"

"Yes, perhaps you can talk some sense into him," Victor said flustered.

"Cam!" Alex said frantic. "Elaina is in Boston."

I froze while Dante stepped beside me and Fabiani stood slowly from his chair.

"Cam, did you hear me?"

"Yes I heard you. Where? How did you find her?"

"That was me, bro," Jared announced through the phone. "The facial recognition alarm went off like crazy. We caught her in three places within the last twelve minutes."

"Thank goodness for your delinquency."

"Anytime, bro," Jared replied proudly. "I'm sending you the images and the locations where she was flagged."

"Dante, would you be able to call in some members of your coven? If we can spilt up into three groups…" I paused, realizing I was overstepping my bounds. "Father, I apologize. I did not mean to take control without your permission."

"I see you want to be a Warrior leader when it suits you."

My hand was pulling at the roots of my hair reflexively. "Father, please…"

"Very well, continue," Victor said over me.

My hands were making fists at my sides as I counted myself down. It was not until I felt Dante's hand on my shoulder did I continue.

"As I was saying, Dante would you…"

Dante squeezed my shoulder again as he nodded. "Yes of course. I will pull in as many as I can. We are not Warriors by any means, but perhaps we can help track Elaina until you can get to her."

"Jared, is the facial recognition still running?"

"Yeah, another alarm will go off if it picks her up again."

"Ok then, I will begin tracking her from the last location and if the alarm goes off again text me immediately."

"Whoa wait a minute, Cam," Alexander interrupted, "you've got to get Brianna out of Boston."

"Brianna is safe at the moment. The priority has to be capturing the threat, which is Elaina. I am the only Warrior here so I must oversee this. Besides, convincing Brianna to leave Boston will not be easy, Alex, and the time I will lose debating with her I could have Elaina in my hands."

Alexander growled softly as Jared answered, "Dude, throw Beebs over your shoulder if you have to…"

"Enough, Jared," Victor said snapping his fingers, "I agree with Cameron. If we stop the threat, Brianna will no longer have to run."

Different scenarios unfolded in my mind while Jared, Alexander, and Father debated heatedly back and forth. Both Dante and Fabiani came closer to the phone, unable to stop their need to mediate. Just as Dante opened his mouth to speak, I held up my hand. "Perhaps we can do both at the same time. Dante, begin calling in your coven members, we need to begin scouring the streets as soon as possible. Alex, of course you are right, Brianna will obviously be safer outside the city. I will call in some help to work on her while we are searching for Elaina. Father, I will keep you abreast of the situation."

Everyone in the room and on the phone muttered acknowledgements as I picked up my cell phone and began to dial.

"Who are you calling?" Fabiani asked.

"Someone both Brianna and I trust."

Chapter Thirty-Two

Brianna

"This is not what I want," Cameron snapped, pulling his hand away from my stomach. "You will be safe here and I will make sure you want for nothing."

"I don't want your money, Cameron!"

"That is all that I can give you now. If you don't want it then you will be left with nothing."

"Don't take it, Morgan," Aidan said behind me, his hand outstretched. "Stay with me. I'll take care of you, better than he ever could."

I turned back to Cameron, seeing now that he had stepped up into the driver's seat of his SUV.

"Aidan's right. He can give you what I can't."

"Or won't," I cried.

"Brianna, stay with me," he whispered into my ear.

I pushed Aidan away as I said, "Cam, I know you love me."

Cameron slammed the SUV's door shut, but rolled down the window. "You must remember, Brianna, I am not who you think I am..."

A second later Aidan stood in front of me, crushing me to his chest and protecting me from the gravel flying everywhere from Cameron's spinning tires as he sped out of the driveway. I pushed and hit against Aidan's chest, trying to get out of his grip.

"Let me go," I sobbed. "Please, Aidan, let me go."

"Allow me to love you, Bri. I promise I will never hurt you."

He lowered his face, his lips resting lightly on top of mine. When I didn't *push him away, Aidan lifted his face slightly, looking deeply into my eyes before he crushed his lips against mine again, forcing his tongue inside my mouth.*

"Morgan," someone said in the distance, but when I tried looking for the voice, one of Aidan's hands traveled to the back of my neck while his other hand traveled down to my stomach. It was a gesture reserved for Cameron, and it felt wrong to have his hand there.

"Morgan!" the voice said with more urgency as the babies stirred underneath Aidan's hand. The initial feeling of bubbles turned into flailing uncomfortable kicks causing me to grasp my stomach in pain while trying to push Aidan away. As his passion increased, so did the babies' violent attack on my insides. Suddenly Aidan gripped the collar of my shirt and ripped it apart enough to expose my breasts to him.

"Morgan! Wake up!"

"Wha?" I whined, unsure of my surroundings or whether I was still dreaming.

"Jesus, Brianna we don't have all day," a male's voice said next to me.

"Fuck!" I shouted, kicking my legs out in front of me, sliding myself further into the bed and getting tangled in the sheets. The room was still dark, which meant it was early, but when my brain finally caught up with me I realized who the stranger was. "Aidan?"

"You're not going to do that head thing to me again are you?"

"It depends," I replied angrily and then was overcome with embarrassment and pulled the sheets more securely around my bare chest. "What the hell are you doing here?"

Aidan removed his baseball cap and began rolling it in between his hands. "Cameron sent me to come get you."

"What? Why?"

"Elaina's somewhere in Boston, and Cameron wants me to get you to safety."

My heart raced the second I heard Elaina's name. Just like every other time in my life, right when things were coming together they had to turn to shit instead.

"Earth to Brianna," Aidan said annoyed, waving his hand in front of my dazed expression. "Seriously, we've got to get going. So put some pants on since I'm guessing you're not wearing any, which by the way makes this whole interaction a little awkward."

"No," I breathed softly. Aidan raised his eyebrows in surprise. "I'm not going without Cameron. I'll stay with you, but I'm waiting for Cameron. If we need to run, we'll run away together."

Aidan's lips disappeared into his mouth as he took in a slow frustrating breath. "Look, Morgan, I'm not here to argue. Elaina's bad news, you know it, I know it. Usually I don't give a shit about anyone but myself..."

"Big surprise," I said snidely.

"*But*, if some crazy bitch was in the same city hunting down my pregnant girlfriend, I'd wrap her up in the sheet she was clinging to and drag her out of the hotel kicking and screaming. Cameron didn't say to do that, but he didn't say not to. So stop being stupid and get out of bed."

Growling and giving Aidan the dirtiest look I could muster, I wrapped the sheet tightly around me and kicked my legs over the edge of the bed. Just as my feet hit the floor a tsunami of nausea came over me. I tried to run to the bathroom, but my feet got tangled in the sheet, causing my knees to hit the floor.

"Garbage can!" I yelled at Aidan who quickly responded and placed the small wicker wastebasket in front of me just in time for me to release what must have been a gallon of vomit.

"I didn't sign on for this," he groaned.

"Then leave," I snapped, my throat burning with bile.

Aidan gave a curt laugh as he removed the trashcan from in front of me, and lifted me gently by my elbow.

"I'll dump the bucket-o-puke, you grab some clothes and change. Then we really have to go."

"Stop being so pushy," I shouted to his back as he disappeared into the bathroom. "I'm not leaving without my stuff. You'll have to wait until I'm done packing."

"Oh no," he replied impatiently and returned to the bedroom, "we're not waiting around while you pack all your girly shit."

I grabbed a pair of my pregnancy jeans from within the armoire along with a soft purple sweater. Comfort would be needed on a day like today. With my outfit in hand I headed into the bathroom, stopping to give Aidan a stern finger in the face. "Now you listen to me, buddy. You have no idea how many times in the last year I've had to leave with nothing and I'm not doing it again. So you're just going to have to deal. If you want to leave so quickly, make yourself useful and grab the red suitcase from the closet over there. I'll be out in a minute."

Aidan screwed one corner of his mouth together while he chewed the inside of his cheek and turned away from me. Not caring what he felt about me, I ducked into the bathroom, locking the door behind me. My back slid down the door, making me catch myself with my hands on the cold tile floor. I may have acted strong in front of Aidan, but the reality of my situation suddenly hit me like a ton of bricks.

Elaina was here. If she found me, my life and the lives of my children were over according to my dreams. Did the scenario in my dream unfold because I chose to stay in Boston or because I left with Aidan? Why couldn't my dreams just put everything out on the table for me? Show me exactly what steps I needed to take in order to *avoid* all the horrible things that might happen to me. Why couldn't they do that? And then there was Aidan. Aidan! The same Vamp who I had just been inappropriate with in my dream, and not for the first time. How could I do that to Cameron, especially after last night?

Startled, I pulled my hand quickly from underneath the sheet, noticing thankfully that my sapphire was still on my left hand. The sight of the ring caused all my emotions to bubble up to the surface. Love for Cameron, guilt for having a dream about another man, fear of being found by Elaina, and lastly terror that my horrific dream would come true. Honestly I hadn't had a dream that had a happy ending and that just sucked. Last night I was foolish enough to think for a minute my life could finally take a turn for the better.

I needed Cameron. I needed him here with me right now. I didn't want Aidan, I wanted my fiancé. Not wanting Aidan to hear me, I balled up the sheet and bit down on it hard while the choking sobs came up from my throat. I don't know how long exactly I sat there on the floor crying like a little girl, wishing and wondering where Cameron was. But then I remembered he said that he wouldn't leave my side unless it was to protect me, and that was exactly what he was doing. That was who he was, that was what he and the Warriors did. And now I was being stupid and selfish, which of course caused another round of sobbing.

"Morgan?" Aidan said softly through the door. "You ok in there?"

"Fine," I choked out, trying to wipe my eyes with the soaking wet sheet.

"Um…well, we really need to get going."

Sighing deeply, I pushed myself up, allowing the sheet to stay crumpled on the floor. Reluctantly I changed into my jeans and sweater, not bothering to look at myself in the mirror since I knew I looked like crap. When I opened the door I found Aidan pacing the floor in front of the bed where my red suitcase lay full and open.

"You really didn't have to pack for me," I said, dumping all my toiletries into the suitcase.

"I was curious about what kind of underwear you wore."

"Disappointing I'm sure."

"A little," he laughed. "Can we go now?"

I nodded. "I just want to call Cameron before we leave. Oh crap my phone isn't charged," I said and grabbed my cell phone from the nightstand, but Aidan quickly took it from my hand and broke it in half. "Hey!"

"No phones, Morgan. Too easy to track you by. Besides you won't be able to get ahold of Warrior boy anyway. No calls when on a mission or some shit like that. At least that's what he told me."

"I hate that rule!" I shouted and watched him throw my cell phone into the garbage. "I guess that means no computer either?"

He shook his head. "Now you're catching on," he replied and grabbed the suitcase from the bed as though it weighed nothing. "From the way Cameron was talking this shouldn't be for too long."

Pushing past Aidan, I gathered a few personal items that were strewn around the room, placing them in my purse before shrugging into my white coat. Aidan stood by the door, sighing and rolling his eyes while I continued to frantically walk from one side of the room to the other.

"I may actually be the first Vampire to die from old age."

"Oh shut up, I just want to make sure I have everything. We are going to stop for breakfast, right? Wait, where the hell are we going anyway?"

Aidan brushed his hair back with one hand and put his baseball cap back on, pulling it down low in front of his eyes. "How does Cameron handle you in more than small doses?"

"You do remember what I did to you in the train station, right?"

"One, we can't stop for food because we *really* need to get away from here and you're taking your jolly-ass time. And two, Cameron told me to take you to Oliver's. Anything else? Or can we seriously get going?"

"I do not care for the attitude, Aidan. I'm human, I'm pregnant, I need food, lots of it and often. And why do we have to go all the way down to Daddy O's? I mean it's not like I don't want to see him, but that's a fourteen hour ride from here. Why do I have to go so far away, how long do I have to stay down there? Why can't I just hide in New York City or something? And why can't we stop for breakfast, I'm really hungry already, I can't let my babies starve for fourteen hours. This isn't fair, I need to call Cameron."

Aidan was frozen by the door, though his posture seemed a little scared of the blubbering pregnant mass in front of him. The adrenaline from being startled awake had begun to drain and now everything was just a little too much for me. Aidan strode slowly over to the minibar just behind me and grabbed the large basket of snacks and fruit that was prominently displayed on the counter.

"Come on, Morgan, please don't cry," he said in soft tone I wasn't used to hearing from him. "I'm sure if Cameron could talk to you he would, but he's probably scouring the city right now looking for Elaina. I'm just doing what I'm told, and I'm guessing he thought you wouldn't mind a visit with Oliver. And since Cameron's loaded we're taking the whole minibar with us so you can eat and I don't have to stop. See, we all get what we want. Ok?" I nodded and wiped my face clean. "All right then, got a bag for this stuff? I'd really rather not have to carry this basket around."

"Suddenly you care about appearances?" I laughed as I walked over to where I had discarded one of the shopping bags from last night.

"Hey, just because I don't dress like Cameron doesn't mean I don't care about appearances. Why bother around you?"

"I think I'm supposed to take offense to that."

"You know what I mean," he replied annoyed and dumped the entire minibar basket into the shopping bag. "You're taken, so I don't have to try and impress you."

"I don't think it would matter, you're really not my type."

"Well at least we have that in common," he laughed as he took the shopping bag from my hand and headed for the door. "Can we go now?"

I nodded, feeling a lump in my throat as flashes of my night with Cameron came to the forefront. Speaking of, I really needed a shower. I actually felt bad that Aidan would have to sit with me in a car for fourteen hours, but that feeling of guilt was short lived when he opened the door and began waving his arms out into the hallway trying to get me out of the room.

The babies began to stir as I stepped toward the door, their bubbly kicks in conjunction with my nervous stomach. Stepping through the door and into the hallway I realized there was something wrong.

"Wait, where's Hugo?"

Aidan turned back around. "Hugo? Big Italian-looking guy?"

"I guess? He's usually by the door."

"He left as soon as I got here. I guess Cameron called him in to help with the search."

"Really!" I replied excitedly. "Oh that's wonderful. What if he was the one who found Elaina! That would certainly put him on Victor's good side and then he'll have to be let back into the coven and then Hugo will be so happy and live happily ever after."

Aidan raised an eyebrow, lifting one side of his cap's brim while he pressed the button for the elevator. "You seriously got all of that from him not being at the door?"

"It's a gift," I said as I prissy-walked into the elevator.

"Oh it's somethin' all right," he laughed as the doors closed behind him and he pressed the button for one of the lower garage floors.

"Sooo…did Cam say anything else? To…me?"

Aidan slowly turned his head. "What, like 'please tell my dearest little poopsie how much I love her.' Are you kidding me?"

"Of course I am," I lied and tried to cover it with an awkward laugh.

From the corner of my eye I could see Aidan shaking his head as I looked to the floor. "Come on, don't pout. He probably didn't say anything because he knew I'd never let him live it down. I'm sure he'll call as soon as he's able and shower you with disgusting romantic gestures."

I smiled weakly. "I wasn't pouting."

"Oh yes you were."

The doors opened to the garage allowing the smell of exhaust to hit my face. I filed in behind Aidan when he stepped from the elevator, following him among row after row of parked cars.

"Where the hell did you park? We might as well walk out of Boston at this rate."

"Um, right here," he said pointing to a silver pickup truck causing me to groan. "Sorry it's not the Vanquish."

"Oh no, that's not it at all. I'm thinking about riding for fourteen hours in a pickup truck."

"I guess neither Cameron nor I thought this one through. It won't take fourteen hours, I promise. I never drive the speed limits. Hell, I rarely drive under ninety," he smiled as he opened the passenger door and gestured for me to get in.

"Try to remember that I can't survive a car crash like you can. I'd like to see my grandfather with all my limbs intact."

I stepped up into the cab of the truck, ignoring the mumbles under Aidan's breath as he shut the door behind me. Only a split second later Aidan was suddenly in the driver's seat starting the engine.

"Aren't you afraid of the cameras catching you doing Vamp speeds?"

"Nah, whatever lazy-ass security guard watching would just think the camera blinked or something. Wow, we're finally leaving, and it only took us five hours," he said before screeching out of the parking space.

"You know, Cam doesn't have the Vanquish anymore."

"What! Why the hell would he ever give up that car?"

"He gave it up for me, I guess. He traded it in so that he could drive me cross-country to the Facility."

"No way," Aidan scoffed. "No way would I ever give up a car like that for a woman. Never in a million years."

"Hence why you are alone. You know, since it's so early maybe I'll just go back to sleep."

"Morgan, I think that is the best idea you've had all morning."

"Oh, wait a minute, do you know how to get to Daddy O's?"

"If you mean Oliver, then yes, I know how to get there. I brought him to you for your Claiming. Not that it would matter. I'm the best Tracker in the world, remember?"

"I thought you and Cameron settled on best Tracker on the East Coast," I said, removing my coat and tucking it into the shape of a pillow on the seat.

"He may have said it, but I certainly didn't agree to it."

"Always a pissing contest, huh?"

"Yep," he replied proudly.

As I laid my head down on my coat my eyes suddenly felt heavy. I felt a slight breeze hit my face as Aidan rolled down his window to pay the garage attendant. Darkness began to fill in around my eyes and I quickly began drifting off to sleep. The last thing I remembered was feeling Aidan's hand pat my arm gently as he said in a soft tone, "Just sleep, Morgan. We'll be there before you know it."

This was probably the only time I would ever do what Aidan told me to do.

Chapter Thirty-Three

Brianna

"Morgan," Aidan said, nudging me awake. "We're here."

"Hmmm," I whined, stretching my heavy eyelids open. The truck began rocking side to side as the tires crunched through heavy gravel. "Where are we?"

The sound of my voice echoed in my head causing it to throb painfully at my temples and forehead. I had to put my hand up in front of me, shielding my eyes from the slim rays of sun peeking through the grayish storm clouds. When the truck came to a stop I didn't need Aidan to answer my question since I recognized the familiar mountains in the distance and surrounding woods. Daddy O's home with full wraparound porch stood only a few feet away looking just as I had left it and as welcoming as ever.

"I slept the whole fourteen hours?"

Aidan smiled as he turned off the engine and began collecting his personal items from the compartments in front of him. "Actually we made it in record time, only ten. I thought for sure I'd need to stop every twenty minutes for a bathroom break. Are you feeling ok?" he asked.

"No, my head is pounding. I think I might have one of those migraine things. I have never had a headache this bad before."

"Well let's get you inside, are you allowed to take anything for it?"

I shrugged. "I don't know. Can you just help me get into the house?"

Before even a second passed, my door was being opened while a shower of black mist brushed across my face. Aidan took my arm and carefully lowered me to the gravel driveway where suddenly hours of missed bathroom breaks hit me.

"Move, move, move," I shouted as I held up my stomach and ran to the house, my head throbbing in rhythm with each step. As I neared the front porch steps I saw the familiar form of my grandfather standing in the doorway, his arms outstretched waiting for the hug that would simply have to wait.

"Be with you in a moment," I said and ran to the bathroom that was just inside the hallway. Thank goodness it was the first door and my pants didn't have a button or a zipper or else I may not have made it.

Through the door I could hear Aidan laughing at me, and the sound of it made my headache worse. For the first time I was thankful that the babies were still. Even the slightest movement right now might make the nausea I was feeling unbearable. This had to be one of those migraines. Why today of all days did my body decide to have one? Like the day wasn't stressful enough already. But I was safe now, in a place where I felt absolutely at home. At least there was a silver lining.

After taking my time freshening up in the bathroom I finally ventured back out into the living room where Daddy O stood looking like a gray-headed elf next to Aidan.

"Sorry about that," I said waddling back over to him, wrapping my arms around him expecting my usual bear hug, but instead I felt awkward in my grandfather's limp embrace. "Are you ok, Daddy O?" I asked as I pulled away from him.

"A 'course, sugar," he affirmed. "Just want to be gentle with ya. You feelin' ok?"

I shook my head slightly and pressed my thumb and index finger into my temples. "No, I have a really bad headache."

"Maybe you need to eat something," Aidan said, walking quickly toward the door and returning with the shopping bag of snacks from the hotel.

"Yeah, maybe that's it. Are you hungry, my darlings?" I said, rubbing my belly but receiving no response. Instead the room began to spin as the blood drained from my head. "I need to lie down."

Aidan's arm came around my back, holding me up against his side while leading me down the hallway to my room. Slowly putting one foot in front of the other I noticed that there was something different, something not right about my surroundings.

"Where are the pictures?" I asked, whipping around to face Daddy O who was just starting to sit down in his favorite chair.

"What pictures, sugar?"

"Wha…what pictures!" My head whipped back and forth doing a double-take like a cartoon character. "The pictures that have been hanging in this hallway for thirty some odd years. Pictures of you and Mama Jo and me."

Daddy O's eyes grew large as he bit his lip several times before answering. "Well…uh…I gave 'em to your mama."

"You did what! But…why? She's not even in them," I screamed, causing my head to pound so hard I thought it would explode. "Tell her to bring them back. I have more claim on them than she does. I can't believe you would do that, Daddy O…I…I really need to lie down."

Pushing Aidan aside I stepped into my old bedroom, looking for more evidence of my estranged mother's thievery. But all was intact, including my thick comforter and plush pillows that were calling my name. I didn't even hear Aidan come into the room after me, but was startled when he was suddenly pulling a thick quilt over me as I collapsed on top of the bed.

"The food bag is on the floor next to you," he whispered as he tucked the quilt in.

"You make it sound like I'm a horse or something."

Aidan smiled as he rose from my side and walked to the door. "Get some sleep, Morgan. And if you're good, I'll give you a good brushing and some sugar cubes."

"Smartass."

"You know it," he winked and shut the door behind him as my eyelids did the same.

It was the smell of food that woke me. My stomach was growling and cramping so hard it made me curl up on my side until it passed. The splitting headache was gone, leaving only a dull ache behind my eyes. My muscles were stiff from the long drive and my perpetual sleeping position, but nothing a nice hot shower wouldn't cure. But before I could even entertain the idea of showering I needed food. My mouth was beginning to water from the smells that were sneaking from underneath my door.

Slowly I stretched up from the bed, kneading my thumbs into my stiff back as I walked to the door and opened it to see the wall in front of me still stripped of decades of family memories. I wanted to rekindle my argument with my grandfather, but I was too tired and hungry to do it right at this moment. Besides he looked too fragile sitting in his recliner reading the paper, a sight that was as familiar to me as my own name. Daddy O looked up from his paper with a warm apologetic smile as I walked down the hall and began to push himself up from his chair.

"Don't get up," I said quickly. Padding further into the living room I could see Aidan in the kitchen standing up against the large center island leafing through a magazine. His greeting smile was soon wiped away when I looked quickly from him to Daddy O and back again.

"If you're sitting there," I said pointing to Daddy O, "and Aidan is standing there, who's cooking in the kitchen?"

Aidan looked confused as I ran into the kitchen. Standing in front of the stove with a small white apron tied over her jeans and red turtleneck sweater was the last person I wanted to see.

"What is *she* doing here?" I said in a nasty tone.

"Now, Bri Bri, that's not polite to say to someone who is making your favorite comfort food."

Shelby turned away from the stove, a fake smile plastered on her face as she walked over to me and wrapped her arms around my neck. The gesture was so uncomfortable and unnatural that I couldn't help but flinch and pull her arms away. For a second she looked angry, but like the Southern woman she was, she shook her head of short blonde hair and acted as though the awkward encounter between us never happened.

"You know, Bri Bri, your face is looking a little puffy. You must be having a girl, they say girls always make you ugly during pregnancy," Shelby said condescendingly as she walked back to the stove.

I gave Aidan a murderous glare, it was all I could do to hold my feet to the floor and not strangle the woman.

"Aidan, I thought no one was supposed to know that I was here. Shelby is the last person that should be trusted."

Aidan opened his mouth, but Shelby quickly interrupted without turning away from the stove. "Bri Bri, I'm right here and I'm not deaf."

"I wasn't trying to be secretive, Shelby," I snapped.

"Ok, ok," Daddy O interrupted and stepped in front of me. "Now, 'Lil

Bri, yur mama's come up here to help take care a ya, and she's makin' one of yur favorites. Now can't the two a you just sit and have a quiet dinner? Fur the sake of an old man, do it fur me?"

Boy Daddy O was pulling out the big guns and I couldn't deny him anything, ever. When I nodded reluctantly he gave me a wink and a quick peck on the cheek before heading back through the foyer toward his chair.

"Wait, Daddy O, you're not eating?"

He laughed while he eased himself down into his recliner. "Sugar, I'm an old man, I ate three hours ago."

Worry must have been plastered on my face since Aidan tapped me gently on my shoulder as he said, "Just remember, it's only for a few days. I'll stay in here with you."

"Thanks," I replied half-heartedly. "Goodness knows what Shelby thinks my favorite comfort food is."

"Grilled cheese and tomato soup a course," Shelby replied as she placed a large plate down on the kitchen island that held a bowl of thick steaming soup and two halves of a gooey grilled cheese sandwich.

"Damn, she's right," I groaned and rolled my eyes.

"Of course I'm right," she said victoriously, "I'm yur mother."

I didn't respond which made Aidan clear his throat and urged me with his eyes to say something.

"Thank you, Shelby."

Having to say it tasted like vinegar, and I could see she was just as unhappy about me using her first name. Seconds later she was flitting about the kitchen making another sandwich for herself while Aidan pulled out one of the stools from underneath the island and gestured for me to sit.

"Has Cameron called?" I asked as I tore off a piece of my grilled cheese and dunked it in my soup.

"Not yet," Aidan replied.

My stomach sank slightly as I placed the sandwich in my mouth. "That can't be a good sign. They've been searching for Elaina all day."

"But it could mean they have her and are interrogating her or whatever it is they do."

"Can I try calling him?"

"He said he'd call as soon as he could," Aidan replied, not hiding his annoyance.

"Oh sure he will," Shelby said snidely from the stove.

"What is that supposed to mean?" I asked as I tore off another piece of my sandwich and dipped it in my soup.

"Alls I'm sayin' is that a man who just sent his baby mama twelve hundred miles away probably ain't too keen on callin'.'"

Aidan placed a steadying hand on my shoulder. "Morgan you look pale."

I could feel the blood running out of my cheeks as I looked at him, only to have to turn quickly away from him and rush to the end of the island. The trashcan's large metal lid clanged loudly on the kitchen floor as I retched embarrassingly into the garbage bag. Thankfully I hadn't eaten much so it was over in minutes and Aidan was quick to take the bag out to the back deck.

Afterwards, I instantly felt better. My stomach and chest felt light, and I was hungry. Perhaps the grilled cheese was too heavy on such an empty stomach. I decided to forgo the sandwich hoping the soup would settle my stomach instead. It took only two spoonful's of tomato soup before I was spitting it up in the sink.

"Not again," Aidan moaned. "I totally didn't sign up for this."

"Then leave!" I yelled before rinsing my mouth and wiping it with a dishtowel.

"Ah Morgie, I didn't mean it like that," he pleaded as he put the garbage can back together.

"I can't help it, Aidan. And don't call me Morgie."

Shelby seemed to be unfazed by the whole fiasco as she cut her grilled cheese in half and sat down on a stool on the other side of the island. "Well, I'm sure you're going to blame this on my cooking."

"Should I?" I snapped, although she didn't acknowledge me in the slightest. Aidan seemed happier for it and pulled me around the island to get some distance between us.

I shrugged out of his grip to step over to the refrigerator, hoping there was something I could keep down. My stomach growled loudly at the sight of a fresh tomato propped up by a jar of mayonnaise. It was a sign from God.

"Brianna Morgan, thou shalt eat a tomato and mayonnaise sandwich," I sang like an idiot and held the tomato and mayonnaise above my head like it was the Holy Grail. Even the babies stirred a little which set my mind at ease since I hadn't felt them all day.

"You're weird," Aidan groaned.

"Get used to it," I laughed.

I was almost drooling while I cut the tomato into thin slices and spread the mayo on the warm toasted bread. The kitchen was quiet while I put my sandwich together with Aidan finishing his magazine and Shelby eating her dinner. There are no words to describe what it feels like to quench a pregnancy craving. It was bliss, complete satisfaction, and a small orgasm all wrapped into one. So maybe there were a few words. The cool tomato was a wonderful contrast to the warm bread and I finished it in a matter of minutes. Having food in my stomach made me feel so good that I had almost forgotten about the earlier altercation. Maybe this night could be salvaged after all.

As was the case many times, one little sandwich wasn't enough for me so I rose from my seat and began to prepare another one. Just as the bread popped up from inside the toaster I heard Shelby mutter something under her breath.

"What was that?" I asked, turning around to see that Aidan was already looking at her with shocked eyes.

Shelby shrugged as she rose from her stool and placed her plate and bowl in the sink. "Just makin' an observation is all."

"And what, pray tell, would that be?"

"Shelby," Aidan warned but she ignored him.

"I was just saying that maybe you should watch how much you eat. Not everyone's figure can bounce back after pregnancy."

My cheeks were beginning to burn with anger. "Shelby, I have to say that it's pretty sad that you don't even know your own daughter is having twins. Of course I'm going to eat more, I'm eating for three. Besides I haven't eaten all day, literally all day. I think I'm allowed a little indulgence at this moment."

"Well then you need to watch yourself even more then with twins. They'll just destroy your body with how big you'll get. I'm just thinking of your best interests here."

I laughed. "You've never done it before, why start now? What could you possibly be referring to?"

"I'm talking about Cameron."

Hearing his name made me freeze and the butterflies start to flutter. "What about him?"

"Now, honey, think of it from his point of view. He's surrounded by female Vampires that will never gain a pound or get cellulite or even a single wrinkle." She pursed her lips together, giving me a sympathetic smile. "I mean you don't want to give him a reason to stray, do you? S'not like he hasn't done it before."

Her words were daggers in my heart. My anger from before drained from my cheeks and once again I became a defenseless little ten-year-old girl. Without saying another word I left the kitchen, trying hard to keep the threatening tears inside. Anger had been replaced with fear and then sadness as I rounded the corner into the living room to see Daddy O sitting unaffected in his recliner. Of all the medical issues he may have had, hearing loss was not one of them. He heard all the things Shelby had said to me and never came to my defense.

I wanted to go home. That used to mean coming here; this had always been home to me. But now home was with Cam, not a place or dwelling, just him. Home was lying in his arms, feeling his cool lips at my temple before I drifted off to sleep knowing how much he loved me. I had gone weeks without that feeling and just when I got it back he's ripped away from me like always.

Tears started streaming down my face as I shut the door to my room and the full impact of the day hit me. I barely made it to the bed before my head started to pound again. Clutching a pillow to my chest I sobbed into its fluffy comfort hoping it would mute the sound.

Only a few minutes passed before there was a soft knock at the door.

"Go away," I sniffled. But my request was denied when Aidan stepped through the door holding a small plate in his hand. "I said go away."

"Unfortunately for you I don't take orders well. I finished making your sandwich. Well, at least I tried to." Slowly he sat down at the edge of the bed, placing the plate next to me. As I took one of the sandwich halves he said, "Your mother is a real piece of work. I thought you two were best friends."

I almost choked on a tomato slice. "Where did you hear that?"

"From her," he replied sheepishly. "Ollie thought you might need a woman around to help you with…well…woman things. And I thought, well she's your mother, what would be the harm. When she got here she kept telling me how close you two were, and how hard it's been for her with you living so far away. I'm sorry, Morgan, I thought I was doing something nice for you. For what it's worth, Ollie's talking to her now. He really wants the two of you to make up."

"It's never gonna happen. There's just too much I can't forgive her for, and she's certainly not sorry for anything she's ever done to me."

"Like what?" he said as he pushed himself up beside me. I felt a little uncomfortable having another man sit next to me in bed, especially in the exact same place where Cameron had been only a few months before. But Aidan seemed casual enough and he was being a friend, an odd candidate, but a friend all the same.

"The story starts before I was born, you're sure you want to hear it?"

"I'm the Vamp here, I've got time on my hands."

"You may fall asleep out of boredom."

"Well that would be a first, but you are a pretty powerful hybrid."

I smiled as he reminded me that I was powerful. Shelby had made me forget all that I had done, all the Vampires I had defeated and even killed. I only needed to deal with her for a couple more days until Cameron came for me. I could do a couple days.

"Ok, then. So let me start with Shelby Morgan, the blood slut years."

Chapter Thirty-Four

Brianna

If I thought my headache was bad my first day at Daddy O's, it was nothing compared to day two. I didn't even leave the bed yesterday because not only was my head throbbing, I had morning sickness that lasted all day and bouts of vertigo. I felt horrible and Cameron still hadn't called which scared the crap out of me. What if something happened to him? Had he told anyone where I was?

My worries brought on fits of hysterical crying and an irritable attitude toward anyone who tried to talk to me. Honestly, I was surprised Aidan hadn't thrown in the towel and just left me here to rot. I certainly deserved it.

But today was a new day and thankfully the room wasn't spinning. Unfortunately I still had a headache, which frankly I was just sick of having. The babies were kicking lightly, announcing to me that they were awake. It was rare that I ever got this far in a pregnancy, so anything these two threw at me I would take gladly. I already knew that this pregnancy was different than all the others, and not the obvious fact that there were two half-Vampires swimming around in there. This one was different because I knew I wouldn't lose them, my father had shown me as much. Having that knowledge took away the stress that always clouded me in the past. I could finally enjoy being pregnant, even if it did bring weird hot flashes and all-day-sickness spells.

"I have been waiting a long time for you two," I cooed to my stomach as I rubbed it softly. They responded by bouncing from one side of my stomach to the other. "Good grief, are we doing laps around the pool?"

There was a light knock at the door before Aidan poked his head in. "You awake?"

"Yeah."

"Is someone in here?"

"Nope."

"Talking to yourself?"

"No," I laughed, "to the babies."

Aidan stepped into the room carrying a breakfast tray which had something awful smelling on a plate. "Do they answer back?"

"Of course not," I replied and noticed their kicking immediately stopped.

"Don't act like it's not a valid question, you never know these days. I would have never thought a hybrid like you could take down an army of Vamps just by doing…well whatever it is you do," he said, placing the tray at the foot of the bed.

"You heard about that?"

"Everyone heard about that. Anyway, I brought you breakfast."

"Is that what that is?"

"Hey, it's not my fault you threw up everything that Shelby made you the last two days. Since you're too sick to make something yourself that means you're stuck with me trying to fake my way through it."

I pushed myself up to a seated position, allowing Aidan to place the tray over my legs. "What a…is this exactly," I asked as I picked at the steaming mystery food with my fork.

"Scrambled eggs."

"They're purple."

"Yeah," Aidan replied while scratching the back of his head roughly. "I think I got the butter too hot and they just did…that."

It was a nice gesture, but there was no way I was going to eat them. Instead I went for the toast that seemed harmless.

"Did Shelby refuse to help you because they were for me?"

Aidan nodded. "Since she's declared she'll never cook for you again she went to the store to get you something for your headache and some bland foods for your stomach."

"I'm surprised Daddy O didn't help you. He used to make me eggs all the time."

"Guess he just wasn't feeling up to it today," he replied dismissively.

"No baseball hat today? Got a hot date or something?"

"If by date you mean watching the great Brianna Morgan puke her brains out all day, then yes I have a date."

"I'm sorry. This must be awful for you."

"Eh," he shrugged, "nothing I can't handle."

"You surprise me."

"How so?"

"Because ever since we met you've been a pompous, egotistical, womanizing jerk."

"At least you recognize my good qualities," he laughed. "I used to be a Gatherer, remember? Can't be a good one without being the pompous, egotistical, womanizing, handsome specimen that I am."

"I thought you got fired from the Gatherers."

"Quit, Morgan, I quit," he replied warningly. "Do you want to try and lay out in the living room? I promise I won't try and make more eggs."

"Let's see what the babies will allow me to do today."

Slowly I lifted the breakfast tray to him before removing the blankets from around me and placing my feet on the floor. Aidan held the tray in one hand as he wrapped a firm arm around my waist, helping me to my feet. After a minute or so of successfully keeping my toast down, Aidan was carefully shuffling me down the hallway one step at a time. Daddy O met us in the living room, a bright smile on his face as he took me from Aidan's arms and helped me the rest of the way to the couch.

"It's good to see ya out, sugar. Still lookin' a little puny though," he said and tucked a warm fluffy blanket over me.

"Today the couch, tomorrow the world," I laughed, although the sudden joy made my head hurt. "I can't believe you let Aidan make me purple eggs. You could have done better than that with your eyes closed, Daddy O."

Daddy O turned uncomfortably in his recliner, his face slightly etched with guilt. "The man wanted to make ya breakfast, and I was busy with my coffee anyway. The boy needs to learn somehow."

"Oh and why's that?"

"To get the ladies of course," Aidan answered smugly as he returned from the kitchen, but turned back around when Shelby walked through the door to help her with the bags in her arms. I guess chivalry wasn't dead within Aidan Pierce.

In contrast, Shelby glared at me before turning into the kitchen. "The pharmacist said she could have acetaminophen for her headache, but nothin' to help with the nausea without a prescription. Sorry, Bri Bri, you'll just have to suffer through it like every other woman in history. A 'course I don't remember ever bein' this sick when I was pregnant. You must just have a weaker constitution than me."

"Or maybe you don't remember because you were a freakin' nut job," I muttered to myself. Aidan laughed from the kitchen, however, I was surprised when Daddy O chuckled as well.

A moment later Aidan handed me a glass of water and two little white pills that would hopefully take away this awful headache. The glass of water was in my left hand and as I drank down the cool refreshing water I noticed my sapphire shining in the morning sun.

"Ohmygod," I spit into the glass. I realized quickly that I needed to stop saying that since both Aidan and Daddy O leapt to my side with worried expressions on their faces. "Sorry. Babies are fine," I announced to their relief. "I just realized I forgot to tell you that Cameron and I are engaged."

There was a loud crash in the kitchen, causing Aidan quirk a smile. "Shelby is obviously very happy for you. I should go check on her."

"Sugar, when did this happen?" Daddy O asked.

"Late Saturday night. It's so new and I've been so sick it completely slipped my mind."

Daddy O lifted my left hand, carefully eyeing my ring. "Mighty nice ring. Is that one a them sapphires?"

"Yes, Daddy O, it's one a them sapphires."

"Only a diamond is a serious engagement ring, Bri Bri," Shelby said snidely as she stepped back into the living room.

"Like you ever got one?" I snapped. "It's what I wanted anyway. I don't need a diamond to prove that he loves me. And if wanting to marry me doesn't prove it to you then he can tell you himself when he comes and gets me."

Shelby looked up to Aidan who stood next to her. "You didn't tell her?"

Aidan sighed as he widened his eyes at her.

"Tell me what, Aidan?"

Aidan bit his lip as he shifted his weight uncomfortably from hip to hip. "Cameron called."

"When!" I shouted as I shot up from the couch, only to catch my head in my hand as the room spun around me. "Why didn't you tell me?"

Aidan's cool hands cupped both my arms and slowly lowered me back down onto the couch. "He called early this morning while you were sleeping. I was going to wake you, but he insisted that I let you sleep."

"What did he say?" I asked softly and slowly opened my eyes. Thankfully the room had stopped spinning, but Aidan's avoidance of eye contact was evidence that whatever he was hiding was pretty bad.

"Oh for heaven's sake," Shelby said flustered as she came around to the edge of the couch. "Cameron's not coming any time soon."

"Shelby enough," Aidan spat. "That's not what he said."

I could feel the tears welling up in my eyes as my nose began to sting.

Aidan took my hand between his own, squeezing it reassuringly. "They didn't find Elaina in Boston. Victor called everyone back to the Warrior manor to regroup. You could be here for another week, maybe more."

"Why didn't he...I can go to the manor, can't I?"

"Victor said no. The manor was breached before, so everyone is in agreement that you're safer here."

"Everyone including Cameron?"

Aidan nodded, and my heart sank. The tears were inevitable and I didn't bother to try and hide them as my head fell into my hands.

"You see, Bri Bri, it doesn't matter if he put a ring on your finger, them Vamps just want one thing."

"Shut up!" I shouted as I clumsily stood from the couch. "Just leave me alone."

"Morgan, wait," Aidan called after me as I padded out of the living toward the kitchen.

"I'm going to make myself some toast, ok? I just need a few minutes, just leave me alone for a few goddamn minutes!"

No one followed me into the kitchen; actually no one made any sound at all. That wasn't what I really wanted either. I needed to cry while I made something to eat and I needed noise out there in order to cover up the sound. After I slammed a couple of cabinets looking for the bread, the TV finally went on and I could get on with my sobbing. Frankly I was surprised the bread wasn't sopping wet once I put it in the toaster. Damn Cameron. Damn Victor! How could they leave me here? How could Cam not come for me, not even dare to tell me himself?

Another wave of emotion came over me, causing my head to hurt and the room to begin to spin again. I grabbed hold of the edge of the counter, anchoring myself in a standing position while salty tears fell onto the countertop below. Next to me the sound of the bread popping up from the toaster startled me, causing my eyes to fly open and notice a red shiny edge of plastic sticking out from underneath one of the shopping bags. Silently I placed my fingers underneath the bag and pulled out a red cell phone. Aidan's cell phone. Aidan's cell phone that Cameron had called earlier this morning. I know Aidan had said Cameron would be using disposable cell phones to call us, but what if he hadn't thrown this one away just yet. Just what if.

Not wanting to be too conspicuous, I opened the fridge and removed the jelly and butter while scrolling through the recent call list. The latest call was from an unknown number, whereas the other calls seemed to be from within his contact list. This had to be Cam. Please, please let it be Cam because if it wasn't, Aidan would be furious at me.

The laundry room was right off the kitchen, and thankfully the door leading into it was open. Quietly I shuffled inside, careful to shut the door behind me softly and slowly release the doorknob until it clicked into place. I couldn't press the talk button fast enough, and my stomach started to churn nervously while the phone rang once, twice, three times, and then finally…

"Hello?" a woman answered.

"Who the fuck is this?" I shouted into the phone.

I could tell the woman was taken aback. "Who were you looking for?"

"I'm looking for Cameron Burke. I was told he was calling from this number."

"Oh," she answered mystified. "He's uh…indisposed at the moment."

I was so in shock that I didn't hear the door open, but suddenly Aidan was yelling at me from behind. "Morgan, what the hell are you doing?"

Before I could answer, Aidan ripped the phone from my hand and ended the call.

"No, wait," I pleaded as I reached across his chest trying to grab the phone back.

"Jesus, Brianna, I can take the snide comments and crying and throwing up, but pulling a stunt like that puts us all in danger. Damn it, woman, you're going to get us all killed."

"I just wanted to talk to him. I wanted to hear his voice, ok? Cameron's the only person I really trust and he's the only one who can make me feel better about having to stay here. So I called the last number and that bastard dares to have a woman answer. For my sake, please let me call again, I need to know who that was. Please, Aidan," I begged, holding my hand out in front of me.

"I told you he was using disposable phones. He could have given that phone away already, and now someone could connect you to my number.

Don't you realize that?"

"No, she knew him, she told me he was indisposed, which means she's near him. Please just let me call again."

"Brianna, you're hysterical. You need to lie down," he said, placing his arm around my back trying to escort me out of the laundry room.

"No!" I shouted and ran out into the kitchen, passing by Shelby as I continued through the living room.

Everyone was calling after me as I rounded the corner to the hallway, and suddenly the walls began to close in around me. A piercing pain shot through my head causing a loud shriek to escape my lips. My feet slipped out from under me and I fell quickly to the floor. But just before I hit the ground Aidan's arms were around me, cradling me to his chest, but I pushed him away as I began to choke on something going down the back of my throat. Aidan responded quickly and lifted me upright, making it easier for me to breathe while I continued to cough. Another second later Aidan shouted something to Shelby who in turn came running towards us with a towel. When Aidan pressed the towel into my face I could taste the coppery tang of blood in my mouth.

Aidan lifted me from the floor, Shelby following after as he carried me into the bathroom and gently sat me on the floor. The two of them shouted orders at one another while I caught a glimpse of Daddy O standing in the hallway, watching at a distance. I removed the towel from my face and was shocked at the amount of blood in the cloth.

"Wh-what's happening?" I stuttered, suddenly feeling light-headed.

Aidan knelt in front of me, placing his hands on either side of my face. "Just stay with me, Morgan. Focus on my voice."

His voice was panic stricken as he placed a clean towel up to my face. I couldn't focus on his voice let alone his face while blood continued to stream from my nose and my head pound as though it was being hit by a meat clever.

"Don't…" I began, unable to finish without coughing.

"Don't what," Aidan said forcefully as he pulled my face up to his.

The room was becoming dark as I panted uncontrollably in front of him. "Don't….drink…my…blood."

But I couldn't tell him why before falling into his chest and allowing the darkness to consume me.

Chapter Thirty-Five

Brianna

I felt cool fingers making light circles on the top of my hand. A part of me didn't want to open my eyes at all. It was surprising how fainting had become a normal occurrence in my life this past year. However, nothing about what had happened before I fainted was normal - the headache, the blood, especially the blood.

"I know you're awake, Morgan," Aidan said softly next to me.

"You know you're not supposed to wake sleeping people," I whined as I rolled away from him.

"Yes, but you weren't sleeping."

"How do you know?" I replied snidely, pulling the covers over my head.

"You stopped mumbling in your sleep."

"Oh heavens. Did I say anything fun?"

"Fig leaf? Fig something or other. You just kept saying it over and over again."

Figs? Why the heck would I be dreaming about figs? My dreams were so weird I didn't even ask anymore, though I couldn't even remember dreaming anything, let alone about figs.

Knowing I would never get back to sleep now, I slowly pushed myself up into a seated position, my back pressed up against the wall with Aidan's supportive arms holding me up from the front while he searched my face with worried eyes.

"How long have I been out?" I asked as blood rushed to my head.

"Almost twenty-four hours. You really had us going there, Morgie." I glared at him from under my brow. "Er, I mean Brianna. How do you feel?"

I took a deep breath in, being sure to fill my lungs as far as they would go. And…nothing. No nausea, no headache, and definitely no blood coming from my nose.

"I feel fine," I answered, but then the tears came. "What's happening to me?"

Aidan squeezed my shoulder. "Nothing's wrong with you, Morgan. You had a nosebleed."

"Aidan, that was not just a nosebleed, just like those weren't normal headaches. What if I have a brain tumor or something?"

"Oh come on, Brianna," Aidan replied annoyed and rolled his eyes. "You do not have a brain tumor."

"How do you know? What if everything I do is because of a big ass tumor in my head? It's slowly eating my brain away and you're sitting there laughing at me while Cameron's off having an affair…"

"Whoa, whoa, wait," Aidan interrupted as he rose from the bed. "Who says Cameron's having an affair?"

"A *woman* answered his phone!"

"Heaven forbid," Aidan shouted dramatically while throwing his hands in the air. "A woman happened to be standing next to a ringing cell phone and you automatically assume he's screwing her? It's craziness like this that keeps me single."

"Oh there are more reasons as to why you're single," I snapped and then began to cry again. "I'm not crazy, Aidan. He's done this before."

Aidan sighed and let the tension fade before he replied softly, "Look, Morgan, I've known Cameron for a long time and I just can't imagine him cheating."

"He kissed another woman. He got caught doing it and says it was under duress, but how do you ever really know?"

"Who was she?"

"A hybrid skank named Nikki."

His laughter sent chills down my spine.

"I'm sorry, it's still hard for me to believe that Mr. Straight-and-Narrow Burke strayed from the reservation, but even more so actually kissed someone named Nikki. What is she sixteen?"

"Stop making fun of me, Aidan," I shouted. "In a few months I'm going to have to raise two little babies and I'm terrified I'm going to have to do it alone. I thought Cameron and I were past this, but what if…"

My words left me and I was overcome by dozens of what-ifs and none of them pleasant. The bed sank as Aidan sat next to me again, causing me to lean toward the edge of the bed and rest my head on his shoulder. Of all the people I knew, Aidan Pierce was the last person I thought I would be borrowing a shoulder to cry on. Even more surprising was when he began rubbing my back in soft circles while trying to silence my sobs.

"Morgan, Cameron loves you. We both know that. He wouldn't have done all of this just so he could go and be with some other woman." I shot up from his shoulder, tears still leaking from my eyes as the thought struck me. Seeing the sudden worry in my face Aidan continued, "He wouldn't, Brianna, you know him. He was so worried about you when he heard what happened yesterday."

"When did you talk to him!"

"Yesterday afternoon. When he heard what happened he called again in the evening, but you were still out cold."

"What was his excuse?"

"He said they were getting ready to go out on some kind of mission and he'd left the phone somewhere. When you called, some other Warrior picked up the phone."

"Who? I want a name."

Aidan rolled his eyes. "I didn't ask. He said he'd call as soon as he was able. Victor was sending them off late last night, but he'll call. Just hang in there, enjoy my company and don't let your mind wander."

I raised an eyebrow at him and shook my head. "Such a stupid boy," I said angrily as I carefully rose from the bed, prepared for whatever would rush over me. But I didn't feel anything. How could I have made such a drastic turnaround in twenty-four hours?

I felt Aidan's arm come around my back, seemingly to help me out of the room but I didn't need help. I wasn't ill anymore, just really moody and still upset about the woman answering Cameron's phone. Aidan could tell me what Cameron said to him until the cows came home, but I would still want to hear it from Cameron himself. Honestly, I just wanted to hear Cam's voice. Yup, I was pathetic. But I couldn't just stand in my bedroom feeling sorry for myself, not because it wasn't good for my psyche, I had to pee in the worst way.

Unfortunately whatever quiet time I thought I might get in the bathroom was negated by a million and one thoughts flipping quickly through my head. Aidan must have thought I had become schizophrenic when I told myself to shut up several times. Not even a soothing hot shower could stop the sound of the unknown woman telling me that Cameron was "indisposed." Just the way she said it made it sound like she was trying to stir up trouble.

When I finally ventured out, I was still in a miserable mood but it was lightened at the sight of my grandfather.

"Well hey there, sugar!" Daddy O said happily as he folded his newspaper in his lap. "Yur lookin' much better."

"I feel better," I sighed as I stretched myself out on the couch. "Sorry if I scared you yesterday."

"Wasn't just me, 'Lil Bri. You gave us all quite a scare. Even yur mama was worried 'bout ya."

I didn't comment since I didn't want to hurt his feelings by telling him that he was completely wrong on that last point. Then speak of the devil she walked in from the kitchen with Aidan close behind her.

"Now, Daddy, don't make it sound like I've never worried about her before. I brought you a muffin, Bri Bri. Don't worry you can eat it, I didn't make it."

I stared at her for a moment, not taking the muffin from her afraid that it would explode, or be full of glass, or be anything other than the delicious chocolate chip muffin that it looked like. She shook it at me one last time before giving up and leaving it on the armrest of the couch. Daddy O gave me a criticizing look over the edge of his paper. She never did things like this, so why wouldn't I think the worst when she did.

Unable to keep my stomach pangs at bay any longer, I unwrapped half of the large chocolate chip muffin and began picking at the top. After keeping down the second bite I really dug in, not even leaving behind a single chocolate morsel. Amazingly having food in my stomach suddenly made my head clearer.

"Figlia!" I shouted, causing Daddy O to crumple his paper, Aidan to leap from the couch, and Shelby to knock over her cup of coffee.

"Damn, woman, what is wrong with you!" Aidan shouted, his brows furrowed in anger and fists clenched.

"I'm sorry! I just figured something out. I wasn't talking about figs in my sleep. I was saying figlia, it means daughter in Italian." Everyone just looked at me with confused eyes. "It's Eris. That's what he calls me. I really need to talk to my father."

Aidan sighed frustratingly. "Morgan, how many times do I have to tell you? You can't use the phone to call…"

"But I don't need a phone to talk to Eris, silly. I think he was talking to me in my sleep, but I've been sleeping so deeply that I haven't responded. He must be worried sick."

Shelby snickered as she walked in from the kitchen with paper towels in hand. "That man hasn't worried about you a day in his life. He's not going to start now."

"How about another muffin?" Aidan interrupted and stood in front of me, urging me not to be baited by Shelby's insult.

"No, I'm good. And do you know why?"

"Please don't tell me," he mumbled.

"Because my father came back into my life and loves me and takes care of me when I need him, and also because I have a stepmother who treats me like her own child, which is more than I can say about the woman who gave birth to me."

"That's it!" Shelby shouted and threw the coffee soaked napkins on the floor. Aidan immediately stepped in front of Shelby as she came toward me. "I came here to help you out of the goodness of my heart and you have done nothin' but be nasty to me."

"Me!" I shouted back, struggling to get up from the couch with my baby belly in the way and taking three tries to scoot myself toward the edge of the couch in order to actually stand. "Since I got here you have made it your mission to make me miserable. Every word out of your mouth is an insult, and there's the biggest difference between you and Eris. He doesn't hurt me and try to make me feel inferior to him. Oh, wait, I take that back. The biggest difference between the two of you is the fact that he never tried to blackmail his way into being turned into a Vampire by attempting to commit suicide and stab your unborn baby."

Shelby's eyes widened, glazed with tears. "It…it's not true," she stuttered. "She told you these lies, didn't she? That woman wants you to hate me. He calls her his wife, but she's just another whore, just like all the rest of them."

"Don't you dare talk about Seraphina like that," I shouted, this time being held back by Aidan as I flailed around him trying to claw Shelby's eyes out. "Sera finally filled the hole I've had in my heart since Mama Jo died. Lord knows you haven't showed me the decency a man gives to a dog. Eris stayed away because he thought by keeping his distance I'd have a chance at a normal life. He even said that if he had known how awful you were to me, he would have taken me away so fast…"

"Never in a million years would he have given up his way of life to take care of you."

"You miserable bitch!"

"That's enough, both of you!" Aidan shouted, throwing his hands out to both of us. "Brianna, sit down, you'll make yourself sick again. And Shelby…"

"Save your breath, blood sucker," Shelby replied angrily and stormed off into the foyer to grab her coat from the closet. "I don't have to stand here and listen to this. You may hate me, Bri Bri, but I am still your mother and whether you like it or not, you wouldn't be here without me. You keep goin' on about how you're nothin' like me and never wanna be. But I hate to break it to ya, Bri Bri, you got in bed with a Vamp just like I did and trust me when I say you're gonna get screwed in more ways than one."

With a flip of her short blond hair, the petite Southern lady slammed the front door behind her and proceeded to spin her tires on the gravel driveway before she sped away.

Personally I thought it was a victory.

"Is that all I needed to do to get her out of here?" I asked victoriously. However, my smile disappeared when I looked from Aidan to Daddy O who seemed less than pleased as he folded his paper and rose from his chair. "Sorry, Daddy O."

"Brianna Marie Morgan, you may not like her but she's yur mama and deserves a little more respect than what you just gave her."

"What!" I said flabbergasted. "She started it!"

"And you finished it. Does that make ya feel any better? Before I die I'd like the two of you to have a civil conversation with each other."

Daddy O tossed his paper on his chair and began walking down toward his bedroom at the end of the hall. Daddy O rarely ever laid into me, but when he did it tore my heart out. The one thing I never wanted to do was hurt or disappoint him and in his eyes I had done both.

Aidan held a tissue in front of me and I took it gladly. My victory against Shelby was bittersweet since Daddy O shamed me into tears. Aidan blurred into the kitchen and returned a half second later with another chocolate chip muffin in his outstretched hand.

"Nothing like family to make you feel all warm inside."

I tried to laugh, but what came out was a snotty laugh-cry causing Aidan to hand me another tissue and sit me down.

"It's times like these I'm happy I have no living relatives."

"It's not fair, Aidan," I sniffled. "Shelby has talked shit to me since I walked through that door and not once has Daddy O said anything to her. Then the one time I stick up for myself and tell the truth I'm the one sitting here crying. This is not how I'm supposed to feel when I come here." Suddenly my stomach growled and I was grateful for the muffin in my hand. "Don't judge me for eating this."

Aidan laughed as I pulled away the paper lining and started tearing into my second muffin of the morning.

"So your middle name is Marie?" he asked as he turned on the TV.

"Actually, not anymore. He must have forgotten in the heat of the moment. When you've been scolding someone with the same name for so many years I guess it's just habit."

"What is it then?"

"Marilena."

"Hmm. That's different. Why change it?"

I smiled. "It was kind of a peace offering to my father. I really do need to talk to him. I can't believe he hasn't been able to get through to me. I guess that means I'm sleeping well." Aidan nodded, although he furrowed his brow a little as if something was bothering him. So in true Brianna fashion, I changed the subject. "So you don't have any family?" I asked as I tore a large piece off the muffin top and shoved it in my mouth.

Aidan focused his gaze on the TV while he flipped quickly through the channels. "Most Vampires don't."

"I know, but were you married?"

Aidan turned his head, his eyebrows raised. "Can you honestly see me married?"

"No," I laughed. "Who Turned you? How old are you? I don't know anything about you."

"I'm actually just a little older than Cameron. And I was Turned by my father," he said, returning his attention to the TV.

"Really? Your father was a Vampire?"

"Why does that surprise you? Have you forgotten your father is too?"

"Oh yeah, duh. I just never think of Vampires Turning their children. Ohmygod, that means you were a hybrid?"

"Tell her what she's won, Bob," he said sarcastically then changed his tone as he noticed the murderous glare I was giving him. "Yes, I was a hybrid before they had a name for it. My mother died when I was young, and my father took me away to raise me on his own. When I was an adult he offered to Turn me, and I accepted."

At the mention of his father I could feel the tension radiating from his body. Of course in my stupidity I didn't lay off. "And he's no longer around?"

Aidan shook his head. "He was killed shortly after he Turned me."

"How?"

Aidan rose quickly from the couch, throwing the remote behind him as he stepped around the couch and walked toward the kitchen. "Not a subject I want to talk about, Morgan."

A few seconds later Aidan came walking back through the foyer with a bottle of dark red blood in his hand.

"I didn't mean to upset you."

"Whatever," Aidan replied dismissively before resuming his channel surfing. Just then a cheerful tune sounded, causing him to pull out his cell phone from his back pocket. With one glance at the number, he handed the cell phone to me and said, "It's for you."

Chapter Thirty-Six

Brianna

"Gin!" Daddy O shouted as he threw his cards down on the ottoman.

"What? How..." I stuttered in disbelief while Aidan chuckled. "Seriously, Daddy O, have you been training with a card shark or something? You've never beaten me at cards."

Daddy O's face fell slightly, giving Aidan an odd worried look before replying, "Maybe I've just been letting you win all these years."

"One more game?"

Daddy O nodded eagerly and gathered the cards from the ottoman and began shuffling. Aidan stood from the couch, reaching into the back pocket of his jeans which now permanently held his cell phone since I couldn't be trusted.

"Aidan here," he answered and then walked into the kitchen.

The butterflies in my stomach started to flutter in hopes that it was Cameron. It had been over a week since I talked to him for the first time, and to say the least it hadn't gone well. We fought over the woman who answered his phone. We argued over the fact that I had tried to call him, which could have been dangerous. And lastly I yelled at him when he told me that I would be staying in North Carolina for another week. Well, the week had come and gone without any news from him.

While I sorted my cards and cherished the sneaky grin across Daddy O's face, the wood floors creaked behind me as Aidan came back into the room.

"Yeah man, she's right here," he said and handed me the phone. He felt my reluctance when I didn't take the phone right away and covered the receiver up as he said, "Maybe it'll go better this time."

I took the phone, and with his help rose from my position on the floor and walked to my bedroom where I could pretend to have some privacy. Once I shut the bedroom door I instantly felt claustrophobic prompting me to open the French doors to let in the cool afternoon air. As soon as the breeze hit my face I was able to put the phone up to my ear.

"Brianna, are you there?"

"Yes, Cam, I'm here."

"Are you feeling any better?" he asked tentatively.

"A little. I had another nosebleed a couple of days ago, but nothing like that first one."

"That's good to hear."

"It's good to hear I had another nosebleed?"

"Uh, no," he replied with a frustrated sigh. "I meant that it wasn't as bad as the first one."

"I should see a doctor, Cam. What if something is wrong?"

"Brianna, I am sure everything is fine. It's most likely the change in altitude."

I sat on the corner of the bed, dumbfounded by his jackass response. "Altitude? Are you shitting me right now? Did you just blame my possible brain tumor on altitude?"

He sighed loudly into the phone. "Brianna, stop being ridiculous. You do not have a brain tumor."

"I'm not being ridiculous, Cam! Something is happening to me and it could be affecting the babies. All I'm asking is to go see a doctor, which is something I shouldn't have to ask for and it pisses me off that neither you nor Aidan seem to care. I'd think you of all people would want to rush me to the hospital."

"Then you are wrong because the last thing I would want is a record of a pregnant woman with twins going to the emergency room. Elaina would be on your trail so fast, and for all we know she has someone already in the vicinity looking for you to emerge from the house. Brianna, I know you are scared but I think you are overreacting. I have very little time to talk to you and I would rather not fight. Again."

I didn't bother to cover up the sound of my sniffling. "I don't want to fight either, but...I want to come home. Aidan drives like a maniac, put me in a car and I'll be at the manor in two days. I love Daddy O, but things just aren't the same here and Shelby is driving me crazy."

"Coming to the manor is not a good idea."

"Why not?"

"Because we cannot protect you here."

"Then let me go to my father's."

"You need to stay where you are," Cameron said in a raised voice.

"Then come and get me!"

"I can't!"

"Don't you use a contraction with me," I shouted back. It was the most pitiful comeback ever, I know this. It seemed as though several minutes silently passed between us, but it was probably more like agonizing seconds.

"How much longer do I need to stay here?" I finally said weakly.

"At least another couple of weeks," he answered flatly.

My cheeks felt hot as his words slapped me in the face. What started out as a few days had now turned into weeks. Not even the November breeze was stopping the walls from closing in on me now.

"Will you at least come see me?"

"That is just not possible, Brianna."

"Just for a couple of days? After everything I've been through the last few months can't you give me a little bit of your time? I don't think I'm asking too much here."

"You are not asking for much, but it is more than I can give you. We are traveling a great deal and I need to be ready at a moment's notice. The sooner we catch Elaina, the sooner we will be together. I really wish you would stop crying, there is nothing I can do about this."

I will concede that my tears were not helping the situation, but his tone was unbelievably cold. In the past, Cameron almost always backed down when I cried, or was at least sympathetic. In this moment he did neither, and it was slowly breaking my heart.

"But we'll miss our first Thanksgiving together."

He sighed again into the phone, making me well aware of how annoyed he was. "Brianna, I have never celebrated Thanksgiving, and of all the things I am doing for you right now I find it upsetting to be made to feel guilty about it."

"Well then why don't you just say what you're really feeling, Cam!" I shouted into the phone as I stood from the bed. "You don't miss me, you don't care to see me, and you're pretty happy with keeping me locked away down here. Ok, I get it. Thanks for another lovely conversation, Cameron. Maybe next time you can wait and call me when you have your head out of your ass and act like the man I fell in love with because right now I have no idea who the hell you are."

I could hear Cameron's voice coming through the phone as I hung up on him, not caring in the slightest what comebacks or apologies he might have had. Frankly I didn't care. I was the one hurting here and he didn't seem to care. So why would I care if he tried to defend himself? Since I became pregnant I had been mad at him more often than I hadn't, and my heart was weary. Still holding the phone in my hand I shuffled down the hallway to find Daddy O and Aidan still playing a hand of gin. Without a word I handed Aidan back his phone and moved toward the front door where I slipped on my sneakers and ducked outside.

The sun was starting to set earlier and earlier each day as autumn began its transition into winter. The air was much cooler now that I was out in the open, however, it still didn't seem to calm my feverish cheeks. As my feet crunched along the gravel driveway, I didn't need to turn around to know that Aidan was walking behind me. Not only by the sound of the rocks beneath his boots, but from the sight of his white halo that was inching closer. What surprised me was his light was different, not only compared to other Vampires, but even from the first time I had seen it in Boston. His previous bright white halo was now milky, cloudy even. Was he ill? But my worries over Aidan's light didn't stop my progression across the driveway and when I reached the road his sickly essence quickly flew past me.

"You running away?" he asked lightly as he slowed to my pace. I shook my head, choosing to keep my eyes on the ground. "That's good to hear. Honestly at this rate it would take you two days to get to the highway." When I didn't acknowledge him, he quickly shifted gears from comedian to concerned friend. "If you're going to stay out here you really should have a coat on."

"I'm fine," I replied and turned down the narrow road. "I just need to take a walk."

"So why all the doom and gloom?"

"As if you didn't know," I snapped as I kicked a small rock down the hill. "He told you that I needed to stay here for a few more weeks, didn't he? That's why you left the room when he called, isn't it?"

Aidan shifted his gaze to the road and shoved his hands into his pockets. "He sent a text last night saying it might need to happen and asking my availability. So when I saw the unknown number I figured it was him and wanted to...I don't know, be prepared for when you flipped out."

"You shouldn't have to stay for this long, Aidan. It's not fair to you either. Seriously, you've become a freakin' babysitter. You have to be going crazy staying here with me."

"Don't worry about me, Morgan. Your family is paying me very well. It's almost like a paid vacation."

I laughed. "I don't think you've been on very many vacations."

"Now there's the smile I was looking for," he said teasingly as he bumped me with his hip. But my smile was gone just as quickly as it had formed and Aidan felt the change immediately. "Are you upset about having to stay or the fact that he's not coming to see you?" My eyes shot up to his. "Sorry, it's hard to turn my hearing off sometimes, especially when I hear you crying."

My emotions were all jumbled up inside me. I didn't know whether to feel embarrassed at the fact that he heard me making an emotional fool out of myself, or be relieved that he seemed to care. When we reached the bottom of the hill, I was suddenly brought to tears and my diarrhea of the mouth began.

"I'm pregnant, for cryin' out loud. This is supposed to be the happiest time in my life, and so far it's pretty much sucked. I've left him twice since I got pregnant, bet he didn't tell you that. And the reason I left was because he was being a jackass and neglecting me and then of course there was the whole kissing Nikki in our bedroom while she was practically naked and now I feel like he's doing it all over again. I know he's trying to protect me, but he can't be bothered to only call me twice in two weeks, and when he does he acts as though I'm the last person he wants to talk to. All I've wanted my entire life was to have a man who loves me and make a family with him. I thought I had that, Aidan. After the hell I endured with my ex-husband I honestly thought I had survived so that I could meet Cameron and have these babies."

Deep heaving sobs began to come up from my chest and only then did I realize that my forehead was resting on Aidan's chest while he gently rubbed my shoulders. Like the other time I had cried in front him, his soothing gestures didn't feel quite right. It just wasn't Cameron.

Not able to take Aidan's touch any longer I turned away from him and continued down toward the main mountain road. Between the stress and the crying, another headache was starting at my temples.

Just as I stepped off of Daddy O's street, Aidan pulled my arm back. "Morgan, I really think we should turn back. It's getting cold."

"Do you know what really makes me upset?" I asked, completely ignoring his statement and causing him to shake his head. "I've been waiting to have a child for almost fourteen years. Fourteen years of trying with a man I hated. Fourteen years of miscarriage after miscarriage and fertility specialists telling me that some people just aren't meant to have children. And then bam, I'm having twins. After years of heartbreak I'm finally blessed with two precious little babies that are miracles. They're such miracles, Aidan, and their father doesn't seem to care anymore. What the hell happened? What could have possibly happened between our last night together and today?" Aidan shrugged, digging his hands deeper into his pockets, being careful to avoid eye contact. "What? Do you know something?"

Aidan shrugged again. "Morgan, I'm really not good at this shit. I don't know why Cameron's being a dick, but he wouldn't have put a ring on your finger if he didn't love you."

But I had asked him. I had proposed to him that last night and woke up to Aidan telling me he needed to take me away. Cam seemed more than happy about being engaged at the time, but what if once everything sank in it frightened him? What if the thought of being married again put him over the edge? Cam fell in love with me first, and since then I have always been the reluctant one, or so I thought. He had changed when I became pregnant, becoming anxious and worried to the point of almost separating himself from me. Suddenly my current situation seemed eerily similar. Cameron was completely consumed with being a Warrior, choosing to keep me away in order to keep his fears and anxiety just as far.

My headache started to grow in intensity as my breathing became shallow. Even being in the open air I couldn't seem to get enough of it into my lungs. I stumbled backwards prompting Aidan to grab my shoulders to stabilize me. The babies started kicking faster and harder than I had ever felt, even creating a burning sensation in my stomach. Between the kicking, the burning, and the headache, the trees and rocks began to blur and swirl around me. The only stabilizing force was Aidan's firm grip on my shoulders, and though his lips were moving I couldn't hear what he was saying because of the ringing in my ears and intensely pulsing headache.

Suddenly Aidan shook my shoulders roughly, bringing my focus to him and noticing that his fangs were extending before my eyes. Slowly I looked down at myself and noticed that my shirt was streaked with blood. I placed my fingers up to my nose and came away with a handful of blood. It was happening again, and at full force with what looked like a hungry Vampire in front of me. Aidan pulled on my shoulders, trying to bring me closer but I struggled against him. The burning in my stomach exploded into every fiber of my body. I didn't even try to focus on his light and simply Pushed with every ounce of energy I had. My eyes flew open at the sound of Aidan screaming in pain and watched him fly backwards at least sixty feet. With the distance between us I scrambled up the hill toward the house. The pain in my head was unbearable by the time I reached the driveway, so much so that once again the scenery around me suddenly looked blurry and unfamiliar.

My knees buckled, causing me to shriek from the gravel digging into them and scraping my palms. The blood draining from my nose began covering the gray rocks under me as I pulled myself along the driveway. I didn't get far before I felt Aidan's arm around my stomach, pulling me up into his arms.

"Stop! Brianna, stop!"

"Get away from me," I tried to shout, but my lack of energy made it sound just above a whisper. "Don't bite me, please just let me go. I can't let you bite me."

Aidan's lips tightened before lifting me up from the ground and carrying me across the driveway and up the porch steps. Daddy O opened the door as we approached, confusion and panic on his face from the sight of the amount of blood leaking down my face.

Aidan quickly pushed past him as we entered the house, but when Daddy O began to follow, Aidan turned his head and shouted, "Stay in here, Ollie."

"I'm sure I can help," Daddy O replied.

"Stay! Here!" Aidan shouted as he ran me into the bathroom and sat me on the sink's counter.

"Don't yell at him," I said with effort. Aidan didn't respond, but merely handed me a towel and left the room. What little energy I had left seemed to be draining out of me and into the white towel I held up to my face, watching it turn red with blood. My head thudded against the mirror behind me as I closed my eyes and prayed I wouldn't pass out this time.

After only another minute or two the pounding in my head began to fade away, so I opened my eyes hoping the bleeding had subsided as well.

"Holy shit, Daddy O!" I screamed as I found him standing in front of me. I hadn't even heard him come into the bathroom.

"Sorry, sugar," he said concerned as he slowly took the towel away from my face. "Just wanted to check on ya."

"How does it look?" I asked weakly as Daddy O pressed his thumbs into my cheeks and titled my head up.

"Oliver, I said to stay out there," Aidan shouted as he stepped back into the bathroom. Daddy O didn't argue when Aidan pushed him in the hallway and then handed me one of my own shirts.

"I said don't yell at him," I said firmly. "He has more business in here than you. I don't have to worry that he'll drain me like you might."

Aidan glared at me from under his brow, his jaw still tightly clenched. My fear climaxed when he took the edges of my blood-soaked shirt and tore it in two, ripping it from my body. By the time I was able to find my voice to scream, he was already shoving my arms into the clean button down shirt he had brought from my bedroom. He allowed me to button the shirt up myself while he placed a clean washcloth under the facet and then brought it up to my face.

"I wasn't going to bite you."

"Your fangs were out and I got scared. How do I know you won't try and bite me now?"

"Because when I left you in here I ran to the kitchen and forced myself to drink half a bottle of disgusting cold blood so that I wouldn't. Sorry about the shirt, I didn't want to take any chances." He was smirking as he rinsed the washcloth again and began wiping my face and neck. "Nice bra by the way."

Enough of my energy had returned to me in order to Push him to the floor.

"Jerk."

"Guess you're feeling better," he laughed as he shook his head and stood back up.

I nodded. "How can I be gushing blood one moment and not the next?"

"Beats me, Morgan. What happened just before that? You were with me one second and then you were off in la-la-land."

Just thinking back to the moment for a second caused the tears to flow again.

"I asked him."

Aidan shook his head. "You asked who, what?"

"I asked Cam to marry me, not the other way around. I asked him that night and then the next day he was gone." I barely got the last words out before I was choking on my tears and the crap running down the back of my throat. I leaned forward to catch my head in my hands, but instead I met Aidan's chest. When my sobbing finally died down he asked, "Do you want me to make you a tomato and mayo sandwich?"

I sniffled and laughed a little at the same time. "See, you're not so bad at this after all."

"Hey now," he replied with a smile, "I have to maintain a reputation here. I don't need crying women flocking to me for comfort. Let's just keep this between you and me."

"Oh because there are so many other people for me to share this with?"

"Well you do have a point there," he laughed, causing me to laugh a little with him. "That's what I wanted to see. I need to make it a point to get you to smile more."

"Just do me a favor, please don't yell at Daddy O like that again. He was just trying to help."

"I'm sorry about that. I don't always handle panic very well."

"Aidan, thank you for everything you're doing for me. I don't say it enough, and honestly I don't want to admit it out loud and puff up your ego, but…you've been…really great. Surprisingly so."

Aidan placed his hands on my shoulders, bringing his eyes in line with mine. "I will do anything you need me to do."

I swallowed hard as his intensity made me a little uncomfortable, especially as images of past dreams flashed in my mind. Aidan released my shoulders and placed his hands on my belly.

"I promise to take care of you little guys, too."

The burning in my stomach came quick and in an instant Aidan was shoved back into the wall behind him, taking out the decorative towel display with him. He looked up at me, his eyes dazed and confused. "What the hell did you do that for?"

I rubbed my belly, feeling the babies kick inside me and then looked back up at Aidan.

"*I* didn't do anything."

Chapter Thirty-Seven

Brianna

Thanksgiving was one of those holidays where I was always jealous of what others had. You would always see pictures of families gathered around a large dining table with smiles, turkey, and an unbelievable number of side dishes. Thanksgiving with Sam was just another miserable day with him. He wanted his wife to cook a traditional meal, but of course nothing with any real flavor. It seemed pointless cooking Thanksgiving for two people, but he insisted. Now that I was free of him, I'm not sure what I thought the holiday would be like. I had been upset with Cameron at the fact that we wouldn't be celebrating together, but really I would still be cooking for myself. Thanksgiving for one. Even more pathetic.

So did I let the fact that I hadn't seen him or talked to any of my other friends or family get me depressed enough to ruin the chance to have a nice Thanksgiving dinner with Daddy O? Yes. Yes I did. Regardless, I was sitting on a stool at the kitchen island crimping my crust for Mama Jo's famous pumpkin pie while watching Aidan try to baste the turkey.

"Son of a bitch," he shouted as the hot juices splattered his face and shirt. Again.

"Now Aidan," I started condescendingly, "what did I say? You need to squeeze the stopper…"

"Before you put it in the juice. I know! My hand just can't seem to remember that until after I'm covered in this crap. Why do I have to do this?"

"Because I've been on my feet all morning cooking a meal I didn't want to cook in the first place, and now my back hurts and my ankles are swollen. So now you get the job of bending down and spraying yourself in hot fat."

It was hard not to laugh at the basting juices dripping from his face. Although this time I quickly looked down at the floor when he took his shirt off, not wanting to gawk at his smooth muscular chest for the second time today. He threw his shirt into the laundry room with the other greasy shirt then ran in a blur to his bedroom and returned seconds later stretching his arms into clean one.

"Don't be mad at me, Morgan. This is all Ollie's doing."

"Don't remind me," I answered and walked over to the cabinets to pull out the ingredients for the pie filling. "I can't believe he pulled the 'I may not have many more Thanksgivings' card. And even more, I'm furious that I have to cook this entire meal from memory since he gave Shelby all of Mama Jo's cookbooks and refuses to let me use them. I could just kill..."

I couldn't finish my statement as the horrible images of me plunging my dagger into my mother's stomach flashed in front of me.

Seeing that I was suddenly struggling with something, Aidan slowly took the ingredients I had piled into my arms and placed them on the counter.

"You need to stay calm," he said in a caring tone, squeezing my shoulder gently. "You've gone a week without a bloody nose. We just need to keep it that way. Ok?" I nodded as he wrapped his arms around me and patted my back. "If Shelby gets out of control, we'll ask her to leave. It's that simple."

"What constitutes out of control?" I asked, stepping out of his embrace.

"Anything that makes you upset or uncomfortable."

"Her saying hello to me makes me upset and uncomfortable."

"Within reason, Morgan. Remember who you're doing this for."

I groaned at him before grabbing the flour and sugar from the counter and placing them on the island so that I could sit and mix the pie filling. I only hoped that I could remember the measurements. This was Shelby's punishment for me insisting that I cook most of the meal since I couldn't eat anything she made for me, although who the hell knew why. So in her mind, if I wanted to make Mama Jo's Thanksgiving it would have to be from memory. I'm sure it would also please the shit out of her if whatever I made tasted awful since I was really flying by the seat of my pants.

"How much longer does this bird need to cook?" Aidan said, snapping me out of another rant inside my head.

"Another couple of hours," I replied and Aidan groaned. "Hey, it's not my fault you bought a twenty-five pound turkey for three people."

"You said buy a turkey, I bought a turkey. You didn't specify the size."

"I'm sorry, Aidan, next time I will remember not to assume you have common sense."

"You're about to lose your baster-boy," he replied, leaning up against the sink across from me, an eyebrow raised and his arms crossed in front of his chest. However, when I pouted and gave him my best doe eyes, he shook his head and melted. "Fine, just don't ask me to shove any more sticks up the turkey's butt."

"They weren't sticks, it was rosemary."

"What business does a stick have up a turkey's butt?"

"It's not a stick," I laughed as I threw one of the leftover sprigs at him. "Rosemary and sage bring flavor to the turkey."

"I think you're making that up."

"Because you have so much culinary experience?"

Aidan pushed himself from the sink and leaned over the island in my direction. "I will have you know that I am a master at making tomato and mayo sandwiches."

"Let's not get ahead of ourselves," I replied and then heard a car pull into the driveway.

"Shelby's here. Now remember, you be nice, she'll be nice."

In order to be nice I'd have to ignore her altogether. I needed to keep my head on straight and concentrate on making this damn pie. My shoulders started to tense when I heard the car door shut. Come on Brianna, one cup sugar, head in the game.

"Aidan," Shelby shouted from outside, "I need help."

"That's certainly an understatement," Aidan mumbled as he left the kitchen.

One cup pumpkin. One cup milk. One teaspoon of cinnamon. As I began to measure the nutmeg, Aidan stepped back into the kitchen, grocery bags hanging from his arms and holding several casserole dishes.

"Stay calm," he warned and placed the dishes on the dining room table. Instead of heeding his advice, I dropped the ring of measuring spoons into the mixing bowl and walked toward the table just as Shelby came through the door with an aluminum roasting pan covered in foil.

"Happy Thanksgiving everyone," Shelby announced happily as she walked past me and placed the roasting pan on the island.

"Shelby, what's this?" I asked as I pulled the foil off the roasting pan revealing a fully cooked turkey. I could hear Aidan groaning behind me.

Shelby turned to me, her eyes blinking widely, trying to look innocent. "Honestly, Bri Bri, I wasn't sure what to expect today, so I just went ahead…"

"But we agreed I would make the turkey and a few sides and you would make all the things that I don't like such as turnips and sweet potatoes. That way I could eat. I've already got the turkey in the oven."

"Yes, but how much longer does it need to cook?" she asked snidely.

I looked over her shoulder and glared at Aidan again.

"Bri Bri, it's almost two in the afternoon. Daddy can't wait that long to eat. Let's just eat now while everything's hot, and you can just put your little turkey away for leftovers."

"But I can't eat anything you cooked," I shouted, unable to keep my anger in check.

Shelby shrugged, keeping her focus on her turkey as she completely removed the foil. "I'm thinking about Daddy right now, maybe you should think of someone other than yourself for a change. Oh, Daddy, there you are," she said, changing her tone quickly when Daddy O stepped into the kitchen.

As she stepped away and gleefully wrapped her arms around my grandfather, my shoulders were met with Aidan's hands as I flung myself in her direction. With little effort he pushed me out of the kitchen, through the laundry room, and out onto the back deck. The cold November air hit my hot cheeks and made me gasp at how cold it had become. I took in gulps of air trying to calm myself down.

"Christ, Morgan, were you seriously going to jump your mother? I told you to stay calm," Aidan shouted at me angrily.

"How can I stay calm when that woman is constantly provoking me? You know she did all of this just to piss me off and bait me and…"

"And she's winning because you're feeding right into it."

"It's not fair, Aidan," I shouted like a child. "How come she gets to control every situation, have the last word of every conversation? I'm just sick of it! I'm sick of how she treats me and sick of having to be in this house and not being able to get away from her."

Aidan stepped closer, tilting my chin up to see his face. "I know you're frustrated. And you're right, Shelby's a nightmare sometimes, but can't you find a way to stand up to her that doesn't involve you diving at her? For your sake and for Ollie's, I implore you to keep calm. I'm not used to begging a woman to do anything, but please just find a way to deal with her that doesn't put you or the babies at risk."

Aidan was right, and I hated that.

"You've *never* had to beg?"

He smiled devilishly. "Never."

I broke out in a smile, shaking my head at his enormous ego.

"Hold the door for me?" I asked rhetorically as I walked back into the kitchen where Shelby was beginning to take lids off of her casserole dishes.

"Bri Bri, where are you going with my turkey?" she called after me as I picked up the aluminum roasting pan from the island.

"Oh don't worry," I responded happily with my fakest Southern smile, "I'm just going to put this right where it belongs."

Holding the aluminum roasting pan by its handles, I continued past Aidan who was holding the door to the outside open for me. I could hear Shelby shouting behind me as I stepped out onto the deck and heaved the roasting pan over the railing and watched it crash messily on the ground below. The animals in the woods would certainly be eating well tonight.

"Was that better, Aidan?"

"Oh, yes, infinitely better."

As we stepped back into the kitchen Shelby stood screaming, turning her body back and forth between me and Daddy O, pointing and accusing me like a spoiled child. "Bri Bri, I cannot believe that...Daddy do something!"

Daddy O held his hands up. "Shelby Jo, what precisely do you want me to do? Go and scrape the turkey off the ground?"

"But I worked hard on that turkey and slaved all morning to make you a good Thanksgivin' dinner," Shelby whined.

Shelby's nostril's flared, her eyes wild with anger over not getting her way. A second later she turned on her heels and went into the living room to pout. Daddy O shrugged and went after her, not sure how to handle the women in his life, and yes it did make me feel guilty that Shelby and I would never have the relationship he wanted.

Aidan came up next to me while I stood silent at the kitchen island, waiting for my heart to stop beating so fast.

"Don't you have a turkey to baste?" I asked without looking up at him.

"Yes ma'am," he replied quickly and turned to the stove and opened the oven door.

"Squeeze the stopper first."

"Goddamn it."

It was hard not to laugh. Again.

Surprisingly it only took two hours for Shelby to stop moping around and grace us with her presence at the dinner table when I finally presented the official Thanksgiving turkey. And just like most Thanksgiving dinners you cooked all day for a meal that lasted maybe thirty minutes. But all in all it was nice to be together with Daddy O on a holiday we hadn't celebrated together since I was young. Truthfully, that was more important than anything else.

When dinner was over, Aidan volunteered to do the dishes, and no one argued with him. My back hadn't stopped burning since the turkey went into the oven, and now it was screaming at me to lie down. Actually, the couch never looked so inviting as it did at this moment, and listening to my body I finally gave in and relaxed for the first time today. I ignored the conversation Shelby and Daddy O were having, and instead chose to sink into my muscles as they began to unwind. Almost instantly the babies started to kick, causing me to smile widely to myself and simply enjoy the feeling of them fluttering inside me. With all the drama of late, it had been a rare occasion to sit quietly and have a moment like this with my little ones.

Just when I thought I might drift off to sleep I heard the sound of a cell phone ringing and knew it could only be one person's. Unable to stop my curiosity I peeked over the back of the couch just in time to see Aidan turn off the faucet and reach into his back pocket for his cell phone. I closed my eyes and strained to hear his conversation. It was difficult to say the least with him talking so quietly, and Shelby and Daddy O in my other ear. However, when I heard the words "she's fine" I assumed that he was talking about me and that he must be speaking with Cameron.

I leapt up from the couch faster than any pregnant woman in history and ran into the kitchen just in time to hear Aidan say, "But she's right here, don't do this man."

Aidan took the phone away from his ear, staring at it in disbelief. He turned quickly around to face me as the floorboard beneath me creaked.

"Brianna, I'm sorry, he only had a second…" he began apologetically.

"It's fine, Aidan," I lied and patted his chest. "You don't need to be sorry, I know he's busy."

"Would it make you feel any better if I told you there were a bunch of voices behind him? He was probably getting ready for a mission or something."

"Aidan, you don't need to explain. Now back to work," I said and winked at him, trying my best to put up a front that I wasn't upset but of course I was. Aidan nodded, squeezing my hand before returning to his dish duty.

With my head down and biting the corners of my mouth to keep my tears from coming, I stepped into the foyer where my feet were met by my mother's. Slowly I raised my eyes to see Shelby shaking her short blonde hair in judgment.

"I tried to tell ya, Bri Bri."

"Not now," I replied and tried to step around her, only to have her step in front of me again.

"When are you gonna start facin' reality? That man ain't comin' for you. So stop this nonsense and start thinkin' about what you're gonna do."

"Shut up, Shelby! Just shut up!"

"Dammit don't call me Shelby, Bri Bri, I am your mother."

"Could have fooled me," I snapped back, but then clamped my lips down from the sudden familiarity.

"Bri Bri, you listen to me, that man is a Vampire. And one thing I know about Vampires is that they don't love anyone but themselves."

"Cameron does love…" but I stopped myself before I could finish. I had dreamt this scene so many times that I couldn't believe it was actually unfurling in front of me.

"He loves this," she said, picking up my arm and slapping the veins on my wrist. "They only care about where their blood is coming from. That's all you are to him, a blood bag, Bri Bri."

"Shelby, please stop. We can't do this…" I pleaded with her, trying to pull my arm out of her grip only making her squeeze harder.

"It doesn't mean anything, don't you understand? He's taken what he wanted. Now he's going to leave you just like your father abandoned me."

"Please, I'm begging you," I said through clenched teeth, looking wildly around me knowing my daggers were safely hidden in my closet, but worried that something else would take their place and still cause Shelby's death. "Shelby you don't understand, we can't…"

"You're going to end up just like me," she interrupted, ignoring my pleas. "Cameron doesn't love you just like your father never loved me."

I shook my head vigorously from side to side and bit my lip, but in the end I was unable to control myself and fell right into line with what I had said to her so many times in my dreams. "Eris loved you and all you could think about was yourself and becoming a Vampire. I doubt you ever really loved him. You just wanted a life you couldn't have. I am nothing like you. And despite what you think I have a man that loves me."

"Then where is he? Where is your precious Cameron?" Shelby smiled when I didn't answer. "You don't know, do you? Trust me, Bri Bri, you can fight it all you want, but you're gonna end up just like me - alone with a baby you don't want."

"That's enough," Aidan growled from behind me. Without any effort he pried Shelby's hand off my arm, causing her to wince in pain. "Now I told you that I'd let you come here as long as you didn't upset Brianna. Now you've just gone too far." Aidan looked past us to Daddy O who was slowly rising from his recliner. "Ollie, I know this is your house, but I can't stand for your daughter to treat Brianna like this anymore. If you're not going to do anything about it then I will."

I turned to face Daddy O, pleading with my eyes for him to stand up for me, but yet again I was disappointed when he simply shook his head, unable to take sides.

Aidan sighed and continued, "Shelby, as long as Brianna is here, you are not welcome. You can visit Oliver whenever Brianna isn't around, and only when I give you permission. Now you have exactly three seconds to get your boney ass out of here before I prove your case that we Vamps only care about where our next meal comes from. Do you understand me?"

Aidan's eyes were fiery with anger and I could see him struggling to keep his fangs from extending. Shelby stood stoic, trying desperately not to show any fear in front of us. With a deep inhalation and her head held high she grabbed her purse from the foyer table and walked out the front door.

"Morgan..." Aidan began, but I was already heading down the hall.

"I just need a minute to myself."

"Sugar, hang on a second," Daddy O said tenderly.

"Don't," I said firmly as I turned to him. "In all my life I have never been mad at you. Never. But right now I can't even look at you because I know that no matter what my mother does or says to me you will never be on my side. You will never defend me when it comes to her. I see where I fit in your life and for the first time I wish my real father was here because right now I don't feel like anyone's daughter. I feel like a stranger in my own family and…I…just leave me alone."

As I turned away from the stunned faces of my grandfather and Aidan, I could feel a thin trickle of blood dripping down my upper lip. I slammed my bedroom door behind me and rushed to the nightstand to grab a tissue to soak up the blood. Thankfully it wasn't much, only a few drops, but it was enough to put me over the edge and send me into hysterics. I knew Aidan could hear me even though I tried crying into my pillows, but I didn't care. Shelby was right, I was alone. I felt as though I had no one, and no one was coming for me.

Burying my face into the pillow I unleashed all of my pain until I came close to hyperventilating and eventually became exhausted. When I finally closed my eyes I thought of my dad. Calling to him, crying for him to find me and talk to me.

"Please, Dad, help me. I need you…"

Sadly, no answer came.

Chapter Thirty-Eight

Brianna

"Five weeks." Block left, right, down. "Two days." Right lunge, duck, kick left, lose balance. "Ten hours." Stab right, stab left, turn, lug stomach around, lose balance. "And thirty-two fucking minutes!" I yelled as I threw my daggers onto the deck. "Sorry, my darlings," I said out of breath and rubbing my belly, "don't ever say that word. And if you do, you never heard it from me."

The weather had turned bitter cold in the last week bringing with it our first snow. Thankfully it wasn't really sticking, allowing me to train on my balcony in the midst of a silent white background. However calming my surroundings were, I couldn't help but be frustrated with how out of shape I was. Of course the extra weight and extension of my stomach was not helping matters, causing me to lose my balance or be unable to get out of my own way. Knowing I couldn't give up, I grabbed my daggers from the deck's floor and began my routines from the beginning.

A few minutes later the French doors leading into my bedroom opened and Aidan stepped out from inside.

"I take it your call with Cameron didn't go well."

"Like you don't know," I replied but chose not to stop punching my daggers into the air. "'Undetermined amount of time', how could you not tell me before I spoke with him?"

Aidan forced his hands into his pockets. "I..."

"Liar!" I shouted before he could even begin his thought.

Aidan raised his eyebrow at me. "You can certainly have this conversation by yourself if you want to."

"No, I'm sorry. I know you're caught in the middle of this thing. It's just...I...he doesn't...oh never mind. I'm not about to bother you with all this crap."

"Oh come on, I love crap. Besides, who else are you going to bother with it?"

I sighed before replying, "He just doesn't seem like himself anymore."

"How so?" Aidan asked curiously.

"Just...you know...distant. Uninterested in anything I have to say, and not worried about the health of our babies. I need to see a doctor, especially now, and all he can say is that..."

"'Women have been birthing babies for thousands of years without real doctors.'"

"Stop eavesdropping."

"It's hard not to. Look, Morgan, you know he's been distracted because he's working really hard to protect you."

"It's not even that, I understand that. There isn't any understanding, or even common courtesy which is so not like him. For example, I told him how bad I felt that we weren't able to celebrate his birthday together and he made me feel like some dumb human wanting to celebrate a Vampire's birthday. He treated me like I was so stupid even thinking about it, even though we celebrated Kyla's birthday just a few months ago. It's just...not like him." Aidan pressed his lips together as he lowered his head apologetically. "See I told you. You really don't want me to unload this on you."

"It's fine, really."

"You know you don't need to feel obligated to stay. I'm sure Cam could find someone else to relieve you of your babysitting duties. Especially now since there is no end date to this horrid arrangement. I feel guilty that you're basically putting your life on hold for me."

"Morgan, I keep telling you not to worry about me. You just need to concentrate on staying healthy and cooking those babies. Besides, who else is going to yell at you about not wearing a coat in the middle of a snow storm? What are you doing out here anyway?"

"Working out for an undetermined amount of time," I answered snidely as I resumed my routine. "With Shelby not around to help with errands and things, you'll be away more I'm guessing. Unless of course you'll let me take your truck once in a while."

Aidan laughed. "Fat chance."

"So with you gone that means I'll need to protect the house."

"Oh I'd like to see you try."

"I've whipped your butt before," I reminded him. "Twice actually."

"But I wasn't attacking you either time. There's a difference between you catching a defenseless Vampire off guard, and one who is intent on attacking you."

"I beat Eris in a battle."

"Yes, but you weren't pregnant at the time. Besides Eris is your father. He's not going to try and kill his own daughter."

"First of all, you don't know my father," I began, and planted my feet in order to glare at Aidan properly. "Second of all, I also took down fifty some odd Vampires that day at the manor. And lastly, I think you hate the fact that a pregnant woman can defend the house just as good as you can."

"Brianna Morgan, are you challenging me?" he asked, stepping in front of me with his arms crossed and an eyebrow raised.

"What do I get if I win?"

"Hmmm…if you win, which I doubt, I will…" he pondered, twisting his lips from side to side, "…take you Christmas shopping."

My eyes widened with excitement at the prospect of leaving the house. "And what if I lose?"

He smiled widely. "If you lose you must always leave the house with a coat on, and the next time you're mad at your fiancé punch your pillow like every other woman instead of whipping knives around. Deal?"

Taking in a deep breath, I shook his extended hand then worried that this wasn't a good idea after all. Aidan released my hand and then slowly Projected away, his eyes being the last to fade away but not before he gave me a sly wink. Once he disappeared I quickly closed my eyes, pushing my mind out in all directions, feeling for where he had gone.

Within seconds I found his cloudy white light flying up from under the far side of the deck behind me. Gripping my daggers firmly in my hands, I took a deep breath before turning around just as Aidan appeared in front of me. Instantly I began plunging my daggers towards Aidan's hands as they blocked my advances while I Pushed his light away from me in short powerful bursts. Aidan's eyes scrunched together with each Push, his blocks becoming sloppy with distraction and pain.

I continued to push Aidan back along the deck until his back touched the railing. A second later he disappeared into black mist causing me to have to catch myself on the railing. Quickly I turned around in time to see Aidan flying at me, fangs exposed and his arms outstretched reaching for my throat. His fingers barely brushed my skin before I jammed one dagger up into his palm, slicing up through to the other side. Aidan flinched his hand up as he yelled in pain, ripping the dagger from my hand as it hung handle down from his palm. His uninjured hand went to pull the dagger out only to yelp from the searing pain of the silver handle burning away his skin. With him off guard, I pulled the dagger out myself and Pushed his light away from me, causing him to skid along the deck flooring that was now becoming wet and slick with the melting snow.

Slowly he turned himself over, being sure to lock his black eyes with mine as he rose from the floor like he was in a slow motion movie sequence. Before my foot could finish taking a step toward him, he was standing inches away, hissing at me with his fangs grazing my lips. With another quick succession of bursts, I Pushed him back enough to be able to extend my daggers in front of me and begin to cut away at the air finding Aidan's arms and hands as he blocked me up, down, and sideways. But then my foot slipped on the wet wood causing me to lose my balance slightly. The spilt second it took for my ankle to twist out and back in was enough time for me to lose my hold on Aidan's essence and allow his arms to come sweeping toward my shoulders. I ducked just in time for him to miss, however, when I tried to turn away from him the size of my belly and the extra weight caused me to lose my balance. This time Aidan was able to wrap his arms around the front of my chest and lift me off the ground. I struggled and kicked my feet at his shins since my daggers were useless. His grip tightened around my chest, but I took as much of a breath as I could, preparing myself for an unpleasant move.

With my breath held tightly in my chest, I exhaled roughly and Pushed Aidan's light away again, throwing him down near the front of the house while I was thrust forward, landing on my knees and catching myself with my hands before my belly hit the ground. Unfortunately the whole ordeal had effectively knocked the air out of me. It was then that my stomach started to burn; my babies knew I was in trouble.

While I rested on all fours, my throat and lungs stinging from the cold winter air, I felt Aidan's fingers brush the back of my neck as he said, "Bri, maybe…"

But that was all I heard before I breathed into the burning in my stomach and sat up as I flung my arms back, Pushing Aidan so hard I actually saw a wave of energy fly out from me. The wave hit Aidan square in the chest, knocking him through the railing of the front porch and landing on the road past the gravel driveway.

Picking up my daggers from where I had dropped them, I lifted myself up from the deck's wet floor, and even from this distance I could see Aidan's eyes flaring with anger as he brushed himself off. It wasn't over yet. He might have been willing to stop earlier, but my last Push had squashed any thoughts of quitting before one of us cried uncle. Or perhaps just cried in general.

Aidan disappeared once again in a cloud of black mist prompting me to close my eyes and feel for where his light reappeared. Just as his light faded away from the road it began to reappear near the far edge of woods to my left. When I turned in his direction, I opened my eyes just as his light faded away again and then reappeared in the driveway to my right. Again, when I turned in his direction he Projected to a position on the sloping ground below. He was testing me, or at least teasing me as he bounced from one side of the yard to the other. Finally his milky white light appeared on the roof directly behind me, inching toward me with silent precision.

Trying to fool him into thinking I didn't know where he was, I leaned over the railing pretending to look for him underneath the deck. I could feel Aidan's light continuing to creep down the pitch of the roof and pause when he reached the edge of the gutter. A second later Aidan leapt into the air just as I turned and held him there with my mind, keeping him steady with my outstretched hand though it was difficult with the dagger in it.

Aidan wriggled and writhed while I held him in the air above me. My head began to ache and I worried that I was overexerting myself. This needed to end. And by the thin black wisps of smoke that were rising from his body, Aidan was certainly trying to put an end to it as well. The pain in my head became sharp and pulsed like lightening, making it difficult to hold him any longer. I could see his light fading as it began to appear at the same time near the railing behind me. With a quick snap I released my hold on him causing him to be thrust into the railing. I grunted through the pain in my head and stretched his arms wide. Using all my weight I jammed my daggers through his hands until they secured themselves deep into the wood of the railing. My belly rested up against Aidan's, the babies kicking at an uncomfortable level. Aidan's fangs were very visible, but his eyes widened as a trickle of blood leaked from my nose and dripped onto his lips.

His teeth ground together while he waited for me to wipe it away, but instead I relaxed my body, giving him permission to taste the power that flowed through me. Within a second my blood disappeared and was replaced with a desire in Aidan's eyes that I couldn't help but notice, and I liked the feeling. I rose from my position and pulled hard on my daggers to free them from his hands. With the holes still healing, Aidan quickly flew from the railing and into my bedroom returning seconds later with tissues.

"I'd appreciate it if you would put those down," he said, gesturing to the daggers still in my hands. I dropped them to the ground as he tilted my chin up in the air and dabbed away the blood from my face.

"I won," I reminded him as he finished.

"And I have the holes to prove it, or at least I did a second ago," he laughed, making me smile as well. As his laugh faded his expression changed once again to one of desire, but it wasn't for my blood. The back of his fingers brushed down my cheek causing my breath to quicken and butterflies to flutter up into my throat. When I didn't stop him, he stepped closer, opening his palm and cupping my cheek. His eyes were burning into mine causing my bottom lip to quiver as he slowly lowered his head, parting his lips as they drew closer to mine.

What are you doing! The voice in my head screamed at me causing me to suddenly break away from Aidan's trance and step back from him.

"I n-need to change," I stuttered and pushed past him into my bedroom, closing the French door tightly behind me. The babies were kicking mercilessly as I sat on the corner of the bed, rubbing my belly and begging for their forgiveness. I was furious with myself for committing almost the same sin against Cameron as he had done to me. How could I have allowed Aidan to touch me like that? It was hard to admit how lonely I was and how distant and cold Cameron was being toward me. I was flooded with doubt and overcome with hormones at the prospect of being shown some kind of affection. Stupid girl.

Not wanting to spend another second remembering the feeling of Aidan's hand on my cheek or the look of his soft lips, I bolted from the bed and grabbed a pair of jeans and a soft sweater before heading into the bathroom to splash some cold water on my face. When that didn't shock the thoughts out of my head I opted for the full blown cold shower.

Finally after several minutes of feeling as though I was being pelted with shards of ice, my head was clear and the babies finally stopped punishing me from within. Moments later I was dry, dressed, and brushing through my tangled damp hair which was in desperate need of a haircut (like that was ever going to happen). My breathing and heart rate were back to normal, though I still couldn't bear to look at myself in the mirror.

I padded back into my bedroom, hearing Aidan and Daddy O mumbling and laughing about something behind me. Through the French door windows I could see that the snow was coming down in greater force. I began to wonder if my first outing in more than a month would actually happen. Not only was the snow a problem, I would be alone with Aidan. Lord give me strength to stay in control of myself.

From the closet I pulled out my fluffy boots and sat on the edge of the bed. Apparently once your stomach got a certain size it was almost impossible to get into a pair of calf-length boots. After almost ten minutes of trying, I laid defeated on the bed with my boots hanging limply from my ankles.

"Morgan?" Aidan asked as he rapped lightly on the door. I tried to get up but was once again hindered by my stomach. I tried rolling over, only to have my long hanging boots knock and twist around one another. The next thing I knew Aidan was lifting me into a seated position. "She can defeat Vampires by the handful, but can't sit up without help."

I glowered at him and removed my arm from his grip. "I can too. I just had some trouble with my boots."

Aidan laughed as he knelt down in front of me and began to pull my right boot up my leg. When I placed my hands on top of his to stop him, but he gently lifted them away as he said, "I'm sorry about before. I shouldn't have done that, it was wrong to put you in that situation. I hope we can just forget it ever happened. I don't want things to be uncomfortable between us."

I nodded silently, unable to form words while he began to pull my left boot up my leg. I was thankful that he was willing to forget what happened, especially since we would be stuck in this house for an "undetermined amount of time." I loved Cameron, even if he was being a jackass. It was only a hormonal moment of weakness, that's all. I didn't have any feelings for the man that was securing my boot up my left calf.

"All right," he said tapping my leg. "We better get going. Shelby will be here any minute. Now don't look at me like that, you know the deal I made and Oliver misses her even though he wouldn't say that to you."

"I wasn't looking at you in any way."

"Bullshit you were."

"Ok, I was. But you're right, it's only fair. Do you think we'll still be able to go out? The snow's getting pretty bad."

"Eh, the truck should be able to get through it."

"Good," I said standing from the bed. "Because I really want to get out of the house."

"And Morgan, I don't care what our wager was, you need to wear a coat in this storm."

"Yeah, no shit. And just so we're clear, just because I am choosing to wear one doesn't mean I'm doing it because you said so."

Aidan glared at me. "I'm going to warm up the truck. Don't come down the stairs without me, they're probably slick. The last thing I need you to do is slip and fall."

I let him walk out the door without an answer, but only because I knew I really didn't have a choice. It seemed funny that I could flail around with daggers in my hands fighting a ferocious Vampire an hour before with no worries, but stairs! They were the real danger. What would I do without a man to help me down three tiny little stairs? Oh deary me, and fiddle dee-dee.

My internal sarcasm made me laugh to myself as I stepped back out on the deck and brought my silver Vampire-death-devices in from the snow and wiped them clean with a tissue. I placed only one back into the wooden holding case, choosing to bring the other along with me on our outing. With my dagger in hand I walked through the living room and into the foyer's closet to grab my white coat. It had been almost six weeks since I had worn it last, I wondered if it even still fit.

As I put my arms through the sleeves I heard Daddy O clear his throat from his recliner. Since Thanksgiving he and I hadn't exactly buried the hatchet. We weren't ignoring each other, but we certainly weren't acting like we usually did. Daddy O was hurt by what I said to him, and I was hurt by his inaction and constant devotion to my mother. We were upset with each other and neither of us thought we were in the wrong and therefore wouldn't apologize. So really it was a draw to see who would blink first. I might be younger, but Daddy O had many more years to hone his stubborness.

Pulling my white coat over my shoulders I was pleased to see that I could still fasten the high breasted buttons, although the front edges of the coat parted where my stomach protruded. It would still work for where I was going, and Aidan would get off my back about it. Grabbing my purse from the foyer table I shoved my dagger inside and gave one last glance to Daddy O who was hiding behind his newspaper.

"Have a good visit, Daddy O," I said, trying to sound sincere.

"Yep, you have fun," he replied from behind his paper. No one was blinking today apparently.

When I stepped out on the front porch Aidan was already standing on the steps with a hand ready to guide me down to the driveway. The snow was indeed heavier, having changed from a soft dusting to blanketing everything around us. Just as my foot stepped onto the gravel, Shelby's car slowly turned into the driveway. Not wanting to give her satisfaction that her visit would upset me, I held my head up high and continued the slippery walk to Aidan's truck, taking pains not to look anywhere in her direction.

Moments later I was being hauled up into Aidan's truck, the heat just beginning to kick on when he closed the passenger side door. I watched as he shook away the snow that rested in his hair while he walked around the truck until he was face to face with Shelby. It was a quick conversation, one that Shelby only listened and then nodded before disappearing into the house.

Finally Aidan returned to the truck, putting his hands roughly through his hair again to brush out the newly fallen snow. And just when he opened his door and hopped into the seat did a headache start brewing. Really?! I battled a Vampire in order to get out of the house. I wouldn't let a stupid headache stop me from going. Suffer through it, Morgan, I thought to myself though it was Aidan's voice.

"Get out of my head!"

"Er...ok. Talking to yourself again?" I nodded, completely embarrassed. "The snow's heavier than I thought," Aidan said as he put the truck in gear and engaged the four-wheel drive. "I take it you don't want to wait until tomorrow?"

"I'm not about to go through you putting my boots on again." He laughed as he began rolling the truck backwards out of the driveway. "So what did you say to Shelby?"

"Don't worry, Morgan, I'm not conspiring with Shelby on anything. I was just telling her we'd be a couple of hours and that she needed to leave once we got back if not before. I'm sorry I didn't ask permission to speak with her, *ma'am*."

I rolled my eyes as we continued down the steep slope of the mountain road. I was surprised that I had to squint to shield my sensitive eyes from the low level light that was reflecting off the snow. My headache was getting worse, and fast. I debated whether to tell Aidan, only from the worry of having a gushing nosebleed either in his truck or in public. But if I told him he would immediately turn us around. Not only would it ruin my day, but it would ruin Daddy O's visit. I hated Shelby, but Daddy O still deserved to see her. Unfortunately she was still his daughter.

Whatever thoughts I had about telling Aidan anything were quashed when we hit a large pothole and bounced through a curve causing my purse to fall into the floor and dump all its contents out around my feet.

"Ah, Morgan, did you bring a dagger with you?" Aidan asked as he watched me clumsily throw all the items back into my purse.

"Of course I did," I replied. "You can't honestly think I'd go anywhere without some kind of protection. I might need to defend myself and I know how, remember?"

"Trust me, my head and hands know you can defend yourself."

Suddenly all conversion ceased when we came upon another sharp downward curve. Even though Aidan downshifted into the lowest gear, we still slid around the corner rather than rolled down it. The snow was so blinding you couldn't see three feet in front of you, but Aidan still trudged down the mountain.

"How did you do it by the way?" he finally said when we came to a straighter road.

"Well, in case you didn't know, Vampires have a weakness to silver…"

"God you're irritating sometimes," he said with a smile as I laughed and then regretted it when my head started to pulse with increasing intensity. "What I meant was when I was Projecting around the yard you seemed to know where I was going even before I fully formed. How's that possible?"

"The same way I knew you were following me in Boston. I could see your essence."

"My essence?"

"Well that's what Lana always called it. Maybe it's your soul, I don't know, it's a bright white light that glows like a halo around your head. Although yours looks a little different than most."

Aidan looked at me through the side of eyes, a slight hint of worry streaking across his face. "Why does mine look different?"

"Beats me."

"It's because I'm such a superior Vampire. That must be it."

"Yeah, Aidan, sure it is," I replied sarcastically.

"And you can see where Vampires are Projecting to?"

"Yep."

"Well it must not work all the time, because you didn't know I was up on the roof until I jumped off."

"You only think I didn't see you. I was waiting for the perfect moment to bring you down without destroying Daddy O's roof."

Aidan shook his head and all conversation stopped when the truck's backend spun out into the edge of the woods. Thankfully Aidan straightened the truck out, but now you couldn't see anything ahead of you but snow. To make matters worse there was a lightning storm in my head, almost to the point of nausea. I had a feeling that in no time I would either be vomiting or bleeding profusely. I'd gotten away from the house for a total of fifteen minutes. Pathetic. This day and my life sucked. Plain and simple.

"Um, Aidan," I said softly, placing my forehead on the cold window, "I don't think I'm going to make it."

"What's the matter? Are you all right?" he asked and placed a hand on my shoulder.

"It's my head. I think I'm getting a migraine again."

Aidan slowed the truck, pulling off to the side of the road. "Well Morgan, not that I'm happy you have a headache, but honestly I'm not sure that if we got down the mountain we could get back up again. This storm has turned bad pretty quickly."

"Just take me home, ok?"

Without another word Aidan did a U-turn and began our trek back up the mountain, slipping and sliding along the narrow curvy roads. Ironically as we got closer to the house, the pounding in my head was lessening. By the time we reached the driveway only a dull ache remained, and all my other symptoms seemed to drift away. I shook my head in frustration, but then flew towards the dashboard when Aidan slammed on the breaks causing the backend of the truck to fishtail widely in the gravel. When my eyes finally opened I saw the reason for his erratic behavior. The screen door to Daddy O's house hung crookedly off its hinges while the front door stood wide open. Instantly my hand went into my purse and wrapped itself around the rounded silver and pearl handle of my dagger at the same time that Aidan's fangs extended.

"There's only one," I said after closing my eyes and seeing only one bright light roaming around the front of the house and coming towards the front door. When I opened my eyes I saw a muscular Vampire step out onto the front porch, blood dripping from his chin down to the middle of his shirt.

"Ohmygod, Daddy O!" I screamed as I opened the truck's door and slid down to the ground.

"Morgan, no!" Aidan shouted and stepped out of the truck.

"You take him, I'll go inside," I said to Aidan without looking at him.

"Wha…"

"Now!" I screamed as I took hold of the nasty Vampire's light and Pushed him hard across the front porch causing him the crash through the railing toward the woods on the other side. Instantly Aidan rushed after him, grabbing him around the waist in midair before flying to the wood's edge. In the next second the two of them were nothing but blurs ripping away at each other.

Not wasting another second I waddled down the rest of the driveway toward the house. As I approached the stairs I could hear Shelby screaming loudly from inside. I tightened my grip on my dagger and stepped inside until I was able to see Shelby standing in the living room, her hands clasped tightly around her mascara-streaked face. She was screaming so loud that her words were incomprehensible and only when she pointed to something on the floor did I continue to creep forward. My nose began to tingle with tears as I stepped into the living room, not yet seeing what she was gesturing to on the floor, but knowing there was an obvious absence among us. Just as I rounded the couch I saw him.

"Daddy!" I screamed over Shelby's wails and rushed to his side, unable to kneel quickly enough and merely falling hard on my knees, letting my dagger clang loudly on the floor as it fell from my hands. Daddy O laid in front of me, shock in his eyes, struggling to take gulps of air while he bled out from a deep, wide gash in his throat.

Quickly I took off my coat and yelled at my mother, "Give me your scarf!"

When she didn't stop screaming I reached up and pulled her down roughly to the floor. The fall knocked the breath out of her but it didn't stop me from pulling the scarf from around her neck. I turned back to Daddy O and pressed the scarf firmly into his wound. Within seconds his blood was soaking through.

"Aidan!" I screamed at the window. Aidan's blood could heal Daddy O. I just needed a little of his blood, Daddy O wouldn't die. He couldn't die like this.

Just then, Daddy O grabbed my hand and I forcibly moved my gaze to his eyes instead of the blood now beginning to pool on the floor. He looked two shades paler than only moments ago, but it didn't stop him from trying to move his lips.

"Don't try to speak. We're going to get help. Aidan is going to help you."

I looked up from him and screamed Aidan's name once again at the window. Daddy O squeezed my hand and I turned back to him only to have my tears fall onto his face.

"Stay with me. Please stay with me," I begged, squeezing his hand and nestling it under my chin. "I didn't mean what I said, I don't care about any of it, Daddy, please. You have…you have to see your great-grandchildren. They need to know you. You're too…important. I need you…Daddy…I need you…"

Daddy O's eyes widened as he struggled to draw breath causing his head to twitch while his hand squeezed mine until my knuckles were almost white.

"No, no, no," I said in a panic, "you stay with me now. Just hold on, Daddy, please, just a little longer. Aidan, help me!" I screamed again although I could still see two bright lights grappling with one another near the woods.

"This wasn't supposed to happen," Shelby whimpered next to me. "No one was supposed to get hurt."

"What?" I snapped at her, but then Daddy O began choking on his own blood. I leaned down to him, kissing his soft wrinkled face, petting his thin gray hair, desperately trying to keep him with me. The blood pooling under his neck spread to my knees and soaked into my jeans. There was too much blood, too much. I just needed a little more time, just a few more seconds and Aidan could stop the bleeding and heal his wound. Blood and time, that's all I needed. Blood and time.

Daddy O twitched one more time and then released a gurgled sigh before his hand went slack in mine. Shelby's screams hit the opposite wall and echoed throughout the house. My head fell into Daddy O's chest, my heaving sobs soaking his shirt while Shelby grabbed and pulled at my sweater's sleeve. I pulled my arm roughly from her grip and tried to sit up only to have my knees slip in the pooled blood and thrust me forward into Daddy O's chest again.

"N-not like this," Shelby mumbled next to me while she rocked back and forth. "They p-promised, no one h-hurt. Not Daddy, not like this. N-no one was supposed to get hurt."

"Why do you keep saying that," I said flatly as I pushed myself up.

Slowly Shelby lifted her head from her hands, her lip quivering while the tears from her eyes finally ran clear following the watery black tracks of her mascara down her neck that was covered in tiny puncture wounds at varying stages of healing. I knew exactly what they were, I had seen the same narrowly spaced holes on my own neck. Images of every encounter that I had with my mother over the last month flashed in my head and in every image she wore a turtleneck or a scarf.

"What have you done?" I growled.

Guilt and shame flooded my mother's face. Shelby's mouth opened and closed several times, unable to find an explanation. Having no patience for her, I grabbed her arm and shook her roughly.

"Tell me what you've done!"

"They just wanted you!" she shouted and ripped her arm away. "No one else was supposed to get hurt. All they wanted was you, it's always all about you," she began, her voice increasing with intensity and anger as she spoke. "This is what *I wanted*. I wanted this life, I was brought to Eris, I bore his child! And all anyone can talk about is you. And why? Who are you? What do you possibly possess that I didn't give you?"

I gritted my teeth as I slowly stood from the floor and crept toward her.

"Everything I possess is from the sweat off my own back, not from you!"

"No one gives me credit for bringin' you into this world," she snarled. "You wouldn't be here if it weren't for me."

"I am here in spite of you!" I screamed at her. "You get no credit because you've done absolutely nothing, and that's what you are, *nothing.* Your whole life you've done whatever you could in order to become one of them, *dead* like one of them. Well let me help you finish what you started."

The words rang familiar as my anger consumed me, but it was too late and my dagger disappeared into her stomach. I hadn't even felt it in my hand, and now only the hilt of it was showing. Shelby's eyes were wide and they burned through me while her blood drained out of her and over my hand, soaking into the sleeve of my sweater.

Shelby's body became limp and fell into me, knocking me back a few steps while trying to hold her weight. With a low scream I pushed Shelby off of me, gripping my dagger tightly as she fell away to the floor.

"Morgan!" Aidan shouted as he ran through the front door, his clothes ripped and torn with bright red gashes healing over. He froze when he saw me standing over my mother's body with her blood dripping from my dagger. "What happened?"

My dagger once again dropped loudly on the floor as I ran to Aidan and pulled him back into the living room.

"Help him, Aidan, please just help him," I begged while Aidan knelt down next to Daddy O, placing his hand on my grandfather's chest. "What are you waiting for! Do something, give him your blood, goddam it," I screamed as I pulled up his shredded sleeve's cuff to expose his forearm.

Gently he turned, apology sinking deep into his eyes. "Brianna...I can't."

"Of course you can, just do it!"

"I cannot help a dead man," he shouted as he stood quickly, grabbing my shoulders firmly.

I limply struggled against him, pushing on his chest and smearing blood across his shirt. Abruptly I stopped, turning my head to see Shelby lying on the floor, blood still seeping from the wound in her stomach and my dagger's silver finish now shining red. Slowly I turned my head back to see Aidan's worried eyes as my brain finally caught up and processed what I had done.

I had killed my own mother.

I killed her just as I had seen in my dream so many weeks ago. But this was no longer a dream. I had killed her. Her blood covered my weapon, the floor, my hand and arm and clothes. It was everywhere and I couldn't escape from the sight of it. Reflexively my right hand flew to my mouth as the sour taste of bile rose in my throat. Without a second's hesitation Aidan lifted me into his arms and rushed into the bathroom where he gently lowered me down in front of the toilet where my stomach retched violently and emptied itself.

My throat burned as I reached to flush my sickness away, and once again I couldn't escape my mother's blood as it streaked the white porcelain where my hands rested. Aidan lifted me from the ground and directed me over to the sink where he turned on the water and placed my hands underneath the stream. Just as the cold water hit my skin my eyes shot up to the mirror where I saw a grisly image of myself. My eyes were puffy and dark as tears cut through the smears of blood on my face and neck. The sight was enough to make me sick again, but Aidan scooped me up and sat me on the counter of the sink with my back pressed up against the mirror. He reached for a washcloth from the linen closet and began wiping my face. With each rinse of the washcloth the water ran a deeper red, staining the cloth until its original color was unrecognizable. Aidan worked silently while the shock of what had happened sank in deeper and deeper, the sights and sounds replaying like an endless movie reel making me oblivious to what was happening around me.

I gasped when Aidan's cold washcloth touched the top of my foot causing me to focus ahead of me. Just past where he stood I could see my fluffy boots resting on a towel on the floor, red boot prints glowing from the white fibers where Aidan had put them before they fell over. My attention moved from the boots on the floor to watching him wipe the blood from my feet where it had soaked through. The sight caused me to finally look down at myself and see that my sweater and jeans were covered in dark red blotches. I lifted the edge of my sweater over my swollen stomach only to find my skin stained red and sticky.

"Get it off! Get it off of me," I panicked as I frantically tried to lift my sweater over my head, but my hysteria only caused me to get tangled within its long sleeves and cowl neck.

"Fuck this," Aidan growled before lifting my sweater off completely. In the next second my jeans were ripped from my body and Aidan lifted me from the counter, swept open the shower curtain, stepped inside the shower, and flipped the water on. Although he set my feet down, his arm was securely around my waist just under my chest where I clung to it while I sobbed and watched the water run red as it swirled around the drain.

Aidan handed me the bar of soap from the tray beside me, but my fingers failed me and it slipped out of my hand only to have Aidan catch it in the air. It was then that he tilted the shower nozzle downward and lowered me to the tub's floor. I laid on top of him while he rubbed the soap on my stomach and then my chest, scrubbing away all reminders of the horrific scene just one room away. When he was finished he threw the soap at the drain and fell to the back of the tub bringing me with him and letting the shower pelt us with steamy hot water.

Not another word was said until the hot water was no more, and only then did Aidan curse softly under his breath. He rose from the tub, effortlessly lifting me to a standing position before taking me out altogether. Having no other choice, Aidan placed me back on the sink's counter where I shivered at the sudden cold. Within seconds he was covering me with towels, rubbing them harshly against my skin in order to warm me.

When I was finally dry he lifted me once more, cradling me tightly against his chest.

"Don't look," he whispered as he carried me through the doorway and into the hallway. I nestled my face into his wet shirt until he placed me down on my bed a few moments later. My body felt numb while I sat and watched him go through my drawers finally handing me a pair of underwear, a random t-shirt, and pajama bottoms. When I didn't take the clothes he offered, he merely placed them next to me. "I am going to change too. If you need me to help you..." I shook my head. "Ok, I'll be right back."

Even after he closed my bedroom door I could hear his wet shoes squeaking on the hardwood floors as he walked to the bedroom next to mine. The old brass bed creaked loudly as he sat upon it, and I kept thinking that if someone were to stand in the hallway and look through our doors we would like mirror images of each other – hair dripping wet, sitting on the corners of our beds, forlorn and too exhausted to be angry or scared anymore. But who would look at us? There was no one left.

I didn't move from my position until I heard the brass bed creak again, meaning Aidan would be returning soon. My arms felt like lead as I peeled off my wet bra and underwear, and slipped on the dry clothes. It was difficult to find the energy to pull the comforter back so I merely climbed to the head of my bed and pulled my pillow to my chest while my legs curled up as tightly as they could.

A few minutes later there was a light knock at the door and Aidan stepped into the room silently. His hair was still glistening from the shower, his torn clothes replaced with another pair of jeans and a white t-shirt. I didn't object when he pulled the comforter down and tucked my legs underneath, being careful to allow me to keep my fetal position.

With a frustrated sigh he melted to the ground and pressed his back up against the side of the bed, letting his head fall back on the mattress.

"Aidan?" I asked through the burning in my throat

"Hmmm?" he replied, keeping his eyes closed.

"Is the Vamp gone?"

"Yeah."

"Is Daddy O really...dead?"

Aidan sighed again as he reached up and curled his fingers around mine. "Yeah."

"What happens now?"

"I honestly don't know."

Chapter Thirty-Nine

Brianna

The house had become colder, prompting me to pull the comforter tightly up to my chin. The light behind my eyes was dark now, meaning that I had slept most of the day and into the evening, though I didn't even remember falling asleep. The needles in my hand made me realize that I'd lost most of the circulation in my right side. Painfully I turned over onto my back and instantly felt the blood rush back into my arm and leg. With effort I stretched my eyes open and found a figure standing in front of the doors.

"Aidan?"

"Has it been so long you do not even recognize me?"

"Cameron!" I shouted with five weeks and two days of desperation as I tossed the blankets off of me. Cameron sat down on the edge of the bed where I struggled to crawl toward him. When I finally reached him, I wrapped my arms around his neck while pulling him into me as tightly as I could. If it were possible I would have pushed my way into his skin to get closer to him.

His touches were light, only grazing his fingers down my cheek. The feeling itself brought tears, making my eyes burn and needing to feel him comfort my trembling bottom lip. He wiped away the tears from my face with his thumbs and I couldn't wait for him to kiss me any longer and brought his lips roughly down on mine almost breaking my teeth. But sadly instead of consuming me with passion he pushed me away slowly, brushing my long bangs out of my eyes and tucking them behind my ear before kissing me gently on the forehead.

"Are you going to take me home now?"

Before the statement was out of my mouth I knew from his squinted eyes that the answer was no.

"Victor has allowed me only enough time to clean up your mess."

"M-mess? How is…t-this my mess? I didn't…"

"Brianna, two well-known people in this town are dead. I might have been able to explain away Oliver, but both him and your mother? People are going to notice her absence and begin to ask questions. What were you thinking?"

"I wasn't thinking, Cameron."

"Obviously."

"Excuse me!" I shouted and stood from the bed. "How dare you…"

"Brianna, you killed your mother…"

"I am well aware of that. What did you expect me to do in that situation?"

"As a Warrior I expect you to be able to control yourself."

"I am not a Warrior right now! I am a very pregnant woman who has been abandoned by her fiancé for over a month who watched her grandfather bleed out on the floor because her bitch of a mother sold her out to some Vampire. And now instead of comforting me over everything I have been through today you are chastising me."

Cameron rose slowly from the bed, his arms stretched out toward me, and like a pitiful child I ran to him.

"I did not mean to upset you."

"I just want to go home," I cried into his chest.

"There is no one there to be with you." I lifted my head, completely confused. "Victor emptied the manor weeks ago. Everyone has been working around the clock to find Elaina and no one can return until she's been found. This may not be what you want to hear, Brianna, but this really is the safest place for you right now."

"But it's not safe, Cam! A Vampire came right through the door and killed Daddy O."

"Yes, and Aidan killed him, and then you killed the threat that brought him here."

I turned out of his arms and walked to the box of tissues on my nightstand since Cameron wasn't helping me to stop crying. With my back turned I said, "So you're just leaving me here by myself."

"You are not here alone."

"But I'm not with you," I replied and Cameron sighed loudly. "Where is Aidan anyway?"

"He's cleaning up the living room."

I jerked my head around so fast my body came with me and I lost my balance resulting in having to put a stabilizing hand on the closet door next to me. Cameron stepped in front of me, placing one hand on my shoulder and the other on my belly.

"Careful now," he said softly.

My stomach sank and fear began to fill me when the heat that normally rose in my stomach at his touch was non-existent. The babies were unusually still in his presence. Had they forgotten him? Or were they just as angry at him as I was? Either way it was too much to handle and I removed his hand and pushed past him toward the door.

Before he could stop me I padded out into the hallway, pulling myself along the wall, afraid of what I might see. But there was nothing. No blood. No mayhem. And even more so, no bodies. If a stranger had walked into the living room they would never had known about the carnage that had occurred hours before. I could hear Cameron behind me, matching my steps as I slowly stepped to where Daddy O had fallen. I rubbed my toes on the hardwood but there was nothing there to feel. Daddy O's spirit didn't magically coarse through me, hell there wasn't even a stain from where his blood had pooled. The absence of everything made me breakdown. He was gone. Erased after only hours.

"Bri," Aidan said as he stepped into the foyer. "You should really be…"

"Where is he?" I sobbed and turned my head in Aidan's direction. Aidan looked awkwardly over at Cameron seeking permission. "Don't look at him! Daddy O is *my* family, you tell me what you've done with him."

Cameron still gave a curt nod before Aidan responded, "I put him and Shelby outside…"

"Outside?" I sobbed and took steps toward the kitchen, but Aidan stepped in front of me and placed his hands gently on my shoulders.

"I was very respectful."

"But it's so cold."

"He cannot feel it," he replied gently. "We cannot keep them in the house, and we need to come to an agreement with what to do with them."

"What do you mean?" I asked and looked between him and Cam.

"One opinion, *not mine*," he stressed, "is to dispose of them completely so there is no evidence."

"How can that even be an option," I shouted as I looked to Cameron since it was obviously his idea. "Daddy O needs a funeral. People need to say goodbye, *I* need to say...I...he...he deserves nothing less."

"Brianna, a funeral is absolutely out of the question," Cameron responded firmly. "Having a public event like that is basically waving a flag that you are here. Besides it would raise too many questions that we cannot provide answers for. We have to dispose of Oliver and Shelby..."

"*Or,*" Aidan interrupted, "I can dig graves on the grounds."

"Which will be seen by neighbors and anyone who passes," Cameron said flustered.

"Not if I dig them under the deck in the back. No one can see around there unless you're actually walking in the backyard and I will make sure that doesn't happen."

Cameron shook his head. "I do not like it."

"You don't have to," I fired back.

"Cameron, Morgan's right. This is her family, it should really be her decision."

"Fine," he grumbled. "I will help you dig the holes."

"Whoa wait a minute," I shouted, putting my hand in front of Cam's chest. "One grave. For Daddy O only. No way are you putting that woman next to him."

"Brianna, you cannot expect Aidan to dig a grave and then dispose of the body of your mother. That's a huge inconvenience."

Rage seared through my body and I could feel the babies begin to stir within me. "Cameron, you should know better than anyone why I don't want Shelby next to Daddy O. Leaving personal reasons aside, she's the reason he's dead! I will not have her lying next to him for all eternity." I shifted my murderous glare over to Aidan but relaxed it since I wasn't angry at him. "Aidan, I'm sorry if this is an inconvenience. Give me a shovel and I'll dig the grave myself."

"It's fine, Morgan," Aidan replied. "I'll take care of everything. Just please, go and rest. We can do a little ceremony of our own tomorrow if you want to. I know it's not the same as a real funeral, but Cameron's right in that we shouldn't do anything to draw attention."

I pushed the tears back, having trouble swallowing the large lump that had formed in the back of my throat. "Thank you," I said weakly as I stepped toward Cameron who in turn stepped in Aidan's direction and away from me.

Aidan scrunched his brows together looking quickly at me and then back to Cameron. "Uh, hey man, why don't you stay with Brianna? I can do this on my own. Besides someone should be here in case I need to leave the premises. That's kind of why I was waiting for you to get here."

Cameron nodded and turned slowly back in my direction, gesturing to the hallway. I must have stood staring at him for half a minute in disbelief at his action before finally shuffling back down the hallway and into the safe haven of my bedroom.

"What time is it?"

"Nearly seven," he replied as he closed the door behind him and sank down on the bed.

"Wait, how did you get here so quickly?"

Cameron stepped around me to a small overnight bag that was sitting on the floor and began rummaging around inside it. "I was in Virginia when Aidan called me."

"How long have you been in Virginia?"

"A week or so," he answered nonchalantly and removed his shirt as if he wasn't ripping my heart out at this very moment.

"You've been hours away for a week and couldn't be bothered to come see me?"

"Brianna," he groaned as he pulled the clean t-shirt over his head and down his chest. "I have been raiding endless homes and warehouses for the last five weeks with barely a minute to even speak to you let alone drive hours to see you."

"You're here now, it obviously wasn't that hard."

Cameron turned around, his lips pursed and an eyebrow raised. "Extenuating circumstances. Being here brings risks, Brianna. Elaina assumes that wherever I am, you will be. Having me actually be with you right now could lead her here. Honestly, Brianna, I just wish you would give me the slightest bit of consideration and think that maybe I too am having a difficult time with our situation."

Bitch, bitch, bitch. That's what you are, Brianna Marilena. A big, fat, super bitch. I rose from the bed and stood in front of him, rising on my toes and kissing him gently on the lips. But instead of returning my kiss, he took me by the shoulders and pushed me away from him. Again.

"Aidan's right, you really need your rest. You've been through a lot today."

Hurt by his action I turned away from him, trying desperately to keep my emotions under control as I walked to my side of the bed. The blankets were still pulled back from earlier and I slipped right into the indentation that my body had already made. Cameron climbed in on the other side of me, tucking me in as I pressed my back up against his side.

This was how we laid so many nights together in this very bed, and yet now we felt like strangers. I might as well have been alone in the bed for all the attention he gave me. This wasn't what our reunion was supposed to be like. This wasn't us. More like it wasn't him. Was the stress of finding Elaina, being apart from one another, and becoming a father too much for one man? Even if that man was a Vampire? I always thought Vampires were invincible, but perhaps they too had their limits.

My worries and endless thoughts were preventing me from relaxing enough to allow sleep to overtake me. Even though I had slept the entire day all I wanted to do was fade away into my dreams that I seemed to never have anymore. I wanted them to take me away from everything that was happening around me.

Only a few minutes passed before my knees started grinding against each other from having pushed the fluff of the pillow to either side.

"This isn't working," I said as I started to pull another pillow between my legs.

"I know," Cameron replied and I froze. "I'm glad you said it first."

I held my breath, afraid of what would happen if I moved a single muscle. While I bit the insides of my cheeks, Cameron continued with, "The time I have had with my coven has made me realize how much I miss being on the front lines. It has been difficult for me to find my balance between my responsibilities to you and truly being an active Warrior. This is what Victor made me for and being around my family this much makes it hard to think about having to give it up. The timing is horrible, I know, but the last thing I want for either of us is to resent one another five or ten years down the line because we felt obligated to stay together for our babies' sake."

As he spoke, I slowly began pulling the edge of the comforter over the side of my face in order to hide myself from him while I bit into my pillow to keep myself from screaming and crying like a mad woman. It seemed so long ago that I had had a dream about him speeding away in his SUV and his spinning tires kicking gravel up at me. But instead he was leaving me in the privacy of my bedroom after seeing me for less than an hour. He was choosing his coven over me and our children. Obviously danger and battle were too much of a draw for him to pass up. I would never be enough for him. If it weren't for my babies inside me, I would rather be lying next to Daddy O in the ground than have to hear Cameron's words.

"Brianna?" he said leaning over me and then touching my cheek. "Brianna, are you asleep?"

When I didn't respond, he rolled back onto his side of the bed, swearing softly under his breath. I kept my eyes closed, although my heart was beating painfully in my chest. It felt as though my ribs would break, though I wasn't sure how much of my heart was even left.

Chapter Forty

Brianna

"Brianna, it's time," Cameron said as he slowly opened the door to my bedroom. The sight of him still made a lump form in my throat. I had woken up alone, which after his statement to me last night, I shouldn't have been surprised.

When Cameron began to turn back around I extended my hand to him, "Cam, wait." Thankfully he stepped toward me and took my hand which I placed softly on top of my stomach. I didn't let the fact that once again his touch didn't generate the heat that it used to stop me from telling him what I needed to say. "I'm sorry about last night. I didn't mean what I said about not being a Warrior. I am, see," I said, pulling up my stretchy shirt's collar to show him my circular gold Warrior pin. "I wear it every day. I am a Warrior, not exactly like you, but in every way I can be. This whole situation has been hard on both of us, and I promise I won't make it any harder by complaining that I'm here because I know you are doing everything you can to protect all of us. And as soon as Elaina is caught and we're together again I will be the best Warrior's wife that you could ask for. I can be wherever you need me to be, we'll figure it out along the way. I love you so much and I am willing to do anything to make this work. Just tell me what you need me to do, I'll change in whatever way in order to make you happy."

Cameron removed his hand from my belly and cupped it around my cheek. "Nothing needs to change in a woman who is so perfect."

His fingers wrapped themselves behind the base of my neck as he tilted my head up to reach his approaching lips. His kiss was very different from yesterday. His lips kneaded and prodded mine to give him more while he wrapped his other arm around my waist and lifted me to a standing position. With both hands he lifted my arms and wrapped them around his neck. His cool breath wisped across my face as my fingers dug into his thick black hair, pulling the short wavy curls.

The babies began to stir when his fingers grazed the side of my breast and traveled down to rest once again on my belly. The feeling of his hand on our children should have felt wonderful and natural, but instead it was uncomfortable since the babies were running a marathon inside me with steel-toed boots. I winced from the pain, causing me to draw back from him enough to see his fully extended fangs. Quickly he lowered his head down to my neck, and just as I felt the tiniest prick on my skin, the babies kicked hard enough to make me gasp and at the same time watch Cameron slam into the wall behind him.

"It wasn't me," I blurted out as he looked wide-eyed around the room and shook his head. My hands went protectively to my stomach knowing that the babies had Pushed their own father away.

"Everything ok in here?"

I looked up to see Aidan standing in the doorway and seeming confused as to why Cameron was half splayed on the floor.

"Yeah, we're fine," I replied flustered. "The babies got jealous I guess."

Both Cameron and Aidan looked at me like I was insane. But seriously, what else was I supposed to say?

Aidan stretched out his hand to Cameron and patted him on the back as he helped him to stand. "We should really get started. I'm not sure how much longer the snow will hold off."

Cameron took my arm and led me out of the room and through the house to the coat closet where I didn't argue about putting on my coat. In fact it was so cold that I even donned a hat, scarf, and gloves knowing that I wanted to be able to stay at Daddy O's resting place for as long as I was able even though it was the last place I wanted to be.

I followed Cameron through the kitchen and out to the large back deck to the steep set of stairs that were anchored to the snow covered ground below. With one Vampire in front of me and one behind, ensuring that I wouldn't fall, I slowly made my way down the stairs and noticed that a path had been cleared of snow down to a fresh mound of dirt located underneath the deck.

I looked up to see Aidan staring sadly back at me. "I'll shovel it whenever it snows so that you can get to him."

It was hard to fight back the tears as I nodded, but I guess today I was allowed to cry as much as I wanted. And even though the path to Daddy O's grave was clear to the wilted grass and gravel beneath, Cameron and Aidan both had their hands around an arm to help me along. When we finally came upon the newly dug grave, I was taken aback by how small it was. Daddy O's actual small stature seemed to always be overtaken by his big personality. Even though I was an inch or so taller, he was always a giant. But now that giant was reduced to a small hidden grave with a boulder at the head with the words *Oliver Morgan* crudely scratched into its surface.

From behind me Aidan unfolded a metal chair, placed it next to the grave, and gently pushed down on my shoulder to lower me in it. Cameron stood next to me while Aidan stepped around to the other side of the grave and clasped his hands together in front of him. "We're here today to remember Oliver Morgan who was a great man to many, a loving grandfather, and soon-to-be great-grandfather. And although…"

While Aidan continued with his kind words my mind shut out everything around me as memories of my grandfather flooded my head.

Age 3:

"Da-e-O, where's Dwight? I tawt you said dis was Dwight's Christmas."

"Naw, sugar," Daddy O *laughed. "The movie's called* White Christmas. *"*

"So when does Dwight come out?"

"Soon, sugar. He'll come on soon," he replied kindly and tucked me into his side.

Age 7:

"Now, 'Lil Bri, what's this I hear about you gettin' into a fight at school?" Daddy O *asked from the front seat while he drove me home from school.*

"Tommy was pickin' on me."

"Now what could Tommy Jacobsen pick on you about so much that ya had to go an hit him in the mouth?"

"He said 'dat I'm a orphan 'cuz my real mama and daddy don't love me. And 'dat I live wif you an Mama Jo 'cuz the hospital made you 'cuz you were bad parents and 'dats what happens when yur bad parents. You hafta

take care of udder kids people don't love."

Daddy O slowed the car and pulled to the side of the road before placing it in park and turning around to face me. "Sugar, now don't go tellin' Mama Jo I said this, but if Tommy Jacobsen said them things then he deserved what ya gave him. Mama Jo and I love you somethin' fierce, 'Lil Bri, and don't you forget that, never, ever, forget that. Yur mama is sick and can't take care of ya right now, that's why you live with us. And no one will ever love you as much as I do. And if that little jerk says somethin' like that to you again, I give ya permission to punch him out again."

Age 16

"This isn't fair, Daddy O! Why do you keep makin' me go back to her?"

"She's yur mama and if I don't send ya back she'll call the sheriff and tell 'em you've run away again. If you keep doin' this they'll put you in juvy and I just can't let that happen."

"You could adopt me. Prove that she's an unfit mother. Anything! Just don't make me go back, please," I sobbed into his shoulder.

"Shh, it's all right now," he said soothingly as he rubbed my back and swayed me slightly. "Sugar, I may love ya like you was my own, but the courts just don't see it that way. They'd rather have ya with yur real mama than an old man like me."

"That's because they're stupid."

"Yes, sugar. They sure are stupid."

"Please let me stay, Daddy O," I cried into his chest.

"Ok now, no need gettin' yourself all worked up. This'll all pass soon enough, sugar, you'll see. How 'bout I make us some hot chocolate and we'll watch Dwight's Christmas.*"*

I lifted my head and wiped my nose with the cuff of my sleeve. "It's the middle of summer, Daddy O."

"Perfect time a year if you ask me," he replied and kissed the top of my head. "Extra marshmallows?"

"Of course," I laughed.

"That's my good 'Lil Bri."

"Bri?"

My whole body shook at the sound of Aidan's voice, startled back into a reality I wish I could escape. "Yeah?"

"Did you want to say something?"

Aidan's voice was gentle, but I could find no solace in his kindness. "Could I have a couple of minutes alone?"

"Take all the time you need," Cameron replied, placing his hands on my shoulders and kissing me softly on the temple.

I reached back and squeezed his hand, looking straight into his eyes. "I only need a few minutes. Then we can…talk?"

Cameron squeezed my shoulder before he turned and walked along the snowless path back up to the house. With the two of them gone it was very apparent how completely alone I was now. My remaining human family was gone, my father unresponsive, and my truelove pulling away from me. If it weren't for the babies kicking inside me I would begin to think my life was pretty much pointless.

Knowing it wasn't good to have the babies out in this weather for much longer I lowered myself to the ground where the gravel dug uncomfortably into my knees as I knelt next to Daddy O's grave.

"It's not even a real grave. Oh Daddy O, I'm so sorry," I choked out as sobs came from deep within my chest. "You…d-deserve so much more than this."

The sobs closed my throat, making it hard to breathe, and the warm tears streaming down my cheeks quickly cooled as winter winds whipped underneath the deck causing my face to burn with cold. I tried wiping the tears away, but more simply made new tracks down to my neck. My knees began to scream at the jagged gravel beginning to pierce through my jeans. Throwing caution to the wind I laid on top of the freshly dug earth like a hysterical grieving woman in a movie. I didn't even care that the front of my white coat was now brown.

"Vampires have ruined our lives, Daddy O. If Shelby had never met Eris, I would never have been born and you wouldn't have been killed. Your life would have been happier." In my head I could hear Daddy O's voice telling me that it wouldn't have been happier because he wouldn't have had me. "I'm sorry for what I said to you on Thanksgiving. I'll never forgive myself…f-for being so stubborn. Why did you have to go…and d-die you…old c-coot.

"You were better than any father could have been to me. You'll always be more than just my grandfather. You're my Daddy O. The only man in my life who didn't leave me or hurt me, you just loved…me. And I don't know…how…I'm going to g-get by without you."

My mouth tasted of dirt as I buried my sobbing face into my grandfather's pitiful resting place. I didn't want to leave but I was frozen and my heart heavy with grief. I needed my bed and my Cam's loving arms in order to survive the rest of the day. As the thought of him crossed my mind I pushed myself up from the ground with a nagging worry. The gravel crunched underneath my feet as I wiped the dirt from my face and coat, only causing it to smear brown streaks into the creamy white wool.

With a very tight grip I climbed up the steep stairs to the top deck and even before I opened the backdoor I could hear yelling coming from inside.

"Don't do this, man," I heard Aidan shout from the foyer as I stepped into the kitchen. "You don't have to do this now."

"I told both of you that I was only here…"

"What's going on?" I interrupted. Both men stopped their arguing and whipped their heads in my direction. I looked down at Cameron's feet and saw his small overnight bag sitting on the floor. I met Cameron's eyes and saw no guilt or sadness over leaving, however, Aidan was furious. His eyes were wild with anger and his chest was even heaving as he looked back and forth between me and Cameron. "I'll get my things."

"Brianna, I don't have time…"

"Cam, it'll only take a few minutes," I said happily, pretending to ignore every negative verbal and non-verbal cue I was receiving from him.

Cameron took my arm, turning me back around to face him. "Bri, don't push this."

"Cam, please," I pleaded as I squeezed his hand to my chest. "Stay another night, just to give us some time to be together and talk."

"I said everything I needed to say last night when you pretended to be asleep. I do not have time to play these games anymore," he responded harshly and ripped his hand from my chest, grabbed his bag from the floor, and walked out the door.

"Cam, wait!" I screamed lunging toward him only to be caught by Aidan.

"He's leaving, Bri. Just let him go."

"I…I can't,"

"Brianna, after everything he's done the last few weeks…"

I pushed him aside and I could hear his frustrated sigh as I walked out the front door.

"Cam, stop, please!" I shouted as I waddled down the stairs of the front porch and slushed through the inches of accumulated snow.

"Brianna, there is no need to keep dragging this out. Nothing is going to change," Cameron said harshly, not bothering to look behind him as he walked to the SUV.

"No, Cam, this isn't how this ends."

"Why not? It's ok for you to leave me, but not the other way around? That's not exactly fair now, is it?" he said as he opened the truck's door.

"Cameron, please don't make me beg. I love you and I know that you love me and that you're scared. But stay, please, for all of us. We can figure something out," I pleaded as I placed his hand on my stomach hoping that the babies would kick. Anything that would remind him of what we were to each other.

"This is not what I want," he snapped, pulling his hand away. "I got you pregnant and I will take responsibility for that and of course ensure the welfare of you and the children. You will be safe here and I will make sure you want for nothing."

"I don't want your..." money. That's what I was supposed to say. I could hear the snow and gravel being crushed behind me and I knew it was Aidan coming to comfort me. Another dream down.

"Brianna, the only thing I can give you right now is money. If you don't want it then you'll be left with nothing."

"Don't take it, Morgan." Aidan said behind me, his hand curling around my own. "Stay with me. I'll take care of you, better than he ever could."

"Aidan's right. He can give you what I can't."

"Or won't," I cried and grasped the truck's door. "Please, Cam."

"Brianna, step away," Cameron said coldly.

Aidan pulled me away, holding my arms down at my side while I struggled against him. "Brianna, stay with me," he whispered into my ear, but I ignored him and lunged toward the truck.

"Cam, I know you love me. This isn't you, you don't even sound like yourself anymore. You are the man I think you are, you are, I know you are."

Cameron squinted his eyes in confusion, but having had this dream several times I knew what he was going to say - *I am not who you think I am.* I knew who he was, he had forgotten. He needed to stay with me and be reminded of who we were together and what we meant to each other.

"Goodbye, Brianna," Cameron said, slamming the door shut and starting the engine.

He didn't roll down the window. He didn't give me once last glance. He simply put the SUV in gear, and rage exploded within me.

"You fucking coward," I screamed and slammed my fist into the window, startling Cameron to attention. "You call yourself a Warrior?"

Through the window I could see Cameron's nostrils flare and his lips drawn tight. Aidan's hands wrapped around my arms again as Cameron began backing slowly out of the driveway. With a quick burst I Pushed Aidan away, releasing me from his grip. Quickly I ripped the sapphire ring from my finger and threw it at the SUV. "Don't come crawling back to me when your little hybrid slut gets tired of you." Next, I reached into my coat and ripped the gold Warrior pin from my collar and threw it at the truck that was now almost to the road. "And watch your back," I yelled as I pointed to him, "Eris. Will. Find. You."

Cameron stopped the truck for a moment and I thought for a second that he might be changing his mind. But as brief as that moment was, in the next he was spinning the tires in the slippery wet snow trying to get into the road causing gravel and a slushy mix of snow and mud to come flying in my direction. A second later Aidan stood in front of me, crushing me to his chest, protecting me as best he could. I didn't push him away or hit at his chest as I had in my dream. I was too tired and angry and broken. So I let him hold me tightly against him while I sobbed into his chest.

When Cameron was no longer in sight Aidan turned me toward the house and guided me up the stairs and through the front door, softly giving me words of comfort, but I couldn't process anything that he was saying. As my anger began to fade, worry and panic began to set in.

"What am I going to do now? How am I going to raise two babies by myself?" I said weakly as Aidan sat me down on the couch before throwing his wet jacket on the floor and turning on the gas fireplace in front of us.

"Morgan, you will not be alone, I promise you. As long as that is what you want."

I wanted to tell him that I would never love anyone again and that I didn't want him putting his life on hold for me. But I couldn't. I was suddenly too scared and felt too alone to push away the only person I had left. It was all too much to take in and I worried about how this much grief and stress would affect the health of my babies. If I were to lose them now, my life would be meaningless.

In my moment of weakness and selfishness I extended my hand to Aidan and said, "Stay with me. Please."

Chapter Forty-One

Brianna

There was only two hours left of Christmas and the day couldn't end soon enough. The holiday reminded me too much of what I was missing in my life now - faith, family, and alcohol. A good night's sleep would be nice, too. Lately I seemed to wake more exhausted than the day before. My pregnancy was certainly beginning to take its toll and I was only in my second trimester. I'd be bedridden by the end of the month at this rate and my depression certainly wasn't helping me.

The morning brought a fresh light snow, just enough to make the day picture perfect for most people, but even sadder for a depressed pregnant woman who lost her family and fiancé a little over a week ago. Six weeks, six days, sixteen hours and thirty-two minutes ago my life turned to crap. Now I was left with a house full of memories, babies that were making me gain weight every day, and a blonde-headed Vampire who voluntarily chose to stay with me in this horrid situation. Stupid choice on his part, but I was thankful all the same.

Since Daddy O's death I hadn't left the house; not only because I was certainly depressed, I was also just too plain scared. The last time I left, two people and one Vampire ended up dead. Goodness knows what would happen the next time. Even the idea of raiding Shelby's house for all the treasures she had stolen wasn't enough for me to find the courage to step out the front door.

So here I was sitting around like a big old cat doing nothing but moping around the house. Even though the TV was on, I wasn't watching. My legs were draped over the arm of Daddy O's recliner while I stared out the window at nothing in particular. Daddy O's impression in the chair had given way to my own since I sat in it almost every waking moment. I still caught myself waiting for him to come in the room and kick me out of his favorite chair. It was an aching desire that kept being unfulfilled as the hours passed.

"*White Christmas* again," Aidan whined as he entered the living room with a glass of milk in his hand.

"Dwight's Christmas," I muttered back, taking the glass from his hand.

"You can call it whatever you want, but after twenty-something times I'm a little sick of happy ever after let's put on a show in the barn."

"It's a hotel. Not a barn," I replied flatly then drank half the glass of milk in one gulp. As the final scene began to fade, I cradled my glass of milk to my chest and turned back to the window. "It's on a loop. Just let it play."

"Ok, that's it," Aidan announced as he dramatically turned off the TV. "No more moping. No more staring out the window for hours on end. And definitely no more *White Christmas*."

"Dwight's."

"Whatever! No more," he said and switched on the ancient stereo next to the TV and turned the dial through the radio stations until he found one playing cheerful Christmas music. When he stepped in front of me, Aidan extended his hand. "Come on, it's Christmas."

"I don't know..." but before I finished, he took my hand and I was being twirled around the tiny living room to the upbeat holiday tune. He caught me every time I lost my balance when he spun me under his arm, and by the end of the song I couldn't hold my smile inside any longer.

"Now there's the smile I've been waiting for," he said looking down at me. The upbeat song changed into a slow depressing one, timing usually only seen in movies, but we didn't stop dancing. My breath became staggered as nervous waves shot through my body. With a gentle hand Aidan pressed me into his chest and led me side to side to the easy beat of the music. Dancing with Aidan was nothing like it was with Cameron. Dancing with Cameron was like being on a cloud...stop it. Don't think about him, don't even mention his name. Push the memory down deep where it can't keep tearing the inside of your heart.

Aidan nuzzled against my cheek as he whispered, "Allow me to love you."

Ah, shit. I didn't respond right away, giving myself a few seconds to swallow the panic.

"Aidan, I don't even know if I can love anyone anymore."

"Bri, I know you see how I look at you and most times I see you looking back at me the same way." Aidan lifted his head to look at me, moving his hand to cup my cheek and stroke my skin with his thumb. "I can be pig-headed and stubborn, but I can love you more than anyone has ever loved you and I will raise these babies as if they were my own. I'm not as wealthy as...*him*, but I have money and we will always be comfortable. Brianna, all I am asking for is a chance."

I bit my bottom lip as Aidan's fingers tangled themselves in my hair finally finding their way to the back of my neck. His gaze had the same intensity and desire as the first time we found ourselves in this position, however, this time I didn't stop him from pressing his lips onto mine. His fingers pulled at my hair while he wrapped his other arm around my waist, pressing me against him as he flicked his tongue against my closed lips. It wasn't that he was a bad kisser, it just felt...well...weird. Maybe if I tried a little harder, relaxed a little. I opened my mouth nervously and instantly he thrust his tongue roughly into my mouth and it made me want to vomit.

I tried making myself breathe a little harder to make it feel more passionate, but the truth of the matter was I felt nothing. Absolutely nothing. Well I couldn't say *absolutely* nothing. My stomach was starting to burn and it wasn't indigestion. The babies were bouncing from one end of my stomach to the other, and it felt like someone had turned the oven on full blast inside of me.

I moaned softly from the increasing pain coming from my belly and Aidan mistakenly took it as a moan of pleasure and began rubbing his hands up and down my body, pressing me even tighter against him. His fingers slipped underneath the collar of my shirt and pulled the strap of my bra off my shoulder. Just as his hand slipped underneath my shirt, the babies kicked me so hard that I yelled in Aidan's face as I grabbed my stomach and flew face forward toward the floor.

Aidan caught me by the shoulders just before my knees hit the ground and lowered me to the floor up against the front of the couch. My eyes were closed while I rubbed my stomach gently, breathing in and out slowly, willing the pain to subside with each breath and begging my babies to stop punishing me.

"Morgan?" Aidan said with a panicked tone while petting my hair with worry. "Brianna, what happened? Are you all right?"

"I'm fine," I breathed out loudly as the burning finally started to cool.

"The babies?"

"They're fine. They're grounded as soon as they're born, but they're fine," I replied and finally opened my eyes to see Aidan's furrowed brow staring back at me. "They just kicked really hard."

"Do you need a doctor?"

"You couldn't take me anyway," I laughed. "I'm fine, really I am."

Aidan sighed and smiled with relief before putting his head down into the crook of my neck. "You scared the shit out of me."

"Out of you! I think I'm the one in pain here."

"Come on, Morgan, you know what I mean."

Aidan's smile fell as his fingers traced the line of my cheek and around the edges of my lips. Taking my chin between his thumb and index finger he pulled my face to his and kissed me once again. Honestly it felt like I was kissing my brother and the feeling was uncomfortable enough to make me pull away.

When he leaned in again I put my hand up to his chest. "Aidan, I…" but he didn't let me finish and tried kissing me again. I shook my head side to side trying to get him to stop, but it only made my face wet as his lips smeared across my face. "Stop, Aidan! I can't do this," I yelled.

"Dammit, Morgan. I thought this was what you wanted."

"Aidan, I…please don't be mad…I…"

"You're still in love with him, aren't you?" he said angrily as he stood above me, waiting for me to answer. When I didn't, he continued with, "After everything he has done to you."

"He's the father of my children, it's…."

"A father who *left* his children. He left you. Left. Do you remember that?" I looked to the floor, avoiding his gaze and his truth. "Well Morgan, I certainly remember. I remember watching him walk right out that door and tell you that all he could give you was money, like you were some goddamn whore. I remember him pushing you out of the way of the truck so that he could drive away after telling you he had someone else. And lastly I remember the agonizing cries coming from your room every night for almost two weeks. That's what I remember. So what I can't understand is how you seem to have forgotten. I am standing here in front of you, begging you to love me and you push me away."

"Aidan, I'm sorry…" I began as he turned and walked around the couch toward the foyer.

"I stayed for you. Not for Cameron, not for the Warriors, you. Don't expect me to keep crawling back forever."

When Aidan opened the front door I panicked and couldn't stop myself from asking, "Where are you going?"

"Hunting. You're not the only one who needs to eat."

The door slammed so hard it made me flinch.

"I hope you're happy," I said looking down at my belly. The babies kicked lightly inside, doing their own little victory dance I'm sure. "Without him, my little darlings, we're really shit up a creek. And unfortunately, I'm not sure I can get up off the floor without his help."

The babies continued to kick inside me as I rolled to my side, raising myself up on my knees and using the couch as leverage to get me to a standing position (which took almost five minutes). It was late, and Aidan was angry enough not to return any time soon so I headed off to bed. Alone. Alone, alone, alone.

As I approached my room the familiar dull ache of a migraine started to hit. A perfect ending to a crappy night. I changed into a pair of pajamas, cracked the French doors slightly for the cool fresh air, and wrapped myself in the fluffy blue comforter. The alarm clock sitting next to my bed seemed to be blazing the time like a beacon into the darkness of my room. I was exhausted even though I had slept on and off throughout the day, but I couldn't relax enough to let myself fall asleep. I couldn't help but continue to stare at the alarm clock burning the time into my eyes. 11:03. 11:04.

Six weeks, six days, seventeen hours, thirty-four minutes. Six weeks, six days, seventeen hours, thirty-five minutes. Just shoot me.

Six weeks, six days, seventeen hours, thirty-six minutes.

Six weeks, six days, seventeen hours,

thirty-six minutes, earlier...

Chapter Forty-Two

Renee

"Re, answer your phone," John slurred and pushed my shoulder. The man was crazy if he thought I would forgive him for waking me up after a night of celebratory sexual debauchery.

Without bothering to roll over, I flopped my hand behind me trying to find the fucking cell phone to shut it up. Of course the minute I got my hand around it the call went to voicemail. Fucker.

Ok then, back to sleep.

"Renee! Answer the damn phone!" John shouted when my cell phone went off again.

"John, I will poison you in your sleep if you yell at me again." Ok, not completely true. I'm really only going to kill whomever is calling me. Putting the phone to my ear I said, "Someone better be dead."

"Since I do not have a heartbeat I am technically dead."

"Cameron! Holy shit, I need to stop answering the phone like that. What…what time is it?"

"Just after six."

"Are you fucking kidding me."

"Renee, I apologize for the hour but I need your help. Brianna might be in trouble."

"What!" I shouted as I sat upright in bed making John flinch and turn over on his other side, cursing me under his breath. "What's going on, what happened? Where is she!"

"Renee, calm down. She's not in any trouble, yet, but…"

"Then why the fuck are you calling me?"

"Has Brianna told you about the Vampire we are protecting her from?"

"Yeah, some crazy bitch."

"Yes, her name is Elaina and she has just been spotted in Boston."

"Holy shit," I said too loud, once again making John curse at me. "So what do I need to do? And more importantly, do I get to have a gun?"

"No, Renee," he laughed. "I need to get Brianna out of the city, but I must go after Elaina. I am afraid that valuable time will be lost by me trying to convince Brianna to leave."

"Yeah, especially since you guys just bought a house. She'll probably want to stay and fight the bitch rather than have to run away again."

"Precisely. I need you to convince her leaving is the safest option. She will not put up as much of a fight with you as she would me."

"That's cuz she knows her place." Cameron cleared his throat, but I knew he was laughing on the inside. "'Kay, so I just need to go to the hotel?"

"Not by yourself. A man by the name of Fabiani will be at your house in about ten minutes to escort you to the hotel and then he will bring you home afterwards. The sooner we can get Brianna out of town the better."

"You seriously think I can get ready in ten minutes?"

"I know you will try."

"Is this Fabiani guy a…you know what?" I whispered.

"Yes he is. You will be well protected."

"I need hazard pay."

"Let me know once you are at the hotel," he said, completely ignoring me, the bastard. "I will text Hugo and let him know you are coming and that you are an honorary Warrior today."

"Well I certainly like having a title. But seriously, hazard pay?"

"Eight minutes, Renee."

"Yeah, yeah. I'll call you later."

As soon as the call ended I flipped the covers off me and leaned over the edge of the bed to find the pair of jeans I knew were hiding on the floor somewhere. When I stood up from the bed I suddenly realized how sore my crotch was. Note to self…do not play ride 'em cowboy when you're completely hammered, you just keep falling off. Damn that last glass of champagne. But overall it was worth it. I was engaged. I finally convinced some poor bastard that I was worth it, and my new engagement ring was shining back at me even in the dark.

"Ya done good, Dr. John," I muttered to myself as I painfully pulled my jeans up. I knew there was a shirt stuffed somewhere under the bed too, but I wasn't about to bend down and find it. When I opened the door to the cubbyhole considered a closet, the tiny light went on and immediately I heard John complaining behind me.

"Re, what are you doing?"

"Er...Brianna's in trouble and Cameron asked me to help get her out of the city. Which when you think about it is pretty shitty since the last thing I want is for her to leave after I finally got her here, but..."

"Whoa, wait a minute," he said sleepily and rubbing his eyes. "If Brianna's in trouble, why is Cameron calling you?"

"Why wouldn't he call me? Men cower before me."

Slowly John rolled over, placing his feet on the floor and pushing himself up to a seated position. He looked incredibly hung over which shouldn't be surprising, truly the man couldn't hold his liquor. He was such a girl sometimes, but he was mine for the rest of my life. That sounded kinda cool.

John groaned as he rolled his chin into his chest and then cracked his neck loudly. "We need to remember not to do ride 'em cowboy when both of us are plastered. It feels like I have carpet burns on my thighs."

"Great choice of words."

"Ok seriously now, where are you going?"

"Jeez, John, I told you. Brianna's in trouble and Cameron needs my help. I'm going to their hotel to convince Brianna to leave the city."

"And why does she need to leave the city?"

"Because someone's after her."

"Her ex-husband?"

"Considering he's dead, no."

"What! Since when?"

Shit. "Forget what I just said. Look, I only have a few minutes until Cameron's friend gets here."

I only got as far as the bedroom door before I felt John's hand on my arm.

"Renee, stop. I know there's more you're not telling me."

"And I don't have time to tell you now."

"If Bri's ex is dead, what kind of trouble could a pregnant former housewife be in?"

"You'd be surprised," I replied and lifted my arm out of his hand, but when I stepped forward he held the door shut in front of me. "Ok fine.

There's this crazy woman whose been chasing Brianna around the country and she's trying to kidnap her so that she can steal Bri's babies. And now that woman is here in Boston and Cameron thinks I'm the only one who can convince her to go. Now can I leave?"

"No!" he said, a little too loudly for my taste and I certainly gave him a look that showed him that and he lowered his voice. "I like Cam and all, but I'm a little pissed that he's asking you to put yourself in danger. Why can't he do this himself?"

"Because he's going after that crazy woman."

"Why isn't he calling the police?"

"Because the police don't handle these kinds of things."

"This is exactly what the police do! I'm not going to let you go out there and risk your life to help your friend. I know you love her, but it is my job to protect you just like Cameron wants to protect Brianna."

"John, I will be protected."

"By Cameron's friend? I don't think so. I'm calling Cameron and then I'm going to call the police. If Brianna is in trouble then…"

"No! John stop!" I yelled as he stepped over to the nightstand for his phone.

"No, Re, you stop! I'm going to call Cam and give him a piece of my mind."

My god he was irritatingly protective. Gently I took his hand and pulled him down on the bed. "Honey, just sit down. I need to tell you something…about Cameron and Bri." John did as I asked, though in total slow motion which was so freaking frustrating. "Ok, so I'm just going to come right out and say it. Cameron's a Vampire."

John's eyebrows only flinched a tiny bit before he began to nod. "Ok."

He was taking this surprisingly well. "Yeah, so he's a Vampire and Bri's half-Vamp because her mother is human, but her father is supposed to be this big bad ass of a Vampire. So anyway Bri's totally like a superhero now and she even has these knives that she whips around."

John got up and began rustling through his green scrubs on the floor.

"Uh-hmm. And how long have Cameron and Brianna been Vampires?"

"Er, I don't know. Wait, aren't you listening to me? Only Cameron is the Vampire, oh and the crazy woman that's chasing Bri around. She wants Bri's babies because they're going to save the world or some shit like that. Which if you ask me, is a bit much to put on the head of a baby, but these Vamps live by a different set of rules I guess."

John stood up from the floor and stepped carefully over to me. "Look into the light for me," he said as he waved his white pen light in front of my eyes from side to side.

"What? Why!"

"Re, honey, I think you might be having a mental break."

"Oh stop your nonsense and get that light out of my face," I yelled and slapped his hand away. "I am not crazy."

"Of course not, honey, you're just sick. I'm going to take you to the hospital and we'll do a full work up…"

"John, I'm not sick and I'm not crazy. I'm telling you the truth."

"Of course you are," he replied kindly.

"Don't talk to me like I'm a lunatic and open your mind for once."

"Renee, I don't…"

"Remember you remarked on the fact that Cameron was cold when he shook your hand? Yeah, well he's cold because he's dead, or kind of dead. Walking around dead. And the times you've yelled at me for eating Cameron's food…yeah…dead people can't eat so Bri and I kept eating for him so that you wouldn't really notice. And remember the first time you met the two of them? That night at my old apartment?" He nodded. "You went into work and Sam came into the ER. Why? Because Cameron beat the shit out of him." And eventually killed him, but I didn't want to blow John's mind even more. Just then I could hear the intercom buzzing downstairs. "Baby, I love you, but my ride is here."

"Renee, wait!" John shouted as I bolted out the bedroom and down the two flights of stairs to the front door.

As I shrugged into my coat I could hear John fumbling around above and then slide down half of the stairs before hitting the first landing. Quickly I turned the doorknob and ran into the foyer of our brownstone before John could stop me. Waving at me through the front door window was a short little man who seriously looked like he just came from the clubs. When I opened the door he instantly thrust his hand in front of me and started shaking my hand.

"You must be Renee, I'm Fab…"

"Yeah, yeah, look, my boy…fiancé is on his way down and he does *not* want me to go and he doesn't believe that you are…er…what you are."

"I'm not sure I follow."

"I thought you Vamps were supposed to be smart."

Just then John came running out the door of our apartment with a dirty gray t-shirt and his pants unbuttoned. "Renee stop!"

"Oh honey, you're here," I said trying to sound surprised and angelic, though I knew he wasn't going to buy it. "John, this is Fab. Fab, this is John."

"Fabi, actually."

John stepped in front of me in a typical protective male way, putting his hands up in front of Fabi. Weird name.

"Fabi, I'm sorry you've come all the way over here, but I'm not exposing Renee to whatever danger Brianna might be in right now. Besides I think Renee is having some kind of episode that requires medical attention."

I rose onto the balls of my feet, rested my chin on John's broad shoulder and looked at Fabi to say, "This would be where you show him some cool Vamp trick or else he's pulling the man card and taking me to the loony bin."

"Oh I see!" Fabi said finally with some recognition on his face. "So John, what's your blood type?"

John shook his head in confusion. "Uh, I'm not sure why that's important."

"Oh it's really important. I prefer A negative, why don't you let me have a taste?" Fabi opened his mouth and with a small clicking noise his fangs shot down causing John to fly back to the wall behind him, almost knocking me down in the process.

"Those are...you're a...holy hell..." he stuttered. "Re, get away...he's a...a."

"No shit he's an 'a'. I tried to tell you, but you thought I was crazy. Now just sit there on the floor while he and I have a little talk. Now Fabi, you're so little and cute I seriously can't believe you're a Vamp."

"Huh, and I seriously can't believe you're trying to fool anyone with that hair color," Fabi replied with tremendous gay-tude. "And not to be rude, but we don't really have time for your little soap opera nonsense. So can we get going or do I need to save the day myself?"

I turned to look at John who was still trembling a little in fear. "Well I like him! Oh, and you didn't hear that about my hair color by the way."

John scrunched his brows together and slowly looked up at me. "You're not a red head?"

"Of course I am. I just don't have a fire crotch. It's a genetic condition." I turned quickly back to Fabi who was tapping his watch. "Bye honey. You might want to go back inside before you freak out the neighbors."

"No, I'm going with you!" John said as he pushed himself up the wall.

"Good thing I bought an extra coffee."

Fabi turned away from the door and both John and I followed him down the stairs to the street where a huge SUV waited with the engine running. Seriously, how did he get around with that thing in Boston? The streets were as wide as my cubbyhole closet for crying out loud.

Fabi stood with the passenger door open, gesturing for me to hop in, but once again manly-man John stepped in front of me. "I'd feel more comfortable if I sat up front."

"Lucky me," Fabi replied, flashing his eyes and checking out my man from head to toe.

John took a step back, stuttering some kind of uncomfortable nonsense, but I pushed him into the front seat anyway. "Sorry, Fabi, he's straight and taken," I said holding up my newly ringed finger.

"I always seem to fall for the straight ones. Why are all the handsome ones straight *and* taken? First Cameron Burke and now this one."

"Well that's a compliment if you're putting John and Cameron in the same category. I mean, ohmygod, Cameron is 'drop-dead-let's-find-out-how-quickly-my-pants-come-off' handsome."

"Re, I'm sitting right here." John chided.

"I know," I replied happily as I hopped into the back seat.

Fabi slid into the driver's seat and then held out a cardboard tray that held two foam cups. "Coffees for the humans. But I'll warn you, I drive pretty fast, so be careful."

Before I could even get the cup out of the tray, Fabi put the pedal to the metal and we were screaming down the street. Literally, John and the tires were screaming at the same pitch.

"We're not going to make it through," John shouted as he pointed to another SUV that was parked almost a foot from the curb, making the street narrower than it already was.

But Fabi didn't seem fazed. "Oh we're fine. I'm a very good driver. Laser-like eyes, I have." As the other truck came closer I found myself gripping the sides of my seat and noticed that John was clinging to the handle above the door. "John, do you think you could hold the steering wheel straight for me?"

"Huh! What?!"

But just as John was beginning to object, Fabi disappeared into a cloud of blackish smoke. John grabbed the wheel and at the same time Fabi suddenly appeared outside next to the other SUV, pushed it closer to the curb and then was suddenly back in the driver's seat.

"Holy shit," I whispered, not caring that my eyes were bugging out of my head.

"I know, right! I love Projection. Coolest Vampire trick if you ask me."

John's hands were shaking as he let go of the steering wheel and tried to open the lid to his coffee only causing it to spill all over the center console. Poor man. Has chaffed thighs, found out Vampires were real, and now can't even enjoy a cup of coffee.

Fabi drove faster than I ever thought anyone could on the streets of Boston, and that's including cab drivers. It only took a few minutes to get to Bri's hotel and I started to feel guilty about waking up a pregnant lady at 6:30 in the morning. Just didn't seem right, but I had a job to do, honorary Warrior and all.

After telling John to zip up his pants, to Fabi's dismay, we piled into the elevator and watched the floors slowly ticked up until we got to the top floor. As soon as the doors opened I knew something was different.

"Where's Hugo?" I asked, looking to Fabi who stepped out ahead of us. "Cameron said he would text him to let him know we were coming."

Fabi shrugged, but kept walking. "Maybe he's waiting inside."

"Hopefully he woke Bri up. I certainly don't want to be the one poking the sleeping bear." Fabi laughed as he pulled a key card from the back pocket of his very tight dark jeans. "So seriously, did you go clubbing all night? And what's with the scarf?"

"Hey girleen, I'm not about to take fashion abuse from someone whose wearing jeans that haven't been washed in days and have probably been rolled up on the floor."

"How could you possibly know that?"

"Comes with the gay handbook. Shall we?"

Fabi slipped the key card into the lock and for some reason John jumped back when the door opened.

"What's your problem?"

"I don't know, I thought something might jump out at me."

"It's a good thing I love you. You could never be an honorary Warrior like me."

Fabi stepped through the door and both John and I followed closely behind only to crash into him when he stopped suddenly. "Do you smell that?"

"Uh…no," I replied and began looking around. "Where's Bri?"

Fabi didn't pay attention to my question and walked to the far left side of the room while I stepped over to the bed that had been left unmade. I looked back at John who shrugged and looked toward the bathroom. Calling Bri's name, I pushed the door open and turned on the light only to look into an empty bathroom.

"Where is she?"

John walked over to a large armoire next to him and opened it to find Cameron's clothes hanging and folded. Nothing of Bri's. There was nothing of hers in the bathroom either.

"Are you sure she didn't leave with Hugo or something?"

Before anyone could answer, my back pocket starting singing and vibrating at the same time. I reached back and put my cell phone to my ear. "Cameron, hey."

"Are you at the hotel yet?"

"Yeah. Bri's not here. Did she…"

"What do you mean she is not there?"

"I'm sorry, did I stutter? She's not here. All her stuff is gone. Did she leave with Hugo or something?"

"Absolutely not. Maybe she needed something…"

"Her stuff is gone, Cameron. What the hell is going on?!"

From the corner of my eye I could see Fabi stepping over to a tall cabinet, sniffing loudly with his nose in the air. Tentatively he placed his hand on the handle of the cabinet and opened it. Suddenly he jumped back when a large dark mass fell loudly to the floor causing everyone in the room to scream. I could hear Cameron shouting at me from the phone but I couldn't find my voice to answer him when a man's head rolled to my feet.

A second later John collected himself and went into full ER doctor mode while he pulled me under his arm and guided me to the bed. Also hearing Cameron's shouts through the phone he took it from me and placed it up to his ear.

"Cam, Cameron! It's John. There's a body. A body fell from a closet. I…don't know who it is."

"It's…Hugo," I whimpered.

"Hugo? Oh no, it's Hugo. What do you mean you need us to clear an area?"

I looked up to John just as confused as he seemed to be at Cameron's request. But a second later there was a flash of black smoke accompanied by a cracking sound and suddenly Cameron was crouched in the floor, catching himself with his hands in front of him. John turned around quickly, placing his arm in front of me as Cameron shot up and walked over to see Hugo lying in a headless heap on the floor. The next second he was walking to the bathroom, looking, searching, and then panicking. He was pacing back and forth, talking so fast to Fabi I couldn't understand him. His movement from one side of the room to the other was making me sick and the panic that was starting to radiate from him was catching.

"Cameron, where is she?" I asked quietly.

"Fabiani, do you smell another Vampire?" Cameron asked, choosing to ignore me. I looked over to Fabi who was cowering over by the window trying to avoid Hugo's body and separated head.

"I do, but I don't recognize it. It took us less than twenty minutes to get here. How did they get her out so fast?"

"Cameron, where is she!" I screamed.

"I do not know!" he shouted.

"You are a deader dead man!"

Chapter Forty-Three

Cameron

Renee knocked John onto the bed as she flew at me and began clawing at my chest while screaming obscenities at me. She was only hurting herself and I did not have the time or the patience but I knew I needed to be gentle with her. Thankfully John wrapped his arm around her waist and pulled her off of me, though her yelling continued.

"What do you mean you don't know where she is! That's your fucking job! To know where she is!"

"Let's just all calm down," Fabiani said from the window, being careful to step around Hugo's dismembered head.

"Calm down?" Renee screamed, turning her venom on the young Negotiator. "What the fuck do you mean 'calm down!' My 'sister' has gone missing and you want me to fucking 'calm down?'"

"Re, honey, please..." John began, only to have Renee hit his hands away.

The cell phone in my hand started to vibrate and Alexander's name flashed across the screen.

"Quiet, everyone," I shouted and put the phone up to my ear. "Alex, Brianna is missing."

"What do you mean she's missing?" Alexander's deep voice elevated with surprise.

"Brianna is gone. Her things are gone, and I can smell another Vampire in here. She must have been taken. Somehow...Elaina got past Hugo...and...they took her. How did no one in the hotel notice a pregnant woman being taken against her will!"

John cleared his throat, "Um, actually it doesn't look like there's been a struggle."

"What was that?" I snapped.

Unfortunately my tone seemed to take John aback. "I was just thinking…that it doesn't seem like there was a struggle…well except for the dead guy. But nothing's overturned or out of place. All her things were packed, nothing seems to have been left behind. I doubt kidnappers would have normally taken the time and care to do that."

"What are you implying?" I growled.

"Uh, I don't know. Just that…there…wasn't a struggle. That's…um…about it."

Turning away from all of them I continued my conversation with Alexander. "Have Jared pull all the video surveillance on this floor for the last hour. I want to know who took her, when, and how in the hell they got her out of here before we did."

"Jared's hacking into hotel security now. But there is something else, Cam. The satellite picked Elaina up a couple of minutes ago at Back Bay station."

"Was Brianna with her?"

"No, I was only calling to give you her latest sighting, but I'll have Jared pull anything he can from those cameras as well. We'll bring in extra techs to go through the video feeds. We'll find her, Cam, they couldn't have gotten far. The first alarms only went off twenty minutes ago."

He was right. Twenty minutes wasn't very long to get into the hotel, get Brianna packed, and leave the city. There was still a chance. So why did I have a sinking feeling in my stomach? I looked back to Renee who was cradled in John's arms and I suddenly realized that Brianna might not be the only one in danger.

"Alex, have Jared ready to present his findings in ten minutes. Father is keeping the line open with Dante, we will conference there."

"Will do, Cam. Talk to you in ten."

"Fabi," I said, snapping him to attention, "do you have a Cleaner crew in the area?" He nodded. "Good. Get them here right away. We need to dispose of Hugo immediately. Hopefully no one has complained about the screaming already. Also, are you all right to drive?"

"Yes, I think so. I'm sorry, I'm just not good with…" he didn't finish but pointed down at Hugo.

"I understand, but I need you to get Renee and John to safety. Can you take them back to Dante's?"

"Cam wait," John began, taking a step toward me. "I should really take Renee home."

I liked him, but I hated the fact that he continually called me Cam.

"John, I am sorry but your home may not be safe. The woman who has been hunting Brianna was just seen at Back Bay station. I do not think it is a coincidence that she was seen only a few minutes from where you live. Please go with Fabiani for now and we will take you home as soon as we determine it is safe."

"Like you would know," Renee said softly but with plenty of venom.

"Fabi, please tell Dante I will Project back over shortly."

"Project from here? Cameron it was dangerous enough the first time, are you sure…"

"Please just go!" I snapped since I knew I would not be able to control my emotions for very much longer. Fabiani nodded quickly, and shuffled Renee and John out of the room. As soon as the door clicked shut I began tearing apart the room looking for anything that would tell me what happened to Brianna.

How did this happen? How in the hell did this happen!

My anger consumed me causing me to grab the large armoire standing against the wall and throw it down into the floor. Wood splintered everywhere as the armoire exploded into a million pieces. I slumped against the wall unable to grasp how my love had disappeared and seemed to have left voluntarily. What would possess her to leave? Was she being a martyr? "Please, no."

The small metal garbage can rolled to a stop up against my hand, having been knocked over by the armoire. I took the can and lifted it upright, only to hear the sound of something hard clang against the bottom. I reached in and pulled out a piece of Brianna's cell phone. It was broken perfectly in half, and from the smell of the other Vampire in the room it was obvious who had done it.

Smell! Damn it, Cameron, get your head on straight. Quickly I shot up from the wall, instantly smelling Brianna's ever present honeysuckle fragrance mixed with hormones. I followed the smell to the door and down the hallway, not caring that I had left a dead Vampire lying in my hotel room. I only hoped that no one had called the front desk due to all the noise. The last thing I needed was to have the police called.

Brianna's smell led me to the elevator where there were thankfully still traces inside the car. I rode down to the lobby of the hotel, but instantly turned back into the elevator when her scent was not even remotely present. Before the elevator doors closed I pressed all three buttons for the garage that was located beneath the hotel. Thankfully Brianna's scent was present on the first garage floor, cutting through the smells of oil and exhaust. I followed her scent over several aisles until it led me to an empty parking spot, the car fluids still fresh on the cement.

Immediately I dialed Alexander and before he could say anything I began shouting orders for Jared to pull all garage surveillance. If we could follow the car, we would find Brianna. At least it sounded simple. I ran to a dark corner of the parking garage and Projected myself without even a full cleansing breath. Fabiani was correct that Projecting at this distance was dangerous, but I had always been able to go farther than any of my siblings. However, I knew full well I was taking a risk doing it twice in a short amount of time and especially without my full concentration. When Dante's red and gold embroidered curtains came into view I felt the back half of my body slam into me, causing me to fall face down at Dante's feet.

"Cameron, my boy, you make quite an exit and entrance I have to say," Dante said as he crooked his arm underneath my shoulder and pulled me up to a standing position. "Victor is still on the phone and the teams are still convened inside if you think they will be of use."

I felt light-headed as Dante led me into the conference room I had vacated only minutes before. Dante had been able to call in a dozen members of his coven in order to help me scour the city for Elaina. Now their presence seemed slightly moot.

"Father!"

"Child! Did you find anything?"

"No. Has Jared pulled the video together?"

"Yes, they are ready for you."

I stood at the head of the large conference table looking straight ahead at the large flat screen mounted above the fireplace that now had a black and white still of Hugo standing outside my hotel room. With all the running back and forth I had not even processed his death with the gravity it deserved.

"Ok, bro, so from the time you left around 3:00am, nothing happens until 5:30," Jared began as he unfroze the video frame, although Hugo stood so still that the only way you knew the video was playing was by the timestamp at the bottom of the screen ticking away. "So here at 5:33:38am we see Hugo lean in toward the door…place his key in the reader…then goes inside, but he never comes back out."

"That is because someone ripped his head off and stuffed him in a cabinet in the hotel room."

"We are speaking of *my* Hugo?" Victor questioned from the phone.

"Yes, Father. I am sorry."

Even though Hugo was an outcast, he was still one of Victor's sires and there was still a bond that was now broken. My father had lost three Warriors in a matter of months – two by death, and one by betrayal. All together it was unheard of for our family.

"We can discuss his death further at another time," Victor pressed. "Let us continue, time is of the essence here."

"Father, I am going to take over for Jared," Alexander's voice vibrated at the edges of Dante's conference phone. "The feed from the traffic cams is finally coming through."

"Fine, fine, please just keep going," I urged without trying to hide my frustration.

Alexander cleared his throat before continuing. He loved me like a brother, but I was treading a fine line. He began fast forwarding the footage while he said, "Once Hugo goes inside we don't see anything until 5:45:13am as you will see in a moment…here we go…we see the door open and a man with a baseball cap exits with a suitcase and Brianna follows after…right here."

"Alex, is there a better angle of his face?"

"Sorry, Cam. This is the best we have. He was obviously avoiding the cameras. We see that Brianna follows him down the hall to the elevators…"

As I listened to Alexander I could not help but hear John's voice in the back of my head pointing out the fact that the hotel room was absent of a struggle. It was difficult to watch Brianna's willingness to leave and even worse, her smile as she followed the stranger into the elevator. At one point my nails began digging into the conference table when she touched his arm and laughed at whatever he was saying to her. If it got any worse I would have to purchase Dante a new table.

From behind me I could hear the front doors to Dante's home open and three sets of shoes tread loudly through the foyer.

"Alex, can you please freeze the frame?"

"Do you recognize him, Cam?" Alexander asked as he froze the scene.

"That's Aidan," Renee said, suddenly standing next to me and pointing to the screen. Quickly I looked back to the screen and saw some resemblance, but looked back at her questioningly. "The hat. He was wearing the same hat the day he found me and Brianna shopping. So...she's with Aidan," she said with a light-hearted, hopeful tone. "No worries then, right? Wires got crossed that's all, just call him and tell him to bring her here."

"Renee," I said gently, placing my hands up in front of me and also noticing John carefully wrapping his hand around her arm. He understood the situation before Renee and realized what her possible reaction could be. "No one called Aidan." I waited a beat, but Renee was still in denial. "He killed Hugo...and...then took Brianna."

Watching Renee's eyes flashed with realization while her breath started to quicken was like watching Devin before he exploded in one of his rages. I wondered how similar their outbursts would be.

"But, child," Victor interrupted, "why would Brianna go with Aidan so willingly?"

"Because *he*," Renee shouted and pointed directly at me, "sent Aidan for her before. You son of a bitch, she trusted him because of you!" Renee lunged at me causing John and Fabiani to hold her around the waist while she hit and clawed at my chest once again. "This is your fault, you bastard. She wouldn't have known him if it weren't for you!"

"Fabi, take her out of here," Dante ordered over Renee's screams.

"If anything happens to her, it'll be on your head, Cameron Burke," Renee yelled as Fabiani pulled her out of the room with John trying to contain her flailing arms. "I swear I will find a way to kill you."

The doors closed securely, but her shouts and threats continued while everyone in the room stared at me, curious to know what I would do next.

"Who was that insolent woman?"

"Father, that was Brianna's closest friend, Renee. She has every right to be upset and nothing she said was false."

"But Cam," Alexander interrupted, "how could Aidan have known your room well enough in order to Project in."

"I do not..." but I stopped. I knew exactly how, and Renee was absolutely right. This was my fault. "The day he brought Brianna to me I had him bring her to the hotel room. He even stood guard until I was able to get there myself. He could have easily taken in enough to Project." And then another thought hit me. "But I think he has been practicing."

"How so?"

"Last night while Brianna was showering she began talking as though someone was in the bathroom with her. I went in, thinking she was talking to me, but…she said she must have been seeing things. What if she was not?" I raked my hand roughly through my hair, pulling at it in frustration and anger at the thought that the bastard was there. "The minute I picked up the phone asking him to help us track Brianna down…"

"Cam, no one is blaming you."

"Well they should. I gave him everything he needed in order to take her, and trusted him so much that I ignored any signs that might have proven he was anything less than what he appeared to be. He was even on the list of those who left Brianna's Claiming ceremony at the time Seraphina stated the threat had left the manor. I know I completely disregarded him because he was escorting Oliver Morgan."

My stomach sank. Not only was Aidan familiar with Brianna, Oliver could be in just as much danger.

"Cam, none of us saw it or would even think that Aidan was ever involved with Elaina. But knowing this, perhaps Aidan was planning on meeting Elaina at the Back Bay station, maybe that's their getaway plan."

"It's a ruse, Alex."

"I don't follow."

"Our attention has always been on Elaina. They knew it and used it against us. They must have known that we were tracking her somehow so they gave us exactly what we wanted – sightings that would turn our complete attention on Elaina while Aidan took care of Brianna. But how? How did they know?"

Dante walked slowly over to my side and placed a reassuring hand on my shoulder. "Alex, could you continue to play the video? Perhaps there are more clues in the footage to come."

Alexander resumed the video and I watched as Brianna continued to smile and talk to Aidan, seeming fully unaware of his betrayal. That was the only explanation I could manage, that she just did not know. She was not emotional or scared, she was merely her usual self. As the seconds ticked away at the bottom of the screen I wished desperately that the video had sound. What was she saying? What was he saying that was making her laugh? Only more things to add to the agony I felt inside.

When the video showed the two of them leave through the open elevator doors, Alexander switched to the video to the parking garage which was grainer than the footage from inside the hotel. But even through the granular black and white video I could decipher my pregnant angel waddling across the parking lot, walking precisely to the same parking spot that I had found empty. However, now the parking spot housed a dark pickup truck.

"Are we tracing the license plate?"

"You can see the footage is spotty, but from various angles we were able to get four out of six numbers. Jared's running what we have now, but no matches so far."

"What about the traffic cameras?"

"Coming online now, bro," Jared announced through the phone. "Hate to say, there's not much but here's what I've found so far." The screen changed from grainy black and white to grainy color footage, though it was only as bright as the street lights made it in the early morning. "I found the pickup truck leaving the hotel garage, then followed it through the street and red light cams. I've tried piecing it together as best I could." The footage jumped and flicked through scenes from multiple cameras projected onto the screen following Aidan's maroon pickup truck through the streets of Boston and then onto a northbound highway. "I was able to follow the truck until they reached the tunnel. I can't seem to crack into those cameras yet but I'm working on it. I've looked at the camera footage that comes out of the tunnel, but there is no sign of the truck coming out."

"What do you mean it does not come out?"

"I've looked at the footage thirty times, bro. I'm telling you a maroon truck doesn't come out of the tunnel."

"Are there off ramps inside that tunnel?"

"I don't know, bro, I just need more time to look."

"How close of an angle are you getting of the cars that are coming out?"

"Only close enough to see the hoods, nothing from the front or side."

"What about other cameras, news cameras maybe, toll booths, they might have different angles?"

"I'm checking into it, but I need more time."

"Brianna does not have any more time!" The room went silent as I pounded my fist into the conference table. I was losing control of myself and quick. It took an incredible amount of energy to push my emotions and anger back down to where I could converse at a more acceptable level. "Jared, I apologize."

"It's ok, bro. We're all feeling the same way. I'll get you everything as fast as I can."

"I know you will, little brother. Could you go back to the frame where the truck is coming out of the garage and just freeze it?"

A second later I was seeing the front of Aidan's truck as it pulled partially out of the garage, waiting for an opportunity to exit.

"Can you zoom in on the passenger side?" I watched as the image became grainer but I could instantly see that Brianna was not sitting next to Aidan. "Where is she?"

Jared continued to zoom in, getting as good of an image through the windshield as possible. "There she is," Jared announced as he highlighted a portion of the frame. "She's lying down, you can see her shoulder."

"She fell asleep in a matter of minutes? Something does not feel right."

"Cam," Alexander interrupted, "look at Aidan." I did as he asked and shifted my gaze to my newly discovered enemy and noticed that he was looking directly into the camera. His right fist was over his heart, and he was smiling. "He is saluting us."

"No," I growled. "He is mocking us. He knew exactly where the camera was and is sending us a message." I paused as undistinguishable grumbles came through the phone. "Has anyone else noticed the timestamps? Jared, what time did the facial recognition alarm go off?"

There was a quick pause while Jared's computer flicked to a different screen showing a black and white still of Elaina. "The photo was marked at 5:52:02am."

"Wait," I shouted as I dug into my pocket for my cell phone. "Hugo was brought down at 5:33. Alex, you began texting me near 6:00am. I texted Hugo shortly after and he texted back. According to the timestamps, Aidan had Brianna out of the city before you even began texting me. If Elaina was a ruse, how was their timing so perfect? How did they know that the facial recognition software would catch her right at that moment?"

"How can a dead man text?" Jared asked.

No one answered, and I sighed before finally saying, "Father, if I may declare, Aidan Pierce is now a fugitive among our race for the kidnapping of Brianna Morgan and is considered to be aligned with Elaina's enemy coven. He is wanted alive unless Brianna Morgan is found beforehand, otherwise mercy does not need to be considered.

"Dante, have the other two teams travel Aidan's route to the tunnel, see if you can discover how Aidan escaped the tunnel without notice and forward any information to Jared. It might be pointless but we need to look at everything.

"Jared, continue looking at the footage and let me know the minute we get a trace on that truck. Also see if Aidan has any other vehicles registered in his name or known aliases. And Alex, find the leak and bring Devin up to speed. If we have another traitor within our midst he should be involved. The timing is certainly not coincidence. We also need to contract with all available Trackers to aid us in finding Brianna. And let it be known that she is the highest of priorities with not only the Warriors' backing, but anyone who wishes to question her importance will have to deal with Eris's fury.

"Father, can you and Dante take the lead of informing the coven leaders of what is happening and that there is a potential delay in the Facility East expansion."

Dante nodded. "We will certainly handle any fallout."

"Father, do you have anything to add?"

"No, child, well said. I believe we have our assignments. I want updates on the hour, not a minute over."

Terse goodbyes were given before the phone lines closed and computer feeds were taken down. Dante stepped to my side, once again placing a comforting hand on my shoulder. "We will give you the room, my boy, as long as you need it."

Dante left through the double oak doors and the remaining Negotiators either followed or Projected from the room in order to embark on what I expected to be pointless journeys. I looked down at the conference table and noticed multiple claw marks I had gouged into the wood along with a round dent from where I had slammed my fist. The sight of them made me angrier so I pushed away from the table and walked around to one of the many conference chairs. As I turned the chair around to face me, Dante's cheery gift bag stared back at me, digging the knife deeper into my heart. I lifted the bag from the chair and sat down in its place. From within I pulled out two small fluffy lambs – one pink, one blue. One girl, one boy. My babies' first toys and I was without them and more so I was without their mother.

"Damn it, Brianna, how could you have gone with him? Son of a bitch!" I swore as I tossed the lambs onto the table. The door behind me clicked closed as the floorboards creaked underneath my unwelcomed guest's feet. "Go away."

"Sorry, Cam, I just…"

"My name is Cameron," I snapped, hating myself the next second. I stood from the chair and kicked the one in front of me to the floor. "John, I apologize," I said and turned to face him. "I just do not know what to do right now."

"Who would?" he replied kindly, shoving his hands deep into the pockets of his jeans. "Look, I didn't mean to disturb you, I just wanted to tell you that Renee didn't mean those things that she said."

I breathed in a laugh. "John Ryan, you are a good man. Do not taint your reputation by lying. You and I both know that Renee meant every word she said."

"She's just upset and when that happens…well she's just so…Renee."

"And she has every right to be angry with me. If Aidan had not pretended to be my friend, I would never have sent him to find Bri and perhaps she would not have gone with him so easily." I took a step back from John, putting my hand roughly through my hair as the anger at myself escalated. "Even further if Brianna had never met me…"

"Cam…er-on, you can't do that to yourself. If this guy was intent on kidnapping Bri, my guess is he would have taken her today whether it was voluntary or not. And I'm not trying to make you worry even more, but the fact that she went peacefully was probably best for both her and the babies considering her medical history."

I sank back into the conference chair behind me, my head falling into my hands.

"Nothing can happen to those babies. Brianna will simply not survive."

"Well, that's what you guys do, isn't it? Save people? You and your brothers?"

I titled my head up, my eyes widening at the realization of everything that John saw today. I stood slowly from my chair, unsure of exactly what to say. "John, let me explain…"

"No need to," he said, taking a tentative step toward me. "Renee told me a little. But it doesn't matter, you have more important things to worry about right now. I just hope that you won't try and kill me off because you think I know too much. Frankly, I'm too scared to say anything to anyone."

"John, unfortunately your silence is expected and necessary. But I will tell you, that both you and Renee will be under the protection of my family. No one will harm either of you while you are in our presence. I can assure you of that."

John sighed with relief. "Look, I know that you are…yeah can't believe I'm saying this…that you are a…Vampire and that you probably have things handled, but if there is anything you need, Re and I are here for you. At this moment, more so me, but she'll come around."

I thanked him as he tentatively shook my hand, his eyes and mind racing with observations and questions at the same time. My back pocket began vibrating and quickly I pulled out my cell phone seeing that it was Kyla.

"John, this is Kyla. I should really take it."

"Of course," he nodded and turned to leave. "Perhaps Brianna will bring Kyla and Renee together after all."

I felt the corners of my mouth curl in a skeptical smile as I placed the phone to my ear, but before I could give her a salutation Kyla was already talking. "How are you doing?"

"How well do you think I am doing?"

"I am just beside myself. I cannot imagine what you are feeling right now."

Hearing Kyla's voice made all my emotions come flooding back, making me sit back down while my free hand rubbed my eyes and temples.

"Please tell me Jared has found something."

"Kyla, I cannot do this."

"Yes you can, Cameron, maybe not alone but you can. The boys are getting the particulars, but we're coming to Boston."

"Who is coming?"

"The family. Eris is going to fly us out today. We should be there this evening."

"Who contacted Eris?"

"He couldn't get through to Victor so he somehow found me. So since I definitely took one for the team today, I am expecting some major thanks and by that I really mean shoes. Now is there a place for us to stay?"

"Dante certainly does not have the room and it is short notice for so many rooms at a hotel."

"Could we rent a house or something?"

Why rent when you owned one, a tiny voice said in my head. It would be tricky to get it up and running in less than ten hours, but it could be done.

"There is a place now that I think of it. I will send the address along shortly."

"Perfect. Is there anything else we can do for you from here?"

"Yes, actually. I am worried about Oliver Morgan's safety. Can you ask Father to send someone to take him and Brianna's mother to the Facility? I think that might be the safest place for them for the time being."

"We'll get them out safe, don't give it another thought. Just a few more hours and we'll be there."

"But if Jared finds something…"

"Cameron, your brothers know what to do."

"Kyla…I…"

"I love you too. We'll be there before you know it."

As I hung up the phone all I could think of was that they could not be here soon enough. I needed my family around me, and in order for that to happen I needed to setup house, which in itself was bittersweet. Not wanting to dwell, I pushed myself up from the chair and walked out to the large waiting area where Fabiani sat comforting Renee while John paced from side to side.

Renee looked up as I stepped in their direction, her glare deadly enough to scare even the most vicious of Vampires. But her contempt for me did not stop my plea. "I need your help."

Renee shot up from her seat, though Fabiani had a light hand around her elbow. "You've got some balls asking me for anything."

I ignored her politely and continued, "My family will be coming in from California this evening and I need help getting the new house in order. We need some basic furniture, two beds for now, sheets, towels and the like. Whatever you can get that can be delivered today."

"You want us to go shopping! My best friend has been kidnapped and you want me to act like nothing has happened. You have no idea what I am going through."

"Do not even begin to suggest that I do not understand your suffering!" I yelled. "Whatever your pain is, multiply it by a thousand and maybe you will begin to feel the agony I am in at this moment. She is your friend, but I have a little more at stake here. All I am asking for is a little help."

"And you will get it," John replied, giving Renee a scolding look.

I reached into my back pocket for my wallet and I began to pull out cash, but then chose to hand over my credit card to John. "I should keep as much cash as I can on me, but Fabi will help you if anyone gives you a hard time using the card or any other roadblocks with getting things delivered today."

"How's that?" John asked quizzically.

Fabiani petted John's arm and winked at him. "They're called sexual favors, honey."

"John, he is kidding," I said giving Fabiani a scolding eye. "You should also stop by the grocery and get the basic necessities since Brianna's stepmother will be coming. You should also get any items for yourselves."

Renee blinked at me in confusion while John asked, "Why…do we need to…"

"Elaina was spotted on your side of the city and Aidan at one point had followed Brianna to your home. The best thing now is for both of you to stay with us so that we can ensure your safety."

"Like you would know," Renee scoffed.

"That is getting old," I replied, unable to ignore another dig.

"Well you're old," she snapped, but then smirked at her weak rebuttal.

"Fabi will escort you back to your apartment to gather some essentials."

Renee stepped forward and grabbed the credit card from John's hand. "And where will you be while the three of us are trouncing all over town?"

"I will be at the house paying off half the city in order to get it up and running with what we need. Hence the cash," I said as I waved the stack in the air. Renee took the money from my hand, removed two hundred dollars and stuffed the cash in her pocket.

With a sly smile she walked past me as she said, "Hazard pay. Now find her Vamp boy, or else you and I are gonna have words."

If only I had to worry about her threats against me. For all I knew Eris was already polishing a place on his mantle for my head.

Chapter Forty-Four

Cameron

The house was furnished. Electric, water, cable, and internet hooked up with the help of an obscene amount of money. There was even food and blood in the refrigerator. Everything needed to set up a home minus a family – my family. I was angry at everything and everyone though I tried desperately not to show it. When the first piece of furniture came over the threshold of the house I had to excuse myself to the patio since I wanted to tear it apart with my bare hands. Brianna was supposed to be furnishing our home, the pieces needed to be her decisions not anyone else's and certainly not because I had failed her yet again. Now she was gone and I had been wallowing outside on the black wrought iron bench for the last eight hours, thirteen minutes and twenty-seven seconds while Renee, John, Fabiani, and Dante took care of all the particulars inside.

The evening had turned cold and was darker than usual because of the looming storm clouds that were swollen with rain but holding firm. Not only did I want the rain to hold so that my family would not be caught in it, but also because I simply did not want to have to go inside.

Since I left Dante's, I had called Brianna's cell phone one hundred and twenty-three times, filling her voicemail box with panicked pleas. I knew she did not have her phone, but hoped that if she was somehow able to check her messages she would know that Aidan was not who we thought he was.

From behind me I could hear Renee's high heels approaching the back door that led out here to the garden.

"Still hiding out here?" Renee asked as she stepped outside, pulling her cardigan around her as she sat down next to me. "It got cold."

"Sitting next to me will not make you any warmer I am afraid."

She laughed lightly and nudged my arm with her elbow. Her tone towards me was drastically different than earlier today, but the holes in my sweater from her nails urged me to keep up my guard.

"I spoke with Daddy O," she said tentatively. "It sounds like he got off ok."

"Yes, I spoke with Connor before they left. He should be landing in San Francisco in the next couple of hours." My index finger began reflexively rubbing my chin and jaw roughly. "Thank goodness he is safe. Though no one, including Oliver, seems to know where Shelby has gone."

"Good riddance, I say. So would Bri…if she…were here." It was hard to keep looking away as she began to sniffle. I reached into my pocket and pulled out my last handkerchief and handed it to her. "Daddy O wants to talk to you, ya know."

My head was shaking before I could answer. "I cannot. I just cannot bear to talk to him right now."

"He doesn't blame you, Cameron," Renee said lightly as she rested her hand on top of mine.

"He should."

"Daddy O cares about you, too. Of course he's freaked out of his mind about Bri, but he knows that you must be going crazy. He would much rather hear about all of this from you than me or Collin."

"Connor," I corrected.

"Does it matter?" she scolded with an eyebrow raised. "Oh and by the way, you owe me a manicure."

Renee inspected the broken and chipped nails on her right hand. I cleared my throat as I put my thumb through one of several holes she had ripped into my sweater. Her smugness of getting a free manicure fell as she watched me find hole after hole.

"Please tell me you at least got that at a bargain basement bin and that it looks amazingly expensive for being under ten dollars."

I started to laugh, but it got caught in my throat as Brianna's voice began singing in my head with things she would have said if she had been standing here. *"Don't worry, Renee, he has fifty more just like them." "Thank you, Renee, now he has one less funeral sweater." "Renee, if you could just go ballistic on him a couple of times a week we'll have him down to a normal person's wardrobe."* Her voice played over and over again in my head causing my jaw to clinch and my teeth to grind.

"Ohmygod Cameron! You're bleeding," Renee shouted as she put the handkerchief up to my eye.

Apparently I was not doing a good job of holding my emotions in as a bloody tear unknowingly leaked from my eye. I rose from the bench, taking the handkerchief from Renee and dabbing my eye clean.

"Ohmygod, you were bleeding from your eye," she said hurriedly as she came around to my side trying to get me to turn and face her. "That's like stigmata or something. Do we need a priest?! Ohmygod wait, can you see a priest? Will holy water kill you?"

"Renee!" I said, raising my voice and my hands in front of her. "I am fine."

"But…"

I waved my hands up in front of her again. "Vampire tears. That is what you saw. I am sorry you had to see it."

"Um…you shed a freaky blood tear and you're sorry?"

"I did not mean to lose control in front of you."

"Jesus, Cameron, if anyone has a reason to be emotional it's you. If you need to have a good cry, then go on and have it. And I promise I won't turn in your man card."

I laughed. "It does not work that way in my family."

"Why's that?"

"If your head is clouded with emotions then you cannot focus on the mission at hand. Showing emotion shows weakness and I cannot afford to have any weaknesses right now."

"Typical male. Now listen to me, Vampy, your baby mama and my 'twin' has been kidnapped and we have no idea where or how she is. We are allowed to be emotional and freak out and flail about if we want to. Let the others do the heavy lifting, you need to deal with what's really happening here."

I turned away from her, heading back toward the house. "I just need to keep moving."

Just as I approached the door to the house, John opened it with a peculiar look on his face. "Oh good, I found you. Your family's here."

"Thank you, John," I said, trying to get past him, only to have him put his hand on my shoulder to stop me.

"The…big guy? He's your…"

"Brother. Well, sort of. Why?"

"He's huge! Re, you have to see this guy…he's like…seriously the biggest guy I've ever seen. I'll admit he's a little terrifying."

John's eyes were wide with fear and it did make me smile. "He may be big, but it is the smaller man with his hair pulled back that you really need to be scared of."

Renee came to stand next to me. "Why? Who is he?"

"Brianna's father," I replied.

"You mean her *father*, father?"

"Yes. And we shall know soon enough if he is going to let me live."

John and Renee both started to laugh until they realized that I was serious and their faces fell at the same time.

"Shall we?" I said nervously and then gestured toward the house. John reluctantly opened the door and I stepped through with Renee in tow. As we stepped into the hallway I could see my sister-in-law gliding toward us.

Kyla's arms wrapped around my neck before she was able to say anything and I let my need for my family overtake me for a moment as I hugged her back. "Thank you for coming."

She nodded into my shoulder and I could hear her sniffling softly. A moment later she lifted her head and wiped the tears away from her eyes until I handed her the popular handkerchief that was still in my hand. From behind me Renee cleared her throat and I immediately opened myself up in order to make the awkward introduction.

"Kyla, this is Renee Snider. Renee, meet Kyla Hunter. Play nice," I urged, stepping out of the line of fire. The two of them sized each other up like formable foes, waiting for the other to break the ice.

Surprisingly it was Kyla. "Nice shoes."

Renee smiled slightly. "Nice hair."

A second later the two of them were sobbing into each other's shoulder. John caught my attention and rolled his eyes before we made our way around to the entryway only to have Alexander walking in our direction.

He shook my right hand while his powerful left arm wrapped around me and patted my back. When he released me he looked past me noticing Renee and Kyla still comforting one another. When he looked back at me he was rolling his eyes as John had.

"I won't even ask."

"How was the flight?"

"Well, we all got a good laugh when Jared had to be transported in a body bag since it was the only way to get him out in the sun. So we have some good mileage on that. But uh…can you do me a favor and stay close to me for a while?"

"Fearful Eris might rip my head off?"

"Cam, I just spent hours hearing what he wanted to do to you. If he were to only rip your head off it would be a blessing."

"Alex, Eris has every right to be angry with me. If harming me brings him some kind of comfort there is nothing that any of us can do about it."

"Don't just lie down in front of him."

"Alex," I began and turned away from him, wanting to change the subject, "this is Dr. John Ryan, Renee's fiancé. John, this is my younger brother, Alex."

John thrust his hand into Alexander's and began shaking it vigorously. "Hi. Sorry for earlier. I didn't mean to…"

"Mutter incoherently while gawking slack-jawed and falling backwards into the stairs?" John froze, completely embarrassed and unable to let go of Alexander's hand. But then Alexander gave a classic smirk. "Don't worry, doc, I've had worse."

John started to smile but it was wiped away along with his breath when Alexander patted him on the back.

"So how come," John coughed, "he calls you Cam and you don't yell at him?"

"Because I battled him and had to repeatedly throw him into a wall before he conceded. Do you want a go at it?" Alexander replied and chuckled at John's expression. He then pulled me through the entryway and around to the living area that had been transformed into our situation room with a long oval-shaped table and large screen TV sitting at its end.

In the minutes that Jared had been in the house he had set up multiple computers, created a more secure network, and was now projecting his laptop on the TV. Heavy plastic cases and cables were strewn all over the floor, table, couch, and the lone club chair that Renee and Fabi had been able to purchase. With the clutter and the number of people in the small room, it was more than full. But the lack of room did not stop Devin from dropping what he had in his hands and coming to my side with words of comfort and encouragement, which was surprising coming from him.

Once Renee and Kyla made their way into the room I decided it was time to make introductions. "Brothers, if you have not already met them, I would like to introduce you to Brianna's oldest friend Renee Snider and her fiancé

Dr. John Ryan. They will be staying here with us until…the threat is gone." And Brianna is in my arms. I could feel a lump forming in my throat so I swallowed hard to push it down and forced myself to focus on something else. "Everyone, this is Dante," I said gesturing to him in the back corner, "the coven leader of the Negotiators and his pupil, Fabiani, preferably known as Fabi," I corrected as he squinted his eyes at me. "Gentleman, and Renee, these are my brothers Jared, Alexander and his wife Kyla, and Devin."

Fabiani's eyes widened at the sound of Devin's name, even causing his head to flinch back slightly. Even though he might have been slightly afraid, it did not stop him from taking the two steps to be next to him and extend his hand. "So you're *the* Devin? The…"

"Warrior Assassin," Devin finished in a flat tone as if he was saying he was Devin the Warrior Accountant. He shook Fabiani's hand and then turned back in my direction. When Devin's back was turned, Fabiani stepped behind him, rose up on his toes and mouthed the words *'Oh my god, he's gorgeous'* over Devin's shoulder. Renee tried to stifle her laugh, but Devin caught wind of it and looked quickly back to Fabiani who had instantly changed his expression.

I turned and gestured to the remaining two people in the room, only one of which was giving me a kind smile. "Renee, this is Brianna's stepmother, Seraphina," I said as I gestured to the exhausted looking French woman. Seraphina did not hesitate for a second and continued past me to place her arms around Renee who had become teary-eyed at the sight of her. Renee hugged Seraphina tightly for a moment but then opened up to look in Eris's direction. "And lastly, this is Brianna's father Eris. Eris, Renee has known Bri…"

"Stop all this nonsense," Eris shouted as he took a step in my direction causing my brothers to all take a step in as well, and John a step back. "My daughter has been taken, and you stand here making introductions like we are at a family gathering. You have things to answer for and you will answer to me personally, Warrior."

"Now Eris," Dante interrupted, "this is a trying time for everyone involved. Perhaps we can all discuss…"

Eris whipped his head around to Dante, a feral hissing sound coming from his mouth. "I have known you since you were reading tea leaves in a back room, Dante, so I suggest you stay out of this. This is between me and the Warrior, and I will speak to him alone."

"No!" everyone in the room shouted at the same time, my brothers taking yet another step closer.

I put my hands up in front of me, begging that everyone calm down. "Eris, we can speak in the master bedroom, it is just down the hall."

Everyone in Eris's path parted to allow him to escort Seraphina toward the entryway. I followed behind them and Devin stepped in line with me.

"I said alone, Assassin," Eris growled.

"That is simply not going to happen," Devin answered firmly.

"Brother," I said gently, squeezing his shoulder, "we shall do what he asks."

I could see the burning worry behind his eyes since he too had heard Eris's threats, but reluctantly he stepped back.

"Heed my warning," Eris began, "any Vampire who dares enter that room will be looking at his feet as his head rolls on the floor."

My family seemed relatively unaffected by Eris's threat, as did Dante, however John and Renee were terrified while Fabiani looked as though he might faint.

I followed Eris into the entryway who surprisingly seemed to know where he was going as he turned left into the master bedroom doorway at the end of the hallway. The room was empty except for a lamp that had been left from the previous owner and my suitcase that contained the clothes I was able to salvage from the shattered armoire. The overhead light fixture was garishly bright and casting ominous shadows on Eris's very angular and angry face. I could see now why Seraphina looked so tired. She had most likely been controlling Eris for most of the day and he was still showing no signs of calming down. I was suddenly stricken with guilt since there was no place for her to sit.

As though she was reading my thoughts, Seraphina knelt slowly down to the ground, staying close to us, but not placing her hand anywhere near Eris who now stood before me.

"You continue to try my patience, Warrior. When I left Brianna in your care you had two jobs – love her, and protect her. Honestly I thought I would never need to worry about the first, yet my daughter escaped to my home for almost three weeks weeping over your negligence of her. And at first I was forgiving since all couples have their growing pains and she was flooded with hormones. My wife and I even encouraged her to return to you, thinking you had learned your lesson, only to receive a call from her telling me that you had carried on with another…"

"It was a misunderstanding…" I interrupted, but was unable to finish as Eris closed his hand tightly around my throat, crushing my larynx and bringing me down to his eye level.

"How dare you interrupt me," Eris growled and then threw me down to the ground where I chose to stay while my throat healed. "I was surprised when she returned to you after your indiscretion, but she seemed happy and who am I to argue with her when she is so blindly dedicated to you. But this," he said and took my chin between his fingers and jerked my head up to look at him. "Having her taken right under your nose by someone you brought into her life is completely unacceptable. Now who knows what they are going to do to her. No wait, I take that back. You and I have seen her dreams, we know exactly what they are going to do and you have helped to make that come true. Now what do you have to say to that?"

"What do you want me to say?" I growled through my clenched teeth. The pain from my healing throat and the pinching of my chin was taking away what little control I had left. He was not telling me anything that had not circled around in my head for the last ten hours, but having them said aloud felt as though each word was slashing a new wound on my body exposing raw bloody nerves.

"I want an explanation, Warrior! I want to know why my daughter is missing. I want to know why you stood in that room as if nothing had happened to her while you made nice with your guests. I want to know how you can lie here and seem unaffected that your children could be literally cut out of my daughter's womb while she screams to be saved. And I want to know why I should not rip you apart piece by piece."

"Then do it!" I shouted back at him, prying his fingers off my chin. "Just do it and get it over with, Eris. I kneel here before you, begging you to do so." I rose to my knees, grabbing his hands and placing them on either side of my face. "Crush it, rip it off, anything to take away the agony that I feel because I cannot take it for a second longer. I have failed your daughter in the most grievous of ways and do not wish to live knowing the torture she will endure from my negligence. So kill me, you want to, I know you do. I am begging you to kill me Eris and let me be free of this torture."

When Eris's hands did not flinch I placed my hands on top of his and began to squeeze, hearing and feeling the bones cracking.

"What is going on in here," I heard from behind me. Eris released my face and began screaming at the unwelcomed guest. With my head still reeling I turned to look at who had entered and became instantly terrified.

"Renee, get out of here," I begged as I crawled in her direction while John pulled at her arm. Renee slipped out of John's grip and stepped further into the room to my horror and knelt in front of me. "Renee, you have to leave," I begged again, trying to push her away but she stayed firm.

"I said I would kill anyone who came through that door!"

Renee stood and held her index finger up in front of Eris. "You said any *Vampire* who came through that door, and I am a living person. So if you go back on what you said, you'll look like a real asshole."

I picked myself up from the floor and stood in front of her protectively only to see that Seraphina had finally come to Eris's side and took in as much of his pain and anger as she could manage. But also seeing her exhaustion, Eris removed her hand from his arm.

"My Sera has endured too much of me today," he said in a softer tone as he petted her cheek and then kissed her hand. "Ms. Renee, you have outsmarted me and unlike some people in this room I do keep my word. You have fight within you, much like my daughter."

"Who do you think she learned it from?" Renee replied. "Look Eric…"

"Erissss," I hissed and stiffened my muscles, ready for Eris to pounce.

"Is that what it is? I swear I couldn't understand what everyone was saying. Look Eris, we're all upset and the easiest person to blame is Cameron. I know I did and he has a ruined sweater to prove it. I think we all, and that includes me, need to give him a little bit of a break." I cocked my eyebrow at her, surprised by her complete turnaround. She shrugged and rolled her eyes. "Daddy O ripped me a new one. He said I was behaving like a 'hellion.'"

Eris took a step forward, jabbing his hand in my direction as he spoke to Renee. "After all he has done to Brianna…"

"And I have atoned for my mistakes," I interrupted. "Despite what you think, I love your daughter…"

"Squeezing your seed into her belly doesn't prove your love, Warrior. And how do we know she loves you if she was willing to leave so easily?"

"Brianna would not have asked me to marry her if she did not love me," I shouted back him, not out of anger towards him, but the fact that I had had the same fear myself.

Renee touched my arm, bringing my attention back to her. "You're engaged? When?"

"Last night, after we got back to the hotel."

"Ok, here's the thing," she began and stepped in front of Eris. "I have known Bri longer than anyone else in this whole house. And I know for a fact that she is scared shitless of getting married again. So the fact that my 'twin' asked Cameron to marry her proves to me that she loves him a heck of a lot and the fact that with your help he was basically 'inflicting' pain on himself over the guilt he feels means that he really loves her too. My suggestion is we all stop trying to prove 'who loves Bri more' and work together to find my twin. Ok?"

"Are your fingers all right? You keep flicking them," Eris said and knitted his brows together. "And why do you keep calling her your twin? I have not fathered any other children."

"One, my finger quotes are my signature quirk, I'm not just 'flicking' them. I'll explain the twin thing later. Just know I might start calling you dad. Ok now, the cute jailbait brother has set up everything in the living room, so why don't we all go out there and listen to what they've found."

It was absolutely a rhetorical question as she flipped her dark red hair over her shoulder and clomped her platform shoes loudly out of the room. Eris did not acknowledge me when he left, although Seraphina gave me a sympathetic nod. While I took a moment to gather myself I could sense John still in the doorway.

"I bet this was not what you thought your day would be like when you woke this morning," I asked, trying to find a lighter tone. I tilted my head in his direction, seeing that I had made him form a crooked smile similar to my own. "Thank you for all you have done for me today."

He laughed. "I still feel pretty useless. And I bet that when you said you would protect Re and me you didn't think she would be throwing herself into danger."

"Oddly enough, I am not too surprised. I am beginning to think that she and Brianna really are twins."

"How's that?" John asked as we both stepped into the hallway.

"Besides Brianna, Renee is the only person I know who has handled Eris and lived," I said and patted John on the shoulder while he turned several shades paler. "Trust me when I say he would have had to go through me and all my brothers before anything like that ever happened."

John's smile was only half-hearted as we entered the living room and Jared immediately shouted, "Bro, please tell Red over there that I am not jailbait."

"Renee, Jared is not jailbait."

"But I am cute," Jared said proudly.

"Shall we look at the video, little brother?"

"Yeah, yeah of course," he said quickly, putting on a more professional voice while everyone took seats around the large oval-shaped table. "Since we've all seen the other footage I'll start with the new stuff."

"I have not seen the footage," Eris interrupted with a growl.

Jared cleared his throat uncomfortably. "Like I said, we'll start from the beginning with the hotel footage."

Jared created his own commentary while we watched Hugo step into the hotel room and never come back out. Minutes later my angel stepped out of the room and I found it extremely difficult to watch. I wanted to look upon her face, but the sight of her continued to tear at my invisible wounds.

"Once they leave the parking garage I was able to track them through the traffic cams, and while on the flight I was able to piece the frames together from different angles. So, bro, you told me you texted Hugo around 6:00am and got a reply."

"6:11am."

"What no seconds?" Jared teased.

"Thirty-two."

"Ok, so at 6:11:32am I found this frame," he began as he fast forwarded through the footage, "and right here at 6:12:58am you can see him throw something out the car window. My guess, he had Hugo's cell phone and once he replied to your text he threw it out the window."

So again, we had nothing.

"Now onto the tunnel," Jared sighed. "We know he went into it, but we don't see his truck come out. Thanks to Dante's guys we know that the maroon truck was abandoned in the tunnel, so I wasn't going crazy after all. But it still leaves the question, how did he and Bri get out. Alex and I think he had another car waiting and did a switch. Without access to the tunnel's surveillance, I can't be sure what they got into."

"Did you..." I interrupted but Jared stopped me.

"It took me forever but I grabbed the license plates of almost all the cars for the next twenty minutes and ran them through DMV and law enforcement. Nothing has come up stolen, and no names jumped out at us but we'll keep digging."

The room was eerily quiet and the air was thick with tension. Unknowingly I was rubbing my chin and bottom lip and it was not until Kyla took my hand away from my face did I realize that I had worn away a small patch of my tough skin. Kyla placed my hand in her lap, patting and squeezing it gently.

"Jared, what about the timing? Aidan had to have had some help."

Jared lowered his eyes and then shared a look with Alexander who took over. "On a hunch we dumped call and text records for Nikki Williams, a.k.a. Nikki Cushlin."

"A.k.a. slutty whore," Renee mumbled under her breath causing Jared's eyes to shoot up in her direction.

"What did you find, Alex?" I asked, trying to pull everyone's attention back.

"Nothing. There wasn't a single call or text," Alex replied causing me to sigh loudly and throw my hands up in the air. "But...wait, Cam, we decided to pull all phone records for the entire manor and we found this."

Alexander gestured to Jared who was reluctant to move, but when Alexander urged him again he pressed a button on his laptop and a woman's whispering voice came through its speakers.

"Hey Dad, it's me. Alarms went off, they've seen E. They're going to Victor and then they'll find Cam. You probably have fifteen minutes. I'll...uh...talk to you soon I hope...um love you, Dad. Bye."

I looked across the table to Jared who was now avoiding all eye contact with me. "She was in your room when the alarms went off, wasn't she?"

"Who?" Renee and Eris asked at the same time.

"Nikki," I answered.

"Are you fucking kidding me?" Renee shouted as she stood from her chair causing it to fall backwards behind her. John pulled the chair up off the floor and pulled her back down.

"But Nikki Cushlin's father is dead," I said, trying to calm the room.

"Either she doesn't know that or she's adopted another," Alexander chimed in since Jared was still being silent.

"Were you able to trace the number she called?"

Alexander nodded. "Do you have your phone?" I reached into my back pocket and pulled out my cell phone. "Type in this number."

I did as he asked and typed in the ten digit number and my stomach sank as a name popped up from my address book.

"Aidan Pierce."

"That's what we suspected, but the number was for an unregistered prepaid phone."

"Aidan Pierce has no children. Why does Nikki think Aidan is her father?"

"Because he's using her just like we were," Jared said, finally lifting his eyes to me.

"I thought you said this Nikki girl didn't have any calls from her phone," Fabiani asked, suddenly reminding me that he was there.

"She was using my phone," Jared admitted under his breath. "She knew I wouldn't be checking my own phone, so she used mine seven times to text or leave quick messages. I didn't know, man, I swear."

My brain could not form words as every piece of information began to fly around in my head while I looked intensely at my youngest brother. He was seeking any sign of forgiveness in my eyes and found none because I did not possess it.

"Does Father know?" I asked, taking my eyes off of Jared and looking to Devin.

"Yes. Father is aware of everything and has assigned Julian to question her."

From the corner of my eye I could see Jared scratching his neck roughly at the thought of Julian interrogating Nikki. Though I could not understand why he cared. The woman had not only betrayed our family, she had used him even more than we had used her. I was surprised that he could feel anything but anger towards her.

"Pardon me, young Warrior," Eris interrupted and gestured to Jared, "is there a better picture of this Aidan Pierce?" Jared nodded and a few moments later Aidan's Gatherer identification photo was displayed on the screen. "Ah, yes. Thank you, little Warrior. You may proceed with your little family drama now."

"Eris," I prodded, "do you recognize him?"

"Yes, but I think it is best if this is discussed in private."

"If you have anything that could help us, say it now."

"Warrior, I do not think you want me to share this in front of..."

"Eris, now!"

The mighty Eris growled at me, his upper lip curling and trying to keep his anger in check. "Fine. This gentleman here, this Aidan, has been in Bri-an-na's dreams over the last few months."

"Wh-what?" I stuttered, wishing I had not pushed him.

"Mia figlia has had a recurring dream where she is arguing with her mother, and this gentleman appears. I have also seen him in different scenarios where he and Bri-an-na are..."

"Stop, stop!" I ordered, not able to hear what I assumed were sordid details. "Did you recognize where the encounter with Shelby took place?"

"I believe it was at Oliver's home in North Carolina."

"Then the dream is meaningless. No one is there, including Shelby."

Eris raised an eyebrow. "I am merely relaying what I have seen. You cannot deny that most times Bri-an-na's dreams are usually correct in some fashion."

Eris was correct, although I hated to admit it. I had even seen Bri's dream where she kills her mother, and it did in fact occur at Oliver's. But it was impossible, it had to be.

"So," Dante said, interrupting the uncomfortable silence that had fallen on the room, "where does all this new information get us? What do we have?"

Renee breathed in a sarcastic laugh. "Jack shit."

Chapter Forty-Five

Cameron

Day three without Brianna and I still found it difficult to stay inside the house for long periods of time. It felt uncomfortable, wrong, like a cheap wool sweater that was too tight and itched incessantly. The only relief I seemed to find was when I would sit outside in the courtyard or out on the second floor balcony just outside our kitchen. The balcony itself was narrow, only big enough for two chairs and a small bistro table, but it had a lovely view of the neighborhood and you could smell the salt in the air from the ocean not too far away.

I have always loved this city, even in its infancy. What I have been unable to understand is why Boston only brings me tragedy? So far all the work Jared had done led us nowhere, though he was not giving up. He followed every red sedan, silver pickup truck, and black crossover as far as the city traffic cameras would get him, searching for something that would give us a clue. But as of yet, nothing. The great Warriors had met their match, and none of us wanted to admit it, most of all Victor.

The whole ordeal was being kept quiet, even from the other coven leaders. Both Father and Dante convened with them yesterday to discuss having to delay the purchasing of the property in Connecticut, making some kind of excuse that the owner suddenly had to go out of the country. Hopefully she had not gotten that far. God lord, what if she has? How on earth would we find her?

"Bonjour," Seraphina's high-pitched voice sang from the opening in the doors behind me.

"Good morning, Seraphina."

"May I join you?" she asked, gesturing to the chair next to me.

"Of course," I answered and mustered a smile as I turned the remaining chair to where she could sit.

"Do you mind if we speak French?" The words in her native tongue flowed like silk across her lips as she spoke in a more relieved tone. "I cannot seem to find the energy to concentrate on my English. It is quite exhausting, I must admit. I am thankful someone in the house will understand me."

"Eris does not speak French?"

She laughed. "He despises the language. I believe it is because of a skirmish he had many centuries ago. He has tried to convince me that he doesn't speak it, but I know he understands me when I curse him."

"A woman could curse a man in seventeen languages and he would somehow know what she was angry about."

She laughed with me as a breeze whistled through the leaves that remained on the tree just at the balcony's edge. Although she did not pull her long white sweater across her I worried she might be chilled, but she merely closed her eyes with a pleasant smile as the wind brushed against her face.

"Are you feeling better?"

"Yes. Thankfully no headache today."

"I believe Dr. Ryan said that you might be having migraines."

"Perhaps my head does not like being away from my island."

"Perhaps," I laughed lightly before another silence settled between us. "May I ask you something?"

Seraphina folded her hands in her lap, lowering her head slightly. "Cameron, I never knew she was in trouble. Eris...he woke me when he realized something was wrong."

"How did he know?"

She sighed and began ringing her hands in her lap. "How does any parent know? He simply had a feeling. Eris has always said that since she was born he has felt Brianna's presence within him, almost a hum in the back of his head reminding him that she is with him. The morning Brianna was taken that feeling simply disappeared."

"He thought she was dead."

She nodded. "It was difficult to get him calm, as I am sure you can imagine. The only thing that comforted him was the fact that if Brianna had been killed, the prophecy would have changed and I would have seen something. I believe that is the reason I did not know she was in trouble. The prophecy is still intact, meaning the babies are still to be born." She paused and cleared her throat. "We just do not know which side will raise them."

"*We* will raise them. Brianna and I," I replied firmly while chewing the inside of my lip. "Eris has not felt Brianna since that day?"

She shook her head. "Something is blocking her from him. When young Jared pointed out Brianna sleeping in the video he knew something very powerful was surrounding her. That is why he has not left our room since our first night here. He has been searching for even a tiny glimmer of her or someone who has seen her, hoping her face appears in their dreams. I have never seen him so tired. Who knew sleeping would be so exhausting and take so much blood. Which reminds me, I need my iron pills."

Seraphina pushed up from the chair and began to step around it when I took her hand. "May I ask one more thing?"

Her voice trembled as she answered, "I wish you would not."

"Why do Brianna's dreams end once Elaina cuts her? Why does she not dream of anything past that day? Why does Bri not have dreams of her with our children that Eris does not put in her head?"

She did not look at me as she answered, "Her dreams have always been warnings. Perhaps she is safe after that day."

"Do you honestly believe that?"

She squeezed my hand as she slowly turned her face to me. "I have to."

I could feel the waves of sadness and fear flowing into her. Quickly I let go of her hand. "I need to feel everything," I said, slipping back into English. "It would just be cruel to add my anguish to what you are already feeling."

"I am stronger zhan I look," she replied. "And since you have not brought it up, I know it is eating away at you, but forget about Aidan in petite's dream. It means nozing."

"Have you ever dreamt of other men?" I snapped and then froze at my forwardness. "Seraphina, I apologize, that was inappropriate."

"Oui, Cameron, I have. Unintentionally of course. It happens, especially when women are hormonal. I have heard zhat zhis is pretty common with pregnant women. I will say it again, it means nozing. She loves you."

"Yet she left with him. What if we are doing all of this to find her, and she simply does not want to be found? What if she wanted him all along?"

Seraphina stepped over to me, wrapped her arm around my shoulder and kissed my temple several times in quick succession. "I have had visions of you by her side since she was one year old, and zhose visiuns have not changed. Do not lose faith in my petite, ok?"

"Wait, since she was one?"

"Oui," she smiled. "You have always been her love, Cameron."

Just then the balcony doors opened revealing a sleepy-eyed Renee in her pajamas, her hair piled messily on top of her head. "I thought I heard voices out here."

"Hopefully we did not wake you," I said, straightening up in my chair.

"No, John's alarm did and then he kept pressing the snooze button, so after the fifth time I hit him and then just got up. Holy shit it's cold out here, Sera aren't you cold?"

Seraphina smiled and patted Renee's hand. "Menopause, ma petite. Tu es faim?"

Renee blinked and scrunched her face. "Please tell me you're speaking another language. Otherwise I think I'm having a stroke or something."

"Seraphina asked if you were hungry," I translated politely, seeing a glaze pass over Seraphina's face making me worried she was getting yet another migraine.

"Sera, I'm hungry if you're cooking," Renee said, wrapping her arm around Seraphina's shoulder and leading her back into the house.

As soon as the doors shut behind them my cell phone was in my hand and dialing the last person I ever wanted to speak to.

"This is Julian."

"Julian, it is Cameron."

"I know."

He was such an ass.

"I am calling to check the progress of your interrogation of Nikki Cushlin."

"I gave my report to Father last night. I am sure he will inform you."

"Can you just tell me what you found out?"

"Father indicated he would call you…"

"Julian! Can you refrain from being a bastard for just a few minutes?"

He paused and the silence tortured me. "She admitted that she was befriended by Elaina while in her custody."

"And?"

He sighed loudly into the phone. "Because of her relationship with

Elaina, she became frightened that we would hurt Elaina which was why she left the message."

"But Aidan Pierce is not her father."

"She believes he is and nothing we did could convince her otherwise."

"Then push her harder."

"You are forgetting your place, Cameron. I do not take orders from you. We pushed her to the edge of what is allowed for her kind."

"Then I request you use non-human protocols against her. She knows more than she is telling us."

"Absolutely not," Julian replied loudly. "We have rules for a reason…"

"Nikki Cushlin is a Healer, she can endure more than most."

"Only Father can approve a request like that and in no way am I going to ask him. If you want to get dirty then do it yourself. I will not get dragged down with you. This is over."

The line clicked loudly as Julian hung up and I wanted nothing but to throw my phone into the building across the way. If I did not possess the hope that Brianna would call me, the phone would be in a hundred pieces.

Just then, the doors next to me opened once again. "Brother?"

I looked up to see Devin staring down at me with a firm expression. "I thought you and Alexander were going to John and Renee's to do surveillance?"

"I was supposed to, but apparently Renee wanted a few more things from the apartment and Kyla didn't believe I was up to the task. She and Alex left a few minutes ago. Honestly, shoes are shoes and Renee is only here temporarily. Why does she need ten other pairs?"

"I am probably not the best person to hold this argument with."

Devin smiled as he stepped out onto the balcony, standing next to me with his hands on his hips. "I didn't mean to eavesdrop, but I couldn't help but hear you say something about non-human protocols? Don't you think you are going a little too far?"

"No," I growled.

"This is so unlike you, Brother."

"If our situations were reversed you would be asking for the same thing."

"Yes, but that is me. You are the compassionate one, the one who actually cares about others."

I stood from my chair. "Not when it comes to this. I will do whatever I need to do in order to find Brianna. I do not care who I have to use, torture or kill in order to find her. Protocols be damned, I want answers from that girl and I do not care if she must shed a little blood in order to get them. Nikki has been playing us since the minute we found her and it stops now."

"If you pursue this, Brother, you must be prepared for the consequences."

Just as I was about to answer, a blood curdling scream came from within the kitchen.

"Cameron! John, get in here!" Renee shouted from inside.

Both Devin and I bolted into the kitchen, the smell of fresh blood hitting us in the face. My eyes widened as Renee waved us toward the edge of the kitchen island with a bloodied hand. I ran to Renee's side, unfortunately slipping on a trail of blood and having to catch myself on the opposite wall. I turned quickly around and fell to my knees next to Seraphina who was doubled over holding her head and screaming in pain while blood splattered on the floor.

"Eris!" I shouted

"Dormir!" Seraphina screamed back, reminding me he was deep in sleep.

"Devin, wake up Eris. He probably cannot hear us."

Devin took two steps toward the hallway, almost running into John who was now standing before us in only a t-shirt and red boxer shorts.

"Cameron, sit her up," he ordered firmly. "Renee, grab some towels."

John knelt down to the floor as I wrapped my arms around Seraphina's waist and pulled her back into my arms. As the back of her head came to rest on my shoulder it was staggering to see the amount of blood that was gushing from her nose. John immediately placed his hands on her face, tilting her head up to look for the source of the bleeding and then looking deep into her eyes.

Renee shoved a wad of paper towels into John's face and he began wiping the blood away from Seraphina's face only to have it flow out again. Just as Eris rounded the corner into the kitchen, his wife began sucking in labored breaths and thrashing against my chest.

"Sera? Sera can you hear me," John said in a calm but raised voice as he continued holding her face, trying to get her attention. "Her pupils are fixed, we need to get her to the hospital."

"No! No! She is having a vision, give her to me," Eris shouted as he knelt to the floor and took Seraphina into his arms.

John placed the paper towels up to Seraphina's face again and began to argue with Eris about taking her to his hospital. Just as it seemed like Devin or I would need to step in, Seraphina took in a high-pitched gasp as if she had been drowning only a moment before. Her eyes were wide with fear as she reached for my arm. "Petite chute."

"You see Brianna?" I shouted anxiously at her.

"Oui," she affirmed breathlessly as she fell back onto Eris's chest.

Renee knelt down beside her. "How do you know?"

Seraphina touched her stomach. "Bébés."

"What else do you see," Eris prompted his wife gently.

Seraphina's breath was still labored as she pressed her hand against her temple. "Elle saigne."

All eyes turned in my direction while I continued to focus on her. "She says she is bleeding," I said confused at first. "You mean Brianna is bleeding!"

She nodded her head but then screamed as another wave of pain shot through her.

"Sera, my darling let me make you sleep."

"Non!" she shouted at the same time John did.

"No! Wait, what? She can't sleep, she might have some kind of neurological damage."

Anger flared behind Eris's eyes and losing all trace of his usual Italian accent he said, "Don't you understand, medicine man? Sera is connected to Brianna at this very moment, a psychic connection. If I put her to sleep I can see what she is seeing."

John stood up from the floor, his frustration beginning to boil over. "No, I don't understand! I have no idea what the hell goes on in your crazy world."

"Aidan. Je vois Aidan," Sera whispered.

"Quiet, everyone!" I shouted and knelt back down in front of her. "You see Aidan?"

"Oui. L'essai de l'aider," she said as she placed her hand up to her bloodied face.

"He is…" I gritted my teeth, "trying to help her. What else, Sera, please. Can you see her surroundings? A building or a house?"

"Maison."

"A house. Good. What else?"

"Une femme."

"A woman? Elaina?"

"Non. Une autre femme de blond."

"Another blonde woman?"

Suddenly Seraphina rose from Eris's chest, squeezing my arm tightly.

"Don't," she said in a voice that was not her own. "Don't drink my blood."

As if all the energy had been drained from her, Seraphina fell heavily against Eris's chest, her head rolling down the side of his shoulder. John immediately pushed me to the side and I gladly got out of his way and walked through the columned archway into the empty dining room just off the kitchen. Devin was right on my heels as I pulled out my cell phone.

"It sounded like Brianna's voice coming out of Seraphina."

"I am well aware of that, Brother," I snapped as I dialed the phone.

"At least we know Bri is alive."

"And bleeding. I am finding no comfort here, Brother."

Devin opened his mouth to retort, but the other lined crackled to life as my Father's voice came through loudly. "Child, do not even begin to ask me about non-human protocols. I do not want to hear it."

"Father, we have had a development."

"It had better be something substantial if you want me to forget the conversation I have just had with Julian."

I looked back at Seraphina, unconscious and a trail of blood down the front of her white sweater. Though the scene in front of me was horrible, even more horrifying was the fact that Brianna was lying in a similar state swollen with pregnancy with Aidan hovering near her while she bled.

"Child?" Victor shouted when I did not answer.

"Seraphina is having empathic visions of Brianna."

"Empathic?"

"Apparently she is experiencing what is happening to Brianna at this moment and it is manifesting itself physically."

"I have never heard of such a thing."

"Regardless, Seraphina is laying here gushing blood and it is Brianna who is experiencing this. That means she is bleeding profusely, Father, and in front of Aidan and others we cannot identify. We have no leads and the situation has obviously become dire. We need to push Nikki harder, she knows more than she is telling us."

"Child…"

"We can no longer treat Nikki as we would other humans."

Devin grabbed my wrist, pulling the cell phone away from my ear and looking firmly into my eyes. "Think about what you're asking. There will be consequences."

I yanked my wrist from his grip and put the phone back up to my ear. "I am formally requesting we use non-human protocols against Nikki

Cushlin."

"You are desperate, child. She does not even acknowledge that she is a Cushlin. What if you are wrong?"

"Of course I am desperate, Father. The mother of my children is bleeding in front of our enemy. What if she were to bleed to death, or even worse have Aidan drain her dry because he cannot stop himself. Either way she could end up dead. The children could die before they even have a chance to live. Please Father…"

"Fine, fine," he shouted over me. "Your request is granted. I will inform Julian to proceed."

"Thank you, Father."

"But any fallout that occurs from this you will be responsible for. Do we understand each other?"

"Yes, Father."

"I will forward whatever Julian discovers, but I want daily updates about whatever Seraphina is experiencing as well."

I did not even get the chance to say goodbye before Victor hung up the phone. Devin was giving me a skeptical eye, but turned away at the sound of Seraphina's voice coming from the kitchen.

"Well that solves the mystery of where Shelby went off to," Renee said looking at Eris as the two of them helped Seraphina to a standing position.

"How is that?" I asked, stepping back into the kitchen.

But it was Eris who answered. "Shelby is with Bri-an-na. She is the blonde woman in the vision. I saw her face when Sera fainted."

There seemed to be no end to the betrayals.

"Cameron, I have ruined your new home," Seraphina said in an exhausted tone.

I shook my head as I stepped over to her, helping her remove her shoes so they did not trail blood throughout the house. "That is why they make cleansers, my dear lady."

"I will bring home some industrial stuff from work. Ah shit, I'm so late," John said flustered, blood staining his knees and smeared across his shirt. He turned to go down the hallway but then quickly turned back around. "I'm sorry, Sera, you probably want to clean up."

"Seraphina," I began, seeing the anxiety in John's eyes, "you may use the master bathroom downstairs that way you can take all the time you need."

She smiled sweetly as Renee led her to the stairs and Eris ducked into their bedroom to gather her fresh clothes.

Devin stepped around me and began searching for items with which to clean the bloody mess on the floor. I could still see a slight amount of shock in the good doctor's eyes as he turned away from me and began walking to the bathroom.

"John, I know this is a lot to take in."

"I was just thinking how weird it was that I need to go to the ER in order to get some normalcy. I've just never...seen..."

"And neither have we. Assuming what we saw here is also happening to Brianna, what would cause that kind of bleeding?"

John immediately began shaking his head. "I have no idea, Cameron. I've never seen anything quite like that. You might see it from someone who's huffing, but usually not even that amount of blood and I don't think Brianna has suddenly taken to sniffing spray paint."

"What else?"

"Er...sometimes brain trauma, or tumors, but again not that amount of blood." He sighed as he looked up at the ceiling, his eyes moving from side to side as if he was going through catalogs of facts in his head trying to find an answer. "I'm sorry. Nothing is coming to mind, but I will do some research. I'll figure it out, I promise I will."

His frustration was evident when he walked to the bathroom and slammed the door behind him. Similarly I wanted to slam my head up against a wall, but my opportunity passed as Eris came out from his bedroom with a clean set of Seraphina's clothes draped over his arm.

"Eris..."

"If I had only killed that woman when Bri-an-na was fourteen I would have saved my daughter years of grief. How can a mother betray her own daughter? My daughter! Shelby Morgan has betrayed Bri-an-na for the last time. And although I would prefer to do it myself, I don't care who kills her as long as that woman is dead by the time this ordeal is over."

I eyed Devin as Eris ran away in a blur.

"Brother, are you going to help me clean this up or not?"

I nodded as I reluctantly took the paper towels from his outstretched hand. "Would you turn him in?"

Devin took a moment before responding, "My initial response is yes of course I would. But then I question if Father would actually do anything about it. Honestly, can you see him order Eris to a stint of board and chains?" I breathed in a single laugh at the thought of it. "Exactly. Perhaps it'll just sort itself out on its own. Maybe Brianna's mother will have a heart attack or something."

"One can hope."

"Yes, Brother, there is always hope."

"Since when do you believe in stuff like that?"

Devin narrowed his eyes and knelt down on the floor. "I can change, Brother."

While Devin and I scrubbed the floors I realized hope was really all I had left. It was a concept that Victor did not really instill in us since we had never had a foe we could not vanquish. Until now. Brianna's kidnapping made one thing apparent – if the Warriors were to survive, we all needed to change. The only constant in the world was change and we had been stagnant. Sadder still, Brianna was our first victim.

Chapter Forty-Six

Cameron

"So how long do you think Aidan has been connected with Elaina?"

I lifted my eyes over the laptop's monitor to see Alexander looking at me quizzically. "I have been asking myself that same question since Brianna was taken." Three weeks, two days, twelve hours, twenty-three minutes ago.

"And you knew him for a while, right?"

"Longer than I have known you, actually."

"I never cared much for him," Devin interrupted as he placed the piece of paper in his hand into a pile and picked up another one to examine.

"Yes, Brother, you always made that very apparent."

"Maybe you should have followed my example."

"And maybe you should stake me through the heart while you are at it."

My tone was not nasty, but I did not need him to make me feel any worse than I did. I had barely fed in three weeks, letting the burning in my throat and ache in my body be a form of punishment. Early last week when my hunger had gotten to a dangerous level, Kyla forced me to get drawn blood from Dante since I refused to feed off someone other than Brianna. When I returned home I was devastated to find Seraphina had had another violent nosebleed and another empathic connection with Bri. I refused to leave the house since.

Just then the sound of someone clumsily trying to unlock the front door came through the living room where my brothers and I sat around the large oval table. Dr. Ryan was home and we all knew the familiar sound. Once John pushed the door open, Alexander eyed both me and Devin, and all at once the three of us shouted, "Clear!"

John ignored us as he bolted into the living room fiddling with the tie of his green scrubs and running to the small half bathroom. It was a ritual that occurred every time he returned from work, no matter what hour of the day it was. In the last few weeks I found that I actually looked forward to it since it was usually the only time I ever really laughed.

Once John disappeared into his sanctuary, Devin brought us back to task. "Brother, in the time you were a Gatherer did you ever hear anything regarding Aidan's performance?"

"No. Why would I?"

Devin shrugged. "Considering how talented he is as a Tracker and comparatively how bad he was as a Gatherer, I thought you might have heard something. Take a look at these."

Devin picked up the pile of papers closest to him and tossed them across the table.

"What am I looking at?" I asked as I thumbed quickly through the pages.

"Gatherer reports for the years Aidan was a member. Now according to these, he had less than a fifty percent return rate."

I flipped back to the beginning of the pile and looked more carefully at the reports for each hybrid he had been assigned to. As I leafed through one after another the same failure reasons were showing up – Unable to Locate; Refusal; Dead. It seemed suspicious and highly unlikely.

"He told me that he was losing too much money being a Gatherer."

Alexander laughed. "Cam, I don't think telling the truth is high on his list. I bet he quit before someone really looked at his record."

While I continued to flip through the pile, I was amazed at the number of failures. "In my three years as a Gatherer I only had two hybrids that refused to go, and even those were at the beginning. Most of these he is claiming he was unable to locate." I threw the papers back down on the table. "Out of the entire country and with nothing to go on he found Brianna in a train station in Connecticut. He found the needle in the haystack. That is what he does. These reports are...nonsense. Hell, even Jazlyn was almost ninety percent successful."

"Maybe," Devin began, "he located them after all, but simply never turned them over."

I froze at first, catching eyes with Alexander and then began shaking my head at how brilliant my older brother was. And subsequently how stupid I was.

"He took his pick of the litter. Keeping those hybrids that showed some skill and then shipping the weaker ones to the Facility. So basically the Gatherers became a recruiting mechanism for Elaina. Perfect."

Flustered, I rose from the chair just as John stepped out of the bathroom, seeming much more relieved at first and then felt the tension that hung in the room. "All I heard was pick of the litter, but I'm guessing you're not talking about cats." Alexander and Devin laughed behind me. "The girls aren't back yet?"

I shook my head as Alexander answered behind me. "I spoke with Kyla a little while ago. Apparently Fabi and Renee were having a little tiff about the flowers so the appointment was running long. But she said they had a successful shopping day, which probably is bad news for you, doc."

Devin cleared his throat, turning our attention to him. "Excuse me, I hate to interrupt, but I do not think it is appropriate to label the group as the girls since Fabiani is indeed male."

"I'm sorry, Devin," John replied. "I didn't mean anything by it. I'm actually very glad Fabi is with them. He's saving me a ton of money with all his haggling. Without him, Renee would be putting us in the poorer, poor house."

"Sorry John, that's probably Kyla's fault too. I'll try and rein her in," Alexander offered apologetically.

"Don't get me wrong, I want Renee to have the wedding she wants, but," John began and looked up at me, a kidding smile on his face, "I don't know, Cameron, we may have to live here with you guys forever."

I gave him a sympathetic smile back, taking another step closer and placing my hand on his shoulder. "Listen John, if you need help…"

"You fucking mother fucker!"

I turned my head toward the foyer just in time to see Jared launch himself in my direction, and subsequently in John's. Quickly I pushed John away causing him to fall backwards over the arm of the couch just as Jared grabbed my shoulders and knocked me to the floor. He got in one good punch to my face before Devin pulled him off of me and thrust him up against the wall on the opposite side of the room.

Alexander hovered over me, extending his hand and allowing me to pull myself up. John still sat in shock with his legs hanging over the arm of the couch while Devin held Jared up by his throat.

"Retract those fangs this instant," he shouted at Jared while thrusting his head against the wall a second time. We all watched as Jared slowly retracted his fangs, though his murderous glare was fixated solely on me. "How dare you fly across the room like a wild animal with your fangs out, let alone while a human is in the room. What the hell is the matter with you?"

As Devin loosened his grip, Jared knocked his hand away from his throat.

"What's the matter!" he shouted at Devin, but then turned his fury back to me. "Non-human protocols? Fucking non-human protocols!"

I eyed Devin who was just as surprised as I was. "Who did you hear this from?"

"I just had a video chat with Nikki who finally healed after everything Julian did to her."

"Since when are you speaking with her?" I growled.

"That is not the point and certainly none of your business."

"On the contrary, little brother, I think it is very much my business. And why are you so upset?"

"Why am I…are you fucking kidding me! We're not supposed to be the ones torturing hybrids. We're supposed to be the ones they can trust, we're the good guys. What you did makes you just as bad as Elaina."

"It was necessary to push Nikki harder."

"Bullshit."

"She did not respond to our other interrogation methods…"

"Then we're not very good at what we do."

My fists clenched and released, trying to keep my composure, though I knew it would not last too much longer. "Without pushing her further we never would have gained the knowledge we did."

"What, that she was sent to get in between you and Beebs? We knew that."

"We *suspected* that," I replied. "You were charged with confirming that, but chose to sleep with her instead and get so close to her that you did not even see what she was doing right under your nose. If anyone should be angry I think it should be me since you obviously cannot do even the simplest of jobs without your cock getting involved."

Jared began laughing, although it was anything but jovial. "You know what? I am sick and tired of the rules pertaining to everyone but the mighty Cameron. You stand there all judgmental when one of us makes a mistake, but when Brianna's in trouble we're all supposed to look the other way when you break the rules. That's fucking bullshit, and you know it."

"I am surprised you even brought up Brianna's name since you seem so utterly devoted to Nikki even though she not only betrayed you personally, but also the very woman you have claimed as your own sister." Alexander placed his hand against my chest as I continued to step forward in Jared's direction. "It makes me wonder if you ever cared for Brianna at all."

Jared lunged for me again as I went for him in retaliation, both of us being stopped by our respective brother's arms.

"You bastard! You know I love Bri and that I have been working my ass off night AND day to find her."

"And with no results."

"Like you do?"

"If we had not pushed your little girlfriend we never would have found out that Elaina has built a new facility somewhere on the East Coast and that Brianna was most likely taken to it. We also confirmed that Elaina is now experimenting on hybrid children and possibly even breeding. And that her ultimate goal is to get her hands on *my* children in order to discover what makes them the key to our future. So yes, I may have pushed the edge of what is right, but I do not regret my decision for a second."

Jared shrugged with a smug smile. "Then really you only have yourself to blame. Nikki may have made a phone call, but you led Aidan right to Bri. So whatever they do to her is on you."

Somehow I was able to rip through Alexander's hold and launch myself at my youngest brother at the same time Devin gave up and let go, choosing to let us kill each other. But just as our fingertips were about to touch, John stepped in between us.

"Whoa, whoa," John shouted with his arms extended out to both of us. "Now come on guys, you're family. Whether or not it's by blood, you're still family and we're all upset about what's been going on. Trying to kill one another is not going to help bring Brianna back any faster. Now can we shake hands and get over this?" Neither of us moved a muscle causing John to sigh in frustration. "Fine then, we'll discuss this like children. Cameron, are you sorry for whatever it is you did to this Nikki girl?"

"No," I answered truthfully.

John rolled his eyes. "Cameron, come on man."

"I am not sorry for it. It produced the results we needed."

"What she needs is therapy, not torture," Jared replied firmly. "After everything that was done to her, she still thinks Aidan is her father. That has to tell you how sick she is. We've done exactly what everyone else in her life has done to her these past few years."

"Jared, we simply did not have the time to coddle her. She needed to be broken."

Jared stepped back into the foyer, shaking his head and grinding his teeth together. "If anyone else besides Brianna had been taken, you never would have given that order, and we all know it. For the second time in a couple months I'm ashamed to call you my brother. You're better than this. We're all better than this and the day our family stops remembering who we are, is the day I stop being a Warrior."

Jared lowered his head and slowly began retreating around the corner to the basement door. I took a step in his direction, but was met with Devin's hand pushing against my chest.

"Just let him go."

"But I need him to understand…"

"Consequences, Brother. I warned you and now you must face up to them."

I nodded and then turned to John who still seemed a little shaken by the whole encounter.

"John, you must never step in the middle of two Vampires like that again."

"I couldn't just let you two go off on each other. Trust me, I've gotten between gang members in the middle of the ER. I can handle you guys," he laughed as he puffed up his chest and flexed his biceps. The tension in the room disappeared as our laughter began to fill it, though mine was only half-hearted.

From above I could hear the sound of dishes and pans being taken out of the cabinets meaning Seraphina was beginning to prepare dinner. While she fuddled around, footsteps could be heard coming down the stairs.

"I seem to have missed the party," Eris said as he came into the room. Seeing him was a rare occurrence, rarer still after Seraphina's second nosebleed attack. And though he looked exhausted and deep purple circles hung under his eyes, he had an odd smile on his face.

"You have news," I said quickly.

He nodded and lowered himself into the nearest chair. "They have a Dreamwalker."

"Dreamwalker?" John whispered as he tilted his head in my direction.

"Yes, Dr. Ryan," Eris affirmed. "A Vampire like me who can control dreams and sleep. Yet this one is very strong. That is why Bri-an-na has been hidden from me, she is being shielded by this Dreamwalker."

"How can you be sure?"

Eris looked at me as though I was the stupidest person in the room. "Obviously he would need to be with Brianna at all times."

"Why is that?"

"Otherwise how would he know she is sleeping? He would need to know when to shield her."

"Eris, there are only a handful of Dreamwalkers in existence. Do you think any of them are capable of this?"

He shook his head. "I thought I knew them all, having come across them at one point or another in my history. However, I am the only Ancient among them and therefore usually more powerful. So whoever this Vampire is, has somehow hidden himself from me and is now very close to mia figlia."

"Perhaps that is how they were able to get her out of the city," Alexander began. "In the video we saw Brianna sleeping in Aidan's truck. There's really no way she would have fallen asleep that easily without help. Plus, Brianna is a smart woman. Eventually she would have started to ask questions the longer Aidan drove. Maybe that is how they are controlling her."

"Only partially," Eris interrupted. "From the visions Sera has had we know she is awake at times."

My hands went through my hair and began tugging at the ends as I circled around the room while my mind was bombarding itself with questions. It was unbelievably frustrating to get answers to one piece of the puzzle, only to have so many more come about.

"Wait," I said turning back to Eris who seemed to be aging in front of me, "how did you find out about the Dreamwalker?"

Eris smiled victoriously again. "They have a traitor in their midst."

"Finally," Devin said sounding relieved. "Someone else has the same problem we do."

"Who is it?" I pressed.

"I do not have a name, and hardly a face. But he is a hybrid in Elain-na's custody."

"Then just have him tell us where he is," Alexander said curtly.

Eris sighed. "This hybrid is only sending me small flashes of information as to not draw the Dreamwalker's attention. He doesn't know how much of the hybrids' dreaming activities are being monitored. It has actually taken me almost a week to get what little I know now. But from what I have attained he does not know his exact location, only that he is in a medical type facility."

Alexander closed his laptop as he said, "But if he's in Elaina's custody how can he be a traitor?"

"I apologize. My weakness is preventing me from thinking straight. The hybrid is not the traitor, obviously, but the Vampire who is helping him is."

"Helping him how?"

"The Vampire told the hybrid how to find me. The Vampire wants to help us find my daughter, and my guess is also to help these hybrids. And no, I do not know why," Eris chided as he pointed to Alexander. "Honestly, I do not care what the Vampire's motives are. I simply want to find my daughter and this seems to be our only connection."

"Did the Vampire identify himself?" I asked, but Eris shook his head. "How do we know this is not a trap? How can we be certain this hybrid and Vampire truly know where Brianna is?"

"Because the hybrid has seen a dark-haired pregnant woman. It was not until I saw the vision myself that I identified mia figlia."

"What have you seen? Why did you not tell us the minute you came down? How did she look? Was she well? Unharmed?"

"The vision was very short, only seeing a quick glimpse of Bri-an-na on a table next to a machine."

"WHAT WERE THEY DOING TO HER!" I shouted loudly enough to cause Seraphina to drop whatever pot or pan she happened to have in her hand.

Eris's lips became tight across his mouth before taking in a staggered breath and saying, "It was not as if she were screaming in agony, Warrior. She was unconscious. I surely do not know exactly what they were doing to her, some kind of...oh...Dr. Ryan...you could be of some assistance."

"Really? How?" John asked hopefully as he took a step forward. Eris did not answer, but merely closed his eyes. A spilt second later John fell to the floor in a heap.

"Eris!" I shouted and went to John's side. "Let the man sit down before you completely put him under. He could have injured himself."

Eris waved away my concern, his eyes still closed as he pushed his vision into John's head. A second later John gasped as he woke.

"Ul-ultrasound," he garbled as he stretched his eyes open and then shook his head vigorously while I lifted him to his feet. "They were doing an ultrasound on her."

"Good man, doctor," Eris announced cheerily as he pushed himself up from his chair with great effort. "Warrior, I desperately need to feed. I am hoping to use the stores you have in the house versus taking from Sera." I nodded without looking at him or being able to stop myself from moving angrily around the room. "Very well then…"

"Eris, I don't mean to interrupt," John began, "the…thing that just happened, making me go to sleep and putting that picture in my head, you did that?" Eris nodded. "And you're saying someone like you may be doing that to Bri but for longer periods of time?"

"John, where are you going with this?" I asked, stopping my pacing for a brief moment.

"Well…Eris's…thing…it affects the brain. If Brianna's brain is being subjected to that kind of strain for eight hours or more a day, every day, that could explain the nosebleeds. Possibly."

"Dr. Ryan, you could be onto something, though it is not necessarily the best of news. However, I will continue to watch for any new messages from this hybrid and provide all of you with updates as I have them. Now Dr. Ryan, you and my surrogate daughter are to be well fed tonight as my wife is preparing a feast to celebrate this joyful news."

"Joy…joyful news!" I shouted. "How can…"

I stared around the room, seeing everyone looking at me as though I was the one being preposterous. A sudden burst of pain came from my throat, making me aware of how much I too needed to feed. Out of pure frustration I fled the living room and opened the front door letting the cold night's air hit my face. I took in gulps of air as I ran down the steps and began pacing the sidewalk in front of my home.

I looked up to the front door when someone called my name and noticed John standing in the doorway, concern etched across his face as he stepped down onto the landing. Immediately I began walking down the sidewalk away from my home, away from everyone.

"Cameron, wait up," John said as he tried to catch up to me.

"John, I suggest you go back inside."

John's hand wrapped around my elbow trying to pull me back, but instead I wretched my arm from his grip and continued to walk away.

"Come on, Cameron, just talk to me," he begged, making me regrettably stop in my tracks.

"What exactly did you see them do to her?"

"What was that?" he asked taking a few steps closer but freezing when I turned quickly around and pounced, pulling him up by the v-shaped collar of his scrubs.

I was panting as I spoke between my clinched teeth, trying very hard to keep my fangs from extending. "What…were…they doing…to her?"

John's eyes were wide and a little fearful as he placed his hands on my shoulders and tried to speak calmly. "I told you, an ultrasound, an external ultrasound."

My fingers curled tighter around his collar. "Were they violating her?"

"No, not that I saw. It looked like she was in her pajamas. They just had her shirt up over her stomach in order to use the machine. Beside bags under her eyes, she looked ok, like she was sleeping."

My knees felt as though they would buckle beneath me. I could not cope with the fact that someone was not only touching her, but examining her without her knowledge. But I knew I could not show such a display, not even in front of John, my friend. A friend who still looked frightened as I held him up by his clothes. Slowly I unfurled my fingers from his collar.

"Go back inside," I said and began walking away from him.

"I'll go wherever you're going," he replied and stepped in line with me.

"Unless you want to take the place of the homeless person I am about to find and feed from, I suggest you go back to the house."

John immediately stopped, allowing me to continue down the sidewalk alone. Just as I approached the corner I was met by Renee, Kyla, and Fabiani, arms full of shopping bags and their cheerful conversation abruptly ending as I pushed past them without a word of acknowledgment.

"Where the hell is Mr. Moody Pants going?" Renee asked.

"I think he's going to eat some homeless guy," John replied.

To which Kyla said, "Well it's good to see him out, but I think we should find Devin. Like, now."

Chapter Forty-Seven

Cameron

"Another homeless person was found dead late last night by police…" the morning anchorwoman announced on the TV next to me.

"Another victim of yours?" Kyla asked smugly as she stepped into the living room.

Without looking up from the email I was writing I responded, "I never killed a first one, therefore there cannot be another."

"You didn't kill him because Devin pulled you off of him in time."

Alexander snickered from across the table while John shifted on the couch behind me, pulling his coat up around his chin.

"Sister, you should really keep quiet while John is trying to sleep."

"I'm not sleeping," John mumbled.

"See, Cameron, he's not sleeping," Kyla replied victoriously as she placed a small gift box next to my laptop.

"I said no gifts," I said, eyeing the box and then the emerald green mini-dress she decided to wear in the middle of December.

"I know you said that, but you have to get a little something on your birthday. So happy birthday, Cameron!" she cheered as she wrapped her arms around my neck.

"Ha…y…ber…ay," John mumbled again from the couch.

"John, you should really go upstairs so you can get some sleep."

He shook his head. "Re's getting ready."

"Yes she is. Today's the big day," Kyla said, clapping her hands softly. "I about had to twist her arm off to make the appointment."

"I am sure you could understand her reluctance."

Kyla huffed as she crossed her arms across her chest. "Cameron, you of all people know it can take two or three months to get a wedding dress in. That's if you find one right away. Goodness, between you and her it's almost impossible for me to keep everyone's spirit up. I mean O-M-G!"

"Oh Ky, you're not starting that again?" Alexander groaned. We had all hoped that she and Jared had finally stopped talking in initials. Of course it would be nice if Jared was speaking to me at all. Even messages from him were given to me through my siblings.

"Kyla, darling sister, all I am asking is that you be gentle with Renee today."

"I am always gentle with her."

"Well that's a lie if I've ever heard one," Renee shouted as she began clomping loudly down the stairs. Renee and John had been staying in our home for over a month now, and I was amazed at the fact that I had yet to see Renee in anything but heels of three inches or more. When she stepped into the living room she was buttoning up her red winter coat over a royal blue sweater. A sweater, mind you, that she had mentioned Brianna had given to her for Christmas two years ago, and one that she wore at least once a week. We all had our ways of keeping Bri close to us.

"Re, honey, love the stiletto boots, but the outfit isn't crying out bridal to me," Kyla said as she futzed with Renee's coat.

Renee simply cocked an eyebrow and a hip as she replied, "And you're still stuck in California. Kyla, you can't wear a teeny tiny dress like that in New England, especially when it's snowing outside."

"But I'm not cold."

"And I'm not 'bridal.'"

With Renee's hands held in air quotes the standoff began between the two of them.

"Ky," Alexander groaned as he tilted his head back and finally noticed his wife's attire, "go put on some pants."

"Alex, I do not need pants. This is how it's supposed to look."

"Sister," I said in a nagging tone as I shut the lid of my laptop, finally giving up on my email to Victor, "you need to blend in while you are here. I know you packed both your black and brown boots, pick one."

"I'll have you know the girl in the picture had booties just like these..."

Kyla's rant continued all the way up to the third floor where we had converted the study into another bedroom for her and Alexander.

"Where is Fabi by the way?" Renee asked as she looked at her watch. "He should have been here by now."

"Date night," Alexander snickered.

"Club Red again? That's four times this week. You'd think Fabi would be a little more creative than that."

Renee stepped further into the living room and sat on the edge of the couch, nuzzling into John's chest as he opened his arms to her. The sight tore at my heart so I turned to face Alexander across the table. "Who is Fabiani dating? Anyone we know?"

Alexander sat silent, his mouth gapping open as he looked at me in shock. "Cam…are you serious?"

"What?"

I looked behind me to see that Renee had sat up and was giving me the same expression. "Seriously, Cameron, where have you been? Fabi is dating your brother."

"Devin?"

"No, Cam, Fabi's dating me," Alexander said sarcastically. "Haven't you noticed that they go out together almost every night?" I shook my head. "Fabi hitting on Devin left and right?" I shook my head again. "Devin laughing and smiling?"

"Obviously I have not, but I cannot be the only one who does not know about this."

"Cameron, even John figured it out."

"Right here, Re," John mumbled.

"Go to sleep, John."

"Devin…and…Fabiani? Together?"

Everyone in the room started to laugh, though Alexander and I stifled ours when we heard footsteps coming up the front steps.

"Speaking of the happy couple," Alexander said under his breath.

A few seconds later Fabiani and Devin came bursting through the front door laughing at something one of them had said while they brushed away the snow from their hair and shoulders. For the first time I saw the happiness in my brother's eyes and could not believe I had not noticed it before. However, as soon as he caught me looking at him the Warrior Assassin returned.

"It's about time," Kyla called from the stairs as she began her dissent.

Fabiani looked up to her, "Nice boots."

"Um, she's copying me today," Renee said as she stood and walked over to Fabiani to model her outfit.

"Dev, why didn't you tell me it was cutie cute boot day?"

"Huh?" Devin asked as he looked at Fabiani and then around the room for help.

"Never mind. Ok ladies, let's get this show on the road," Fabiani announced, seeming just as excited about shopping for Renee's bridal gown as Kyla was.

"Wait," Devin interrupted as he placed a hand up in front of him, "I wasn't aware there was an outing today."

"Aw, the little Warrior misses me already."

Devin changed his posture uncomfortably as he said, "All I am saying is perhaps I should provide some extra security."

"Uh-uh," Fabiani replied waving his finger at Devin. "I am the only sausage in this Italian restaurant. Now go on and do your manly Warrior work, we have an appointment. Come on ladies."

Renee walked to the coat closet by the front door and shoved one of her extra coats into Kyla's resistant arms. With Fabiani holding the door, the two ladies stepped out – Kyla hopeful and excited, Renee reserved and apprehensive. Fabiani, on the other hand, winked and waved as he ducked out the door. I could not help but notice Devin watch Fabiani walk down the front steps and catch up with the ladies walking in the lightly falling snow.

Devin's ogling did not go unnoticed by Alexander. "So when are you two picking out curtains and china patterns?"

Alexander immediately began snickering at his own joke, and honestly I could not help but join in. Although I was laughing more at Devin's confused expression than anything else.

"I assure you I would never have a reason to pick out curtains."

"Oh come on, Dev. You might as well admit you two are..."

"I suggest you hold your tongue," Devin threatened. If looks could kill, Alexander would be missing his head. "You are lucky that the good doctor is asleep and does not know what you are implying."

Behind me John started to laugh softly. "Yeah I do."

"No. You don't," Devin said sternly.

John opened his eyes, finally giving up trying to sleep. "We are talking about you dating Fabi, right?"

A chill went through Devin's body, fury filling his eyes as he looked from me to Alexander and back again while his chest started heaving. "Who...which one of you..."

"Brother! Brother, calm down," I said, putting my hands up in front of me. "We have said nothing."

"Then how…why would he think…"

John leapt up from the couch but chose to stand behind me. "Devin, sorry, I thought it was common knowledge."

Devin's chest began to calm, but his face was strained with worry. "It is nothing. Father wanted to make sure we cultivated good relations with members of Dante's coven."

"I'm sure you're cultivating something."

"Alexander, cut it out," I warned. "Devin, we are all family here. You never need to hide who you are in front of us."

Devin tightened his lips, lowering his head slightly before stepping closer and looking at me under his brow. "I feel guilty."

"Why?"

"It is wrong of me to find happiness amongst your sorrow."

I paused for a moment before squeezing his shoulder tightly. "Brother, do not forgo anything with Fabiani on my behalf. If Brianna were here she would be thrilled. As am I, you deserve to be with someone just as much as anyone."

"Oh, are we discussing the Assassin and the little Negotiator?" Eris said from the corner of the room as the black mist of his Projection dissipated around him.

Devin threw his arms up, walking away and shaking his head in disbelief.

"Assassin, you and I can be very much alike, and I will tell you that once you find that one person who can temper your violent ways, do not let them go."

"With all due respect, Eris," Devin replied, "it is my job to be violent."

"Ah yes, but not twenty-four hours a day. My Sera has taught me that balance is the key. Of course what do I know, I am only four times your age. What wisdom could I possibly bestow?"

All eyes were wide and looking at Devin for a reaction, but surprisingly there was none. In the past Devin would have been flying across the room, no matter if it was Eris in his way. Maybe Fabiani was already teaching him something.

"But I am not here to discuss the Assassin's love life. Dr. Ryan, I was wondering if you perhaps had any more of those migraine pills."

John nodded as he stepped back over to the couch and began rifling through his coat. "I remembered to bring home some more samples. Is Sera having one now?"

"Yes," Eris answered.

"Another nosebleed?" I asked.

"Only a slight one a little earlier. No more than a dribble."

"A vision?"

"No. Not this time. Although I may have the beginnings of an early Christmas present for you."

"Elaina's hybrid has contacted you?"

He nodded. "Like I have said before, small bits of information here and there, but put it all together…"

"And? Do we have a location? A date? Time?" I pressed as I stood directly in front of him.

"And…" he responded calmly, lifting his brows and widening his eyes, silently telling me to be patient, "we should begin pulling any forces together in order to recover my daughter somewhere around the Christmas holiday."

"Christmas! But that is over a week away. So much could happen until then. Push back on this hybrid, and subsequently her traitorous Vampire and tell them we want answers now. I am tired of being strung along for weeks at a time."

"Warrior," Eris replied, "personally I choose not to punch a gift horse in the mouth. Since my connection with this hybrid is all we have to go on, we are unfortunately at his mercy unless you and your family can pick up Brian-na's trail."

"But Christmas…"

"I know, Cameron," Eris interrupted, keeping his voice calm and squeezing me firmly by the shoulders. I was in slight shock hearing him call me by my real name. "I know you long for her to be with us, as do I. But we must wait."

"Why?" I asked pathetically, feeling as though all my energy was draining out of me.

"From what I have gathered, it appears that Elaina herself will be in the vicinity at that time. You could potentially kill two birds with one stone."

With a sigh, I acquiesced. "We will speak with Victor about pulling Warriors in the area. We should probably start to congregate now so that we do not bring attention to ourselves."

"Good thinking, Brother," Devin said behind me. "I will take the lead on handling logistics with Father. We definitely should use Warriors outside of the manor. If the Warrior headquarters suddenly emptied out at once, I am sure Elaina's people would notice."

"Brother, you make a good point," I began. "I know they say Nikki is responding to treatment, but in no way do I trust her. She cannot be tipped off in any way that we are getting close to finding Brianna. That means even Skylar cannot be brought in the loop, or any one close to him as they might divulge information unknowingly. In addition, tell Father that all conversations between Nikki and Jared should continue to be supervised. We simply cannot screw this up." I paused, suddenly exhausted as a large weight began bearing down on my shoulders. "I just want this to end."

"Warrior, we all do," Eris said in a gentle tone. "We are almost there. We only need a little more patience. Smile, things are beginning to look up."

Such things should never be said. Just as the last syllable sounded from Eris's mouth, a blood curdling scream came from upstairs. Eris disappeared with a loud snap as he Projected quickly from the room. The rest of us ran hurriedly up the stairs, including John who was still coming up them as we approached the source of the screaming.

When I opened the door to their bedroom, Seraphina was sobbing as she knelt on the floor while Eris held her tightly around her shaking shoulders. "Il est mort."

"Who is dead," I shouted as I ran into the room coming on the other side of Seraphina, my brothers circling around us while John knelt in front of her trying to get a look at her face.

"Sera, who is dead? Tell us, my darling," Eris urged when she did not answer.

John began shining his pen light into Seraphina's eyes. "Her eyes are fixed and dilated again. Is she having another one of those visions?"

"Of course she is!" Eris screamed. "Please, my darling, tell us something."

Seraphina's tears were streaming down her face as she began rocking back and forth. "He is dead. She is so sad, he is dead."

"Who, darling, who?"

"I do not know," she replied and then took in a deep gasp as she began speaking to the floor, as if someone was lying there. "No, no, no," she shouted, though in a voice resembling Brianna's as she began stroking an invisible person in front of her. "Stay with me now...just a little longer...Aidan help me!"

Once again her scream sent ripples through the house as she collapsed forward into John. Quickly Eris took her by the shoulders and rolled her on her back into his arms. Sweat was beading up on her forehead while tears still leaked from her eyes. Crawling towards her I continued to press, "Seraphina, please tell me. Who is dead?"

She shook her head as she continued to cry. "I do not know."

"Did you see him? What did he look like?"

"Y-young," she stuttered. "Brown…hair. I have never seen him before."

Just then Seraphina arched her back as her eyes began to glaze over again, her body jolted forward to a kneeling position as she sobbed into the floor. Suddenly her head jerk to her left, looking directly at me as she once again said in Brianna's haunting voice, "What have you done?"

"W-what?" I said in surprise as I fell backwards, landing against Devin's shin.

"Tell me what you've done!" she screamed again, her eyes boring holes mine.

"Seraphina, I…is this you? Or Brianna? What is happening?" I asked frantically as Devin cupped his hands under my arms and lifted me up. Seraphina's glare followed me as I rose and then began rising herself.

"Everything I possess is from the sweat off my own back, not from you!"

It was as if Brianna was in the room – crying and yelling as anger overwhelmed her.

"I am here in spite of you," she screamed, jabbing her finger into my chest.

"Bri please," I said breathlessly.

"She's not Bri, Brother. Focus," Devin said in my ear as he pulled on my shoulder.

I wretched myself from his grip and stepped closer to Seraphina. "Brianna, I am so sorry. Help me…"

"Well let me help you finish what you started," Seraphina growled as she reached back and plunged her right fist into my abdomen as if she was stabbing me.

Devin pulled me around him, throwing me to the floor as Seraphina once again collapsed. Resting on all fours, I could not seem to keep my stomach from retching dry heaving breaths. Everyone was seeing to Seraphina behind me, and all I could think about was the fact that Brianna was devastated by the death of a person we did not know and then turned around and possibly killed someone else. The things she was saying tore me apart. She was in so much pain and there was nothing I could do because I was a failure, a disgrace to her and my family and even my unborn children. And what of them? Would this amount of stress and trauma be harmful to the babies? What if she were to lose them? What if Brianna went into pre-term labor? What would they do with her? The questions continued to pile up as the familiar feeling of anger and panic filled every muscle in my body.

"Cam?" Alexander said tentatively as he wrapped his hand around my arm only to have me thrust it away.

"I need some air."

The room and the hallway outside were a blur as I ran out and down the stairs. When I rounded the corner to head out into the courtyard I stopped abruptly at the basement door. I realized I needed something other than air. I wrapped my hand around the door handle and began my dissent down into the musty basement. Once I reached the bottom of the steps I walked toward the small stone room that had been turned into a makeshift bedroom for Jared.

My youngest brother was splayed out on the twin sized bed, his chest hanging off the side with his face being propped up on his laptop. A large monitor was set up behind the computer, a short snippet of the highway footage replaying a ten second loop. There were dark purple circles under his eyes, much like mine.

I kicked the edge of his bedframe causing his head to jerk slightly, his eyes trying to stretch open.

"Get up," I growled at him.

Jerking awake he kicked wildly to the head of his bed, pressing his back up against the wall. His face was tied up in all kinds of emotions. At first he was startled, then confused, and then just plain angry.

"Dude, what the hell? It's the middle of the freaking morning and I totally don't want to talk to you."

"Pack your things."

"Wh-what? Why!"

"You are going home."

Jared pushed himself up from his bed, his black t-shirt wrinkled and twisted around his waist. "What, I finally call you out on your shit and you send me home? Is that it?"

"Not at all," I replied, trying my hardest to sound like Devin which would make Jared even angrier. "Father and I are disappointed with your performance, and therefore we are pulling you."

Take the bait, take the bait, I willed into my brother's eyes.

"You can't do that. You can't make me go."

"Actually, I can. This is my house. So get back in the body bag you came in, your flight leaves in an hour."

"No way. I'm not leaving until Bri is found."

"Since you have not brought anything new to the table, and now that Eris has an inside connection, you are no longer needed. Leave this to those who really care about finding Brianna."

Jared took a step forward, his fists clenched at his side. "I'm pretty fucking tired of hearing you say shit like that. You know how much I love Beebs and I am doing everything I know how…"

"But that is the problem, Jared," I interrupted. "It is simply not enough. Look at it this way, by going home you get to spend more time with your mentally ill traitorous girlfriend." Jared took another step toward me, his lips taught across his teeth. Keep coming, little brother, just keep coming. "If you leave quietly, once Brianna is returned to us I will make sure she never knows that you chose a piece of ass over her."

I watched my brother crouch down and then leap across the room, hitting me square in the chest. The pain was a welcomed feeling. It was what I wanted, and I hoped Jared would not see through me. As my back crushed the wall behind us, Jared's face was only inches from mine, his fangs fully extended. I had hit a nerve and that was my purpose, but it simply was not enough. So I laughed.

"Is that all you have," I teased. "No wonder Father has kept you from missions these last six months. You are a liability more than you are a Warrior."

Jared's anger exploded as he grabbed me by the throat and then threw me into a perpendicular wall. Purposefully I stayed crouched on the floor until he leapt on top of me, hitting and tearing at my face and arms. But it still was not enough; I needed to feel more pain.

With three quick jabs into his gut, I lifted him off of me just enough to adjust myself upright and kick his legs out from under him. As he scrambled back up to me I began taunting him, calling him a weakling and a disgrace, even though I was truly talking about myself. As my taunts became even more hurtful, his hits became harder. It was working. At least initially. As he continued to beat on me I could feel his fatigue begin to set in. The timing between punches was getting longer. I needed to keep up his anger before the others came and put a stop to this.

In the spilt second between hits, I thrust my elbow across Jared's face, hearing and feeling his nose break before he collapsed onto the floor. He stayed there for a moment, touching his nose and seeing the blood come off on his fingertips. With a feral hiss he launched himself on me again, but I caught his chest with my foot and kicked him away. He rose and pounced, only to have me push him away again. On his third attempt I let him come after me, his hand grabbing my face and crushing it against the wall, this time breaking bones in the back of my skull.

A second later Jared's fangs were deep inside the side of my neck, tearing and pulling at nerves and muscle, but it did not stop my taunting. "Is this what you did to Brianna that night you attacked her?"

Jared's growl vibrated into my neck and chest just before he ripped out the right side of my throat and spit it out on the floor. The pain was excruciating but I did not fight back. Jared rose from the floor, taking my right leg in his hand and swinging me across the room causing my shin to break away from my knee and hang crookedly off the side of the bed. Jared once again leapt on top of me, punching me incessantly across the face, hardly letting a second pass between hits.

"Harder!" I growled at him as my mouth filled with blood. He obliged, this time breaking my nose and cheekbone in retaliation. "Harder!" I screamed at him again, and I could hear the sound of the others coming down the second story stairs. "Do not stop now! Do it! Do it!"

Jared hit me across the face one more time and then he stopped abruptly, his face changing from anger to confusion in a millisecond. Before he could say anything, Alexander and Devin burst into the room. Alexander wrapped his arms around Jared's waist, and lifted him off of me, although he put up no fight. Devin stood between us, his eyes widening at my injuries, and then looking murderously in Jared's direction.

"Someone better start talking," he shouted loudly as more footsteps stumbled down the basement stairway.

"Cameron's gone fucking crazy," Jared shouted back, trying to push Alexander's arms away.

"From what I see, it is the other way around," Devin scolded back, shaking his head as he looked back at me. My wounds were slow to heal because of my lack of blood, and my body was burning and twitching as muscles and bone struggled to stitch back together.

Just then, John came shuffling into the room, panting loudly as he held himself up in the doorway. "You guys are definitely proving to me that I need to work out more. Is everyone...holy shit, Cameron!" Immediately

John came to my side, taking care to avoid my broken shin lying at a ninety degree angle in front of me. "I'll call for an ambulance," he said as he patted his pockets for his cell phone.

"That won't be needed," Devin said firmly as he took John's cell phone from his hand.

"But Devin, look at his leg? It's practically amputated. He also has a broken nose, cheek, and a giant hole in his neck."

"Does he really?" Devin questioned as he pointed past John causing him to turn back around. The look on John's face was priceless as he watched my nose pop back into place at the same time the cuts across my face began to mend. "Jared, I want an explanation."

"But I…" Jared started.

"Brother," I interrupted softly, having trouble speaking smoothly while my sunken cheek began to repair itself along with my throat. "This was not Jared's doing."

"You hit yourself, and broke your own leg off?"

I sighed, trying to look around John to see Devin better, however John merely moved with me, his eyes mesmerized by my healing wounds. "No. I mean I made him do this."

"How did you make him?"

"By provoking him."

Devin threw his arms up. "Why? What would possess you to…"

"Did you not see the pain that Brianna was in? One person is dead and she might have just killed someone else."

"That does not mean you can go around…"

"I cannot take it anymore!"

My outburst caused everyone in the room to take a step back, and John to fall over all together.

Jared took a step around Devin. "Dude, were you trying to get me to kill you? Like some assisted suicide shit? I should break your other leg, ya bastard."

"I am sick of feeling this way. The sun comes up on another day without Brianna and I want to slit my throat, anything that would take this god awful feeling away."

Devin let a tense silence fall upon us before saying, "From now on, Brother, you will not provoke anyone in this house to inflict pain upon you. In fact, no one else will hit, spit, bite, growl, or even look at each other sideways while we are all still here together. Lately it seems like Alex's full-time job is pulling the two of you off of each other."

Jared started laughing. "I think you've got us mixed up with you and Fabi." Devin narrowed his eyes at Jared. "I thought you said no growling."

"Help your brother," Devin snapped. "Alex, you're with me. We need to have a conference with Father."

A second later Devin stormed out of the basement, Alexander shrugging and following after. John was comatose as he watched the last of my throat piece itself together. Reflexively I rubbed at my neck, feeling the tenderness of new skin.

"You got me good, little brother."

"I shoulda realized what you were doing. I've just been so mad at you..."

I held my hand up. "I knew that and I used it. Used you. I am a horrible brother. I am sorry."

"Me too, bro. I mean look at my room, who's gonna clean this mess?"

I laughed. "You are of course."

"Why me?"

"Because you decided to use my leg like a baseball bat."

"Speaking of," John interrupted as he pointed to the one break that had still not healed. "Can I at least set it or something? My medical OCD is kicking in."

"Don't worry, doc. It'll snap back any second. It's actually pretty cool to watch," Jared said as he plopped down next to me on the bed.

"It won't heal crooked like that?" John asked with amazement.

"Well you are about to see," I said, feeling the strain in my muscles and burning in the bones of my leg as they began to stretch and stitch back together. Then with a loud crack, I howled in pain as my tibia snapped back into place under my knee.

"See! Wasn't that awesome!" Jared cheered as I panted next to him.

John's eyes were as big as silver dollars. "Do they have Vampire morphine or something?"

"In this moment I truly wish they did," I replied while my knee and calf continued to burn.

"Sorry, bro, what you really need is some Vampire anti-depressants."

"John, what are you doing?" I asked.

John looked up quickly, his eyes flooded with guilt at getting caught looking up the cuff of my pants. "Sorry. You have no idea...this is...can I please look?"

Smiling, I pulled up the pant leg of my dark jeans, letting him watch the last section of skin knit itself together, leaving only a wide red line around my calf where the bone had torn through.

John brushed his fingers lightly over the tender red skin. "What I wouldn't give to see your blood under a microscope."

"And a mad scientist is born," Jared teased.

Again John looked up guiltily. "Sorry. I've seen someone come into the ER with a break like this and the person basically has a leg full of titanium rods. You just…grew new bone and tissue in minutes. Can you imagine the possibilities for modern medicine?" He paused. "Oh my god I am a mad scientist."

"May I ask what happened with Seraphina after I left? Did she come to?"

He nodded. "She still couldn't identify the person who died, and Eris did his…thing and didn't recognize him either."

"And the person Bri stabbed? Did Sera see who it was?"

He nodded hesitantly. "Eris said it was a woman…who looked like…" he sighed, "Bri's mom."

"Shelby?" I whispered stunned.

"That's what Eris said. Sera's really shaken up, I think she's still having residual visions. Wow…I can't believe I just said that. My life has really taken an odd turn."

"Whoa, wait a minute. We think Bibi killed her mom?"

"Think? Unfortunately, little brother, we are relatively sure about it," I responded and turned back to John. "Did Sera see anything else?"

John nodded. "Snow."

A second later and without being prompted, Jared was typing on his computer.

To say that Devin was angry with me was an understatement. He was furious at my behavior, though I did take slight offense since he had done similar things in the past. When I brought that fact to his attention he reminded me that I was supposed to be the "composed" brother. Since the day Brianna left I could hardly consider myself composed.

Jared had forgiven my awful comments since I was only trying to provoke him and I in no way meant them. I think it was also because he felt a little guilty for beating me so badly. Hopefully we were even now. The only good thing to come out of this awful morning was the fact that it had been snowing in Boston at the same time it was snowing wherever Brianna was. Jared had immediately pulled up weather maps and revealed that five states within New England were affected by storms. The area was still big, but it was a thousand times smaller than what we had previously. It was a start.

After my outburst downstairs I guess you could say I was grounded. Fabiani had convinced everyone that a night at Club Red was needed to take the edge off. I, however, was required to stay home and babysit the humans. The bottle of blood I was drinking had gone cold over an hour ago, but that did not stop me from continuing to nurse it – another term of my grounding, the bottle needed to be empty by the time Devin returned.

The twenty-four hour news station switched to another program when I heard the sounds of someone padding around in the kitchen, opening cabinets and taking items out of the refrigerator. A few minutes later that same person was slowly coming down the stairs.

"I thought I heard the TV on down here," Renee said as she walked into the room, eventually melting into the couch next to me.

"Did the television wake you?"

"Nah," she replied and took a large sip of her white wine. "Just couldn't sleep. You?"

"I rarely sleep. Besides I do not have a bed to sleep in."

"That's your choice. I told you Kyla and I could go and pick out something. You'll need to put furniture in there eventually."

"It feels wrong to do it without her," I said into my glass as I forcibly swallowed the foul red liquid.

"I know the feeling," she said under her breath while eyeing my glass as I took it away from my mouth. "Is that blood?"

"Yes."

"Can I have some?"

My head flinched. "No."

"Please?"

"No."

"Just one time."

"Renee," I warned.

She rolled her eyes and took a sip from her own glass. "I was just curious. You know it almost looks like red wine."

"That is what Brianna used to say," I said with a small laugh, but then a heavy silence fell between us. "I heard you found a dress today?"

"Kyla really does have the biggest mouth of anyone I know."

"She was surprised you did not purchase it."

Quickly she looked away, trying to hide the fact that she was wiping away a tear from her eye. "Like you said, it feels wrong to do this without her."

"Bri will understand, Renee. You have a time constraint…"

"John and I had a fight," she interrupted. "That's why I couldn't sleep."

"A fight about what?"

"Everything."

"That certainly narrows it down," I replied.

"Tonight when we got in bed I told him I wanted to postpone the wedding and he just freaked out. I can't get him to understand that I really can't do any of this without Bri. I just feel so friggin' guilty every time I pick something out because she should be there. Today was just…awful. I put the dress on and looked in the mirror and just started crying. Fabi and Kyla thought I was crying because I had found *the* dress, and that was it at first and then I couldn't stop because all I wanted was my friend standing in the mirror crying with me. That was the moment we were supposed to share together, you know? I'll never get that back."

Seeing Renee cry was like watching my angel cry, and I could not help but open my arms to her. Putting her glass down on the floor, she crawled across the couch and placed her head in the crook of my neck.

"You really are cold," she said as she moved her head from my neck to my shoulder.

"Vampire."

"Doesn't Bri ever get cold?"

I shook my head. "Hybrids are not as warm as humans. So she does not seem to feel the temperature difference as much, or at least she does not complain about it."

"You have to find her," she cried into my shirt.

I squeezed her tighter into my shoulder as I replied, "Eris thinks we might have her back by Christmas."

"Really?" she whimpered as she looked up at me.

"He seems to think so. If Eris is right, and Brianna returns to us by Christmas, there is no reason for you to postpone the wedding."

"You're siding with John now?"

"I am pretty certain that if Brianna returns home and you have canceled the wedding because of her, she will be devastated."

"So what are you saying?"

"I am saying," I began gently, "to tell John to forget what you said about postponing the wedding and order that dress."

She shook her head. "I really can't. It's too expensive. John would freak out even more than he already is."

"But is it the dress you want?"

"I'll find something cheaper."

"Renee, when you saw yourself in the mirror could you picture yourself marrying John? Right in that moment, did you see him standing next to you in his tuxedo vowing to be with you for the rest of your life?"

Although my statement invoked more tears, it also brought on her sarcasm. "You really do sound like a girl sometimes. Doesn't matter what I saw, I can't afford it."

"What if it were a gift?"

She paused. "From whom?"

"From me and Bri. It could be our wedding gift."

"No."

"Why not?"

"Because it isn't right."

"Who says?"

"I didn't tell you I couldn't afford the dress just so you'd buy it. Good grief, we've only known each other for a few months and I have done nothing to deserve something like that."

"Renee, you and I may have only just met, but you have known Brianna for many years and you have always been there for her. And if that was not enough, you and John picked up your lives at a moment's notice because of this situation. Let me do this for you, not only to celebrate your wedding, but to show you my appreciation for your help and understanding during this whole ordeal." Renee sighed and started to open her mouth but I interrupted with, "It can be our secret. Ours, and of course Bri's."

Her mouth twisted back and forth as she considered the offer, but it was not until she sighed deeply did I know she had accepted. "Fine, but I will get the dress the day you get furniture for your bedroom. My twin needs a bed for when she comes home."

"You have a deal."

With a sudden burst of energy, Renee wrapped her arms around my neck, but then a second later pushed away with her eyebrows scrunched together.

"Speaking of gifts, you never opened yours?" Renee asked and pointed to the small gift on the oval table next to us, exactly where Kyla had placed it this morning.

"I told Kyla I did not wish to celebrate my birthday."

"Too bad," she said angrily as she rose from the couch, grabbed the present, and pushed it into my hands. "I helped make that thing, so you better open it."

"A homemade gift?"

She shrugged as she sat back on the couch. "Kinda. Just open it."

Reluctantly I untied the stiff blue ribbon and began tearing away the thick silver wrapping paper. The thin box underneath was white and plain, nothing that would instantly give away what was inside. Removing the lid and lifting away the white tissue paper, I revealed a small rectangular pewter frame. At first I thought I was looking at the picture insert that came with the frame, but with a second glance I realized I was looking at the familiar ultrasound photos of my little ones. Baby Boy and Baby Girl Burke. Our babies.

"I noticed that the ones in your wallet were getting all crinkly, so I had John pull some strings with Bri's doctor and print some new ones."

"This is the best present anyone could ever give me," I said as I brushed my fingers down the glass.

"And you can just keep replacing them as you get new ones until they're finally here and we'll have ten million pictures all over the house."

Feeling the emotions swell inside me, I clamped my right hand over my mouth, clawing and digging into my skin to get them to disappear. But every second I stared at my children the pain deepened. I felt Renee's hand begin to rub my back, obviously seeing my internal struggle. A few moments later she leaned over the other side of the couch and retrieved a box of tissues from the end table, then took the frame from my hand.

When I looked at her she merely held out a tissue and said, "We never did have that big cry. Don't worry, it'll be our little secret."

"I will hold you to that."

Chapter Forty-Eight

Cameron

It was Christmas day. A wedding dress had been ordered and the master bedroom was now furnished. Beyond that it had been agreed on by the entire family that no gifts would be exchanged this holiday. Our gift would be Brianna's return and restoration of the Warrior coven's reputation. The main worry of course being that if the Warriors cannot protect their own, how would they protect everyone else? There were many of us asking the same question.

But all questions aside, today we would be battling to bring my angel home. At this moment I was staring at myself in the full-length mirror, tugging at my black t-shirt collar and adjusting it underneath my protective vest for the sixteenth time. Nothing seemed to look or sit right from my combat boots to my hair and I had been fussing with everything for over an hour.

In the mirror I looked behind me to see the new bed and dark satin embroidered bedspread Kyla had helped me pick out. All I could think about was that I hoped Brianna would like it. Truly there were only three permanent items in the entire room – my framed ultrasound photos placed on a night table, and the two stuffed lambs that Dante had given the babies. Everything else was returnable. The thought of Bri lying in that very bed in a few hours made me start raking my hand through my hair again to get the blasted curls to lay right in the back.

"Bro, you look fine," Jared said as he entered the bedroom in his matching black battle gear. "Not to say you look as good as me, cuz no one can pull this outfit off like I do."

"You are just lucky our gear does not require a bowtie because you would be shit out of luck, little brother."

"Ouch!" he whined, rubbing his chest as if I had hit him. "You know you're starting to get a foul mouth. Today it's shit, and last week you actually referenced my cock. You're not being a good role model, and you know kids like me are so impressionable."

I shook my head as I began pulling at my comm's throat strap and clasping it around my neck, then unclasping when I realized it was twisted, clasping it again and then noticing in the mirror that the microphone was facing out instead of in. Just then, Jared's hands pulled mine away from my neck and unclasped the throat strap a final time, eyeing me humorously in the mirror.

"Yep, it's a good thing Dad doesn't make us wear bowties with our battle gear because right now I don't think you could tie your own shoe," he said smugly as he untwisted the strap and clasped it around my neck successfully.

"I can too. My boots are triple knotted."

"Not double, not quadruple. But triple, huh? Is that the magic number?" I exhaled a slow breath, realizing for the first time how much tension I was keeping built up inside. Jared grasped my shoulder firmly as he looked me in the eye and said, "We're all nervous, bro. But you have to stay cool, ok? We've got a great team assembled and we've all done our fair share of rescue missions. Once we know where Bibi is, extracting her will be a piece of cake."

"But what about after?"

"After what?"

"You are correct, we have all done extractions, but we never know what happens after. We leave that to someone else. What if..." I began, but turned away from him and began to pace around the room. "What if she does not want to come home? What if she no longer wants to...be with me?"

Jared did not answer, prompting me to turn around.

"Oh I'm sorry, bro, did you want me to react to that horse shit?"

"Thank you for turning my anxiety into a joke."

"Oh come on man," he huffed. "There's no reason to get all worked up now over it. We don't know what to expect. None of us do. So you can't start worrying about all that crap now. You need to concentrate on getting

Bri back, and then whatever happens afterwards we'll deal with it. All of us. We're all here for Bri, and on occasion you."

I laughed lightly, releasing another layer of anxiety with my breath. "Is everyone in place?"

"Yep," he nodded. "Connor has the bulk of the team outside the city. Fifteen in total with four different style vehicles to help us blend in. We have two SUVs waiting outside for the nine of us and that includes Fabi, Kyla, John, and Eris's driver Vlad."

"He does not like to be called a driver."

"Oh that's right. The tool likes to be called a transportation specialist," Jared mocked as he rolled his eyes. "So yeah, we're all just waiting on you so we can meet Connor at the rendezvous point."

I exhaled a final breath. It was finally time, and I was so nervous I thought I might actually rip my skin off, which would be disappointing in some respect since it would merely grow back. After six weeks and six days she would finally be in my arms, her long dark hair splayed across my chest while we lay in our bed, the heat coming off her pregnant stomach as it pressed against my skin, and lastly the sound of Brianna's voice whispering that she loved me as her lips grazed mine. The thoughts were enough to send me into the floor with the weight of my desire and need for her. As I took steps toward the bedroom door I could hear shouting coming from the living room just down the hall.

"What is going on out there?" I asked as I turned to see Jared checking himself out in the mirror.

"Oh, Red is throwing a tantrum because she's not going with us."

"But I talked to her this morning. She seemed fine staying here with Seraphina and Dante."

"Yep, well..." he dragged out as he fixed his hair and winked at himself in the mirror, "that was this morning. Her shit is literally hitting the fan. I mean seriously, you're going to need to buy a new fan because, well, it's covered in Renee's shit."

"You can be so vile sometimes."

"Hey, I learned it from watching you, you cock-sucker. No, wait sorry, I'm confusing you with my other brother, De..."

"That is enough," I warned firmly before giving him a little hit in the arm and leaving the bedroom. When we came around the stairs that rose to the second floor we became witnesses to the scene that I was sure my neighbors could hear quite well. Renee's face was almost as red as her hair, and unfortunately John and Devin seemed to be taking the brunt. Honestly, I was very proud of my brother for maintaining his patience, however, it was short lived the minute he saw me. With a quick flick of his finger he was demanding that I step in.

"Renee, whatever is the matter?"

Renee whipped her head around and I could see now that her eyes were red and puffy, most likely from crying. Kyla was trying desperately to soothe her by placing her hands on Renee's shoulders, but Renee was having nothing of it.

"I've changed my mind, Cameron. I want to go too," Renee said demandingly.

"Renee, you and I talked about this…"

"I don't care, I want to go."

"No," I replied firmly, which only caused her eyes to flair and her posture to straighten.

"Why not!"

"Because it is too dangerous."

"Then why does he get to go," she shouted and pointed to John.

I paused for a second, giving her a moment to breathe and to slow down the pace of the argument. "Like we discussed this morning, John is going because Brianna may need medical attention. Now I can afford to lose a man or two protecting him, but I cannot have two humans to worry about."

"But…but I am her family. I need to be there and you can't stop me."

"He may not," Eris said as he stepped off the stairs next to me, Seraphina walking just behind him with a holstered broadsword in her hand. "But as your surrogate father I will put my foot down, my dear. What may happen tonight is no place for you. It is for your own protection that you stay here with Sera. And who knows, maybe even Dante could give you a free palm reading."

With tears in her eyes, Renee bolted from the room and ran down the hallway towards the master bedroom with Kyla sympathetically running after her. Dante was glaring at Eris from across the room. There was definitely history between them that none of us knew, and frankly we did not have the time for such drama. We had more than enough to handle.

The room was suddenly quiet and all eyes looked to me for what to do.

"We should get a move on if we are to meet Connor and the team in the next thirty minutes. Then we will wait for Eris's hybrid to make contact on Brianna's exact location. Correct?" I asked looking directly at Eris.

He nodded. "Yes. We will be given the location and additional instructions within the hour." Eris turned proudly to his wife as he said, "Sera, my darling, I am going off to battle. I need my sword."

Seraphina smiled as she fastened the long sword's wide leather strap around Eris's waist and placed a thin lacey handkerchief into his hand before kissing him. It was a scene from medieval times, and it made my heart ache.

"Let's do this!" Jared shouted enthusiastically, breaking up the awkward moment.

Devin followed Jared out the door with Fabiani close on his heels, looking excited about going on his first Warrior mission. John, on the other hand, looked as though he was going to be sick. In the last six weeks I had mostly seen him in hospital scrubs, but today he looked like one of us in black cargo pants, black shirt, and protective vest, though I smiled at the messy way his pants were tucked into his boots.

"Nervous, John?" I asked as I waved him toward the door.

"Give me gangs and gunshot wounds, amputated fingers and suicides gone bad, and I am good to go. But put me in a civil war between Vampires, and…yeah I'm a little more than nervous."

"John, I promise you will not be expected to do any fighting. As soon as we have Bri you are coming home with her in the car. No reason to worry."

"Has anyone ever puked during one of these things?"

I smirked. "Funny enough, Brianna has vomited while the fighting was happening around her. So if you do get sick, you will be in good company."

He laughed nervously just as Renee began to run back down the hall.

"You're leaving already?" she asked teary-eyed as she ran to John and wrapped her arms around his neck.

With a heavy heart I watched their embrace, and then glanced at Kyla who was giving me sympathetic eyes. Turning away from her, I trudged down the slushy wet stairs outside. My brothers and Vladimir had congregated on the sidewalk, our two large SUVs somehow parked conveniently in front of the house.

"Alex?" I asked pointing to the two trucks. "On tonight of all nights, how did you find two consecutive parking spaces directly in front of the house?"

"Good luck?" he answered with a sheepish grin.

"Try again."

Vladimir stepped forward, putting a defensive hand in the air. "We were just playing a little game of Find-Your-Car-On-The-Streets-Of-Boston."

I quirked my eyebrow. "You moved two cars without anyone noticing?"

"Technically three," Alexander chimed in. "The little one was like moving a toy car. I'm sorry I won't be around to watch the people roaming around trying to find their cars. Vlad says that's the best part."

I opened my mouth to speak, but Eris shouted behind me from the stairs, "Vlad, it is time, my old friend. My daughter awaits."

Vladimir nodded to his employer, and quickly ran to the driver's side of the first SUV. Behind Eris, Kyla was leading a nervous John down the front steps while Seraphina waved from the top landing.

Just as I turned to walk toward one of the vehicles I heard, "Cameron, wait!"

Slightly startled I turned back in time to see Renee fleeing from the house and running clumsily down the icy front steps. As soon as she hit the sidewalk she ran to me and hugged me tightly, burying her wet face into my neck as she sobbed, "Bring her back."

"I will," I replied softly as I gently placed my arm around her.

"Keep John safe, ok?"

"With our lives."

Renee unwrapped her arms from my neck, and lowered herself to the ground as she said, "You come back, too."

"Everyone will come back, Renee. This is what we do."

She nodded, wiping the tears from her cheeks. "Yep, I know. Just don't choose today to suck at it."

"Ah, there is the Renee I know."

She forced a smiled as she backed away from me and gave John one last kiss before she made her way up the stairs.

"Hey Red, where's my hug?" Jared asked with his arms out wide in her direction.

Renee did not turn around as she replied, "Bye, jailbait."

"Ah cumon, Red. It's because big John's here, isn't it? Don't worry, I'll getcha when I get home. Ow!" Jared shouted as he rubbed his arm from where Devin had punched him.

"Thanks, Dev," John said gratefully to which Devin gave him a nod.

"All right, are we done with all this horseplay?" Eris asked annoyed. "Warrior, you are with me. Vlad will be driving."

I nodded and took John by the shoulder. "John and Jared, you will also come with us."

"Aww," Jared whined, "I wanted to go in the fun truck."

"Which is why you are going with us."

"You're not my dad."

"Thank goodness," I teased as I pushed him up into the truck. "Uh-uh, third row, little brother."

"Why?"

"So that John will not have to fight off anyone who comes through the back window."

"What?!" John answered with worried wide eyes as he sat in the backseat.

Jared leaned over the second row seat, grabbed John by the shoulders and began shaking him teasingly. "Just the beginning of your initiation, man. You're lucky though. Dev threw me from a twenty story building, and then made me battle against four other Warriors. At least all you have to do is get through one night without getting killed."

"Enough, Jared," I warned and shut the passenger door.

John leaned over to me, "You did say Bri threw up at a battle, right?"

"Yeah, totally right next to me," Jared answered instead.

Eris turned around in the front passenger seat as Vladimir pulled the truck away from the curb. "She did no such thing. A daughter of Eris would never vomit during battle."

"She sure as hell did!" Jared replied and then began to recap all the details of that day. Whereas Jared concentrated on remembering Brianna's one embarrassing act, I had always remembered her bravery and perseverance on that day. When we traveled down the streets of Boston toward Connor's convoy I prayed that those same qualities had kept her alive and well these last six weeks. I did not want to lie to Renee, but god forbid something did happen to my Bri, I too would not be returning. It was that simple.

"Oliver Morgan, please."

"I am sorry sir, there is no one by that name at Facility West," the young receptionist answered.

"Madelyn Forebush, then," I pressed with little patience.

The receptionist sighed loudly into the phone, and then canned hold music came over the line while she transferred me. I was standing at the edge of an abandoned field about fifteen miles outside of the city where we had met up with the other convoy. Eris was sitting in the SUV scanning "frequencies" for a message from the mysterious hybrid/Vampire duo. It had been over an hour and I was not the only one who was going stir crazy. Some of my other siblings had begun to grapple in the snow.

Suddenly the music stopped. "Merry Christmas, this is Maddy and why are you interrupting my holiday?"

"Because, Maddy, I am looking for Oliver."

You could hear a pin drop on the other line. "Mr. Burke?"

"Ms. Forebush."

"It is about time you called us...well I mean Ollie of course. Let me transfer you to his room."

I cleared my throat. "Why not just hand him the phone?"

"How could I do that?"

"Because I am sure on this lovely holiday that he is next to you since I know for a fact that the two of you are practically living together."

"But...how..." she stuttered.

"Jared can be jealous when it comes to you, my dear."

"That little brat. Hold on a minute, Ollie's right here."

The phone shuffled hands before Oliver's distinct voice came over the line. "It's 'bout time ya called me, son."

"Oliver, I do apologize. I have had a...difficult time these past weeks, but it is no excuse. I know this is just as hard for you."

"Not so bad now since you all are headin' off to git her, right? At least that's what Renee was tellin' me."

"Yes...we simply have no details as of yet. Oliver...I am so sorry."

"Now, now, son, don't be gettin' all sorry. Only time you need to be doin' that is if sumin' else happens to my girl. And that ain't gonna happen, right?"

I sighed. "I hope not, sir. I will be sure she calls you as soon as she is able."

"Ah-yght, but I want a call from you as soon as you have her. Ya hear? None a this waitin' 'til the last minute 'cuz yur afraid a me. I'm just a little ole' man."

"But I feel so…"

"Son."

"I should have…"

"Son!"

"Da!" I replied in a pathetic and panicked tone. "How do I get through this, Da."

My term of endearment had not been used in over three hundred years, but Oliver always brought out these feelings in me. It was a name I called my own father when I was older.

"You don't need help, son. You got everythin' you need inside ya. We all have faith in you and them Warriors. Maddy an I been prayin' all day and we'll keep on doin' so. The only thing that'll getcha in trouble is that head a yours. Be that man I met at my house who had a strong head on his shoulders and was confident as all get out. Now you go find him, and bring me back my girl."

"I will," I replied, taking in a deep breath and trying to shake the demons that had dug their claws in me.

"Da, huh? Is that what I am to ya now?"

I sighed in embarrassment. "It just came out, Oliver, I will not…"

"I like it. Yur my son, I'm yur Da. I'd rather be that than you always callin' me Oliver."

"Yes, Da," I laughed lightly.

"We'll be prayin' and waitin' for calls. I do love ya, son. Good luck."

"Calls are forthcoming. Love to you and Madelyn.

"Take care, son."

"You too. And Da, thank you."

When the line went dead I could hear someone coming up behind me causing me to turn around and see the small frame of Fabiani standing in front of me with Devin a few steps behind.

"I didn't mean to interrupt, but do you have a second?"

"Of course," I replied and placed my phone into one of the many side pockets of my pants. "Has Eris heard anything?"

"Not yet," Fabiani answered lightly. "Actually, I wanted to talk to you about Brianna's reentry."

"Reentry?"

"Cameron, you need to remember that we don't know what she's been told or even what has truly been done to her."

My body began to tense up as I inhaled a slow breath, but Fabiani put his hands up to warn me to stay calm.

"Cameron, you need to have patience."

"Patience with whom?"

"Right now, with me," he laughed, and then changed back to a serious tone. "Listen, I only mean that we do not know what to expect from Brianna because we know so little about what she's been through. She may be hysterical or she may be raging mad or even catatonic. I just want you to be prepared that this may not be the reunion you have been imagining. We all need a little patience and play everything by ear once we see her. But don't worry, I will be there to help you both."

"Thank you, Fabi. Despite Devin's protests I am very glad that you are here."

"Protests! What protests!" Fabiani squealed, losing all of his professional tone causing Devin to glare at me.

While the two of them bickered I saw the one person I was truly hoping to see walking through the snow-covered grass. "Eris!"

"Yes, Warrior, it is time."

Devin instantly put his hand over Fabiani's mouth. "Where is the extraction point?"

"About four hours from here in New Hampshire. There is an opening in a wooded area a few miles from where she is being kept. We are to leave in roughly ten minutes in order to get to the rendezvous no earlier than midnight."

"Why no earlier?" I asked.

"Our Vampire contact will ensure that our entry into the area will be clear."

"What about Brianna?"

"Brianna will be brought to us unharmed between midnight and 1:00am."

Without another word I started walking back to the cars, Devin and Fabiani following in line behind me.

"Devin, tell Connor that once we get close to the extraction site the convoy should leave the vehicles behind and follow us on foot, this many cars will attract attention."

"Yes, Brother."

"Warrior," Eris cried out, "I am not finished."

I dug my heels into the snow and turned quickly around. "What else is there?"

"I have made a deal."

Devin stepped ahead of me. "A deal? A deal with whom?"

"With the Vampire who is helping us."

"It was not your place to make deals…" Devin continued angrily.

"It certainly was my place," Eris shouted back. "My daughter, my connection, my deal."

"It's fine," Fabiani said as he stepped in between the Assassin and the Ancient. "Eris, what is this deal?"

Eris took a moment, allowing his anger to subside slightly. "The Vampire bringing Brianna to us is not to be harmed at any point during the exchange. That is the deal I made. There will be no retaliation against this Vampire, and in return the location of Elaina's current holding area will be revealed to us. Therefore, I expect all your Warriors to abide by this, do we understand? No one will jeopardize getting my daughter back. Understood?"

Fabiani looked each of us in the eye, warning us silently before he answered, "Eris, no one will jeopardize tonight's mission. The deal seems fair, right gentleman?"

"Yes," Devin and I answered together.

Within minutes everyone was packed inside their assigned vehicle, and we were finally on the road, *finally* bringing me closer to my missing angel. While the others in my SUV made small talk, I was praying. More like psychically trying to relay a message - *I am coming, angel. Hold on, my love, I am coming.*

Chapter Forty-Nine

Brianna

"I'm awake, I'm awake," I whined to the tiny babies doing backflips in my stomach. At first their kicking seemed far away, like in a dream, but almost as if a dark veil was being lifted I could feel them moving at an uncomfortable level. When I pushed up from the pillows my stomach growled painfully. It was the first time I had had a late night craving. Lately I had been sleeping so heavily that even when I woke I was still groggy and sluggish. Sitting on the edge of the bed I felt more alert than I had of late. Of course I had only been asleep for an hour and a half, though the dark winter sky made it seem much later than it really was.

"It's only 11:30, kids. Do we round up to say this is a midnight snack?"

The babies continued their bouncing, so much so that I had to run to the bathroom with only a second to spare before I peed my pants. Oh the joys of pregnancy.

Once again my stomach growled loudly when I stepped out of the bathroom. The house seemed stark and cold when I walked into the living room. The combination of the pitch black sky and the bright silver moon reflecting off the snow cast a gray light into the house, taking away its usual warm and comforting charm.

Before going into the kitchen, I peeked out the living room window to see that Aidan's silver pickup truck was still parked in the driveway. At least he hadn't gone for good. It had been a terrible evening; one that exhausted me both emotionally and physically. I really couldn't believe I was awake right now. When my stomach growled yet again I padded into the kitchen and immediately went to the pantry for something salty.

"Pretzels?" There was no response. "Chips?" Still no response, prompting me to dig further into the shelves. "Pretzel chips?"

One side of my stomach started to flutter, so at least one of my babies was happy. As I pulled the box of pretzel chips from the pantry I was hit with the flash of headlights pulling into the driveway. In an instant I fell to my knees, knowing it wasn't Aidan. Quickly I pushed my back up against the kitchen's center island, and opened my mind up to see the area around me. In the direction where the car had pulled in there was one bright white light. Vampire. Shit, shit, shit, shit.

Where was Aidan when I needed him? Could it be Cam changed his mind? He was the only other person who knew I was here. Right?

Too curious for my own good, I crawled around the island and hid in the shadow between it and the sink. I peeked around the edge of the island in order to look through the dining room window and I could see the dome light of the car blink on. Even through the tangled legs of the dining table and chairs I could clearly see the platinum blonde hair of a woman. As she stepped out of the car and shut the driver's side door my stomach sank as I stared upon the one person I feared the most. Elaina.

My bottom lip instantly began to tremble at the sight of her. Several of the windows in the living room and dining room were left cracked at my urging since the fresh air helped with my nausea. Way to go Brianna, now she'll hear your every move.

I scanned the yard once more and to my relief I could see Aidan's milky white halo coming up the hill on the side of the house, walking right toward the driveway. I was about to speak into his head to warn him that Elaina was here, but at the last second I stopped myself. The problem was he wasn't running or charging, he was simply gliding up to the front of the house. He must have heard the car pull in, and there was no way he didn't see her as she stood in front of her car. He did know who she was, didn't he?

But another second later my question was answered as he approached her and said, "Damn woman, it's about time you got here."

"You know I despise when you call me *woman*," Elaina said in her high-pitched voice.

"But Lainey, you are my woman."

In a split second Aidan was standing right in front of Elaina, his hand wrapped around the base of her neck as he pressed her up against the side of the car and kissed her passionately. My mouth dropped open as I tried gasping for air that wouldn't come. Tears flooded my eyes as the taste of bile rose in my throat. Hanging on the cabinet door opposite me was a dishtowel which I grabbed to muffle the sounds of my hysterics at seeing Aidan, a man whose lips had been touching mine only hours before, kissing the woman who wanted me dead and my children to be hers.

What the hell was I going to do? Not in a million years did I see this coming. I was wracking my brain trying to figure out what cues I had missed. When had Aidan betrayed me? Or even Cameron? How far back did the deceit go?

There were so many questions that it was almost impossible to keep them straight with the noises coming from outside. I tried not to watch the two of them grinding up against the car while they tugged at each other's clothing. Finally, Elaina dropped her leg that had been wrapped around Aidan's waist and pushed him gently away.

"Miss me?" she cooed as she brushed her lips lightly on his.

"Oh Lainey, you have no idea," Aidan replied as he tried getting back into her embrace.

But instead she walked around to the passenger's side door and retrieved two bottles from within the car. "So how is the prisoner?"

"As oblivious as ever."

"Madly in love with you yet?" she asked snidely as she placed the two bottles on the hood of the car.

"Almost. Why? Are you jealous?"

"Do you want your delivery or not?" Elaina said and pointed to the bottles on the hood, one of which was clear but was filled with a thick red liquid that looked a lot like blood. "Remember, the clear one is L's, the green one is Gorum's. Green for Gorum. I figured that would be easy enough for your tiny oversexed mind to remember."

Aidan turned on the charm as he walked over to the other side of the car, smiling and pinching at Elaina's sides. "Come on, Lainey, you know how much I've missed you, but this was the plan. Remember?"

"Yes, the plan that you came up with."

"And you agreed to, baby. Now I know you didn't come up here just to deliver my blood, anyone could have done that. You came here because you missed me, too."

Elaina's will weakened when Aidan placed his hands on her hips and leaned his head into the crook of her neck doing things I was glad I couldn't see. When he raised his head, she brought his lips back to hers and off they went again. There was no way I could cross in front of the foyer without them seeing or hearing me. I was screwed.

After several more minutes of making out like teenagers, it was Aidan's turn to remove his lips from Elaina's.

"I am sick of Vampire blood, what do you say we go hunting? There is a town only a few miles away?"

Yes. Leave, damn it. Leave, leave, leave. Agree with him, Elaina. For the love of god, leave with him.

Finally, "But what about *her*?"

"Who, Morgan?" Elaina nodded in annoyance. "I put her to sleep a couple of hours ago. She won't even know we're gone."

"But if I'm delivering blood tonight, that means you're getting close to losing control on her. We can't take the risk, Aidan."

"I'll let you see her if you promise to come hunting with me. You can see for yourself that I still have control."

What? Er...what? And what the hell? But I didn't have time to process anything else once Elaina nodded her head to the agreement and they both turned to walk up the front steps.

Thinking quickly, I slid around the island thanks to my jersey pajama pants and smooth hardwood floor, and crawled to the refrigerator just as I heard their footsteps come up onto the porch. I grabbed the box of pretzel chips from where I dropped them on the floor, and opened the refrigerator doors.

"Morgan!"

I screamed as the pint of ice cream I had just grasped in my hand went flying in the air and splattered on the floor between my feet and Aidan's boots.

"Jesus! You scared the shit out of me!"

"What are you doing up?" he asked angrily as he bent down to pick up the ice cream from the floor and placed it on the island next to us.

"I was hungry," I answered with the biggest doe eyes I could manage. "The babies were kicking me so hard and my stomach started cramping I was so hungry, but I was still half asleep that I don't even remember how I got in here and then I found myself standing in front of the pantry and couldn't decide if I wanted salty or sweet so I started to go for both, hence the chips and the ice cream, and that's when you decided to..."

"Ok, ok, I get it. You were hungry," Aidan interrupted. Finally my diarrhea of the mouth actually did some good. "Now get back to bed."

"Can I take my ice cream?"

"Yes, fine. Take the damn ice cream."

"O-k," I answered nervously and took the pint from his hand. "I just need a spoon."

"Oh for fuck sake, I'll get the spoon, just go."

Without waiting another second I walked to my bedroom, scanning the house and finding Elaina's light positioned in the corner of the front porch. Not wanting Aidan to hear my breath catch, I quickened my steps down the hall.

Just as I began tucking my feet into the bed Aidan came into the room, a spoon extended toward me. "Your spoon, your highness," he said grudgingly and sat on the side of my bed near my feet.

Carefully I took the spoon from his hand, once again trying to hide the fear that was beginning to creep back up to the surface. We sat quietly as I forced spoonful after spoonsful of ice cream into my mouth. It was probably the only time in my life when I didn't enjoy it.

When I finally placed the container on the nightstand, Aidan stood quickly from the bed. "Are you done?"

"Uh…yes."

"Good. Go to sleep, you need your rest."

"Aidan, wait," I said, touching his arm as he went to take the ice cream. "I want to talk to you."

"Morgan, it's late," he growled.

At the same time I could feel a twinge of pain in my head, like a headache about to begin. Was this what he meant by controlling me? Not having the time to figure it out I shook my head and pulled his arm closer to me. "Aidan, please, I'm trying to tell you I'm sorry."

"Sorry for what?"

"For what happened before. Can…can you sit down?"

With a reluctant sigh he sat back down on the bed. "Ok, I'm sitting."

As I placed my hand on top of his, pulling on it to set it in my lap, I said a prayer deep within my soul asking my babies' forgiveness for what I was about to do.

"Aidan, I have only been with two men my entire life. One who abused me, and the other…" I cleared my throat and swallowed down the real emotions that were still raw. "Well, the other who just ripped my heart out of my chest."

"Bri, why are you…"

"I do have feelings for you."

Aidan shook his head as he removed my fingers. "Don't do this. I know you don't mean it."

"Yes I do," I replied and threw the comforter off of me and crawled toward him, placing my hand on his thigh. "I just…I need to take it slow. It's not that I didn't want to kiss you, I did…it's…I got really nervous and Cam is still messing with my head." Aidan shrugged my hand off his leg, and began to rise off the bed when I placed both hands around his face and pulled him back down to me. "Help me forget him."

I closed my eyes when I saw Aidan come towards me, I could only hope that it looked like I was swooning. His lips were uncomfortably cold and his tongue easily slid into my mouth. It took all my strength not to vomit. My stomach was churning, and the babies furiously fluttered inside. Aidan's fingers reached up to my face and then combed deeply into my scalp, bending my head back to expose my neck.

My heart started to beat wildly at the thought that his fangs would pierce me, but instead his cool tongue licked up the side of my neck before he brought my face back to his. I tried to look aroused, though I most likely looked like I was having a seizure. He slipped his fingers underneath the thin strap of my camisole top, pulling it down off of my shoulder. This was my test, I could see it in his eyes. He was skeptical about why I was in the kitchen and was probably worried about why he was unable to "control" me. If the plan was for me to fall in love with him, I had to convince him even if my body was completely revolted by the idea.

Placing my hand on top of his, I pulled my camisole down further, exposing my breast to him. As he cupped it with his hand, he squeezed it tightly, once again looking for a reaction. With my heart practically beating out of my chest, I brought his head down to my chest. Aidan wrapped his arms around my back as he took my breast into his mouth and laid me down onto the bed. I stared at the ceiling while he groped and sucked on me, finding the numbing solace I hadn't escaped to since I was with Sam.

The numbness in my brain was finally traveling down my body, although I could still feel the babies moving inside me. I turned my head to allow the pillow to catch the tear that was leaking from my eye while Aidan continued what he must have assumed was pleasuring me. Eventually he relinquished his attack on my chest and stretched himself long ways against my side as he pressed his lips firmly on top of mine, forcing his tongue roughly inside. His hand moved away from my breast, gliding his fingers in tiny circles across the top of my stomach, caressing my babies in such a way that I could feel my blood rising within. I was reaching my limit.

While he continued thrusting his tongue inside my mouth, his fingers traveled down to the base of my stomach, playfully tugging at the waistband of my pajama bottoms. Just as his fingers slid underneath my pants I reacted by grabbing his wrist and pulling my lips away.

"Slow, remember?" I said through labored breath.

Thankfully he nodded, kissing me lightly on the nose. "We have time. We have lots of time."

I smiled and grazed his cheek with my fingers though I felt that at any moment I would be sick. With another kiss, Aidan lifted my camisole back into its proper place and raised the comforter for me to get inside. Once tucked in, I rolled onto my side and tried to withhold the shiver going through my body when he draped himself over me.

"You need to sleep now, ok?"

"Mm-hmm," I answered sleepily and tucked the pillows underneath my head. "You'll stay with me?"

"I'm not going anywhere," he replied as he petted my hair and kissed my bare shoulder. "Goodnight, Morgan."

"Goodnight, Aidan."

As I closed my eyes I could feel the same sharp pain begin to tug at the edges in my head. Though I was still very conscious, it seemed like the thick sluggish veil was being placed back over me. What made me even more nervous was when I heard the French doors creak open and Elaina's light appeared on the other side.

"Elaina!" Aidan whispered. "You can't be in here."

"Why? So that I don't see what you're doing with her?"

"Lainey, cut it out. She threw herself at me, what was I supposed to do? It was hard to keep her hands off of me. You know I hate having to do this."

Lying sack of shit.

I could hear Elaina's heels clicking on the hardwood floor as she walked around to my side of the bed. "Oh I am sure this must be so difficult for you."

Aidan stretched his arm across my body and pulled her down to him. "Baby, you know you are the only woman for me."

"Because I'm the only one who'll put up with you."

"And vice versa," Aidan replied, his tone changing quickly.

The bed rocked as they kissed across me. I realized now I was in hell.

That's where I was, lying in hell while two devils made out over me.

Finally the heavy breathing stopped and Elaina said, "I want you."

"I want you too, baby."

Oh good god.

"Take me right here. Right next to her."

Please don't. There's no way I won't throw up.

"I need real blood first, baby."

"No."

"Elaina…"

"Aidan, she already woke up once."

"She woke up because the brats inside her got hungry. She's eaten, and now she's sleeping. She won't wake up while we're gone and I promise that when we get back I will fuck your brains out right on this bed. Come on, baby."

"I want proof she won't wake up."

What? Breathe, Brianna, breathe.

"Fine," Aidan answered as he took my arm, bringing my wrist to his mouth. With a soft click I knew he had extended his fangs and quickly realized what his proof would be. I clamped my jaw shut a second before his fangs sunk into my wrist and he began drinking from me. When I didn't stir he removed my wrist from his mouth, but Elaina grabbed my arm and licked the wounds shut.

"Mmm, just as sweet as I remember."

"Do you have your proof? Can we go now?"

"You have security?"

"Don't I always?"

Elaina sighed as she said, "Fine." Just then my face was shadowed by her thick blonde hair as she leaned into my ear and whispered, "I hope my voice haunts your dreams and you can hear me as I tell you that I have won. You are mine now, and soon enough even Seraphina will join you up on my wall and no one, including your pitiful father, can do anything about it."

My blood ran cold at the sound of my stepmother's name coming from Elaina's lips. I suddenly realized that by opening up to Aidan over the past months I had inadvertently told Elaina how to find Sera. Oh my god, what have I done? What else did I divulge? Who else did I screw over?

As if I wasn't struggling enough with the situation, Elaina began pulling back at the comforter and shifted herself from my face to my stomach, lightly scratching her sharp nails across my skin. The babies instantly began to kick and I could feel the heat rising from inside which meant that at any moment Elaina could go flying across the room.

Please stay calm, I urged my babies. Though I was scared shitless I knew she wouldn't hurt me, at least not yet. Elaina needed me. She needed me to carry these babies a little while longer. Don't Push her my little ones, she's almost gone.

"Hello my little darlings," Elaina cooed as she brushed her face against my stomach. "It's your Mama Lainey. We will meet each other soon."

"Yeah, unfortunately," Aidan scoffed. "Ready?"

I had to bite the inside corners of my cheeks as Elaina placed the comforter back over me and her heels clicked back around toward the French doors. A second later the door creaked shut and the room fell silent. I followed the white lights as they ran from the house and faded away in the distance. When I couldn't hold my breath any longer I began gasping for air and sobbed into my pillow. My hands instantly began rubbing my belly, feeling the babies fluttering wildly inside.

Ok, now count to one hundred and keep searching for their lights, a voice shouted in my head. They could turn around any second and I needed to calm down in order to think of a real plan. One, two, three…

"She is not your mother," I whispered to my babies as the pain in my head began fade. "I will always be your mother." Four, five, six, seven. "She will never get her hands on you. Never!"

Eight, nine, ten…

Chapter Fifty

Brianna

So I only got to thirty-two before I couldn't stand it any longer. Bonnie and Clyde, a.k.a Elaina and Aidan, hadn't come back and I was crawling out of my skin lying in the bed. I dressed warmly, though cursed my belly for not fitting inside my coat any longer. The last few minutes had been filled with silent panic as I raced through the house looking for a phone that worked, but none of them had a dial tone. Even Daddy O's two-way radio down to the neighborhood boys didn't have a power cord. Just more to add to the list of things I didn't notice.

The only things I was leaving with were my daggers and the harness. I couldn't afford to bring anything that could drag me down, who knew what I would run into. But this time I wasn't leaving behind just stuff. I was leaving Daddy O and family keepsakes without a guess of when I'd return.

I shook my head, knocking out the emotions that could get me and my babies killed. Ok Bri, now get your head on straight and start thinking like a Warrior. Aidan and Elaina had fled down the main side of the mountain where the neighborhood boys lived, so they were out of the question. The Miller's tree farm was only a mile or so south. The distance would be tough with the snow, but there was really no other choice since Aidan's keys were nowhere to be found. After grabbing my hat, gloves, and wrapping a scarf around my neck, I walked through the kitchen and into the laundry room. Before opening the door to the outside, I scanned the area one more time looking for any Vampires in the area and thankfully found none.

The bitter mountain air hit my face the minute I opened the back door.

This would be brutal, and was probably the stupidest thing I could do but I couldn't wait here in the house like a sitting duck. When another cold wind whipped around the back deck, my feet pushed me forward to grab hold of the railing as I slowly made my way down the steep deck stairs.

I was only halfway down when my eyes were met with a young dark-haired man who came around the side of the house, his eyes widening at the sight of me. What frightened me was that his black eyes, pale skin, and absence of a jacket over his short sleeved shirt made me think Vampire, but he had no white halo around his head. What was he? And how in the hell was I going to get around him?

As he stepped up on the first step I drew one of my daggers and held it firmly in front of me. Instantly the young man held his hands up.

"Ok, ok, let's just calm down and get you back inside," he said evenly as he took another step up.

"Don't take another step," I shouted and jabbed my dagger out in front of me. "I am not afraid to defend myself."

"Look, just go back inside and we'll forget that this ever happened."

He took another step up and I jabbed my dagger at him again.

"I am not going back into that house. Now why don't you step back and forget you ever saw me."

"I'm afraid I can't do that. You are going back inside and I will use force if I have to."

A woman began laughing from the side of the house. "No you won't," she said mockingly as she revealed herself. "You have a direct order not to harm Brianna Morgan, so really she's going to call your bluff."

"Jazlyn, what are you doing here?" the young Vampire asked, and I was thinking the same exact thing. The ex-Warrior stood at the base of the stairs, a white skintight patent leather jumpsuit zipped tight up to her neck. With the exception of the lack of exposed skin, it was interesting to see that Jazlyn's affiliation with Elaina hadn't changed her sense of style. Even more interesting was the fact that she too did not have a bright white halo, and I knew for a fact that she was a Vampire. Had my powers stopped working in the last hour?

Jazlyn pushed the young man aside as she came up the stairs toward me. "I am here to check on the prisoner of course. Me and Brianna go way back, don't we?"

"Get away from me," I growled, almost losing my balance on the stairs and having to stabilize myself with the railing.

"What, no hug?" Jazlyn replied as she pouted condescendingly.

"Ok, enough of this," the young Vampire interrupted. "I'm calling Aidan."

Jazlyn whipped around to face him. "Oh no you don't. Elaina specifically said they were not to be disturbed this evening."

"Well I work for Aidan, and he said to alert him if anything happened."

"You may work for Aidan, but Aidan works for Elaina and I am her second in command. So that means when they're not here, you work for me. Now stand down," she growled and turned back to me.

From over her shoulder I could see the other Vampire remove a phone from his pocket. "Screw you and your power trip. I'm calling Aidan."

Jazlyn rolled her eyes and she sighed loudly. "Don't say I didn't warn you."

"Warn me about what?"

Jazlyn crushed her right hand around mine and thrust my arm forward, guiding my dagger around and straight across the Vampire's throat. His body fell onto the stairs and slid down to the ground, splattering the bright white snow with dark crimson blood. Jazlyn finally released my hand and instantly it began throbbing. Jazlyn followed me as I staggered backwards up the stairs trying desperately to Push her as hard as I could but there was no reaction whatsoever.

"Stay away from me!" I shouted as my back pressed up against the house and tried Pushing her once more.

This time the corners of Jazlyn's eyes twitched. "Trying to do your little parlor trick?" I bit my lip to get it to stop quivering as Jazlyn hovered over me, the tip of her nose rubbing lightly against my cheek. "It. Won't. Work."

"Why not?" I asked stupidly.

Jazlyn straightened her posture. "You showed all your cards that day at the manor. Elaina may be evil but she isn't stupid. But apparently you are since you seem to have no idea what I'm talking about." I shook my head. "During the battle at the manor you took down the Vampires, and only the Vampires. With that little tidbit, and everything else you decided to spill to Aidan about your gift, you gave Elaina basically everything she needed in order to protect us against you."

"H-how?"

"Hybrid blood. Everyone who is to be close or come in contact with you must be given large amounts of hybrid blood. Seems to have worked so far," she said tapping her temple.

"But I could P-push Aidan."

Jazlyn rolled her eyes. "Aidan's a whole different story, which I don't have time for. Now come on, we have to get going."

"Going? So you can turn around and kill me yourself?"

"I came here to take you to your father."

"Bullshit. This is another trick," I said as I held my dagger back up in front of me.

Jazlyn took my right hand once again and crushed it while bending it backwards and this time making my dagger fall into the snow on the deck.

"If I wanted to kill you, I would have already. You need to trust me."

"Why should I believe you? You're the one who led Elaina straight to me. You betrayed your own family, why the hell would you help me now?"

"Because I am not who you think I am."

"W-what did you say?"

Her statement slapped me in the face, especially since I had been used to hearing it come from Cameron's mouth in my dreams. She had even almost broken my hand like I had seen so many times.

"I am not the evil person everyone thinks I am. I made a mistake and I am trying to make it right," she answered angrily as she looked at her watch. "I am running out of time to get you to your father before he starts charging through the woods and ruins everything." When I didn't move she bent down and picked my dagger up from where it had fallen, letting it sear the skin on her hand as she handed it to me. "Please."

Watching as whispers of smoke continued to rise from her hand, I pulled my hat further down over my ears and took the dagger from her, wiping it clean with my glove before sliding it back in its holster. "You'll need to help me."

I barely had enough time to wrap my arms around Jazlyn's neck before she scooped me up and jumped over the deck railing, landing quietly on the ground below. The wind felt like sheets of ice slicing my skin away layer by layer as Jazlyn raced into the woods.

"Where are we going?"

"Shh!" she snapped, but then whispered, "We have to get past the perimeter guards first. Tell me when you can see them."

"But...I thought you said everyone had hybrid blood."

"Only those who were close to you, not the perimeter guards since they're deep in the woods, though they're probably closing in on us now. Have you ever tested how far you can see Vamps?" I shook my head and she rolled her eyes. "Stupid brother. Even Elaina has tested you more than my fam…the Warriors have. Just whisper when you see them, otherwise we won't have surprise on our side."

"Well if you hadn't taken the hybrid blood, I wouldn't have to whisper at all."

"Do you see them yet?" she asked annoyed as she continued to glide over the snow, barely leaving footprints.

I closed my eyes and instantly saw three bright lights converging on us. "They're coming, three of them," I whispered as I pointed in their directions.

Jazlyn nodded and kicked her speed up a gear, angling our direction toward the furthest Vampire. She nuzzled her mouth near my ear, "Are they following?" I paused, but then nodded as the three lights stopped and then changed direction. "Tell me when they're close."

We continued are trajectory and the Vampires were catching up quickly. When I could see their lights in the distance with my eyes opened, I nudged Jazlyn and once again indicated their position. Carefully she lowered me down in front of a thick oak tree. "Stay."

Without waiting for an answer, Jazlyn sprinted ahead a few yards and darted up a tree without making a sound. Then, we waited. It was awful. I stood behind my tree, dagger drawn and watched the Vampires slowly come closer. Finally the Vampires were within several feet of where Jazlyn was located. This of course was the precise moment a stick decided to break underneath my foot.

Suddenly the three Vampires changed their direction to come toward me. Jazlyn saw their sudden change and proceeded to kick a large branch down from her position in the tree, causing it to crash loudly on the ground below.

"Up in the trees!" one of them yelled, but only two of them went in Jazlyn's direction, the other staying in a path towards me.

Just as the two Vampires approached Jazlyn's location, she leapt from her position, tackling them from above like a white flying squirrel. However, my concern couldn't be with them, but with the third Vampire that was steadily getting closer.

The Vampire made a wide circle in front of me, and for a minute I thought that perhaps he would miss me altogether. Oh, but of course my stellar luck had to come into play. He was standing only a few feet away when one of the Vampires battling with Jazlyn howled in pain causing my Vampire to look in that direction and find me crouched down. He showed his fangs as he hissed and ran in my direction.

Instantly my stomach started to burn on one side where one of my babies began kicking. Apparently he or she wanted to help. Flipping my dagger to hold it by its blade, I whipped it at the Vampire while pulling his light forward to ensure it hit him. Underestimating my strength, the Vampire not only got pulled into my flying dagger but flew into me, knocking me backwards into the thick tree. The collision knocked the breath out of me and I panicked over the babies' safety. Instantly the Vampire's hands went for my throat. Why did they always go for the throat?

I grabbed at his hands in a panic, but knew it was pointless. My dagger still stuck out from the middle of his chest, so I pushed it in further to his responding agonizing screams. His distraction was enough time for me to grab the dagger in the lower holster, however, he caught my arm as I swung it around and thrust it against the tree causing the dagger to fall to the ground.

My head already ached with fatigue, but the fire in my stomach felt as though it would burn a hole from the inside out. Having no other defenses, I placed one hand around the Vampire's neck, the other flat against his face, and Pushed. I groaned through clenched teeth as I put all my energy behind keeping his light in front of me while my power fed through my fingers. His skin burned underneath my palms making him release my throat and pull at my wrists. The more skin he touched, the more he burned.

The burning in my stomach began to work its way up my chest, and I knew from experience that this would be the extra burst of energy I needed. As the burning came up my throat, I breathed deeply into it and exhaled all the power within me. A wave of energy came out of me and down through my arms and fingers causing the skin of the Vampire's neck to tear away. With one last Push, I pulled at his light, stretching it past his shoulders until his skin finally gave way and his head ripped away from his body.

Immediately I dropped his head in the snow, unable to stop his body from slumping against my chest and sliding down my stomach, streaking my white coat with his blood. The weight of his body caused my knees to buckle and fall into the snow as well. From behind me I could see a white form moving towards me. I never thought I'd be happy to see Jazlyn.

"Get him off of me," I pleaded as the babies kicked uncomfortably within me.

Jazlyn obliged and pulled the Vamp's body to the ground and rolled him over onto his back. "Do you want the dagger?"

I nodded as she helped me to stand and then bent over to pull the dagger out of the dead Vamp's chest. Jazlyn didn't make me scour the ground for the other one, but instead burned her hand on the rounded silver hand and tossed it in my direction. I grabbed it from the air and slid both daggers into my harness. Seriously, I was the biggest badass pregnant lady there ever was. The thought of which, must have made me pose.

"Are you through?" Jazlyn said snidely.

"I literally just ripped a Vamp's head off with my bare hands. Can't I have one moment?"

"No," she replied plainly and looked at her watch again. "Come on, we only have twenty minutes."

A second later I was scooped up once again and we were running through the woods, but at a slightly slower rate from my fear of the babies being jostled more than they already had been. After only a few yards I asked, "What made you realize your mistake?"

The corners of Jazlyn's lips tightened before she answered, "Elaina started experimenting on kids."

"What? When?"

"The last few months. She even turned one of her warehouses into a full-fledged medical research lab not too far from here."

"Near here!"

"It's relatively new," she interrupted, completely ignoring the fact that I was freaked out by the fact that Elaina had an establishment so close to my grandfather's home. "She began targeting hybrid women who already had children. But it wasn't until Aidan told us that your babies were showing abilities from the womb that she started breeding. Between that and seeing what she's been doing to the children, I realized I needed to do something."

"Now you realized?" I said angrily. "It wasn't when she started killing and torturing hybrids? Not when her cronies invaded the manor and Jared almost died? It's ok for Elaina to kidnap me and endanger *my* kids, but she starts hurting others' and you grow a conscience? Christ, you turned on your own family for what? A title from a sociopath?"

"Look," she began and stopped in her tracks, "my maker, *my family*, didn't give a shit about me. For three hundred and twenty-five years Victor barely gave me the time of day. Everyone always joked that Cameron was his one mistake, but Victor treated me as though I was. No matter what I did, Victor ignored me, and my family disrespected me. Elaina gave me what I needed. She made me feel wanted, she gave me a purpose. And yes, her methods are vicious, but we know more about hybrids now and what they're capable of because of her."

"That's the biggest copout I've ever heard. You are just as bad as she is."

Jazlyn placed my feet on the ground and turned her back on me while she tugged on her long hair in frustration. "I am doing what I can to fix this, don't you see that? The minute I decided to help you I put a price on my head. Every time I contacted your father I not only put my life in jeopardy, but the life of the hybrid that was willing to help me. The longer I stay alive, the longer I have to tear apart Elaina's organization from the inside." She whipped around to face me, "I am not the person my family thinks I am. If Elaina finds out what I am doing I'm dead, and I am ok with that. In the end I want my father to know whose side I was really on in the end."

For the first time in my life, I felt sorry for Jazlyn. The thought was so foreign.

"I promise he'll know."

"I doubt Father will even believe you," she replied as she picked me up once again and began running.

My lips were unbelievably numb, but I still managed to say, "I'll make sure he listens. Even Cam said..." I cleared my throat, "even he said you had a caring side. Like that time you stayed with him when those people raided Victor's home."

"I'm surprised he even remembers that."

"Yeah, well he does. Even though the bastard seems to have forgotten about everything else."

Jazlyn looked down at me, squinting her eyes in confusion. "Brianna, I don't know all you were told or exposed to down here, but just know that not everything is what it seems."

It was the second time Jazlyn had spoken familiar words to me and once again I thought about how my dreams had mislead me. For once couldn't they just spill everything out and the people that will really say things to me truly say them! My head ached enough, I didn't want to have to drudge through past dreams which I thankfully haven't had in months. "Put me down."

"What?"

"Please just put me down," I said raising my voice and kicking my legs. With only a loud sigh Jazlyn placed me down on the ground where I instantly began to pace and take in deep breaths even though the frigid air made my lungs sting. "Sorry, I just need a second."

"It's fine, we're only a few miles away. Can you see your father? He should be up in that direction," Jazlyn said as she pointed straight ahead.

I closed my eyes and my head pounded in protest as I stretched my mind in the area ahead of me. It didn't take long to see the massive white glow in the distance and as I opened my eyes it almost looked like there was a sports arena in the distance.

"Were you expecting just my father?"

Jazlyn's eyes widened, her fingers tangling themselves in her hair. "Hope was more like it. How many are there?"

I shrugged. "I won't know until we get past that hill, but it looks like a lot."

Jazlyn sighed as she closed her eyes while worry and fear crossed her face. "Let's just hope your father is a man of his word."

"Huh?" I asked but she didn't answer as she scooped me up once again and ran quickly over the hill bringing us only a mile or so away from the bright white Vampire lights.

"Can you see them now?" she asked softly, fear still evident in her voice.

I nodded as I noticed one light brighter than all the others standing in front of the crowd. From the brightness of the light alone I knew it was my father. "I can see my dad, but there's probably another fifteen or twenty behind him."

Jazlyn cursed under her breath as she continued forward. "Tell your father you're here."

I nodded and focused on the brightest light in the crowd. *Daddy?*

"She is here!" I heard my father shout.

Jazlyn slowed our progression when we were roughly fifty feet away and lowered me to the ground behind another wide tree.

"Shit!" she whispered as she looked around the tree.

"What?"

"They are all Warriors. He even brought Devin! There's no way I am getting out of here alive."

"Look, if my father made a deal with you…"

"Sorry to have to do this, Brianna."

"Do what?" I asked as she stepped forward and then disappeared behind me, crooking her elbow around my neck and pushing the tip of a small knife into my back.

"You are my insurance policy. I won't hurt you as long as they don't hurt me. Understood?"

"Ye-yes," I stuttered.

"Tell them we are coming out."

Dad, we're coming out. Nobody move.

Jazlyn and I stumbled forward over the snow and uprooted branches hidden underneath. I could hear grumblings from the opening in the woods ahead. A few moments later I could see the face of my father, his hair tied back as usual although he was wearing a black Warrior's uniform instead of the linen shirt and pants I was used to. My heart grew just seeing him. Unfortunately my joy was short lived as Jazlyn pushed me fully out in the open and I saw Cameron standing just behind Eris.

"What the hell are you doing here?" I asked nastily. But my statement was ignored by all when they realized it was Jazlyn holding me and every Warrior around us flinched forward.

"Do not move!" Jazlyn screamed as she moved her knife from my back and held it against my stomach. "Eris, we had a deal."

"Yes we did," Eris nodded and held Cameron back by the chest, although Devin was still gliding forward. "Warrior, you promised to keep your men in line."

"You did not tell us you made the deal with Jazlyn!" Cameron shouted.

"I told you I did not have a name. Regardless, I made my deal and you agreed to it."

"But she is the one who betrayed our coven and brought Elaina to Brianna in the first place. Devin has the authority to kill her on sight. That makes your deal moot."

"No it's not!" I screamed, pulling Jazlyn's elbow completely from my neck and causing all the Warriors, including Cameron to stare at me with wide eyes. "You have no idea what Jazlyn's gone through to get me here and the dangers she faces when she returns. If anyone jumps out of line I swear I will Push you so hard you won't know your own name! Besides, my father keeps his word," I said and then glared at Cameron. "Unlike some people."

Cameron's face scrunched up in shock as his mouth opened to say something, but Eris said, "My daughter is right. I am a man of my word, however, the deal was to return her unharmed," he said pointing at my abdomen which I realized was covered in blood.

"It's not mine!" I shouted. "Jazlyn protected me, I swear. Now tell them about where Elaina's holding the kids." Jazlyn didn't answer, still on the defensive with her former brothers surrounding her. "Jazlyn!" I shouted over my shoulder, shaking her to attention and whispering, "Show them you are more than they think you are."

Slowly Jazlyn lowered the knife from my belly, but still kept me as a shield. "Elaina has built a medical plant seventeen miles northeast of here. Their guard is weak on the east side because it is the only side of the building without an entry. The wall is only made up of cinderblocks, so nothing that Alex can't break through," she said with a slight smile that wasn't returned.

"Where was Brianna kept?" Cameron asked.

"You've forgotten already?" I asked angrily. Cameron flinched his head back and blinked several times before looking behind him at a shrugging Jared.

"What about Elaina?" Devin asked as he came to stand next to Cameron.

"She is in the woods somewhere hunting with Aidan, but I do not have a precise location or when she'll return."

"Do not think that Eris's deal holds after you step into those woods. If we come across your path, we will not restrain ourselves."

"You will have to catch me first," she replied and then was a whisper of wind disappearing in the woods behind me.

Only another second past before I ran to my father's arms, my stomach of course getting in the way, but it didn't stop his kisses on my cheeks and forehead before squeezing me tightly against him. I had only known I was truly in danger for a little over an hour, but as he held me I found myself weeping in his arms. While he gently rubbed my back, I felt another set of hands caress my arm and begin petting my hair. I looked up from my father's chest to see Cameron standing next to me, looking pleadingly into my eyes and smiling.

"Don't touch me," I snapped and smacked his hands away from me. Cameron backed away with shock plastered on his face.

"Bri, what is wrong?" he asked weakly, looking awkwardly around at the Warriors surrounding us.

"Like you don't know? What are you doing here anyway? Is it out of guilt? Did my father threaten you or something?"

"Love, I do not know what…"

"I don't want to hear it!" I shouted and pushed past him. "Dad, can we get out of here? Please!"

"Y-yes, of course. This way," Eris said and directed me toward an SUV where Kyla stood with a nervous looking Dr. John. "Vlad has heated the vehicle for you, and Cameron and I will escort you back home."

"I'm not going anywhere with him," I yelled. Eris stopped, surprised by my statement which seemed odd since he must have known what Cameron had done. Didn't he? I even looked around at the other Warriors, seeing Jared and Alex looking at me with peculiar expressions.

When I looked back at my father, he had nothing but confusion on his face while Cameron pressed his lips firmly together, his fists clenching. What was his problem? Finally, a short, thin Vampire came to stand in front of me.

"Brianna, do you remember me?"

"Only Fabi Fabulous could get away with making the Warrior uniform look that good."

He smiled and took my hand, taking the lead of bringing me to the SUV a few feet away. Kyla didn't wait another second before she came barreling towards me, almost knocking me over as she hugged me tightly. When she finally released me, she and Fabi placed their arms around my shoulders, directing me to where Dr. John was standing.

"You did say the blood wasn't yours, right?" Dr. John asked, looking nervously down at my coat.

"Oh for heaven's sake," I said while taking my coat off and throwing it on the ground. "It isn't mine. I'm fine."

"Let me be the judge," he replied as he took a pin light from his pocket and began waving it in front of my eyes. "How have you been feeling? Any...unusual symptoms? Illnesses?"

"John, come on, I'm fine, just cold," I responded annoyed as he began feeling the glands in my throat.

"Brianna, let him check you over," Cameron said as he came to stand in front of the truck's opened passenger door.

"Seriously, why do you care?"

"Why would I not care?" he replied angrily, causing Fabi to place a hand on his shoulder.

"So you're choosing to care about me now? Performing in front of the family, is that it? Just go, I know you don't want to be here."

"I am not moving until John checks you over."

"Well I'm telling you I don't want you here."

"Ok, enough you two," Dr. John said and tugged my chin back in his direction. "Bri, answer my questions please. Any headaches, unusual nausea, cramping, back pain? Anything out of the ordinary?"

Still panting with anger I finally answered, "A few nosebleeds and some really bad headaches. But I feel fine, just really tired."

"Eris, I want to take her to the nearest hospital so they can do a full work up."

Eris nodded and everyone began to disperse when I put my arms up. "Wait, wait, no. I'm not going to a hospital. John, I'm fine."

Dr. John sighed as he pursed his lips. "Brianna, will there ever be a day where you will let me be your doctor?"

"Not when there are children and hybrids that need your help more than I do. That's where you need to go."

Dr. John looked over my shoulder. "Cameron? I'll do whatever you want me to do."

I placed one hand on Dr. John's chest. "You're going up there to help those kids and I'm getting in this truck and going home. That's what we're doing. Do we all understand?"

Everyone nodded slowly, including Dr. John, prompting me to get into the SUV where heat was coming full blast through the vents. My father came around to the other side of the truck and sat next to me while Vlad sat waiting behind the steering wheel.

"John," Cameron said plainly, "you will stay here while we invade the compound, then we will have someone bring you up to help as needed. Fabi and Kyla, can you also escort Brianna home?"

I sat in the backseat of the truck while Cameron spoke, using the rest of the energy I had not to breakdown in front of him and keep my eyes forward. I was suddenly so tired that my anger was fading and all the raw emotions I had suppressed for over a week were coming back up and it was painful.

Kyla climbed into the front passenger seat while Fabi filed into the third row behind me. I was still focusing on looking out the windshield when I suddenly felt a cool hand resting on top of mine. Slowly I turned my head to see Cameron leaning into the truck as he gently squeezed my hand.

"Whatever your feelings are about me, I love you, Brianna. I will see you at home."

"Why are you doing this to me?" I asked as a lump rose in my throat.

Cameron paused, and then kissed my temple as he said, "I do not wish to cause you any pain, my angel."

A second later he shut the door causing Kyla to swing around in her seat. "Brianna Morgan, what the hell is the matter…"

"Kyla," Fabi interrupted, "give her some time."

Kyla huffed and turned back in her seat.

"Can we please just get out of here?" I begged while leaning forward and squeezing Vlad's shoulder.

"Certainly," Vlad answered cheerfully and put the truck in gear. "I told you all you had to do was call me and I would take you home."

My nose tingled with oncoming tears. "You're a bit late."

"So are you," he chided as he looked in the rearview mirror.

I turned to face my father. "Where are we really going?"

"To your home, daughter. Where else?"

"My home? What home?"

Eris scrunched his brows together. "In Boston, my darling. Your home in Boston."

"There is no way I can survive a fourteen hour drive." Everyone in the car turned and looked at me, Vlad even slowed the car and looked in the rearview mirror. "What? Why is everyone looking at me like I have lost my mind? I'm pregnant, tired, killed two Vampires, have a headache, hormonal, pregnant, tired, and did I mention tired?"

"I do not..." Eris began but was interrupted by Fabi who placed a hand on his shoulder.

"Eris, I am sure you planned in stops along the way. There is no issue in stopping overnight if Brianna needs it. Correct?"

I could see that Fabi was leading my father, but I couldn't understand why. Nothing about this evening seemed to be clicking.

"Of...of course not?" my father stuttered. "I mean yes, of course we can stop when you need to. Vlad, carry on please. The sooner we get home the better."

Vlad obliged by speeding out of the field and through the bumpy dirt road that eventually turned into pavement within minutes. About that time, Kyla Projected herself next to me, and I melted into her arms.

"Dad, just put me to sleep, ok. And keep the dreams away. I don't need to see more horrible things than I already have tonight."

He nodded as he brushed my cheek. "I will, my darling. But soon we will need to..."

"Tomorrow. We can talk about everything tomorrow." Or the next day, or the day after that.

Chapter Fifty-One

Cameron

As I watched Brianna's SUV pull away I wanted to thrust my fist into my chest and pull out my heart. Perhaps I could even get Jared to break my leg again. Even though Fabiani had warned me, never could I have imagined my reunion with Brianna would have been this bad, and there was obviously no time for an explanation. Not that Bri would have given me one I am sure. She seemed convinced I knew so much more than I did.

When the brake lights of the SUV were halfway across the field I turned toward the crowd of Warriors listening intently to Devin's instructions about raiding Elaina's new base of operations. When I came to stand next to him he paused for a spilt second, seemingly surprised that I was still here, however, not as much as I.

"Anything to add, Brother?" he asked in a guarded tone.

I nodded. "Jared and Connor, you two are coming with me. We are going to check out where Brianna was held. Brother, you can contact us once you have overtaken the compound and we can meet up there."

"Very well," he replied while the other Warriors looked at us. "Is there a reason all of you are standing around?"

A dozen Warriors startled to attention, and scurried to gather in their assigned groups.

Devin squeezed my shoulder once again as he said, "Be vigilant."

"Be strong," I replied.

"And unleash the fury of the Warrior inside of you."

"Dad says it better," Jared said as he came to stand with us.

"We'll work on it," Devin said annoyed and then punched Jared in the shoulder before walking away.

"Ow! Why am I always the one getting hit? This is brother abuse and I'm not gonna take it anymore. When a Vamp says no, he means no." Jared looked for a laugh, but none came. "Ok, yo Connor! Let's go!"

A second later Connor was jogging in our direction and patting me on the back. "You ok, man?"

"Hardly," I replied honestly. "Please tell me you have your lucky ear."

Connor smiled wickedly, reached into his pocket, and pulled out a shriveled ear that he had ripped off one of Elaina's Vampires. "Of course I do. It's starting to smell, though."

"Shit man," Jared said looking at Connor in disgust and holding his nose. "Throw that thing away. It smells like ass."

"More like ear," Connor teased causing the two of them to laugh until they saw my scowl. "Sorry, Cameron. Do you know where we're going?"

I shook my head. "No. I was planning on following Brianna's and Jazlyn's scent through the woods and see where it takes us."

"And what'll we do once we get there?"

"Hopefully kill Elaina and Aidan."

"Awesome!" Jared shouted as I began walking toward the woods with him and Connor in tow. When our running was at a full gait Jared came up next to me as he asked, "So what was up with Beebs?"

I simply shook my head and then banked to the left as the scent changed direction.

"How can you piss off a woman when you haven't seen her for weeks?"

"Can we not talk about it right now," I snapped and began to run ahead of him.

The woods whipped past while snow dusted up behind us as we followed the zigzagging pattern Jazlyn had traveled. Roughly ten miles in, the wind brought with it a smell we all knew too well.

"Is that Vamp blood?" Connor asked from behind me.

"I believe so," I replied as a stronger wave of the sickly sweet smell hit me. Quickly we came upon two dismembered Vampires, limbs scattered crudely in the surrounding snow staining the ground dark crimson red. While Jared and Connor surveyed the scene I followed the smell a few feet forward to where a third Vampire laid, his head crudely ripped from his body.

I could hear my brothers coming towards me as I tilted the dead

Vampire's head in my direction, stunned by the burns on his face.

"What happened to him?" Jared asked as he knelt down opposite me.

"I think this is Brianna's work."

"Dude! Since when is she able to do that?"

"If she touches you while she Pushes it can burn your skin."

"Yeah, but it looks like she ripped his head off."

"Or Pushed his head off. I am assuming this is the blood that was on her coat."

"So even though she's preggers, she's still a kickass Warrior," he laughed proudly.

"I do not see the humor, little brother," I growled, causing his face to drop. "She could have injured herself, or worse the babies."

"Buuut...she didn't. Now come on..." he began, but both of us stood quickly, ears perked as shouts came in the distance. Not even a second passed before Connor was next to me and the three of us were once again running at full speed, being careful to keep our approach as silent as possible.

Less than two minutes later we were standing several feet away from an opening where a lonely house rose from a steep slope, and where a thin female Vampire dressed in a white jumpsuit stood at the edge of the woods with her back turned in our direction. We did not need to see her face to know it was our traitor sister, though now she seemed more like a double agent which in itself caused me some internal turmoil.

Just past Jazlyn, midway up the back lawn was Elaina looking like a referee between Jazlyn and Aidan who stood above on the back deck of the house. The sight of him made me flinch, making Jared clamp down on my arm and then point across me to two other Vampires coming around the corner of the house.

"Do not blame this on me, Aidan!" Jazlyn shouted. "You had only one guard on her! Even a child could have gotten away from that pitiful excuse of a Vampire."

"For all we know you unlocked the door!" Aidan shouted accusingly in return.

"I believe it was *your* idea to leave the house, Aidan, so perhaps you wanted to let her escape."

"Stop it, both of you!" Elaina yelled back. "We need to stop blaming each other and find her! She couldn't have gone far. Now Aidan where could she have gone?"

"I can sense she went through the woods. That way," Aidan said as he pointed straight in our direction. It was time to act, and fast.

I pointed to Connor and then to the two unknown Vampires, and he nodded. Next I pointed to Jared and then to Elaina, to which he flinched, surprised I would give him the queen. But I wanted Aidan. Jared then pointed to Jazlyn and I paused for a second before shaking my head. Once again he flinched, so I shook my head again. I saw the look he and Connor shared, but I was adamant in my decision.

Just then I noticed Jazlyn look slightly over her shoulder and shift her weight. At first it seemed like nothing, a normal movement in a fit of anger as she and Aidan continued to spit insults and accusations at one another. But then I realized that by moving to her left she gave us a better angle at our targets.

"You know what, Aidan," Jazlyn shouted up at him, "why don't you come down here and face me like a real man."

Even from my obstructed view I could see Aidan's anger flare in his eyes. A second later he disappeared in black smoke, Projecting himself to Elaina's side but continuing his approach towards Jazlyn, successfully bringing him closer to us. Looking side to side, I gave the signal to my brothers to go in three...two...one...

In a mix of black mist and blurring black uniform, the three of us burst through the woods while shots from Jared's gun rang in the quiet night. Aidan's face was priceless as I tackled him square in the chest. We flew into one of the support beams of the deck causing it to crack and the corner of the deck to slump.

My fangs were already extended and deep in Aidan's neck when I thrust a thin silver knife into his gut. He wailed as I tore further into his throat and he began ripping at my shirt finally planting his elbow into my neck. I fell slightly, but came up and back slapped Aidan across the face causing him to fall to the ground. Grabbing him by his shirt, I thrust him up against the struggling deck post enjoying the sight of blood trickling down his lip. I took pride in hitting him across the face again, and again, the skin of my knuckles cracking at my ferocity.

Next my hands went for his throat, ready to tear his head from his body, but his hands grabbed at mine, a devilish smile coming across his face as he grunted through his clenched teeth, "I...can see...why you keep...Bri around."

"Do not even say her name," I shouted as I brought his face up to mine.

"She tastes so good...in more ways than one."

I could see the pleasure in his eyes as he made the crude remark, and unfortunately the spilt second I relaxed my concentration over what he meant he took the small knife from his stomach and jabbed it into the side of my throat. I fell to my knees as Aidan scurried to my left, screaming orders at Elaina to Project.

"I can't!" she screamed as Aidan grabbed her hand and they began to run toward the front of the house, Elaina ripping the sleeve off her shirt to reveal two bullet wounds in her shoulder.

As I pulled the knife out of my neck I looked over to Jared just in time to see Jazlyn launch herself at him feet first, wrap her legs around his neck and spin him upside down on the ground. One of her signature moves. Running to my brother's aid, I was stopped short when Jazlyn picked up Jared's gun, pointed it at her own forearm, and shot.

"Fucker!" she growled through her teeth and threw the gun onto Jared's chest. Even Jared froze in place, his hand not knowing if he could really take the gun or not. As she placed her hand over her arm she looked up to me and whispered, "You can either kill me, or go after them. But if I live I can still help."

Jared rose from the ground, his gun pointed at Jazlyn and looking between the two of us. "Why shoot yourself?"

"I didn't trust you to miss. I have my battle wound so no one will suspect me as long as Connor kills those two over there."

With a deep conflicted breath I nodded and began to retreat toward the front of the house. "Come on, Jared."

"Are you serious?" Jared yelled.

"Those silver bullets will not stay in Elaina for long. Come on!"

As we came upon the front lawn, Jared continued to run but turned around and shot two more rounds hitting Jazlyn in her chest and shoulder.

"What?" he shrugged as I glared at him.

"Was that necessary?"

"Absolutely. It has to look real, right?"

Not wanting to entertain my brother a second longer, I pulled all of my concentration into tracking where Aidan and Elaina had gone. We quickly crossed the driveway and headed into the woods located across from the house. As we followed their scent you could hear Aidan and Elaina shouting at one another regarding getting the bullets out of her arm.

"You got two shots in and you missed?"

"Only because Jazlyn hopped on my back right when I pulled the trigger, then I had to fight both of them. Damn Jazlyn fights dirty."

"She always has," I replied, having to shake off the emotional demons of having Jazlyn back in the Warriors' court, if she truly was. But before I could ponder on that fact a second longer I saw a flash of blonde hair dart behind a tree. "There!"

Jared fired off another shot, just missing Elaina as she fled from the tree with Aidan's fingers still digging into her shoulder. There was a slight embankment ahead, and using the slight elevation I launched myself into the air flying almost seventy feet down on the severe angled slope and landing only inches from them.

"Shoot them!" I shouted over my shoulder to Jared who was only a few feet behind me. However, just as Jared took aim, Aidan looked back and flung his hand out in front of him as a piercing pain took control of my head and caused me to fly backwards into my brother. I had been Pushed. By Aidan. It was not as painful as when Brianna did it, but it was familiar enough to know that Aidan had acquired the power from Brianna's blood, making his earlier statement even more maddening.

Jared pushed me off of him and forward into a run just as Elaina lifted her bloody burning fingers in the air. "It's out!"

"Jared!" I screamed as I launched myself in the air, pulling out the small silver knife while shots rang in the air around me. Elaina disappeared before one of the silver bullets cut through the black smoke of her Projection. Aidan looked up at me with a vicious smile as his face and shoulders began to fade away. As my body began its descent to the ground I extended my silver knife towards Aidan's calf only to fall through a cloud of black smoke and plunge the knife into the frozen ground beneath.

I had failed. Again. I pounded the ground and screamed into the depths of the earth.

"I'm sorry, bro," Jared said as he extended his hand and lifted me from the ground.

Not wanting to say a word on the matter, I slowly began my way back towards the house where Brianna had been kept. The run back seemed so much longer as thoughts and images flashed in my head, analyzing every mistake, every misstep. How would I explain to Victor that I let our enemy slip through my fingers? Literally.

Within minutes Jared and I were at the front of the house, and now that I had a moment to actually look at the building it seemed eerily familiar.

"Connor!" Jared shouted.

"Back here," Connor replied from somewhere behind the house.

"You ok back there?"

"Yeah…I…just looking for my lucky ear."

"Just follow the smell, man," Jared laughed.

"All right, all right," I interrupted. "Connor, check the grounds, and I mean for more than your ear. Jared and I will take the house."

Jared broke away and began inspecting the two vehicles in the driveway while I stepped through the front door of the small ranch-styled house. It was as though I was transported to North Carolina - a living room to my right, the small foyer opening to the kitchen on the left, a center island with two stools tucked underneath where I could visualize Oliver Morgan sitting and drinking his coffee. Not everything was exactly as I remembered, small decorative items were missing like pictures and other wall hangings, but the layout and large furniture was all the same. Why would they recreate a generic version of Oliver Morgan's house? Not only would Brianna have seen the differences, but she had to have known she was not in North Carolina. Right? I had hoped that when we found Brianna our questions would be answered, not continually added to.

Stepping down the hallway I made my way to where I believed Brianna's bedroom should have been, and to no surprise as I stepped through the doorway I was met with another almost perfect recreation - similar bedspread, small nightstand with tattered books, even the French doors on the opposite wall. Brianna's distinctive scent saturated the air. This was where she had stayed for the last six weeks, and although the room was nothing like the prison setting I had imagined, it gave me no comfort.

The sheets and comforter were tossed back, exposing a depression in the mattress from where Brianna must have slept. Her scent mixed with fruity shampoo filed my nostrils as I placed my head on her pillow. When I turned to face her nightstand on the opposite wall I was hit by another familiar scent. It was the same smell that had been left in our hotel room that day. The same smell I had just chased in the woods. It was Aidan's. He had been lying in this bed. Next to my Brianna.

Not only had he fed on her blood, had he slept with her? How could she? How could Brianna turn to another man after such a short time? "And with my children inside her!" I shouted out loud as I leapt from the bed and threw the mattress through the French doors.

"Dude!" Jared yelled as he ran into the room. "What the hell?"

"I think Bri has…" I began, but then stopped myself. My chest was heaving like Devin's usually did, and Jared stayed quiet knowing the signs. "Did you find anything?"

Jared's eyes were burning a hole in the side of my face since I refused to look at him. Finally giving up he said, "I ran the license plate numbers from the two cars. The license plate on the truck isn't registered, but using the VIN number I found that the truck was stolen. And the convertible belongs to, get this, Shelby Joanne Morgan."

I whipped my head around. "Well that is interesting. Anything else?"

"I found two bottles of blood on the hood of the car. Both smell like Vamp blood. What's Shelby Morgan doing with bottles of Vampire blood?"

"I do not think Shelby was actually driving the car. The blood is curious though. Make sure we take it with us." He nodded as I turned toward the closet and found Brianna's red suitcase, actually my suitcase.

"Watcha doin' with that?"

I opened the suitcase and began to toss clothes from within the closet inside. "Brianna obviously left all her things and we should bring them back with us. Start grabbing whatever is within that dresser."

"I love my Beebs, but no way am I touching her underwear."

"Then go and get all her things from the bathroom. It's right across the hall."

"Really? How do you know that?"

"Jared, please just do it."

"Not until you tell me what's up your ass all of a sudden."

"Not now."

"Jesus, Cameron…"

"I smelled Aidan in Brianna's bed. Happy? I think the two of them were sleeping together. Brianna wanted nothing to do with me when she saw me tonight. Aidan and Elaina got away…again. So far this evening has been a disaster and I seriously have no idea what to expect from Brianna once I get home. Weeks of worrying and pining for her seems to have only been one-sided and…what am I going do?"

My brother's eyes were kind as he patted my back reassuringly. "Ok. Tonight's sucked, I'll give you that. But there's no way Bibi slept with Aidan. No way. It may look that way, but you don't know for sure. This whole situation is fucked up and there has to be an explanation. We just haven't found the key yet, but we will. We always do, don't we?" I nodded. "Right, or else Dad will eat us alive. And I mean that literally. Now come on, let's finish this and get out of here."

I nodded again as he left the room and came back a short time later with various toiletries in his arms and threw them into the suitcase along with the clothes I was able to stuff inside.

"Hey Cameron," Connor shouted from outside. "There's something out here I think you should see."

"We will be right there," I replied and then looked to Jared as I zipped up Brianna's suitcase. "You get the blood and I will meet you outside."

Jared disappeared once again into the hallway as I grabbed the suitcase before stepping through the shattered French doors and leaping down to the ground below with Connor just inches away.

"What's with the mattress?"

I ignored him. "There was something you needed me to see?"

He nodded and gestured for me to follow him around to the back of the house where Jared joined us a second later. We followed Connor underneath the deck to where a boulder sat oddly at the head of what looked like a freshly dug grave. The words Oliver Morgan were scratched into the face of the boulder and the smell of decomposition was rising from the large mound of dirt.

"I brought Ollie to the Facility myself. As far as I know, he's still there," Connor said next to me.

"He is," I replied.

"Then whose in there? 'Cuz it's someone, you can smell it," Jared said as he waved his hand in front of his face.

"There is only one way to find out," Connor answered as he picked up a shovel that had been discarded a few feet away and extended it in Jared's direction.

"Why me?"

"Because you're the youngest," Connor answered smugly.

Jared looked to me to defend him.

"Sorry, little brother, you are the youngest."

With a groan Jared reluctantly took the shovel from Connor's hand and began to dig near the headstone. Less than thirty seconds later a woman's face was looking back at us, her features still relatively preserved due to the cold.

"Who is that?" Jared asked as he dropped the shovel at his feet.

"That is Shelby Joanne Morgan."

"Oliver told me he hadn't heard from her for a few weeks," Connor began as he knelt down beside the grave. "Even with the cold temperature she's only been dead a week, maybe two."

"But why is she in a grave marked with Oliver's name?"

"Another question to add to the pile."

Just then I could hear the crackling of a voice coming through Jared's earpiece. "Yeah, hold on," he said as he touched the microphone at his throat. "The other team has overtaken the compound. Devin wants to talk to you."

"Have him patched through," I replied as I handed Jared the suitcase and stepped out from underneath the deck. "Go ahead, Brother."

"Did you find the house?"

"Yes, but it has only created more questions. What is your situation?"

"We are starting to explore the building, but have hit a snag and could use your help as well as John's."

"We are almost done here anyway. What is your location?"

"A couple of miles east from you. We have turned on the security floodlights, you should be able to see us."

I jumped up onto the deck above and could easily see bright lights rising from a peak in the distance. "Yes, I can see you. I will have John brought up, and Jared and I will be there shortly."

"Did you find Aidan or Elaina?"

"They got away."

There was a short silence on the other end before he said, "Just get up here."

I could tell he was not happy, but at least there was some success tonight. As I jumped back under the deck, Connor and Jared were hunched over the grave having removed more of the soil that was on top of Shelby.

"Bro, she was stabbed," Jared said while pointing to a hole in Shelby's bloody sweater. "Looks like Sera's vision was right."

Wanting to change the subject I reached down for the suitcase that had toppled over and handed it to Connor.

"Connor, I need you to take this suitcase and those bottles of blood back to the convoy, then gather Dr. Ryan and bring him to Elaina's compound. Send the Warriors watching him back here and have them search for any other evidence they think might be of some use to us."

He nodded as he took the two bottles of blood into his arms. "What are we going to do with this place?"

"Destroy it."

"What about Brianna's mother?"

"She is already dead and there is no way we can transport the body without raising suspicion. Burn the house, make sure she is in it and disintegrate the bones afterwards if need be. No one discusses her death, make sure everyone is clear about that. I will speak with Oliver personally and…make up something."

Connor headed to the woods while Jared and I began running up the mountain toward Elaina's compound. Jared remained quiet, allowing me time to process the questions that were piling up. As the lights of the compound came closer I could see Devin standing in front of the building while other Warriors were subduing several of Elaina's Vampires on the lawn.

"Good work, Brother," I said as I ran up to him.

"We are still searching the compound," he began as he turned and gestured for me to walk with him into the building. "We are going room to room and we have found a handful of medical staff, human mostly, and most of them are here under duress."

"It sounds like you have everything under control. What do you need my help with?"

Devin inhaled slowly as he licked his lips. "We believe we found where the hybrids are being held, however, a hybrid child is preventing us from entering."

"How old is he?"

"I don't know, a medium-sized child."

I smiled as I continued to follow him down several sterile looking hallways. "Brother, I am surprised that you could not get through a medium-sized child."

"I could have, but I am trying to be…"

"Less Devin," Jared laughed behind me.

"Jared," I warned, and then turned back to Devin. "Who is with the child now?"

"Alex."

"Alexander! For goodness sake, Alexander is almost seven feet tall. The child must be terrified."

"That's what I was going for, but the child just started swinging his knife around. I was afraid he'd hurt himself, so that's why I called you. Also, the child is refusing to talk to anyone but Eris. So I am hoping you can get around that peacefully. Honestly, I am only going to humor the child for a few more minutes."

"Good to know, Brother," I smiled.

Moments later we came upon the child who looked roughly eight or nine years old. His dark hybrid eyes were wide with fear though he continued to hold a small knife in front of him. Surprisingly enough it was similar to the knife that I had stabbed Aidan with, and similar to the one Jazlyn had held to Brianna's stomach. In other words, it was Warrior standard issue.

With a gentle tap on the shoulder I gestured for Alexander to go with Devin. The young boy's extended hand was shaking as I came closer to him.

"Hi there," I said to the boy softly and knelt down in front of him.

"Are you Eris?" he asked nervously.

I shook my head. "My name is Cameron, but Eris is a friend of mine. Are you who Eris has been speaking with?" He nodded slowly. "So by the look of that knife, and the fact you know Eris, that must mean you know Jazlyn."

He nodded again. "She gave me this knife for protection. She said it would hurt Vampires."

"Jazlyn is my sister," I said though Jared gave a smug snort. "So if you can trust her, do you think you can trust me? I only want to help, just like you helped Brianna."

"You mean the lady with the big belly?"

"That'd be her," Jared laughed just as Connor and John came down the hall.

"What is your name?"

"M-Mikey," he replied, allowing me to take his wrist and lower his hand.

"So Mikey, how exactly did you come to see the lady with the big belly?"

A devilish smile came across the boy's lips. "Toby dared me that I couldn't sneak out and get us pudding snacks."

"I used to love those," Jared said behind me.

"Yes, *Mikey*, so you were able to sneak out one night and..."

"Well...I got lost and I heard some people coming so I went into this room and that's where they brought the lady. They caught me and made Jazzy take me away. I thought she was gonna take me to the bad room, but she didn't. That's when she showed me how to talk to Eris."

"But kid," Jared interrupted, "did you ever get the pudding? Please tell me you got the pudding."

"No," Mikey replied sadly. "Toby keeps pickin' on me about it."

I waved my hand at Jared to get him to stop interrupting. "Mikey, you were very brave and we could not have done any of this without you. Now this is my friend John," I said gesturing behind me as John stepped forward. "He is a doctor. Do you think you can let us in so he can see if anyone needs help?"

"I guess so," he replied as he stepped past me and grabbed John's hand. "Come on, I'll take you to the mommies first."

"The mommies?" John asked curiously, looking around at the Warriors around him.

Mikey nodded as he pulled him toward two white doors. "Yeah, the mommies with the babies in their bellies."

John's surprised and worried expression matched mine and my brothers' as he was led away by little Mikey. The three of us stepped in line to follow when we were stopped by Alexander shouting behind us.

"Cam!" he said as he waved me towards him. "I need you to come with me. There is something you need to see."

"Right now?" I asked, but he nodded. "Fine. Connor, find the other doctors that Devin has detained and have them help Dr. Ryan assess the hybrids. Also coordinate with tech ops to get as many Cleaners as we can up here. They will need to do a lot of Glamouring on the humans. We also need a full count on how many hybrids there actually are and develop a plan to transport them out of here."

"Anything else?"

"Yeah," Jared answered, "find that kid some pudding."

Connor rolled his eyes as he turned away and we began to follow Alexander through more winding white corridors. Eventually he pushed opened a steel swinging door walking us through a room with a long metal table and various surgical instruments strewn across the counters. At the end of the room was a thick vault door that was now open with three Warriors standing in front of it to block whatever was inside.

"Alex, what is in there?"

"You'll see in a second," he said as he waved the Warriors out of the way only to have them close ranks behind us.

"Lanashell," I said breathlessly, hearing Jared's intake of air at the sight of a woman who was usually immaculately dressed with every hair in place, stretched out on a table with ragged thin pieces of fabric covering her private areas. Silver cuffs locked her arms and legs to the metal table along with multiple thin silver chains stretched across her abdomen. "Jared, go get John and bring him back here."

Lanashell's eyes widened. "I was not aware of the Dreamwalker."

"One even more powerful than Eris. Did you see anyone else having blood taken?"

"No," she answered sadly as John began pushing on her arm. "But I am guessing if you haven't found him, he or she gave blood willingly."

"It also means we still don't know who this Dreamwalker is," Devin said and looked me dead in the eye. "Brianna could still be at risk."

"When is she ever not at risk," I mumbled.

"So now what?" Jared asked.

Lanashell groaned. "There is one last tube, doctor."

"Ok, Lana. Deep breath in," John said. "Exhale and I'll pull."

"And Lanashell," I interrupted, "yell as much as you want."

Chapter Fifty-Two

Cameron

Brianna was lying in our bed in the same position she had been in for almost three days, and in the same pajama pants and white camisole that was too short to cover her bulbous stomach. Her feelings of anger toward me had not changed, and she refused all help I tried to give her since I came home. She was weak and easily fatigued, only getting up to go to the bathroom, and even then with someone else's help. But that all stopped today.

Brianna could not ignore me any longer; frankly I felt I had humored her long enough. I understood that she had been through a traumatic ordeal, but I could not tolerate her usual avoidance of uncomfortable things. She loathed me, and I wanted to know why. We were not two teenagers who could simply breakup. We had a home and two children on the way. We had a life together. If she no longer wanted to be with me then so be it, but I deserved an explanation. And if her heart had truly left me for another, she had to tell me to my face.

Just then Brianna stirred underneath the sheets that were tangled around her legs. She rubbed her eyes as she yawned and then turned over, kicking the sheet away from her body. Her hand grazed over her stomach, pulling at my heart since I wanted to do the same. Then her face fell when her eyes came into focus and noticed that I was sitting in a chair at the corner of the bed.

"Re?" she moaned loudly.

"Renee and John moved back to their apartment last night."

Brianna's lips tightened as she took in a slow breath. "Kyla?" she moaned again as she lowered her legs toward the ground and began pushing herself up to a seated position.

"Kyla and Alexander have gone out for the day."

"Sera..."

"She will not come." Brianna opened her mouth to speak again, but I rose from the chair and offered my hand as I said, "Nor Eris."

Brianna's nostrils flared as she glared at me and knocked my hand away. "I will do it myself then."

Slowly she pushed herself up from the bed and my arms were ready to catch her, but she did not fall and her look towards me was smugly victorious as she walked toward the bathroom alone.

Once she shut the door I Projected upstairs to the kitchen where Seraphina was already putting the finishing touches on Brianna's breakfast tray. I no longer questioned how she seemed so in tune with her stepdaughter. She gave me a charming smile as she slid the scrambled eggs from the skillet onto Brianna's plate when Dante and Eris came back into the kitchen from the balcony. If anything, perhaps Dante's purple suit would make Brianna laugh.

"Good morning, my boy," Dante said cheerily as he began shaking my extended hand. "I take it Brianna is awake."

"Yes sir. And still wanting nothing to do with me."

"And that is why I am here," he replied as he squeezed my shoulder. "I do want the two of you to try and resolve this on your own. However, I will stay close in case you get into trouble. Oh, and Eris, it is important for you and Seraphina to stay out of the situation."

"Yes, yes," Eris groaned.

"Dante, I will plant his feet to zhe floor if I have to," Seraphina laughed as she handed me Brianna's tray.

Dante followed me down the stairs to my bedroom where he gave me a hopeful smile before I sighed and ducked inside. Brianna was easing herself down on the bed as I placed the tray near her feet. The blood drained from her cheeks right before my eyes, her fingers going up to her mouth as though she would be sick. Quickly I opened the draw to the nightstand next to her and pulled out a stack of her favorite crackers. She looked up at me, surprise hidden in her eyes as she took a cracker and began nibbling on the corner.

"Could you...get rid of the eggs?" she asked as she placed her fingers underneath her nose. Within a second I was handing the plate of steaming eggs to Dante who was standing in the hallway. When I stepped back into the bedroom, Brianna had pushed further onto the bed, propping the pillows up behind her and taking another cracker from the stack. "Tell Sera I'm sorry. The smell was just…ugh I can't even think about it."

"I am sure she will understand. Is there something else I can get you instead?" I asked as I pulled the comforter over her legs.

Her eyes caught mine and held them for a moment before she said, "Why are you here?"

"This is our home, Bri. This is where I am supposed to be. Angel, we need to talk."

"There is nothing more to say."

"No, Brianna, there is plenty to say."

"No, *Cameron*, I'm simply telling you exactly what you told me. You made your choice perfectly clear."

"But…Bri, I do not know what…"

"Look, I know my father's here and that you're worried that he can hear you. So I'm telling you now, you don't need to pretend anymore."

I exhaled loudly. "I am not pretending…"

"Let me get this out," she said in a raised voice. "I know this is not what you want. I just need a few more days to recover from…well whatever it is I'm recovering from, and then my family and I will be out of your hair."

"Brianna, I do not want you out of my hair!"

I instantly regretted raising my voice and it was obviously Dante's cue to interrupt since he slowly opened the door and stepped inside the bedroom.

"Dante?"

"Good morning, Brianna. You are looking better every day."

"Th-thank you," she replied self-consciously and pulled the comforter up over her chest, but then looked Dante over. The sheen of his suit certainly got her attention. "I don't mean to be rude, but well, I'm pregnant and have lost all my manners. Why are you here?"

Dante smiled. "I am here to help you work through what happened to you. There is so little we know about…"

"Well why don't you ask him?" Brianna said as she pointed accusingly in my direction.

Dante gestured for me to sit and reluctantly I obeyed as he said, "For now I only care to hear your version of the events starting with the day you left Boston with Aidan."

"Really?" she replied annoyed with a raised eyebrow.

"Humor me," Dante smiled.

With a sigh, Brianna tucked the comforter between her arms and placed her hands on top of her large stomach. "That morning Aidan woke me up telling me that Elaina was spotted in Boston and that Cameron had asked him to get me out of town and take me to Daddy O's."

One question answered, she really did think she was in North Carolina, though the accusation that I had sent Aidan made my body flinch.

"And what happened once you got to your grandfather's?" Dante asked lightly.

Brianna quickly brushed away a tear that had streaked down her cheek. I went to rise from my chair, but Dante stepped in front of me and took a tissue from the box on the nightstand and handed it to her.

"Nothing really. Shelby...uh, my mother, was there. Daddy O had asked her to come up and help out, which of course was just a nightmare because we fought the entire time. Even the babies knew she was trouble."

"How is that?" I asked looking around Dante only to see a scowl on Brianna's face.

"Because I threw up everything she made me. Which is exactly what I told you when you finally decided to call."

"Bri, I never..." I began and stood from my chair only to find Dante's hand planted in my chest, prompting me to sit back down.

"Now Brianna," Dante said in a calm voice, "Dr. Ryan mentioned you had some headaches and nosebleeds. Did you ever find a pattern to when you would get them?"

"Not really. Sometimes I got them when I left the house. I couldn't even get three miles down the road before my head would start to pound. Well...except that last night. Huh, that's weird. I never thought about that until now. But...the nosebleeds would just come on all of a sudden. Once when I left the house, another time I was just really upset and walked to my room, and the last time..." she paused, "...the last time I had Pushed Aidan."

"By Pushing, I am guessing you mean your gift?" Dante asked and she nodded. "Ok then, what happened after that?"

Tears began to form in her eyes and it was becoming even harder to stay seated. "Aidan said to hell with Cameron's rules and that he would take me Christmas shopping." Dante gave me a curious look over his shoulder as Brianna continued, "But I got a really bad headache so we had to turn back and when we got there…" she paused as she took another tissue from the box that Dante held out in front of her. "…we pulled in the driveway and there was a Vampire already there. I went inside while Aidan handled him and that's when I found Daddy O…dying. He was…bleeding and I…couldn't stop it." Brianna cleared her throat, looking up to the ceiling to prevent more tears from falling as she tried to gain her composure.

"Do you know how this Vampire found you?"

"My mother. At least at the time I thought it was just her. Now I'm beginning to think that Aidan was in on it too. I found bite marks on my mother's neck. They could have easily been Aidan's. I…just didn't think it was possible at the time."

"What happened to your mother?"

Brianna's breath became staggered as she said, "I…killed…her. I stabbed her right after Daddy O died. Her betrayal was what got Daddy O killed, and…and I lost it…I just lost it."

Another question down, though it did not make the situation any easier.

"After that everything really turned to shit," she said angrily as she shook her tears away. "That's when *he* finally graced me with his presence and not ten minutes after burying Daddy O did he decide to take his coward ass home and leave me with Aidan who, by the way, turns out to be Elaina's lover. Thank god for my father and Jazlyn, or else who knows what they would have done to me."

"Now wait a minute," I shouted as I jumped from my seat, effectively startling Brianna and having Dante place his hand against my chest once again.

"Cameron, you will have your turn," he warned.

"No, I will not have her think of me this way for a second longer."

"You know, Cameron, none of this would have happened if it weren't for you," Brianna said in a nasty tone.

"Me? How is this my fault?"

Brianna's eyes grew wide. "You made the call! If you hadn't called Aidan, none of this would have happened!"

"I called Renee!" I shouted.

"Wh-hat?" she stuttered, as new tears started to form in her eyes.

I felt Dante's hand on my shoulder, warning me, though it was difficult to use a calm tone. "Our last night together you asked me to marry you, and I vehemently said yes. I made love to you until the early morning hours, kissed you and the babies goodbye, and left for Dante's. When I learned of

Elaina's presence in Boston I called *Renee* thinking that she would be the only person who could convince you to get out of the city. If I had only known you would be so trusting of any man who walked in the door..."

Dante squeezed my shoulder so hard that my knees bent from the pain.

"Brianna, I think what Cameron is failing to say is, what made you trust Aidan so fully?"

"Because he did. He sent Aidan to find me the first time. Why wouldn't I trust him? He told me Cam was too busy and pulling in all the help he could to find Elaina and I didn't question it when I saw Hugo gone."

"Hugo is dead, love," I responded calmly. Brianna's brow scrunched together, her mouth left slightly slack. "Aidan killed him and stuffed him in a closet in our hotel room."

Brianna took in a slow deep breath, her face beginning to show signs of exhaustion already. She spoke very softly as she said, "But if you knew...when did...if you called Renee...I'm so confused. If you found Hugo, why did you leave me with Aidan? Why didn't you come sooner? Christ! You knew where I was."

I knelt down beside her, placing my hand on her forearm. "Brianna, I know this may be difficult to understand, but you have not been at Oliver's..."

"Cameron, I think I know..."

"They built a replica of Oliver's house," I interrupted. "Angel, we found you in New Hampshire, about four hours away from here." She began shaking her head, unable to settle in with all the truths that were now being handed to her. "Think about it, love. You even said to your father that you were surprised you slept the entire trip home. It was because it was only four hours versus fourteen. Try and remember if there were things about the house that were different, or missing..."

"No. No, I grew up in that house. There were things that have been there for fifty years, antiques, pictures..." A thought or memory passed across Brianna's face, a sudden glimmer of recognition. "Wait...the pictures in the hallway, Mama Jo's cookbooks. Daddy O said Shelby had taken them...but everything else...how..."

"Lanashell," I said as I curled my fingers around her hand that was shaking on top of her stomach. From the corner of my eye I could see Dante backing out of the room.

"Lana's been working with Elaina all this time?"

"No," I replied as I rose from the floor and sat on the edge of the bed, my hand still wrapped around hers. "Elaina kidnapped Lanashell the day she resigned from the Facility. They were drawing her blood and giving it to Aidan so that he could use her mind control power. They built a replica of Oliver's home and used Lanashell's blood to show you the details."

"But how did they get Daddy O? He kept telling me he gave things to Shelby and that's why they were missing. Ohmygod, we have to go back up there."

"Why?"

"Daddy O's there. He's buried up there, it's not where he belongs. We have to go get him!" she shouted as she pulled her hand out of mine and ripped the comforter from around her.

"Bri, wait," I said quickly, taking her by the shoulders. "Oliver was never with you."

"Cameron, he bled out right in front of me."

"A man bled out in front of you. With Lanashell's blood they made you see your grandfather. Bri, I assure you he is safe and has been in good hands since you were taken. He speaks to one of us every day."

Brianna's bottom lip trembled as tears crested her lower lids. "Daddy O's...not...dead?" I shook my head. "Why wasn't that the first thing out of your mouth!"

"Well...I..."

"Wait a minute! So I didn't kill...I didn't kill Shelby?"

My face fell and my delay in speaking gave Brianna her answer, causing her jaw to flex wildly as she bit away at the emotions raging inside of her.

"My love, I do not have words that can express how sorry I am for what you have gone through or how much anger I feel towards your mother. Bri, she was their insider. I am sure she provided added details about the house and Oliver. She was the only one who knew him well enough to make sure you absolutely believed you were in North Carolina with your grandfather."

Brianna's eyes became heavy as she leaned into me and tucked her head in crook of my shoulder. "How long do you think she was working with them?"

"At least a few weeks before you were taken, probably more. We found her home in North Carolina almost completely cleared out, and one of the teams found a small cottage near where you were being kept that we think she stayed in. Someone was even using her car. We found it in the driveway at the house."

"It was Elaina. She came over that night, it was the first time I hadn't slept through the night and I caught them together, Aidan and Elaina. He played me, Cam. He got me to open up about everything and he used it against me. I told him what happened to make me go to Boston. It was…" she paused and I could hear her heart start beating rapidly as she slowly lifted her head from my shoulder. Anguish was written on her face as she said, "Oh-my-god. I didn't talk to you did I?"

"No, love."

"You were never there, were you?"

"No, love," I replied, brushing the back of my hand down her tear moistened cheek and worrying over the guilt I saw in her eyes.

"I'm…I'm so sorry, Cam. I thought it was you. They made me think it was you," she sobbed into her hands.

Thinking the worst and trying to keep my emotions in, I rubbed her back gently as I said, "Just tell me what happened. Be honest, please I need to know."

Brianna lifted her head, tears streaming down her face as her breathing became staggered making it almost impossible to understand her. "I…I kissed him…He looked just like…you…I kept trying…to get… you…him…to. I'm going to be sick," she mumbled as her face turned green.

Without a second's hesitation I lifted her into my arms and ran her to the bathroom, setting her down gently on the floor and holding her hair back while she emptied her stomach. I did not think her time away could be even worse than I had already imagined.

When she finished, I wetted a soft washcloth and wiped her face while I asked, "This impostor, did you make…did you have sex with him?"

"No," she whimpered. "I just kissed him and…he slept in the bed, but nothing happened. I swear, I thought it was you. You have to believe me."

"I do," I answered.

I rinsed the washcloth and rung out the excess water before throwing it across the room and watching it splatter against the wall. At that moment I was overtaken by frustration, and yes, anger. I stood with my back to Brianna, one hand propping me up against the wall while the other raked through my hair.

"Did anyone else sleep next to you?"

Brianna's breath caught, causing me to turn around and face her.

"Cam…"

"There is no point lying, Bri. I smelled him in your bed," I said angrily.

"Cameron, please it's not what you think," she pleaded as she pulled on my arm to help her to stand.

"What I think is not the issue. What I know is that I went through torture every day I was without you. What I know is that I thought about you and our children every minute of every day and agonized over what they might be doing to you. What I know is that it took less than seven weeks for you to turn to another man."

"That's not what happened," she shouted as I stormed past her into the bedroom.

"So he just laid there, nothing happened?"

"Yes…I mean no…"

"It's hard enough to forgive what you did with my look alike, but there were no mind games when it came to Aidan. How am I supposed to feel about that, Bri?"

"Cam, please! You have no *idea* what I went through these last few weeks. You knew I was taken, I didn't! I thought I was losing you. You never wanted to talk to me and when you did you were such a jerk."

"It was not me!"

"Fine, *him!* When *he* talked to me, which was hardly ever. One time I stole Aidan's phone and called back a number I thought was yours and a woman answered. I thought you were having an affair which was why I was being made to stay where I was. Don't you see? I told Aidan what happened with Nikki and he used it against me. After Daddy O died…the fake, the fake Daddy O died, the fake Cameron finally came. He said such awful things to me. I'm sorry, it was your voice telling me you didn't love me anymore. Your face that had absolutely no caring for me and you left me, just like in my dream. My last memory of you was pushing me out of the way so that you could drive away.

"After you…he, after *he* left, I could barely get out of bed. I had no one left. Daddy O was dead, I killed my mother, and you left me. I was alone except for Aidan. He was all I had and he preyed on that. I was so lonely and depressed that yes, I let him kiss me and when he tried to take it further I pushed him away because deep down inside I still loved you."

"So you only kissed him?"

Brianna's heart started racing, giving her away before she ever said a word. "The first time."

"There was a second?" I asked and sat on the edge of the bed, completely defeated as I held my head in my hands. It was more than I could take, knowing that my children stirred within her as she did things with other men made it almost unbearable to look at her as she stood sobbing in front of me.

"The night I left, I woke up in the middle of the night. When I went into the kitchen I saw Elaina and Aidan, and I realized I was in trouble. He wanted to go hunting, but she wanted him to prove that I wouldn't wake up while they were gone. I only had a few seconds so I had to convince him that I hadn't seen them and get his mind on something else so I...pretended to...want him."

I lifted my head. "Did he touch you?" She nodded reluctantly. "How far did it go?"

"Pretty far," she answered as she began to choke back her sobs. "It was awful, Cam. It was like...being with Sam all...over again."

"You let him drink from you."

"Not by choice. I just needed him...to believe...so that he would leave. I...I kept thinking about you and the babies...begging for forgiveness. Please Cam, I did the only thing I thought..." but her sobs became overpowering and I caught her in my arms just as her knees buckled from underneath her. She clawed and pulled at my shirt, pulling me closer to her as she cried into my chest. "Forgive me, Cam. Please forgive me for what I did. I love you, I do. You have to believe me."

"Shh, angel," I said as I tucked her head underneath my chin and began rocking back and forth. "I am sorry, angel. So, so sorry. I do believe you, I love you so much, Brianna. Please believe me when I say that."

Just then Eris opened the door to our bedroom, but stepped aside to allow Seraphina to run into the room and wrap her arms around Brianna's huddled mass. Eris walked slowly to my side, a sympathetic look on his face as he knelt down as well, placing one arm around Seraphina and the other around me, bringing the four of us together in a complete circle. "Now we can all heal together."

Eris was right, there was healing that needed to happen. We had reached our lowest point so we could only go forward from here and I refused to let it go any other way. Never again would another man touch her. Never. As possessive as it sounded, she was mine and no one else's. I would kill whoever tried to come between us again. My death list was growing, and the first name on that list now started with A.

Chapter Fifty-Three

Brianna

Yesterday all the truth came out, and my eyes were still puffy from the amount of crying. My nerves were raw and my heart heavy with guilt. Guilt over being intimate with multiple men. Guilt over not seeing all the little things wrong with Daddy O and the house. Most of all, I felt guilty for not believing in Cameron. But as was said to me many times yesterday, between the isolation, manipulation, and mind control, it was no wonder I fell into their trap so easily. It didn't change the fact that I had thrown away my ring and my Warrior pin. It also didn't change the fact that the trust Cameron and I had worked so hard for now had to be rebuilt.

But, I was hungry and my pregnancy-enhanced sense of smell was telling me that Seraphina was working hard. I threw the blankets off of me and slowly got out of bed. Knowing there were Warriors going in and out of the house, I couldn't stay in my pajamas. After throwing on a pair of sweatpants and a large zipper hoodie, I padded out of my bedroom and down the hall to the sound of several people talking over each other. When I reached the foyer I could see the long oval table in the living room surrounded by almost every male Vampire I knew. Even Jared was hiding in a dark corner of the living room with a wide smile as he caught me peeking into the room. Cameron was leaning his chair back on its rear legs while listening intently to those who were speaking, but Jared caught his attention and gestured his head in my direction. Cameron turned too quickly and lost his balance, causing the chair to crash loudly on the floor and break into several pieces underneath him.

While the room erupted in laughter he scrambled to his feet and within seconds he was standing in front of me with nervous energy as he carefully took my hand. "You are going to laugh at me too?"

"It's not often that you're the klutz. Usually I have that covered."

With a smile he leaned in and kissed my forehead, bringing his wonderful autumn smell closer to me. "Did you sleep well?"

"A little better every day," I replied truthfully as I took a step away from him and waved to those in the room.

"Child? Cameron? What is going on?" Victor's said from the conference phone in the center of the table.

"I didn't mean to interrupt," I whispered in a worried tone, though Cameron shook his head.

Jared stood from his seat in the corner as he said, "Sorry Dad, Bri just walked in. We need to take a hug break."

With an apologetic smile to Cameron, I shuffled across the room to where Jared's expectant arms were extended in front of him.

"When did you guys get back?" I asked as I squeezed him tightly around the neck.

"Super early this morning. Sure did miss ya, Beebs. We all did," he said and then gestured behind me to Devin and Alex who were now standing from their seats. Seeing them now, I hadn't realized how much I missed them too.

Devin broke from his usual uptight demeanor for only a second as he hugged me. Alex, on the other hand, was extremely boisterous as he lifted me off the ground and squeezed me to him, though it wasn't all that close since my beach ball sized belly was between us.

When he put me down I looked around the room and asked, "No Kyla?"

"Uh…shopping…with Renee actually," he replied uncomfortably and I tried not to sigh or look upset.

Victor cleared his throat over the phone. "Are we done hugging?"

"Sorry, Victor," I apologized, hearing the annoyance in his voice. "I'd hug you if you were here."

"Thank you, my dear, and I would hug you back. Hopefully you will come and see us out here soon."

"Well you could always make that sooner if you came and visited us. Your grandkids will be here before you know it," I said, knowing Victor was still upset that we were making a life outside of the manor.

"Yes, well, we will see. May we get back to the debrief?" he grumbled in his raspy voice.

"Yeah, sorry about that. I was just following the smell of food. Upstairs, right?"

Cameron nodded, though he looked at me and then back to the table with a conflicted expression.

"I can take her," Fabi said cheerily as he rose from his chair and I noticed that his hand lingered on Devin's shoulder.

Cam stole one last kiss before Fabi pulled me away and we began the harrowing task of going up the stairs, even though Fabi did offer to carry me. But honestly I had been in bed so much that walking felt good to my stiff legs.

"So, Fabi Fabulous, how long have you and Devin been dating?" I whispered.

Fabi's head whipped around so fast I thought it might come off. "Whatever are you talking about," he whispered back.

"Oh don't even try and deny it."

Fabi pursed his lips as he stopped on the stairs and placed his hand on his hip. "Everyone here knows what's going on, but he keeps insisting that we deny everything. He's such a...a..."

"Stupid boy?"

"Exactly!"

"Sorry to tell ya, honey, most Warriors are. Not that it makes the situation any better, but Devin was with his last boyfriend for three years and no one knew. So if everyone here knows you're dating, that's saying something. It also means he's slipping a little, probably because he likes you so much."

"Of course he does, I'm a catch," he said proudly and we continued up the stairs. "I'm not staying in the closet for anyone, not even for Dev. I should be on display at all times."

"You're so cute."

"I know, it's a gift."

"Petite chute? Is zhat you?"

"Oui, ma mere," I replied to Fabi's raised eyebrow. "What?"

"You're just full of surprises."

Finally reaching the top of the stairs I replied, "I only know five words in French, those are three of them. Don't be too impressed."

"Honey, the fact that you're actually growing two humans inside of you makes me automatically impressed with you. I'd be too scared that one day they'd start clawing their way out..."

"Thank you...Fabi. Let's just add to the nightmares I already have."

Sounds and smells from the kitchen drew me away from the stairs towards Sera who was standing in front of the large stove flipping a batch of pancakes on a large flat griddle. "You have good color today, ma petite chute. I hope you are hungry, I promiss, zhere are no eggs today."

"Sera, I promise to eat everything you give me, as long as I can make a tomato and mayo sandwich too. These kids crave them every day, I can't help it."

As I stepped around the island and began looking in cabinets for bread, Sera shooed me out, but not before giving me several kisses on the cheek. "Out, out. Sit, sit. Eat, eat."

"Yes, yes. Ok, ok," I teased and stepped to the kitchen table that was covered in plates of cut fruit, bacon, and now steam buttery pancakes. "Where's Dad?"

"Resting," she answered as she began slicing a tomato and making my mouth water. "He has been monitoring you very closely these past three nights."

"I know. I can see him in every dream I have. It's getting a little creepy."

Fabi rubbed my arm sympathetically. "It's only because he's so worried about that other Dreamwalker. He's never had to worry about someone surpassing his ability. I think he's a little self-conscious."

"You can say zhat again," Sera replied. "Voila! One tomato and mayo on toast for mes petits-enfants."

"Sorry Sera, too advanced for me," I laughed as I practically ripped the new plate from her hand.

Sera sat in the chair next to me, fixing a plate of her own from the spread she had made. "Petits-enfants means grandchildren. Don't worry, you will be bilingual soon enough, as will zhey. Look how much you know so far."

I raised a brow at her as I tried swallowing a large bite of my juicy sandwich. "Oui, ma mere," I said sweetly, leaning my head on her shoulder. The feeling of her soft aging skin and the smell of her hand lotion as she patted my cheek made my eyes water.

"Petite chute, why zhe tears?"

"I'm just happy I have you in my life," I answered, lifting my head from her shoulder and feeling the tears dripping from my eyes.

"Is zhat all?"

"I'm sorry," I whimpered.

"You have nozing…"

"Yes," I interrupted, "yes I do. I just feel so bad…"

"Petite, we talked about zhis last night."

"I know but I'm still so mad at myself about telling Aidan who you were. He knows you're married to Eris which means Elaina knows. She'll know how to find you now. I'm so sorry…"

Sera pulled my face back up to hers as I broke down. "You did nozing wrong. I cannot run from Elaina forever, I longer wish to. Zhere is so much life I have missed by hiding."

"I can't believe I was so stupid," I cried as I leaned into her shoulder. "I will never forgive myself if something were to happen to you because of what I said."

While I continued to cry in her shoulder she patted my head and back, shushing me softly when another set of arms curled around us.

"I can't be the only one not crying," Fabi wept into the back of my shoulder. "And I'm sure Sera will agree you weren't stupid. You couldn't have known."

"Zhat's right," Sera replied as the three of us released each other and wiped tears from our eyes. "You are lucky to be alive, petite chute, very lucky. I know what it feels like to be under Elaina's spell. But I zhink zhat it is only fair for you to tell her where I am since I told her about you so many years ago."

"I didn't do it for payback…"

"Of course not, you love me too much," she replied calmly.

"I do," I sniffled. "You're the only mother I have left."

As tears began to fill my eyes again, Sera pushed my plate closer to me and began piling food onto it. "No more talk, eat, eat."

I could hear the emotion in her voice too. I went to grab the napkin that was next to my plate, but Fabi took it before I could get my hand on it and immediately began crushing it into the corners of his eyes.

"Fabi, are you ok?"

"Yes," he sniffled as he took the bloody napkin away from his face. "I just can't help…oh the whole…you're all I have left…oh it just turned me into a hot mess. And that plate is reminding me I haven't had bacon in fifty years."

"I was wondering how old you were," I laughed, trying to keep my own emotions at bay.

"I know. I have such a baby face. Devin's really robbing the cradle, the man's practically ancient. Oh no offense, Sera."

She smiled as she began dousing her pancakes in syrup. "None taken. I am very proud to be the only living wife of an Ancient Vampire."

"Wewe?" I asked stupidly with a large bite of my tomato sandwich in my mouth and then tried very hard to swallow. "Ugh, sorry. Really? Is that true?"

"Oui. Not zhat a few have not married before. Ancients can be…"

"Difficult?" I said with a raised brow causing her to smile slyly back at me. "So what makes someone an Ancient? I mean beside the obvious age thing. Where's the line drawn?"

"You could think of it as anyone your father's age and greater. Eris is one of the youngest, I believe," Fabi replied allowing Sera to chew her food while she nodded.

"So Victor isn't an Ancient?"

Fabi shook his head. "No, but his maker is. With the exception of Eris, the other seven keep to themselves, really. You never see them getting involve in today's skirmishes or politics. Master has met a few of them over the years, have you Sera?"

"I have not. Eris has of course, zhough not often. Zhey tend to look down on him."

"Because of his violent tendencies?" I asked snidely before shoving the remaining piece of my sandwich into my mouth.

Sera pursed her lips as she tentatively said, "No, it is more because he cannot prove his lineage." I scrunched my brows questioningly as I began chewing on a piece of bacon. "Eris cannot prove who his maker is, or more so his fazer's maker."

"No one ever found him?"

"He has no idea what he even looks like. I know he would never admit it, but sometimes I think he regrets not having his maker to guide him during his early years."

"I can't quite picture Dad with a mentor."

Fabi shrugged next to me, "Maybe if his maker had been around he wouldn't have the history that he does."

I raised an eyebrow at him and Sera even laughed softly under her breath. "Yeah, I have a pretty good feeling that wouldn't be the case."

"Why's that?"

"Eris's father bartered one of his daughters in order to be Turned, and then ended up draining the other. It's why Eris killed him."

Killing one's parent seemed to run in the family, I thought as I cleared my throat.

"Oh," Fabi replied awkwardly as the front door downstairs opened and a gush of cold air flew up the stairs. "I love when a distraction comes at the right moment."

I laughed as I heard the familiar voices of Renee and Kyla coming up the stairs. Renee's red hair came into view over the top of the banister, her smile and eyes growing bigger when she saw me sitting at the table in the kitchen.

"So you really are alive!" she said cheerily as she clumsily crested the stairs and shifted a long garment bag in her arms. "For a while I thought we would have to wheel a bed down the aisle in order to get you to the wedding."

"Ha! You still may. My stomach isn't going to get any smaller."

Kyla came to stand just behind Renee's shoulder, garment bags also strewn over her arm. "It's good to see your sarcasm wasn't affected while you were gone."

"You two expect me to be happy that you're doing all this wedding planning and shopping without me?"

"Bri," Renee said with dead eyes and her hip popped, "there are so many inappropriate comebacks I could say at this moment, but your hormones will make you cry and then everyone will feel even sorrier for you than they already do, and now that you're back I'm trying to make everything about me as much as I can."

"Hey now, *Twin*, if you don't start being nice to me I'm going to make it a point to push out these babies as I'm walking down the aisle."

"Nice to you!" she shouted, pretending to be offended as she held up the garment bag in front of her. "Who has been searching the city for pregnant lady bridesmaid dresses? Oh wait, that would be me." Kyla nudged Renee's shoulder. "And Kyla. Obviously."

"Do I get to see the dress? Or are you expecting me to wear that bag?"

Renee quirked her lips over her teeth as she unzipped the black garment bag and revealed a large shapeless black dress. She twisted the dress back and forth, allowing all of us to see the movement of the skirt.

"Bri, why are you crying?"

"You're making me wear a garbage bag to the wedding."

Chapter Fifty-Four

Cameron

"Damn it," I cursed under my breath as I stared at the sparkling diamond ring that was stuck at Brianna's knuckle. She had thrown her sapphire ring and Warrior pin away in a fit of rage, but even before she had divulged that information I had noticed it was missing. Kyla was thrilled when I asked her to help me pick out something new, a true engagement ring. Things between us were beginning to settle back in, and though it was presumptuous of me, I had hoped we could go back as far as being engaged again. However, neither Kyla nor I accounted for Brianna's swollen fingers.

Carefully I removed the ring from her finger and ran into the hallway just as Kyla and Alexander were opening the front door for Eris and Seraphina.

"Kyla! It does not fit," I said, holding the ring out to her.

"But she and I have the same ring size, it fit perfectly."

"Her pregnancy has caused her fingers to swell. What do I do?"

"A chain, perhaps?" Seraphina suggested.

"A chain?"

"Oui! She could wear zhe ring around her neck."

Before I could answer, Kyla took the ring from my hand and disappeared up the stairs. I looked to Seraphina and asked, "The swelling will go down though, correct?"

"Oui," she replied with a sweet smile. "At least I believe so. Zhe ring is beautiful."

I shrugged with uncertainty. "I hope Bri likes it. I am afraid she will think it is too big of a diamond."

"Ha!" Eris laughed as he walked toward the door. "A woman may complain initially, but once that diamond is on her finger nothing is ever too big. Am I right, Alex?"

Alexander nodded as he laughed. "I definitely have to…"

"Disagree," Kyla interrupted from the top of the stairs. "That's what you were about to say, wasn't it, honey?"

Alexander cleared his throat and gave me a haggard look. "I'm sure you saw my answer before I said it, *honey.*"

With that, Eris escorted Seraphina outside with Alexander following close behind. Kyla squeezed my arm gently once she stepped onto the landing and placed Brianna's engagement ring into my hand with a shiny white gold chain threaded through the middle. I sighed as I stared at the chain and ring, upset that Bri would not wake to the ring on her finger as Kyla and I had planned.

"Smile, Cameron," Kyla prodded, "she's going to love the ring and what it means, not how it's given to her."

"I know. I just wanted everything to be perfect."

"And it will be. The two of you just need to relax and be yourselves, and remember what you are to each other. Just be Bri and Cam, that's all. The rest will fall into place on its own."

I nodded, though hardly confident. She kissed my cheek before stepping outside and I heading back to my bedroom where Brianna still slept peacefully. I lifted and stretched the chain wide trying to figure out how I could get it around her neck without waking her. When it was obvious that the chain wouldn't go over her head, I unlatched it and tried threading it through her hair which made her moan and bury her face further into her pillow. With a sigh I opened the drawer to my nightstand and tucked the ring and chain back into the small black ring box.

"Morning," she said, surprising me and making me slam the drawer.

"Good morning, angel. Did I wake you?"

She shook her head. "The babies started kicking. They must have known you were here."

I leaned over her, placing my hands on her distended stomach and kissed my children as I whispered, "I thought I told you two to let your mother sleep."

Brianna giggled, causing her stomach to bounce under in my hands. "I don't think they'll ever let me sleep. You're lucky, you don't need it."

"Go back to sleep, love. There is nothing you need to be awake for."

She shook her head again. "I'm too hungry. Besides I told Daddy O I'd call him this morning."

"You do remember the time difference."

"What time is it here?"

"Almost 10:30."

"So four hours behind means," she paused as she did the calculation in her head, "that means he's been up for a half hour already and will be thinking of ways to hide the fact that he and Maddy are shacking up."

"All right, angel. Make your call, but try to be understanding. I will get you some breakfast. Do you have a craving?" And please let it be something that has instructions, or comes out of a box since Seraphina is not here.

Brianna bit her bottom lip as she thought about her options. "I know I keep asking for them, but I really want a tomato and mayo sandwich. I seriously have dreams about them, just ask my dad."

I laughed as I kissed her forehead. "One tomato sandwich coming right up."

"Make it two," she replied quickly and I laughed. "Don't judge me. I'm eating for three you know."

"Yes, love. Even the grocer is well aware you are eating for three."

She did not respond verbally, only with a raised eyebrow and pursing of lips. I could feel a slight pulling in my head, meaning if I did not apologize soon I might just find myself on the floor.

"I am teasing, my love. I would bring you five tomato sandwiches if you asked for them."

"Well that might not be too far off."

"You know I am rarely able to say no to you."

"I think it's what makes us work."

I took her hand and placed it over my heart. "Our love for each other is what makes us work."

She smiled as she pulled my hand down from my chest and placed it over her heart instead. I leaned down and sighed at the feeling of her warm lips against mine. Just as she was about to open her mouth to me, her stomach growled loudly causing the intimate moment to be lost as we both laughed lightly. With one more kiss I was out the door and up the stairs to figure out how in the world I was going to make a tomato and mayonnaise sandwich.

As I approached the kitchen counter I noticed a sheet of white paper sitting on the granite countertop. Although I could not recognize the handwriting, I knew it was a note written by Seraphina as it gave instructions on how to make Brianna's number one craving besides guacamole, which I was thankful she did not ask for. First item on the list, two slices of bread. Check. Second, place bread into toaster. Ahh. A toaster. Admittedly, I have never used a toaster, but really how hard could it be. Figuring that the two slices of bread went into the two slots at the top of the machine, I successfully placed the bread inside and pushed down the lever which I quickly noticed caused the coils inside to glow red and begin to emit heat. Toaster, mastered.

Next item, slice a tomato. Should be easy enough. Just as I placed a tomato onto the cutting board, Fabiani walked into the kitchen and dramatically threw a manila folder down on the counter.

"What is that?" I asked, jutting my chin toward the folder.

"Brianna's copies of all the paperwork for the sale of her house in Connecticut. Dante wanted to formally thank you for getting her to sign everything. He knows this is still an adjustment period for her."

"Trust me, she was more than happy to get the property off her hands," I replied, though I was taken aback by his businesslike tone. He was usually so lighthearted and relaxed, but it was more than evident that something was bothering him.

"Master has also included a list of candidates for the director's position and a listing of the other staff that need to be hired. He would like to start interviews within the next month or so."

I opened a drawer in front of me in search of a knife. "Why would Dante be giving me a list of candidates?"

Fabiani knitted his eyebrows together. "Because you're helping with the staff selection."

"I am?"

"Er…yes? The director, assistants, medical staff, drivers, basically everyone."

"This is the first I have heard about it."

"Well don't shoot the messenger. Master said he and Victor agreed to your services a couple of days ago."

"I am sure it is just a formality. I have not spoken to my father in several days," I said as I picked a sharp knife out of the drawer. "Are you and Devin going out for the day as well?"

"As if!" Fabiani shouted. "Mr. Assassin and I are professionals from here on out. Negotiator and emotionally repressed Warrior, that's what we are." Fabiani took a small side step into the hallway. "You hear me, Mr. Assassin!

Done, finished, never to see me again. Leaving you to roam the world alone and wonder what life could have been like." Fabiani turned on his heel and headed down the stairs. "By the way, Cameron, your toast is burning."

Suddenly startled back into what I was doing I turned around to see smoke coming out of the toaster. Quickly I popped the toaster's lever upwards causing the two slices of charred bread to shoot up in the air and be caught by Devin who was suddenly standing next to me.

"This doesn't happen when Seraphina makes it," he said condescendingly as he placed the black toast in the garbage.

"Thank you, Brother, for your commentary. I was a little distracted by the scene that just played out in my kitchen. Would you care to explain?"

"It is times like these I wished my relationships were still in secret."

"Yes, but would you be happy?" I asked as I placed two more pieces of bread into the toaster.

"Happier than I am at this moment? Yes. Over time, it is hard to say."

"I thought things were going well," I said, handing him the knife and pointing to the tomato on the cutting board. He shrugged and took the knife while I located the mayonnaise in the refrigerator.

"Things were ok, I guess. But remember I told you about the assignment Father gave me in Oregon?"

"Yes, and you are taking Jared home with you."

"Right. So last night I told Fabi I had to leave for a job and that I would probably be staying in the manor for a time. Then he started going on about how he could not wait to see the Warrior manor and finally meet Victor face to face."

"And you got scared."

"I did not!" he shouted, bringing the knife down forcibly, slicing the tomato in half, and wedging the blade in the cutting board. When he finally looked up at me, he sighed and shook his head. "Fine. I got scared. Happy? Does it make you happy that the Warrior Assassin was afraid of what a five-foot-six-inch, one hundred and forty-five pound Vampire would do in front of Father and the other Warriors?"

"Brother," I said calmly, placing one hand on his shoulder, "this is not as new to Fabiani as it is for you. But I think Father would understand. In all actuality it should not matter, you are still the same Warrior Assassin you have been for the last five centuries."

"Your toast is burning again."

"Damn it!" I shouted as the smell of burnt bread wafted through the room once again. "What am I doing wrong? I'm going to need to go to the store if this continues."

"Maybe you should call Seraphina."

"I will not let a puny kitchen appliance get the best of me."

"Looks like it already has."

"And I could say the same for you and a one hundred and forty-five pound Vampire." Devin punched me in the arm in response, causing the burnt toast I had in my hand to crumble in pieces to the ground. "See, same old Assassin."

Devin's tight grin fell as I began picking up the pieces of toast on the floor. "I told Fabi that I would be embarrassed if he came to the manor."

"Brother," I sighed.

"I know. He turned around and looked me dead in the eye and said that I couldn't be any more embarrassed than he was of me being an assassin." Even a human could have heard a pin drop in the silence that fell between us. Slowly Devin picked up his knife again and began slicing one of the tomato halves into thin perfect slices. "I don't know how a soldier and a peacemaker can ever be together, and I simply don't know how to be anything else than the Warrior Assassin."

"That's not true," Brianna said as she crested the top of the stairs in her pajama shorts and red zippered hoodie, seemingly unable to make up her mind if she was hot or cold. "You're a kickass trainer, and from the look of that tomato, a great sous chef."

"Angel," I said rushing over to her, "you should have called me. I would have brought you upstairs."

"Cam, I'm not an invalid," she said and then waved her hand in front of her face. "What's burning?"

"Cameron is trying to make toast," Devin laughed.

"Oh, Cam," she whined as she stepped around me and headed into the kitchen. "Where's Sera?"

"Brianna, I can handle making you breakfast without Seraphina's help."

"Apparently not. You have the setting on the toaster all the way up, that's why it's burning."

Devin laughed again. "The Warrior may have mastered the toaster's mechanics, but failed because he couldn't read."

"Brother," I growled, "I am sure there is somewhere you need to be."

"Not that I know of."

Brianna snorted as she turned the knob of the toaster down and then placed two pieces of bread into the machine. "I think he's saying you need to go and talk to Fabi."

"How do you know about that?" Devin asked defensively.

"I was eavesdropping," she shrugged as she walked around the island and sat on one of the stools hidden underneath. "You should talk to him and apologize."

"I tried. He told me we were through."

"He just wants you to be able to admit you're with him when you're outside of this house."

"What does Fabi expect me to do? Announce it to the world? Hold hands with him in public and show affection like the two of you do?"

"Yes!" she answered.

"That isn't going to happen," he replied firmly.

"Then you will never be happy, Devin. If you can't be comfortable with yourself, you will never be able to be with someone else."

"Why is this so hard? I am surrounded by my siblings who have mates and everything comes so easy to them."

"Brother, every real relationship takes work and compromise. Look at what I went through to be with Brianna. You of all people know the struggles she and I have faced since we met. But we have faced them together and compromised with one another along the way."

"That's right," Brianna chimed in. "Cameron's only taken up half the closet instead of the whole thing like at the manor."

I narrowed my eyes at her smiling face and was rewarded with a kiss on the cheek. Devin sighed as he wiped his hands on a dishtowel lying on the counter and stepped from around the island.

"Speaking of the manor, have you spoken to Father about what your plans are now that Brianna is back?"

"My plans have not changed, Brother. We plan to stay in Boston," I replied as I widened my eyes at him, trying silently to get him to leave off.

"Yes, but when I spoke with Father last night he was saying how with all your involvement these last couple of months that you might have changed your mind about…"

"Brother, we can talk about this later."

"No, Brother, we cannot. I am leaving tonight and Father wants an answer."

"Answer on what?" Brianna asked as she looked up at me with worried eyes.

I paused before I reluctantly answered, "The morning you were taken I was in the middle of relinquishing my seat on the Elite Council. Father had threatened to remove me from the coven altogether."

"And crush Father's dreams about having the two of us lead the Warriors in the future," Devin added, making me clinch my fists at my sides and want to hit my brother in the jaw.

"Cam? Is that true?"

My hand relaxed at the sound of her voice and I squeezed her shoulder gently. "We can talk more about it once you have eaten. Brother," I said sternly as I turned in his direction, "now I am telling you that you have somewhere else to be."

"You know Father, he won't wait long," Devin said flatly and made his way down the stairs.

"Go and talk to Fabi," Brianna shouted after him.

"I'm going, I'm going," he mumbled before the front door shut behind him.

Brianna smiled as the toast popped up from the toaster. "Babe, you did it!"

I shook my head as I took out the toast and placed the last two slices of bread inside the toaster for Brianna's second sandwich. Turning back to the island, I dipped the knife into the mayonnaise and began spreading it on the warm toast as I said, "It is not my fault I have never cooked in my long life."

"Trust me, you're not the only Vamp who's burnt..." she began, but quickly bit her lip.

"Did he used to make these for you?"

Our eyes met and I instantly felt horrible for asking the stupid question at the sight of the guilt on her face.

"Sometimes. He...he had to because I kept throwing up anything that Shelby made me and I was so weak..."

"Bri angel," I spoke over her as I stretched over the island and placed my hand on top of hers. "It was insensitive of me to ask. I am still...adjusting."

She squeezed my hand and then released it in order to put me back to work on her sandwich.

"So where is everyone?" she asked as she began looking at the papers in the manila folder that sat next to her.

"Alexander and Kyla are escorting your parents on a tour of Boston," I replied and placed several slices of tomatoes onto the toast, feeling extremely accomplished. "What is that look for?"

Brianna closed her jaw and blinked several times. "Sera left the house?"

I nodded as I took the fresh toast from the toaster. "Yes. She became very animated last night after you went to bed and planned her attack on the city. I think you have liberated her, my love."

"Wow. I really am speechless," she replied and reached for her sandwich, only to be stopped by her stomach. Her bottom lip instantly jutted out in an adorable pout. Not wanting her to suffer a second longer, I placed the sandwich on a plate and slid it across the countertop before going to work on sandwich number two.

"So what's this?" she asked as she took a bite of her sandwich and then lifted the piece of paper that listed names and positions for Facility East.

"Apparently Father and Dante want me to help in hiring the staff at the new Facility."

"Really?" she replied. "You need drivers? Why?"

"Since the new location is not particularly close to an airport or train station it was determined that it would save time if drivers were to meet the Gatherer's instead of having them drive all the way."

"Then I have the perfect candidate," she said, wiping a dollop of mayonnaise from her mouth.

"You do?"

"Yes. My friend Jonah."

"Jonah?"

"Yeah, Jonah, my driver in Connecticut, remember? He's perfect for the job, and he lives in the area."

"Bri, I think they want to consider Vampires for the job."

"Having been a new hybrid, Vamps can be intimidating. It might be nice to get a ride from a human to help you ease into the situation. Just promise me you'll talk to Dante about Jonah. That's all I'm asking," she said sweetly as she placed the paper back into the folder and closed the cover.

"Yes, love. I will."

"So with Devin gone, we have the house to ourselves?"

"Jared is in the basement of course, but besides that, yes we have *our* house to ourselves until everyone returns for your appointment at the hospital. You are seeing Dr. Taylor today, remember?" She nodded as she continued to eat her sandwich. "Did you have something in mind until then?"

She swallowed with effort before saying, "I was thinking we could go downstairs?"

"Lay out on the couch?"

"Blankets and pillows?"

"Watch your mindless reality television shows."

She laughed. "Usually I would say yes, but I think we have a lot to talk about."

There was nothing worse than when a woman said you had a lot to talk about.

"Shall we?" I said as I placed her second sandwich onto her plate and tried not to show an ounce of fear.

Slowly we went down the stairs together, and within minutes she was stretched out on the couch, her plate balanced on her belly while she ate. I took the soft white blanket that was strewn across the opposite loveseat and tucked it around Brianna's legs and then fluffed several pillows to prop up against her back. When I sat down next to her, she instantly removed the pillows and climbed backwards to the edge of couch and across my lap.

"Much better," she sighed happily as she placed a pillow behind her head against the armrest.

"So my love, what is first on the list of discussion topics," I asked, pulling the blanket back up around her legs as she balanced the plate once again on her belly.

"I've been meaning to tell you that I like the furniture," she said as she popped the last bite of her first sandwich in her mouth and then picked up her second.

"It was Renee and Fabiani's doing, mostly out of necessity. You can change whatever you want, that was our deal."

"No," she swallowed, "I like it. Except, can we move the conference table upstairs to the dining room or something?"

"Angel, we can move the table to the roof if you so wish it."

"Crazy thing is you'd probably do it. No, I like what's here, I just want to add to it, move a few things around."

"We can move things to your heart's desire. Is that it?"

She laughed. "Hardly."

"Ok, next topic," I said and then decided not to breathe at all, it was easier not to let out a sigh that way.

"Names."

"Names?" I replied with the small amount of air that was left in my lungs.

"Mmm-hmm. For the babies."

I could feel the corners of my mouth almost touching the lobes of my ears. "I love this topic. So where do we start?"

"I think we should start with boy names."

"It sounds like you have some ideas."

She nodded. "Well I've been thinking that his father has a beautiful name."

"You want to name our son Cameron Jackson…"

"Junior," she interrupted. "We could call him CJ for short."

"Absolutely not," I replied firmly. My skin was crawling, though Brianna's entire face furrowed into a frown. "Love, I want our son to be his own person, not be constantly compared to me or feel that he has to live up to me in some way just because of a name. Besides I do not want anyone to call my son CJ."

"You could have just said no."

"Fine. No, my love."

"Ok then, what about naming him after your father?"

"Vic-tor?" I said slowly and dripping with confusion.

"Ohmygod no," she laughed. "I meant your real father. Thomas." My pause caused her to think I was vetoing yet another suggestion. "Look, I'm just thinking it would be nice to honor our families a little."

"Thomas has potential," I smiled.

"Ok, little girl names," she said happily as she bite into the last half of her sandwich.

"Maybe we should go with your theme and name her after your grandfather."

She paused, a sliver of tomato hanging from her bottom lip as she said, "Oliver?"

I shook my head and laughed. "We are not very good at this. I meant the feminine version. Olivia."

Brianna's eyes widened at the sound of the name. "Can I call her Livy?"

"Yes, you can call her Livy."

"I like it. Olivia Burke, it has a ring to it. Ok, next topic."

"Already?" I asked. She nodded as she shoved the last of her sandwich into her mouth and placed the plate onto the floor. "Should we not discuss middle names?"

"They'll come in time. We need to keep pushing through or else I won't remember everything we need to talk about."

I hoped for my sake the other topics were similar to the last two. She took a deep breath before she spoke, making me believe she wanted to discuss something other than what color to paint the nursery.

"Don't leave the coven."

My eyes blinked several times, unprepared for those words to come out of her mouth. "Bri, whether I leave the coven is not necessarily my choice."

"Victor's mad because you won't be in the manor anymore, it's just one of his tantrums. He doesn't mean it."

"Father has no use for me just as a Warrior. I was not chosen for my fighting skills like his other children. My purpose has always been for strategic purposes on the Elite Council, and in order to be on the council you must live in the manor."

"Do you want to leave the coven?"

"Of course not," I replied, my chest suddenly heavy with the realty.

"Do you want to lead the Warriors?"

I sighed. "I never wanted to, but at times I seem to just sink into the role. More so, if I refuse to lead, then I will be responsible for killing my eldest brother's lifelong dream. But being here with you, in our home, it feels right. This is where we are supposed to be, not in the manor."

"But you have a bargaining chip."

"I do?"

She released a long sigh, keeping her eyes on her stomach as she said, "Agree to lead the Warriors with Devin."

"What!" I said too loudly, startling her slightly.

"But Cam just listen…"

"No. It is not what I want for our family."

"Cameron," she said calmly as she placed my other hand on top of her stomach. "Victor isn't planning on you taking over right away I'm sure. Promise him that when it's time, you'll lead the Warriors with Devin as long as you can stay here in Boston for the time being. We both need to admit that," she paused, "I'm not always going to be around. You should have something to go back to after I'm gone."

It was a topic that she and I had never broached, mostly because neither of us wanted to come to terms with her mortality. It made me wonder if her dreams and her recent brush with death brought the worries to the forefront. Since I met Bri, I never pictured my life without her at my side.

"There is a way for us to always be together."

Brianna's chest fell, as did her face. "Cam…I…I don't want to be a Vampire."

"O-oh," I stuttered, never thinking that would have been her answer.

"It doesn't mean I don't love you, Cam."

"I know you love me, Brianna."

She sniffled as she placed her hand back on her stomach. "I need to be a real mother to our children. I want to breast feed and be able to take them outside during the day and…and not worry about eating them if I get low on blood. I just can't ever be afraid of hurting our babies…I could never live with myself."

"Then we could wait until the children are grown."

"And be frozen when I'm almost fifty? No way. I…I need you to understand why I can't."

I paused, looking deeply into Brianna's dark eyes, unable to grasp that at some time in the future I would not be able to look into them again. But the tears that were now filling her eyes made me have to push down any selfish emotions I felt in this moment. "I do."

Knowing she did not fully believe me, but wanting to change the subject again she said, "Next topic?"

I nodded.

"I feel like such a snitch, but last night I caught Jared talking to Nikki on his computer. Did you know he was talking to her?"

"Unfortunately, yes," I sighed as I scratched my fingers through my hair. "But they are monitored at all times."

"For real this time?" she asked with a raised brow.

"Nikki is monitored twenty-four-seven. Father is not taking any chances this time."

"Victor won't forgive Jazlyn, but he'll forgive Nikki?"

"Jared has made a convincing case that she is a victim of circumstance and manipulation."

"And skank-alation," she replied flustered and crossed her arms in front of her chest. "She's just playing all of us."

"Yes, angel. We are all waiting for her next move, but we will be watching this time. It is simply too dangerous for her to be out where we cannot monitor her."

"It just makes me so mad that Jared is still in love with her after what she did to us."

"It is not real, Bri. Not like us."

"Right, not like us," she replied and brushed the back of her hand down my cheek. "Only one more thing to talk about, I promise."

"Oh good, I think there is a marathon of that housewife show I would like to get started on," I said sarcastically, getting Brianna's narrowed eyes in response.

"Actually, I wanted to talk about this," she said as she put her hand into the front pocket of her hoodie and pulled out the ring box that was supposed to be in the drawer of my nightstand.

"Where did you find that?"

"I was talking to Daddy O and needed a piece of paper so I looked in the drawer."

"And you started snooping."

"And yes, I started snooping."

"Did you open it?" She shook her head. "Truly?"

"I swear."

I took the box from her hand and slowly opened it to reveal the platinum set four carat round diamond between two tapered diamond baguettes. Brianna tangled her fingers around Kyla's white gold chain that dangled over the box's edge while she gawked at the ring in the center.

"When did you get a ring?" she asked, finally looking up at me.

"The day after you came home without one." Her face fell slightly, still guilty about throwing her sapphire away. "I told you I wanted to get you a diamond anyway."

"It's huge."

"I knew you would say that. You can always pick out something else…that is, if you still want to…"

"I didn't say I didn't want it. I want it, I want it on my hand right now."

Only the left side of my mouth lifted into a smile. "You see, love, the ring was made to the same size as your sapphire, but your fingers have swelled since then. Seraphina suggested the chain."

"Can you still put it on?" she said as she held out her left hand.

With absolute relief I took the ring from the box and slid it down as far as it would go on her left ring finger. Taking only a second to look at the ring she placed her hands on either side of my face, the white gold chain brushing my cheek and chin as she brought my lips down onto hers. It was not until her stinging hot tongue surged into my mouth that I felt my control begin to waiver. Suddenly my fingers were pulling down the zipper of her hoodie, exposing her usual thin white camisole.

Rising up from her lips, I stared deeply into Brianna's eyes as I slowly pulled at the edge of the camisole, lifting it up to fully expose her pregnancy. A heat instantly stirred under my hand as I placed it on her stomach, and I could even feel the babies' soft kicks from inside her.

"I want you," she said breathlessly as her hands disappeared underneath my shirt.

"Not nearly as much as I want to take you."

"I haven't showered though."

"Has that ever stopped me before?"

"Have you gotten over your fear of putting a dent into our children's heads?"

Pulling my shirt over my head, I threw it over the back of the couch as I stretched alongside her. "I believe you told me I was not well-endowed enough for that to happen."

With a seductive smile Brianna unbuttoned my pants as she said, "I could have been wrong. Let's take a look and find out."

Chapter Fifty-Five

Brianna

"Are you ready for this, love?" Cameron whispered in my ear as he wrapped his arms around me from behind.

"Yes...n-no..." I stuttered.

Bulldozers and a wrecking ball sat on the front lawn of my former Connecticut home. It had been three months since I sold my home to the coven leaders and in that time building permits and snow delays continued to push the demolition date until this freakishly warm week in March. Almost all the winter's snow had melted, leaving only small dirty mounds near the streets. And even though it was stretching up to sixty degrees, it felt like summer after all the single digit temperatures we had had this winter. So much so that I was wearing capris pants and a short sleeved tunic after a long harrowing debate with Cameron this morning.

To put it lightly, I was ginormous. There were so many stages in my early pregnancy that I thought for sure there was no way I could get any bigger, or my ankles even uglier as they transformed into canned hams. But as every week passed I was a little bigger, a little slower, and scarily enough a little hungrier. Snacks were as common as the Braxton-Hicks contractions I'd been having for the last month. It was only five weeks until my due date, although no one thought I'd make it that far. Lying in bed was the norm these days so the fact that I was sitting here in Connecticut was really by the grace of God, and many an argument with Cameron. Not only did I want to see the last evidence of my life with Sam destroyed, I wasn't going to miss Renee's bridal shower. I had missed enough of the wedding plans. Besides it was my duty as maid of honor to throw a shower, even if Renee's mother decided to take complete control. Not that I want to sound bitter.

"Earth to Brianna," Cameron said in my ear as he squeezed my shoulders.

"Sorry, babe, just spacey today," I replied as I patted his hand and began playing with my engagement ring that was hanging around my neck. "Is there any more of that maple cake?"

"I would be surprised if there was," he replied with my favorite crooked smile. "Mable sent you out with extra supplies for the ride home, but I think you ate most of it before we got here."

"That's not true!"

From behind me I could hear a deep guttural laugh near where our SUV was parked. When I turned my head I noticed Alex's chest disappearing into the backseat and then coming out with one of the small red tins that Mable had given me this morning when we left her bed and breakfast.

"Bri, you're in luck," Alex shouted over the construction noise. "There's one piece left."

Really? How did I let that happen?

Devin, who was standing to my left, grunted disapprovingly as I took the tin from Alex's hand. "Brianna, the more weight you gain, the tougher it will be to get back in shape. Perhaps you should lay off the snacks."

"Well *perhaps* you should shut the f..."

"*Brianna*," Cameron warned.

"If Dev is switching places with you for a week, he better learn what not to say to a very pregnant woman."

Devin took a step forward and turned to face me head on. "Brianna, I didn't mean to offend you. I was merely saying that if you continue to..."

"One more word and you will be face down on the ground," I said nastily.

Alex and Cameron tried unsuccessfully to stifle their laughter while Devin pretended to be cross with me. "It's a good thing I like you."

"Ditto," I growled kiddingly and narrowed my eyes. "It's ok, Dev, you can admit how much you missed me."

Devin harrumphed, crossing his arms in front of his chest, but then unable to stop the tight smile from forming. Since New Year's there had been a strict rule of two Vampires on Bri at all times. Ok, not *on* me. Not even Cameron could get on me anymore. Since it was difficult for everyone to be away from the manor for such a long period of time, the Warriors were on rotation in Boston. The only constants in the house were my parents, Kyla, and Cameron. That was until today. Once the demolition was underway, Cameron would be leaving me for the first time since we had been reunited. Neither of us liked it, but we didn't really have a choice. Victor had made it clear that Cameron was to return home in order to discuss the terms of how they would work together outside of the manor. It was a big adjustment for everyone, especially Victor.

Just then all three Vamps around me puffed up their chests, ears perked as they turned toward the sound of an oncoming car in the distance.

"It's not an SUV," Alex said first.

"Can't be one of ours then," Devin answered after.

"Definitely not," Cameron said as he took a step into the road. "That is a 1969 Camaro."

Alex whistled as the nose of the car finally came into view. "Camaro Z28, 302 cubic inch V8 engine."

"Five speed manual transmission, 290 horsepower," Devin finished.

"It better not be silver," I said through my teeth.

"With two black racing stripes up the front," Cameron cooed, echoing the dreamy looks on his brothers' faces.

"That little shit!" I shouted as the silver muscle car slowed and crunched over the ice that remained on the side of the road. Cameron whipped his head around with a questioning look. "It's Jonah."

"Jonah? Your Jonah drives a car like that?" Alex asked with a seed of jealousy.

Cameron looked back at the car as if in a trance as Jonah exited the car. "I will give him cash today for that car."

"It's Sam's old car."

Cameron's face fell. "You had to ruin my dream."

"Sorry, babe."

"Wait a minute," Cameron said coming back to reality, "you sold Jonah *that* car for a dollar!"

Suddenly I was despised by three men.

"Hey now, it was mine to do with as I pleased so I did. The little shit told me he was going to sell it. Stay here, I need to yell at him first."

I stretched out my arms and allowed Cameron to lift me from my chair. With a huff I waddled slowly away to the snickers of Devin and Alex and even Jonah, though he tried to hide it behind his fingers. I only took a few more steps before placing my hands on top of my stomach and waited for

Jonah to complete the distance between us.

"So do you actually have a sister? Or did you just play me like a schmuck in order to get that car?"

Jonah extended his arms out wide. "Of course I have a sister, you know I'd never lie to you." I let him wrap his arms around my neck though I didn't hug him back, causing him to step back. "Ah Bri, come on. My mom took one look at the car and wouldn't let me sell it. At least not yet. I think she likes riding around in it as much as I like driving it."

"You're still a little shit, but I'm glad you came."

"Well, you said you had a job opportunity, and considering how I've hated every other client I've had since you, I need a new job. Besides I wanted to see you and see you and see you. Seriously, how are you standing right now? You're enormous."

"Jonah, the fact that you live in a house of women, I'm surprised you don't know you should never tell a woman she's enormous."

"Sorry, you're just…so…how are you not falling forward."

I growled under my breath and gave him an evil eye. "Do you want the interview? Or do you want to keep wearing that monkey suit you have to call a uniform."

I could feel Cameron approaching before his arm draped over my shoulder. "I heard the words enormous and falling forward, so I thought I should come over to offer some protection."

Jonah's face instantly flinched. "I would never…"

"Oh no, protection for you…from her," Cameron replied with his crooked smile, placing his hand on my stomach and giving me a hot flash.

"Cameron, this is Jonah. Jonah, meet Cameron."

Jonah extended his hand and Cameron shook it carefully. "Nice to meet you, sir. Can't tell you how happy I was when Bri told me you two worked things out."

"Not as much as I," Cameron replied, releasing Jonah's hand and then kissing my temple. "So Brianna tells me you are one skilled driver."

"Er…yes?" My eyes shot open causing him to clear his throat. "I mean yes. Yes. I have been a chauffeur for only six months, but put me behind the wheel and I can drive anything. Is that the job? You need drivers?"

Cameron nodded. "We are building a training facility and we will need people to pick up our recruits and bring them here. The job is pretty simple, but we need to have people we can trust to keep our business confidential. And if the need occurs, outrun the law if necessary."

"Cam," I sighed and smacked him gently on the chest. "Don't scare him."

Cameron laughed, making Jonah relax a little. "I am only kidding, Jonah. But if you had to, would you?"

Jonah shrugged. "As long as I get paid on a regular basis and don't have to wear a uniform, I'm pretty much up for anything."

"Good to hear," Cameron said as he patted Jonah on his shoulder. "Before the demolition gets under way, how about we go and introduce you to Dante. He will be overseeing the actual facility."

Cameron gestured across the wide lawn to where Dante was flitting excitedly between several bulldozers. Today he felt it fitting to wear a lavender polyester jumpsuit accented with a red ascot flapping at his neck.

"He's the boss?" Jonah asked softly in shock.

"Yes," Cameron answered cheerfully. "His outfit is rather tame today, actually. But do not let it throw you, he will see through anything you try to put past him."

"What Cameron is trying to say," I said, rolling my eyes, "is just be honest. Dante cares more about getting to know you. Don't try and be more than you are, just be yourself. He'll find it refreshing."

Jonah looked at me out of the side of his eye. "Thanks for the pep talk, mom."

"Older, wiser sister," I corrected and pushed him away to follow Cameron across the yard.

A few feet away Alex caught my attention and waved me back over to my chair and patted the seat. "Brianna, come sit down before you go into labor. I left my catcher's mitt back at the manor."

"You and I both know they don't make a baseball glove big enough to fit your hand."

"She does have a point," Devin chimed in with a shrug.

But before the two of them could get into a friendly tussle, a large SUV crested the hill and eventually parked in front of Jonah's Camaro. Even from my chair roughly fifty feet away I could see the glowing red and orange hair of my two best friends sitting in the front seats. You couldn't even see through the back of the SUV since it was filled to the brim with all the bridal shower gifts from the day before. Honestly I was surprised there was enough room for John and Fabi in the back seat.

Renee's fire engine red hair blew in the wind behind her as she trudge over to me and I knew I was in trouble by her tight lipped expression. "Nice twin you are! You left me high and dry with my mom! I should revoke your maid of honor status."

I could feel the babies stirring inside me. The babies created a freakish heat when Cam touched them, but whenever they heard Renee it felt as though they were going to kick a hole through me.

"Re, the last time I checked, your mother was *your* mother. And if you didn't notice, she was more than happy to get me out of her house."

"That's because she's threatened by you. She thinks I love you more than her."

"You do love me more than her."

"Duh," she replied and rubbed her hand over my belly. "But she can't know that. Hi babies! Auntie Re still loves you, even when your mama abandons me."

"Where are you going to put all of that stuff," I said gesturing to the SUV.

"Most of it's going in your basement."

"Since when?"

"Since you have free space and we don't."

"Don't you bring your hoarding into my house."

Renee squinted her eyes up at me because of my tone. "You doing ok?" I nodded but she knew I was putting up a front. "When's Cameron leaving?"

"Vlad is waiting at the airport for him. He said he had to leave once the demolition was underway. So…not long."

She squeezed my hand and looked across the lawn while the others gathered behind us. "Who's the hottie talking with Dante and Cameron?"

"That's Jonah. The kid I was telling you about."

"Boy, he makes me want to be a cougar."

John cleared his throat somewhere behind me. "Re, you do know we're getting married in a week."

"Yeah I know," she replied without an ounce of apology.

A few minutes later Jonah was jogging back up the lawn towards us with a peculiar smile on his face. I looked over to Kyla who was standing next to me, and stretched my arms out. Carefully she lifted me to a standing position just as Jonah came to stand in front of me.

"Bri, wow," he began excitedly, "that was the weirdest, but greatest, interview ever. How can I ever…seriously stop doing nice things for me. My tab is way too big. First the car, now maybe a new job…"

"Whoa, wait a minute," Renee interrupted and pointed to the Camaro, "that's not '*Sam's*' car is it?"

"Re, I told you I gave it away," I replied.

"Damn, twin! You give his prized car away and sell his house to your new fiancé, talk about 'revenge.'"

"And Sam didn't deserve it?"

"Oh of course he deserves it. I find it fan-fucking-tastic, but a little sad that we'll never get to see the reaction on his rotten cock sucking face."

Jonah stood frozen in front of me. "Jonah, this is my foul mouthed friend Renee, scarily enough one of the godmothers to my children."

"'Kay. I'm kinda scared to ask who the other godparents are," Jonah said, looking oddly around at the group in front of him.

Kyla crooked her arm around Alex's large bicep and said with immense glee, "That would be us! I think it's the perfect balance."

Jonah laughed lightly under his breath. It was in that moment that I realized Jonah seemed completely unfazed by Alex's size, or any of the other strange and unique qualities of my family and friends. For that alone he should be given the job, but we would know soon enough since Cameron began walking up the front lawn.

Jonah turned nervously in Cameron's direction and even I had a hard time figuring out if he had good or bad news from his expression.

"So Jonah," Cameron began in a very formal tone. "Dante would like to offer you a driver's position, head driver actually. You would be responsible for the fleet of vehicles, schedules, and logistics."

"What about salary?" I pressed.

Cameron raised an eyebrow at me, but then turned his gaze back to Jonah. "Salary would start at $50,000."

"Holy shit!" Jonah shouted, skipping backwards with a short victory dance before straightening up and stepping back into our circle. "Sorry. Really? Like, for real?"

Cameron smiled. "Do not be fooled, Jonah. This will be a full-time job, sometimes more so. For a while you could be on call twenty-four-seven."

"*Buuut,*" I interrupted again, "once Dante hires other drivers he'll have a regular schedule with most nights free and at least two days off. He needs two weeks paid vacation, and everyone will need to be understanding of his class schedule. He needs to finish school. Oh! And he gets access to the Facility's medical services when needed."

Jonah's jaw hung open while Cameron crossed his arms in front of his chest and quirked his lips. "Does Jonah need anything else, love?"

"And no uniform."

"Fine," he replied with a crooked smile. "Jonah? What do you say?"

"When do I start?" he asked excitedly.

"Today actually," Cameron replied, giving me an apologetic look. "I need a ride to the airport, and we can talk more specifics about the job. Sound good?"

"Heck yeah!" he shouted as he shook Cameron's hand and waved happily over to Dante who was stepping away from the wrecking ball.

Everyone behind us cheered as the trucks began to move closer to the house, and Cameron wrapped a protective arm around me and escorted me back to my canvas chair. With every stone crushing blow the wrecking ball made through the house I felt a little bit of the remaining hold Sam had on my life crack and float away. It was amazing that the amount of hate and pain held within those walls couldn't even begin to match the amount of love that Cameron and I had for each other. This was truly my revenge.

After several minutes my mansion in the Connecticut hills was no more and Cameron was squeezing my shoulder, making my stomach feel like the pile of rubble in the distance. Carefully he took my hands and lifted me from my chair, wrapping them around his neck and gliding his hands down my back. With the size of my belly I could no longer tuck my head underneath his chin, so instead he leaned his head down, his dark curls tickling my cheek as he nuzzled my ear, making the tears hard to hold back.

"It is only four days, love."

"I know," I sniffled, taking the opportunity to take in his rustic scent that I loved so much.

"I knew you would cry, but it always tears me apart."

"I'm...sorry.

"You have no reason to be," he replied softly. "Four days will go by in a flash. I meet with Father, pack our room up, gather Oliver and Madelyn, and then I will be back in your arms. You will hardly notice I am gone."

"Don't forget my pictures," I reminded him for the millionth time, even though he never pointed it out.

Cameron stood straight, placing his hands on either side of my face. "I will miss you every minute we are apart, and I will long to feel your warmth in my arms," he said and gave me a single kiss on each of my eyelids, leaving my lips for last. "And what is the awful password you came up with if anyone comes to you saying I have sent them to take you away?"

"Pickles," I smiled through tears. "Sorry, babe, it was my stranger-danger password with Daddy O. There's no way I would ever remember another one, I can barely remember my name these days."

Cameron kissed the tip of my nose. "Brianna." Then my forehead. "Marilena." Then my lips. "Morgan-Burke."

"A hyphen?"

"Just making sure you know you have options. One last kiss, love."

This kiss was soft, but filled with promises and longing, and too short.

With tight lips and a reluctant expression on his face, Cam took a step back and walked me over to where Devin and Alex were leaning against an empty SUV.

"Brothers, I am leaving what I hold most dear in your care."

"And we will protect her with our lives, Brother," Devin replied with an absolute certainty.

"Let us hope it does not come to that," Cameron said with a hint of worry in his voice. "Jonah," he called over to the other SUV where everyone else had gathered, "are you ready, kid?"

Jonah took his keys from his pocket and shook them in the air as he jogged over to us. "Yes, sir. I'm guessing you don't mind going in the Camaro?"

Cameron opened his mouth to speak, but I put a hand to his chest. "Remember, Cam, the car is Jonah's now. So don't go pissin' on the tires."

Cameron pursed his lips tightly at first, but then they melted into a crooked smile as both Devin and Alex laughed loudly behind us. "Come Jonah, we must go. And on the way I can tell you a little more about Facility East and those who you will be working for."

Jonah nodded, not seeing the sly smile Cameron was giving him as he hugged me. We all knew what Cameron meant. The real test would be how Jonah reacted to learning that Vampires truly existed and that he would be working for them.

"Fifty bucks he completely freaks out and kicks Cameron out of the car," Alex laughed as we watched Cameron and Jonah walk to the Camaro.

"No way!" I answered and turned around to face both of them. "Jonah has a way about him. I'll bet you fifty dollars that he doesn't freak out and they just keep driving."

"Deal. Now you don't mind if I carry you over there, do you? With the way you walk these days it will take you twenty minutes to waddle over far enough to where we can see them drive away."

I shot a nasty look to his pleasant smiling face, but didn't object when he lifted me into his massive arms and carried me over to where the rest of our family was milling around the grill of the loaded SUV. When Alex put me down he updated everyone on the terms of the bet, and like curious kids we all huddled together and peeked around the side of the SUV when the Camaro roared to life.

We watched as Jonah pulled a U-turn and began heading down the narrow country road, but just as the car was about to go down the hill and disappear from our view, the brake lights suddenly illuminated and the car swerved to a stop.

"Here it comes!" Alex cheered with anticipation.

Keep going Jonah, just keep driving, I kept thinking. But at that moment the driver's side door burst open and Jonah jumped out of the car, his hands pulling at his hair. A moment later Cameron stepped out of the car, his arms stretched out over the roof looking as though he was pleading with Jonah to get back inside. While we continued to watch the scene play out, Cameron gestured down the road in our direction causing Jonah to look at us.

"Everybody wave," Fabi erupted and we obeyed by waving or giving thumbs up or any other positive and encouraging hand signal we could think of. The gesture seemed to only make Jonah even more confused as he kept looking between us and Cameron.

"Poor kid," Dr. John said shaking his head. "I've been in his shoes. You seriously have no idea which way is up and everyone around you seems so calm."

"Ok then, everyone stop," Fabi chimed in again. "Maybe we're coming on a little strong."

We stopped waving, but we continued to watch as Cameron slowly made his way around the trunk of the car, eventually coming alongside Jonah who didn't back up or run down the street like I'm sure his feet wanted to do. With a pat on the shoulder, Cameron continued to speak to Jonah and eventually led him to the passenger side of the car and allowed him to melt into the seat. After Cameron closed the passenger car door he walked back around the rear of the car, looking at us and shaking his head before disappearing into the driver's seat. Within seconds the brake lights disappeared and the back tires were squealing on the asphalt before the Camaro finally disappeared over the hill.

"I believe the bet is a draw, Alex," Devin said backing away toward our SUV. "Jonah was frightened, but they ended up driving away, which is exactly what we should be doing now."

"Yep, Devin's right," Renee said as she looked at her watch. "We have a fitting to get to, people! Let's not putz around. Bri, wanna come with us?"

"Um…that's ok, there's more room for me in the other truck."

Renee huffed as she walked over to the driver's side of the bridal shower clown truck. "Fine, but Dev, don't drive like an old lady. We have an appointment in two hours and I'm not waiting for you to catch up. Ok, let's move it, people, we don't have all fucking day."

With that I turned and waddled back to the SUV where Devin was holding the backseat door open for me. "I have never driven like an old lady."

"Of course not, Dev, she's just a little high strung at the moment," I said, patting him on his tight jaw.

"I am surprised you are not going with them."

I laughed. "Renee, I love. Totally-stressed-out-week-before-the-wedding-Renee, not so much. I'm on edge as it is right now, I don't need her barking at me too."

"I thought you might be a little…emotional?" he said, questioning his word choice as he lifted me into the backseat. "There is a surprise on the seat next to you."

While Devin closed the door I looked to my left and saw a rectangular red tin sitting beside me, similar to the tins that were discarded on the truck's floor. I placed the tin on my belly shelf and opened the lid to find a layer of maple cake squares.

"Where did you get these?" I asked as Devin climbed into the driver's seat and started the engine while Fabi climbed into the front passenger seat.

Devin put the truck in gear and pulled it away from the street. "While everyone was watching the demolition I checked out that kid's car and saw the tin inside."

"You stole it?"

"No!" he said offended while looking at me in the rearview mirror. "I told him it was for you and gave him twenty dollars."

"Devy," Fabi said tenderly as he touched Devin's hand that was resting on the center consol. "How sweet of you to do that."

"Not really," Devin answered flatly as he gunned the gas. "I knew Bri was hungry and I didn't want to hear her complain for two hours."

"Ah, there's the Devin I know and love. Uh…why are we going so fast?"

"Because I'm racing with Renee."

"Does she know that?"

"I am sure she knows now."

"Devin, I swear if you make me go into labor I will Push you so hard your head will explode. So unless you want these babies to be born in the backseat, I suggest you slow down."

"Brianna, I assure you I am an excellent driver."

"Devin!"

"You are taking the fun out of everything."

"I'm a mother, that's what I'm supposed to do."

"Let's get this over with," Jazlyn shouted as she leaned over me, covering me with her long thick black hair.

Tears streamed down my face as I stared into Jazlyn's black Vampire eyes. "You're just like her," I whimpered helplessly.

Jazlyn's eyes narrowed slightly before she nuzzled into my ear and whispered, "Not everything is as it seems."

Jazlyn's grip softened as she lifted her veil of hair from around my face, just in time for me to see Elaina raise the knife above her head. A second later Elaina thrust the knife down toward my stomach just as Jazlyn pushed off my wrists like a tigress and tackled Elaina into the wall across the room. Quickly I dug my heels into the floor and pushed myself backwards, but only seconds later the back of my head slammed on the floor as a blurred hand thrust against my chest. Stars were circling in front of my eyes as Aidan's snarled expression focused in front of me. His left hand clamped down around my throat, holding me down on the floor while he held Elaina's knife at my stomach.

"One way or another I always get what I want," he said with a wicked smile stretched across his face while the tip of the knife pierced my skin and began cutting up the length of my stomach. My screams were caught in my throat while my insides burned with pain from the knife. But through the pain I Pushed, and Pushed, and Pushed until my head ached, but Aidan didn't flinch, not one little bit.

Suddenly Aidan released my throat and shoved his hands into my stomach. I screamed in agony while he rummaged inside me, but it seemed no one could hear me.

"Wake up, Brianna! Wake up!" I screamed to myself.

A wicked laugh came from Aidan's lips as he said, "Stay, Morgan, keep on dreaming. We're about to get to the good part."

"NO!" I screamed as I lifted myself up, flinging my arms out in front of me and Pushed at anything and everything in front of me.

I opened my eyes in time to see Devin and Fabi fly backwards into the opposite wall of my bedroom. The light from the hallway flooded into the room and over Alex's large shoulders as he knelt on the floor, holding the edges of the doorframe to keep himself from flying away as well.

My Push died and all three Vampires crumbled to the floor. I didn't try and hide my sobbing as I brushed my damp hair from my sweaty face. Devin was the first to stand from the floor, but his head jerked up as he sniffed the air loudly.

"Brianna, there is blood," he said as he quickly turned the lamp on next to me.

"No, no, no, no," I cried and put my shaking fingers between my legs but came back with a clean hand. "I don't...I don't know where it is."

Devin squeezed my arm as he said, "lie back, and let me take a look."

I did as he asked and felt Alex's arm catch me before I hit the pillow as he climbed up on Cameron's side of the bed.

"I'm sorry guys, I didn't mean to hurt you."

"No apologies necessary, Brianna," Devin replied as his attention focused on the underside of my belly. "Fabi, can you get me a clean wet cloth."

"Dev, what is it?" I asked as Fabi jetted into the bathroom.

"Just a little bit of blood breaking through the skin. Did you scratch yourself while you were sleeping?"

"Is it a straight line or an upside down T?"

"Straight line," he replied as he took the washcloth from Fabi and began cleaning the blood away.

"I've never drawn blood before," I whimpered, covering my eyes and letting the tears fall through my fingers.

Alex squeezed my hand. "Was it the knife dream with Elaina?"

"And Aidan. He was the one cutting me this time. It seems to be the only dream I have anymore."

Devin pulled my top back over my stomach and now that he was standing up straight I noticed that he was only wearing pants.

"I thought you might want some water," Fabi said sweetly as he stepped forward with a glass in his hand wearing only a black t-shirt and a pair of bright red plaid boxers.

"I didn't mean to interrupt anything," I laughed as I gestured between the two of them and took the water from Fabi's hand. I think both of them would have blushed if they were able.

The water was nice and cold as it traveled down my sore throat, and the tears didn't come again until I heard the sound of my stepmother's voice.

"Petite?" she called in a worried tone as she stood in the doorway.

The men in the room backed away when Sera glided into the room and sat on the bed with her arms around me, allowing me to rest my cheek on her shoulder letting my tears soak into her soft pink robe. She cooed words I couldn't understand for several minutes as she petted my hair and wiped my cheek, but it was no use.

"I'm so tired," I said breathlessly as I lifted my head from her shoulder.

"Zhen rest, petite. Rest now."

"No, I mean I'm tired of sitting around and waiting for my dream to come true."

Devin stepped forward. "Brianna, we will not let it happen."

"Dev, in all the times I've had that dream, never once are any of you around."

"Then we will never leave your side, no matter where you are," Alex chimed in from behind me.

"And constantly look over my shoulder? Live in fear every second of the day? I just can't do that, Alex. And even if we somehow bypass what I keep dreaming about, Elaina and Aidan are just going to come after my kids. I can't do that to them, they deserve a better life than that."

"Then what do you suggest, Bri?" Alex asked in a frustrated tone.

I paused as I looked at each person in the room, seeing both fear and curiosity in their eyes. Taking in a deep breath, I finally said, "Use me as bait."

"Absolutely not!" Alex shouted.

"Alex, listen…"

"No. We're not even going to discuss it."

"Discuss what?" Kyla said through the door with my father behind her.

"Oh hi, Ky. How was Club Red?" I said trying to take the heat off of me.

"Daughter, what is going on?"

"Brianna!" Kyla shouted. "Are you out of your mind!"

"Kyla, stop looking ahead and let me explain," I pleaded.

"Enough," Eris said firmly. "Explanations need to start now."

Alex came around the bed and stood next to Kyla who was fuming with her arms crossed in front of her chest. "Sir, Brianna is suggesting that we use her to lure Elaina."

"Mia figlia," was all I understood before he began shouting in Italian and pointing accusingly at the others in the room.

Fabi, in his t-shirt and boxers, placed his hands up in front of him and yelled over the angry shouts in the room. "Everyone needs to calm down." When they didn't, "I said stop it right now before I start clawing everyone's eyes out." The room went silent. "Thank you. This is Brianna's life, and she is allowed to have a say in how she protects herself and her children. And of the little time I've spent with her, even if we say no, she'll find a way to do it herself. Now, let's all take an unnecessary breath, listen to what she has to say, and find ways we can help."

I waited a beat before I finally said, "Right now, we don't know where or how Elaina will take me." I held up my hand in Alex's direction when he took in a breath to speak. "And I'm sorry, Alex, but my dreams come true for the most part, so somehow she does get to me. So why not be prepared, let's bring her to us. We'll control the circumstances of where I'm taken and then someone can follow us to their headquarters. Not only could we take Elaina down, but also Aidan and a bunch of their followers."

"But Bri, honey, how do we do that?" Kyla asked while Alex paced next to her.

"Kyla is right, figlia. I am sure a cunning Vampire like Elaina would surely notice a troop of Warriors following after her and could decide to harm you before we could get to you."

"Then everyone stays back far enough to where they won't see you..."

"Brianna," Devin interrupted, "if we are too far behind, how would we know where they are going."

"Because I could tell you," I answered and pointed to my temple. "If one person could stay within a mile or so, I could tell them every turn she takes, then that person communicates to the team further away."

"But where would we even do it, Bri? We're always around you, they would notice if we suddenly just left you alone."

"It wouldn't be weird if it happened at the wedding," I mumbled, unable to look at anyone in the eye. "We would all be there, and I could believably say I needed to duck out and take a rest or something."

"Brianna, in order to take on Elaina, we would need more than the Warriors in this room," Devin said, taking a step closer.

"And only Father can approve a mission like this and give us reinforcements," Alex said angrily.

"Then I'll get it from him," I shouted back.

"No you won't," he replied, "because it will never get that far. This is madness. Devin, tell her." All eyes in the room moved to Devin who stood stoic with his arms across his shirtless chest. "Devin! If you're seriously considering this, then you are just as out of your mind as she is."

"Remember who you are speaking to, Alex," Devin warned. "Brianna's plan has some major advantages for us."

"But the risk…"

"There are risks in every plan," Devin interrupted causing Alex to growl and punch the air. But Alex's anger didn't seem to affect Devin so he continued, "Now Brianna, I will volunteer to be your contact and feed your location to the team, providing we get approval from Father. That is, of course, if Eris doesn't insist on taking the task."

My father shook his head. He was definitely quieter than I expected him to be. Eris turned his head, his eyes filled with guilt that I didn't understand.

"Dad, what is it?"

"Daughter," he began, but then paused and looked to the floor. "For most of your life I have never been there for you. And now that a crucial point comes along, I wish that I could be broken in two in order to protect both you and Sera."

"Darling, do not worry," Sera said softly next to me.

"She's right, Dad, I'll be fine. Stay with Sera, she'll need you with Elaina being so close."

"Petite, no…"

"Ok, excuse me," Kyla chirped with a little bit of attitude and sounding way too much like Renee, "how does Elaina get the information about the wedding?"

"Because we have someone who will tell her," I replied.

Kyla took a moment to think about it and then said, "Nikki?"

I nodded. "I know she keeps swearing up and down that she's come to our side, but does anyone in this room really believe that?" No one moved. "If she's really with us, then this will be her chance to prove it. Which brings up another point, we need to keep all of this from Jared. And also from Cameron."

Alex laughed with his back to the rest of us, though it wasn't a humorous one.

"Alex," Devin began, "you and I both know that Cameron would give us away. There is no way he would be able to act naturally in this situation. Elaina will be looking for anything that would tip her off that we know her plan, especially from Cameron. Now looking at the hour, this is usually when Father spends time alone in his office, so it will be the best time to contact him without drawing Cameron's attention."

"I will help you, Assassin. I can represent Bri-an-na's interest in this," Eris said before cupping my face and kissing my temple. He looked at me intensely for a moment, seeming to want to say something, but unable to find the words and choosing to follow Devin out of the room.

Fabi turned on his heel and stepped toward the door as well. "Well I think I'll go and find some pants."

"Oh Fabi Fabulous, you even make a t-shirt and boxers look stylish," I said.

Fabi posed in his best pageant stance. "It's a gift."

Once Fabi left the room, Sera pulled me into her arms and my head instantly fell onto her shoulder. "Petite chute, would like a hot cocoa?"

"Yes, please," I replied, feeling suddenly exhausted.

Sera started to rise but Kyla stepped in front of the bed. "I'll make it for you, Sera. I've seen you do it enough times," she said and stepped away, but then turned back around. "Bri, you know I love you, but sometimes you ask way too much of those close to you. This won't end well, I can feel it."

Without sticking around long enough for me to respond, Kyla disappeared through the door leaving only Sera and I on the bed, and an angry Alex who was now standing in front of me.

"Alex," I whined as I pulled him down onto the bed, "please don't be mad at me."

"I gave Cam my word that I would protect you with my life and when he finds out that I knew about this plan, he will kill me. I am certain that he will literally rip my head from my shoulders. And if we don't get to you in time, Elaina could do the same to you, if not worse."

"Then don't be late," I said teasingly, but he wasn't having any part of it. "Alex, I'd rather do this on my own terms than wait for Elaina to jump out of the shadows. We had warnings last time and we didn't do anything. Let's not make the same mistake."

"Bri, things go wrong all the time. Cam would never forgive me. I would…"

"Bri, you didn't see Cam when you were away. This will kill him."

"If this works, Elaina will be gone and we can all live our lives in peace. I wouldn't be doing this if I didn't trust each and every one of you to protect me. We can do this, Alex, please tell me you understand."

Alex rubbed his face in frustration and answered, "I don't, Bri. But if Victor approves this I will crash through every wall in Boston to help you. You know I will. Not only for you and Cam, but I'd really like to be an uncle."

Tears filled my eyes and overflowed down my cheeks as I hugged the gentle giant.

"The kids will love their Uncle Alex," I replied and wiped my cheeks.

Alex chewed his bottom lip and rose from the bed, avoiding eye contact with me as he left the room. Sera kissed my temple and patted my arm. We sat quietly for several minutes though we could hear a lot of hustle and bustle from other parts of the house. While Sera sat watching me, tenderly brushing away stray hairs from my face, my brain was at war with itself.

"Sera," I began and her eyes instantly became glassy with tears. "Mom. In all your visions, you've never seen me with my children, have you?"

Both of Sera's lips disappeared into her mouth as she tried holding her emotions inside. "No, petite. I have not."

I took a deep breath in, blowing it out slowly as my heart began to race. A tear finally escaped down Sera's cheek, and mine weren't too far behind as I asked, "Is all of this just pointless? Am I putting everyone in danger just so I can delay the inevitable?"

"If you zhink zhis is what is supposed to happen, zhen why are you fighting so hard? What are you fighting for?"

"I want to see my children! I want to see their faces, hold them and show them that for one moment I was their mother. In the dream, I never see them. I never get to tell them how much I love them and that I fought so hard for them. I need them to know that I didn't just lie down and die."

"Zhen don't," she said in a tone so fierce I almost thought she'd been possessed by my father. "My visiuns change, so zhis time *you* make zhem change. Keep fighting for what you want and do not let anyone try and stop you. You have so much of your fazer in you, so use it to take down anyone who would step in your way of being a mozer to your bébés. Comprends?"

The bedroom door creaked open over Sera's shoulder, the hallway light casting an orange glow into the bedroom as Kyla stood frozen in the doorway with two mugs in her hand. "Hot…chocolate…anyone?"

Chapter Fifty-Six

Cameron

"So who gets your quarters now?" Connor called from my wardrobe room, the room I was already starting to miss. With every box of my clothes Connor took out of the closet and brought downstairs to storage I felt myself being tugged in its direction. Many of the items had been with me for centuries, carefully preserved and protected wherever our home base was located. Although I missed her dearly, I was happy Brianna was not here. Not only would she be laughing at me, she would be astonished at the amount of clothing I had hidden in various compartments within the closet itself.

But as Connor screeched packing tape across yet another box, I peered down at the porcelain frame in my hand. It was the photograph of me dancing with my love on the night of her Claiming. She had only reminded me to pack it fourteen times, and I knew it was not only because she wanted to see a slimmer version of herself, it was also the only picture we had together. Even though we would obviously show up in them, Vampires were not the biggest fans of pictures, especially in today's world. There was too much risk of exposure. People would notice you did not age throughout your photos, or even have the slightest change in your appearance. But with the sad total of three frames wrapped in bubble paper, I knew some things needed to change. I wanted to fill my new home with pictures of Brianna and the children. It seemed so human, so natural. I think Bri and I deserved a little of that in our lives.

"Hey man, did you hear me?" Connor asked as he stepped through the archway carrying a tall wardrobe moving box.

"Yes, sorry. Father said he would keep it as guest quarters for when my family and I visit. He has even talked about transforming the sitting room into a nursery."

"That's wild. The Warrior manor will have a nursery. It sounds so weird," he laughed as he dropped the box on the floor. "But I guess having kids around will be pretty normal once you start running the show."

"H-how is that?" I asked, almost dropping the porcelain frame.

Connor suddenly looked just as uncomfortable as I was shocked. "Well...you know."

"Enlighten me."

"Come on, Cameron, it's all over the coven. We all know Father's training you to take over."

I shifted uncomfortably, deciding to place the frame in the box before I broke it and had to suffer Brianna's wrath. "Father is grooming Devin as well."

"Yeah, figured that too."

"Since none of us have mentioned a thing about this, how does the entire coven know?"

"Cameron, at times we may be thugs, but we are not stupid. Father doesn't let anyone talk to other coven leaders or handle Warrior business. It was pretty obvious things were changing with all the Facility East business."

"Nothing is happening any time soon, so try and keep the rumors to a minimum. Ok?"

"Sure. Of course if I were to get these sweet quarters I could ensure that..."

Raising an eyebrow, I crossed my arms in front of my chest. "And this is how you want to start my reign?"

He laughed, picked up the wardrobe box again and walked toward the door. As he approached, the bedroom door swung open and Skylar missed running into the large box by inches. "I was told Connor was in here."

"I am," Connor replied from behind the box.

Skylar narrowed his eyes, waiting for Connor to put the box down, which he did not since he liked to torture Skylar just as much as I did. "Connor! Put the goddamn box down."

"Ok, ok. Calm down," Connor replied condescendingly. "This is a free coven, I can hold a box if I want to."

"Not when Father is looking for you."

Connor's shoulders slumped as he set the box out of the way and gave me quick finger salute goodbye. "Later, man."

Connor disappeared through the doorway, leaving Skylar and I with an awkward tension. "So now you are using Connor to do your grunt work?"

"Skylar, I do apologize, you were busy. At least you were supposed to be. Where is your charge?"

Skylar's face turned into a snarl before saying, "I wouldn't know. Nikki is no longer my responsibility. I guess Father doesn't tell you everything after all."

His pompous expression made me want to punch him in the face, but he left too quickly and unfortunately he did have a point. I was unaware that he was no longer watching Nikki. Begging the question, who was?

Before the thought prevented me from finishing my packing, I folded the lid to the cardboard box in front of me and stretched the tape over the top. As I carried the sealed box over to the pile in front of the fireplace, someone cleared his throat from inside the wardrobe room.

"Hey, bro!"

"Jared?" I asked, turning around and seeing my youngest brother hiding in the shadows of the closet. "What are you doing in there? More so, why are you awake at this hour?"

The early morning sun was pouring through the windows, brightening up the room and illuminating a tremendous amount of dust floating in the air that had been kicked up from all the moving and packing. Not wanting to keep the awkward distance between us, I stepped into the closet.

"I couldn't help it, bro. I just wanted to say thanks for whatever you did," he said enthusiastically as he wrapped his arms around me and slapped my back roughly.

"Jared, I do not know what you are referring to," I replied taking a step back.

Jared's head flinched back in surprise. "You worked your magic with Beebs. I couldn't believe it when she called me this morning."

"Stop, Jared, please. I have no idea what you are talking about."

"Oh," he said slowly, his eyes widening even further. "Bibi called me this morning and told me that I could bring Nikki as my date to the wedding."

"*My* Bri, said this?"

"Yeah," he replied in happy relief, oblivious to my own surprised tone. "This is great, bro. With you and Beebs accepting Nikki, that means everyone else will follow. I...I know things between you and Nik are weird with what she did to you and then you getting Dad to torture her, but all under the bridge now. Right, bro?"

"Jared, I...I am not exactly sure..."

"Hello? Anyone in here?" a woman's voice called from inside the bedroom. And even with my back turned to her, the smell of oranges solidified that Nikki had just stepped into the room.

"Yeah, Nik! In here," Jared called over my shoulder and gestured for her to come into the changing area.

Every nerve in my body fired as she hugged me from behind, wrapping her arms around my neck and nuzzling her face in between my shoulder blades. "Thank you, thank you, thank you, Cameron!"

Carefully I removed her arms from around my body and turned in order to take a step back and see her straight on to prevent any more sneak attacks.

"Nik, get this, he didn't know. It was all Bri. I told you things would turn around eventually, didn't I," Jared said as he picked Nikki up by the waist and twirled her once around.

"What a morning," she replied almost breathless. "First Victor takes off my restrictions, then Brianna calls and invites me to Boston..."

"Hold on," I interrupted, "Father has lifted the restrictions?"

Nikki smiled with relief. "I can finally see my boyfriend without Skylar watching us all the time."

"How happy that must make you both," I tried saying with as little condescension as possible while I hid my clenched fists behind my back. "Now, if you two will excuse me, I actually have a meeting with Father that I must get to."

"Yeah sure," Jared nodded and patted me on the arm. "Nik, I'll see you back downstairs?"

"You got it, baby," she replied in a sickie-sweet tone before she kissed him. I thought for sure I would be the first Vampire to vomit at that moment.

Once Jared Projected away, I gestured Nikki out toward the bedroom since there was no way I would trust her to leave the room herself. Silently I followed her through the room and as we approached the door I went to the small table just to the side and opened the slim top drawer, removing from within it a key. In all the time I had stayed in the manor, I had never needed to lock the door to my bedroom, but with Father's recent decision to let Nikki roam free I felt I had no other choice.

I ignored the questioning look Nikki gave me as I locked the door and gave her a curt nod before I Projected myself outside of Victor's office. Without knocking I bolted into the room finding it empty. My stomach sank slightly, but I quickly turned and began walking through the main corridor of the manor where various Warriors were walking and mingling about. As I approached the grand foyer I noticed Skylar leaving through the front door with Connor only a few steps behind him, each with heavy packs strewn over their backs.

"Connor!" I shouted, causing him to stop. "Where are you off to?"

Connor paused, looking nervously out the front door. "Uh...a new mission. I just got finished meeting with Father. He's sending me and Skylar out to do some preventative work back East."

"Oh," I replied, struck by the fact that Father had not mentioned any of this to me when I met with him early this morning. "Where was Father when you left him?"

"He was in his quarters a few minutes ago."

"Thanks, Connor," I said stepping past him, but then turned back and hit my fist across my chest. "Good luck."

Connor saluted me back and we parted in opposite directions. As I traveled down the winding stone hallways I could not help but think how everything seemed to have turned upside down in the last hour.

"Father!" I said as I entered Victor's room. For obvious reasons, Victor's quarters were the biggest and grandest in the manor. A large sunken sitting area was directly in front of you with a large stone fireplace and two long couches that faced each other. The large canopy bed was on an elevated level two steps above that curved around the second half of the room. Creamy white curtain sheers hung from the tall glass doors that opened up to a wide terrace looking upon the manor's grand gardens.

Since the doors were open, I stepped out onto the terrace to find Victor sitting at a small round mosaic top table with a wine glass of blood in his hand, his white Roman-style robes draped around him.

"Hello, child," he said with his back still to me.

"I am surprised you are awake and enjoying the morning's sun."

"And yet you still thought it a good idea to barge in unannounced?"

His raspy voice had a bit of sting to it as he took a sip from his glass.

Ignoring his warning I came around to the other side of the table and purposely blocked his view of the garden. "Father there is something I need to discuss with you."

"Yes, child, as do I. I wanted to inform you that I will be coming with you and the others to Boston on Thursday."

My rigid defensive stance melted completely. "Father, I have been begging you to visit for three months now. Why the sudden change of heart?"

Being sure to draw out my curiosity, Victor took a long slow drink of blood. After licking his lips he said, "Brianna called me this morning."

"She seems to be doing a lot of that today."

"Yes well, we had a lovely conversation and she brought up a very good point."

"And what was that?" I replied since I thought I had made every point possible in the last three months.

"These little twins will be the first and possibly only grandchildren I will have. And Brianna made me aware that they could be born within the next few weeks and I would hate to miss such an experience. I want to make sure those children know that Eris is not their only grandfather, therefore, I cannot lock myself out here. I have even started a list of names I thought the children could call me and those that would be unacceptable." There was an odd smile on Victor's face, one of adoration as he pulled a piece of paper from within his robe and with the sun's rays shining through it I could see two lists, each with half a dozen options. "For example, Pop-Pop, Grand Pappy, or Gampy, are unacceptable."

Pushing the humor I found in it aside, I cleared my throat and sat in the chair opposite him. "Father, it has been brought to my attention that you have taken away all restrictions on Nikki Cushlin."

Victor looked up from his list. "That is correct."

"I have also found out that she too is coming to Boston, and I know that only you could have given her that kind of permission."

Victor slowly placed his glass of blood on the table and tucked his list back into his robe. "Now that you have agreed to eventually take over our coven you believe you can question my decisions?"

"When it affects the safety of my family and fellow Warriors, I do."

"Brianna does not seem to feel the same way about Nikki anymore. Since most of Nikki's grievances were against her, I believe if she can find a way to forgive, so can we. Skylar and Jared have monitored Nikki for months and nothing has come of it." I stood abruptly from my chair, turning to look out over the garden and concentrating on the fountain that bubbled in the distance. Victor's chair scraped loudly against the concrete floor and a second later he was lightly patting me on the shoulder. "Child, I know this is difficult for you, but it is time for us all to move on."

I stepped away from Victor, letting his hand drag down my arm as I walked around the table.

"Father, there are times that I just do not understand you," I said in a frustrated and almost angry tone. "Hugo made a greedy mistake, using the very skills he was Turned for, and yet after fifty years you never forgave him. Jazlyn made a horrible choice and she has now admitted as such. She saved Brianna's life and even placed her own life in danger in order to help us. And yet, you have not forgiven her. But Nikki…"

Victor held his hand up to stop me. "Child, in a few weeks' time you will have two children of your own. And with all the love I have for you, I hope that you are never betrayed by your son or daughter, for the hurt is infinitely more painful. But if you are, perhaps you will understand my ways a little better. Now, if you don't mind I would like to go to bed."

Victor walked past me and shut the tall glass doors behind him. He was officially closed for business.

Walking down the dozen cement stairs, I stepped onto the soft grass of the gardens where plants and flowers were at the beginning stages of budding. When I reached the fountain, I sat down on its ledge and pulled out my cell phone.

"Hey babe," Brianna's warm voice came through the phone. Just the sound of it almost made me forget the upheaval her phone calls had made this morning. Almost.

"Is there anything you want to tell me, love?"

There was a pause. "I love you?"

"Not nearly as much as I love you. But try again."

"I can see your son's foot sticking out of my stomach. It's freaking me out a little."

Bri was playing dirty by using the babies as a distraction.

"And how do you know it is our son's foot?"

"Because it's sticking out on the right side and that's where the ultrasound showed him today. He really doesn't have anywhere else to go."

"And how is our daughter?"

"She's hitting my ribs like a xylophone right now. How were your meetings with Victor?"

"I should ask you the same thing."

"Ok, here's the thing…"

Chapter Fifty-Seven

Brianna

"They're here!" Kyla shouted from the foyer.

"Ada's home," I whispered to my babies as I rubbed my very bulbous belly. Now four days of prepping myself to lie and keep things from Cam would be put to the test. My guilt was definitely punishment for what I was going to do in two days, and even though Cameron loved me I hoped he would be able to forgive me. The babies kicked as I wobbled out from my bedroom, my flip flops snapping against my heels as I traveled to the foyer.

Kyla was already at the front door with a tuft of fluffy gray hair sticking up over her shoulder.

"Ky, please don't suffocate my grandfather," I laughed as Daddy O's wrinkled smiling face glanced around Kyla's arm.

"Well, sugar, look at you," he said with his short arms out wide.

"Yeah, look at me, a whale that used to be your granddaughter."

Daddy O laughed and barely got his arms around me. "You'll always be my 'Lil Bri."

My Daddy O was finally here and my heart felt so warm, as did my stomach all of a sudden. Just then it felt as though the babies were trying to leap out of me, causing me to lurch forward into Daddy O and catch myself on the banister next to me.

"I'm ok, I'm ok," I assured Daddy O and then looked up to see both Kyla and Maddy with panicked looks on their faces. "Apparently they really want to meet their great-grandfather."

Daddy O gave me a worried smile but then scolded my belly. "Now you youngins need to stay in there until yur mama says it's time to come out. I'm not goin' anywhere."

"Daddy O!" Renee squealed as she ruined the hardwood on my stairs with her ginormous heels.

"If it ain't the bride to be," he said as he stepped up on the stairs.

"Well he's certainly not talking to me," I said sarcastically as Maddy stepped toward me. Even after an eight hour flight, her short gray hair was perfectly coiffed and not a wrinkle in her slacks and silk blouse. My arms immediately went around her neck. "Maddy, it is so good to see you."

Maddy broke away from our embrace and patted my stomach gently. "I am honored to be here, Miss Morgan. And may I say how happy I am for you and Mr. Burke."

"Maddy, when I'm in your house you can call me Miss Morgan, but when you're in mine you have to call me Brianna. Or else I'm going to pull the Madelyn card."

"I see pregnancy has not taken away your sense of humor."

"It's about the only thing that hasn't been taken away."

Maddy squeezed my hand and patted my stomach once more. "It is all worth it in the end. I can assure you of that."

"So Daddy O, who's the new chicklet?" Renee said loudly from the stairs.

I could hear Maddy's breath catch in her throat, but I smiled warmly to ease any fear she had. "Maddy, this is the bride Renee. She's the rudest, most inappropriate person I know, and she's one of my dearest friends. Just ignore most of what she says. Daddy O, I hope you're hungry. Sera's been cooking all day just for you."

Daddy O snapped to attention and reached over the banister for Maddy's hand. He led her up only two steps before Jared came through the door carrying several bags which were immediately dropped to the floor.

"That's all right, Ollie, I'll take it from here," Jared insisted as he pulled Maddy away and whisked her up the stairs to the second floor. Daddy O looked at me over his shoulder and shook his head, knowing there was nothing he could do but smile and laugh. But without missing a beat Renee crooked her arm around his and escorted Daddy O the rest of the way.

From behind me, Kyla rested her head on my shoulder. "Jared's here without Nikki?"

"You think I'd let that snake in my house? She's at the hotel where she needs to stay and do her dirty work without any of us around her."

"Boy you're deceitful when you want to be."

"Probably the only thing I learned from my mother. Speaking of, can you go upstairs and keep Daddy O off the topic of Shelby? I don't need anyone slipping up and telling him the truth. Oh, and can you make sure my dad behaves? This is actually the first time he and Daddy O have been in the same room together for more than five minutes."

Kyla crossed her arms and sank into her hip. "Anything else?"

"Just keep remembering how much you love me."

Without another word, she kissed my cheek and flew up the stairs just when Cameron and Victor came through the door. The sight of Cam made breathing easier, but I chewed the inside of my cheeks in order to prevent from blurting out everything that I was keeping from him. Without making it too obvious, I tried concentrating on Victor who surprised me with his blue jeans, black t-shirt and black blazer. I was so used to seeing him in robes, and today he looked like everyone else. But even with his casual attire, he still exuded a tremendous amount of power and regality.

"So this is it, Father. What do you think?" Cameron asked nervously.

Victor looked around the foyer and then took several steps to poke his head into the living room. "Small, but charming. Just like my lovely new Warrior," he replied with a wide smile as he opened his arms to me.

I laughed. "Not sure who you're looking at, Victor. There's nothing small about me."

Victor timidly reached his hand near my stomach, but then retracted as he asked, "May...may I touch them?"

Without answering I grabbed his hand and placed it on top of my stomach. I waited for kicking, jumping, heat, cold, something, and even Cameron peeked over his father's shoulder with curiosity. But I shook my head at him, worried that Victor might be upset by the lack of movement by the twins. However, when I glanced down at him, Victor was smiling and mesmerized by my stomach. And then, he giggled.

Cameron's eyes flinched. "Father?"

Victor straightened, removing his hands from my belly. "Do they do that to everyone?"

"What is that, Father?"

Victor looked back at Cameron and then to me. "Oh nothing. Do I get a tour of the rest of the house?"

"Of course, Father..."

"I am sure Brianna can handle the tour while you finish unloading the cars," Victor interrupted.

Cameron looked at me longingly, but knowing he couldn't get around Victor's suggestion he merely called up the stairs to Jared to come and help him, which of course Jared complained about.

When the two of them were out the door, Victor took my hand. "Is there a place we could go and talk?"

I nodded and led him down the hallway and through the door to the small courtyard outside. Not waiting for me, Victor stepped over to the wrought iron bench and brushed it clean of a winter's worth of debris and dirt.

"Knowing my child, we do not have long before he comes to find you. So I will keep this brief." With a supportive arm he lowered me to the bench, surprising me with his gentleness. "Skylar and Connor have set up a home base near the reception hall for the wedding and have been doing surveillance for the last several days. To prevent suspicion within the manor I have asked five other Warriors living on this coast to join us. Vlad, your father's man, has also volunteered to help so we should be fine in our numbers.

"Devin will be your point person once you have been taken from the reception site. Connor has suggested, and Devin has agreed, that in order not to be seen by Elaina or possibly any reinforcements she may have, he will follow you by rooftop jumping. Most people look behind them for cars, or people running through the streets, no one ever remembers to look up. This should also make it easier for you to communicate with Devin using your gift since hopefully he will be the only Vampire traveling on the rooftops of Boston.

"Once it has been determined that all of Elaina's followers have left the reception site, Alexander will bring Cameron in the loop, and the Warrior team will come after you. Cameron and Vlad will be charged with getting you out, and the rest of the Warriors will take down Elaina's coven. Eris, myself, Kyla, and Fabiani will stay at the reception site to ensure the safety of the guests."

"What about Jared?"

Victor sighed. "It pains me to know how necessary it is to keep my young Warrior in the dark. But just as I will have to accept his anger, I hope that you will be able to accept any fallout between you and Cameron that may occur as well."

"I am," I lied and he knew it.

"With all the business out of the way, I want to express my concern for your safety since I know I cannot change your mind. This mission has probably been the test of my long life. I found myself feeling an emotion I have not experienced…well ever in fact."

"And what is that?"

"Guilt. If anything happens to you as a result of my approving this mission not only could I lose you, I could lose my grandchildren and in turn lose Cameron. I have never had to take these things into consideration before."

I placed my hand on top of Victor's. "Well, if we don't screw it up, you won't lose any of us."

"Spoken like a true Warrior," he replied, narrowing his eyes and giving me a sly approving smile.

"So what did happen when you placed your hand on my stomach?" Victor looked away, another sly victorious smile on his face. "My belly, my kids, you have to tell me."

Victor laughed. "Nothing sinister, I assure you. More of a feeling, really. I touched your stomach and my body was suddenly flooded with warmth. I felt…"

"Loved," I replied with tears in my eyes as I rubbed my belly. "They were showing you how much they loved you."

Victor's jaw flexed several times, his eyes purposely looking away from me. "I am sure they do that with everyone."

"No, actually. They seem to have a different reaction with everyone. Usually I'm the victim of their love fest."

Victor became silent, still avoiding all eye contact. Sometimes even the biggest Warrior could be brought down at the prospect of being loved. After several moments he cleared his throat and reached into the pocket of his black blazer. "I heard from a beautiful orange-headed bird that you had lost something, but were too scared to tell me."

I looked down at his extended hand to see the outside floodlight reflecting off a small gold circular pin clasped between his thumb and forefinger. My fingers trembled as I reached to take it, but then I shook my head. "I…can't."

"Why forever not?"

"Did Kyla tell you how I lost mine? I didn't believe in the coven, or you, or Cameron. I just threw you all away."

Victor placed the small pin into my palm and closed my fingers around it. "Brianna child, being a Warrior is not about wearing a pin. Honestly I believe you and I are the only ones who even wear it on non-formal occasions. I have never doubted my choice to make you a part of our coven. You are a Warrior through and through, my dear. You challenge even some of my greatest children with the amount of bravery and perseverance you have. So please do not get hung up over a pin. I believe Jared is on his eighth or ninth. One, he told me, he dropped in a toilet. Now what he was doing near a toilet I will never know, and I prefer it that way. But as I was saying, pin or not you are a Warrior because it's in your heart. Your plans for Saturday more than prove that you are…right. I do think hydrangeas would look nice in the far corner."

"Huh?"

Victor ignored me and looked over my shoulder. "Child, how nice of you to join us."

I turned toward the house and saw Cameron opening the outside door with a questioning look. "I am surprised to find you out here."

"Well you see, child, I was just telling Brianna how lovely the house is."

"You have only seen the outside, Father."

"Yes," Victor replied as he rose from the bench and extended his hand to help me up, "but you can tell so much about a home from its grounds. Shall we go back inside? I am sure your guests are wondering what has happened to their hosts."

Victor quickly disappeared into the house while I waddled to the door. Cam's crooked smile inched up the left side of his face as he said, "Please tell me you have been resting and letting everyone else handle all the preparations for this evening?"

"Like Kyla and Sera would let me do anything."

Cameron placed his hands on either side of my face, kissing me with his open mouth, but nothing long enough to start anything. When he pulled away, his crooked smile was making my heart beat faster.

"That's enough of that," I warned as I put my finger up to his lips. "Will you carry me upstairs?"

"Angel, I have been waiting four days to carry you anywhere."

Within seconds I was nuzzled into Cam's chest while heat rose quickly from my stomach as the babies pushed against me at every angle. The babies seemed to have missed him as much as I had. When we reached the top of the stairs we came up to what was becoming my favorite part of the house. The big dining table that was formerly in the living room was now in its proper place in the open dining area to our right. The small table in the kitchen had been removed and replaced with a plush couch and two thick arm chairs. Instead of a kitchen, we had created a hearth, a place of comfort for everyone whether they ate or not.

Daddy O and Maddy were seated at the island with Sera placing plate after plate of food in front of them while gabbing with Renee and Kyla. Jared was catching up with Alex, Dr. John, and Devin while Victor spoke with Fabi and Dante. It was almost the Thanksgiving that had been taken away from me this year. Though there were only six people who would be eating, Sera made enough for an army and all of it was Daddy O's favorite foods. It was an attempt to butter him up since he and my father would be together, though there was no "together" about them as the evening progressed.

Daddy O stayed glued to his stool while my father stood within the open balcony doors watching the others around him mingle. Eventually I left Cameron's side and crossed the room to stand next to Eris and also to feel the cool air coming from outside.

"Why are you over here by yourself?"

"But I'm not, I have you," he replied. "Besides, I am thoroughly enjoying watching Victor's reactions to Dante's outfit."

I peered over to the opposite corner of the kitchen where Victor and now only Dante stood in deep conversation. As I watched them, I could see Victor steadily stealing glances at the royal blue sequined suit jacket and matching skinny cut pants with a long thin black silk scarf hanging from his neck.

"It takes a very confident man to wear the things he does," I said, making my father smile. "Seriously, Dad, why are you standing away from everyone?"

He pulled at the tie in his hair, making his wavy brown hair fall around his shoulders. "I am giving your grandfather the space he needs. I know he despises me, though I am happy to see him getting on with Sera."

"Daddy O doesn't hate you."

"He does not like me either," he replied, caressing my cheek with his index finger. "Do not worry about me. Go and entertain your guests."

And so I did. It was the perfect homecoming and open house for our extended family. After several hours all the food had been eaten and goodbyes were beginning to be expressed. Victor and Jared escorted Maddy back to the hotel which was a surprise since I assumed she was staying with Daddy O here at the house. Dante gladly followed Dr. John and Renee home while Fabi and Devin went on their first double date with Alex and Kyla, but only once Victor was a safe distance away. It was good to see that Devin was at least trying, even if it still wasn't in front of Victor.

Cameron had insisted on cleaning the kitchen after all of Sera's hard work, and my father graciously escorted her down the hall to their room. While Cameron began feverishly washing dishes, I took a seat next to Daddy O on the comfy couch and rested my head against his shoulder.

"Thanks for coming out here, Daddy O. I know how much you hate to fly."

He kissed the top of my head. "Well, sugar, I had to come and meet my 'lil chiluns."

"You know that Maddy didn't need to stay in the hotel. I know you guys are shackin' up."

"Language, little girl," he warned.

"I didn't swear," I replied as I lifted my head from his shoulder.

"Granddaughters aren't allowed to talk about their grandfather's new…" he cleared his throat.

"Girlfriend, Daddy O. She's your girlfriend."

"Again with the language, 'Lil Bri. She is my lady friend and she is tryin' to be respectful."

I squeezed his hand. "Daddy O, I like Maddy, always have."

"She cares for you too, and doesn't want to be throwin' anythin' in your face that might upset ya."

"You guys don't need to hide from me. I really am happy for both of you. Once everyone goes back to San Francisco, tell her to come and stay with you here until the babies come."

He smiled and patted my hand gently. "Well there's another reason she wanted to go back to the hotel tonight. There's somethin' I want to talk to you both about. That means you too, son."

Cameron turned the water off and dried his hands with a dishtowel, all the while giving me a concerned look. Once Cameron sat on the arm of the couch, Daddy O took his handkerchief out of his pocket and dabbed his forehead before his face settled into a stern expression.

"I know that I'm an old man and that I live in the sticks, but I'm not stupid."

"Daddy O what are you…"

"I know there's somethin' y'all aren't tellin' me about what happened to Shelby Jo. I didn't want to talk about this over the phone, so I'm askin' ya now to start tellin' me the truth."

Instantly my throat became dry and my nose began to tingle. I knew if I opened my mouth that I would completely breakdown. But thankfully Cam came to my rescue.

"Da, it was the truth when we told you that Shelby was another unfortunate victim of Elaina."

"Yes, but you said she was taken. Now before Connor an them took me out to California, we went to her house and all her things were gone. Nothing was ransacked or broken, so unless her kidnappers let her take her time to pack everythin' I think there are some things y'all aren't tellin' me."

Cameron inhaled in order to speak, but I reached for his hand and squeezed it. "S-shelby..." I stuttered and then cleared my throat to start again. "Well she...she..."

"Da, what Bri is trying to say is that Shelby went to the enemy willingly. I know this may be difficult to understand, but there are Vampires who have the ability to trick the mind into thinking that it's seeing people and places that are not really there." Daddy O knitted his brows together. "When Brianna was taken, she was made to believe she was in your house in North Carolina. Shelby gave them all the details they needed in order to make that successful and we believe they promised to make her a Vampire in return. Your daughter aligned herself with Elaina and betrayed your granddaughter for the most heinous and selfish reasons."

Daddy O let out a deep sigh and I could see the conflict brewing behind his eyes. "Then how did she really die? I believe I have a right to know."

My grandfather was looking me dead in the eye. If I lied to him, he would know. He always knew. I could feel the warm tears dripping from my eyes as my lower lip trembled. I couldn't say it. I couldn't tell him what I had done. He could very well walk out of my life once he found out.

"Da, please understand..." Cameron began.

"I killed her."

But the words didn't come out of my mouth. The three of us turned our heads toward the edge of the kitchen, and standing stoically in the hallway was Eris. A silent moment passed before Daddy O stood from the couch and took a step toward my father.

"You? You killed my Shelby Jo."

"Dad, no."

"Oliver, my daughter has been protecting me knowing that if you found out what I had done it would fuel your hatred for me even further," Eris said, completely stripped of his accent.

Daddy O took another step forward. "You'd already taken her innocence and her sanity. Ya had to go an take her life, too? How much more are ya plannin' on takin' away from me? At my age there ain't much left."

"Sir," Eris began in a caring tone that even I had seldom heard, "there will come a time when the wound is not so fresh, and we can speak candidly about the time Shelby spent with me so many years ago. But in regards to her death, Shelby went to attack Brianna and I got in her way. Unfortunately my anger caused her death. I refused to watch her hurt our daughter once again. I know this does not excuse what I have done, but I am sorry for how much I have wronged you."

Daddy O didn't say a word. After staring down Eris for several seconds, he turned back to me and kissed my forehead. "'Night, sugar. 'Night, son."

"Goodnight, Da," Cameron replied and enjoyed the hug he received.

Daddy O passed Eris without acknowledging him and walked silently to his bedroom down the hall. Cameron lifted me to my feet and I waddled over to my father and kissed him on the cheek. "Thank you."

"I will always fall on my sword when it comes to you. Let this be payment for all the other times I was not there for you when it came to your mother."

"I love you, Dad."

"Daughter, you will always be my greatest achievement. You are braver than I ever could be and...I am very proud to be your father," he said and then cleared his throat. "Now Warrior, get my daughter off to bed. She needs her rest with the busy days ahead."

Eris raised his brows to me with his hidden meaning then turned and walked away toward his bedroom.

Cameron came up behind me and snaked his arms around my waist, resting his hands on my stomach as he nuzzled his face into my neck. "Are you all right, love?"

"I can't believe Eris did that," I sniffled and wiped my eyes quickly.

"Your father has come a long way in the last year," he replied and lifted me into his arms. "And though he and I do not always see eye to eye, I agree with him that you need to be in bed."

I smiled as I nuzzled into his chest. "Da?"

His laugh rumbled in his chest. "It just sort of happened while you were away. One night I just started calling him what I had my father."

"I thought you called him Ada."

"I did for a long time, but then it went back and forth between the two when I got older. Since I met your grandfather he has reminded me of my real father. He does not seem to mind, and I have to say I rather like calling him that."

"And I'm sure he likes hearing it. He's never had a real son-in-law, and goodness knows my father will never fill that role." Cam kissed my temple as I yawned widely. "Maybe tonight I will actually get some sleep. I always sleep better when you're in the bed with me."

"From here on out, when you fall asleep I will always be lying next to you," he said as we traveled slowly down the stairs.

"Don't make promises you can't keep, Cam."

He narrowed his eyes and bore his gaze into mine. "I will always be next to you. When you fall asleep, when you wake, there I will be. And soon enough our children will be. It is all coming together, my love. Our life together is finally coming true. We just need to start enjoying it."

The faith in Cameron's eyes made the guilt almost unbearable, but thankfully the sight of our bedroom filled with tall boxes created a wonderful distraction.

"So how many of these are mine?"

"That one…I believe," he said pointing to the smallest box of the bunch.

"I see a storage unit in your future, Mr. Burke."

He sighed. "Yes, love."

"Did you remember my picture?"

"Yes, love."

"Wanna make out for the ten minutes I'll be able to keep my eyes open?"

His crooked smile was his only response.

Chapter Fifty-Eight

Brianna

The day of the wedding had arrived. My head was heavy with a thousand bobby pins holding my hair up in big curls while the black chiffon tarp they called a bridesmaid dress didn't do anything for my figure. I was still a very fat pregnant lady in fancy looking flip flops, and trust me, it was a battle to get them. The bride wanted me in heels, but that simply wasn't going to happen. So we compromised - I could wear blinged-out flip flops if I wore the necklace Renee had picked out for me versus my engagement ring that usually hung on a chain around my neck. Renee's reasoning – it picked at my chest and made it red, which it did. The reason according to moi – my ring was bigger than hers.

Regardless of ring size, Renee looked beautiful, more like breathtaking. Her rich red hair was pulled back in a side chignon and the color popped against her light skin and white sheath wedding dress that wrapped her curves in sparkling lace. But now all the wind had billowed out of the bride's sails, in fact she had gone catatonic in the last half hour.

Kyla was still fidgeting with Renee's hair and make-up, basically anything to keep her mind off of the mission. I had chosen to count the petals in my bouquet and try not to worry how I would accomplish what I needed to do with the amount of pain in my back. However, I couldn't figure out what was worse, my back pain or the non-stop high pitched cackling of Renee's mother and her four sisters. The bridal suit wasn't small by any means, but the five ladies seemed to suck out all the oxygen in the room.

Just as I finished counting the petals of the peonies in my bouquet, Fabi came through the door in his pristine dark suit and lavender tie.

"Good news, the groom has arrived. He looks great, has the rings, and smells quite nice. And yes, I know that because I did smell him up close and personal, but I think he's used to that from me by now."

All the ladies in the room laughed, however, Renee was still non-responsive which seemed to irritate Fabi since she was usually the person who kept his shtick going.

"Almost everyone is seated, so that means we can start getting into place," Fabi announced, but Renee only blinked slowly in response. "And I'm sorry to tell you Re, but your dinner will be one lobster short since I took it and shoved it up my…"

"Fabi!" I warned loudly, which startled Renee back from wherever she had been.

"Wh-what?" she said, looking around the room and finally meeting Fabi's gaze.

He smiled and took her hand. "It's time to get married, honey."

Renee shook her head nervously, diverting her eyes to the floor. Kyla gave me a concerned look and I gestured for her to help me up from my chair.

"Ky, why don't you and Fabi take the family downstairs and get them seated. We'll be right behind you."

Both of them nodded and herded Renee's mother and aunts out of the bridal suit, though Renee's mother was not very happy about leaving. Once everyone was out, I turned back to my friend and saw a rare sight. Renee looked terrified.

"Ok Re, why do you look like a cat that's about to be put in the bathtub?"

She laughed nervously, faking a smile as a small tear leaked from her eye. In a weak voice she asked, "Am I doing the right thing?"

Now, what I wanted to say was, *"You made me get into this dress and be your maid of honor at eight months pregnant, and now you're having doubts? No way, girlfriend, I will duct tape you down to a rolling chair and shove you down the aisle if I need to."*

But, I took a breath, centered my thoughts, took her hand and said, "Renee, you have never hesitated one second since you've been with Dr. John. He asked you to move in, bam, you did. Then he asked you to drop everything and move to Boston, bam, you did that too. And I was there when he asked you to marry him, and…"

"Please don't say bam."

I stuck my tongue out. "Bam, you said yes. So why in the world are you hesitating now?"

She put her shaking hand up to her eyes to dab away another tear. "All of a sudden it's here. The rest of my life with one person, right here. And it doesn't help that Mom and my stinking aunts keep whispering about how long we're going to last. Aunt Kitty thinks I'm pregnant and that's why we're getting married so fast."

"Are you?"

"No," she growled with her famous dead-eye look. "I even heard Mom say that she was happy that John and his parents were paying for the wedding so that she didn't have to waste her money on something that wouldn't..."

"Re, stop. Your mother's a moron."

Renee's tears instantly stopped and she broke into a real laugh, one that came from the soul and seemed to lift her spirit.

"Look, honey, here's how I see it. Did you guys move fast? Yes. Are you doing things in the right order, unlike me? Yes. Does Dr. John absolutely and positively love you with all his heart? Yes! And the fact that he's still around, even with all the crap that's been thrown at him the last few months, truly makes him a keeper in my book. So pardon my language, but screw your mom and your aunts, and anyone else who dares to come to this wedding and talk smack about you two."

I took her hand and pulled her out of the chair and looked her firmly in the eye. "When you get into the aisle, just look at John. Don't look at anyone else. Just find him and trust me, the love you'll see behind his eyes will bring you down the rest of the way."

With a few more tears, she wrapped her arms around my neck and hugged me tightly.

"I wish my dad was here," she sniffled.

"He is, honey," I replied. "He's watching."

"This is why you're my maid of honor."

"Of course I am. Your twin will always be your maid of honor, even if she ends up having her own twins during the ceremony."

"Yeah, please don't do that. Today is really my day."

"And the bridezilla returns," I laughed as I pulled her toward the door.

"The what?"

"Er...nothing. Let's go get married!" I said with a big fake smile as she narrowed her eyes at me.

"Wait, wait," she said as she squeezed my hand and pulled me back, her face suddenly very serious again. "I...I just want you to know that I wouldn't have...if you weren't back with us, if Cameron hadn't found you...I would have postponed the wedding. I never would have gotten married without you here. I need you to know that."

I patted her hand. "Damn right you wouldn't have. But you do know that I am not getting married until you're eight months pregnant so that you can know what this feels like. I need *you* to know that."

We left the room arm and arm and laughing as we rode the small elevator down one floor to the large open ballroom where the ceremony and reception would be held in front of a wall of windows with a stunning backdrop of the city. The guests applauded while I wobbled down the aisle, and I had a sneaking suspicion that Jared had started it. But once I was in place everyone gasped when Renee stepped into the aisle, the shear chiffon and lace train stretching out behind her as the romantic lighting sparkled off the sequences hidden all over her dress. Just as I had told her to do, she immediately looked at Dr. John and all her nerves melted away from her face, helping her to walk confidently down the aisle to the man she loved.

Vows were said, rings exchanged, and finally a kiss before the newlyweds fled down the aisle to the sound of applause. Apologizing once again to the best man for having to walk with me, I took his extended arm and we followed the bride and groom. As I slowly wobbled down the aisle it was wonderful seeing all the faces of my family smiling back at me. But even funnier was seeing bubbly Dr. Cathy Taylor clapping even harder as I passed. Apparently she and Dr. John had a bet going as to when I'd pop, and Dr. Taylor thought for sure the wedding would send me over the edge. For more reasons than one I prayed that the good doctor was wrong.

While couples enjoyed cocktails and appetizers, the ballroom was transformed from a twinkling romantic ceremony setting to a posh nightclub. There was no formal sit down dinner, though there were tables scattered around the outside of the dance floor. Renee and Dr. John had made it clear that they wanted a party, not a stuffy dinner. Now don't get me wrong, there was food. Everywhere. Dance, drink, talk, and eat. That was the theme, and it was the party of the year. To prove my point, even Devin was on the dance floor, though I'm not sure that what he was doing could be classified as dancing and neither would Fabi by his expressions.

With my ankles the same size as my calves, and the pain in my back, I could really only handle one dance with Cameron and he could tell that I was upset about it. To make me feel better, when he noticed that I couldn't get enough of the scallops wrapped in bacon, he paid the waiter forty dollars to keep my plate full of them and whatever else I might possibly crave. Yet another thing he did for me that made the guilt monster pound a hammer into my heart.

"Are you all right, love?"

"Huh? Why?"

He shrugged. "You were staring."

"I told you I love the way you look in a suit."

"Yeah, bro. I know my heart always goes pitter pat when you wear a suit," Jared said sarcastically across the table.

Our family had commandeered one of the larger round tables near the back of the room, although now everyone except me and Cameron, and Jared and Nikki were on the dance floor, which wasn't necessarily ideal.

"Now Beebs, you didn't say anything about how I did on my tie," he said proudly as he slid his hand down his crumbled and crooked superhero tie.

"That's because it looks like a three-year-old tied it, Jer. I thought you were taking lessons from your brother."

I smiled at my joke, but I was the only one. Jared looked awkwardly at Nikki as he squeezed her hand and leaned in to kiss her cheek. I looked at Cameron whose eyes were slightly widened.

Did Nikki tie his tie? I said in his head, and he nodded slightly causing me to sigh and roll my eyes. I had enough on my mind that I didn't need to deal with Nikki's bullshit, especially considering she very well could have turned against us all. Again.

"Cam, what time is it?"

He looked toward the front of the room and narrowed his eyes to the city skyline where the moon shown just above one of the buildings across the street. "Almost 11:30."

"How do you do that?"

He shrugged and leaned in as he whispered, "Vampire."

Placing two fingers up to my lips, I kissed them and then placed them on his lips. "Love you."

He took my hand away from his mouth and held it to his heart as he leaned down and kissed my stomach on each side – one for each baby. And with a sinking feeling, I knew it was time to begin breaking his heart.

Looking out at the dance floor, I opened my mind and thankfully found only the Vampires that were ours. I Pushed a message telling everyone it was time and like a well-choreographed dance number they divided themselves casually to their designated positions. Devin and Fabi left the dance floor altogether so that Devin could change in a room near the roof where I could "see" him. While Sera asked Daddy O to dance, Eris broke away to ensure that those not involved in the mission were kept occupied and away from the second floor. Alex and Kyla came walking toward our table and everything from here on out hinged on two things.

The first one, was mine. "Hey Jer, Daddy O finally let Maddy go. Why don't you go and ask her to dance?"

Without even looking at Nikki for approval, Jared shot up from his chair and walked over to Maddy who was making her way to our table. Although she didn't know it, there were many eyes watching Maddy, waiting to see if she would say yes and I sighed with relief when she nodded and headed back to the floor with her hand wrapped around Jared's arm.

The second task, and the most important, was assigned to Kyla. Once she and Alex reached the table, Kyla broke from her husband and extended her hand out to Cameron. "Come on, Cameron, let's show these people how you really dance to this kind of music."

"Dearest sister, I wish I could. But I am taking care of my angel."

Kyla, knowing that the entire plan hinged on keeping Cameron away from me, threw her hands up dramatically then grabbed Cameron's arm and pulled him out of the chair causing my feet to fall heavily to the floor.

"It's not like her ankles are going to get any smaller. Now come on," she said, not giving him any other choice but to go with her to the dance floor.

Alex sat in Cameron's vacated seat, giving me a nervous look. With a nervous look of my own I slowly released my breath while my feet searched for my fancy flip flops that were hiding somewhere under the table. Once I had slipped my feet into my shoes I turned in my chair to face Nikki who was sitting behind me. She was looking around the room nervously as though searching for someone, which we all hoped was exactly what she was doing.

"So Nikki," I began, "are you having a good time?"

As I addressed her, her eyes began to sparkle while a smile stretched up her face. "Yes I am. This is the best wedding I've ever been to."

"Good. I'm glad you were able to come with Jared."

Nikki rose from her chair and sat in a chair next to me. "I just want to thank you for inviting me. Jared and I both know it was you who pulled all the strings to get Victor to let me come. I know you and I will never be best friends..." she said and if I had been drinking milk, it would have come out of my nose, "...but I'm hoping that we can be good acquaintances, for Jared's sake. I know I don't deserve it, but it will just make it easier for Jared not to feel so torn all the time."

"Nikki, I love Jared as if he was my own brother, and I think I speak for everyone when I say that none of us want to see him get hurt. He's the baby of the family, and you can't hurt the baby and not expect a punch in the face."

My eyes were blazing into hers and she caught every ounce of my meaning.

"I don't want to hurt him."

"Then don't," I warned, in a way, giving her an out for whatever aid she's given Elaina tonight. I watched as she licked her lips nervously while her nostrils flared with emotion. For a moment I thought perhaps I could get her to confess her sins, and maybe even help us. But the connection we had broke when Fabi came to stand over my shoulder.

"Well this looks like a conversation I don't want to miss," he said. Nikki's eyes fluttered as if she was awakened from a trance and leaned herself away from me with her arms crossed in front of her chest. Fabi squeezed my shoulder as he pointed out to the dance floor. "I didn't know Cameron could dance like that."

I peered around Fabi's side and watched Cam and Kyla twist and twirl to the big band song that was blasting over the speakers. "Neither did I, but since both of them were alive when the jitterbug was invented, I'm not surprised they're that good at it. Just looking at them makes me tired," I said as I stretched my arms above my head and yawned.

While Fabi continued to look out at the dance floor I gently asked in his head, *Is Devin ready?*

Without looking back at me he nodded ever so slightly. Opening my mind once again, I Pushed at its edges, stretching it out like tentacles up to the top floor where I saw Devin's light looking like it was floating a hundred feet above me. I took one more deep breath and extended my hands out to Alex who took them immediately and lifted me from my chair.

"I think I'm going to go and put my feet up in the bridal suit."

It was hard not to crack at the sight of Alex's lips twitching as he said my own words to himself. We had practiced this exchange several times. "Do you want me to escort you?"

"No, I'll be fine. It's right upstairs next to the elevator. And don't let Cam go running up there, I want him to have some fun too. Just send someone to come get me when Renee and John are getting ready to leave."

Alex nodded and squeezed my hands too tightly. I waved to Fabi and to Nikki, giving her a small smile which she did not return. Well fuck you too, I thought and waddled to the elevator. When the elevator doors closed in front of me, I thought for sure I would throw up. My back was aching, but when the elevator slowed and the doors prepared to open, the left side of my stomach started to burn.

"What's the matter, baby girl?" I whispered and rubbed her side of my belly. Of course she didn't answer, but the burning didn't subside.

Stepping out of the elevator, I kept my hand on my stomach and stepped over to the bridal suit just ahead on the left. When my hand folded over the doorknob, my shoulders were suddenly crushed from behind. Reflexively I held my stomach tightly from underneath as I was roughly turned around and slammed back into the door, knocking my breath out of me. When I finally found the strength to open my eyes Aidan was standing in front of me, his fangs drawn as he pressed my shoulders and back into the frame of the door.

Aidan's here! I said in my head to Devin several floors above.

I started to gasp but swallowed it, trying to hide the fact that I could see a halo of light shining around Aidan's head. But instead of his previous milky white color it was bright hybrid red. I was prepared for Elaina's minions to have been drinking hybrid blood. What I didn't expect was that I would be able to see their essences. The continued burning of my left side made me think that my daughter alone was responsible for my ability to see the red halo glowing in front of me. Could it be that my son had been responsible for the aid with the Vampires?

But I couldn't ponder on the gifts of my babies since Aidan leaned in closer and began grazing his fangs against my lips.

"I missed you, Morgan."

"The feeling isn't mutual," I grunted back as the bones in my shoulders began to creak under his pressure. "Now let me go, I don't even have to scream in order for the Warriors to hear me."

Aidan sucked in a mocking breath as he shook his head. "I wouldn't do that."

"Why not?"

He released my left shoulder and trailed his fingers down my cheek causing me to flinch. "Well there aren't just Warriors downstairs, are there?" Aidan tilted his head down, brushing his nose against the lobe of my ear. "Ollie and Sera are down there. Renee is dancing with her new husband. It would be a shame to see her get her throat ripped out on her wedding day and stain that pretty white dress."

I tried moving my head away from him, but Aidan took my chin between his fingers and put us nose to nose.

"What do you want?"

"What I've always wanted. You," he said and placed his hands on my stomach. "And them."

"Don't touch me," I said as I pushed his hands away.

Aidan took me by the shoulders once again and slammed me up against the wall, making stars sparkle before my eyes.

"I will touch you anyway I please and you will come with me," he growled as he pressed his forehead against mine letting his fangs graze against my skin.

"And if I don't?"

"Then you might as well wave goodbye to everyone you love downstairs."

"You're going to take on a room of Warriors?"

"Do you honestly think I would come alone?"

I swallowed slowly as I reached out with my mind to the surrounding areas, seeing if I could use the same technique I did when I searched for Vamps. Quickly I caught the sight of a dozen or so red halos floating in the stairwell behind Aidan's shoulder. I concentrated on finding Devin's white light above me, though my head was already starting to ache.

Elaina's Vamps in the stairwell, I Pushed and hoped that he heard me.

"Come on, Morgan, this is where you either decide to come with me, or I have your entire family killed," Aidan said with a devilish smile.

"If I go with you…" I paused for dramatic effect, "you promise you won't hurt my family?"

While Aidan pondered his answer, the stairwell door opened behind him and Nikki stepped into view.

"Dad!" she whispered harshly. "We have to go! Cameron will come up here any minute."

Aidan kissed me on my cheek as he said, "I will make you so happy."

"You disgust me," I replied and looked over his shoulder at Nikki, unsure who I meant the statement more for.

"We'll have the perfect little family."

"You, me, and Elaina? The three of us in bed together?"

Another wicked smile stretched across his face. "Three in a bed is never a crowd for me. Now before we go..." he said as he ripped the necklace from my neck, and then patted me down uncomfortably, "...we don't want to take any chances that those Warriors put any tracking devices on you."

Not waiting for any comeback he took my arm and pulled me from the wall. Nikki looked nervous as we came closer to her and I gave her the dirtiest look I could muster though all I wanted to do was rip that bright red light from her head.

Aidan led me through the door and as we entered the stairwell Elaina's Vamps were scattered on the stairs above us and below.

"There's no way I can go down those stairs."

Aidan lifted me into his arms. "It's ok, Morgan, you don't need to be embarrassed about wanting to be in my arms."

The other Vampires snickered as they closed ranks around us and Aidan began running down the stairs.

Going down the stairs. A dozen Vamps around us and Nikki, I Pushed at Devin, watching his light get further and further away. With only being able to communicate one way, I kept praying that Devin was hearing me.

Nausea was beginning to set in as we circled down thirty floors. In my head I was sending the floor numbers to Devin, and when we reached the bottom, the Vamps in front of Aidan opened a door which led outside to a narrow side street where the wedding limo idled against the sidewalk.

As we approached the limo, the passenger door was opened from the inside and Elaina's corn colored head peeked out with a wide victorious smile.

"Brianna Morgan, how nice of you to join our party," she said as she ducked back inside.

Aidan lowered me to the ground and grasped the back of my neck while Nikki came around us and climbed inside the limo. Holding me firmly against his chest and squeezing me around the throat, Aidan put his lips to my ear and whispered, "No funny business. If we so much as see anyone following us I will rip those brats out of your stomach with my bare hands and make you watch as I drain each of them dry. You understand me?"

I nodded nervously and concentrated on the white light atop the skyscraper next to me. *In the wedding limo. Others behind us looking for Warriors following.*

Still holding me by my throat, Aidan lowered me into the limo, finally succeeding after several attempts. Once he closed the door he took a seat next to Elaina on the long bench seat while Nikki sat at the opposite end, her arms crossed in front of her chest while she looked pensively out the window. Someone looked a little guilty.

The limo pulled away from the curb and the true test of my gift was about to begin. Placing my elbow up on the window, I closed my eyes and began nervously picking at my lips. Devin's light was moving slowly across the top of the building as the limo crawled down the street.

Turning right onto Kilby Street.

Like a bird gliding over the skyline, I could see Devin leap over to the next building.

Elaina began to cackle to my left, making my eyes fly open in her direction. "Ah, Aidy, our little mother looks frightened. Make her feel better."

Left on State Street.

Aidan quirked a smile. "I can't wait for my Nikki to have a brother and sister to play with."

I rubbed my belly protectively, noticing for the first time since we began traveling down the stairs that my stomach was no longer burning. The red essences of those in the limo were fading, though Devin's light behind us was burning bright. My baby girl's power was draining and I worried it had something to do with the cramping that was now occurring at the base of my stomach. It was Braxton-Hicks, I thought to myself, that's all, just like every other day.

I looked across the limo to Nikki who was still looking nervously out the window.

"But Nikki already has a sister, don't you?" Nikki snapped her head back to me, her eyes suddenly glassy with tears. "Does she know what you're doing? Did you even see her after she got burned? She's still recovering, fighting every day to survive. Is this how you want her to remember you?"

I barely got my words out when the cramping in my stomach intensified. I held my stomach tightly and tried concentrating on Devin's light floating in the air behind us instead of the growing pain from within.

Left, Tremont Street.

Softly and slowly I began breathing through the pain while Nikki glared at me from the other end of the limo. "Shut up! You know nothing about my sister!"

"That's right, Morgan, you know nothing about my other daughter," Aidan replied smugly.

"You're so full of shit," I shouted, letting out a big breath as the cramp finally released. "And Nikki, what about Jared? For some reason he loves you, and this will crush him."

"Shut up! Just shut up!" Nikki shouted and then looked back out the window while trying to conceal wiping away a tear.

"Both of you need to shut up," Elaina shouted.

"What do you want from me?" I asked, surprised at the exhaustion already in my voice.

Elaina smiled as she licked and then bit her bottom lip with excitement. "I have waited a long time for you and those babies."

"They're just babies. What powers could they possibly possess…"

"Powers?" Elaina laughed. "You think this is all about powers? Please! I have found hybrids with almost every power conceivable and I have tasted every one of them. I could care less about powers. This has always been about the future of our race. These babies will be the first of their kind."

"W-what do you mean?"

Elaina lifted a single eyebrow. "So it seems that I'm not the only one Seraphina likes to keep secrets from. You mean to tell me that after all these years, she's never told you?"

"Told me what?"

Elaina smiled wickedly at me. "I remember it as if it were yesterday. My young naïve little prophetess came to me brimming with excitement as she said, 'The Vampire race will change for all time because there will be a hybrid unlike any other. Her name will be Brianna, a daughter of Eris, and her children will be Vampire but human all the same.' So don't you see, Brianna, you will be the first in our race's long history to give birth to Vampires."

My hands froze over my stomach. "It's not true."

Elaina pouted at me mockingly. "Oh my dear, but it is. Not only will your children change how Vampires are created for the rest of eternity, but they will be stronger and more powerful without aversions to silver or sun. They will truly be Vampire hybrids but with more of the Vampire traits within them instead of being mainly human like the pathetic hybrids we have now."

"If you've been waiting all this time for my children, why torture all those other hybrids?"

Nikki looked over at Elaina through the side of her eye, seemingly looking for an explanation as well. Elaina stretched her right arm up and over Aidan as she rested her head on his shoulder while she spoke in a tone as if we were having a conversation about her new nail color.

"Like I said, it has always been my mission to find ways to make our hybrids reach their full potential."

"By electrocuting them!" I shouted, noticing a shiver go up Nikki's spine, though Elaina remained calm and showed no emotion whatsoever.

The limo slowed as it prepared to turn. *Right onto Park*, I Pushed to Devin, almost forgetting what I was supposed to be doing.

"Sometimes you need to use extreme measures in the name of progress."

"You turned them into wild animals."

"Yes, but stronger wild animals," she replied with a sly smile.

My back started feeling as though it was being squeezed in a vice as another contraction began. I was beginning to worry that this wasn't just Braxton-Hicks. Brianna Morgan's luck and unbelievable timing strikes again. You have to be freaking kidding me! Now I was conflicted with the decision to stop this now, or wait it out. If this was just Braxton-Hicks, the mission would be a failure. But if I was in actual labor, it would be hours before anything really happened. So the question now was, could I make it through the pain without tipping them off?

Trying to breathe through the new round of pain I asked, "Why did you have to start experimenting on kids?"

Elaina shrugged. "They were my plan B."

Her nonchalant tone made me want to stab her in the eye with my dagger, if I only had it. The contraction started to fade and I was able to tell Devin we were turning left onto Beacon Street. It seemed that Elaina was taking me to the Back Bay area of the city.

Without any prodding Elaina continued with, "You see, my plan for you has evolved many times over the years. At first I wanted simply to kill you, fear of change you know. But Sera continued to tell me about what your children would be able to do. That's when I decided I would simply kidnap you and raise you as my own. However, that was a little easier said than done. Sera fled and Eris kept you very well hidden. I had almost given up hope of ever finding you when Jazlyn came over to our side and told me Eris had sent a Gatherer after you. Of course I never expected you to fall in love with your Gatherer, especially one who was also a Warrior. That just made my job even harder.

"So then my experiments on hybrids became even more intense, trying to make an army that could go against the mighty Warriors. But after the attack at the manor I abandoned my efforts on the hybrids and decided to change tactics. If for some reason I couldn't get my hands on you, I would find a way to do it myself. There has to be a logical reason for why your children will be born Vampires because let's face it, you're not that special."

"My babies are NOT Vampires!" I shouted angrily and too loud for the close quarters of the limo. "I've had a dozen ultrasounds and my babies are nothing more than human."

Aidan snickered. "Oh yeah, Morgan. Every human baby can attack Vampires from within the womb."

Suddenly I was overcome with fear and dread. I knew my children would be hybrids. I wasn't, however, prepared for them to be anything else. Vampire babies? How could that even be possible? What would I do, how would I raise them, would they grow into adults, how could they be Vampires if I've heard their heartbeats? The questions just kept coming and coming and my bottom lip was trembling from the absence of answers.

"Why? I don't understand why," I whimpered.

In a second's time Elaina rounded on me, straddling my large belly and pressing my shoulders firmly into the leather seat just as another contraction began to rip through the lower half of my body.

"Why?" she shouted. "Why! We are the most dangerous of all creatures yet we hide and cower in the shadows because our elders say so? Well I didn't agree to that, I deserve better. We all deserve better! Bringing our race out into the open and elevating us above humans where we belong is my destiny." Elaina's hands moved off my shoulders and onto my stomach. "And these babies are the ones that will turn the tide."

Feeling violated, I tried moving her hands off my stomach which was pointless. "Don't tou…ow-oooowwww," I groaned loudly as the contraction took hold of me.

Elaina knelt in front of me as I dug my nails into the leather seat, waiting for the contraction to pass. Elaina's hands went back to my stomach as she looked at Aidan. "She's going into labor," she said excitedly and then looked back to me. "You're in labor, aren't you?"

I didn't answer, but the harsh exhale through my clenched teeth probably gave me away. Elaina leapt to the far side of the limo and banged on the divider. A second later the divider slowly rolled down revealing someone other than the limo driver I remembered from earlier this evening.

As Elaina continued shouting orders to the driver, I weakly focused on Devin's light that was still flitting in the distance, though I found it hard to concentrate through the pain.

Can't...wait...labor...turning on...Aaarrrr, "-rrrlington Street!"

I gasped as the limo went quiet with all eyes on me, but then gasped again as Devin's light flew backwards and then fell to the ground. Oh dear lord, what had I done?

Just then a walkie-talkie somewhere within the vehicle crackled to life. "Someone just fell from a building! We just saw someone fall from one of the buildings, but they're running to a truck behind us. We have a tail, repeat we have a tail!"

Aidan rose from his seat, his fingers splayed tensely as he came to stand hunched in front of me. He was going to rip my babies from my stomach just like he said he would.

He reached his hand back.

"NO!" I screamed. "No Aidan, please!"

The corners of his lips curled into a wicked smile as his splayed hand wrapped into a fist right before cracking it loudly against my cheek. My head whipped around, blood spurting from my mouth onto the window. And then...darkness.

Chapter Fifty-Nine

Cameron

"Cameron!" Renee squealed as she flung her arms around my neck. Her breath was heavy with alcohol and out of necessity I had to place my arm around her back in order to keep her standing. "So you're like my best-friend-in-law, no wait! My twin-in-law," she slurred.

John sighed behind her as he too kept a protective arm around her. "Have you met my drunk wife?"

"I am not drunk!" she shouted, but was muffled by the uncomfortably loud music being pumped through the room. Renee removed her arms from around my neck and melted back into John's chest as she giggled. "You called me your wife."

"That's because you are my wife. My very intoxicated wife."

"Well I had to drink for the both of us," she said with a pout.

"And you have accomplished that."

"No alcohol for you tonight, John?" I asked as I looked around the room for where Brianna had gone off to since she was no longer sitting at our table.

"Just a small glass of champagne earlier. I need to stay sober just in case."

"Just in case of what?"

John shifted awkwardly as Renee began to slide in his arms. "Well you see, Cathy and I have a bet on when Bri will drop. After Cathy saw her going down the aisle, she thought for sure it would be soon, she said it was a gut feeling. So I'm staying sober because someone will have to drive drunkzilla here to the hospital. That is until ten o'clock tomorrow morning because that's when we're leaving for our honeymoon. Right, Re?" he warned.

"Yeah, yeah. Going on our honeymoon no matter what. No matter if my niece and nephew are born, my new husband will drag me away to a tropical island and not let me come back until it's over. Blah, blah, blah, wa, wa, wa. Speaking of, where is my twin?"

"I was asking myself that same question," I said pulling anxiously at my jacket's cuffs. "I am going to go look for her. Will you excuse me?"

Not waiting for an answer I walked off the dance floor making my way over to the back table when Fabiani came to walk beside me and crooked his arm through mine. "Hey handsome."

"Fabi," I nodded curtly, but did not slow down. "I really do not have time to flirt with you at this moment. I am looking for Brianna."

"She's with Devin," he said as he pulled my arm toward the elevator.

"Why is she with my brother? Is she all right?"

"As far as I know. Actually Alex needs your help with something…"

I pulled my arm out of his grip. "Fabi, I do not have time to help Alex. Where did Brianna go?"

"I told you," he answered calmly, "she's with Devin. Now I'm telling you, Alex needs your help. It'll only be a minute." With surprising strength, Fabiani pulled me into the elevator and waited for the doors to close. "Do you remember where the loading dock is?"

"Yes," I replied, though thoroughly confused.

"Good. Project there, that's where everyone is. Do it now."

Before I could ask any questions Fabiani disappeared into a cloud of black mist and I had no choice but to do the same since the elevator was already in motion. Picturing the loading dock surrounding me, I took a cleansing breath and willed myself away. A second later the black mist began to dissipate from around me and Victor began to focus in front of me. Once I had fully formed I realized he was in full Warrior gear standing in front of two black SUVs. Alexander was standing just behind him, also now in Warrior gear, with Connor and Skylar on either side. Seeing the two of them made my stomach sink into my knees since both of them were supposed to be on a mission and Connor seemed to have difficulty keeping my eye contact.

"What is going on!" I yelled looking back at Victor.

"I warn you to keep your voice down, child," he said with a raised brow.

"Five days ago a mission was commissioned and approved for the abduction of Brianna Morgan."

"What!" I screamed as I flung myself at Victor but was held back by Alexander, but it did not stop my arms from searching the air for Victor's throat. "What have you done! How could you do this to her, to one of your own Warriors. To my children!"

Victor stayed frozen in front of me, not flinching in the slightest. "Considering the mission was commissioned by Brianna, and that she voluntarily took the hand of Aidan Pierce this evening, I am not the one to spew your anger at."

"Wait...what?!"

"You are wasting time, child. Now I urge you to get into the vehicle to help retrieve Brianna. The others will bring you up to speed." Victor opened himself up so that all the Warriors could see him. "As always, be vigilant, be strong, my children. And unleash the fury of the Warrior inside you. Now get moving!"

Everyone but me beat their fists against their chests and dispersed between the two SUVs. When I past Victor without acknowledging him, he pulled my arm, but I stayed with my back to him.

"Good luck, child."

"Go to hell."

Victor pulled on my arm roughly and turned me around to face him. "You have every right to be angry, but as your leader and your maker I am telling you that you need to think like the Warrior I made you to be. Do not let your emotions get the better of you."

"You may have very well sent my family to their deaths. I would never knowingly put another's life in danger, especially a woman in Brianna's condition."

Victor's grip loosened. "When the time comes, you can run our coven the way you see fit. But for now, get in the truck."

Victor turned me back around and shoved me toward the SUV. Connor had taken the front passenger seat while Alexander climbed into the backseat. I took the seat next to him and the truck lurched forward before I was even able to shut the door. It was the first time I noticed who was actually driving.

"Vladimir, from your presence I am to assume that Eris is also in support of this ridiculous plan."

Vladimir peered in the rearview mirror and caught my gaze. "I will always volunteer when Miss Brianna needs help."

Connor bent down into the floor in front of him and came up with several black colored items in his hands.

"We brought your gear," he said as he turned toward the backseat and handed me my personal Warrior uniform.

I took the clothing from him and threw it in the floor. "Have you and Skylar been here all week? Is this the mission Father sent you on last minute?"

"Cameron, I'm sorry. I couldn't…"

"You flat out lied to me! You looked me in the eye and lied to me!"

Connor turned back to look out the windshield while Alexander put his hand against my chest. "Cam, don't blame Connor. We were all under orders…"

"And you," I growled as I knocked his hand from my chest. "I am not sure who I am angrier with right now – you or Brianna. I entrusted you with the lives of my unborn children, and this is what you do? We have never had secrets from each other. Of all my brothers who would understand…"

"I was against this from the beginning, ask anyone! I know that if our roles were reversed…"

"But your wife would survive a hell of a lot better than mine."

Alexander shifted in his seat although he did not have room to really move. "Cam, I tried, you have to believe me. I have never yelled at Bri the way I did that night. But once she had Eris and Devin's support…"

"Wait, where is Devin?"

Connor lifted a tablet in the air with the GPS tracking system that we used lit up on the screen. "He's a street ahead of us, but you should be able to see him…right about…now!"

Connor pointed through the windshield as we turned onto State Street and right at that moment I saw a dark figure leap across the distance between two buildings like a gazelle. Reaching down into the floor where I had thrown my gear, I picked up my communication device and strapped it around my neck. "Is his comm open?"

Connor nodded his head. "Brianna is telling him where they are going, and he's communicating it us, plus we obviously have a GPS on him."

Placing the earbud into my ear I said in a terse voice, "Brother!"

You could hear the wind whispering through his microphone while his voice bobbled as he ran. "She's fine."

"How could you do this to me!"

"Brother, I do not have time to argue. There's a van…" he paused again and this time the distance between buildings was greater and he looked as though he was running in slow motion across the void.

"A dark colored van?" Connor asked as he pointed out the windshield.

"Yes. Those are Elaina's Vamps. I counted them as they came out. Three more with Bri in the limo."

We followed the van at a safe distance, watching to see if the van veered away from the route Elaina herself was going. When we turned onto Tremont Street I could see the limousine they said was carrying Brianna. It took almost every ounce of control I had not to jump out of the SUV and attack it. Just then, I was suddenly hit by the absence of an important member of our family.

"Where is Jared?"

The truck became very quiet and Alexander looked down at his hands. "He was not brought into the loop about the mission."

"Why not?"

He sighed. "Because we knew he would have prevented us from setting Nikki up." I shook my head slightly, not quite understanding his meaning. "Nikki proved to us this evening that she is still in contact with Aidan and Elaina. We gave her an opportunity to vindicate herself, and she failed. Which in all actuality was what we wanted, otherwise we never would have been able to draw Elaina out and control Brianna's abduction."

Realizations were beginning to flood into my head. "Is that why Brianna suddenly invited Nikki?" He nodded. "And why Father lifted all her restrictions?"

"Yes, and then Nikki fell in line with everything we wanted her to do."

I raked my hands through my hair knowing how hurt Jared would be, especially after thinking we had all finally accepted Nikki. Feeling antsy and not knowing what else to do, I pressed the microphone of my comm unit. "Brother, anything?"

"No," he answered curtly.

The leather upholstery was ripping under my nails as I dug them into my seat. The next few minutes were torturous as we drove slowly from one red light to the next, bumping and bobbing along the crowded streets. Vladimir was being cautious of not drawing attention to ourselves, keeping safe distances between cars, not running lights or hitting pedestrians as they crossed the streets in front of us. It was a busy night in the city, which seemed to be somewhat of an advantage to us since it was difficult for a limousine to hide in the crowded streets.

Finally, the sound of wind came through our earpieces. "They're turning right on Park Street."

Vladimir responded by turning onto Park Street and eventually onto Beacon. Instead of fleeing the city altogether Elaina was winding further in, meaning she had established a headquarters in the area. Though it was hard to admit, but if this plan ended everything tonight it would be a relief. Could a conclusion to what seemed like an endless battle seriously be within reach? Could Brianna and I have a life with the children that did not involve looking over our shoulders at all times?

Devin sucked in a quick breath, and then another, and then another. "Br...bro...brother," he stuttered between breaths. "Something's...off."

Everyone in the SUV tensed, and Connor began communicating with Skylar in the SUV two cars behind us.

"What is off, Brother," I replied, trying to sound calm.

There was a pause as he leapt across another building. "I am getting...hit...Pushed, like Brianna does, but it's...different. It doesn't *feel* like her. It's not as...potent? More raw? I can't describe it, but...it's not Bri."

"It's the children," I replied breathlessly. Alexander turned and looked at me questioningly. "We kept it to ourselves, but Brianna told me that while she was held by Aidan the children showed similar gifts to her own. If they are doing this, then Bri must be in trouble. We need to get to her now, screw taking down the coven. The two most important members are in that limousine, we need to take them down now and get Brianna out of there."

Connor nodded and pressed his comm, "Skylar, we're going in. Take the van, we'll go after the limo."

From behind us you could hear the other SUV's engine rev and a horn blare as they cut off another car in order to catch up with us.

"Devin," Alexander began.

"Got it," Devin cut him off. "I'm going down there...ah...wait...she's saying..."

But he was unable to tell us what Brianna was saying since the next second everyone was yanking the ear buds out of their ears because of Devin's shouts. I looked up at the building ahead and watched as he flew backwards across the roof, tipped over the ledge, and fell down toward the ground.

Feet down, feet down, I said to myself continuing to hear his screams through the ear bud hanging on my shoulder.

"Feet down, Devin!" I yelled into my mic when he was only several feet from the ground, and a second before he hit, he pointed his feet down. Pedestrians in the area screamed and fled from the sidewalk, their cell phones drawn and pointing toward Devin's landing site. A second later Devin was bursting through them and toward our moving vehicle. I rolled down my window and extended my hand. Devin leapt from the street and grasped my arm, allowing me to pull him up onto the running board.

"Thank you, Brother," Devin said gratefully, though his face was strained.

"Do not thank me yet. I am certain you will be on the internet within the next five minutes. The Cleaners will have their work cut out for them tonight."

"*That* was definitely Brianna."

I let go of Devin's hand, yet he held onto the SUV by the luggage rack railings above.

"What happened?"

"Brother, I think she's in labor."

My jaw clenched tightly and suddenly my bottom lip was stinging in pain from my fangs extending. Victor's voice was echoing in my head, telling me to be a Warrior instead of an angry and worried lover. Brianna needed a Warrior and I needed her, which meant I had to flip the switch.

"Uh, gentlemen," Vladimir began, "I think they know we're here."

I leaned toward the center of the vehicle and looked through the windshield in time to see the dark van slam on its brakes, causing the other cars to swerve in various directions. As we approached, the van cut sharply in front of us causing Vladimir to bank to the left in order to avoid it.

Devin was not prepared for our SUV to swerve so drastically and he lost his grip on the railing. Lunging out of the window, I caught Devin by the forearm although his legs dangled behind him near the back tires. Devin ground his fingers into my forearm, ripping through my white dress shirt until he found my skin. Vladimir's driving skills were being tested as the van continually made him swerve all over the road, making it almost impossible for Devin to get his footing.

With my torso hanging out of the window, I could see our other SUV riding up on our tail. "Skylar!" I shouted through the wind, though I knew my throat mic would pick it up. "Take the driver." Through the windshield I could see Skylar nod in the passenger seat, disappear and then reappear crouched in a cloud of black mist on the roof of our SUV. "Brother, take everyone else!"

Skylar leapt from the roof of his SUV and at the same time I gripped my brother's arm tightly as I swung him like a pendulum toward the enemy van. Both Warriors flew through the air, Skylar less than a foot ahead and landing on the roof of the van, kicking his legs up and swinging them through the driver's window. Devin tipped his foot off the hood of our SUV, launching him forward head first through the back window of the van.

The van began to swerve in sharp movements, but Vladimir wasted no time pulling out into the opposite lane of traffic in order to get around it. We all knew that the Assassin was in that van and within minutes there would only be two Vampires still alive, and they would both be Warriors. Our secondary SUV stayed with the van while Vladimir crossed back into the appropriate lane just as the limousine turned down a street several lights ahead of us.

"Vlad!" Alexander yelled as he pointed to where the limousine had disappeared.

"I see them," Vladimir replied calmly. "No need to shout."

"Go, go, go, go," I kept muttering underneath my breath. I knew he was doing everything he could, but we simply were not catching up fast enough and the headrest of Connor's seat was paying the price as I kept pulling out handfuls of foam. Vladimir was certainly pissing off every driver in Boston, but no one or no traffic law would stop him from getting us to that limo.

Clipping a parked car, Vladimir turned us onto the street that the limousine had disappeared down and then he was suddenly slamming on the brakes, causing me to fly over the center console. The one-way street was at a standstill, car and trucks parked at odd angles with smoke still rising from the road where their tires skidded across the asphalt.

I bolted out of the truck and ran down the sidewalk at a human pace that would not bring too much attention. The traffic was backed up almost the entire length of the street, and at its end where it dumped onto a busy intersection was the limousine parked at a wide enough angle to block all cars from passing on either side. Three of the doors were left open, the inside dome lights casting thin columns of light onto the pitch black street. Pushing past the outraged onlookers I knelt inside the limo and found it empty, as I fear I would. I stepped further inside the limousine and the only thing I was grateful for was the noticeable absence of fluid. If Brianna was indeed in labor, her water had not yet broken, though I could not say she had been left unharmed. I could smell her blood and as I looked to the door I saw it splattered on the window.

Just then Alexander wrapped his large hand around my arm and pulled me from the inside of the limousine. "Cam, come on! We can't stay here."

"This is your fault, Alexander!" I shouted and pushed him away.

"Cam," he said loudly then stepped back to me and whispered, "put your fangs away. We don't have time for this. They couldn't have gone far without being noticed, they're carrying a pregnant woman for goodness sake."

"Exactly!" I shouted again, fighting to pull my fangs back up and pushing Alexander so hard he fell back into Connor's arms. "She's pregnant, Alex, and now might even be in labor! Never in a million years should she have been in that limousine. And I should have NEVER been kept in the dark on this."

"She and father knew you would say no…"

"Of course I would! As you should have said in my stead."

"I did! There is only so much I can do when…"

"I do not want to hear it," I snapped at him. "Find Devin and the other team. We need to gather back at the wedding reception."

"Wh-what? Why?" Alexander stuttered, but Connor did not wait for an explanation before he started spitting orders over the comms.

"Not that I owe you any explanation, but not only was Brianna inside that limousine, but so was Nikki, you can smell her rancid citrus perfume. We need to go back to the reception and get Jared because months ago he placed a subcutaneous tracker on Nikki and that might be the only way to find where they took Brianna."

"We were not aware that Nikki had a…"

"Maybe if you had brought me into the loop you would have."

"Cam, come on. Don't be like this."

Glaring at him I turned away and began walking back down the sidewalk toward our SUV where Vladimir was directing traffic to help those reverse down the street.

I stopped just before I stepped up into the SUV and turned back around to see Alexander looking defeated with his shoulders slumped and Connor striding just behind him. "And the two of you will update Father. If anything happens to Brianna or my children I will kill all of you, one by one, I swear I will. And if Brianna gets herself killed I will never forgive her. Never!"

Chapter Sixty

Brianna

My eyes were closed, but I could feel cool fingers gliding across my cheekbone. I remembered the exact moment when Aidan's fist came in contact with my face causing blood to splatter on the window. I was, however, surprised I didn't feel any pain as someone caressed my cheek again.

Oh shit! Really, Bri? Really? Open your damn eyes. Someone is touching you for crying out loud.

With a gasp I opened my eyes and the beaming white light all around me was blinding except for the shadow that was being cast over me. I looked up to see a small statured man stood in a crisp white suit. His skin was dark, almost sun burnt, while his dark hair was cut to the skin several inches above his ears then faded up to a very square shape.

I placed my hand over my eyes to protect them, and with a snap of his fingers, the white light faded and transformed into grayish clouds. He extended his hand and lifted me to a seated position on the glass bench I was lying on. My hands instantly went to my stomach, now suddenly noticing that my large belly was gone.

"I'm dreaming, aren't I?"

He nodded with a curious smile, but said nothing.

"That must mean you're the other Dreamwalker."

Again without saying a word, he bowed deeply keeping his creepy smile stretched across his face.

"Who are you? What's your name?" He waved his index finger at me, clicking his tongue with disapproval. "I heard Aidan and Elaina one night. Isn't it something like Golek? Gordon? Gollum? No, wait. That's Lord of the Rings."

The silence was killing me, as was his annoying smile.

"For goodness sake, what do you want?! Just tell me so we can move on and I can figure out how to kick your ass."

The mystery man unbuttoned his jacket before sitting next to me on the bench, which I have to say was becoming uncomfortable, even if it was a dream.

"You have the fight of your father in you," he finally said. His voice was as creepy as his smile. The tone was thin, raspy, and didn't seem to match his body. It was a voice that you would expect to come from a person who lived their entire life in a cave. Ohmygod, like Gollum from The Lord of the Rings.

"You know my father?" I asked and he gave a slow nod with a raised brow. "Then you know that if he finds you, you're a dead man."

His laugh echoed among the darkening clouds, seeming to mimic his changing mood. "Eris cannot touch me. That was more than evident a few months ago. My blood alone kept him from penetrating your mind, and that was under Aidan's control. With me inside your head, you are all but lost to those around you."

"What is it you want from me? Why align yourself with morally corrupt evildoers?"

So apparently even in my dreams I could sound like a complete idiot.

"Money," he replied flatly.

I paused and even took a double take as I scrunched my face. "Money? That's all?"

"Money tends to fuel most of us morally corrupt evildoers."

"That can't be all. You didn't give your blood away for almost two months just for money."

He shrugged. "You and I have a commonality."

"And what is that?"

He clicked his tongue again. "Not yet. I think it makes our story more exciting. Don't you think?"

"So now what? You keep me in this dream state until they kill me?"

"That all depends on you, Brianna."

The way he said my name made my skin crawl. "So you do want something."

"Nothing in life is free."

His black eyes burned into me as a corner of his lips lifted into a devious smile, the clouds around him darkening to the point I thought we would be drenched in rain at any moment.

"Just tell me then. There's no need for all the dramatics."

"I want Eris."

"You want Eris? What the hell does that mean?"

"What do you think it means?"

"It could mean a lot of things. It could mean you want him to give you swordplay lessons. Or, maybe you've been secretly in love with him all these years and you want me to set up a meeting. But I hate to tell you that he doesn't swing that way..."

"Silence!" he yelled as he pushed me flat against the bench. *"I am owed a debt, and he is the only one left to pay it. So you will tell me where he is."*

"Or what?"

"Or," he began in a voice raspier and scarier than before, *"this is how you will spend the rest of your short life. However, if you tell me where Eris is, I will release you."*

No he wouldn't. I'd met enough morally corrupt evildoers to know they never kept their end of the bargain. What scared me even more was the fact that I knew in reality I was somewhere lying unconscious, and possibly in the midst of labor. I had no idea who was with me, or what was being done to me. I needed to wake up, but if Eris couldn't penetrate this guy, how would I?

"So?" he hissed. *"Are you going to give me your father?"*

"You don't know me very well."

"I know you better than you think," he replied.

"Well if you did, then you'd know that I would fight to the death to protect those I love, and strangely enough that now includes my father. If you want him, find him yourself. And I hope you do and that I'm there to see it because I want to be there when he rips your friggin' head off."

Before he could respond I placed my hands on either side of his face and funneled all my strength and power into my fingers and Pushed him. He screamed and hissed as my fingers burned into his face. The gray clouds around us began to crack and shatter like glass. Honestly, I was surprised that this was even working, but as I continued to shoot my power into him, his face began to crack like the clouds and light shot from within him while he screamed and labored for breath.

"You...cannot...hide from...me," he stuttered. "I will...haunt you...forever...and your children..."

My fingers glowed with extreme power and with one final Push the entire scene around me exploded into a brilliant light...

I opened my eyes and I was instantly hit with a pulsing pain from my cheek and eye, but then a second later my entire lower body was cramping. Another contraction. I hadn't even been conscious to begin to time them. I reached down near my thighs and felt no wetness between my legs. My water hadn't broken yet. Was that good or bad?

I tried taking in slow controlled breaths. Breathe through the contraction, they said. Just breathe through it and it'll pass. Were they freaking kidding me! How do you just breathe through this....ow, ow, wow, wow, shit, shit, shit, holy holy shit shit, Cam, Cam, Cam, Cam, where are you!

Better question, where was I? Placing my hand over my mouth, I panted through the pain for another minute or two, hoping that my fingers would muffle the sound of my moans. When the contraction finally started to pass I began reflexively rubbing my belly, silently telling my babies that everything would be ok, even though I wasn't sure if I believed it myself.

As my hand glided over my stomach, I realized that I wasn't feeling the silky chiffon of my bridesmaid dress, but a soft cotton material which sent a chill through my entire body. Slowly I pressed myself up to a seated position, trying to get my bearings in the pitch black room. There was only a sliver of moonlight coming through a crack in the draperies that had been pulled over the only window.

My hands searched the air for any piece of furniture around me, hoping for a table or a lamp, but I found nothing. Cautiously I placed my feet down onto the floor and pushed myself to stand. With one arm holding up my stomach and the other searching in front of me, I made my way over to the window to open the drapes. There was no way I would be able to find a light switch without a little help, and the window was currently providing the only source of light.

Just as I reached out to grasp the drapery, my foot caught on something hard causing me to lurch forward into the window. I whipped the draperies open to see what I had tripped over and had to cover my mouth to stop the scream from coming. A man in an electric blue suit lay before me, blood staining the white shirt and scarf surrounding the silver knife sticking out of his chest. Scratches covered the dead man's face, but I could still see Dante through the dried blood. Tears dripped over my fingers as I thought of him. Sweet, calm, loving Dante. I couldn't believe he was lying dead in front of me. Why did they kill him? Why was he here? Wherever that was.

With the curtains open I could see a lamp to my right so I quickly turned it on. I looked around the room and noticed the walls covered in framed awards and certificates as well as pictures of Dante shaking hands with almost every famous world leader since photographs had been invented. Suddenly I knew where I was – Dante's home, his headquarters. But I didn't have the time to grieve for Dante, it would have to wait. I needed to get out of here, and even though I roughly knew the layout of his house, I had no idea how I was going to get out besides the front door. Looking around the room I saw no phone. Knowing I was probably going to hell for what I was about to do, I apologized to Dante before kneeling awkwardly next to him and rummaging through his pockets for a cell phone. Nothing.

Frustrated and fearful tears began streaking down my cheeks. I didn't have a plan for this. I didn't know what to do or how to tell anyone where I was. As a last ditch effort I closed my eyes and scanned my surroundings, looking for any Vampire in the area that I could speak to. But again, nothing.

I placed my hand on the left side of my stomach. "Baby girl, can you help mama again? Please little one, I need your help."

There was no response, no kick, no movement of any kind and I certainly couldn't see any red lights floating around me. My baby girl was probably rolling her eyes and saying, *Geez, Mom, I'm kind of busy trying to be born at the moment. I can't really be bothered right now.* She was still in utero and already giving me attitude.

If I could only see where my captors were, then maybe I could get out of here, but without my daughter's gift it was no use. If only Dante were alive I could give him my blood and he would be able to see them, like Cameron had. The ability seemed to be in my blood, but only available to those who drank it. Not by the person it was currently flowing in and who could really use it right about now.

Then the thought hit me. The ability was available to those who drank my blood. Drank, my, blood. I needed to drink my own blood.

Gross.

With no other ideas and worrying that my captors would come barging through the doors at any moment, I took the letter opener on the desk and punctured the side of my palm. Letting a few drops of blood bubble up and drip down my hand, I took in a deep breath and released it as I placed my lips to the cut.

The coppery taste filled my mouth, and it made me think about how different the taste was compared to my father's. Then the fact that I was now comparing blood, I dropped my bloody hand and tried not to vomit. Strangely enough, even though the amount of blood was small I could feel it trickling down my throat. I waited several moments, keeping my eyes closed and concentrating on the area around me. Just when I thought my blood had failed me I saw flickers of red at the edges of my mind.

I concentrated on those lights and watched as they brightened and took shape around me at different levels. There was only one light on the other side of the door. Others were congregated on a slope, possibly the grand staircase that led to the first floor. Another large grouping had gathered right below me, maybe in the waiting area in the front of the house. The backside of the house, however, seemed to be almost completely bare. If I could get my guard away, perhaps I could sneak to that side of house and get to a phone. That was the goal and really the only option.

Ok. Plan set. And oh my fucking god you've, "Got to be kidding me," I shouted as my body was racked with pain. The contraction had come on quick and strong, taking me completely off guard and I was unable to keep myself quiet. The door opened and closed behind me, and through the pain I could see my guard's red essence coming toward me. Roughly he grabbed my arm and pulled me upright. He stared at me for a brief second then reached for the radio that was hanging from his belt.

"Oh no you don't," I hissed as I took hold of his essence and whipped him down to the ground causing him to land in the center of Dante's bloody chest. I slumped over him while he thrashed against Dante's dead body. My Push seemed to intensify as the contraction did, but finally my muscles began to relax and I could feel exhaustion begin to set in.

Losing a second of concentration, the Vampire reached behind him and grabbed a handful of my hair. I squeezed his light like a vice, making him release his hold on my hair and allowing me to reach up to the top of Dante's chest and pull the knife out of his heart. The Vampire rolled over, opening himself up to me as my hold on him lessened. I plunged the long knife toward his chest but his hand caught my wrist and held the knife away. Within seconds my arms were already burning, there was no way I would be able to keep this up. Holding the knife near his heart I pulled his essence toward me. The silver sunk into his skin like it was made of butter and within three seconds the knife came through the other side.

"That's for Dante, you son of a bitch," I growled as I pushed his slumping body away from me.

When the contraction finally passed, I crawled to the couch and used its different levels in order to get standing again. I allowed my body to take a five second break before pushing my feet toward the door and peer into the hallway where there were two doors. Thankfully it was empty so I crossed to the end of the hallway. The first was a linen closet. The second, a narrow twisting staircase down to the first floor. It looked like one you'd see in a horror film, but honestly I didn't have any other choice. Besides being afraid that arms would suddenly break through the stairs and bring me down to hell, I was a little worried that I wouldn't fit around the sharp narrow L-shaped curve halfway down. But again, I had no other choice. It was either go down the creepy stairs, which all horror movies warned against, or go back to Dante's office and wait for whatever torture Elaina had planned for me. Looks like I was going down the creepy stairs.

As I approached the halfway mark, no zombies burst through the boards and my stomach just barely made it around the corner. When I reached the bottom, I slowly opened the door, carefully peering around before entering the room. The tall windows on either side were left exposed and silvery moonlight cascaded inside making it easily recognizable. It was Dante's conference room. I had been in here, even sat at the conference table, although all the furniture in the room had been removed or pushed up against the sides. Looking around, once again there was no phone, no electronics whatsoever. The entire room had been stripped. There was only one way to get out of this room and that was through the sliding double doors across the way, and with my eyes closed I could see a flood of red light on the other side. Looking out the window next to me there was at least a six foot drop to the ground. Could I make it without injuring myself or the babies?

There wasn't time to ponder the matter since at that moment the entire house erupted in shouts and sounds of footsteps running above me. Rising up to my toes, I unlatched the window and propped myself up onto the wide window ledge. I rose up to my knees and opened the window as high as it would go. Just as I swung my legs over the ledge, arms came around my stomach and threw me roughly to the floor knocking the breath out of me.

Two Vampires stared down at me and shouted words I couldn't understand from all the ringing in my ears. A second later, a hand came over the shoulder of one of the men and yanked him around. Aidan stood next to him and punched him right in the face.

"What did E, say? Gentle hands, morons. At least until the brats are out of her," Aidan shouted. "Now pick her up."

The two Vamps scurried to attention and placed their arms under my shoulders, lifting me to a standing position while I flailed and screamed and kicked, basically having an all-out fit. I tried Pushing the red lights away from me, but my strength and power were fading quickly.

Aidan took my chin between his fingers as he said, "Don't make me give you a matching black eye, Morgan. Now keep still."

"No! Never," I shouted and continued to flail about. "I will never stop..." But my words were cut short when my legs and feet suddenly became wet. I looked down at the floor and saw the puddle of fluid. It was the first time I had truly looked down at myself and noticed the white gossamer nightgown I had been changed into which was soaked with blood from my tussle with the Vamp upstairs and now amniotic fluid.

It was coming true. The dream to end all of my dreams was finally coming true. Hadn't I learned? No matter the amount of planning and precautions and reinforcements, my shitty dreams came true and this was evidence.

Hot tears streaked down my face as I looked up to see Aidan with a wicked smile on his face. He snapped his fingers and the lights in the room were flicked on while members of Elaina's coven filed inside and positioned themselves around the room.

"In some ways, Morgan, you make it so easy for us."

In the full light the room was suddenly picture perfect with my dream from the red and yellow draperies to the large fireplace. I wanted to bang my head against the wall for not recognizing it before. Without the conference table in the center, the room looked completely different and I didn't remember the drapes being those colors when I was here last. It still didn't make me feel any less stupid.

Another contraction began to set in causing my breath to quicken, and this time I didn't try to cover up the sounds of my pain. The two Vampires on either side of me continued to hold me up even when my toes curled and my knees went out. The room became crowded as Elaina's followers formed a semi-circle around me. There had to be at least thirty of them and my agony seemed to excite them.

To my left several Vamps parted ways and Elaina entered with an air of tremendous power. She must have changed at some point since she was wearing what she had in my dream, her black leather vest and skin tight leather pants. Elaina smiled victoriously as she came to the center of the room, her followers on edge for her to break the intensity in the room.

"My friends," Elaina began in a soft tone, "we have had a long journey together. And those of you standing in this room have never given up the faith that one day *we* would hold the upper hand above the leaders who would oppress us. That *we* would see the new dawn of our people, and that *we* would be the ones to take our race out into the open and into a new age. For tonight our future begins, my friends. Because with patience comes victory!" Elaina shouted as she flung her arms in my direction.

The chandelier shook slightly above me from the Vampires shouting and banging on the floor and walls, all hailing their leader's capture of me. Lowering her arms, Elaina slowly made her way over to me, the roar of her followers still drowning out my groans. Her fingers trailed over my swollen cheek and then brushed away the sticky wet hair from my forehead. "It is time, little mother."

"NO!" I screamed as Elaina directed the two Vampires to lower me to the ground.

"It is time to bring these babies into the world," Elaina shouted triumphantly to the cheers of her followers. She snapped her fingers and Jazlyn stepped out from the crowd, a gold jewel-crusted dagger in her hand.

"No, no, no," I pleaded on my knees. "Please, Elaina, the babies are already coming. Just let them come," I sobbed. "Just let them come on their own, please. Please, for the love of god DON'T DO THIS, PLEASE!"

Elaina ignored my screams and took the knife from Jazlyn who then came around me and took me by the shoulders. I kicked and screamed as she forcibly lowered me down to the floor. Elaina raised the white gossamer gown over my stomach, her eyes widening as she tickled my skin with her nails. I flinched and kicked at her, grabbing handfuls of the gown and trying to pull it down.

"Hold her down," Elaina commanded and Jazlyn obeyed by holding my wrists above my head. My sobbing screams were completely uncontrollable. I knew what was going to happen, my babies would be cut out of me and I would be left to bleed out and die.

I flinched at the touch of the cold blade pressing against my skin. "This will hurt, my little hybrid," she cooed.

I continued to scream and writhe, kicking my legs out around me when another set of hands grabbed my ankles and clamped them tightly together. Over my belly Aidan's eyes were boring into mine.

"Let's get this over with," Jazlyn shouted as she pressed down on my arms, making the bones in my wrists creak under her pressure.

"What's the problem, Jazlyn," Aidan snickered. "Can't bear to see what your deception has produced?"

"Screw you," Jazlyn fired back. "At least I didn't sleep my way to my position."

"Quiet!" Elaina shouted, throwing down the knife and slapping both of them across the face.

Aidan looked like a wounded bird while Jazlyn narrowed her eyes and gave a steely look.

"Just kill her, Elaina," she said. "We have no time for ceremony. You know the Warriors will be looking for her. They could be here any moment."

"You would know, you traitorous bitch!" I spat in her face. "You never deserved them. They knew you for what you were, that's why they always hated you."

Jazlyn's lips tightened and almost disappeared into her mouth as she leaned over me causing her thick hair to cover me in a black silky curtain. "Just...shut up."

"You're no better if you let her do this. You're just like her," I whimpered, but my words triggered a sudden recognition.

Jazlyn's eyes narrowed slightly before she nuzzled into my ear and whispered, "Not everything is as it seems."

When she lifted her head slightly, she winked. My eyes widened with a sudden hope. Jazlyn's grip softened as she flipped up her veil of hair just in time for me to see Elaina raise the knife above her head. I screamed as I watched Elaina thrust the knife down toward my stomach but she froze when the room's double doors burst open. Everyone turned toward the doors in shock as Cameron stood fuming in the doorway. His white dress shirt and pants were in severe contrast to the solid black Warrior battle gear of the dozen others behind him.

"CAMERON!" I screamed so loudly I thought my throat would bleed. His head whipped around and in the same moment Jazlyn pushed off my wrists and leapt over my head, tackling Elaina into the wall across the room.

Just then Eris leapt over the crowd of Warriors with his broadsword held above his head as he soared in the air. Before he hit the ground, and with only two swipes of his sword, he sliced off the heads of three Vampires that stood in his way. When the heads hit the floor the entire room exploded into battle, and Aidan released my ankles to join in. Digging my heels into the hardwood floor I scuttled backwards until my back hit the wall.

A second later Cameron's terrified face was hovering over me while his arms wrapped around my legs and back. I reached up to put my arms around his neck when Aidan suddenly wrapped his arms around Cameron's chest and pulled him upright. Cameron grabbed at Aidan's forearms, but Aidan plunged his fangs into Cameron's throat, tearing and ripping violently at his skin.

"Cam!" I screamed, reaching out towards him, but he waved my hand away.

"Do it, Bri!" he shouted as he tried prying Aidan's fangs from his neck.

"Remember I love you."

"Always...do," he stuttered, grabbing hold of Aidan's head and then shouting in agony as I grasped his essence and Pushed him across the room taking out two other enemy Vampires with them. But after they fell to the floor I couldn't see them among the Vampires from both sides clashing in the middle of the room.

Devin was whipping around gracefully while Alex blew through the room like a bowling ball. My father was moving through the room so fast that light was barely able to reflect off his sword. To my right I saw a flash of blonde hair as Jazlyn threw Elaina into the side of the tall stone fireplace. Elaina hissed and clawed at Jazlyn's face, drawing small drops of blood before the wounds healed on their own.

While I watched the greatest cat fight of all time, from the side of my eye I saw a blur coming toward me. Quickly I diverted my eyes forward just in time to see Nikki coming at me with the jeweled dagger gripped firmly in her hand. My hands jutted out in front of me as she hovered over me and pressed the dagger down near my heart. I ground my teeth together as I held her arms away from me, struggling with the strength she possessed.

"D-don't...do...this Nikki," I grunted.

Nikki's face contorted as she pressed harder into the dagger, the tip of which pricked against my skin. "This will make...him love me."

"He's...not your...father...Nikki. He used...you."

"Not true," she replied, a small tear forming at the corner of her eye. "He searched…for me. Saved…me."

"Look at what…he made you do. Did you want…to do…those things…to Cameron?"

"No," she answered and stopped pressing on the dagger. "But…I had to or else…"

"Or else he wouldn't love you? Is that how a real father acts? Ransoms his love unless you make a whore out of yourself?"

For the second time that evening I had Nikki in my grasp, but a piercing shriek came from behind her. Nikki looked over her shoulder and opened herself up enough for me to see Jazlyn plunge a knife into Elaina's heart. Elaina's eyes widened in shock as blood trickled from her mouth while she gasped for air. Jazlyn ripped the knife from Elaina's chest and sliced it across her throat, severing her head cleanly. Elaina's decapitated body slumped to the floor, blood dripping from her head that Jazlyn still held by the hair.

In less than a second's time, enough time for Jazlyn to exhale a relieved sigh, Aidan stood behind her, grabbed her hand that held the knife and dragged it across her own throat. Jazlyn's head was held on by only a thin flap of skin, and her body convulsed as she slid down the wall. She wasn't dead. Aidan had made sure that she died a slower, more agonizing death.

Aidan stood looking back and forth between his dead lover and her dying killer. His chest was heaving, his fists opening and closing with anger. Suddenly his eyes caught sight of me and he began stomping over in my direction.

Nikki stood from the floor, the jeweled dagger still in her hand. "Aid…Dad, it's true, right? You are my father. I wouldn't have done all this if…I'm your little girl, aren't I? Just like you said."

Nikki sounded as pitiful as she looked begging for Aidan to love her like the father she so desperately wanted him to be. Her hopeful face fell as Aidan's mouth turned into a vicious snarl.

"No daughter of mine would ever be as pathetic as you," he said in a nasty tone. Then in a quick motion he took the dagger from Nikki and backhanded her so hard she slid across the floor and into the wall several feet away, crumbling into an unconscious heap.

From somewhere deep within me, I released a cry so loud the walls seemed to vibrate. My entire lower body felt as though it was being squeezed in a garbage compactor, making me curl up into myself. Aidan seized the opportunity and forcibly turned me onto my back.

"Morgan, I told you if you made trouble I would rip these brats out in front of you. And I always get what I want," he said as he held the dagger above his head.

"Jared!" Cameron shouted from somewhere in the room, and suddenly two shots rang out in the room, hitting Aidan in his back with only one bullet coming out through the top of his chest.

Aidan slumped over slightly, obviously stunned by the silver bullets in his body, but he was still alive. The contraction was still going strong, but suddenly I could see a faint glow of red light circling Aidan's head. Just as Aidan reared back with the dagger again I took hold of the faint red halo and flung my hands out in front of me. Though I was Pushing him away, he was digging his feet into the floor and leaning against the invisible link between us. The dagger was inching closer to my stomach as I breathed into my power and struggled to hold him away from me.

Suddenly a sharp pain came from deep inside me, making me lose my concentration for a split second and lessen my grip on Aidan. Unfortunately the slip up was enough time for the dagger's tip to pierce my skin. My entire body seemed to be screaming in pain, the sound of which was coming out of my throat. Knowing I had only enough strength to hold him for a few more seconds, I stiffened my hands and clamped down on his red essence with my mind. Aidan's groans turned into agonizing screams as I lifted his light above me, my hands and arms shaking from the strain of his weight. With a scream of my own I flung my arms over my head and pulled his light along causing the dagger to drag up my stomach as he sailed above me and through the window.

Glass shattered all around me, making me curl into a ball on my side. My hand flew to my stomach and I gasped at the searing pain. I didn't need to see my hand to know there was blood. Between the pain of the contraction and the large gash stretching up my stomach, I stayed curled up on my side. If anyone else came for me I was done for. I was tired, hurting, bleeding, and in labor. What else could happen to me? I just wanted to lie here and cry.

Suddenly hands grasped me around my shoulders and carefully turned me over onto my back. Cameron's face was panic stricken as he looked down my body. Quickly he ripped the dress shirt from his body, lifted the gown over my stomach, and pressed the shirt into my wound. I gasped from the pressure and then moaned as the contraction seemed to peak. My hand didn't even have to search for his as his fingers were suddenly tangled in mine and allowing me to squeeze them to the point a human man's would have broken.

Cameron rested his cheek against mine. "Breathe, love. I am here, just breathe."

"The babies…they're coming," I whimpered.

"I know, angel. Just concentrate on my voice, and breathe."

I did as he said but, "Well don't stop talking!"

His strained laugh pelted my ear. "If I were not so scared right now I would be furious with you."

"That's better," I groaned. "Yelling at me makes me feel so much better."

"Promise me you will never do anything like this again. You promise me right now."

"Can't…promise…having babies…right now."

"And you would be having them in a hospital if you had not devised this horrible scheme and kept things from me."

"Fine…I promise…I'll never go off with…evil Vampires when…I'm eight months pregnant…happy?"

My grip on his hand lessened as the contraction finally passed. Cameron lifted his head to look me in the eye, a hundred emotions passing over his face before pressing his lips against mine, fear and anger radiating from them as he kissed me a dozen times in a matter of seconds.

"Figlia," my father said suddenly next to me, making me flop my head around to the other side. "I should have come with you, oh mia figlia…" Eris continued his thought in Italian as he kissed his way up my swollen cheekbone, and within seconds the throbbing pain was subsiding.

"Dad," I replied, sounding drunk with exhaustion, "when you flew up…with your sword…you looked so badass."

Eris looked over at Cameron. "What is badass?"

Cameron smiled slightly. "It is a compliment, sir. Now have Vladimir bring the truck around."

Eris nodded while I was lifted from the floor. Cameron took a step toward the door when I pressed my hand against his chest. "Jazlyn."

He looked at me with sad eyes. "Devin is with her, there is no coming back from her injury."

Slowly Cameron turned toward the large fireplace where Devin was kneeling beside Jazlyn.

"Devin," I said, making him look over, "she leaves as a Warrior."

Cameron turned back around but I continued to watch over his shoulder as Devin formed Jazlyn's hand into a fist and placed it over her heart. However, I looked away when he held her face between his hands. I didn't need to see what happened next.

"Alex, with me," Cameron said as he stepped around the bodies that scattered the floor.

"We won?" I asked breathlessly.

"Yes, love. Only one got away today," he replied. "We will get him too. I swear to you we will."

"Promise me that when you do, you will rip him apart piece by piece until he begs you to kill him and then let him bleed out one drop of blood at a time until he feels every ounce of pain he has put us through."

The left side of Cameron's mouth lifted into his beautiful crooked smile. "Now you really do sound like a daughter of Eris."

Chapter Sixty-One

Cameron

"Just hold on to me, love," I said to Brianna as she tucked her head into the crook of my shoulder. Dante's conference room was covered in dead members of Elaina's coven making getting Brianna through the room without jarring her slightly difficult. A few of our group had sustained injuries, including myself, but our wounds were healed or in the process of.

Finally stepping out into the decorative waiting room, Fabiani was bursting through the front door, a few unknown members of his coven right behind him.

"Where's Master?" he asked with panicked eyes.

I shook my head, but Brianna answered in a breathy exhausted tone as she pointed up the stairs. "He's upstairs, in an office or something."

Quickly the small group of Negotiators flew up the stairs in a blur while I headed for the door.

"He's dead, Cam. They killed him," she whispered and broke into tears.

I squeezed her arm and leg lightly where I held her. "Shh, love. We will grieve for him, but later. We need to worry about you right now."

As we made our way down the front stairs, Vladimir was pulling up in the SUV while Eris directed us toward him. The SUV slammed to a stop, and immediately Eris was pulling the backseat door open, but then eyeing Alexander.

"Warrior," Eris said placing a hand up in front of me, "with this amount of blood do you trust your brother?"

"As much as you trust Vladimir, if not more."

"Very well," Eris nodded as he ducked inside the truck. "Vlad, to the hospital and don't spare the horses."

"Horses? What are you talking about," Brianna moaned.

"Well, my angel," I began, hoping I could distract her while I shifted her in my arms, "for most of us we had to use horses to get around. If you overexerted the horses over long distances they could die from exhaustion. So by saying not to spare them…"

"Ok, I get it, I get it," Brianna shouted painfully as Eris took her under her shoulders and pulled her inside while I stabilized her legs and bleeding stomach. The movement was painful and she did not hide it from us.

Once she was finally seated next to Eris, I jumped in next to her and the truck lurched forward. Now that we were all in a closed confined space, the smell of Brianna's blood was overwhelming, prompting Vladimir to roll down all the windows without being asked. Looking down at Bri's stomach I was nervous about the amount of blood that had already soaked through my dress shirt.

"Angel, I need to look at your wound."

Carefully Brianna lifted her hands from her stomach and I removed the bloody shirt. The long laceration looked roughly half an inch deep and was still seeping blood. I extended my fangs and bit into my wrist, squeezing the puncture wounds to draw the blood. Brianna clamped down on my forearm as it hovered over her stomach.

"No!"

"Bri, the wound is too deep for me to…"

She shook her head vehemently, looking almost terrified. "No! Too close to the babies. I can't have any Vampire blood near them…we don't…know…oh holy hell here comes another one."

Bri's jaw clinched as she exhaled loudly through her clenched teeth. I took her hand and noticed a heavier flow of blood was coming from her wound.

"Eris, your shirt," I demanded. "Bri, angel, try not to bear down, it is making you lose even more blood."

"Do YOU want to go through this instead?" she shouted angrily as Eris placed his ripped dress shirt over her bleeding stomach.

Knowing it was the contraction talking and not my Bri, I disregarded her tone and kissed her temple. "Squeeze my hand instead, love."

Bri clamped down on my fingers as the SUV came to a stop. Brake lights were everywhere with traffic inching slowly through the busy city intersections. Just as I was about to say something to Vladimir my right leg started to vibrate. Reaching into my pants pocket I pulled out my cell phone which was flashing John's name on the screen.

"John!"

"Hey, where are you guys?"

"John, I apologize. Brianna has gone into labor…"

"Yeah man, I know. We're at the hospital already."

"What?" I asked and looked over at Eris who was shaking his head. "How did you…"

"Sera told us that Bri went into labor so we all rushed to the hospital. Cathy has everything ready, how did we beat you here?"

"John, it is a little more complicated than Bri just being in labor. I do not have time to explain how it happened to her, but she has a deep vertical laceration over the top of her stomach and the bleeding has not stopped."

There was a pause. "How far apart are her contractions?"

"Four minutes and twenty-seven seconds, give or take."

"Give or take, what? A millisecond?" When I did not respond he cleared his throat and continued. "Ok, we'll prep an operating room. Just come to the ER bay, we'll have someone waiting for you. Get here as soon as you can."

That was easier said than done since the truck stopped once again causing Vladimir to hit the steering wheel in frustration.

"Vladimir!" I shouted. "Screw the traffic lights, we do not have this kind of time!"

"What do you want me to do? Get out and push? If you haven't noticed there are wall to wall cars."

"Then go on the sidewalk for all I care!" I shouted back.

"Shut up, shut up, shut up you goddamn stupid boys," Brianna screamed at the two of us as the climax of her contraction overtook her. "Never mind, go on the sidewalk. I can't have these babies in the floor in front of all of you. I'll never be able to look at any of you in the eye ever again."

Everyone in the SUV laughed tensely. Reaching into my pocket I pulled out Brianna's handkerchief and wiped her sweaty brow. The light finally turned green, and suddenly Alexander unbuckled his seatbelt.

"Stay close," he ordered at Vladimir.

"Warrior, what are you doing?" Eris shouted.

Alexander turned to the backseat with a quirked smile. "Going out to push."

The cars ahead of us slowly began rolling forward and Alexander took position behind them. As we crossed the intersection, Alexander grabbed the bumper of the car in front of him and shifted it to the right side and out of our way. Vladimir sped up and stayed unbelievably close behind Alexander, just as he had ordered. Car after car was moved away, almost hitting other cars that were parked alongside the sidewalk.

Alexander waved us through the next intersection into the thinning oncoming traffic. As we sped across the center, a white pickup truck came barreling right at us from the other direction.

"Ohmygod!" Bri screamed next to me.

The pickup truck's headlights flooded the inside of our SUV as the driver blared his horn. Vladimir pressed on the gas and swerved at the same time the pickup truck was suddenly lifted into the air. Alexander stood underneath the truck, holding it up on his shoulders like Atlas held the world while he leapt over our SUV and landed on the other side.

Once across, the traffic thinned and there were no cars in front of us. Vladimir sped up once again, and seconds later the front passenger seat was filled with a large cloud of black smoke.

"That was fun," Alexander laughed once he was fully formed.

Brianna tried to laugh along with the rest of us, but groaned instead through her exaggerated breathing.

"Alex," I began, "you will be responsible for the bill from the Cleaners on that one. Father will be furious."

"Totally worth it, Cam. Good driving, Vlad."

I could see Vladimir roll his eyes in the rearview mirror. "I am trying to figure out why you Warriors are so surprised that there are other Vampires with skills."

Alexander was taken aback. "I didn't mean it like that."

"And obviously Warriors do not have senses of humor."

"Can we stop the nonsense and get to the hospital, please!" Brianna shouted.

Eris patted her other hand. "Daughter, we are almost there. Almost there."

Once again I wiped the sweat away from her forehead and kissed her temple. I gave a cautious look to Eris when I noticed that blood had soaked through the shirt that he was holding against her stomach. Even through the dark cabin of the SUV I could see that she was losing color in her face as she rested her head on my shoulder.

"I saw him," she said weakly.

"Saw who, love?" I replied as my finger grazed her cheek.

"The other Dreamwalker."

I looked across her to Eris whose eyes were as wide as mine probably were. "Did you recognize him?"

She shook her head.

"Show me, daughter. I need to see his face."

She lifted her head up slowly, shaking it again. "But he could get to me again."

"He will not get through me, I promise. Picture him in your head now, and I will put you to sleep for only a moment and bring you right back. He won't even know you're under. Are you ready?"

She nodded and closed her eyes, squeezing my hand tightly before Eris closed his eyes as well. Brianna's hand went limp for less than two seconds before she opened her eyes again. Eris flinched as he opened his eyes, worry and surprise creasing the corners of his eyes.

"Do you know him?" I asked.

"He seems familiar," he answered stiffly and turned to look out the front of the car. Apparently it was a conversation for another time.

Brianna returned her head to my shoulder and I could not help but keep kissing her temple and hair.

"You are doing great, angel."

"It hurts, Cam," she whined weakly.

"I know, my love, but we are almost there. The hospital is just ahead," I said pointing to the hospital lights in the distance.

"Alex?"

"Yes, Bri?" Alexander replied, turning around to face her.

"Did Cam yell at you tonight when he found out what I'd done?"

Alexander smiled slightly. "Yes he did. He also threatened to kill me, just like I said he would."

"Cam, you should apologize."

"You should apologize to me first, my love."

"Why?" she replied, lifting her head from my shoulder.

"Do you have any idea what you have put me through this evening?"

Her eyes became watery with tears. "Babe, I'm sorry."

Kissing the tip of her nose I said, "You are forgiven. But you can never do anything like this to me again."

"I already promised I wouldn't."

"Yes, you did and I will keep you to your word."

Brianna tilted her head and lowered her lips softly onto mine. "I love you so muu-cho caliente here comes another one," she yelled as another contraction took hold of her.

I brushed away the hair that had fallen into her eyes while trying to help her breathe through it. "Not as much as I love you, angel. And in the next few hours we will have our own little family. This is it, love, you changed it, you changed everything."

She nodded, though she kept her head down while she exhaled loudly through her pain. Tears dripped from her eyes and onto our clasped hands as the SUV turned into the grounds of the hospital.

"John said someone would meet us at the Emergency Room bay," I said to Vladimir.

A minute later we were turning at the Emergency Room sign and out in front were two male nurses standing next to a gurney while Renee, still in her wedding dress with a tux jacket draped around her shoulders, was jumping up and down and waving. Vladimir pulled up alongside the gurney and before the truck came to a complete stop I had already opened the door and was jumping down onto the pavement. The two male nurses came up behind me, one beginning to tell me that they would take Brianna from the car, however, before he could even finish his statement, my arms were under her legs and around her back.

"Hold on, love," I warned, making Brianna hold her stomach painfully while I slid her along the length of the seat. The male nurses directed me to the gurney and helped me lower her down, though none was needed.

"Bri! What the hell happened!" Renee shouted as the nurses turned the gurney toward the automatic doors. "Sera just told us you were in labor."

"Believe me, I am," she replied through her clenched teeth, but eventually let out a high-pitched moan when we entered the hospital.

"But...where's this blood coming from? And when did you change into this nightgown?"

"Renee, please. Explanations later," I said to her over Brianna's stomach. "Where is John?"

"John and Cathy are waiting for you upstairs...but, seriously what..."

"It was...my fault," Brianna answered as she exhaled in staggered breaths.

"Just breathe, Brianna. You can tell her everything later." As we approached the elevators I looked up to Renee, "Eris, Vladimir, and

Alexander will need to be shown where to go. Can you do that for me?"

She nodded as she tugged on her bottom lip with her teeth. "Yeah, I can do that. Everyone else is already up there." Renee put her arms through the tuxedo jacket that was hanging on her shoulders, and tightened it around her as she walked back from where we had come. Suddenly the sound of her high heels on the tiled floor stopped. Renee whipped herself around and looked me straight in the eye as the nurses steered the gurney into the elevator. "She's gonna be ok, right?"

I nodded, thinking to myself she had to be. The elevator doors closed, and just in time for Brianna to let out a wail that sent shivers through my body. Both nurses and I were coaching Brianna through her contraction while the elevator slowly went up to the second floor. Her moans continued as the elevator doors opened and the nurses pushed her down the hall to a large waiting area where Kyla, Seraphina, Oliver, and Maddy stood from their seats. Brianna waved weakly as we passed and all eyes were large with worry.

I followed the gurney into a narrow room with several large sinks and stacks of green medical scrubs folded on shelves against the wall. Brianna's fingers slipped out of my grip when one of the nurses pushed the gurney through a parallel door and the other placed a hand on my chest.

"Wait here," he commanded. He was completely unaware that I could snap his hand right off. "Someone will come out shortly."

Shortly? What was shortly? A minute? Two minutes? I had never been in a hospital. Was it bad etiquette to burst through the wall?

Before I could test it, John came in from the operating room with a mix of excitement and concern as he patted my back. "I won't ask how you are."

"Do I have to stay in here?"

John quirked an eyebrow as he grabbed a set of mint green scrubs from one of the shelves. "Of course not, what is this the dark ages? Wait, were you alive back then?"

"No," I replied in frustration as I took the scrubs from his extended hand. "So...I get to be with her?"

"Of course you do."

"Do you have another color I could wear?"

"Nope!" he answered happily as he stepped on a pedal in front of one of the sinks and began cleaning his hands and forearms with a small scrubber. "Don't forget the little hat and booties. Do you have a cell phone on you? Not only are you going to want to take pics of the babies when they come out, but I'm going to want to get a picture of you in this getup."

Reluctantly I pulled the green cotton shirt over my head. "Is this how you always are in a crisis?"

"Yep! It's why I'm a good ER doc. So here's what's happening," he began as he rinsed his soapy arms, "Bri's being prepped for an emergency C-section. The laceration she has is pretty long, but not dangerously deep. Cathy's going to get the babies out first by making an incision at the base of Bri's abdomen, then we'll stitch her up. She's going to have a wicked scar, but I'm sure you can afford some plastic surgery, unless you can help her with that."

I pulled the hideous green pants over my tailored suit pants and cringed. "So the babies are all right?"

John stepped off the sink's pedal and began wiping his arms dry. "Cathy is taking a look now but I'm sure they're fine. She's one of the best OB's in the Northeast, so if either baby is in distress she'll get them out quick."

"You will be helping as well?"

"Yep!"

"You seem very excited about that."

"It means I get to see my godchildren before Renee does, of course I'm excited." John stood with his hands held in front of him as he stood at the door of the operating room. "Wait, there's going to be blood in there, are you going to be ok?"

"Yes, I can control myself."

"Ok then. Don't forget the hat and booties," he gestured with his eyes.

I did as he said and followed him into the operating room where Brianna had been transferred to a large table, her distended and bare stomach exposed while intravenous tubes were connected to her arms.

"Where's Cam?" Brianna asked a passing nurse in a weak voice.

"Right here, love," I replied going to her side. One of the female nurses placed a small rolling stool at the head of the table and gestured for me to sit. Brianna lifted her hand and I squeezed it tightly as I kissed the tops of her fingers.

"Nice hat," she mocked and I ignored her.

"Are you in pain?"

She shook her head. "Anesthesia is a beautiful thing."

"Don't worry, Mr. Burke," Dr. Taylor said from the opposite end of the table, "we've given Brianna a spinal block. She won't feel anything during the procedure."

The room was organized chaos with both doctors and nurses rushing around making preparations for Brianna's surgery. Only five minutes passed and all the instruments had been laid out, everyone gloved and masked, and a blue medical drape hung in front of Brianna's chest. My lips seemed glued to her temple, but I took in a gasp at the sudden overpowering smell of iodine.

"If it's too hard for you to be in here…"

"I will rip my nose off before I leave your side," I whispered firmly.

"Ok kids," Dr. Taylor said from behind her mask, "are you ready to become parents?"

Tears instantly began trickling out of the corners of Brianna's eyes and I caught them with my index finger. "I think that is a yes," I answered while John gave a shout of joy. "Bri, you have made John a happy man."

"How's that?" she replied emotionally as she wiped another tear from her cheek.

John leaned around the drapery separator and said, "Because you're finally letting me be your doctor."

"Well just this once," Brianna replied with a light laugh.

"Ok Dr. Ryan, since you insisted on being in here you better get to work," Dr. Taylor announced as she took position near Brianna's lower body. "Besides, I won the bet so you're basically my bitch."

"Cathy, please. You need me here because I'm better and faster at suturing than you are."

"Well tonight we have our work cut out for us. So do you kids want to give us the lowdown on how you get a gash like this at a wedding?"

Brianna did not miss a beat. "I was trying to shave my legs for you, Dr. Taylor."

Dr. Taylor laughed. "You're sweet. Suction," she ordered, and shortly after you could hear Brianna's blood being sucked away through a tube.

It was times like these I regretted being a Vampire. No one should be able to hear the tearing of your lover's tissue as well as the smells coming from an open wound. But Dr. Taylor's next statements made it all worth it.

"Ok kids, this is where all returns become null and void. John, you ready?"

He affirmed as he held a medical blanket across his arms. Brianna squeezed my hand tightly just before the room was flooded with the sound of a baby crying.

"Hello baby boy!" Dr. Taylor announced as she lifted my son into the air and then into John's arms.

Brianna's cheerful sobs challenged my son's, and I even found myself biting the insides of my cheeks in order to prevent bloody tears from rolling down my face. John wrapped the baby loosely in the blanket and placed him on Brianna's chest. As soon as her fingers touched our son's face his cries ceased, his large dark eyes mesmerized by hers.

"Hello Jackson Thomas," she cooed as she kissed his forehead.

Digging underneath my scrub pants, I reached into my suit pants pocket and retrieved my cell phone. Brianna looked up at me as I framed the perfect picture of my love with our newborn son in her arms.

"He's so beautiful," she cried.

"Well he's going to have some competition," John said as he stretched another medical blanket between his hands.

One of the nurses removed Jackson Thomas from Brianna's chest, and I instantly stood from my stool causing Bri to put a hand on my arm. "They have to check him out, babe. They'll give him back."

Reluctantly I sat back down on my stool.

"Here comes baby girl," Dr. Taylor announced, and the anticipation started once again. I watched as she lifted our daughter from Brianna's womb and placed her in John's arms, but quickly she and John turned their backs.

"Is she out?" Brianna looked up at me with a crinkled brow.

"Yes, but…"

"Why isn't she crying?" she said in a panic. "Is she ok? Why isn't she crying, Cam!"

Finally my little baby girl coughed and then began wailing loudly. John turned back around, wrapped our baby girl as he had Jackson, and placed her in Brianna's expectant arms. "She's fine, Bri. She wanted to make a dramatic entrance that's all."

Brianna let out a snot-filled laugh. "She's thirty seconds old and already scaring me to death."

"John, I need you," Dr. Taylor said urgently.

"Ok Cathy, let the battle begin."

While the doctors began stitching Brianna up, I took one last picture before kissing our baby girl's wet little forehead. "Welcome to the world, Olivia Sera."

Olivia's cries turned from terrified to almost cooing. She had instantly become a daddy's girl. But as they had done with Jackson, they took Olivia away. Once the baby was off her chest, my lips were crushing Brianna's, though her lips responded weakly.

"Suction," Dr. Taylor ordered.

I lifted my head and gently caressed my Bri's brow, noticing the visible exhaustion on her face. "You are amazing."

She smiled faintly. "I am?"

"You created two of the most beautiful babies I have ever seen in my life," I said and then nuzzled against her ear, "and I have lived a long time."

"I had some help," she replied as she combed her fingers through my hair. "They came from good stock."

"Cathy," John said in a questioning and firm tone.

"Yeah, I see it."

"Do you want to switch?"

"No, just keep going. More suction please."

Their conversation suddenly caught my attention. The cheerfulness that was previously in their tones had been stripped away. The smell of blood was filling the room and being sucked away more frequently. I looked down at Brianna and noticed her face becoming very pale.

Brianna blinked slowly, and her grip on my hand lessened. "Cam?"

"Yes, love?" I replied, trying to keep my worry out of my voice.

"Thank you."

"For what, angel?"

"Bursting through my front door that day."

I brushed away a few strands of hair from her face. "You are...welcome?"

Brianna smiled weakly. "If you hadn't..." she shook her head slightly, her eyes struggling to stay open. "I love you so much."

"Suction, dammit, I can't see," Dr. Taylor demanded.

Something was terribly wrong, and I could see it burning in John's eyes as he stared down into Bri's abdomen. I squeezed Brianna's hand and began brushing my fingers over the soft hair at her scalp. "Bri," I said firmly, "I need you to fight like you have never fought before. I need you, love. Our babies need you too."

"I got to see them, Cam. In all the dreams I never got to see them, but this time I did."

I shook my head wildly. "This is not your dream, Brianna. You changed it. You made up that terrible plan and changed everything, you changed the ending."

She blinked slowly, letting her head fall slightly to the side. "We can never really change it. They still come true, no matter what we do. But I got to see the babies, I…just…wanted to…see them."

Brianna's breathing became shallow as her eyelids drooped heavily.

"Bri? Bri!" I said and slapped her cheek roughly when the sound of the heart monitor began beeping erratically. "John!"

John looked up to the heart monitor, but ignored me. "Get the crash cart."

"What!" I shouted, knocking the stool to the floor.

"Let us do our job, Cameron," he warned.

I shook my head and placed my wrist up to my mouth.

"Cameron! What are you doing?!"

"She needs it, John. I can help."

"No!" he shouted in reply and left Brianna's side to pull me away from her. "Give us a chance. We just need to find the source of the bleeding. Now step away, Cam."

"My blood can help heal her."

"And if it doesn't?"

"Then I'll Turn her."

"What!" he shouted, causing someone to drop a tray of instruments. "She doesn't want that!"

"How…how do you know that?"

"Because she told Renee. And if she told Re, then I know you two have talked about it."

"But it may be the only way."

"But it's not what she wants to be! Think of her right now."

"I am!"

"Then let me do my job!"

The heart monitor's sporadic beeps turned into a single long tone. John turned away from me as he shouted, "Paddles now! She's flat lining!"

A shout escaped my lips that was so loud and piercing that one nurse fell into another. John went right to work rubbing the heart paddles together while the nurses lowered the medical drapes around Brianna's chest and prepared her body to be shocked.

"Clear!" John shouted as he placed the shock paddles to Bri's skin, making her chest jerk up and flop back down on the table. The heart monitor sputtered up and down frantically while a nurse placed a mask over Brianna's mouth and began squeezing air into her lungs.

Dr. Taylor continued to frantically pull a thin piece of suture wire in and out of Brianna's abdomen trying to seal the wounds inside. There was a steady flow of blood being sucked out of Bri's body. One of the nurses hung several blood bags, however, it seemed that as quickly as it was going in, it was coming back out.

"Clear!" John shouted again when the heart monitor flat lined again. Everyone working on Brianna jerked away before John shocked her, but stayed away when he upped the voltage and shocked Brianna again, and then again.

My body felt numb. I was watching Brianna's life fade away. "John, leave me with her."

"No!" he growled as he threw the shock paddles to the ground and began pumping Brianna's chest with his hands. "She doesn't want it!"

"She is dying, John! I cannot help her if she dies!" I shouted and took a step toward him.

"Stay back, Cameron!"

John continued to pump at Brianna's chest. I did not need to hear the flat line tone of the heart monitor to tell me it was not beating. Eventually Dr. Taylor stopped suturing and placed her tools away, but John kept beating on Brianna's chest even when the nurse removed the breathing mask. The room became quiet except for John cursing under his breath, begging Brianna's heart to start again.

Dr. Taylor pulled at John's arm. "I'm calling it, John."

"NO," John growled with clenched teeth and shrugged her hand off his arm. A crack came from Brianna's chest, a broken rib. It was the only sound coming from her body now.

"Dr. Ryan!" Dr. Taylor shouted and forcibly moved him away from Brianna's side. John stared at her with wild eyes, his chest heaving uncontrollably. "It's over, John. We did everything we could. I'm calling it."

John shook his head. "Please don't."

"I'm sorry," she replied tenderly and then looked up at me. "I'm so sorry. Time of death, 3:37AM."

John screamed as he thrust the crash cart against the wall and stormed across the room, splaying his arms out against the wall and hanging his head. The nurses quickly and silently removed the remaining wires and medical instruments from Bri's body and covered her with a medical blanket, being sure to leave her face exposed.

Dr. Taylor stepped over to me and patted my hand gently. "You can stay with her for a little while. Eventually someone will take her downstairs. I am truly sorry, Mr. Burke."

Dr. Taylor's eyes were glassy, though her tone was professional. After patting my hand one last time she left swiftly with the nurses behind her. John was still holding himself up against the wall while I stood frozen in the same position I had been in for the last twenty minutes while I watched my beloved's life drain out of her.

Several minutes passed in silence before John finally pushed himself off the wall and turned to face me. He looked at me with his fierce blue eyes, his chest still heaving. "I thought...I've brought people back from worse...everything was fine and..."

"Get out," I said in a weak voice.

"I'm sorry, Cam..."

"I said get out!"

John lowered his head as he walked toward the door. "I'll let everyone know."

After the door shut behind him I could hear metal crashing against the floor and walls in the next room as John wailed in anger. I continued to gaze down at Brianna, her face looking more peaceful than it had in almost a year. Was this supposed to be my solace? My love was finally at peace? A peace that could only be found in death.

My knees finally gave out and I melted into the small stool next to me. I sat next to Brianna, brushing my fingers across her forehead and cheek. She was already colder and her skin felt odd with the lack of response. I lowered my head and nuzzled up against her neck where blood no longer flowed underneath her skin. My chest began taking in quick breaths making my ribs hit against the cold metal table. My breath became faster until a ferocious roar rose from my chest and burned my throat before bouncing loudly off the walls around me.

When I lifted my head, several bloody tears dripped down onto Brianna's face. I stared down at her, finding myself waiting for her to wipe them away.

"Wake up, Brianna," I urged her softly, and then anger began to build inside of me again. "Open your eyes, damn it! Never have you ever let a tear stay on your face, not in the time I have known you. Now wake up, Bri. Wake up!" I shouted at her, kicking the stool out from under me and slamming my fist down on the metal table.

"You survived fourteen years of hell with Sam and you leave me after less than a year? No! No! This is not how this ends. Brianna Marilena

Morgan I demand that you wake…"

My voice cracked as I slumped over her and rested my cheek against hers. I was screaming at her pointlessly, knowing I would never see her beautiful dark eyes or hear her voice again. She had thanked me for saving her from Sam, and for what?

"If you had never taken my hand that day…" Coppery tasting tears filled my mouth as they flowed from my eyes. "I cannot do this, Bri."

I lifted my head to see that Brianna's face was stained with my red tears. Reaching into my suit pants I pulled out my handkerchief and carefully wiped her face clean, a red tint still visible. "How can you leave me like this? How do I raise our children without you? I cannot do it…I cannot…I will not."

With a sharp click, my fangs extended and I brought my wrist up to my mouth and bit. I squeezed my wrist and placed the dripping blood into Brianna's mouth. The puncture wounds on my arm closed quickly, prompting me to bite at my wrist again, tearing at the skin and squeezing more thick blood into her mouth. Seeing no response I stepped over to her side and removed the sheet that had been laid across her body. With her stomach no longer distended with pregnancy or stretched open for surgery, the combination of the laceration from Aidan's knife and Dr. Taylor's incision made the shape of an upside down T on her lower abdomen. It was similar to the ones that her dreams had burned and carved into her.

Maybe it was a sign. My fangs tore two long channels down the length of my forearm and I allowed the blood to drain into Brianna's wounds. Before the channels could close, I bit deeper into my arm, tearing away chunks of skin and muscle, and letting the blood continue to flow into her. After several minutes my left forearm was nearly torn through to the bone when I decided to bite into my right. I would give Brianna every ounce of my blood if it would help her.

My fangs sank into the wrist of my right hand when someone cleared their throat in the room.

"Child?"

I looked up to see Victor standing with Eris just behind him.

"Father…" I replied weakly.

"What are you doing, child?" he asked gently as he slowly stepped around the metal table, choosing not to look down at Brianna's lifeless body.

My arm burned as it began to heal and stitch itself back together. "I was giving her my blood."

"Child, she is…"

"Help her," I said and grabbed his wrist. "Your blood is stronger than mine, help her, please Father, help her." When Victor did not move I looked over to Eris. "Please, you have to try."

Before the words were out of my mouth Eris was ripping at his arms and draining his blood into his daughter's open wounds. Victor grabbed my shoulders and pulled my attention back to him.

"Child, you need to accept that Brianna is dead."

"No," I replied adamantly. "Our blood heals, Father. Yours and Eris's even more than mine. We can heal her, Father, if you just…"

"Cameron!" Victor shouted and squeezed my shoulders even harder. "We cannot help those that are dead, you of all people know this."

A lump formed in my throat at my father's statement. The flashes of Chloe's and Christian's lifeless bodies were now meshed together with Brianna's. "Am I cursed?"

"Of course not, child. If anyone is to blame for this it is me for I allowed her to go off on that mission."

"It would have not mattered, Father. Brianna was never supposed to live, was she, Eris?"

Eris looked up at me, new red tears flowing down the tracks the previous ones had left behind. "No," he replied softly, his accent stripped away. "Sera never said one way or another, but after years of seeing glimpses of her visions I pieced things together. I think we were all hoping that if we changed things enough, a new future would be written."

Brianna's words echoed in my ears. "'We can never really change it. They still come true'. Those were her last…" words to me. Last words. Her lips would never utter a single word again. She would never call out to her children. She would never make our family laugh with her wit. And she would never say my name or tell me that she loved me ever again.

I did not feel my knees buckle until they cracked against the floor. Victor's arms caught my shoulders and held me upright to his eye level. "Child, you have two little ones who need their father. You need to pull yourself together."

"Why would she be brought into my life only to be taken away so soon?"

"I do not know, child. It is cruel and certainly not deserved. But you need to think of the children now."

"I cannot do it. I will be useless to them. I am useless without her."

Victor lifted me to a standing position. "You are my child, my Warrior, a favorite son. You were not useless before her, and you will not be useless now. Do not let Brianna's sacrifice be in vain, and do not let her death take you away from your children's lives. They deserve better than that. They deserve the man their mother loved."

Victor's words were sobering and painful. I looked over at Brianna's lifeless body one last time and touched her hand gently.

"Someone will need to find Dr. Taylor and the nurses. They heard me say some things that could create some questions."

Victor nodded. "I will see to it. The family is waiting outside. I know they will want to see you."

Reluctantly I stepped past him, my silent heart tight and pulling me back to Brianna's side. I stopped at the operating room door and ripped the green scrubs from my body revealing my black suit pants and white t-shirt which I now noticed was smudged with blood.

Looking over my shoulder I caught Victor's gaze and asked, "Will you still give her your blood?" Victor sighed. "Please? For me, for her. Please. In my entire service to you I have rarely asked you for anything. I am only asking for this one thing and I shall say no more and accept what I must."

Victor sighed again and then nodded curtly as he extended his fangs and bit into his wrist. I turned and left the room, having to step over the carnage of shelves John had pulled down on the floor before leaving the operating area. The air in the hallway was lighter, though my chest was still tight. I looked down the hall to see our...my...my family sitting and standing in various positions while they comforted one another.

Alexander was the first to see me and I could not bear to see the sorrow in his eyes. Kyla was sobbing into his chest but he still opened his arm to me.

"Cam..." Alexander said sadly as he placed his thick arm around my shoulder. "I should have...stopped her...or..."

"No one could have stopped her. We all know that. I am sorry for what I said earlier tonight..."

"No, I deserved it. If I...hadn't..." Alexander's chest began heaving as he struggled to keep rare emotions inside.

"Alex, with or without you everything would have played out the same."

Alexander still shook his head while Kyla's sobs intensified. Jared sat on a couch behind them, his face buried in his hands until I came to stand in front of him. He rubbed his eyes before looking up at me, tiny red lines staining the outside of his eyes.

"This is bullshit, bro," he said as he looked back down at the floor. "Beebs is…she's supposed to be here…she's my…Bibi was my…"

"And you were her brother," I finished as I patted his back.

"You're my brother too," he said softly. "Whatever you need…"

I nodded and allowed him to melt back into his seat, his head returning to his hands. The only person left in the group was Seraphina whose side was stretched over the arm of the couch while her face was buried in the crook of her elbow. I knelt in front of her, placing my hand lightly on her knee. She lifted her head, her eyes swollen and red though from natural clear tears. Her breath became staggered at the sight of me, emotions and tears overwhelming her. She patted my hand gently, but she was unable to form words.

"Eris is with her," I told her, and she nodded gratefully.

"A-t-elle vu les bébés?"

"Y-yes," I stuttered through the lump in my throat, "she saw both babies. She was so happy."

"I…thought…if she fought…against what I had foreseen…zhen zhings would be different…I told her zhey would be different…"

I placed Seraphina's shaking hands in between mine. "They were different. Brianna saw her babies, which she said in all her other visions she never did. So you did change things."

"Not enough," she wept.

"It was enough to let her…die…in peace."

Kyla released a wail behind me, and I could see Jared's shoulders shaking.

"I loved her as my own."

"And you were the mother she had always longed for."

Seraphina wiped her face, and as I stood from the floor I noticed Madelyn walking swiftly toward us from the other end of the hallway. She paused when she saw me. I was already tired of seeing the look of sympathy in everyone's eyes. I began walking toward her when she extended her arms and wrapped them around me. She released me a few moments later, crooking her arm around mine and guiding me down the corridor.

"Where is Oliver?"

"Down this way. John secured a private room for you and the family in order to see the children. Ollie and Renee are with them now. They are beautiful, Mr. Burke, both of them are just so beautiful."

My feet became heavy as I thought about seeing my children without Brianna. They would live a life without knowing how truly miraculous she was and that their lives, our lives together, would never be whole without her. Could their tiny heads fathom what they had lost?

"Mr. Burke," Madelyn said as she patted my hand and pulled me to a stop, "from experience I know there is nothing that I or anyone else can say to you that will take away the pain you are feeling right now. People are going to say they know what you're going through, but unless they've lost someone like you have, they have no idea. I've buried a husband, a daughter, and a grandson, and I know that right now you feel like there is no air and even if there was there would be no purpose in breathing it in. It may not seem like it, but eventually, unfortunately not any time soon, that feeling passes a little every day. Ollie and I both know what this feels like, and we're here for you in whatever capacity you need us. You just need to ask."

Unfortunately I was familiar with this dreadful feeling. It was almost as if my body was being enveloped by an old friend, but one that suffocated you in your sleep.

Madelyn pulled me to the end of the hallway until we reached a set of glass doors that led to a narrow balcony looking out onto the city. The hallway continued to the right and as I peered down the new corridor I noticed a man crouched down in a huddled mass on the floor. A second later the man began banging the back of his head against the wall. It was John, still in his scrubs that were streaked with blood.

"He'll never forgive himself," Madelyn said nudging me. "Not unless you forgive him first." I gave her a challenging look, which she returned twofold. "He knew Ms. Morgan's wishes and he held his ground even when things took a turn for the worse. John did what he knew was right, and he shouldn't be punished for it. He'll have to live with the guilt for the rest of his life. I think that's punishment enough, don't you?"

John's head fell back into his hands, his shoulders shaking as he wept. Madelyn prodded me forward, gesturing her hand in John's direction. My feet stumbled over each other at first as I shuffled down the hallway. John's head shot up as I approached and then pulled himself up against the wall. His eyes were red and swollen, his cheeks still glistening with tears. We stood silently in front of each other for several moments, neither of us sure of what to do or say. Finally John took a step back and then turned to walk away.

"John, wait..."

He paused but kept his back to me. "Cameron, nothing I say will ever…" He sighed as he turned back around, unable to finish his statement and found it difficult to make eye contact. "I should have just let you…"

"No, you were right," I admitted reluctantly. "Brianna had told me that she never wanted to be Turned. I never thought I would lose her…" I gritted my teeth and cleared my throat, "…lose her so soon."

"Cathy and I did everything we could. If Cathy hadn't pulled me off I would still be there pumping on Bri's heart but…I know it'll just be easier if I stay away. Lord knows I'm the last person you'll ever want to see again."

Wrapping my arm around him, I could hear his sniffling in my ear as I slapped his back several times. "You were the first to hold my children, John. You cannot stay away, you are family, their godfather. You have to be in their lives."

John slapped my back in return and pushed himself away as he wiped his face clean. "Maybe you could tell that to Renee. I think she's finding it hard to be married to me right now."

"Where is she?"

"In there," John replied and pointed to a room door directly behind me. "Ollie's in there too. I had the twins brought in after their checkup. The nurses know not to disturb you, at least for a couple of hours."

"Did they pass?" I asked, creating confusion on John's face. "My children, did they…pass…their exam?"

John's face relaxed. "With flying colors. They're perfect, Cameron. Absolutely perfect."

My chest released an enormous sigh of relief. "Thank goodness for that."

John patted me on the back one last time before I turned and stepped inside the hospital room. The room itself was painted a cheery yellow, the smell of disinfectant still in the air. Renee stood in front of the window in her sparkling lace wedding dress and did not turn around when the door closed behind me. She was swaying ever so slightly and I could see the edge of a thin blue blanket peeking over her left arm.

Oliver sat in a tall rocking chair next to the empty hospital bed. He held a tiny pink wrapped bundle in his arms while he wiped the corner of his eye. He gazed up to me for a brief moment, but then the tiny bundle in his arms stretched and yawned, bringing Oliver's attention back down to my precious baby girl. My tiny Olivia.

"She looks just like 'Lil Bri when she was born," Oliver said weakly. "That just makes 'dis even harder."

"Did they tell you her name?" I asked, not able to move any closer.

Oliver nodded. "They did. I'm honored, son."

"Da, you were the most important person in Brianna's life. The one person who loved her unconditionally. We…" I paused with stabbing realization, "I…I am honored that you are in their lives."

Oliver swallowed hard as he slowly rose from the rocking chair, cradling Olivia in his arms. "Son, you were the most important person in her life. Pretty sure I lost that title the day you two met. You gave her the two things that were always missin' in her life."

"I did?"

"A course, son. You loved her somethin' fierce, and you gave her two a the most beautiful babes I ever seen."

Oliver carefully shifted Olivia and placed her gently in my reluctant and shaking arms. It had been several centuries since I held a baby, let alone my own. That scared me most of all. This tiny baby girl, who felt as light as a doll, was mine. The small pink hat fell from her head showing a flash of jet black fluffy hair. She was a part of me; I could see it plain as day. It was not until she stretched her eyelids open and stared at me with big dark eyes that my stomach dropped. Not only was she a part of me, she was even more so and heartbreakingly a part of her mother.

Absentmindedly I walked to the empty rocking chair. Olivia stared intently at me as I sat down. I knew it was impossible for a newborn to focus her eyes, but it was as if she knew me. She knew I was her father.

"She's definitely got her mama's eyes," Oliver said sadly. "Feels like just yesterday I was holdin' 'Lil Bri in my arms and she was lookin' at me the way Olivia's lookin' at you right now."

"Da, I am so sorry."

Oliver shook his head. "Son, I'm the one who's sorry. I…I musta done somethin' in my life to deserve all my girls bein' taken away from me." Oliver took his glasses off and rubbed his eyes as he walked toward the door.

"Without Bri," I began, causing him to stop with his hand on the doorknob, "what happens with you and me?"

Oliver placed his glasses back onto his face and looked firmly into my eyes. "You are still my son, and I am still your Da. And hopefully I'll last long enough for them chiluns to call me Daddy O. Nothin' changes, son. I can't lose the only family I got left."

Without another word Oliver left the room, closing the door softly behind him. The air in the room was thick and tense, and made worse by the fact that Renee had not moved from the window or said a single word. She was oblivious to her surroundings and stared blankly out the window while holding a sleeping Jackson in her arms. I looked from her back down to Olivia who was still staring at me with her mother's eyes. Suddenly the air in the room was no longer thick, but absent all together. Looking at my daughter had suddenly become painful and felt as though there was a jagged piece of glass cutting and tearing my heart into pieces. Unable to take Olivia's gaze any longer I carefully placed her into one of the two bassinets.

"I couldn't hold her for long either," Renee said without taking her eyes from the window. "She'll always be compared to her mother. It's not fair that everyone will see her and think of..." Renee stopped herself from saying Brianna's name and through the reflection of the window I could see her nostrils flaring as she sniffled.

"None of this is fair, Renee."

"Yeah, no shit," she replied flatly. "This was all she wanted, you know? Even before she met you, all she ever wanted was a family. And now that she finally got it..." Renee paused again, this time taking several moments before being able to continue. "Why her, Cameron? Of all people, why the...fucking, fuck, fuck, did it have to be her?" Renee went quiet once again, letting her anger die down before turning toward me and saying, "Would you like to hold your son?"

"He seems fine with you," I replied nervously.

Renee ignored me and stepped in front of me. "Little Jackson is a snuggler already. I think you should see for yourself."

Carefully Renee placed her hand underneath the tiny bundle and transferred Jackson into my arms. His eyes stretched opened sleepily as my elbow came to support his head. As I cradled him to my chest he began nuzzling his face against my shirt. "He is a...snuggler? Is that what you called him?"

Renee leaned down and petted his capped head before kissing his forehead. "Little snuggler with a kickass name. You guys did good. Livy and Jack. I like 'em."

"Jackson and Olivia."

Renee rose and popped her hip, showing a bit of her true self. "Uh, godmother here. I get to call them what I want."

"Speaking of that," I began, causing Renee to squint her eyes. "You and John, and Kyla and Alexander are all the twins' godparents."

"Yes...and?"

"Although Brianna and I trust Kyla and Alexander implicitly, we...we had talked that if anything ever happened to both of us, and the children were still young, that we would want...if you were able of course...we would want the children to be with you and John."

Renee was silent for only a moment, her expression unreadable. "You want us over them? But they're..."

"The children would be more than provided for."

"Christ, Cameron, I don't care about that. I meant, they're Vamps."

"Yes, but you and John are human. You would be able to bring the twins some semblance of normalcy, something that my family cannot give them no matter how hard they would try. I know this is a horrible time to discuss this, but...but I do not want to leave anything to chance. I cannot even predict what else might happen and I need to know the children will be taken care of."

Renee sighed as she pursed her lips and flared her nostrils with emotions. Finally, "Of course we'll be there for whatever Jack and Livy need."

Renee squeezed my shoulder before turning and walking around the bed. But before reaching the door she paused and looked back to me. "But Cameron, you can't let anything 'happen' to you," she said firmly with her finger quotes. "You're the only parent they have now. They shouldn't have to have me and John as consolation prizes."

Renee skirted out of the room, and I was finally left alone with my children. The feeling of emptiness was overwhelming. This was my life now. A single father of two children. An ungrateful man who was lucky enough to have two beautiful babies, and yet all I wanted was my lover and partner to be lying in the hospital bed next to me. She should be here instead of me. My children deserved to know the warmth of their mother's loving arms instead of the cold stone feeling of mine. They needed to hear their mother's calming voice and the magic of her soothing touch when they were scared or hurt. What did I know about raising a child? What could I possibly give them? I was useless, empty. Brianna had always filled the void and made me a better person. She turned me from a Vampire back to a man. Without her I was nothing, and my children deserved more than that.

Just then Jackson stretched his right hand free from inside his swaddling blanket revealing five of the tiniest fingers I had ever seen. His fingers flexed and searched the air until they found my index finger and wrapped themselves around it. Suddenly an intense heat began to spread down my hand and up my arm, eventually traveling across my chest and feeling surprisingly familiar.

"So it was you doing this from inside your mother," I cooed.

The heat began to recede once Jackson released my finger and rubbed his face. Instinctively I gently removed his hand to prevent him from scratching himself and quickly he wrapped his hand around my finger once again. Just as it had before, a heat traveled down my arm, but instead of stretching across my chest it soared up my throat. It had been scratchy beforehand because of my lack of blood, but now it was burning so badly that my fangs extended immediately.

I removed my finger from Jackson's light grip and the burning instantly faded away. Jackson, however, began to wail. His entire body was shaking as his cries bounced off the walls around us. A second later Olivia joined him. Their combined cries in the small hospital room was enough to make my ears bleed.

"What do you need?" I asked looking between the two of them in a panic and then shouted at the door. "Can...can someone help me?"

The children's cries became more intense and sounded desperate. However, over their screaming I could hear someone press down on the door handle and all I could think of was that I was saved. But just as the door opened slightly, a flash of Renee's sparkling dress peeking through, I heard Madelyn's voice tell her to stop.

"He needs to learn how to help them himself, sweetheart."

"No, Renee please," I begged as Renee pulled the door closed. "Please, Renee come back! What do I do? Please someone tell me what to do!" No answer came and the children simply kept screaming in agonizing tones. I shifted Jackson higher in my arms and pleaded with him. "Are you hungry? Is that what you need? Tell me, son, please. Somehow please tell me."

He answered by screaming louder. I looked around the room for something I could feed him when I realized I had no idea what I would have given him. Babies drank from a mother's breast, beyond that I knew nothing, had nothing.

The children's cries were ringing painfully in my ears to the point I felt ill. The ache in my body was spreading along with the burning in my throat making me want to crawl out of my skin.

"Brianna, help me," I begged as the children's cries became unbearable. I placed my fist up to my mouth and began biting into the knuckle of my right index finger in order to stop from screaming. My fangs were still extended and pricked the side of my hand. A droplet of blood dripped down my chin, but that was not what made me pull my fist from my mouth. It was the fact that in an instant the children stopped screaming.

I looked down at Jackson whose lips were slowly opening and closing as if he was suckling. In my shock at the sudden silence I neglected to move my bleeding fist that was hovering over him and a tiny drop of blood dripped onto his bottom lip. I watched as he sucked in his lip and cleaned it of my blood. A second later he began smacking his lips together and when nothing came into his mouth his wails began again.

Not knowing what else to do, I punctured a hole in my index finger and then placed it in my son's mouth. His gums tickled and massaged my finger as he sucked the blood into his mouth. A thousand voices rang in my head, screaming at me to stop what I was doing, but yet I did not draw my finger away. I could feel the blood receding from my veins causing my body to burn even more. I looked down at my son who was finally calm with his eyes becoming heavy with satisfaction.

"Jackson Thomas," I cooed at him softly, "named after your paternal grandfather, your true paternal grandfather, that is. And on the insistence of your mother you are also named after me, although I will admit we fought a little on that one. You come from a line of Burke's who originally settled in Maryland, but then eventually moved to Massachusetts in an area outside of Boston in the mid-1700's." Jackson's sucking became weak so I carefully removed my finger from his mouth and received no protest, just the sight of his sleepy eyes. "Our family had always been farmers until I broke away and left for the city to make a different life for myself. But now we belong to a new family, a larger and older family of Warriors who hail from all over the world and protect humans and Vampires alike. And though at some point they may all compare you to your father, you must always remember that you are your own person with your own dreams and I will always support you in whatever it is you want to become. You are my most precious son, Jackson Thomas."

I lifted his tiny head and kissed him gently on his warm forehead. Carefully I shifted him in my arms and placed him inside the empty bassinette next to his sister. Olivia's eyes were open and oddly expectant, and once again it was like looking at a baby Brianna as I pulled her into my chest.

As I had done with Jackson, I punctured my index finger and brought it up to Olivia's mouth. She instantly began sucking and I was surprised at the difference in strength compared to her brother. She was definitely an eater.

"Olivia Sera, named after two very special people in your mother's life – your maternal great-grandfather, and your maternal grandmother. Two people who saved your mother in more ways than one, and on more than one occasion. Your mother's side of the family settled in the beautiful mountains of North Carolina, and I am sad to say that is all I know. I kept thinking I had more time to find out these things, or at least your mother would be here to tell me. I...I think you will miss out most of all having to grow up without your mother because she was...amazing. She wanted both of you so desperately...I wish you could have seen her face light up every time she talked about you or saw you on the ultrasound. I will never tell you the horrors of your mother's past, but I will say that I believe she fought to stay alive for as long as she did in order to have you.

"And though your brother may share my name, I am afraid it is you who will always have a greater burden of being compared to your mother. But just as I said to your brother, you always need to remember that you are your own person with your own hopes and dreams and...I...will make sure everyone in our family reminds you of that. Because...I...I may not always be here to tell you."

My daughter chewed on my finger as though her life depended on it. I was happy to give her everything. I would give both of them the only thing I had left to offer - my blood. An early activation, I rationalized. I could not see myself being alive in twenty years in order to do it. In some ways I already longed for a true death. My body seemed to already be so close with the tremendous burning eating at me from the inside out.

With surprising effort I removed my finger from Olivia's mouth, though she still seemed hungry even after she had taken more blood than her brother. I placed Olivia back into her bassinette and looked down on both of my children. My precious ones. Olivia and Jackson. Livy and Jack.

Just then my pocket began to vibrate and I pulled out of my cell phone expecting it to be Devin, having chosen to stay at Dante's to help sort out the mess. But instead the name that flashed across the screen made my hand almost crush the phone to dust. I accepted the call and pressed the phone up to my ear but found myself unable to speak at first.

"Sorry old friend, did I catch you at a bad time?" Aidan's cocky voice rang through the phone.

"You are a dead man."

"Well you got me there, I actually am dead. So is your wife, I hear. Or was she still your fiancée, or maybe just your baby making whore."

"I will rip out your fucking throat," I growled but soft enough not to startle the children.

"Problem is, *old friend*, you actually have to find me first."

"I will find you and I will kill you for what you have done to my family. Do you hear me? I will rip you apart piece by piece and make you watch, I will torture you until you beg me to rip your head off and even then I will drag out your death until my father and brothers pry me from your bloody corpse."

"Now is that any way to talk in front of your children?"

My head whipped around. I rushed to the window and found no one, not even a building across from where I was, only manicured hospital grounds. When his wicked laugh came through the phone I knew he was torturing me and I had easily let him inside my head.

"Since you seem so hell bent on killing me, I'll give you one shot. One shot to prove you're the big bad Warrior you think you are."

"I am not falling for your tricks, Aidan."

"Well, that's your choice. Try and kill me now, or look over your shoulder for the rest of your children's lives. It's up to you."

"This is your way of drawing me out of the hospital so you can try and take the children."

"I want to see what is more important to you. Revenging your lover's death, or protecting your newborns. Thirty minutes, underneath the Mystic River Bridge in the Inner Harbor. If you don't come alone I'll know, and if you don't show up the game simply continues."

The phone went dead. I looked down at my precious ones now asleep and unknowing of the dangers that still surrounded them. I had less than thirty minutes to decide whether or not to open my children up to that danger now for a short time, or for the rest of their lives. As the call screen faded away I found myself staring at the picture I had taken of Brianna with our baby girl on her chest. I flipped to the next picture and my heart broke at the happiness in Bri's eyes as she held Jackson for the first time.

This was not a choice of what was more important to me. Not only would killing him now revenge Brianna's death, it would solidify my children's safety forever. It was the only choice and it most likely meant my own death since I had hardly any blood left in me.

Leaning into the bassinettes I kissed my sleeping babies goodbye.

"I love you, my precious ones. Your mother and I love you very much, and I hope that one day you will understand the sacrifices we made for you, and why."

Feeling the emotions well up inside my chest, I bolted from the room and was met by most of the family standing in the hallway.

"Stay with them, please. I need to…" I turned and began walking down the hallway after I glanced at Kyla's unfocused eyes. "I need to take care of something."

"Cameron!" Kyla shouted behind me. "Alex, don't let him go!"

"Everyone must stay with the children!" I shouted over my shoulder as I continued down the hall.

Jared and Alexander caught up with me quickly and both placed a hand on my shoulders.

"Cam, stop. Where are you going?" Alexander asked pulling me back slightly.

I shrugged his hand off my shoulder. "I am meeting Aidan, and I am going to kill him."

"What? When?"

"Now. I have thirty minutes to get across town."

"Whoa, bro, you can't leave your kids here," Jared said stepping in front of me, but then had to walk backwards when I proceeded forward. "Just tell us where you're meeting him and we'll go."

"No. If anyone else besides me comes he will know. I may not get another chance like this. Now get out of my way."

"Cam, this is madness," Alexander said as he pulled me over to the wall, but I twisted out of his grip and tried pushing him away. I was so weak that I barely pushed him at all, but I still continued down the hall to where it opened into the waiting room where my eldest brother was now approaching us.

"Dev! Thank god, Cameron's lost his mind," Jared said from behind me.

Devin was walking straight at me, a concerned and worried look on his face. "Brother, I just heard…" he began.

But I stopped him and tried to walk around him. "This is not the time."

Devin grabbed my arm as I passed and pulled me back to stand in front of him. "It's not true."

"What?"

"Brianna is not dead, Brother."

I lunged at him, only to be stopped by Alexander.

"Seriously Dev, what the fuck?" Jared objected.

"Guys! Guys!" John said in a soft but warning tone as he ran to our group. "Let's take this outside. We're in the maternity ward, they call security at the drop of a hat."

John urged us toward the glass doors that led out to a narrow balcony. I tried to step around Devin again, but both he and Alexander shuffled me through the outside doors and tossed me toward the balcony's ledge.

"I do not have time for this!" I shouted and lurched forward only to be stopped again. "What is it you do not understand? I have a small window of time here…"

"To do what, Brother?"

"To kill that son of a bitch! Brianna is dead because of him and he is threatening my children. I will not miss this opportunity and I will go through every one of you if I have to."

I took the two steps to the door and Devin grabbed my forearm forcefully causing me to grind my teeth from the pain. I looked down at my forearm and watched my skin flake away as Devin's thumb rubbed against it.

"Jesus, bro, what the hell's wrong with you?"

Devin whipped his head up and squinted his eyes at me. "This happens when you have little or no blood left in your body. Brother, what have you done?"

Giving up and seeing that my chance to confront Aidan was slipping through my fingers I confessed. "When Brianna died I was desperate. I drained myself on her wounds."

So I only partially confessed.

John stepped forward, a disappointed scowl on his face. "Cameron, I thought we understood her wishes…"

"John, please not now," I begged. "Brother, just let me avenge her death."

"Cam," Alexander answered instead, "you wouldn't last five minutes with him in your condition."

"Yeah bro, you goin' off and getting yourself killed will do nothing to stop Aidan and it certainly won't do your kids any good to become orphans on their birthday. I know what it's like to grow up without parents, do you seriously want your kids to end up like me? Think about it, man."

"Yes, Cam, think about what you're doing. Brianna would not want you to leave the children like this. We all need to grieve and honor Brianna properly…"

"But we don't! That's what I have been trying to tell you!" Devin yelled.

"She's not dead."

"Devin stop," John warned angrily. "It's not funny. Cameron and I were both there. We saw her..."

"Brother, listen to me," Devin interrupted and squeezed my shoulders tightly as he looked firmly into my eyes. "You of all people know I have always been able to feel when someone's death is upon them. I would have known if Brianna would lose her life, I would feel her death now."

Slowly I pulled my brother's hands from my shoulders. "Brother, she is dead. And I more than anyone wish you were right, but I gave her my blood as did Eris and Father. Brianna did not heal because she was already gone. Please Brother just..."

"No!" Devin shouted as he pushed me away from him.

My three brothers and John started shouting at one another as my back rammed into the railing of the balcony. While they argued I turned around to look over the balcony's view. The street lights were beginning to fade as dawn loomed in the distance. The crisp spring air stung my nose as I inhaled deeply, causing the back of my head to pulse. My need for blood was becoming dire and though I hated to admit it I doubted if my weakened body would survive a fall to the ground in order to escape my brothers. Reflexively I began massaging my temples, but the dull pain began to grow legs and travel to the front of my head. I gripped the railing tightly as the pain made my knees weak.

"Cam?" Alexander said, placing a hand on my shoulder when my knee hit the ground.

"My...my head."

"You need blood, Brother," Devin said as he extended his fangs.

I reached up and grabbed his arm. "Brother, no. Not here. There are too many people around." The words took effort as the pain filled my head and seemed to drag me forward. "Is anyone else feeling this?"

"Feeling what, bro? You look crazy right now."

I pulled on Jared's outstretched hand as a shockwave of pain shot through my body. Jared wrapped his arm around my shoulders and lifted me to a weak standing position. Suddenly I knew this pain. The sensation was impossibly familiar. "It...it feels like...her."

"Who, Brother?"

Slowly I looked up to Devin. "Bri. It's her. She's in my head. No one else can feel it?"

"Cameron, don't do this, man," John pleaded.

"I can feel her, John."

"Cam, it's probably because you need blood," Alexander said as I stepped through the glass door back into the hospital.

The pain in my head was sharp as the florescent lighting hit my eyes. My shoes slipped on the tile floor as I scuffled along down the hallway towards the operating room.

"Cameron, wait!" John called from behind me alerting the rest of the family. "Where are you going?"

"Brianna needs me," I called back as I reached the operating room door. John's hand covered mine as I closed my fingers around the door handle.

"She's not in there."

"Wh-where is she?"

John's face dropped. "They took her away a while ago, Cameron. She's in the...morgue."

"Where is that?"

"The...the morgue? It's downstairs, but you can't...Cameron, wait!" John shouted after me as I ran to the stairwell.

When I reached the door I looked back to see my brothers, John, and now Renee running and shouting after me.

"Cameron, what the hell are you doing? You can't just go and leave the babies..."

"Bri's not dead," I said through the pounding pain in my head and started down the stairs.

The others were shouting behind me, John being the most vocal, "Alex, you can't let him do this."

"Well doc, doesn't look like we have much of a choice."

"But you need an ID card to get through the doors."

"Then I suppose you should give it to him, otherwise he'll just break the doors down. Or at least he'll try. Just get him through so he can see he's wrong and stop acting like a lunatic."

"I can hear you!" I shouted up to the landing above.

"I hope you can, bro," Jared responded, "because it's true. You are acting like a fucking lunatic. I'm surprised Dad isn't chasing you down right now."

Ignoring him, I continued down the final set of stairs and was then stopped by the basement security door. I looked up to see John running down the stairs with his ID card in his hand. Alexander and Devin were right on his heels while Jared was carrying Renee in his arms, most likely at her insistence.

John held his ID card just above the reader and I could see the reluctance in his face.

"John, please," I begged. "Let me find her. I am not crazy."

John sighed as the card reader chimed and the locks released. As soon as the door opened, a wave of energy flew down the hallway and effectively took down the four Vampires standing in its path. John and Renee stood over us stunned. Devin lifted me from the floor and held me upright until my legs regained their strength.

"Dev…" I said breathlessly.

"I told you," he replied in a cocky tone.

"But how?"

"We will know soon enough. Now come on."

Devin took my elbow and guided me down the hallway with John leading the pack. As we approached the second door marked "Morgue", a short bald gentleman came out from within his office.

"Dr. Ryan, what are you…you can't bring all these people down here," said the bald man.

John stopped, a panicked look on his face, but Jared stepped forward and took the bald doctor by the shoulders. "Don't worry, doc, I'll handle this."

As Devin and I passed, I could see the bald doctor's eyes begin to glaze over while Jared Glamoured him with something I could barely hear over the ringing in my ears. But I swear I heard the words – bikinis, nurses, and booze. The bald doctor scurried down the hallway toward the stairs and it was very clear that we needed to help Jared with his Glamouring skills.

John once again held his medical ID over the card reader but before he scanned it he looked at me intensely. "Ok, I'm risking my job here. So we'll go in there, find out where she is and then we'll leave. Two minutes, tops. Do we understand each other?" When I did not answer him his eyes flared in an anger I had never seen in John Ryan in all the time I had known him. "Cameron, I need to know you understand what I'm risking here! We can't keep dragging this out. Do-you-understand?"

But before I could answer him, a loud bang came from inside the morgue. Through the windows of the doors you could see the wall of small rectangular steel doors of the refrigeration unit shake. When a second bang came from inside, John dropped the ID card on the floor. A third bang came a second later but this time a steel door located in the center of the wall became misshapen, dented from a blow from the inside.

John stood frozen, prompting Devin to rip the reader from the wall and manually open the double doors. The doors gave way just as another loud bang sounded and then the misshapen steel door flew across the room right in our direction.

"Look out!" I shouted as I ducked to the ground. Devin pulled John to the floor while Jared pushed Renee up against the opposite wall. Alexander, on the other hand, thrust his large first forward and punched a hole through the steel projectile.

We all took a second to look at the metal door spinning around Alexander's wrist when a terrifying scream rang through the room. I whipped my head back around in time to see hands coming around the sides of the rectangular opening. Slowly I stood from the floor, watching as the hands stretched to arms and shoulders and eventually the face of a shrieking Brianna as she pulled herself out from inside the refrigeration unit.

The white sheet that had been draped around her was being pulled away from her bare body as she clawed her way out. Rushing over to her, I placed my arms under her shoulders and pulled her free while she continued to scream and flail wildly around. Once she was on the floor I tried wrapping the thin white sheet around her, but her hands fought me and then hit me forcefully in the chest.

"Brianna!" I shouted as I slid back across the floor. I dug my fingers into the floor creating ten claw marks in the tile to prevent me from crashing into everyone like a bowling ball. "Bri, calm down!"

Brianna stood from the floor, clumsily trying to keep the white sheet wrapped around her. Her hair was matted in various directions while her skin looked pale and flawlessly smooth. Through the sheet I could see that she had regained her pre-pregnancy figure and all signs of the butchery she had endured had disappeared.

Everyone stood in awe as they gazed upon my love shaking in front of them.

"Holy Mary Mother of Martha," John whispered just before Renee fainted in his arms.

"C-Cam?" Brianna finally said with a trembling bottom lip.

Slowly I rose from the floor, being careful not to startle her in her present condition. Hearing her voice seemed to make everything around me disappear. Brianna was standing in front of me. My angel was both alive and dead, and standing before me by some unexplainable miracle.

"Everything will be all right, love."

Brianna pulled the sheet tighter around her body as she looked uneasily at her surroundings. "I'm cold, Cam. I'm so cold."

"Probably 'cuz you've been in a freezer," Jared muttered under his breath and then received a shot in the arm from Alexander.

"It will pass," I said gently and slowly walked toward her.

Brianna's chin began trembling along with her bottom lip. "Everything looks so…so different."

"That won't pass," Jared kidded again.

"Jared, shut up!" I shouted.

Brianna rubbed her hands down the front of her abdomen and was suddenly in a greater panic.

"The children are fine, angel," I said before she could run and she looked up to meet my eyes. "Jackson and Olivia are perfectly fine and healthy."

Brianna's chest began to heave and she grabbed her throat. "Cameron, where am I? Why do I only have a sheet around me?"

"Jesus, Beebs, that's what you're curious about? How about…" But Jared did not get to finish his statement since Devin rounded on him, making him scurry back against the wall and take Renee out of John's struggling arms. "You wouldn't hit a guy holding a red-headed unconscious bride would you? Wait a minute, I take that back, you probably would. But can we concentrate on Bibi right now?"

Devin shook his head and turned back toward the front of the room where Brianna was slowly piecing things together. "I remember Dante's, then the car ride to the hospital."

"Yes, angel," I nodded slowly.

"Then Jackson came, then John put Olivia on my chest, then…then…" Brianna's eyes searched the floor as if they held the answers. Suddenly her eyes flashed up to mine. "Cameron, what have you done?"

"Angel, listen to me…"

"What-have-you-done!"

"It should not have worked, I was desperate. We were all desperate. You should not even be standing here, my love."

"But I am!" she shouted and making the edges of my mind flinch from the Push I was not completely convinced she knew she was projecting. "Am I…am I a…a Vam…a Vampire?"

"Yes, love, but…"

"NO!" she screamed and Pushed me back several paces. Her cries continued as she sank into the floor, red tears leaking from her eyes. Brianna wiped her cheeks with her hands, smearing the bloody tears across her face.

She looked at her red stained hands and began sobbing even more hysterically.

I knelt in front of her, placing my hands on her shoulders as I said, "Please understand, Brianna, you were dead. At least the machines said you were. I…I could not be without you and I went…mad. I gave you my blood, almost every drop of blood I had. And then your father and Victor came in and saw what I was doing. They too gave you their blood and by some miracle…"

"But look at what I am," she cried as she wiped her cheeks again and held out her bloody hands to me.

"You are alive, that is what you are."

From underneath my fingers I could feel a growing heat rising from Brianna's skin. With tremendous speed Brianna rose from the floor and a wave of energy exploded from her body sending all the Vampires soaring in the air and through the back wall into the bald doctor's office on the other side.

Jared hissed as his arm was met with a stream of sunlight coming from the narrow windows near the ceiling of the office. Quickly he scurried back into the hallway where the sunlight did not hit. With a sudden horror my eyes followed the beams of sunlight as they flooded through the large hole in the wall and into the morgue.

"Brianna!" I screamed as I tripped over the rubble with Devin and Alexander close behind. The sun burned my neck as I stepped through the hole and standing directly in the sun's bright beam was Brianna. Her hands and arms cut through the sunlight like swords of shadow, but she did not burn. She took a step forward into the thickest part of the light and let the sun shine brightly on her face. And still, she did not burn.

Jared stepped through the double glass doors, amazement and jealousy on his face. "Now that's so not fucking fair."

Devin stepped up behind me, gazing at Brianna over my shoulder as he whispered, "Apparently Eris was right."

"How is that, Brother?"

"Brianna obviously is the one who changes everything."

Epilogue

Eris

"Victor, I have to say I am not sure why people make such a fuss over taking care of babies. It seems so intuitive and simple, do you agree?"

Victor looked up from my grandson, Jackson, who was sleeping in his arms. "Yes, Eris, I have to say I do agree with you. They simply seem to sleep. But I do think we are doing a banner job at taking care of them so far. Don't you agree?"

I nodded courteously as I wiggled my finger that was being held by the newborn Olivia. "I do agree, Victor. But do you think perhaps our body temperatures are making them cold?"

"Perhaps another blanket?" Victor suggested as he placed Jackson upon the hospital bed.

"Wonderful idea, Victor," I replied, placing Olivia down next to her brother.

Gently I placed a protective hand over both babies while Victor took two more blankets from the pile that had been stacked on the counter on the other side of the bed. I watched as Victor spread out each blanket one at a time and swaddled each of the babies like my Seraphina had showed us. Two minutes later we were once again sitting in our opposite chairs and gazing down at our grandchildren.

"I have to say, Eris, it has been both a trying and emotional day. Though we had some good luck there at the end."

Having my daughter resurrected was a bit more than good luck. It was a miracle, and one that no one could quite explain.

"I wish my Bri-an-na could see it that way. She is still quite upset at your Warrior."

Victor lifted his eyes slowly with a warning. "And us, Eris. We must always remember we gave her our blood, too. Perhaps my child's blood would not have been able to Turn her by itself."

"Yes, but I like to blame your Warrior. I feel it is my job as his future father-in-law."

"So I have gathered," Victor replied in a less than polite tone. "But what do you make of her absence of sun sensitivity?"

"I do not know what to make of it."

"I wonder what else she will surprise us with."

"Only time will tell, I suppose. I mean, her insensitivity to sun has never been seen, who knows what else could be different about her."

Victor leaned in, lowering his voice slightly. "Has Seraphina," he paused, "*seen* anything?"

"Unfortunately my Sera has seen nothing. Bri-an-na being a Vampire was never in any of her visions so all of this is as new to her as it is for everyone else. I am sure it will be the twins who occupy her visions now. And no, I will not comment further," I interjected as Victor opened his mouth to speak.

A silence fell between us until the door to the hospital room slowly opened and my wife floated into the room.

"Bon journo, mia bella," I said with all the love I had within me as I did every time I saw her. "And how did the new grandmother sleep?"

Seraphina smiled widely as she strolled to stand between me and Victor, placing her hands on the covered heads of the twins and kissing each of them gently. "It is hard to sleep when zhe babies are so close. I cannot get enough of zhem."

As Seraphina sat on the bed I carefully transferred Olivia into her waiting arms. It was hard not to look proud as my wife held her granddaughter, her namesake. She had sacrificed and lived through so much throughout her life and there were few times I had ever seen her as happy as she was now holding the new tiny life in her arms.

But her silent joy was interrupted by Victor. "So Seraphina, now that your grandchildren have safely arrived, I suspect you will want to stay close to them?"

Sera looked up from the baby, a coy smile stretched across her face. "Oui. But why are you concerned?"

Victor knew he had been caught. "As you know, we are building a new facility in Connecticut, on Brianna's former property actually. Facility East should be operational within six or seven months, but we are needing someone to run it. I have looked over countless resumes and histories, but I cannot help but think you would be perfect for the position."

Sera's lips twisted around her teeth as she thought about the offer, but then shook her head.

"Or perhaps the responsibility could be split between you and Eris, as long as you control him, that is."

I scoffed at Victor's accusation. Honestly, when had I ever been out of control when it was not warranted? My wife looked at me with curious eyes and within them I could she was now considering the offer more seriously, but was looking for my approval.

I placed my hand on her leg and gently kissed her arm. "My darling, there is no need to seclude yourself any longer, not with Elaina dead. This could be the adventure that she took away from you so many years ago. I will support whatever decision you make, but it must be yours."

Sera licked her lips nervously as she turned back to Victor. "I will zhink about it. It would make it easier to see zhe bébés."

"This is true, my darling. I do not know how I will ever get little Olivia Sera out of your arms."

Sera looked up at me and smiled lovingly for a moment. But then the smile fell as she read my face and seemingly stole my thoughts right out of my head as she had done for over thirty years. "Zhere is somezing troubling you."

"Isn't there always?" I replied. "With everything that happened today I have not had the chance or the heart to discuss this with Brianna or the Warrior."

"My child has a name, Eris."

"Yes, Victor, I am aware," I answered dismissively. "As I was saying, when we were fleeing from Dante's, mia figlia confided in us that she had seen the other Dreamwalker."

"He was among Elaina's followers?" Victor asked.

I shook my head. "No, apparently he had come to her in a dream, under his control of course. I was unable to ask Bri-an-na how she came to escape his control, but she did allow me to look into her subconscious and see what he looked like."

"Did you recognize him?" Victor asked, excitement building in his voice.

Sera could see my reluctance and squeezed my hand that still rested on her thigh. "Yes. I had almost forgotten what he looked like until he shimmered to life in Bri-an-na's mind."

"For goodness sake, Eris, are you going to tell me who it is or do I need to draw blood?"

I sighed as I finally admitted, "Bri-an-na saw my father."

"I thought you killed your father."

"Oh yes, I certainly did. I killed him the day after he Turned me."

"But he is alive?"

"No, no. No Vampire can heal from their head being cut off."

"Then if you killed your father, how is Brianna seeing him in her dreams?"

"I asked myself that same question before the chaos of this morning occurred and I had almost all but forgotten about it until only moments ago. There are only two individuals who knew what my father looked like. Myself, obviously, and then," I paused for dramatic effect in order to irritate Victor, "there is my father's maker."

"So you believe that your father's maker is the Dreamwalker that has been tracking Brianna? And he, for some reason, has taken the form of your father when he shows himself," Victor said in a mocking tone.

"It would make sense since he is the only other person who knows what my father even looks like, and second, he is the only other Dreamwalker of our time who is stronger than me. It would explain why I have never been able to penetrate his hold on my daughter. And as for taking my father's form, I am assuming he wanted to send me a message, and also I am sure his true form would have been slightly frightening to Bri-an-na, from what I remember of my father's description. I would consider him an ancient of the Ancients, barely resembling a human."

"So with Brianna now being one of us, and no longer dreaming, do you still see him as a threat?"

"He certainly will not be a threat to her, but who is to say the twins are not susceptible."

The room became quiet. Sera kissed Olivia's tiny head before transferring her back to my arms and walking around the bed to the counter where various baby items sat. Eventually she began pouring a white powder into a small plastic container they called a bottle, a device with which to feed the babies. Oh the inventions they had come up with.

"My darling," I called to her, "I am not sure the twins are hungry."

As the words came out of my mouth Olivia began to whine and Jackson's cries were not far behind.

"As always I stand corrected," I responded, causing Victor to laugh smugly.

Suddenly Victor jerked his hand up near his face, a drop of blood dripping from his index finger that had been in Jackson's mouth. Victor's eyes flared at me before looking back down at Jackson and lifting his thin upper lip to reveal two tiny fangs extending from his gums. Instantly I looked down at Olivia who also had two small sharp fangs extending down from her upper gum.

Victor's eyes widened as he said, "How has your daughter accomplished this?"

I shook my head as Seraphina turned around with two bottles in her hand, and I was surprised at the absence of shock on her face. When had she known about this? More importantly, why did she not tell me?

"Is this how the children save our race?" I asked as I took one of the bottles from Sera.

"Time will tell. Zhey have a few years to just be zhe precious bébés zhey are."

"But how many years," Victor pressed.

Sera gave her classic coy smile, the truth hidden behind her eyes and never coming past her lips. "Time, Victor. Let us give zhem zhe gift of time. Zhey already have enough to contend with."

Victor smacked his lips in frustration and chose to concentrate on putting the bottle into Jackson's mouth. My darling wife smiled as I transferred Olivia once again into her arms, allowing her to feed her granddaughter. I did not need for Sera to tell me how many years my grandchildren had until the rest of the prophecy would come to pass, for I knew. I had seen flashes of it in Sera's dreams though I did not let on. I knew that the precious babes before me would have less than four years before they would be tested beyond any other child their age.

In the end it would determine whether our race survived as it always had or would be changed forever.

STAY TUNED FOR BOOK THREE IN THE

Blood-Borne Series

VISIT **WWW.CR-QUINN.COM** FOR THE MOST UP TO DATE
INFORMATION ON THE BLOOD-BORNE SERIES

Acknowledgments

When I finished *A Midnight Bloom*, I put it away and thought I'd gotten this crazy need to write a book out of my system. But after only two weeks I couldn't stop thinking of Brianna and Cameron, and I thought, why not? Let's see what happens. Unfortunately 670 pages happened. As I worked through *A Blinding Winter*, I kept cursing myself and wondering why I can't seem to write shorter books. Let's see how book three goes, but there isn't much hope.

None of this would be possible without the constant love and support from my husband. I'm sorry for the endless nights of me staring at a computer, but you told me to keep going. So it's really your fault.

Thank you to Ashley, the original Twin, and my sissy, Kelsey, for pushing me to keep going on this journey and for being my readers these last few years. Your opinions and support always help me when I doubt everything from my book cover to a character's name. And thank you for having five of the most beautiful nieces and nephews in the world who always make me smile and provide me with endless inspiration.

About the Author

C.R. Quinn is a budding author whose prior accomplishments include a bachelor's degree in Biology, surviving the corporate world for over fifteen years, and a singer/dancer/actor in community theatre. She lives in Connecticut with her husband, and is lucky to be the stepmother to two wonderful children. With two books of *The Blood-Borne* series complete, a third on the way, she's looking for a title for the next series with her fabulous cast of characters.